**THE WEL...**

Book One
Rape of the Fair Country

Big Rhys and Griff were resting Mo and my father on the Brynmawr Corner. There we formed up and went into town. Down North Street we went, past the people huddled on the doorsteps of the Row, and I knew in an instant something was wrong, for the women were wringing their hands and weeping. The crowd parted as we reached it, and my father, soaked with blood and rain, walked through it to our front door. Twm-y-Beddau was there beside my mother. Edwina and Jethro stood nearby. There was a smell of burning in the air and ashes were hot under the feet.

'They came back, Hywel,' said Twm-y-Beddau. 'They flogged you first to be sure of it, they said. My woman has your food. Dai Pig is alive, although they looked at him twice, mind.'

This was the law of the Scotch Cattle. Every stick of furniture was burned, every possession except the clothes we stood in, Edwina's Bible, food and money.

# THE WELSH TRILOGY

Book Two
Hosts of Rebecca

In the light of the Corpse Candle I saw his face, eyes bulging, jaw dropped for the scream.

Flat on my belly now, wriggling towards him, grasping the tuft-grasses, the hair of the peat bog, and I reached him in pistol shots of cracking ice.

'Granfer!' I cried, but he gave no answer. Not a sound he made standing there to his waist in bog, with one hand gripping a bottle and the other hand pointing to Tarn. The fingers I clutched were frozen solid. Preserved all right was Grandfer but not in hops as he'd planned it.

Preserved by peat for Cae White's generations. As I snatched at his belt he slipped from my sight and his soul flew up to Bronwen, his lover.

And the peat bog sighed and sucked in hunger.

**THE WELSH TRILOGY**

Book Three
Song Of The Earth

Looking back, it might not have happened had Dewi been home and the shifts stayed normal. But with the heavier stall of the two, Dada linked with me, and left the inside one for Ifor, Billie Softo and Jed Donkey.

It was a mistake, for there wasn't two ounces of brains between the three of them.

Alehouse Jones, who was in the next stall, said it was a bellstone. Manuel Cotari, the Italian, said it was a face-slip that trapped them first, then took the roof. To this day Owain and Phylip Benyon reckoned that Billie was clearing the gas with a cover board and candle, like I used to do, and the stone dropped as Ifor came in with Jed Donkey.

Whatever it was, it laid sixteen tons on them, and when they roped Ifor's feet for the haul-out he would not come, said Albert Crocker, for his arms were wrapped around Billie Softo.

'She liked that,' said my father. 'Miss Carey liked that . . .'

**Also by the same author,
and available in Coronet Books:**

The Fire People
Land Of My Fathers
Rogue's March
This Sweet And Bitter Earth
Peerless Jim
Rape Of The Fair Country
Hosts Of Rebecca
Song Of The Earth

# The Welsh Trilogy

## RAPE OF THE FAIR COUNTRY
## HOSTS OF REBECCA
## SONG OF THE EARTH

---

# Alexander Cordell

**CORONET BOOKS**
Hodder and Stoughton

First published in three separate volumes:

*Rape of the Fair Country* © G. A. Graber 1959
First published in Great Britain in 1959 by
Victor Gollancz Ltd
Coronet edition 1976

*Hosts of Rebecca* © G. A. Graber 1960
First published in Great Britain in 1960 by
Victor Gollancz Ltd
Coronet edition 1976

*Song of the Earth* © Alexander Cordell 1969
First published in Great Britain in 1969 by
Victor Gollancz Ltd
Coronet edition 1976

This edition 1986

**British Library C.I.P.**

Cordell, Alexander
The Welsh trilogy.
Rn: George Alexander Graber   I. Title   II. Cordell,
Alexander. Rape of the fair country   III. Cordell,
Alexander. Hosts of Rebecca   IV. Cordell, Alexander.
Song of the earth
823'.914[F]        PR6053.067

ISBN 0-340-38933-8

Printed and bound in Great Britain for
Hodder and Stoughton Paperbacks, a
division of Hodder and Stoughton Ltd.,
Mill Road, Dunton Green, Sevenoaks,
Kent (Editorial Office: 47 Bedford
Square, London, WC1 3DP) by
Richard Clay (The Chaucer Press) Ltd,
Bungay, Suffolk

To my wife


'Pay ransom to the owner
And fill the bag to the brim.
Who is the owner?
The slave is owner,
And ever was.
Pay him.'

Emerson

# Book One


# RAPE OF THE FAIR COUNTRY

# CHAPTER ONE

## 1826

THAT JUNE stands clear in my mind.

For apart from it being the month Mrs Pantrych went into the heather with Iolo Milk and had her second in January, it was the time my sister Morfydd stopped going steady with Dafydd Phillips and put him on the gin.

Very strange, all this, for never a drop passed Dafydd's lips before he set eyes on Morfydd, and with poor Mr Pantrych dead eight months everybody knew Iolo was the father, for not a child in his family had run its full time.

A terrible girl for the men was Morfydd, especially in summer when there was a bit of life in them, and if ever a man was dangled on a string it was Dafydd. Fresh from Bangor, he was, following the iron up to the Eastern Valley, and mad for my sister the moment she bowed back at him. Terrible to see somebody get it so bad; wandering around town hoping for a glimpse of her, not knowing if he was in Brecon or Bangor. Off his food, too, so his mam said; making up poetry and going to Chapel to pray for her soul, while Morfydd, like as not, was up on the mountain with her new boy from Nanty, deep in the corn or down in the heather, fretful because it was Mothering Sunday.

It was a good summer that year. The days passed in rich splendour, with the corn so thick and tall around Bwlch-y-drain farm that the tenants could not open their gate for carts. The nightingales sang loud and clear in the moonlight, something that had not happened since the industry came to town, and every morning I climbed to the crest of Turnpike and looked over the golden valley of the Usk to watch the mountain change from brown to green as the sun got going.

From the day I was four years old my father took me up to The Top on his morning shifts at the Garndyrus furnaces; on his back at first, but later we walked hand in hand. But he would leave me on the crest of Turnpike because of the swearing men. And I can see him now, waving as he walked round the Tumble. Home to Mam, then, and in later years to school; sitting by windows hoping for a furnace flash, every inch of me up in the heat and glare of the iron. First out at the school bell, race to Mam for tea, and away up to The Top with me. There I would wait for him until darkness; lying on my back listening to the drop-hammers of the Garndyrus forge or watching the kingfishers sweeping their colours over the brooks.

There is no green on the mountain after dark. Sulphur is in the wind then, and the sky is red with furnace glare all over the ridges from Nantyglo to Risca, and when the night shift comes on the world catches alight. From the valley comes the singing of the Irish and the screaming of the babies they have nineteen to the dozen. The lights of the Garndyrus Inn go on, the workers crowd in for beer, and an hour later hell is let loose with their fighting. But not my father, who could hold his beer with any man on the mountains. He preferred to come home to a decent supper and listen to my mother's gossip; of how Mrs Pantrych ought to be ashamed of herself for going big in the stomach unwedded, or grumbling about the prices in the Tommy Shop, and if ever a man wanted transporting it was Iolo Milk, for if he was not the father of Gwennie Lewis's first as well as Mrs Pantrych's second she was very much mistaken.

"Hisht, Elianor," said my father. "Not in front of the children, please. There is enough wickedness for them to pick up in Town without hearing it at home."

Sit chewing, with your elbows on the table and listen to grown-ups. Very pleasant is the scandal when you are seven years old. Watch Morfydd's dark, lazy smile, Dada's frown, Mam's little red hands cutting bread or sweeping the big black kettle from the hob. Hear the spit of water from the spout, the dying sigh of scalded tea in the pot. Bustle, bustle goes Mam, her mouth a little red button, well up on her dignity.

8

"No good blinding yourself to facts, Hywel," she says. "That Iolo Milk is a bad one, and never again will he enter this house while I have growing daughters. Three times today he has looked through the window and knocked once on the door."

"A scandal, pestering a decent household," says Dada.

And there sits Morfydd with a face of innocence, eyes to tempt a saint, but she winks at me over the brim of her cup.

Terrible to have a loose sister.

"Speak to him, Hywel," whispers Mam. "Something will have to be done or I cannot face the pastor at Chapel next Sunday."

"Aye," sighs Dada. "Where is Edwina?"

"Down at the Company Shop, but back this minute."

"There is a girl to give an example," he says, and glances sideways at Morfydd. "Strong for her Chapel is Edwina, a daughter to be trusted, with no men trailing her like rams. So let me say something that is on my mind, eh, Morfydd? Iolo Milk do not pester this house for nothing, so any girl of mine seen with him on the mountain leaves home quick, and Iolo Milk goes six feet down without a service. Do you understand, girl?"

"Yes, Dada," says Morfydd.

"Then do you mind me."

This takes the smile from her face, which is a pity, for Morfydd is beautiful, especially when smiling. But a clean-thinking man was my father and determined in his manner. The way he caught my mother was determined, too. It was at the Cyfarthfa Horse Show that he bowed to her and her sister, and when the fair was over he invited them home in his trap. Not a word passed between the three of them on the ride, Mam said, and when they reached her father's manse Dada handed them both down, bowed and was off. She thought it was the end of him and went to her room and wept for hours. But a week later he was back outside her gate. Straight up to the front door he went and asked for her father. Ten months later Mam had been signed for, sealed, and had delivered her first in our two-bedroomed house in town.

9

"Good God," says Mam. "Here is Iolo Milk now. Speak to him, Hywel."

"Aye," says Dada.

"But no violence, mind."

"Just man to man, girl. Do not bother yourself."

Very smart is Iolo, with his black hair plastered down and in his new coat and trews, with the carnation he wears in his buttonhole especially for ladykilling. Bang, bang on the door. There he stands, six feet two of him, cap in hand, white teeth shining.

"Good evening, Mr Mortymer," said he.

"Good evening, Iolo," said Dada. "Very fancy you look in that new suit. Up with the chest to show it off, man—in with the stomach by here," and he tapped it. "Aye, very smart you look. Courting, is it?"

"No violence, remember," breathed Mam.

"God forbid," said Dada. "Is it Morfydd you are come for, Iolo?"

"Please God," whispered Iolo, "and with your permission, of course."

"For a little stroll up the mountain, is it?"

"Just a stroll, Mr Mortymer. No harm in a bit of a stroll, you understand, with a maiden as respectable as your Morfydd, not like some I could mention."

"Back before dark, is it, Iolo?" asked Dada.

"Aye, indeed, and the lighter the better, see, when a decent girl is involved. Back in half an hour, if you like, Mr Mortymer, if that suits you better."

"It do not," said Dada. "Head on one side, if you please, for I have been puddling all week and I cannot see in this light. Bend a bit, too, for you have grown inches since I saw you last. And smile, man, do not look unhappy."

And Iolo, the fool, held his chin up, beaming.

One hit and he was out, flat out in the yard, with his hands crossed on his chest and ready for burial.

Good God.

"And me a deacon," said Dada while the women screamed.

"This house is open to Christians, Chapel or Church of England, but pagans and fornicators stay without."

It is good to be sleeping with your sister, with your feet where her knees begin. We always kissed Mam goodnight in the kitchen, but my father came in later with the lamp. And I can see Morfydd now, hear her sighing after her fourteen-hour shift down the Garn pulling trams—reaching up for Dada's kiss. Then, when he shut the door we would settle together in the belly of the bed. With the house gone quiet she would whisper:

"Iestyn, you asleep?"

Lie quiet and see her rise in the blankets, careful of the squeaks, for ours was a bed you would not sell to the devil for courtship. One eye open, watch her slip out. Up goes her flannel nightdress and she is there in buttoned boots; on with her dress, a comb through her hair, and away through the window she goes like a witch on a broomstick.

God in heaven, you think, one day that girl will be as full as Mrs Pantrych. For you have heard Mam say this in the kitchen. Scramble out of bed and run to the window. She is climbing the mountain stained silver, her hands searching for a hold, her long black hair streaming out behind her. Shiver, and listen. An owl hoots from a thousand feet up. Morfydd hoots back. Iolo Milk is up by there, lying on the tumps, smiling at the stars; responsible for the next generation of furnace workers if he has his way, says Mam.

And there is Dada in the room next door, snoring his way up the path to heaven, while Morfydd, his beloved and eldest, goes hand in hand with Iolo Milk to the gates of hell.

# CHAPTER TWO

ON MY eighth birthday my father put my name on the books of the ironmaster and took me to work at the Garndyrus furnaces. It was either the furnaces or the Abergavenny Hiring Fair, and I chose the furnaces, for some of the farmers were devils with the stick. Starting work at eight years old was late to begin a career, for some of the children in town began work at seven, or earlier. Take Sara Roberts—she was about my age but she had been chipping the rock from the iron vein since she was five, and Ieun Mathers lost one foot under a tram at five and the other when he was six. Still, there was no comparison between my family and the likes of these. The Roberts sat a long way behind us in Chapel for their father was a plain limestone digger, work that could be done by the foreigners, and he took home a bare three pounds a six weeks. My father, on the other hand, was a forge expert lent to Garndyrus by Mr Crawshay Bailey of Nantyglo, and was paid twice as much. So the fourpence a week Sara took home made a deal of difference.

Grand to be pulling on your trews of a winter's morning with the frost making you hop. Dada and I were due on shift at first light, so I hopped quietly, for fear of waking Morfydd. She scrubbed at the manager's house in Nantyglo until ten and then went down the Coity Pits getting coal and seeing to the children in charge of the doors. They thought a lot of Morfydd in Nanty, I heard, for she had quick fingers with bleeding when the children were caught in the trams, and she could deliver a baby underground as well as any doctor. She lay in the bed now, her face white and her hair flung black over the pillow. Downstairs Dada was hitting the tub, making the noises of a man being drowned, next door Mam was snoring. The moon was putting his fingers round the room as I pulled my shirt tail between my legs. With my boots in my hand I got to the door.

"Iestyn."

I turned. Morfydd was sitting up.

"Up The Top, boy?"

"Aye," I said, dying to be gone, for I could hear my mother stirring in the bed next door and if she came down there would be talk of my first day at work and what has he got in his eating bag and has he washed and combed his hair properly.

"Wait, you," said Morfydd.

"To hell. I am late already."

"Come over by here," she said.

Sighing, I went round the bed and her hand went under my shirt.

"Where is the vest?"

"Dada does not wear one. It holds the sweat."

"On with the vest I knitted you last week or you do not leave the house alive," she said. "Too young you are to be going up The Top. What time is it?"

"Six o'clock," I replied.

"Six o'clock and a child goes to work. A plague on the whole bloody system. . . ."

"Swear and I tell Dada," I said.

"Tell and be damned," said she, climbing out to the boards. "You at work first light while the brats of ironmasters eat at eight before riding."

Her face was dark with anger as she reached for the long drawers and pulled them up her legs. Up with her nightdress, a lift to her breasts to give them a start for the day, on with the ragged dress now, pulling in her waist with her leather tram-towing belt, and she whispered to herself, her eyes large and bright with growing anger. "See now, if there is trouble on these mountains then I am having a hand in it, for there is not a man in town with the belly to shout." She hit me across the ear. "Go then. Be like a sheep. Go to work years too early and draw starvation pay, but come back here weak in the chest and you sleep under the bed with the china, is it?"

"To hell with the bed, I will sleep with Edwina," I said, and I went through the door and down to the kitchen like a rabbit.

My father was kneeling by the grate blowing flames into the fire. Edwina was asleep under the table, her naked arm lying across the boards like an accident. The kettle was in tears on the hob and bacon sizzling in the pan. Dada did not turn as I entered.

"Trouble with Morfydd, boy?"

"Aye. Because I am going up The Top."

He sighed. "Take no heed, I expected it. The Scotch Cattle will be enrolling Morfydd before she is much older." Smiling, he gripped my arm. "Not much there in the way of muscle, but the furnaces will put it there, and quick. Away and wash now."

Lovely it is to plunge your body into frosty water when rime is lipping the tub, to know the shock of lost breath and fight to get it back. Trickles of freeze run down your blue chest and soak the waist-towel; splash and thresh about and take great breaths of the white mountain mist. Down into the lungs it goes, making the blood run in hot agony; rub, rub with the towel and sing for courage. No hair on the chest or belly like Dada but it will come after a month of Garndyrus where grown men die in the heat and frost, says Morfydd. Cross the legs for the towel is soaked and letting it down to the privates.

"*Bore da' chwi!*" shouts Twm-y-Beddau, the coal-trimmer from next door. Naked as a baby he is and his children throwing buckets at him.

"Good morning!" I shout back, shivering.

"Up The Top today, Iestyn?"

"Aye, aye!"

"Good lad. Dead you will be before you get there, whatever!"

Up with the dry towel and pull it like a saw across the back. Shout, dance, sing, and heat comes from the agony of the morning. On with the shirt, pull the flap between the legs and go like Risca for the door before the fingers of frost have you back. Change your mind and race down the garden. Fling open the door and Morfydd is sitting on the seat.

"Good God," said she, "is nothing here private?"

14

"Quick, you, or I will do it in my trews."

"Do it and to hell," said she, "I was here first. Hie, back here this minute!"

Her hand went for the vest. "Right," she said.

Off with her, on with me. I watched her go to Dada by the kitchen door.

"Dada," she said, "Iestyn will not wear the vest I knitted special and it is cold enough for furs."

There is a bitch for you.

"Vest on," called Dada, "and buttoned at the top, please, and be so good as to shut that door."

Two sheets of *The Record*, read one, use the other, and away.

Morfydd felt me for the vest when I got in, but I had no time to be angry for my lips were wet with the smell of bacon in the pan.

There is good to be a pig and give such joy. No smell like you in every corner of the house; up in bed with Mam, opening Edwina's eyes, tickling the end of Twm-y-Beddau's nose —out of the window and straight up the mountain to the heaven all pigs go with nothing on their conscience. Edwina put her face from under the table, blinking.

"Good to see you," said Dada. "And remember that you are supposed to be cooking the breakfast. Outside with you and wash your hands and sharp to table, please."

There was never any strictness in my father when he spoke to Edwina. She crawled out on all fours and smoothed back her long white hair from her face, smiling.

My second sister, Edwina, was nearly thirteen then.

To make a picture of her would need the hand and eye of a London artist. She was beautiful, but the serenity in her face, pale and proud, was something more than beauty. Her eyes were the palest I have ever seen, slanted so high at the outer corners that they turned the gaze of strangers. Mystery, deep and pure lay in Edwina, and when she was in school no other child would sit with her for fear of the *tylwyth teg*, the supremely fair and terrible ones who lived at Elgam Farm.

She touched my hand as she passed the table and I drew it

back as if scalded. The hurt lay in her eyes, but I could not help it. All the people in town treated her the same, and little wonder. Rub shoulders with a *tylwyth teg* on a Sunday and the coal face might have you on Monday. Look one in the eyes, and watch for your toes in a tram, and more than one God-fearing man has had molten iron over his hands for calling goodnight to footsteps he believed to be human.

A white girl, Tomos Traherne, our preacher, called her once, which is only another name for wickedness.

Edwina's eyes were big at me as she went out to wash, and she smiled so gently that I knew she had something under her apron that would come out at breakfast. But I did not worry for I was into the bacon now and packing bread in after it, thinking of the trams running the finished iron down the mountain to the canal at Llanfoist and through the arched bridges to Newport.

But she had her say at table. Morfydd was cutting bread, Dada sipping his tea. I knew something was coming by the rise and fall of her pointed breasts and the quickness of her fingers.

"Yes, girl?" asked my father, not looking at her.

Edwina swallowed hard, shivering. God knows why she was scared to death for he never laid a finger on any of us.

"True, is it, that Iestyn starts work today?" she said.

"Aye. And what of it?" he asked his tea.

She screwed her hands. "The English preacher do say he is going up years before time."

My father blew steam from his tea. "Does he now?"

"Aye. And I heard him tell the owner straight that it is terrible to see the little ones on The Top in winter and that heaven has no place for the father who sends them there."

It was out. Sweat sprang to her forehead and she closed her eyes and wiped it into her hair.

"Excuse me," I said, getting down. "I will start going."

"Wait, Iestyn." Rising, my father went to the fire and lit his pipe. "Let us be clear, Edwina. Is it the English preacher saying this or my daughter?"

"Little matter," said Morfydd with a sniff. "Everybody in

town is thinking it." She washed that down with tea. "Including me."

"Good," replied Dada. "Now let it be said without English preachers and owners."

No nerves in Morfydd. She smiled dangerously, her dark, rebellious eyes lifting slowly. "*Diawl!* Too young he is, and you know it. We are not like the Hughes or the Griffiths—a penny a week less and they starve." She cocked her thumb at me. "You send a baby to work in iron in a house that is already taking thirty shillings a week. It is not Christian."

Dad blew out smoke. "Take my shift at the forge today. Dressed in trews you might run the house better, I doubt."

"Easy to say, but no answer," said Morfydd, and pushed her chair back and stamped to the fire.

"O, please, do not quarrel," begged Edwina, gripping herself.

"Shut the snivelling. It do gain nothing," whispered Morfydd. "I say a bitch on every man who sends a child under ten to work with fire. God help us, the owners will be snatching them from their cradles soon, and that is not the only injustice. Half the town is in debt to the Company Shop and the other half starving. The place is in rags at the height of winter. Over the Coity in Nanty we work like horses and here we live like pigs, and when Hill says grunt we grunt. . . ."

"It is written," said Dada. "As poor we must labour."

"Aye, labour, and sweat by the bucketful. Right, you! Does Tomos Traherne tell you what else is written? Suffer little children and such is the Kingdom—that is written, too, he says. But Sara Roberts chips the ore when she is not as high as His knee. Little Cristin Williams is buried with cold and Enid Griffiths gets the iron over her legs at nine!"

"As poor we are born to suffering," said Dada quietly.

"Whisht!" cried Morfydd. "Suffering all right and called early for the Kingdom, by order of the masters and the preachers who take their money, eh? Listen! The God of Traherne is a pagan Christ. Sick to death I am of the bowing and scraping and tired enough to sleep for a month, and if Iestyn goes to Garndyrus he goes without my permission."

17

"This has been a long time coming out," said Dada.

"But not soon enough," breathed Morfydd, her eyes on fire. "If there is not a man with the belly to lead us we can soon find another out of town. Mr Williams comes from London to speak to us and there is not a soul at his meeting . . ."

"Wait. What do you know of Williams?"

"That he stands for fair wages and decent hours like the workers are fighting for in London."

"You have been to his meetings, then?"

"Yes, and not ashamed of it."

"Nobody says you should be, but you will keep his talk out of the house or find another place to live, for I will not have it used as a political platform. Save your speeches for the mountain, and do not blame me if the Baileys run you out of Nanty, for they are dead against lawyers."

"The Baileys have more friends than they think," whispered Morfydd.

"O, Morfydd!" breathed Edwina, her hands clasped.

"Yes," said my father. "For I am a worker and a good worker knows his place, and perhaps you will tell me what we would do without the Hills and Baileys, who have put their every penny into these mountains and are entitled to something back, even at the cost of sweated labour."

"And perhaps you will tell me what they would do without us," shouted Morfydd. "The masters of these towns are bleeding us to death, and if Williams had his way he would kick the backside of every ironmaster from here to England."

"Easy in front of the children, please," said Dada.

"Labour indeed! Crawling through the galleries where the masters would not rear their pigs, and them sitting in the middle of their Company Parks paying wages in kind and their prices in the Tommy Shops higher every month!"

"Finish now," said Dada.

"God help me, I am not started," said Morfydd. She swung to me. "Away to Mam and say goodbye, Iestyn, and remember that it was your father who sent you to work years before your time for pigs of ironmasters who have money to burn."

"Enough!" roared Dada, and hit the table with his fist in a

18

sudden fury that sent me from the table and scrambling up the stairs.

My mother was sitting up in bed as if awaiting me.

"Trouble downstairs, is it?" she asked.

"Yes," I replied. "About the ironmasters as usual, but finished now. I am going to Garndyrus this morning unless Dada changes his mind."

"He will not change it. That Morfydd will get us hung with her speeches and shouting."

"Chipping the ore first," I said, "and then on the trams with the Howells boys to learn spragging. Away now, is it?"

My mother nodded as if not seeing me, and the lovely smile went from her face. I will always remember my mother as I saw her then, for beautiful she looked with her long, brown hair over her shoulders. A noble face she had, with the stamp of the manse on it. You could see she was not born at a tub. Pick, pick went her fingers on the blankets, always a sign of trouble with her. I was half way through the door when she called me back.

"Iestyn, bad times are coming, Dada says, and money will be shorter. Another little one is with me. Clothes will be needed, extra milk and food. That is why you are going up early to Garndyrus."

Swollen in the waist she had been these last few weeks and sickness with her in the morning, which I had heard was a bad sign. A terrible business it was when these babies came, with Wicked Gwennie Lewis in a bother with deacons and Mrs Pantrych the scandal of the neighbourhood. And when Dathyl Jenkins caught her first the sidesmen pulled her out of the front row at Chapel and chased her up the mountain with Bibles and sticks. Morfydd lived in dread of having one, for I had often heard her praying about it. And here was Mam smiling and nodding about it as brazen as the foreign women.

"Good God," I said.

Often I had seen the Irish women in town, big in the hips and stomach, setting out for Abergavenny market with their baskets. Mrs O'Reilly for one. There is a size for you is that Mrs O'Reilly. Down North Street she goes like a ship in full

19

sail, with the wind under her skirts and her bonnet streamers fluttering, rosy face glowing, smiling one way and bowing another, not giving a damn for her trouble, though every soul in town knew it was Barney Kerrigan, Nantyglo. Then Dathyl Jenkins, the daughter of Big Rhys, I saw once in the Company Shop. Happy as sin and as pretty as a picture looked Dathyl that morning—lifting her stomach sideways to get it through the crowd and pushing the people about with it inside and chattering like a magpie. Mervyn Jones Counter had something to say, as usual:

"There is healthy you look, Dathyl Jenkins. Three of a kind you are having, is it?"

"Two for Crawshay Bailey and one for Will Blaenavon, I am thinking," said Dathyl. "Marrying, we are, next Sunday at Brynmawr, so Will says, thank God."

"No chance for Chapel, then?" asked skinny Mrs Gwallter with her nose up.

"Dead I will be before I enter Chapel," said Dathyl, putting her stomach on the counter. "Brynmawr to make it respectable, says Will, and to hell with Tomos Traherne and the deacons."

"A loaf of bread," said Mrs Gwallter, "and two penn'orth of accidents, please. A terrible thing it is, Mervyn Jones, when a woman does not know the father."

"Worse when she does," replied Dathyl, giggling as Mervyn cut the meat. "All bone and muscle is Will, but I would not give your Mr Gwallter bed room," which put the other women into fits.

But Dathyl did not marry at Brynmawr or any other place, for Will was absent at the altar. Sorry in my heart I was at the time, for all the town was talking, saying it was this one and that one, and Owen Howells had a finger in the pie unless Morfydd was mistaken, although Big Rhys, Dathyl's father, laid poor Will out for burial in the Abergavenny Fountain and his three farmer friends beside him.

And now Mama.

"Well," said she now. "What is it thinking?"

"Sorry I am," I said. "Will there be trouble for you?"

Her eyes went big, and she began to laugh, making the bed shake. She put out her arms and held me tight, laughing in tears, as women do.

"O, Iestyn," she said. "So small you are to be working for me while I lie here like a lazy old lump. Listen, boy. The tales they tell you in town are nothing to do with your mam, for I am respectable."

"Good," I said. "Now I am from here."

But she caught my hands. "Take care on the mountain, boy. Keep clear of the trams and away from the horses, and try to stay out of the wind, eh?"

I kissed her and was down into the kitchen before she could wink. Morfydd, her face still flushed with anger, was waiting with a scarf she had knitted for herself.

"Round here, you," she said, tying me up and tucking in the ends. "Freeze if you must but do it in style." She gathered my things from the table. "Eating-bag, tea-bottle, vest back on, hair combed, scarf. Right now, away!" She pushed me through the door. "No fighting with the men and keep off the women."

"I will pray for you," whispered Edwina.

"Aye," said Morfydd. "Very warm he will be after prayers. Move your backside, boy. Dada is waiting and scared to death of being late."

She tried to kiss me but I pushed her away and ran into the dark street. My father had already left the Square, and I could hear his iron-tipped boots ringing on the cobbles. Gasping, I joined him with a quick upward glance, knowing he was frowning.

"Only one way to go to work, Iestyn—early. Please remember it."

"Yes, Dada."

"Which shows respect for the man who pays you—Mr Crawshay Bailey of Nantyglo, who has been kind enough to take you on his books and lend you to Garndyrus."

"Very kind," I said.

We clanked on past Staffordshire Row. The moon was bright and full and shivering with frost and the stars over the mountain looked cold enough to faint from the sky. My father said:

"You are going to work before your time because of a new baby coming, do you understand?"

"Aye. Mam has told me now just."

"A bit of a surprise for you, eh?"

"I heard the people talking but did not believe them," I replied.

The little shuttered windows leaned over us. Chinks of light shone from slits in curtains, yawns came on the wind.

"Iestyn," said my father. "Some things you must know when starting work. Tonight, when we get home, the new baby may be with Mam. Do you know how it will come?"

My face went hot despite the cold, and I was thankful for darkness.

"Aye," I said. "Out of the stomach, and with pain."

"Well done. And do you know how the baby was put into Mam?"

We took the middle of the road now for Mrs Tossach was pouring slops from her window.

"Yes," I answered, wishing myself to the devil. "It was put by the seed." A funny time to talk of such things on a first day at work, I thought.

"Well informed, you are," said he. "Who told you this?"

"Mr Tomos Traherne, preacher, and Moesen Jenkins, the son of Big Rhys."

"There is a mine of information. And does Moesen Jenkins know who put the seed into Mam?"

"Aye," I said. "Iolo Milk."

"Good God," he said, and whistled long and clear at the moon. "Did he explain when it happened?"

"Yes," I said. "On the outing to Abergavenny you were on day shift and Iolo Milk partnered Mam and they went up the mountain together. . . ." I stopped, suddenly fearful of his anger, and gripped my hands in my pockets, swallowing dry in the mouth.

"Continue," said Dada. "Do not spare me."

22

"And the seed from the heather went under her skirt and into her, because it was spring."

This had a terrible effect upon him. He went double and pulled out his handkerchief and put it around his face and made strange sounds.

"Is it sad with you?" I asked.

"Upon my soul!" he answered, and blew his nose like a trumpet. "It is a pity to spoil your innocence. You have many things to learn, Iestyn, and in good time I will tell you them. Meanwhile do not talk of Iolo Milk and your mother in the same breath, and give me the name of any man who does. But one thing I will tell you now, Iestyn, for you are going to work with men. A child comes from a woman with enough pain to kill a man, and from that part of her body that is sacred to God, for He sent His Son that way. Are you listening?"

"Yes."

"So you will close your ears to rough talk about a woman's body, and scorn men and boys who speak of it with foul jokes. For if you heed the things men say on the mountain you will be telling the secrets of your mother, and I will disown you for it, and so will God. Do you understand me, Iestyn?"

"Yes," I replied, hot as fire.

"Swear if you like up there. A bloody or two is good for a boy, but not at home or in front of women, or I will have you for it."

"Yes," I replied.

"Fight if you like, but not for sport, and then only with boys bigger, or I will start fighting. Girls are working up at Garndyrus so do not wet before them or drop your trews before them like some men do, but treat them as your sisters."

"Yes, Dada," I said, knowing that he was very firm on this point.

"Nobody to see, my son," he said then, taking my hand. "Two men together go easier up a mountain."

The town was beginning to wake. The houses were bright in moonlight, their little square windows white with frost. A

23

baby was crying in the house of Evans the Death, and I thought of him lying upon his back, his beard staining the blanket—dreaming of corpses, no doubt; of little Mrs Timble who would not put her knees down, said Morfydd, and Butcher Harris who burst. Next door Marged Davies was getting dressed without bothering to pull the curtains, and pretty she looked standing by the candle, waving her arms into her bodice, trembling her pear-shaped breasts. Enid Donkey was standing in the shadows of Shop Row, getting into her nosebag, Mervyn Jones Counter was scratching in his books in the window of the Company Shop. Everybody was getting up now; pots clanging for breakfast, smoke curling from chimneys. Little Willie Gwallter was shouting for his turn on the seat, crossing his legs on the pavement. Wicked Gwennie Lewis was feeding her baby on the bed. Dogs were barking, cats being booted, babies being scolded for wetting the beds. And poor Dafydd Phillips lies stiff in his straw, longing for Morfydd no doubt, for his mam is shouting her head off for him to get up for shift. On we went to Turnpike. The clamour of the town died. On to the mountain along the icy road that led to Garndyrus.

# CHAPTER THREE

A FINE looking lad was Moesen Jenkins, son of Big Rhys, tall and straight for his ten years, with a handsome face and dark lashes to his eyes. He looked up as if expecting me as Idris Foreman led me into the cave near the Garndyrus Inn, and rose, leaning against the rock wall with his hands in the tops of his trews. Eight other children were working there, chipping the rock from the iron vein, going faster when they saw Idris, who paused, his eyes on Moesen.

"New boy, Iestyn Mortymer," he said. "Come to work like the rest of us, and no fighting, mind."

"Fighting? *Diawl!* This one is a friend of mine," said Mo, his eyes glinting. "How are you?"

"How are you?" I said, wondering if it was best to hit him flat and have it over and done with.

"Pleased I am to hear it," said Idris with a hitch at his little fat stomach. "Responsible to the Agent is anyone found fighting, to say nothing of the toe of my boot into two backsides. Start here, young Mortymer. Sara Roberts has two hammers as usual and she will lend you one."

I knew Sara. She was about seven years old and lived in the Tumble houses with her mother, father and little twin brothers. She was dressed in rags, not clothes, and the holes in her mam's black stockings showed her knees and ankles caked with dirt, but pretty, she was, with her dark hair hanging either side of her face. Her eyes were big as she smiled up at me and threw me the hammer. Most of the other children were from the Tumble, too, but some from the Bridge Houses that the ironmasters had walled up for homes; arches where the trams rumbled overhead and the smoke-pipe went through the sleepers above. Ceinwen Hughes, for example. She had lived in one since the day she was born six years ago. Now she sat beside Sara, trying to lift her hammer, for until she could lift it she drew no pay. Her mother had taken the molten iron over her shoulders and had been lying in straw since spring, so Mr Hughes got Ceinwen signed on because there was nobody at home to take care of her. She had seen this winter through so far, but according to Morfydd she was weak in the chest and would not see another.

Sitting down beside her I got busy chipping.

"First day at work, eh?" said Moesen, thick in the throat, for we passed each other in the street like hackled dogs since our fathers had fought near Cae White months back.

"Aye," I replied, "or you would have seen me up by here before."

"You will have your belly full before you are finished."

Sara said, "Do not mind him, Iestyn. It is not so bad with Idris Foreman in charge, although the last one was a bastard with the stick," and she pulled down the neck of her dress and showed me the bright red weal over her shoulders. "But Moesen's father had him coming out of the Drum and Monkey and put him flat and kicked him over to Pwlldu where the colliers saw to him proper."

"Which will happen to more than one I could mention," added Mo, glowering at me.

The trams were going past the entrance, bringing limestone from the Tumble quarries and furnace slag to the Garndyrus tips and the foreign women on the ropes were grunting a song as they pulled them up the pitch. No ribbons in their hair, these women, but their plaits held down by string; sweating like animals and cursing for colliers, with the muscles of their backs bunched and shining with sweat and their breasts as flat as a man's through too much tram-towing underground.

Hundreds of strangers had come to Garndyrus since the Works opened under Hopkins and Hill. Sara's father was one. He had walked from Aberdovey with Sara strapped to his back and the twin boys in his arms while his wife carried the bag, but he was respectable, every inch. The foreigners were different. The masters imported them in hundreds, bringing some from Ireland as walking ballast to live like pigs in the little fenced compounds of the valleys.

The sun was rising now and Idris came in to turn out the lamps. I was shivering to have the bones from me, and many of the younger children were in tears. The wind was whistling into the cave, bringing slag dust from the furnace trams, my breath was misting in the frost and my fingers in agony.

And Moesen Jenkins was after me from the start.

"Iestyn Mortymer," said he, showing me his hammer. "You are a pig and your dada is a pig, and a little tap with this hammer would stir your brains if you had any."

The other children turned up their faces at this, but I just went on chipping, so he said:

"Any trouble from you, Iestyn Mortymer, and I will have you in lumps and dangling from hooks."

"Aye?" I said.

"Aye," said he, "for pigs do hang from ceilings and so will you."

"No trouble from me," I replied. "I want my wages for a new baby coming, and sent home the pair of us if we are found fighting."

"Frightened, he is."

"Shut it and quick," said Sara, her blue face going up. "No fighting in here with the little ones about." She smiled at me and I saw her teeth missing in the front. "Can you fight, Iestyn Mortymer?"

"Aye," I replied, "and no need for hammers."

Moesen made a rude noise with his mouth.

Sweating, me. My heart hitting away under my vest.

"Hisht, Mo!" whispered Sara. "He will have you for it if you do not shut it."

"And quick," I said. "Foreman or no bloody foreman."

Mo sighed at the ceiling. "Twt twt," he said in pain. "There is going to be a bother soon, for I do not stand much from kids," and he got up, unbuttoned his trews—and did it against the wall like the men, watching me over his shoulder.

"Away with that," shouted Sara, "or I will have it flat with this hammer. Shame on you, Moesen Jenkins, for piddling in front of the children, and I will report it to Idris Foreman."

"That is what I think of his dada," said Moesen, putting it

27

away, "and I will do it again as soon as I can over the whole family, for they are a disgrace to a decent community, says my mam."

Too much. The sight of him sitting there in his dirt brought me upright. The furnaces were in blast now, belching as the puddlers tapped them, and the cave was swirling with smoke and steam. Bright flashes lit the shadows as I took off my coat. I tried to remember all the things my father had taught me—bend forward, left hand out, right fist high; keep the hands loose until the strike, hit on the twist with the shoulders, not the arm. A stone in the way now. I kicked it clear, circling Moesen who was sitting cross-legged.

"Up," I said.

Moesen climbed up slowly, his eyes lazy, his white teeth shining. He was two years older than me and inches taller. Ceinwen began to cry and Sara snatched her clear, and the other children dropped their hammers and ran deeper into the cave.

No fool was Moesen, for he came from a family of mountain fighters. Once I had watched him fight in the street. He had the brute strength of his father in him, but not the science of my father who had taught me the value of the long, straight English left that knocks a hooker off balance and leaves him open for the following right. On tiptoe now, I waited for Mo to rush. The knuckles of my left hand were tingling. Nothing like a hit on the nose to make a man angry and a boy cry, says Dada.

Science, me. But not a patch on Sara. She was between us when she saw we meant business, holding us apart with her little fists bunched.

"Right, you," she said. "No kicking on the ground, no thumbing in the eyes, no butting with the head or scratching. A fair fight or not at all, boys," then one of her hands went right, the other left, and the furnace-grit she was holding sprayed into our faces, blinding us.

"And anyone who tries at me gets the hammer," said she, and sat down and went on with her chipping.

Well.

Moesen and I clapped our hands to our eyes and hopped like country dancers, and the tears streamed from us while we called her all the bitches in creation.

"Water in the tin down by here," said Sara, "and any fighting in this cave will be done by me in future."

Groping, we knelt together, splashing the water into our eyes and cursing.

"There is a bloody hag for you," gasped Mo at length. "But I will have you up on the mountain, Iestyn Mortymer, or die doing it."

"Seven o'clock up by Balance Pond," said I, "and I will flatten your nose for you."

At midday the iron bar was beaten for dinner.

Down with the hammers and away we all went, Sara leading, to the furnaces glowing red. The workers were streaming in along the tram roads; mule drovers, limestone carriers and ore tippers, and all gathered around the furnaces, their hands outstretched to the heat.

My father did not go to the furnaces. I found him sitting alone on a tram with his eating-bag open and his tea-bottle steaming. Good it was to see him there, and I noticed many of the younger women giggling and nudging each other for glances at him, smoothing back their hair and putting years on themselves, but my father had eyes only for me.

"Well," said he. "How is the first day going?"

"Fine," I said, climbing up beside him. "Working with Sara Roberts and Mo Jenkins chipping the vein for Number Two Furnace, and a bit of it in by here." I touched my eyes.

He looked hard at me. "Is it cold with you, boy?"

"Enough to freeze you solid, but no matter. There are many younger than me."

He bit deep into his loaf and chewed, looking at nothing. Then, "No trouble with little Mo Jenkins, remember."

I could not lie to him. "No fighting after tonight, Dada." I went at my eating-bag.

"For God's sake," said he. "You do not waste much

time," and he drank, wiping his mouth with his sleeve. "When is it?"

"At seven o'clock, up by the Balance."

He groaned. "Hell and fury, we will be getting a name for pugilism. Come and get warm, then, or you will be nicking some muscles," and he shouldered his way through the crowd and pulling me after him to the hearth of the furnace.

"Back, there!" shouted a ladle-man, and the crowd spread to a wide circle to watch the liquid iron coming out.

Great is the ingenuity of man that he digs rock from a mountain and boils it into iron.

The firebox door swung back and there was a blaze of white heat as the flames curled up in smokeless red and gold. The people shielded their eyes from the glare as the plug was knocked out. I saw the lip of the moving iron, sheet-white at first, reluctant as it struck the misted air. Steam rolled as it took its first wet breath from the mountain; a hiss, a sigh, and it was down, down, a writhing globule of red life flashing at the plug. Black it turned, the white water in pursuit of the impure in the sand-mould; popping, cracking, its fingers diverting into flaring streams. Flame gathered along the moulds and a shining bed expired into a mist of purple, growing rigid in shape and colour to live for a thousand years. The furnace roared, the sand-mould hissed. The plug was sealed. The firebox belched relief.

It was dark in the cave by four o'clock and Idris Foreman came in and gave the stick to an Irish boy who was not working. After he had gone Ceinwen Hughes fell asleep against the wall, but we did not wake her, and Brookie Smith, a gipsy boy, stole what was left in my eating-bag—Brookie Smith, the bastard son of an Abergavenny trader, who two months later starved to death on Christmas morning. The hours dragged by in fear and shivering, with some English gentry peeping into the cave at the little Welsh workers. My hands were blistered and there was blood on my hammer when Idris Foreman hit the bar at half past six.

"Up a dando!" cried Sara, and was away with us after her.

But at the cave entrance I remembered Ceinwen, and went back. She was still asleep against the wall, her legs blue to the thighs and her breathing a whisper.

"Come, you!" shouted Moesen from the entrance. "No hiding and running for home, Mortymer."

"Ceinie is asleep in here," I called. "Does she stay and freeze to death?"

It was then that I saw the good in him. "Eh, dear!" he whispered, peering. "Wetted herself, too, poor thing, and she is soaked. There is a pity. Warm her by the furnace, Iestyn Mortymer, and I will run to the forge for her dada."

It was evil-black outside, with sleet coming down and the wind doing his tonic-solfa around the damped-down furnaces. Number Two was still glowing bright as I carried Ceinwen from the cave and laid her at its base. I was rubbing her legs for warmth when Idris Foreman came back and laid his stick above the ringing-bar.

"What is happening here?" he asked, peering.

"Ceinie fell asleep, sir," I said, "and frozen to an icicle, and Mo Jenkins has run to fetch her father."

Idris sighed and sat down on the slag beside me. "He is wasting his time, then. Doing extra time is Mr Hughes for losing a day with his dying wife. Wonderful men are our employers, but if I had my way I would burn the tails from every ironmaster between here and Cyfarthfa." He lifted Ceinwen and took her closer to the fire. "Whee!" he said, "cold is this baby. Terrible that children are allowed into this hell in winter."

"No choice for Mr Hughes, sir," I said, growing confident, "with his wife caught by the iron and nobody at home to take care of Ceinwen."

"Aye," replied Idris thoughtfully. "No hope for any of us, I am thinking." He rocked the child against him. "Unless we are saved by a Union half the workers of the iron towns will be six feet down and none of them working."

"My father does not care for a Union," I said. "Loyalty to the masters is what counts, he says."

Idris looked at me sharp. "Aye? And if your father says

jump into the firebox of this furnace, young Mortymer, would you do it?"

I did not reply, and he smiled at me. I saw his big teeth broken and yellow and his little eyes gleaming from the sagging folds of his blistered face. Clearing his throat he spat past me.

"Young you are yet, Mortymer, and not enough brain grown to put your heart right. But when you are warm in your bed tonight give a thought to the mother of this child and ask the Christ if it is right that she should be burned to the lungs and lie in straw while her baby freezes in a tunnel."

I played with slag, uncertain, giving quick glances at his face.

"Speak up, boy," he said. "Straighten out your tongue, for we may need you to free this God-forsaken country."

"What is a Union?" I asked.

"God help me! Do not say it has not been explained to you?"

"Plenty of trouble in our house about it, but no explanations," I said.

Idris looked at the sky for words, then said carefully, "If a man were to thrash this child with only you near to stop him, then you would ask my help to put him down, and that would be a Union. But first we would talk with him, to save fighting."

"My father speaks of Scotch Cattle," I said. "What are they?"

"If I refused to help you save this child and you were to drag me from my bed and flog me and burn my furniture because I would not help, then you would be like Scotch Cattle."

"They are wicked, then," I asked, fearful for Morfydd.

"Dung, and the spoilers of our cause. For a Union is built upon comradeship and is formed for negotiation, not violence. But mark me! Since the owners reject negotiation, violence will come. Blood will be spilled on these mountains before they are finished."

Footsteps hammered the grass and Moesen ran up.

"Mr Hughes says to hold Ceinwen by the furnace until eight o'clock, sir," he gasped, "and he will see you square for it in the inn next pay day."

"Right," said Idris, "but not for payment, so back with you and tell him to take his time."

"We are in a hurry," said Mo. "But he promises to come by eight o'clock."

"What hurry? Women before twelve years old, is it?"

"To fight, sir," I said. "Up by the Balance at seven."

"*Dammo di!*" said Idris. "But it is legal enough to tear each other to pieces in private time, so go. And if you fight like your father, Mortymer, I will be happy to carve Mo a coffin, big as he is."

We left him rocking Ceinwen on the slag. He began to sing as we climbed the tram road to Turnpike and his voice was bass and pure in the blustering wind.

Fighting by the Balance Pond was the custom, and everything there being convenient for bruising: near home in case a man had to be carried; a gallows head with an oil lamp on it so you could see who you were hitting; and three feet of mud for the loser.

I was shivering as I ran to my father who was waiting there, but not with the cold.

"Sink him quick, boy, for the love of God," said he, "for I am damned perished."

Big Rhys Jenkins and some of his criminals from the Drum and Monkey bar were there, huddled against the sleet. Moesen was stripping off his coat.

Off with Morfydd's muffler, away with my coat, shirt off, start on the vest.

"Vest on," said Dada.

Tighten the belt to hold up the trews, for there would be hell to pay rent to if they dropped while fighting. Ready, I turned. Moesen was stripped to the waist, looking as big as a man, his brown body shining under the flickering lamp.

"Ten minutes, is it?" asked Big Rhys, very polite.

"Five," said my father. "Two years and six inches, what more do you want?"

33

"Five, then," replied Rhys. "Quite enough time to bury the Mortymers," and he pushed Mo forward. "Into it, the pair of you."

"Hammer the nose," whispered my father, holding me under the flaps of his coat. "A fine straight nose, that, for the English left, and a bend in it will help his looks."

Helped by the toe of his boot I stepped out to meet Moesen.

The mountain grass was wet against my back with the first blow of the fight. I stared at the faint stars, shook my head and climbed up. Mo came in like a tram, fists flailing, but I stepped away and he went past, fighting himself, to wheel and come in swinging.

"Left," called my father, but Mo had already taken it in the mouth and I felt the glorious pain in my knuckles as his head snapped back. My head was clearing now and I stood on tip-toe shooting lefts through his swings while he stayed, flat-footed and grunting.

"Nail him!" yelled Rhys, and Mo leaped in, his fists thumping against my body. We stood shoulder to shoulder, hitting at everything and mostly missing, and then Mo lowered his head and charged.

"Uppercut," said my father, and I dropped my right and hooked it up into Mo's face. He staggered, and I swung the same hand at him and caught him flush in the mouth. Blood spouted down his chin and as his jaw dropped in pain I steadied my hands and hit him left and right in the body before knocking him flat with a swing to the face. Turning, I walked to my father's knee.

"Heaven help us," said my father. "Are we staying here all night?"

I looked at Moesen. He was crawling to his father on all fours, wondering if he was in Garndyrus or China. As he dragged himself up Big Rhys called "Time", and he staggered and turned, jumping after me like a mad thing, but I had a left in his eye before he could blink and another on his nose when he did. His face was dancing before me in the swinging light of the lamp, sleet flying across it, and I saw his eyes, suddenly

34

bright and alive and the blood streaming over his bared, white teeth. The wind buffetted us as we circled, looking for openings. I tried a long right, but he ducked it and hit me about the body with vicious little punches that drove me against Big Rhys. Rhys held Mo off with one hand and pushed me clear with the other, and for thanks I hit his boy twice with my left before he could settle himself for his rush.

"Again," said my father, and I did so, knocking poor Mo sideways.

A terrible thing is this English straight left. The tap-tap of it is maddening to a grown man, let alone a boy who cannot keep his temper. Moesen was crying with rage and pain, and he came in upright, hooking to have my head off.

"Now," called my father, and I stood my ground and let fly at Mo's chin with every ounce of my strength. He took the blow full on the point and dropped flat upon his face and lay there, sobbing and clutching the grass. Rubbing my knuckles I turned and walked back to my father.

He called to Rhys, "Mr Jenkins, I say finish this. He is bleeding like a little pig and he has the courage of a lion."

"To hell with you, Mortymer. He has another minute to go, and he will last it!"

"There is a swine of a father," whispered Dada. "You will handle it, then. Take this boy as you would Edwina. Waste the minute by keeping him off. Hit him down again and you will have me to fight after. Do you hear me?"

Moesen staggered from his father's knee and wandered towards me, but he suddenly gathered his strength and rushed, hitting me solidly for the second time. The gallows light swung across the sky and I tasted the sweet salt of my own blood. In he came again, crying aloud, but I danced away. The light was gleaming on the little bunched muscles of his body and in desperation I drove at them to check his next rush, but the blow never reached him. Instead, I saw the swing of his boot, and bent. The boot took me in the side, pumping out my breath in one long gasp. And the next kick caught me in the mouth.

Very pleasant to be floating in a dream and to wake in your

father's arms. The wind was rocking us and crying in dark places. It was warm and comforting under his coat. I looked around. The light of the gallows was directly above me. Big Rhys, Mo and the Drum and Monkey men had gone.

"Very handy you are with fists," said my father. "But you will rarely fight with gentlemen. Next time I will teach you how to miss their boots."

"Christ," I said. "There is a tooth missing," and felt my mouth.

"Two," said he. "I have another in my pocket, and please do not take the Lord's name in vain. Up on your feet now; do not make a meal of it."

I looked at him as he brushed water from his eyes. "Up a dando!" said he. "We will go to our graves sitting by here. All right for you, mind, for you have been kept warm fighting. And your fight, remember, not mine, for Mam plays hell with pugilists. You will make the excuses for being late at supper."

"That will be worse than boots," I said.

A strange thing happened then. My father kissed me.

"I am freezing solid," said he. "Look, I am streaming from the eyes." And he wandered about, kicking at stones and cursing while I pulled my clothes over my aching body.

A first day at work to remember, this one. A bleeding nose, a tooth in one hand, another in Dada's pocket, and a boot in the belly.

There's a mess to take home to Mam, and all for twopence.

# CHAPTER FOUR

I⊤ is strange that memory will fade on some things and hang like hooks on to others.

Jethro, for instance, was different from the rest of us, and I will always remember the hell of that first twelve months when he took my place as baby in the house. There was no sense in his behaviour; bawling all night if he was in any bed but my mother's, and half the day out of temper. Every doll in the place was pulled to ribbons, not a plate left unsmashed within his reach and rivers of blood would have flown had he got his hands on a hammer. Nothing was sacred. Mam had him on the breast all that year and when he could not get at her he was fishing down the front of Edwina and Morfydd.

But in the eyes of my parents Jethro could do no wrong.

"The devil himself," hissed Morfydd, "but with the tail in front. Now do you listen to that palaver!" And she thumped over in our bed and hit the pillow and pulled the blankets up round her ears.

I could hear Mam walking the boards next door with Jethro screaming on her shoulder and my father and me due up on furnace shift at six o'clock.

"Listen," said Morfydd.

"Hisht, my little one, my precious," said Mam. "Wind it is, Hywel. Wind in my precious baby."

"Then up with it, woman," said Dada, groaning.

"Hitting him for holes now, mind."

"Then feed him, girl. I expect he is empty."

Mam sighed. "Empty? *Diawl!* Tight as a ball he is, for he has been at me hours."

"Wind it is, then," said Dada. "A little drop more will clear it."

"If I have it," said Mam.

37

The old bed grumbles as Mam climbs back in, with Jethro still screaming to wake our dead grandmother.

"There, there," whispered Dada. "A fine man he is going to be, Elianor. A fighter for his rights, eh? All this good food you give him. Hand him here, girl. Now! On this one, my son. No, Elianor, the other, there is none in that old thing, girl. Hisht, Jethro, Mama says the other. On you, my pretty little fighter."

Silence. Mam sighs like the well of life going dry, and Morfydd rises in the bed.

"The damned little glutton," she said. "A bull calf it is, not a baby," and she hit the pillow and buried her face in it.

The bitter winter went by without a nudge of the elbow in our house, but some were not so fortunate. Sara Roberts lost one of her brothers with cold and Ceinwen Hughes died with the chest, and a blessing that, said Morfydd, for Mr Hughes had enough to do to care for his crippled wife. Mrs Pantrych had another, making three, and Gwennie Lewis had her second on her father's birthday and went to live in the disused ironworks in town for scandal.

I remember, too, the cold of the early morning tubs, with the wind coming down the Coity tearing at my trews; the frosty walks home from Garndyrus with my father; the dreary quiet of Hush Silence Street and the little square windows loaded with ice; the lights coming from the Drum and Monkey where the men were putting away the beer and quarrelling about Unions. The wind whistled to take years from your life when you returned with bread and meat from the Shop. But the coldest man in town that year was Dafydd Phillips.

Went mad for Morfydd did Dafydd that winter. Terrible to see him mooning around hoping for a glimpse of her with his blue nose sticking over the top of his muffler and coughing to have ribs up. Here he comes again. Peep through the curtains, wait for his knock, go like Risca to the front door. Open it.

"Morfydd says she is out, Dafydd Phillips."

And over my shoulder he can see Morfydd spitting on the iron and going at my father's Sunday shirt.

"Morfydd!" he calls, sending up steam.

"Shut that door!" she cries from the kitchen. "It is having the legs from me with draught."

"Sorry, Dafydd Phillips." Shut the door in his face, back to the window seat with me, and watch her.

Queer, I thought. Here is a man in trouble, and Morfydd does not raise a hand to him. But if a little one is coming in town, even with a foreign woman, Morfydd reaches for her shawl and goes to help, cursing for ten. A burn, a furnace scald will bring her. When a coal-trimmer lost his leg in a tram last spring she trimmed the stump with scissors, stopped the bleeding and tied the bandages—in her nightdress, because the man would have no other touch him. Morfydd would go to a dog in need, but Dafydd Phillips could cut his throat on our doorstep and get no more than a blink.

Here he comes again, shivering to lay his bones out.

"Down with that curtain," she said, "or we will have him head first through the window."

"He is dying for you," I replied. "And his mam says he has not eaten solid in years."

"Open that door and you die with him, then," said she, and she spat on the iron and whistled at the steam. "There is mad to expect a girl to go courting in snowdrifts." She sang then, with a voice like an angel.

"Never mind the hymns," I said. "The devil has a place for you."

"And blister in very good company," said she. "Some I know will fry very brown."

Bang, bang. On the back door this time.

"I will go," said she, taking the iron. "Like the rest of them, he will have his chance in the spring."

God knows what she did to him but he went off howling and missed shifts for a week.

The spring is a madness that comes into grown-ups when the sun comes up warm over the mountain. One has only to go a mile from town to see what they get up to. Always in twos, they are, sitting in the heather away from eyes. She is saying no and doing a giggle, and he is trying it on and getting nowhere, although she is hoping he will. Worse still up on the Coity, Mo Jenkins says. Things get busy away from the deacons, for dozens are ferretting about in hedges, and stop-its and pleases are going on all over The Top down to the Puddler's Arms on the road to Abergavenny.

But Dafydd did not have to wait until spring. He had his feet in our house in mid-winter, by special invitation from Dada.

A fair-looking chap was Dafydd Phillips, wide in the chin and brow, and with hair I had always wanted for myself, black and straight and flattened down either side with water. Well set up, too, for somebody half starved, with bull shoulders on him and a nose that had seen trouble in its time, by the look of it. He came through our front door like a man to the gallows, screwing the peak from his cap while his mam, a ferret in widow's weeds, was elbowing his ribs to keep him upright.

"Well!" cried Mam in astonishment, for she was not sup-posed to know of the visit. "Look you, Hywel, who has come visiting. Mrs Phillips and Dafydd!" And she took the door back on its hinges. "Come you in. Half frozen you look, and no wonder with the weather we are having!" She bustled the pair of them into the kitchen, laughing and chattering, but I knew she was wishing Mrs Phillips to the devil because Mam was Chapel and Upper Palace and Mrs Phillips was Church and Perpetual Fire.

My father rose and gave his fine bow and Dafydd gave it back, his face as red as a turkey's wattle, and Edwina did her new English curtsey with her eyes cast down.

"Edwina," cried my mother, "bring up the chairs to the fire. Iestyn, down with Jethro and fill the kettle sharp. Come close to the fire, Mrs Phillips. We will soon have you warm, *fach*."

"Morfydd is up at the Shop for the groceries," Dada was saying as I got back, "but home this minute, Dafydd, so make yourself comfortable."

Yes, I thought, make the most of it because brooms and hooves will be in here within the hour. Back to my corner I went and got Jethro on my knee again and listened to their chattering. Hypocrites, all of them, saying things to keep the conversation going—Mam raking at the fire and talking nineteen to the dozen over her shoulder, Mrs Phillips laughing and running her finger round the furniture for dust, and my father smiling encouragement at Dafydd who sat white-faced and staring, as still as a man with a stroke.

"Right, is it, that you are working at Nanty now, man?"

"Yes, Mr Mortymer," replied Dafydd, hooking at his collar.

"Phil Benjamin's shift at the Balance?"

Poor at the English was Dafydd, being Bangor born and bred, and his face was agonised. "Aye," said he, understanding.

"They say he is a hard master."

"The harder the better for Dafydd," interrupted his mam. "Industrious, that is the word for him, Mr Mortymer, and ambitious—take my word for it. Finish up well the way he is going. Know you Caradoc Owen, foreman?"

My father nodded, sucking his pipe.

"Great things Mr Owen has in store for Dafydd, mind. Soon he will be taking Benjamin's place, for it is a pit that needs handling and brains, and you are not backward in that respect, eh, man?"

"No," replied Dafydd, looking as brainy as an egg addled.

Dada said, "Caradoc Owen goes hard for a Union, lad. Do you agree with his views?"

"Whee!" said Mrs Phillips, "that is easily answered. No son of mine would join a Union and still live under my roof, Mr Mortymer." Her thin face twisted up. "It is discipline the workers are needing, as Mr Crawshay Bailey says. . . ."

"That is what Bailey says, but what about Dafydd?"

Dafydd straightened and took a breath.

"As strong against a Union as you, Mr Mortymer," said his mother. "I have heard your words about loyalty repeated in town and I agree with them. And it is the same with the Benefit, mind! Nothing but an excuse for drinking."

"Do you agree with Owen's views, Dafydd?" asked Dada.

Dafydd opened his mouth.

"Enough of old Unions and Benefits," said my mother, "for I can hear Morfydd coming and political talk puts the house up the chimney. Iestyn, out to the back and meet her, for fifteen shillings of groceries do take some handling," which was meant to lift Mrs Phillips' eyebrows, and did. She held out her hands for Jethro as he waddled past, but I lifted him and gave him to Dafydd, for there is nobody like Jethro for making friends with a pair of Sunday trews.

"Here with him this instant!" cried Mam in panic. "A soaking boy is this one, and you in that fine new suit."

Morfydd's footsteps were coming nearer as I shut the back door and went to the gate. The stars were like little moons in the darkness, for the night was black with him and freezing, but flashing red and hot over The Top towards Merthyr, and Nantyglo was smouldering crimson on the clouds. In the shadows I waited until the mist of Morfydd's face took shape. Frost was upon her hair and her eyes were dark smudges in the white loveliness of her cheeks.

"Good evening," I said.

"Good God," said she. "Why all the politeness?"

I held the gate open and she came in backwards with the baskets.

"What time is it?" she asked.

"Six o'clock just, and hurry with the food for Mam is waiting to lay supper."

"Then he will be here any moment," she replied. Suddenly she knelt and swept her arms about me, her eyes large and shining. "O, Iestyn," she said, "because I love you best you will be the first to meet my man. Richard Bennet of London I am marrying, and he is coming in a minute to speak to Dada."

Well! There is a situation.

One of them inside asking for the hand and the other coming in with the bride.

"Sad, are you, boy?" she asked, wrinkling her eyes.

"Why should I be?" The spit was suddenly dry in my mouth, but she was not having me as easy as that.

"Because I will be leaving?"

"Go when you like," I said. "I am not worried."

"O, my precious," she whispered, pulling me against her. "Be happy for me. Do not be like that."

A footstep clattered on the frosted road.

She rose swiftly, patting her hair. "Richard! It is Richard!" she said, dreaming. "Ah, but you will love him as I do when you know him. Listen, he is coming!"

I watched her. Her hands were clenched by her sides, her shawl was over her shoulders to show her hair. With the mist of her face turned up, she waited. Beautiful, she looked, with her eyes wide and her parted lips showing the straight white lines of her teeth.

He vaulted the wall as if he owned the place and she ran into his arms. Motionless, they were; as still as black rocks with the stars behind them. Miserably I turned and kicked at a stone, and it rolled with a clatter and hit our shed.

"What was that?" His voice was deep.

"Only Iestyn, my little brother," she whispered back.

He moved to me, his hands on his hips. "Well, well," he said. "The first of the family, eh?"

I looked him over. He was nearly as big as my father. His hair was black with curls and his face square and strong. He stooped, moving easily from the waist, and I sensed the power in him.

"Good evening," he said, and out came his hand. "I have heard a great deal about Iestyn Mortymer."

His words were level and smooth, like most English. There is a horrid way of speaking—every word deep and pure, but without music.

"Richard is shaking hands, Iestyn," said Morfydd in a panic.

Tired of holding it out he leaned against the wall beside me. "Has your sister told you about me, Mr Mortymer?" He was dead serious.

"Aye, now just."

"About us marrying?"

I nodded.

"And what do you think of it?"

43

I searched his face for a smile and found none. "Not much until I have seen you in the light," I said.

This must have been funny to an Englishman, for he brought up a knee and rolled his backside against the wall and bent and brought the laugh deep from his stomach.

"Hush, Richard!" breathed Morfydd. "You will have my father out here!"

This straightened him, his hand to his mouth. Gasping, he said, "My! This is a cool little customer. Are they all like this in your house?"

"My dada is cooler," I said sharp. "And I am not a bloody customer!"

But this only put him into stitches again.

"Iestyn!" snapped Morfydd. "Please do not be rude! Mr Bennet is only trying to be friends."

"Then let him try it on Dada and see where he lands."

"Great Heaven! He's a little spitfire, isn't he? Do they come any bigger?" I heard him say as I rushed past them to the gate.

"Do not mind him, Richard," said Morfydd with hate in her voice. "Only a kid he is, and jealous—do not mind him."

At the gate I fought back the flood of tears that threatened me. I knew I had lost her. No fear of her going to Dafydd, but I knew she would leave me for this one. He would take her away and put her to the tub, and his vests and shirts would be on her line, and there would be no sound of her in our house, no place laid at table. Many men had owned Morfydd, I had heard say, but this one would take her. And then I remembered Dafydd Phillips, and to this day I do not know why I called, "Morfydd!"

Arm in arm with him at the back door, she turned, came back, and stooped. "Finished I am with you, Iestyn! Do you hear me? Finished! Swearing at Mr Bennet!"

"Do not take him in there," I said, looking away.

"*Duw Duw!* Head of the house as well now, is it?"

"Do not go in," I repeated. "Dafydd Phillips is in there, by special invitation from Dada."

"Dafydd Phillips?" The chap had been dead twelve

44

months the way she said it. Then she folded her arms and tapped her foot and made no eyes to speak of. "There is a damned cheek!" she said. "And what has he come for?"

"To ask for a girl in marriage, but no chance this side of heaven with the flies buzzing round her like a jam pot."

"Whee!" She put her hand to her face. "That was nearly a step in the wrong direction."

"Aye," I said. "No good at making speeches, is Dafydd, but by the look of his nose he would stuff this new one up the chimney."

"I do not think so," she replied. "But it was kind of you to warn me, Iestyn." She bent, kissing the air with her lips. "There is friends we are again, boy. I will send Richard away. Will you come in with me, my lovely?"

You can hate people one moment and die for them the next.

I turned my head when she kissed him. But even as she reached for the door he was standing there as if she had taken his legs with her.

"Away!" I said as I passed him. "Not a chance in a hundred, man. There has been a couple of thousand here before you."

This set him off again, double bass. Morfydd waited until he had vaulted the wall before she opened the door. I saw my father's quick frown, Mam's anxious look and the radiance of Dafydd's smile as we entered.

"What have you been doing the pair of you?" asked my father. "Eating the groceries?"

"No," I replied. "That excited she is. She has been curling and combing and making herself tidy for Dafydd Phillips."

After cleaning Dafydd down and swabbing up the pool, Mam took Jethro to bed for punishment, leaving my father to carry on the conversation. Edwina was sitting in her corner reading the Bible, as usual, so I helped Morfydd lay the table.

I was sorry for Dafydd sitting there in soaked misery; hanging on to Morfydd's every word as she cut the bread, but wild horses would not have dragged from him a word of complaint as his mother did all the talking.

"There is pretty you look tonight, Morfydd," she said. "And very handy about the house, too, I am sure."

"But politics will be her downfall," said Dada.

"Love her, Mr Mortymer, there is none of us perfect, and even Dafydd has his faults. Three times to worship every Sunday—Church of England, see, to follow his English father, God rest him. Saw you at Chapel Easter Sunday, Morfydd—remember?"

"Yes, Mrs Phillips, but I have not been there since."

"There's bad! A wife should be humble on her knees before the Lord before she can hope to be obedient to a husband, eh, Mr Mortymer?"

My father smiled. "Obedience and religion are not Morfydd's virtues, I fear, but she is good at public speaking."

"No path to heaven that, though. The soul of woman is black with sin from birth, and only regular Chapel can save it from the everlasting fire."

Dada said, "That is open to argument, Mrs Phillips, for I have known deacons who were criminals and drunkards who were saints. Have you strong views on these things, Dafydd?"

"It is a person's beliefs, sir," said he with deep humility.

"And yours, Morfydd?" asked his mother thinly.

Morfydd was still cutting the bread. She raised her dark eyes, shook her head, and went on cutting.

"Come, Morfydd, you must have views, girl."

"Aye," whispered Morfydd, "but not for airing."

Dafydd shifted his feet, sweating. "Leave it, Mam," he said. "It is not important."

"Come, come," said his mother. "We have a right to know the family we are marrying into."

I looked at my father. His long legs were thrust out. Puffing at his pipe he was staring at the ceiling with his shoulders hunched, a man awaiting an explosion. Morfydd pushed away the bread and put the point of the knife into the board.

"First prove that there is a God by example, Mrs Phillips," she said, "and then I will pray to Him, for there is little enough

46

example given by Chapel botherers, and some wailing in church who would be better lifting elbows in the Drum and Monkey. . . ."

"Steady, Morfydd," said my father, and I saw Dafydd close his eyes in agony.

"And another thing, Mrs Phillips," went on Morfydd. "There are a few things that need putting right with churches and chapels to my mind. So let us all pray the way we like and behave the best we can, and if the God you worship is as good as you say we will all land in the same place. Away, Iestyn. How the hell can we have supper without cups?"

"Well!" said Mrs Phillips, her jaw dropping.

"Aye," said Morfydd. "And knives, too. Are we going to tear it?"

"Things are becoming clear at last," said Mrs Phillips. "Then you do not believe in God, woman?"

"Mam," begged Dafydd, "it do not matter."

"Do it not? Would you marry into a godless house, boy?"

"Mind your words, Mrs Phillips." Morfydd levelled the knife. "There is one behind you into her Bible and another upstairs the most God-fearing woman in town, to say nothing of deacons and pew collectors, so do not be too sharp."

"But you do not believe—answer me!"

Morfydd did not move. Her eyes were narrowed and glittering and her hatred of hypocrites was filling the room. "You will not trap me into rejecting the One I fear, in case He do hear me, Mrs Phillips. The views I hold upon religion are mine but I do not fling them over town three times on Sunday and bury them the rest of the week." She came closer. "If there is a God on these mountains then He must be sleeping. Six years I have worked under the Coity, and there is no sign of Him there. No sign that He looks into pits where children fall under trams or sees a girl of nine caught by liquid iron. God is all right in the sun for the likes of you, Mrs Phillips, for you have never been six inches underground or within a yard of a furnace. And while the masters sing their prayers for higher profits in the place you call God's house, you will never find me with them except for weddings and christenings, and

47

the last christening was Easter Sunday," and she picked up the knife and went at the bread as if she had an ironmaster roped to the table.

Mrs Phillips was already on her feet, tightening her bonnet streamers. "Come, Dafydd, I have heard enough," said she, trembling. "There are enough God-fearing young women in town without seeking out pagans!" On with her gloves now, stretching every finger, fussy little swings of her hips, her mouth a button seeking words she could not find. Then, "And you, Mr Mortymer—you tolerate such views in your house, and you a deacon?"

My father rose. "I have cared for her body until now and my wife has taken her soul to Chapel, Mrs Phillips. Morfydd is eighteen now. Better to let your boy see her in this light; that is why I sat quiet."

"Pleasant to have met you, I am sure," said she. "Say your piece, Dafydd, and show me to the door."

He had been stretched on the rack of words, allowed no questions, no replies. Head and shoulders above the skinny woman before him he looked at Morfydd with the look I have seen in the eyes of a sheep nailed to the board, awaiting the knife. At the door my father gripped his shoulder and turned him.

"Better this way, Dafydd," he said. "If they had agreed on religion it would have come to murder when they got to politics. Do not lose sleep on it, boy."

My mother came down from Jethro a moment after they were gone.

"Away so soon?" she asked, surprised.

"Aye," replied my father. "Congratulations for working it so well, you are sharper than I give you credit for."

"And not even a bite of supper for them?"

"The truth cooled her," whispered Morfydd, staring at the table. "And good riddance. I would not have that for a mother-in-law if it was the last one living."

"Oi, oi!" exclaimed Mam as she sat down to table. "Religion, was it? They come in their droves, Hywel, but we will be searching the mountains for a savage before we wed this one."

"It was cruel, cruel!" whispered Edwina, clutching her Bible, and I saw her eyes bright with brimming tears.

This put a silence on the meal for Edwina never had views on anything.

Nobody was happy that night. Everybody, including Morfydd, I think, had Dafydd in mind.

Later I remembered that it was the meeting of the Benefit Club. I had fourpence in my pocket and another ninepence under the bed saved for Christmas. Nothing like banners and singing to take away bad spirits, the Benefit says.

Away out of this, I thought. Away up the mountain for a walk in the frost and a quart of beer with Mo Jenkins, me.

# CHAPTER FIVE

A NEW summer swept over the mountains bright and hot. Dandelions and meadowsweet grew in clusters along the banks of the Afon-Lwydd, where the last speckled trout fought a passage through the pollution of the industries, and the fields were yellow with celandine and buttercups.

Moesen and I, firm friends now, did well that year. Apples had been taken from Coed Eithin Farm in daylight, for Grandfer Trevor Lloyd was as weak in the eyes as a bat in sunlight. Honey had been lifted from Will Tafarn's hives and trout tickled from the Usk under the nose of the bailiff. All these things were sold at cut price for everybody was saving for the annual outing to Newport, and it was only fair that the tight-fisted ones should pay their share towards treating the poor. Little Willie Gwallter, for example; he had a new suit especially for the occasion, bought by Tomos Traherne, the preacher, out of subscriptions, and his father walked him three times round town so nobody would miss seeing him, although you could not see Willie for suit until he raised his cap.

Other important things happened that summer. The masters raised their prices at the Company Shop and dropped wages all round, several more cottages were built in North Street where people were living seventeen to a room, cholera broke out at Risca, and Mr Snell, the English seller of coloured Bibles, began to court Edwina.

A little crow of a man this, thirty if he was a day, with a wig to cover his baldness; a red nose that curved down, a red chin that curved up, with a little hole for a mouth in between, and every inch of his five feet two in the service of his Maker. He was a wandering preacher collecting for the poor, but I had heard my father wonder how much of it the poor received. Most respectable, was Snell, and learned, with fasting on fast days and fish on Fridays and God Save William the Fourth.

"Eggs you will be having with that in bed beside you," said Morfydd. "*Diawl*, Edwina! Get a fat little hen from Shams-y-Coed's and you will make your fortune with poultry. Surely it is a husband you are wanting, not a bantam cock?"

Sitting in my father's fireside chair with my eyes closed I breathed noisily, my ears shivering.

"No body to him, I know," replied Edwina, "but he has goodness and faith. Brainy, too, mind, and a scholar."

"Aye?" answered Morfydd. "I would rather have stupidity if it kept me warm in bed, for brains can be damned freezing things. Not that I can read much myself, but I could not stomach a Lesson for breakfast and supper, and that is what you will have from Snell."

"You are hard on him," came the gentle reply. "It is not every day of the week that a girl is followed by a gentleman out of Eton."

This even opened one of my eyes.

"What is that?" asked Morfydd.

"A place where they learn to read and write and speak languages."

"A school, is it?"

"A school where hundreds of men live together and they won the battle of Waterloo. On the playing-fields, at that."

"Be damned," said Morfydd. "It was fought in France and Grandfer Shams-y-Coed ran the cannon balls down the Blorenge Incline for it. Spinning you a fine old tale is Snell."

"Fought on playing-fields," said Edwina, "so do not believe all they tell you."

"Good God," said Morfydd.

"And very good friends with the Duke of Wellington, too, so kindly give him a little more respect when next you see him."

Which shows what you can learn when you pretend to be sleeping. Very interested in history I was at this time, and

51

pleasant to have this fact straightened out at last, for the English were a mile in front of the Welsh when it came to education.

What with battles and Etons, Edwina was getting in a bad way over Mr Snell. She got up now, sighed and ran her hands over her slim body. A fine figure had Edwina, smaller around the waist in inches than my father was around the neck, but good over the shoulders, and the summer dresses she wore were stretched tightly across the tips of her breasts. Now she stood before the looking glass, smiling and combing and tying coloured ribbons in her hair.

"Educated or not," said Morfydd, "by the time he was plucked he would not make a Christmas dinner. You will sleep with him one day, remember. Eton or not, a husband expects more from a wife than cooking and cleaning."

"Whee, there is terrible!" said Edwina, and she turned and squeezed herself like a tap-room barmaid. "And you not married, either! How do you know what a husband expects?"

"Oi, oi," whispered Morfydd. "It is amazing what some girls know, even if they have not been to an altar, but do not get me on my favourite subject or I will talk all night."

I risked a peep at her. She was lying back in her chair, her eyes half closed, her breast high and full, her expression, brilliant with memories, changing from amazement to pain as she sighed and stretched herself in long, feline grace. She looked as Delilah must have done on the night the roof came down.

"*Whisht!* It is wonderful," she breathed.

"What is wonderful?" asked Edwina sharp.

"Never you mind," said Morfydd, pulling her skirts down. "Yes now, this business of husbands. It is experience you are wanting, Edwina. You cannot go rushing into marriage without a walk or two up the mountain to get the lie of the land, for do not think men like Snell are backward; he may be a rough old lad in a bed. Remember that boy from Gilwern?"

"Lemuel Walters?"

52

"Aye, Lemuel. He was the same as you. Shy and nervous he was, as jumpy as a grasshopper, but he was a different chap after I had sat him on the mountain for a couple of Sundays running, and now he is a terror."

"And Willie Bargoed. Him too?"

"Do not talk to me about Willie Bargoed!" This sat Morfydd up. "Very innocent looked Willie when I took him up for lessons, but he had the skirt from me in under a minute, and . . ."

I was breathing so hard that I nearly dropped off.

Squinting from under my eyelashes I saw Morfydd's eyes full on my face.

"Asleep, he is," whispered Edwina. "Dead to the world. O, tell me more, Morfydd, for Mr Snell will be having me in the marriage bed any time between now and a year last Sunday."

"Not if Dada has a say in it. *Diawch!* If that thing over there is asleep, then I am twice buried. Both ears flapping from the moment we came in." She caught me by the ankles and heaved me to the floor. "Out of that chair and lay the table quick, and a word to anyone of what you have heard and I will damned fry you!"

"I have as much right to know things as Edwina," I said.

She hit me sideways. "*Duw!* Hark at the innocent! With the company you have been keeping lately you could teach me a thing or two. Who was walking round the Tumble last Sunday with Polly Morgan Drum and Monkey?"

"She is not my girl," I said, hot.

"Pleased I am to hear it, and the moment she is I will be on her doorstep, for this is a respectable house. Keep clear of that one—leave her to Mo Jenkins, for the pair of them come from gutters, and mud always sticks."

"Hush!" warned Edwina. "Mam is coming!"

As I laid the table I thought about Polly Morgan.

Pretty was Polly, thirteen years old, with a figure that turned the eyes of grown men, let alone boys like Mo and me. Her dark hair hung in plaits to her shoulders; she had a fussy little swing to her hips when she walked, a neat little waist, and enough for a grown woman above it, and her lips were high-curved red and half open, as if in the hope of a kiss. Polly had been on my pillow since the night I went to buy whisky for medicine purposes, though Mam drank most of it in tea.

"Good evening, Iestyn Mortymer," said Polly. "There is a stranger," and she leaned her elbows on the bar counter and hunched her shoulders, bringing the shadows deep in her breast.

"Good evening," I said. "Two pennyworth of whisky for medicine purposes, please," and I pushed the bottle towards her.

"Who for?" she asked.

"For my father," I said.

And then she smiled. "Do not come that old tale, boyo. Drink will be the end of you—sinking quarts down at the Benefit, is it? Next you will be sleeping with Wicked Gwennie Lewis, who is not half so wicked as me."

There is forward for a bare thirteen.

"Two penn'orth of whisky," I said. "And a little less old tongue with it, please."

"Phew!" said she. "Independent, eh? But a pretty boy you are, Iestyn Mortymer, so you are forgiven. For some time now I have had my eye on you, so if you fancy ten minutes in a haystack a handful of gravel at my window will always bring me out, never mind the neighbours."

"According to the deacons you are a harlot, Polly Morgan," I said, "and doomed to everlasting fire, so give me the whisky and I will get from here."

"Aye," said she, drawing it and winking over her shoulder. "Fry, I will, so I am making the best of things before I blister. Very disappointing, you are, Iestyn. Many men would pay a sovereign for me, but for you I would be wicked free, and do not look so saintly."

"I am too young for women," I replied, sweating, and reached for the bottle. But she caught my fingers, and the touch of her hand, so smooth and strong, was like a burn.

"Blessed are the fornicators," she whispered, "for the others do not know what they are missing. Nobody would be the wiser, see? Round the Tumble at eight o'clock next Sunday night and grow up two years older?"

"I will not be there," I said shivering.

"If you are not you will be the first to stay away," and she leaned over the bar and kissed my lips.

So Polly Morgan was on my pillow and it took six weeks to get her off.

Clutching the whisky I ran home, cursing her, and that night I went with Edwina to a Reading to cleanse my soul. But the next Sunday I was walking round the Tumble above Garndyrus and came across her lying in a sheltered place with her skirts above her knees and showing her red garters.

"Good evening," said she, sitting up. "For one who is not here you are pretty well on time. Up a dando!" And she kicked up her legs and got to her feet. "Lead the way, Iestyn Mortymer, for there is not enough quiet here for girls as wicked as me."

"You first," I said, every nerve trembling. And away she went along the tram road, swaying at the hips and smiling over her shoulder.

What is it that flashes into a man so that the swish of skirts is music and half an inch of petticoat makes his head spin? Before me were the high-buttoned boots, the skirt, then the waist swelling to shoulders where the black plaits bobbed, and the fragrance of her drifted into my face. There is a fragrance about women that does not come from bottles. My mother smells of lavender from the little bags she stores with her aprons; Morfydd smells of thyme she gathers for the meat, and Edwina of cowslips she puts into her hair. Polly Morgan smelled of heather that Sunday, which is a smell of wildness and freedom; as if she had made her bed in it and bathed herself in mountain springs and pinned wild herbs on her petticoats. The path was lonely and pure with sunlight. Above us reared the mountain with its gorse fanning live in the wind and below us the valley of the Usk lay misted and golden at the foot of Pen-y-fal. On we went until we reached an opening in the rock face. Taking my hand she drew me within it, swung wide her skirt and lay down on the high grass. Quite still she lay, eyes closed, waiting.

"Down by here," she said, patting the grass, eyes still closed, and I obeyed, sitting cross-legged, wondering what to do.

"Well," she said at length. "Unless somebody starts something wicked soon I am off from here to find somebody who will." But still I sat.

"O, Iestyn," she whispered, and rolled towards me, reaching out, her lips pouted for kissing.

And then it happened. The water came down first and then the bucket and we were swamped in rivers that ran down our necks and sent us gasping, soaking us both head to foot. Furious, I struggled to my feet. Mo Jenkins was lying on the rocks above us, grinning.

"Quite still!" he called, and down came a bucket that bowled me over and sent Polly scampering and cursing to tarnish altars.

"And I come next," said Mo, leaping from rock to rock like a deer. "Very kind of you, Iestyn, to get across my girl, so now I will smash your face in, and Polly goes home without trews."

Very fast I went along that tram road, for Mo had long since outstripped me in strength and size, and the last I heard of Polly Morgan was her trews pinned to the signpost of the Drum and Monkey.

"*Polly-Without-Trews?*" whispered Edwina now.

"Aye," said Morfydd in disdain. "Pinned to the Drum and Monkey with *Iestyn Mortymer* chalked underneath, and it took me a ladder to rub it out."

I was hot enough to catch fire, believing the secret firm.

"There is a scandal!" breathed Edwina. "What if Dada finds out?"

"He will find out soon enough if anyone breathes a word of

what he has heard in here," said Morfydd. "Sharp with that table, Iestyn, and do not forget to offer to wash up after."

I was half way through laying the table when my mother, father, Jethro and Tomos Traherne came in.

"No table ready?" asked Mam, her eyebrows up. "No beef cut, no butter? One would think we were in debt at The Shop, and us with a visitor to talk about the outing."

And in he came.

A man and a half was Tomos Traherne; black-bearded and grizzled in the cheeks where years of coal had cut their pattern. He dwarfed my father in size and the town by the ferocity of his faith. Powerful upon a hassock he did good work in the name of the Lord, but on his feet he was the most dangerous man in town, where his thunder boomed over the valleys in pursuit of urchins, harlots and ironmasters. Like the martyrs of old, he had suffered, and wrote religious pamphlets since the night Will Blaenavon parted his hair with a quart bottle and threw him out of the Lamb Row public and his pamphlets after him.

"Sit you down, Tomos," said my mother, and he threw his coat tails before him and eased his great shining backside into the best chair. Perched there, his little black eyes swept the room above his steel-rimmed spectacles.

"Where is Edwina?"

"I am here, sir," said she, stepping into the lamplight.

"Happy art thou in the service of the Lord, child?"

"Happy indeed, sir."

"Right, you! Judges eighteen, verse two. Recite!" Squinting down, he began to fill his clay.

"In those days there was no king . . ." began Edwina.

"Eh? What is this?" He stared at her and smoothed his stomach with great, ponderous hands. "Think, child, think! 'And the children of Dan sent of their family. . . .'"

"'. . . five men of their coasts,'" chanted Edwina, "'men of valour, from Zorah, and from Eshtaol, to spy out the land, and to search it; and they said unto them, Go search the land:

who, when they came to mount Ephraim, to the house of Micah, they lodged there.'"

"Good God," said Morfydd.

"Amen," boomed Tomos. "Excellent, excellent!" And he brought out his little black book and put her name down.

"Do not spoil it by examining the other two," said Mam, coming in. "One is a pagan and the other is following her example, from what I hear lately." She looked at me and my heart stopped beating.

"Stay for a bite of supper, Tomos?"

"Just had my supper I have at Mrs Evan's, God bless her."

"But stay for another, for you are welcome," said my father at the door. "We have slices of good roast pork and beef needing a home, Tomos."

But his hand was up and Tomos shook his head. "Everything in moderation, Hywel. As you know, I am not a man of gluttony, which, according to the Book, is one of the sins cardinal."

And him with belly enough for six suppers.

"O, stay!" whispered Edwina from her corner.

"For you, my child, yes," said Tomos, relieved. "Lay another place at table, Mrs Mortymer, and I will do your cooking justice if only to please the children." His little eyes switched to me as I sidled up with his knife and fork.

"Aha! Iestyn!" And I was lifted bodily and put upon his knee. I heard Morfydd's giggle, and hated her, for if there is anything indecent in this world it is one man sitting on the knee of another.

"One question well answered and your name is down for the outing," he said. "Bear ye one another's burdens . . ."

"And so fulfil the law of Christ," I said, scrambling away.

"There is a surprise," said Dada. "We will have a monk in the house before we are finished."

"And Morfydd?" asked Tomos. "What will Morfydd answer?"

"Good on the Ten Commandments, mind," said Edwina warmly.

"Right, then. One of them from you, Morfydd, which is asking little enough considering you are the eldest."

"Thou shalt not commit adultery, Tomos."

"Amen," said Tomos without a blink. "But another would have been more appropriate in a house mothered by such virtue."

"You can have the ten," said she with a sniff, "but I am not bothered if I go on the outing or not. I have plenty to occupy my time."

"So I hear, child. But you will go if only to keep you from wickedness."

"Well," began my father, clapping his hands, "in with the meat, Elianor, for the righteous need feeding as well as the unbelievers, and Tomos looks starved. Will you sing and play for us, girl, while we eat?"

Sweet was my mother's voice that night. The lamplight shimmered on the strings of the harp as they vibrated under her fingers.

Plates pushed away, we listened, for it was not possible to eat when my mother made her music. O, beautiful is the harp and a woman's voice singing with the wind sighing in the eaves and hammering in the chimney! Morfydd was motionless, her eyes lowered. Edwina took Jethro upon her knee. My father was in a holy silence, and Tomos, face turned up, was plucking deep in his beard. And when the song was ended I saw tears in my father's eyes.

"A beautiful song, Elianor," he said deeply. "There is a woman for you, good in cooking, milk and music. Search the mountains for a voice so pure and the world for such goodness."

"Amen," said Tomos, going at his beef.

"O, get on, get on, Hywel!" cried Mam, scarlet now.

"A candidate for the contralto competition, think you?" asked my father. "Charlotte Guest is giving a golden purse next Eisteddfod at Abergavenny, and we could do with the money."

"With you collecting the bass oratorio and Owen Howells winning the tenor, aye, it would be fine to win the contralto purse as well," said Tomos. "Yes, I will have her entered."

"You dare!" said Mam. "My singing is confined to the house. I am not making a public exhibition of myself like Mrs Gwallter and others I could mention."

"Whee!" exclaimed Morfydd. "Flat at the top and sharp at the bottom, and better noises do come from Irish bagpipes."

"The Book is open," said Tomos. "Please do not slander Mrs Gwallter or any other neighbour, Morfydd. Quiet now, all of us, and let me call upon this house of love the blessing of the Almighty God who fashioned it and sustains it in peace and joy. A prayer of thanks to Him, then, each in his own way," said Tomos, "for the brave people of this town, and this house in the Square."

And Morfydd reached out and gripped my hand under the table.

But I washed the dishes just the same and was there with the rag long after the house was quiet.

I was surprised when my father came down into the kitchen and helped me finish them. His eyes were smiling as he said:

"Iestyn, it is a father's duty to talk to his son about women. Earlier today I had decided to ask Tomos to do it for me, but since the Drum and Monkey is involved in this discussion, I think it had better be done by me, for he might be too hard on you. Do you understand?"

Floors swallow people in books. In life they stay solid. I stood before him with the shame flooding to my face and the sweat breaking out in every pore. He put his hand upon my shoulder and gently pushed me into a chair.

"It is not too bad," he said, grinning. "More than one I ran down a tram road before I was your age, but I was careful to make sure it did not get round town. But now to the point—do you remember I raised this subject on your first day at work?"

"Yes, Dada," I said, my eyes down.

"Face me, Iestyn. Do not make it hard. What do you know of these things?"

60

"Not much," I replied.

"Why did you run Polly Morgan, for instance?"

"To find out," I said, boiling.

"About women? Surely you know much already. Have you never seen Morfydd or Edwina unclothed?"

"Morfydd once, when she was not looking," I said.

"And seen that she has breasts, like Mam, where she will one day feed her children?"

"Yes," I replied.

"And that she is rounder in the hips and a very different shape to us in front?"

"Yes," I said.

"Listen," he said, "I do not intend to do you drawings. You have noticed, for a start, that women have nothing, yet it is from that part of a woman that her children come, do you understand—that you surely know, Iestyn."

"Aye," I said.

"Why run Polly Morgan, then?"

"Because I wanted proof."

"Good," he said. "Now tell me, boy. Is it not true that from the exact spot where a seed is planted in ground the plant comes forth?"

I nodded after some thought.

"Then so it is with a woman," said he. "The woman is the soil and the man is the planter, and the seed springs to life within her and comes forth as a plant—a child."

"Yes," I said.

"Do you remember your Bible—*In The Beginning. . . .*"

"Yes, Dada."

"For in the beginning God created Adam," my father said, "and gave to him a mate whom He called Eve, and He created Eve from a rib He took from the body of Adam that she should be his companion, friend and lover, as your mother is to me."

I asked, "Was it the same with the Lady of Bethlehem, whose husband was Joseph, and who brought forth the Lord?"

"No, Iestyn. That Lady was entered by the Seed of God,

not of Joseph—something special, it would need, to make the Son of God, you see?"

"Aye," I answered, becoming interested. "And I would have liked to come that way."

"Why?" he asked, eyes narrowed to the lamp.

"Well, it do seem indecent otherwise. I can understand people like Gwennie Lewis and Mrs Pantrych being shameful, but I hate to think of it with Mam."

This put him on his feet again. "Listen, Iestyn. One day you will know that nothing done by a man and woman married is shameful, if it is done with love. For if our mating is devised by God how can it be indecent? To run a woman for peeps as you ran Polly Morgan is indecent. And to take a woman to bed and divide her body for the seed is a thing commended by God, if done in marriage. But if it is done after drink, say—up on the mountain or round the Tumble with looks over the shoulder, and with a single girl or another man's wife, then it is a disgrace, and God will turn His face from you, and so will I."

"Yes, Dada."

"And the child of such a mating will be damned. Now one more thing before we finish, boy, and then to bed. Is Edwina, who is older than you, as strong?"

"No."

"Right, then. It is to us that God has given the greater strength—to support and uphold women, who are weak. Who, then, made Gwennie Lewis wicked?"

"Men," I said.

He sighed deep. "At last we are learning. And who is making Polly Morgan wicked these days?"

"Mo Jenkins."

He drew himself up. "And how do you stand in the judgment?"

I flicked my eyes to his face and lowered them.

"Good," said he. "Remember, Iestyn, all women are pure until defiled by men of wickedness. So give respect to women, boy, for their bodies belong to the Lord, and are precious to Him as the bodies of Morfydd and Edwina are precious to me. So let us hear no more talk of Polly Morgan Drum and Monkey or hell will come loose in the house."

He got up and ran his fingers through his hair. "A good boy you are for listening, Iestyn. I am going under the table tonight. Away next door to Mam. She is waiting for you."

"To sleep with her?"

"Aye." He sighed. "That is her sole contribution to this conversation."

"Dando!" I said. "Goodnight, Dada."

My mother was waiting with the Cyfarthfa blanket well back.

"Dada told me to come," I whispered, throwing off my clothes.

"Did you understand what he told you?"

"Aye, but I knew most of it before. Over a bit so I can get in."

"No shirt?" said she. "There is indecent. Never mind, it is only your old Mam."

Her arms went about me and she sighed deep in her throat.

# CHAPTER SIX

SINCE THE age of six, when I was old enough to go on the annual outing, something always happened to stop me: spots, fevers, threats of the cholera in one shape or another, which made me unpopular with Morfydd who had to stay home to nurse me.

But nothing happened to stop me in the June I was thirteen.

On the great morning everybody gathered at the top of Turnpike and walked down to the inn. The Garndyrus Benefit band was there; furnace-men, colliers, quarrymen and limestone carriers in Sunday suits with their wives and children adorned in best dresses and lace, even if it meant going twice into debt at the Shop. Outside the inn Billy Handy Landlord was rolling out the beer, barrels for the men, bottles for the women and small beer for the children, and Rhys Jenkins and a few other roughs were rolling on their feet before we had moved off.

"Into the trams!" bellowed Tomos Traherne, who had been in charge of annual outings for the past ten years, and I took my family to the road.

"Lead the way, Iestyn," said my father, "for I would rather trust the women to you than those pair of hot-heads the Howells," and my heart nearly burst with pride as I handed my mother and sisters in while my father, Bennet and Snell climbed up in front. Elot, my new tram-mare, was a little delicate with the wind that morning for Mo Jenkins had mixed sulphur with her oats, so I tethered her behind the tram and away we went, spragging down the line, making a rare speed while my father roared encouragement and the women screamed.

"Faster, boy, faster!" shouted Richard.

"O, Hywel!" screamed Mam, "for God's sake stop him!"

"Iestyn, do not be a damned maniac!" shouted Morfydd, clutching at her bonnet, and Edwina used the chance to faint away into Snell's arms. On, on, rumbling and swaying down the Govilon Incline we went like demons until we came to the cable-engine.

"O, heavens!" whispered Mam, patting herself. "There is a madman. In several pieces I am. Hywel, hand me down from this contraption."

Mr Gwallter and Dic Shon Ffyrnig were the cable-men that morning, and they turned our tram and shackled it up and we sailed down the Blorenge bowl, pulling an empty tram up. Down to the Llanfoist Wharf we went, where a gang of broody Irish were waiting by a string of barges, and into them we went as excited as little children. The band came down next, with the beer and food after them, and Will Blaenavon and Rhys and Mo began to load it aboard while the children garlanded the barges and horses with summer flowers. Tomos Traherne climbed on to the prow of our barge and lectured us on how to behave in Newport; urging us to keep away from the gin-shops and beer-houses, which, he said, were the scourge of a decent community, and a special warning to the pugilists about hitting out Redcoats all the time Irishmen were plentiful. Then he read out the addresses of the chapels and churches and begged everybody to attend the singing competition to be held in the public hall, and God help anybody not in a fit state to leave Newport Docks by eight o'clock. Prayers, then, and thanks to the ironmaster who had given a sovereign or two to make all this possible, and Tomos blew on a horn. The horses were whipped up and away down the canal we went with our barge leading.

Wonderful to be moving on water. The silky movement is a drug to the senses when you are lying along the prow of a barge watching the water-lilies and bindweed waving. Soon Pen-y-fal and the Skirrids were well behind us, and the sun, streaming down through the avenue of trees, cast golden patterns on the barges. On, through the drain locks, into the drone of bees and the skimming dragonflies. There is peace for you, lying half asleep after being up since

65

midnight, quivering with the dreams of the happiness to come.

And it came sooner than a soul expected.

*"Diawl!"* whispered my father. "There is an anxious lot!"

"Trouble, by the look of it," said Richard, getting on to his haunches. "Now whose idea was it for the Mortymers to travel in front?"

"Whee!" whispered Morfydd, staring ahead. "Trust Iestyn to mess up anything he organises."

"Spread your stays, Elianor," said Dada. "Trouble is upon us."

"Calm, everybody!" shouted Tomos Traherne from the next barge down. "It is the worthless sent by the devil to provoke us to violence, but we will receive it with dignity. Calm."

"To hell with that," said Richard. "I am receiving no turnips with dignity for I have stopped too many in Covent Garden," and he reached into Mam's basket and brought out a tomato.

"O, Richard, do not provoke them," said Mam while Morfydd was giggling herself double. "Do not provoke them, but do as Tomos says, boy."

Fifty yards ahead the arched bridge was crowded to the footwalks with more Irish than in Dublin, all chattering like monkeys and making rude signs and stacking the parapet with everything man has been able to throw since the creation. Nearer we came, our old horse plodding to a carrot one of them was holding. Louder and louder came the chatter from the bridge and higher went their piles of vegetables, and three little boys were lifted on to the parapet and stood there like sentinels of fate, undoing the buttons of their trews to give us a dousing.

"Good God!" said Morfydd, "here is a cloudburst coming," and she opened her parasol while Mam fought for room under it. Helpless, every one of us, for so grave and determined those little boys stood, holding them up and waiting for the right moment. My father was pressing his sides and

66

rolling with laughter and my tears were blinding me at the sight of Edwina's face and old Snell comforting her.

"Leave them to me!" shouted Snell suddenly, getting on his feet. "There is goodness even in Irish and I am used to handling violence," and he flung his arms wide and appealed to their better natures. But Will Blaenavon was more practical.

"Do not distress yourselves, my little ones," said he, jumping from the prow of the next barge down with his arms full of turnips, "for the committee of the annual outing has provided for all possibilities. Six each, and throw to kill, mind," and he poured them into our laps. "And lend me your knife, Iestyn. I am having those little pinkles on a pin for trout fishing if I die threading them."

"O, Will!" giggled Mam, shaking and streaming tears.

Our barge was rocking with laughter until the Irish let fly, and the first swede dropped took Snell in the chest and bowled him in head first while Edwina screamed and held on to his ankles.

"*Diawch!* There was a shot for you," said Dada. "Iestyn, Richard—up by here with you and let us get organised. Napoleon is finished, but we are still good for others," and we scrambled up beside him in a hail of rotten cabbages and stood over Morfydd's parasol and let go with our turnips. Everybody on the following barges was at battle stations now, and parties had landed ashore bringing armfuls of root crops from poor Grandfer Shams-y-Coed's fields. Hunting horns were shrieking, whistles blowing the alarm and the band had its head well down into its collar, playing *Welsh Heroes* fit to stir Owen Glyndwr from his ashes.

Ten yards from the bridge and the Irish opened fire in earnest, shouting every war cry between Dublin and Belfast, and as we drifted under the bridge the little boys let it go. We took it point blank. Buckets came from that parapet. And there was just time to take a breath before we got it from three more little boys standing on the other side. The Irish were here in strength, crowding the towpath, and with two of them feeding our barge-horse we seemed likely to stay for hours. The Irish confetti rained down, with Irishmen stripping half an acre of field and starting on another. Besides, the law of gravity was a taking a hand, and if the field lasted much longer they seemed sure to sink us.

"A landing-party!" shouted my father. "Follow me every man who can stand!" and he leaped ashore blowing shrill notes with his fingers. Crowds followed him, Richard and I leading. Up the towpath we went, opening our shoulders at anything in sight. The Irish flew up the bridge and we stormed after them with Owen Howells and Griff supporting the charge with the big bass drum and blasts on the trombone. Good parents are the Irish. They packed their brats on the hump and fought like cats, but as we closed the range they wilted and broke. Up the mountain they streamed with the Welsh after them, running hand in hand with little Irish toddlers.

Laughing, triumphant, we came back to the barges. Mam and Morfydd were still sitting under their ragged parasol. Edwina had got Snell from the water and was dabbing at him with a little lace handkerchief. We got the barges lined up again and threw out the vegetables, washed in the canal and whipped up the horses. The sun streamed down, the air was sweet with smells of summer. Out came the beer, the home-baked loaves, cheeses and the women's parsnip wine, and we drank and feasted our way to Newport under the alders, singing and whooping every yard of the way. Good neighbours are the Irish in many respects, I say. There is nothing like a good fight to give a start to the day.

Viking and Dane, Roman and Spaniard have thundered into Newport with sunlight gleaming on spur and mace, for Cardiff is a farming town and never worth its capture. Chained slaves have toiled in the galleys of conquering fleets that came with bloody pennants from the Channel to the North Sea to rape the women and slaughter the men, but the lot bundled together never caused the stir in this fussy little seaport as we mountain ironworkers sailing in by barge for our annual outing. Twenty-two barges, every one decked from prow to stern with ribbons and wild flowers; a brass band letting fly and the banners of the illegal Benefit Clubs waving in the faces of scowling Redcoats. Past moored ships we went; barques from the West Indies with their smells of Eastern spices; alongside white-sailed schooners with prows of sweeping dignity to the tumbledown poverty of the waterfront and the crowded jetties where whole families jostled for position to see us march by. Urchins who had not seen a bath since the midwife danced alongside catching the food we threw; ancient faces peered from little square windows, shouting and laughing, for a town in the clutch of the English is happy at a show of spirit. Groups of Redcoats leaned idly on muskets with watchful, nervous glances at the mad Welsh workers.

There is a place for you, this Newport! London is only half the size, for nobody is fool enough to believe all the English tell you. Great stone buildings dominated by the Westgate, big enough to frighten a countryman to death; broughams, traps, carriages, dog-carts on the streets with fine ladies and gentlemen bowing this way and that and spotted dogs running between the wheels. Dandies by the score, drunkards, men on horseback with a superior air; beautiful girls in hooped dresses walking daintily under frilled parasols, and everybody going about their business with a rush and tear that left me breathless. Richard and Morfydd were first off the barge and were away to visit some of his English friends. Edwina and Snell got into a trap to find the nearest Church of England where he could borrow dry clothes. Mo was ready, his face full of wickedness, and we were off.

Everybody in Wales must have been in Newport that day, for Dock Street was as packed with people as herrings in a barrel. Beggars sat in the gutters and pulled at me for money: men from the French wars, mostly; arms off, legs off, some with their faces shot away. Crippled children sat in the laps of verminous old hags; old men, too tired to die, stooped weakly on sticks. And the streets were filled with vendors and criers, gentry and workers standing shoulder to shoulder. Sailors from the East were there with parrots in cages; mulattos, gipsies and freed slaves from Bristol, as black as watered coal. Bears were being led on chains, carts loaded with merchandise. Fiddles were going, drums being beaten and dogs howling to kicks. The crowd was even thicker in the Fair, the stalls end to end, with people shrieking in foreign tongues, begging us to buy. Wool stalls, flannel stalls from Abergavenny; poultry benches with scraggy necks swinging; stalls where bootmakers were at work, spitting out the nails and hitting them in like lightning. Ostlers were there leading fine Arab stallions splendid with medallions. Here the gentry were buying, their hands heaped with golden sovereigns.

"A penny for anything you like!" cried a voice, and even as I turned Mo tossed her one and she caught it and ran like a hare, shrieking with laughter, without showing an inch of petticoat.

"Damned little bitch," said Mo, blazing.

"Aye, but serve you right," I said. "This is the city and you are caught too easy for my company."

"Come, you," said he. "I will show you things you do not know. Two women in Dock Street who do it with boys half price and I am not paying more than threepence, mind."

"Not me," I said. "I have two shillings to spend and I am taking something back from this fair to remember it, not pox."

"Eight and sixpence!" roared a voice from the crowd, and I shouldered my way through the people to see what was selling.

"Do not go too close or they will have you," said Mo. "I am off after that little bitch to get something for my penny. Hell, I will cross her in daylight."

"Nine shillings," called another.

You can always tell a gentleman by the cut of his coat. This one was tall and lean, with narrow calfskin trews buttoned at the knee and gaiters under, and there was elegance in the spread of his fingers as he helped his fine straight nose to snuff.

"Ten shillings!" This one was beefy, his red face sweating

beer; a farmer by the bulge of his belly and his grin was wide and stained with nicotine.

"Eleven," said the gentleman.

"Eh!" said the farmer. "You have backed the wrong horse this time, my lad, for I am bound to go higher to get what I want for Lancashire. Fifteen shillings, and hand the boy down to me, Mr Poorhouse."

"Fifteen shillings for a boy like this is a scandal!" cried the skinny, mop-headed auctioneer. "With no mother or father to snatch him from your kitchen and half a loaf a day will keep him. Come, twenty!"

"Fifteen," said the north countryman, "and not a penny more." He grinned as the gentleman walked away and slapped his leggings with his whip.

"Dewi Lewis down to Mr Winstanley for fifteen shillings," said the auctioneer, and pushed the boy down the steps. Dressed in the rags of the dock urchins, he stood against the farmer's stomach, his head low, his hair over his face.

"This Lancashire gentleman do beat me," said the auctioneer. "Always gets what he wants."

"Aye, and fifteen shillings to my account, if you please, for I have not stopped buying today."

I watched Pig's eyes as a girl was pushed on to the platform. She was about my age, noble in the face and clean, her ragged dress tight about her waist. Her dark hair she wore over her shoulders like the Irish, her legs and feet were bare.

"Two pounds," said Pig, "and give her here."

The crowd murmured. White-faced women were moving angrily in the crowd. The girl looked down at Dewi Lewis, swept back her hair and joined him by the farmer.

"That will suit me," said Pig. "One for the yard and one for the house," and gripping their shoulders he took them away.

Sickened, I watched the buying. The poor, who had been keeping the poor, sold them. Mothers sold their sons for hire, fathers their daughters, and the orphanage sold its children in droves of ten. Older, I fought my way out of the crowd and came face to face with Mo.

"I got that little bitch," said he, radiant. "I caught her under a cart up by the bull-baiting and tickled her up the drawers before she bit me, look you."

He held up fingers. I turned away.

"What is wrong, man?" he asked, frowning. I jerked my head at the hiring platform.

"Why, that?" He hit me sideways. "You can see that any July at Town Hall Abergavenny—no need to come to Newport."

"What the hell is wrong with you today?" asked Mo.

"Shut your stupid face."

"Come to see the ships, then?"

I slouched through the streets with my hands in my pockets.

"Come and have a grown woman in Dock Street?"

I looked at him, hating the sight of him.

"You are a boot-faced bloody Puritan," said Mo. "Weak in the belly, in tears at the hirings and not enough in your trews for pike-bait."

"I am too young for grown women," I said.

"Right, you. Thirteen, is it? Too young? My grandfather Ben was into his first at eight."

"Aye, and look at him now at eighty."

"Lend me sixpence, then."

"Not if it is for whoring."

"Sixpence more and I can go on the ships."

"Threepence to go on ships—there is the notice."

"Bloody old skinflint."

"But better than a fornicator. So get from here before I drop you, for the sight of you makes me sick."

"Away, me," said Mo. "I will find a man for a friend and go into Dock Street."

"Then go," I said, kicking at a stone.

Disgruntled, unhappy, I went behind the stalls to the entrance of the Westgate Inn, to watch the gentry coming and going. I felt, leaning against the great stone wall, a sudden excitement, a strange presentiment of violence. The square before me was dense with people, a swaying mass with raised fists. The crowd began to chant in Welsh as a trumpet sounded. Hooves clattered on the cobbles. The people, violent with noise and activity, suddenly parted. A troop of fifty Redcoats clattered through them, glorious in pageantry, and marched towards the inn entrance with muskets at the ready. Insults were flung after them in Welsh and English, sticks were raised, but the soldiers marched on steadily with a horseman at their head; men of Brecon Garrison, the thorn in the side of Merthyr and Dowlais. Wheeling to their officer's command, they formed themselves four deep in front of the Westgate, and turning, faced the hostile crowd.

"Trouble in Merthyr again, see?" said a man near me.

"Taking no chances," said another.

"They burned the Court of Requests once and they will burn it again, for Dic Penderyn."

"And blood is running in the gutters. It could be the same here in Newport."

"Aye? It takes men like the Crawshays to bring about a misery like Cyfarthfa, but we would knife their kind in Newport."

"Out of it, you," said a soldier, and gripped me and flung me headlong from the doorway. Tripping, I lost my balance and fell, rolling to the heels of the soldiers with the steps of the inn immediately before me. Hands clenched, I was upon my feet seconds before the gentleman from the hall reached me. He came running, a man of strength by the litheness of his step. He was dressed in black, with buttoned cloth leggings. No dandy, this, for all the lace at his wrists and throat, and his smile was ready and kind as he stood clear while I brushed the dirt from my Sunday suit.

"Are you hurt, lad?"

"No," I said, blazing.

"Good. You were watching the gentry?"

"Aye," I replied. "And no harm in that."

He sighed. "Cats may look at kings, it is said. But the working boy who looks upon gentry without a pull of the forelock can be taken and flung into the gutter, eh?"

73

I looked at him, turned to go, and swung back.

It was his eyes.

Small and keen they were, set close in his strong face; eyes of steel that flickered over me, beautiful one moment, fierce the next. Shining, they penetrated, and held me.

"Where are you from, lad?" The eyes swept quickly around.

"Garndyrus, sir."

"The annual outing?"

"Aye."

"Then you will know a man named Richard Bennet?"

I nodded, wonderingly.

"You could find him now?"

I nodded, staring.

"Then be so good as to find him quickly and give him this." He brought an envelope from his pocket and put it into my hand.

"Who shall I say, sir?"

He smiled. "There is no need for names, lad." He tossed me a sixpence and I caught it and dropped it into my pocket.

"As sharp as you can," said he, "for it is important."

Turning abruptly, he ran up the steps into the Westgate.

I went to find Richard Bennet but found Dafydd Phillips instead; standing outside a beer-house, full to the back teeth by the look of him, and grinning like a dead sheep. I took a chance.

"I am looking for Morfydd," I said, keeping a safe distance. "Have you seen her?"

"Aye," said he, rocking.

"My father wants her quick," I said. "It is a matter of life and death."

"Like Merthyr," said he, very sober. "The Highlanders went mad there. Women and children were shot down, they say. But like the other agitators Mr Richard Bennet is nowhere to be found when John Frost needs him."

"John Frost," I repeated, going cold.

"Aye. Very distinguished you are becoming carrying messages from the leader. And very foolish of him to send his messages with hundreds watching, thank God for him. Come with me."

"Where are you taking me?" I demanded.

"To Bennet. To hell with Morfydd for once."

Elbowing his way through the crowd he took me back the way I had come, past the Westgate where the people were still jeering at the soldiers guarding the entrance, and turned up Stow Hill. Half way up the hill two fat women were fighting in a circle of cheering men, scratching and tearing at each other, their rags hanging down over their waists and their slack breasts swinging. This delayed us. We turned into a side street. Slum alleys here where mangy dogs nosed garbage bins and skinny children raised their heads from doorsteps. Through the alleys we went with Dafydd not giving a backward look, although I kept my distance in case he was up to tricks. And then he stopped.

"The third door from here," he said. "An hour back I followed the pair of them. Bennet's friends, mind, it is all very respectable, so do not be shy." And then he put his hands over his face and sobbed like a baby. "O, holy God!" he said.

"Dafydd, Dafydd," I replied, sick of him, "go back to your beer and forget her for she is mad about him. You are worth something better than old Morfydd."

This got him into his stride again, blowing and bubbling and bringing me from patience, for beer has several ways out of a man and one is through the eyes, says Dada.

I hit his arm. "Come now, do not be soft. Hang about here with Bennet sober and you will have a hammering. Go down to Dock Street with Mo Jenkins and find yourself a sand-rat and you will feel happier in the morning."

This brought him steady and he stared, disbelieving his ears.

"O God," he said, breathing hard. "From the mouth of a child! Should I debase myself with a hired woman? Seven times seven will you burn, Iestyn!" He caught my arms, pulling me closer. "You wanted Bennet. I brought you to him.

75

Speak to her, boy. Look, I beg you. Tell her I will work for her, that I will go blind for her. O, great Jesus, do pity me! Listen!" He shook me to make the sense of it. "Bennet will go from here sharp. Tell her I will wait by Stow Corner to take her to the singing. O, Iestyn, tell her?"

"All double dutch to me," I said. "But I will tell her. Now go from here sharp before that door opens and he flattens the pair of us."

Away he went along that alley beating lightning.

Trembling, I went to the door and fisted it. Footsteps sounded. A shadow fell across the glass. A woman, tall and thin and dressed in widow's weeds, opened it. She had the face of a starved ghost, hair to match and hands for gripping tombstones. But behind her was a little polished hall and table with flowers in shining brass. I took off my cap.

"I am looking for Mr Richard Bennet, who is visiting here," I said.

She smiled then, and there was sweetness in her lined old face. "If you are a friend of Mr Bennet then no need for introductions, young man," said she. "Please bring your lady in."

I gripped my cap, frowning, went in and closed the door behind me. The eyes of the old woman were sightless.

"No lady?" she said. "There is a pity. Never mind. Sit you down and examine the comforts of this place. Mr Bennet is entertaining a woman, but he will be down when he is finished with her. A house for courting this, to be sure, but count upon it that only the respectable are made welcome, so if you bring a lady you can be sure of good clean bundling with tea brought up when you ring for it. Shall I give a name?"

"No name," I said huskily. "But if you will please give Mr Bennet this envelope I will go from here," and I pressed it into her hand.

"Stupid I am," said she, chuckling. "But a boy you are, I hear, and too young for courting. First the eyes go and then the ears. Poor old Olwen. Aye, I will give him the letter. Will you see yourself out?"

"And thanks," I said, shivering. "Good day, ma'am."

76

I went to the door and opened it, but impelled by a greater power than decency I slammed it and stood in the hall, watching her high-buttoned boots climbing the stairs. Then, on tiptoe, I followed her until my eyes were level with the landing. Taking a tray from a table she pushed the bedroom door wide and went within. Trembling, I looked into the room beyond her.

I saw a window with sunlight streaming through it on to the crumpled coverlet of a wide bed. Richard Bennet was sitting on the edge of it, dark-handsome in tight satin trews and his white, lace-hemmed shirt open to the waist. He sprang up to take the tray, and then I saw Morfydd.

She was lying on the bed as bare as an egg, singing and smiling and waving around her head the nightdress Mam had missed the day before yesterday, looking as flushed and happy as a bride of ten minutes and twice as healthy.

"Whee!" she cried in ecstasy, "here is the tea!" And she kicked up her legs at old Blind Olwen who thought she was dressed for bundling.

Away, me. Down those stairs on tiptoe like something scalded, through the door and along the street like a hare. Dafydd Phillips was waiting at Stow Corner and flung out his arms to catch me, but I was through him, down the Hill and between the women who were still fighting in ponderous swings, into the shadows of the silk stalls and the seething, jeering mass of the crowd, in search of a haven of decency.

At four o'clock I went to the public hall. I saw my mother and father pacing about, agitated.

"There is a good one," said Mam, hugging me. "Have you seen Edwina? The singing is soon to begin."

"Gone for dry clothes," I said, "but if I know Snell they are on their knees to bishops."

"Morfydd and Richard?" asked my father.

"Visiting friends, I hear—no sign of them."

"O, damn!" said he. "Here is me practising for the last six months and growing horns and not a daughter to hear me sing Handel."

"A scandal," said Mam, patting him. "Your father all ready to lift the bass cup and half the family absent. I will warm the breeches of the pair of them if they are late. In with you, Hywel boy, and sing despite them, and do not go flat on the lower registers."

Along came Owen Howells, the tenor entry from town, and Griff, his twin brother.

"How are you?" cried Mam. "Very confident you are looking, Owen. All ready, is it?"

"Aye," said Owen, "but not at my best, see?" And neither did he look it, for his new jacket was ripped and his nose was across his face, and Griff was not much prettier. Beggars for bathing their back teeth and fighting were the Howells.

"It is his top set, you understand," explained Griff. "An Irishman caught him with a boot and they slip at the best of times."

A good tenor was Owen, but he had never been the same in the upper registers since Will Blaenavon removed four of his front ones over eighteen rounds last summer, and it is one thing to have a plate made by a London dentist but another to sing in public with one made by Dic Shon Ffyrnig, blacksmith.

Yes, tuneful was Owen, but voice for voice he was no match for my father. A fine fierce tone had Dada, with a double bass echo that could be heard in Swansea when he got going; rough and vibrant, he was, with his air going in like church bellows. Bass is the voice for a man; a voice with mud on its boots and a smell of sweat and tobacco about it, and all tenors should be in skirts, especially when they go falsetto, for which they are shot in the Italian opera, Dada says.

Into the hall we went now, Mam leading as usual, and many of the gentry like Prothero and Phillips looked down their noses at the rough ironworkers. Lady Charlotte Guest was up in front, bowing this way and that, she and Sir John being the richest ironmasters in Wales, Owen said—people who could buy up the Baileys with the spare change in their pockets. We took our seats in an unholy quiet and I noticed

78

Redcoats standing in the corridors. My father leaned over to Owen.

"Plenty of military, eh? Trouble in Merthyr, I hear."

"And Dowlais—that is why Sir John Guest is not here and Lady Charlotte is. Very good at scampering is Charlotte when there is trouble."

"Truck trouble again," whispered Griff. "Rioting in the streets and fighting with the Highlanders. We will give them bloody kilts if they come to Garndyrus."

"Prices up and wages down," said Owen. "It is an Act of Parliament to ban the Shops that is wanted, but half the Members pay our wages and the other half sell the goods. What this country wants is an armed rebellion, for it is people like the Guests who are bleeding us."

"And the Irish by the look of you," said Mam, "so enough of politics or we will finish up in carts to Monmouth."

"But he is right," whispered Idris Foreman, tapping us from the seat behind. "All right for the Guests to give money to music, but they are bleeding us dry. Killed more people they have than ten days of the French wars; emptied more sleeves and tied up more trouser legs than six iron-masters put together. The trouble with Lady Charlotte is that she plays the Christian while Bailey plays the devil, which is more honest."

"Quiet!" whispered Mam, smiling kindly at the big hats coming round and the stares for silence. "A real lady is Charlotte, so not a word against her, please."

"To hell with you," said Idris, very hot. "She buys a house in England for thousands of pounds—somewhere to run to from the cholera in Dowlais—but not a hundred pounds will she spend for a new water supply."

"Remove your chops from my shoulder this minute," said my father. "And do not say to hell with my wife or I will have you in bits. Music it is, not politics, this afternoon, and the soldiers are watching us."

God Save The King, then, done on trumpets and drums with Mam and Dada hauling the Howells twins up on their feet as fast as they sat down, and Idris Foreman

79

making rude signs at the soldiers. Very ashamed I was of my town.

"It is this top set that is worrying me," said Owen.

"Knees back, please," said Morfydd, coming in. "I will sit by Mam."

"There is a wicked girl to be late," said my mother, looking daggers. "Where is Richard?"

"Called away on politics and would not say where he was going, so I am not interested much."

"That is a change," I said. "Sharp enough on other people's business usually."

"You shut it," said Morfydd, flaming. "Richard's business is mine now we are going to marry."

"Thank God," I said. "Not before time."

"Hisht!" breathed Mam, for the big hats were coming round again and a Newport bass was into Handel's test piece and raging the nations together three bars ahead of the harpsichord.

"Where is Edwina?" whispered Dada, his finger up.

"Gone to church, is it?" asked Mam.

"Started for church," I said to her, winking.

"And what do you mean by that?" asked Morfydd, pale.

"Where sisters start for and where they end up are two different things. We are not all so daft as we look, mind."

"Eh! Soon I will brain this damned kid!" said Morfydd.

"Quiet, the lot of you," hissed Dada. "It is bad manners and making it hard for the singer."

"Hard for him?" said Owen in misery. "Worried to death I am."

"What is wrong with you?" asked Morfydd, leaning.

"It is this top set," whispered Owen, rattling it. "I caught an Irishman and they are swines for swinging the boot. As sure as fate it will drop during 'Rest in the Lord' Top C."

"*Duwedd!*" exclaimed Morfydd, and went double, holding her stays.

"Mr Owen Howells of Garndyrus," shouted the adjudicator on the platform, pushing the Newport bass out of it.

"Good God," whispered Owen, white as a sheet.

"'Rest in the Lord', is it?" asked Morfydd, swaying and bubbling.

"Aye," said Griff. "Bring up your knees, girl, away I am quick."

"You stay!" said Morfydd sharp. "Would you desert him in his hour of need?"

"That is what Bennet has done to you," I whispered.

"Carry on, carry on, make a good coffin," said she, scowling. "I will have the skin from your backside when I get you in the house!"

"O, for Heaven's sake!" breathed Mam.

Up to the platform went Owen like a man to a gibbet while everybody clapped in recognition of last year's champion, but Griff had his hands over his face.

"Blood will run in the gutters if that top set drops," said he. "He will have every Irishman with boots from here to Killarney."

A harpist for Owen this time, one with a beard to his waist. The mountains could have toppled then and nobody noticed it as his thick old fingers ran swiftly over the strings. Owen braced himself and took his last breath. Three years running we had taken the tenor cup to Garndyrus. Terrible to lose it through an Irishman's boot.

"Mr Owen Howells has changed his mind because of an indisposition," shouted the adjudicator after a lot of nodding and barging on the platform. "'Comfort Ye My People' he will sing instead," which brought the place down, for anything Handel is popular with the Welsh. So we started again and tidy it sounded, and very apt, said Morfydd.

Brave was Owen. The pure notes flowed out despite his split lips. He did the Comforts all right and was proceeding to New Jerusalem when bedlam was let loose. The doors came open and the mob came in with sticks and boots and hit the military right and left for what was going on in Merthyr. Seats were going up and sticks coming down as my father gathered us and raced for the door, taking time to lift the bass cup as he ran, being still champion. Owen kicked the harpist flat and picked up his cup while Griff tripped the organisers who tried to stop him. Down the corridor we went with the women screaming until we reached the Garndyrus contingent, who had run to save us. With half the elders of the town in pursuit we made for the fair stalls where the crowd was thickest.

Very successful was that day in Newport, with two cups to our credit and not having to sing for them. A much happier day than in poor Merthyr where the Highlanders went mad and shot down the rioters for burning their debt to the Shops.

*Listen!* Otters are barking along the Usk. The June moon is flashing and the arched bridges step over us all the way from Ponty. Faint is the singing of the night-shift Irish as the homecoming barges drift under the shadows of the mountain. The barge-men are astir, yawning and stretching. Women begin their chattering, tired children their crying. Ropes are coiled for flinging, windlasses turn in shrieks as Llanfoist Wharf comes flaring through the mist. To the hostile stares of the Irish who pelted us, we help our women out and into the trams for the climb back to Garndyrus.

The night was black with him, but the canal flares were alight for the night-shift Irish loading limestone for Hereford Tram Inn. Stripped to the waist, every one of them, despite the frosty June. Good breasts on them, some of these Irish girls, with waists like Edwina's and long, black hair flowing over their shoulders, and enough tricks in them, says Mo Jenkins, to satisfy a good Welshman, though hell was let loose if one of them came full, with Paddy this and Paddy that knocking out the locals with knobkerry sticks, trying to find the father, and more than one lump they raised on Iolo Milk.

*"Phist!"* whispered one, lying in the heather clear of the bank. Very pretty she looked with her hand up, begging, and the other holding her baby for milk, feeding it in Foreman's time and God help her if she was found there.

At the foot of the Incline an empty limestone tram was going back up and I jumped it and lay there watching the stars step over the trees as it climbed. How pure is a cold evening when you are lying in a tram climbing up the face of a mountain! The loveliness of God's earth comes into you, its beauty new in the phantom shapes of trees in moonlight. There is a smell of sweetness from the branches and nightingales are singing above the rumble of the tram, and you begin to compare this beauty with the lives of humans and the messes they get into, for Morfydd was on my mind. And half the mess is caused by this baby business, which, according to what Mo Jenkins lets loose at times, is not very attractive. And even when you have babies there is a bother feeding them, like the Irish girl feeding hers with one hand and begging with the other. Better, I think, to lie in a tram watching the stars go by in the brilliance of summer moonlight.

# CHAPTER SEVEN

NEXT SPRING I joined the Benefit Club and went into politics, which were coming more popular that year, and with good reason. Cholera was sweeping the mountains, coming from Dowlais, it was said, because of the water pollution. It got through Merthyr and along The Top, killing hundreds, and picked off a few in our town, and they were felling the trees in Clydach Valley for coffins. The prices in the Tommy Shops were going up monthly because the price of iron in foreign markets was coming down, according to the owners, although what one had to do with the other only St Peter knew, said the pamphlets. Men with big families to feed were fainting at the furnaces and falling under trams and the secret Union was calling for strikes and the workers for armed revolution.

Yes, politics were popular, outright criticism of Church and Throne rampant, and Bennet was at pains to say where his sympathies lay, which did not please my father.

"It would have been more honest had he said he was in politics," said Dada one night.

"Do you splash your business all over town?" asked Morfydd.

"A mention would have been polite," said my mother. "We have enough trouble getting a living as it is without you marrying into a working-class Union, and a London one at that."

"Safe houses make cowards of us," replied Morfydd, set for a fight as usual. "But trouble is coming and we need men like Richard and Frost to lead us."

"There is a trouble-maker," said Mam. "Williams, Partridge, Frost—all tarred with the same brush. They will lead us to transportation before they are finished."

"Mr John Frost is a very fine gentleman," I said sharp.

"Hush, Iestyn," whispered Morfydd.

My father frowned at me. "And what do you know of Frost?"

"Only what I read in *The Merlin*."

"Confine it to that. There is not enough room for two anarchists in this house." He levelled his pipe at Morfydd. "Listen. This town works for one of the best masters on the mountains. If I worked in Merthyr, Dowlais or Nantyglo I would have need of a Union. But under Mr Hill I hold no brief for Benefit Clubs, National Unions or Charters that will never be obtained, for the men who make these organisations are of the same greed as their masters. Those are my views, now away to your torchlight meeting, but do not expect me to fight for you when the military pack you and your friends in carts for Monmouth."

"And what of Jethro and Iestyn? You have seen your generation go from bad to worse under the English. . . ."

"And it would probably be worse under the Welsh all the time we are sitting on iron and coal—as for Jethro, he must manage in his generation as I have managed in mine."

"A selfish, cowardly view," whispered Morfydd. "This house has no manhood, and I would be better out of it."

"Then go!" Suddenly raging, my father rose and flung down his paper. "As soon as you like out of it, for I am sick to death of your politics and slanders. Every day it is the same—Lovett, Frost, Williams. Pigs of ironmasters and starvation wages. Not a single word of loyalty, not one of religion. You would be better on your knees thanking God for what we have given you than whipping the house into a ferment."

Threats to leave from Morfydd. Go, and to hell, from Dada, with Mam sitting behind her spinning-wheel putting in one here and one there, her eyes brimming with tears and saying she had something to do with the pair of them and God knows who is right.

Sick at heart, I left them. Every family was quarrelling then —the old people talking about the good old days and loyalty to the masters and thank God for being hungry. The young people were creeping over the roofs at night to attend the torchlight meetings where men like Bennet, missionaries from the new London Union, hammered into them William Lovett's four demands from Parliament, which were the aims of the Union. The old generation was deaconing in Chapel, bowing to Royalty and keeping the bishops in finery. The new generation was forging pike-heads and moulding iron shot for the little square cannons, and God help the Members of Parliament if the Four Points of the Charter were not granted. A printing press had been dug into a mountain cave and every week a pamphlet circulated denouncing the masters; telling of the prosperity of the iron trade and why wages should be raised and how much Robert Thomas Crawshay had put into his bank since a year last Friday, and the number of singles and twins a wicked old man of commerce was paying for already.

Very informative were those pamphlets, very dangerous, said my father.

And on the barren stretches of coastline from the West Country up to Newport arms were being landed by night.

It was cold for spring that night. A lot of Irishwomen were standing around the Company Shop looking at the food and watching Mervyn Jones hopping about inside and smiling his rhubarb smile, always a sign that he was giving underweight. Next door the Drum and Monkey was packed to the windows with men, and more going in from shift. Billy Handy, landlord of the Garndyrus Inn, was slapping the backs of others going in for their pay.

"Room inside for another," said he with a wicked wink. "But since they are handing out money for work you can make home, for it is something the Mortymers have never been guilty of."

"Had mine," I told him, for still being on the Nantyglo books we were paid out at Garndyrus with Crawshay Bailey's money. "And knit your teeth before you lose them."

A cheeky little face had Billy Handy, I thought. Very pleasant he would look with no teeth. He was to be my first man; I had always fancied him for laying out. Not much taller than me he was inches broader. I hated Billy Handy because he was beer mad. It was said that he had a nice little bit tucked away, too, every penny made out of misery. Get into debt at his inn and he would have the trews from your sister-in-law for selling in Abergavenny market. He was also a pig-sticker, slitting them for money and enjoyment; a man who worked in hot blood through a season of pigs and then beat his breast in Chapel and called down blessings on his innocent soul.

The masters always paid out in the beer-houses. In our town they sometimes paid in silver, but Crawshay Bailey of Nantyglo paid in brass, coins he minted himself, and if a man wanted silver to spend in the open market he paid Bailey six-pence in the pound for the privilege. The Bailey coins could only be used in Bailey's Shops, where the prices of goods were often thirty per cent higher. The secret pamphlets were against payment of wages in the beer-houses, for the beer-houses were owned by the masters, too, and their pay-masters always arrived late so that a man could drink on credit for hours before getting paid, and then be too drunk to count it. There was the time when Big Rhys Jenkins drew what was left of his six weeks' pay at two o'clock in the morning and rolled home drunk with thirty shillings in his pocket. Few of the workers were any good at figures except my father, and he worked out that Rhys must have drunk two hundred quarts that pay night. Had he drunk twenty he would not have been standing, so the rest of the money must have been shared between paymaster, landlord and master.

Above the hoarse shouting and laughter of the men inside I heard dice being rolled and remembered that it was Benefit Club-night. Later, there would be a visit from the Garndyrus Benefit and a fight and a smashing of windows, so I put my hands in my pockets and walked on.

Will Tafarn, I saw first. Along the top of North Street he came rolling and singing drunk. Not a hair on his body had Will, for the furnace blow-back that had twisted his mind had stripped him. Belching, he swayed before me.

"Fifteen pints tonight, Iestyn Mortymer. By Heaven! Little Will can still sink it, eh? And a good little hazel stick to have the backside from that woman of mine, is it?" and he lifted the stick, his one eye shining from his white, scalded face.

"She is minding her children, Will," I said. "Not a man but you has touched her."

"She-cat!" he whispered. "The moment my back is turned a tom is between her, so tonight I will bitch her."

Laughing, waving the stick, he was off, for tonight was pay night, and it was a pay night when the molten iron came from the furnace bung like a shaft of fire and took him in the face. And when they doused him with whisky at the Drum and Monkey and carried him home and put him on his bed his wife's brother was in it, visiting from Risca. . . .

So every pay night Martha Tafarn had it black and blue in exchange for the money. I gave her a thought as she watched from her window with her three children locked in the bedroom.

Little Willie Gwallter was out with his mam and I stood aside and knocked up my cap to her.

"Good evening, Mrs Gwallter, good evening, Willie."

"Good evening, Iestyn, *bach*. Seen my husband, have you?" Thin and pale she was and worried about the drinking.

"No, Mrs Gwallter," I lied, for I had just seen Gwallter parting his beard in the Lamb Row Public and pouring in a quart without a swallowing.

"Looking for him, see," she said. "Here is Willie and me without a crust of bread in the house and not a penny to bless us. A pig of a man is Mr Gwallter on pay nights but good otherwise, mind. Never a finger he puts on wife and child, like some I could mention," and she nodded at Will Tafarn who was crawling home, lashing the gutter with his stick. "Aye, a happy family, the three of us." She sighed at the moon and I took the chance to get a penny into Willie's hand. "Only on dirty old pay nights when Mr Gwallter do sink it. *Ach y fi!*"

"Goodbye," I said, raising my cap, and she hurried away

88

dragging Willie after her, his big, hungry eyes sending thanks over his shoulder.

I walked on. Many of the Irish were coming down from the Tumble, wild in their shouting and singing. Big men, they were, many of them bearded, with their little shrivels of wives and women hanging on their arms and everyone swearing to rise Satan's eyebrows. It was as dark as curtains in Rhyd-y-nos Street, for the women of our town were hard against street lamps, and right, too. It is not every wife who wants the neighbours to count from upstair windows the value of her basket after a visit to the Company Shop, with the shillings and pence in the back pews of Chapel on Sundays.

A little friend I found on the street, shivering to have her teeth out. Hungry days for humans, these, but hungrier still for dogs.

"Oi oi," I said, "has your old mam dried up? Have to eat, *fach*." I gave her bread I had been carrying for days, and if she had eaten that month I doubt it.

"With me?" I asked her, and her little brown tail went round. A glance up the street and I was away heavier, for if a well-covered bitch crossed the path of the Irish on a pay night she was likely to end in a pot at mid-month. Under my coat with her, button it tight, good evenings and good nights right and left to neighbours, for sure as fate if you hate the bloody sight of them you will meet twenty, and away went the pair of us down to the Company Park for a look at the gentry.

When I got to the corner of Queen Street I heard the sound of the Benefit Club procession. In no time it appeared, with Billy Handy striding at its head, the swine, waving the colours on a stick. On either side of him were the torch-bearers, and one was Mo Jenkins.

"Hoi, Iestyn!" yelled he.

"Go to hell," I said.

But this was a fine procession. Owen and Griff Howells were blasting on tenor trombones. Mr Gwallter had the big drum on his stomach, hitting it for holes, and Will Blaenavon was puffing deep with him on the bass horn. Next came the flutes and whistles and Mr Roberts on the ophiclyde and hard behind him Iolo Milk with the serpentine, ending with Evans the Death on Enid Donkey and Phil Benjamin hanging on to her tail. Pretty good it sounded, too, considering most of them could hardly stand. Behind came a crowd like the French Revolution with sticks and staves and banners, making enough commotion to bring out Brecon Garrison. Mo scrambled a path through the crowd and gripped me.

"Come on in, man—do not stand there gaping."

"What is happening?" I asked.

"Hang me for a bastard," said Mo. "This is the Benefit. Round the town twice and then to the Drum and Monkey for a talk to by the Union speakers."

"Finish up in Monmouth, all of you," I said.

"Free beer afterwards, mind!"

"My father will see me and hell will set alight."

"In this crowd? Easier to nip a flea in a wig-sack. Here, take a swig of this to cheer you up for you look miserable to death," and I swigged twice at his gin bottle and the little bitch popped out and sniffed it and sneezed.

"Up with it again," said Mo.

It is amazing how nice raw gin can taste during a procession.

"Will Tafarn is back home beating his wife," I said.

"Aye," said Mo. "I have just heard her howling. Back with that bottle. *Diawl*, there will be a row when your dada smells your breath and thank God I will not be there at the slaughter."

"To hell with my dada," I said.

Wonderful is the feeling of just getting drunk. And there is nothing like marching with comrades, either, for the tramp of boots on a frosty road takes a swing at the senses when the shoulders barging you are the shoulders of town brothers and the band you are marching to is the best in the Eastern Valley. Down Heol-y-nant we went with every window in the place going up and bedsheets and tablecloths waving out.

"Down with your cap, Iestyn," whispered Mo. "Your mam is up at the window."

"Room for her," I said. "Tell her she is welcome."

"Quick!" hissed Big Rhys, and he heaved up his belly and

pulled me under his flaps. "She will have your father out and half the town will be mutilated," and the pair of us walked past my house with Big Rhys bowing this way and that, his thighs hitting me in the behind.

The door of the Drum and Monkey was wide open as we wheeled up by the market place and tramped in. Down went the instruments and straight up to the bar went the band, hammering it for beer. Polly Morgan was too slow by halves and Will Blaenavon lifted her into the crowd for kicking out and began to draw the jugs. Amazing how attractive women look through neat gin. Very severe about Polly Morgan I had been since the night of humiliation, but she would not have stood much chance now. Over our heads she went, upright one moment, head down the next, with her legs bare to the waist and screaming for a pig-sticking. Out she went sharp, for a room of Benefit drinkers is no place for a woman; nor Irish either, come to that, and a pair of Kildare men went after her with Gwallter's boot behind them. Will was serving foaming jugs and Mo got two and was through the legs of the crowd to our corner.

"Down with this, boyo," he whispered. "You are not a paid-up member, see, and it is asking for a ducking."

I had just got my teeth into it when Dic Shon Ffyrnig the Chairman came up with a book and pencil. "A shilling for membership, if you please, or out on your ear and Mo Jenkins with you for introducing a scab."

"He has money to pay, I doubt it," said Billy Handy, "so let the chairman see the colour of it or I will be happy to kick him out."

"A shilling," I said, counting it out. "And do not forget the receipt." A look of wonder on their faces then, for I do not think they had a shilling between them, and if mine went into the Fund for Children it would be a surprise. Often my father had said that more money went up against the wall of Dic Shon Ffyrning's house than ever reached the Benefit Funds. No sight of a receipt, anyway, and next moment Dic Shon was up on a chair patting his belly. A good talker this one, with a plum for a face and a watch-chain over his waistcoat like the

chains around Parliament. "Gentlemen, gentlemen," he began. "Wonderful it is to have for each other this great com-
panionship, and very happy is your chairman to welcome you
to this glorious anniversary of the Benefit," and he lowered his
face and threw out his palms and blessed us. Very holy, it all
was.

"And wasting our bloody time, too," roared Owen
Howells. "Union men are speaking on the Coity tonight and
here we are listening to speeches from tap-room barristers who
can do nothing but spout about benefits."

"To hell with the Benefit," bawled Griff the Twin. "I am
for a Union."

"And me for a Charter," cried Owen. "A Union first, perhaps, but Lovett's Four Points eventually, and down with the
Benefit."

Dic Shon Ffyrnig spat. "From the mouths of sucklings,"
he cried. "Shut the trap and quick. I, Ffyrnig, have been
calling for a Union of workers before the pair of you were on
tits, and I organised this Benefit before you knew there was a
bloody mountain—so remember it."

"And feathering your nest with the funds," shouted Owen.
"To hell with Benefits, I say—a lot of damned subscriptions
and nothing coming back."

Most grave was this, apparently. The men went quiet.
Terrible to see the look on Ffyrnig's face, for the remark
had cut him to the quick. "Am I to understand," he began,
"that I am being accused by hints of confiscating public
money?"

"Aye," I said without thinking. "A shilling I paid minutes
back and still no sign of a receipt," and I was sharp back to my
corner with Mo after me.

"The boy is right," said Mr Gwallter. "Take Afel Hughes
here. Pounds and pounds he has paid into this Benefit, Ffyrnig, yet his wife is still with the Irish in straw and his Ceinwen
girl six feet down, eh, Afel?"

And Mr Hughes nodded, his eyes bright in his gaunt face.
Never touched a drop, did Hughes, and very strong for the
Benefit.

"But Afel Hughes has not paid six months yet," cried Ffyrnig. "Can I draw money from stone, think you? Upon my soul, gentlemen, I am not a magician to rise sick women from straw and dead children from graves. Fifteen pounds we have in the funds, and how far will that go if the owners put us on the blacklist or discharge labour? How far will it go if we decide on strike action tonight? You have an excellent example of defeat through lack of funds in Merthyr, who could have won her case through the courts had she had the money to pay lawyers."

"She would have needed millions to oppose Crawshay, so talk sense," said Big Rhys. "How do the funds stand, you say?"

"Fifteen pounds," said Ffyrnig.

"There is a queer figure," said Will Blaenavon. "And ten shillings might have saved Ceinie Hughes. Where are the shillings and bloody ha'pennies?"

Bedlam.

Dic Shon Ffyrnig stamped upon his chair. "Order, order, gentlemen. Mr Handy, kindly serve the members with another round, for it is beer we are needing to make us sociable."

"To hell with the beer, it can come later," said Big Rhys, pushing to the front. "Not a good man at figures, I am, but it do strike me that fifteen pounds is a small amount for the members to have saved over six months, and with the greatest of respect, Mr Ffyrnig, I would propose that somebody outside the Benefit and good at sums like Hywel Mortymer should have a look at your accounts."

"Over my dead body," shouted Ffyrnig, blue round the chops. "Mr Billy Handy has signed my accounts and I will not have scum like Mortymer near them, for he is not even a member."

"It is the principle with Hywel Mortymer, not the penny a week," said Big Rhys, "and sorry you will be for mentioning names in public, Ffyrnig, for Mortymer's boy is here and his father will come and squeeze subscriptions from your belly and cut off your privates for roasting."

"Aye," said a voice.

93

Six men stood at the door. Never have I seen their like for size and ferocity, but never in dreams a man like Dai Probert, their leader. He could have given my father a foot in height and another across the shoulders. He was ragged, one arm bare. The bearskin around his waist dangled to a point at his feet. His face, like Will Tafarn's, was parched by a furnace blow-back; one eye, criss-crossed with scars, was a red socket. In his hand he gripped a cudgel, and around him pressed his supporters, every man armed with iron spikes for leg-breaking. Mo put his elbow into my ribs.

"Scotch Cattle," he whispered. "Under the table with us quick, for now there is going to be trouble. Come to enforce Union membership, see?"

Very cheeky was Big Rhys, his father. With one hand in his belt and the other dangling his drinking-mug, he sauntered towards them.

"Nantyglo, is it?" he asked, innocent.

"Aye." The Bull looked past Big Rhys, adding the strength of the Benefit.

"Then get out," said Rhys. "When we form a Union it will be from this town and no invitations sent to Nanty."

"Before we damned move you, Dai Probert," added Owen Howells in his light fighter's voice.

Probert grinned. "Backward in this town and no mistake," said he. "Talking about Benefit Clubs and a penny a week and living on the blood of the workers in Blackwood." Thrusting Owen and Rhys aside he walked up to Dic Shon Ffyrnig, caught him by the watch-chain and pulled him from the chair. "Too much Benefit membership and too little Union will be the death of a few of you before you are finished." He threw Dic Shon away and he stumbled the length of the room and landed in the arms of Afel Hughes and lay there, staring and trembling. Probert turned to Big Rhys. "And you," he said. "Clever with your mouth, eh? Get out, is it?"

"And quick," said Rhys, "or we will have the six of you in salted hams and hanging from hooks."

Mo whispered, "Listen, you! My father is after him. Watch now, for he has always wanted a Scotch Cattle Bull."

94

"And bloody got one," I said. "If he puts a finger on this boy he will be slabbed for burial."

"Do you stand for a Union, man?" Probert asked Rhys.

"No," said Rhys, "and I will trim the chops from any man who does, so make a ring and take your guard."

"Is it clean in here?" asked Probert, looking around.

"As clean as a nut, boy. To a finish, is it? I am no man for breathers if I fight for William the Fourth."

"Right, you," said Probert, untying his bearskin. "To the grave, if you like, and when I have done with you I am breaking the legs of every man in here who does not show a Union card."

"First one down gets hobnails," said Rhys, circling, his left hand out. "God help you, Probert, for you have tangled with a professional." His left came out, smashing into the big man's face. The room was silent. There was no sound but the creak of the boards under the feet of the fighters. And then, with a look of terror in his eyes, Big Rhys dropped his fists and stared at the window.

"Good God," he breathed. "The Military!"

Like a top Dai Probert spun, and Rhys was into him with a terrible right-hander that laid open the bone above his single eye. Arms waving, he dropped. The boards shuddered under his twenty solid stones. Rising to his knees, he knelt there, shaking his great head. Blood dripped, splashing.

"Dirty swine," said Probert.

"Aye," said Big Rhys, still circling. "I will be as dirty here as you have been in Blackwood. Up, you big cow, and I will hand you more than you would have from a Carmarthen slaughterer."

"Very handy is my dada with Scotch Cattle Bulls," said Mo.

And as he spoke the door opened and Idris Foreman stood there, half the size of Rhys Jenkins. His eyes took in the scene.

"Dai Probert, eh?" said he. "Up to your tricks here?" His little wrinkled face moved from one to the other. "Big heads and no brains, and no loss to the Union either of you. Away to the counter and drink together and learn sense." He waved his arms in a sudden anger. "All of you back to the bar!"

"There is a pity," whispered Mo. "Bleeding to death he was, and in his shroud in two minutes. Never mind, we will have him after the speeches." He jerked his thumb. "Guests are coming tonight, see?"

"Guests?"

"Your sister!" hissed Mo. "Look you, boy!"

With the bitch held tightly against me I watched Morfydd follow Bennet through the door and into the tap-room. Pale and sad she looked; beautiful in her black, full-skirted dress and her long hair tied with blue ribbons. My father was right, I thought. This was the end of her, for it is one thing to spout fireside politics but another to shout them in public with Redcoats sewing their ears to keyholes and agents of the gentry lying flat under floorboards.

Idris Foreman jumped on to a chair. "Gentlemen and ladies," he began. "Tonight being the feast of the Benefit and a special occasion, I have brought from Nantyglo a guest speaker from the National Union of Working Classes and Others, so give him a fair hearing. For whether you vote for the Benefit Club or the Union one thing is certain—it is time to unite under one flag, so pay heed to suggestions," and down he jumped and up got Bennet ready for fighting. Moans and groans left and right now, for there are enough Englishmen as agents, collectors, schoolmasters and reformers without having to stomach them as friends of the Welsh.

"Go north and see to them up in Lancashire!" shouted Rhys.

"A fair hearing!" roared Idris Foreman, and we all went respectable and quiet, for Idris was big in the Union.

"Gentlemen," began Bennet. "As Idris here has told you, I have been sent by your English brothers to unify working-class labour under a single flag. . . ."

"Ay," said Owen Howells, "a bloody red one and to hell with you for we are not having foreign interference in home affairs."

"A white one," said Bennet. "And when it turns red you will see me sharper out of collective bargaining than any man here. As for home affairs, you have none, nor are you entitled to any while you sit and whine about exploitation. Are you the only victims? Christ, but I wish you were, for the Union's task would be easy! The exploitation of the workers runs from north, south, east and west to every corner of the country. The evil forged by Throne and Church dominates our towns as well as yours, and while we are making the weapons to fight it you are sitting on your backsides paying pennies into Benefit Clubs."

"This is insulting!" cried Dic Shon Ffyrnig, shocked.

"Shut it!" shouted Idris Foreman. "It is the truth."

"The truth or not," said Big Rhys with a chuckle. "It is sedition and very handy. Let us hear more, Englishman."

"You shall," said Bennet. "The Throne is in hand with the Church and the Church is in hand with the Devil. And while the bishops are gabbling the sanctity of the monarch in the eyes of God the monarch is frittering away fortunes amassed by the starvation of factory children. A pleasant union, this one. Then the monarch blesses the bishops and grants them palaces earned by the rent of prostitution. To make my position doubly clear to you, I say down with the king and off with his head and roast the devils of the Church alive as you once did in old Carmarthen."

"Good God," said Owen Howells.

Very respectful was the Benefit now, as befits a tap-room listening to first-class sedition, for a word outside and Bennet would have stood for hanging, drawing and quartering.

"Yes," said Bennet. "Good God. It is time somebody spoke the truth for it has been whispered around corners far too much in Wales. There is too much spouting in private and too little action in public, which is a shame to a country that gave birth to Owen Glyndwr. There is too much self-pity, too, if nobody minds me saying it—you are not the only ones exploited by my countrymen. Slaves are still being sold in Bristol by men who go on their knees in church. Do you beat your children to save them a flogging by the factory overman? Are your little ones plunged into water to revive them and keep them at the machines? Are they beaten and starved before their mothers? For all this happens in the mills

97

of Lancashire. Do you keep foster-mothers in milk to suckle the babies of the poor because the mothers are too starved to bring forth milk? Do not stare at me. Go down on your knees and be thankful you are Welsh and pay your pennies into drunken Benefit Clubs and to hell with anyone else, eh?"

"Mark your words," said Billy Handy.

"And you your tongue before I come down there and pluck it out," cried Bennet. "For it is the likes of you and Ffyrnig I am roasting. The Welsh Benefit Clubs were founded upon friendship by saints, not men, but they have been murdered by men like you, their funds stolen and their principle of common decency depraved. You take the money and give back nothing. You are the tools of the masters, worse than scum. And yet you have served us. Men like you have proved that the Benefit Club is not only useless but the coward's cure of an ill. Yours is a defence against the filthy conditions, not an attack. The Benefit Clubs are being abandoned throughout the land as useless, the Union is taking their place. And from the Union will spring Lovett's Charter of decency. . . ."

This brought cheers. Many were strong for the Union's new Charter, especially men like Afel Hughes, who were all for cannon and gunpowder under the Houses of Parliament, all Members present.

"No longer will you be driven to the polls to vote for Whig or Tory according to the whim of your masters," shouted Bennet. "Your Union will give you secret ballot, paid Members of your choice, not the lackeys of the aristocracy who make laws to suit the Throne."

The beer was going round now and everybody chattering, always a good sign for a speaker. Bennet had got them going and he knew it. His fist was swinging an inch from their noses. "And next will come adult male suffrage—the right of every man to vote—for why should the policy of the country be formed by a privileged few? These are the aims of the Union —attack, not defence, so away with your Benefit. Wind them up, share what is left of their funds and pay your penny to the Union which stands for the comradeship of men irrespective of creed or colour. Force the masters to new conditions of labour, make them disgorge their profits. Live for your Union—die for it if needs be, and it will be the guardian of your new generations!"

Bedlam now. Typical of the Welsh, this; to hell with him one moment, follow him to the scaffold the next. The door came open and Dic Shon Ffyrnig went through it sharp and Billy Handy was only spared because he was holding Benefit money. Mugs were going up and drinks going down and everybody shouting and fishing out pennies for the new Union. I saw Morfydd's eyes glowing as she took Bennet through the door and Idris Foreman only stayed long enough to issue Union cards. Very happy it all was with Scotch Cattle slapping each other's backs and roars of laughter as jokes went round. And then it happened. Dai Probert's mug went up as Big Rhys cracked him solid with the right. Across the room he staggered, hit the wall and sat down.

"Changed my mind, see," said Rhys. "I am not drinking with Scotch Cattle, and it do seem a pity to let a good fight go by."

Dead silence, and Mo whispered, "Now's our chance, boyo. Here, take this chair leg. Down among their legs and hit their feet from under them."

The men were dividing, the Cattle to the right of the bar, the town men to the left. Nobody shifted then until Afel Hughes took off his glasses—always a sign of trouble. Over in a corner Evans the Death was slipping little bands of iron over his knuckles. And as Will Blaenavon leaped the counter with a barrel-tapper in his fist, the Cattle rushed with Probert leading.

*Well.*

If the ancient Welsh had fought the Romans as we fought the Blackwood Cattle that night the devils would never have built Caerleon. Men went down like pit-props. Afel Hughes was flat before he got his glasses away, with Mr Roberts on top of him. Big Rhys had got Probert on his knees again and Griff Howells was hitting everyone in sight, while Owen caught a Cattle the prettiest left hook I have ever witnessed, laying him quiet and ready for burial. Dirty Billy Handy had another by the fork of his trews, screwing hard while the devil danced like a Scot and screamed at the ceiling until he was backed through the door and kicked into the gutter. A dirty fighter was Billy Handy, for a man's privates are entitled to respect, especially when fighting. Mo and I were crawling among their legs now, tapping the unconscious ones to make sure and cracking at the shins of the living. I was helping Mr Hughes find his spectacles when I came face to face on all fours with Billy Handy as he was reaching up for another set of trews, so I swung my chair leg and hit him out. Never have I heard such a commotion. Men were slipping on broken glass and the seats of trews were cut to tatters. Big Rhys was giving Dai Probert the hobnails and he was bellowing to deafen—size ten, took Rhys, and every kick was going well in. Will Blaenavon was slumped in a corner, Mr Gwallter was flat on his back with Mr Roberts and two Scotch Cattle under him, and Owen and Griff Howells were into one another because of the shortage. But every enemy was down and out when Polly Morgan threw a stone through the window.

"The Military!" she screamed.

"Excuse me," said Mo, "I am getting from here," and he pushed me aside and kicked his way through the nearest window with me after him followed by the others, for it is amazing how the dead will rise and walk when the Military get among them. There was a crowd of Chapel people outside wagging their heads and slapping their Bibles and I was straight through them, up North Street and down High Street to the safety of the tombstones. There, under cover, I straightened my clothes and brushed myself down, then, hands in pockets and whistling, I made my way home and vaulted the gate at the back.

My father was leaning against the shed, pipe in hand, looking at the moon.

"A little activity in town tonight," said he, very formal.

"Aye," I replied. "Sickening, it is—always the same on Benefit Night."

"Did you see the procession?"

"*Jawch*, no! I have been walking from Abergavenny."

"Then you have not seen the Military in town?"

My face showed wonderment.

"Come then," said he. "I was thinking of a stroll up the Hill. We will watch them looking for the trouble-makers," and he smiled and took my arm and steered me through the gate.

Up North Street we went in the moonlight. There was a crowd of drunken Irish outside the Drum and Monkey and the mounted Redcoats were plunging among them, looking for disturbers. The Chapel people were still outside Staffordshire Row muttering and scolding, and Tomos Traherne was among them.

"Fighting and drinking, as usual," he told my father. "The drunken Benefit plagueing the town on its feast night. But agitators visited and Union cards were issued—to say nothing of sedition and the king's name spoken in defiance." And he bowed deep and grinned at me. "Very happy I am to see you safely with your father and away from such evil. Good night, Iestyn Mortymer."

"Very pleased with you is Mr Traherne, it seems," said my father up by Cae White.

Gapers here; all the neighbours in the kingdom, whistling and chattering like monkeys, and isn't it a scandal and not fit for decent people, with fingers wagging and tongues raised and giving it to everybody from the Mayor of Abergavenny to William the Fourth. I blew my nose to cover my face when I saw Polly Morgan giggling, and when I took my hand down I came face to face with Billy Handy and Dic Shon Ffyrnig. White as a sheet was Billy from the chair leg I had caught him, but he smiled sweet and pure and bowed low to my father.

"Good evening, Mr Mortymer," said he.

"Good evening, Mr Handy."

"A pleasant evening it is indeed, Mr Mortymer, dear me."

"To be sure, Mr Handy," replied my father.

"Too pleasant for neighbours to be mixing with Scotch Cattle Bulls and anarchists and hitting each other out with chair legs," said Dic Shon Ffyrnig, and he lifted the cap from Billy Handy's head and the lump I had raised was as big as a duck's egg and sparkling.

"Solid oak chair legs," said Billy Handy, glum.

"But we will have the bastard, mind," said Dic Shon, "and begging your pardon for the language, deacon."

"And quick," said Billy Handy. "Marked I am now, but in bloody strips he will be when we catch him, and iron bars it will be, not chair legs, eh, Iestyn Mortymer?"

"Indeed," I said.

On we went and turned down High Street.

"A terrible thing to strike a man down with a weapon," said my father, "even a man like Billy Handy. And thankful I am that my son has no need for such treachery, which saves me the bother of flogging it out of him with a mule whip, for if there is a man I cannot stand it is one who hits from behind."

"Aye," I said, sweating.

Crowds of people were huddled outside the school, most of them nodding and bowing to my father most respectfully, and from them came Mr Gwallter, one eye shut tight, blood down his muffler, and stinking of beer to strip varnish from pews.

"Take my hand, Mr Mortymer!" cried he, swaying. "I am one of the Benefit who hit out the Cattle, and proud of it, not skulking. And if my little Willie do grow like your Iestyn, with the courage of a lion and fists to match, then thank God for him!"

"Aye," said my father, handling him gently aside with the smile he always kept for those of poorer intellect. "Home to your wife now, my good man."

"Not like you for drinking, of course," went on Gwallter while I cursed his soul into everlasting hell, "for Iestyn can sink them, and I know you never touch a drop. But for fighting he stands proud with you, man. After the show he put up tonight I would back him against Big Rhys Jenkins."

"Good night, Mr Gwallter," said my father, pushing him aside firmly, and we walked on with my body going colder every step.

"A terrible man for the beer that Mr Gwallter," said my father when we got clear. "He is dazed in the head with drinking and fighting—getting you mixed up with Mo Jenkins, no doubt."

"Aye," I replied, shivering.

"For Mo is strong for the Benefit processions and its feast nights."

"Yes," I said.

"And you were nowhere near the Drum and Monkey but down in Abergavenny, if I remember?"

I closed my eyes, dripping.

Not a word from either of us as we walked on. I gave quick glances at his white shirt. Very sick I felt. It was the first time I had lied to my father, and by the look of him now it would be the last.

"Dada," I said, stopping him, "I have been drinking with Mo Jenkins at the Benefit and round town in the procession and hitting them out with chair legs."

"Well done, my son," said he without a blink. "Never let a Judas betray you, for I would rather lose both hands than hear you repeat a lie. A good boy you are, Iestyn."

There was never a relief greater than mine. "Thank you, Dada," I said.

"But the lie has been told, if not repeated," said he, "and it is demanding punishment. Home now, the pair of us, for a hammering you will not forget this side of Christmas."

Mam was sitting at the fire, going hard at her spinning-wheel when we got in. Edwina, behind the door, was reading the Book. Not so much as a blink from either of them as I came by, and I knew that in this room, not an hour before, I had been tried, convicted and sentenced.

"Into the bedroom," said my father. "Drunkenness and fighting must be stamped out in a decent family before it takes a grip."

"O, Hywel!" sobbed Mama then.

"Silence, woman," said my father. "What would you have me breed—drunkards, rowdies and chair-leg fighters? Out of the house if you cannot stomach it."

A lonely place is the stairs when they lead to the place of punishment, each one creaking like a tumbril. Into the bedroom now. Sit on Morfydd's bed and await the persecutor. Up like lightning as the door comes open. But my mother stands there.

"*Cariad Anwyl!*" said she, choked. "Terrible that our dada is going to lay hands on you, the first of the family."

"Do not upset yourself," I said. "It is me who is having it."

"O my precious," she breathed, "it is the drinking, see— not the silly old Benefit or the fighting, for drinking is the devil incarnate in a house, so have the thrashing just to please me, is it?"

There is a damned woman for sense.

"Downstairs fast," I said, "before he has the pair of us with the same fist."

Downstairs with her, upstairs with Edwina, all her coldness gone, weeping to float ships.

"Iestyn!" she sobbed. "O, Iestyn."

Pitiful are women, one moment stern and cold, the next wet with tears and sympathy. Shivering is in them, a blueness of the face, and trembling hands; loving, yearning, protecting. Weak to bring a man to weakness, and out of patience.

I preferred my father.

Slam went the back door, slam went the kitchen door.

"O, Hywel!" cried my mother, and caught at him.

"Away!" he roared.

Up the stairs now with a giant's tread. The door of the room nearly came from its hinges.

"Out of it," said he, twisting Edwina away.

Slam went the bedroom door to bring down plaster, and he faced me.

"Right, you," he said. "I will give you chair-leg bloody fighting."

Aye. Pretty good reason to remember the night I went into politics.

# CHAPTER EIGHT

BEER AND politics have something in common, I found. Men get drunk on both. All that year it was mountain meetings and Unions, Benefit Clubs and secret pamphlets. All over The Top from Hirwaun to Blaenavon the towns were going on fire with the politics; sending their deputations to the ironmasters demanding higher wages and lower Tommy Shop prices. But masters are no respecters of the workingman's rights when the Irish are waiting in their thousands to slave till they drop for a pound of potatoes. The trickle from Ireland widened into a flood that threatened to sink Welsh labour for a generation. But the Welsh and the men of Staffordshire were key men, and they knew it. Soon the tram road men came out, then the forge workers and the rollers. When the puddlers threw down their tools the strike spread like a fire over the mountains. Furnaces were blown out in Risca and Tredegar at the start of winter, mills were broken in Dowlais and tram roads levered up in Nanty. Armed meetings were held in mountain caves and lonely inns. Weapons were being forged with masters' iron in masters' time. The uneasy peace in my town could not last. In the grip of snow, up to their middles in debt to the Company Shop, the men in a body came out on strike.

Sad was my town that winter. The warm red glow was gone from The Top and the moon hung brilliant and cold over the mountains, glinting on the little square windows of the frozen houses, for one in twenty had a fire. The peak of Pen-y-fal and the ridge of the Blorenge were crystal white, guardians of the blackened furnaces of The Top, where the children of the valley Irish, always the first, had begun to die.

But there was food in Heol Garegog, said Tomos Traherne, and the rest of the town starving to death. Food in plenty, thanks to Iolo Milk, for to give the chap credit he always feeds what belongs to him, whether entered in Chapel records or not.

Have a peep through Mrs Pantrych's window for proof. Amazing, said Gwennie Lewis. I cannot believe my eyes, said Mrs Tossach. Tread gently in the snow.

Come nearer.

Here is Mrs Pantrych, beaming, wheezing, large about the stomach with her, busy round her kitchen. In the family way again is Mrs Pantrych; fetching them out as fast as rabbits, says Mrs Gwallter.

"Any day now, Ifor boy," said Mrs Pantrych to her eldest.

"That will be a load off my mind, Selwyn," she croons to her youngest. "The head is well down, girl—waiting for my sign," she tells her Betti.

Six little Pantrychs sitting at the table, backs straight, knives and forks up like Highlanders' bayonets, every one the image of Iolo Milk.

"Hurry, Mama!"

"Hungry as hunters."

"Let us have it now, girl—never mind the basting."

"Good God," said Ivor. "How much longer?"

Bang bang on the cups, roll the plates around, kick him under the table, somebody has her by the hair. Up a dando, boyo! *Phew*, there's a stink! Blodwen is doing it in her trews again—off with them quick, lads, and out of the window for airing.

"Eh dear," whispers Ieun, staring out.

"What the hell has happened now?" asks Mrs Pantrych.

"Blodwen's trews, Mam. I have dropped them on Grandfer Ffyrnig, look you."

"Good grief! Were they wet or full, then?"

"Full," shouts Mrs Shon Ffyrnig from downstairs, hands on hips in the yard. "Who the hell is dropping full trews on Grandfer Ffyrnig?"

"If the old fool dozes in snowdrifts he do deserve to be spilt on, and anyway, the cobbles do belong to the upper storey, and I can show it in writing," says Mrs Pantrych.

"Indeed," sayd Mrs Shon Ffyrnig. "Then these trews stay here on Grandfer's head until he wakes up, and then you will have bloody cobbles."

"Do not mind her, Mam," says Ieun. "Let us get on with the dinner. She is only jealous because we are eating, see?"

Round comes Mrs Pantrych, kneels by the oven, sweating like a puddler and looking twice as healthy.

"Hurry, Mama!"

"Get it on the table, girl."

"I haven't eaten in weeks," says Shoni, "and here I am with chicken. Good old Iolo Milk!"

Open comes the oven, out comes the joint now, brown and sizzling. Six little mouths water as she sharpens the knife. Now for the slicing, good thick portions, tender as a lamb and cutting twice as tasty.

"There is a fine little chicken," says Mrs Pantrych.

"Aye, better than Christmas, Mam. The parson's nose for me, is it?"

"Where is the bloody thing?"

"Language, language," says Mrs Pantrych. "This is not Mrs Ffyrnig's house, mind!"

Munching, crunching, drooling at the mouth, the six little Pantrychs dine. Sweating, sighing, fat Mrs Pantrych watches.

"But no parson's nose," whispers Betti to Gwyn. "There's queer. . . ."

"Aye, girl. Never seen a chicken with a curly tail like this. . . ."

"Eat up, my little ones," Mrs Pantrych beams. "Never mind the tail."

A winter bitch and a spring chicken taste alike on strike. . . .

Will Tafarn has eaten all the honey in his hives, and now he has started on the sugar, for the breadwinner must be fed. Comfortable in his chair Will faces Martha, his wife. His good eye shines at her, the other winks red from the scarred turmoil of his face. The willow stick in his hands is a bow of gold.

"Are the little ones asleep, my precious?" he asks.

"Sound," says Martha. "God be praised."

"Praised indeed," says Will, and raises his burned cheeks—riven by the iron splashes they levered out in six-inch strips. "A good woman, you are, Jezebel," says he, which is not her name but the one by which he calls her. "These are the days of the lost, Jezebel. Yet I, the fruitful labourer, am full while thunder and lightning strikes in the houses of the ungodly. Amen."

Martha raises her face. She is young, perhaps thirty; her hair is white, her beauty gone. "Food, Will," she says. "Not for me, for my children; food for the love of God!"

"Aye, girl. Two sacks of flour are under the boards right by here where I am sitting. Happy, happy is the man who rejoices in such beauty as yours, Jezebel, for in this pit of misery it upholds him to bear all that the Big Man sends, aye!"

"Will!" She is upon her feet now, pleading above him.

"Hisht, girl!"

"Will, they are weeping upstairs, they are weeping!"

"*Hisht*, or you will have the neighbours in. The children will be fed, but all in good time. First you will read to Will?"

And Martha puts her hands over her face.

"Read, my precious?" softly, soothingly, he pleads.

Silence, except for sobbing.

"*Duw Mawr!*" His voice is a scream, the stick is high. "Christ, but you shall read!"

"What verse, Will?"

And he answers, "May the starving die because of their iniquities, and may the Man of the Lower Palace possess them. Judges nineteen, chapter nineteen. Read!"

The Book divides to its worn place, and Martha Tafarn, knowing the words by heart, turns down her face, saying, " 'And it came to pass in those days, when there was no king in Israel, that there was a certain Levite sojourning on the side of Mount Ephraim, who took to himself a concubine out of Bethlehem-judah. And his concubine played the whore against him, and went away from him. . . .' "

"And the name of the Levite, woman?" asks Will through his teeth.

"Mr Will Tafarn of Carmarthen," says Martha.

"And the name of the concubine, woman?"

"Mrs Martha Tafarn, whose name is Jezebel."

Will smiles and lowers the willow stick. "Read," he says.

" '. . . And divided her, together with her bones, into twelve pieces, and sent her into all the coasts of Israel.' "

"And why such a punishment, answer me?" He leans, peering.

"Because she was a whore, because a man made sport with her in her husband's bed, a harlot, even as I, Martha Tafarn, who has brought forth bastard children."

"Amen," says Will. "Off with the dress."

She always gets it worse on strike pay nights, says Mrs Watcyn Evans next door.

And it was a pay night when Will came home on fire.


Up at the top of North Street there is a light in a window. Wicked Gwennie Lewis is dry of the milk for her third, and she sits on the bed with her first one buried, her third one screaming and her second lying beside her, white as a sheet.

"It is finished," says Gwennie, pressing her breast. "There is a stupid flat old thing that once was the pride of the county —not even a dew drop to wet it," and she takes a breath and tucks it into her bodice. "*Dammo di!* There's a life!" And she bends and kisses the baby. "Sinking my pride for you, boy," she says. "I am off to Mam to see if she has any to spare."

Her door opens, the store-room of the disused ironworks. Light floods the snow. Hugging her sack over her shoulders she bends into the wind on her way down the Hill.

"Good evening, Iestyn Mortymer."

"How are you, Gwennie Lewis?"

"I am off," says Mo, and goes, running.

"What the hell is wrong with him, then? Does he think I have the cholera?" asks Gwennie.

"He is late for his supper, girl."

"Good God," says she. "Are people still eating supper?"

109

Her face is pinched and pale, the shadows under her eyes deep, the cheekbones proud. "Well, are you, Iestyn Mortymer?"

"Well enough, but getting poorer, like the rest."

"Too poor to spare a penny for me?"

"Aye. Nothing, see—not a farthing—given it all to my mam."

"Mean swine," says she. "And talking of pigs, is Dai Two still living?"

"Only just. They are sticking him tomorrow."

She tosses her head. "*Diawch!* When the town is six feet down and the undertakers dead the Mortymers will still be feeding. Keep your penny and to hell with your pork," and down the Hill she goes to the house of her father. She knocks, crying:

"Mam! Dada!"

But the door does not move, the blind does not turn.

"You are wasting your time there, girl," says a voice. "They are keeping their word never to see you again, so do not lower yourself."

It is Billy Handy come from Garndyrus, smelling of ale, and the prints in the snow behind him are cloven hooves.

"Two children starving," sobs Gwennie. "One short of bread and the other of milk. O, Jesus, pity me, Billy."

"Thank God for me," says he. "Very strange, it is, for I was just walking up to your door."

"With food, Billy?"

His cap comes off and he bows low, squat and black against the snow. "With money, girl, look!" And the silver leaps in his hand.

"Not with you, Billy Handy, not for two-pounds-ten!"

"Not that much money in Nanty, Gwennie. Have a bit of sense, woman. Even Crawshay Bailey is going to a shadow, they tell me. One and sixpence?"

It was a criss-cross baying moonbeam of a night, with the wind wolf-howling around the crooked shadows of the squatting house, a night of witches and besoms and brooms and curses, when Gwennie Lewis bared herself to Billy Handy on the pee-soaked bed of the ruined ironworks, for money, in strike time, to keep her children fed.

Tread softly over the snow of the town on strike, do not disturb their sleeping, six to a bed for warmth. The only people eating are the masters and the parsons, who have never gone hungry yet. But Tomos Traherne, the lay preacher, is doing well on his knees and very powerful with his blessings, and Evans the Death is making his fortune, for the Truck Shop has run out of coffins and shrouds. Hold your breath outside the window of Five Hush Silence Street or Mrs Gwallter will see you. Look down the moonlight into her room. There is no fire, no lamp; frost is shining on their boards. Mr Gwallter, up to his elbows in his trews, face deep in his beard, is getting it, and Tegwen Gwallter is in form.

"Damned loafer, damned pig! A fool I was to give you a second look!"

"Tegwen!"

A long-tongued shrew of a woman she is, with a white, peaked face and a body as a broom, but he loves her.

"Six weeks now! Six weeks, and our Willie has gone to a skeleton, all because of pride . . .!"

"Tegwen, would you break me?" he whines.

"Break you? You fat, pot-bellied swine! They are crying out for puddlers up at Nanty and you sit here idling without a glass of water in the house—flooded your belly with beer when you had it—remember? Throwing it around at the bloody politicians of the Benefit, and where has it landed you?" She leans towards him with hatred in her eyes. "In the gutter where you belong, Gwallter. Do you hear me—in the gutter!"

The old chair creaks as Gwallter rises, and the seat of his great backside, shining with grease, fills the window. Lumbering, he reaches the wall, fingers spread, and leans against it, shoulders shaking. Six feet five, he is; four hundred pounds of iron he can carry on his back. He weeps, whispering, "O, merciful God, save us!"

"Blasphemy now, is it?" she breathes. *"Uffern dân!"*

"Tegwen!"

"Up to Nanty this moment," says she. "And back tonight with money or by God I will go running to Billy Handy and do the same as Gwen Lewis."

The Scotch Cattle were waiting astride the road to Nanty that night, and they strung Gwallter up, stripped off his clothes and flogged him with willow sticks to the bone, and not a sound he made, they say, not a tear he wept.

Cold in our house, too, come to that, with no fire and Morfydd gone to live in Nanty. My father, mother, Edwina, Jethro and me sat around the empty grate on the last night of the strike, and the voice of Tomos Traherne was weak.

" 'Why art thou cast down, O my soul?' he asked, 'and why art thou disquieted within me? Hope thou in God; for I shall yet praise Him for the help of His countenance. In God we boast all the day long, and praise Thy name for ever. Selah. Wherefore hidest Thy face, and forgettest our affliction and our oppression? For our soul is bowed down to the dust; our belly cleaveth unto the earth. Arise for our help, and redeem us for Thy mercies' sake. Amen.' "

Amen.

# CHAPTER NINE

AFTER SIX weeks the men got up from their hunkers and their wives and children drove them back to work under the masters' terms, as always. This was the strike that was going to change things, but it did nothing for our house except keep Morfydd from home. After the strike she had left us for a room with a widow woman in Nanty, it was said, but I knew she was living there with Bennet. The end of the strike on masters' terms was a moral victory for my father, of course, but he was dying inside for Morfydd, my mother said. Every night he sat by the window with the curtain pulled back, watching the road; shrugging his shoulders every time her name was mentioned, as if he cared little if he saw her again, but he was a year older with every month she was away. Little else happened that year. Dai Two Pig was reprieved even as Billy Handy was sharpening the knife, for word came that the strikers were breaking. Gwennie Lewis's second passed on to Bethlehem despite the money from Billy Handy, and Sara Roberts lost her other twin brother. By early spring the furnaces at Garndyrus were flaring again and the Irish had their wakes and buried their dead.

Most Sundays, when the women had no jobs for me, I fished the Usk down at Llanelen Village.

Out of bed at first light, me. Crawl from under the table—for Edwina and Jethro slept together in Morfydd's room now—dress in the kitchen and away out of the back door and up the mountain in the cold, spring sunlight.

The hills were April-misted, the old sun red and rosy after his winter sleep. Up to the tram road, down the middle of the Blorenge to Llanfoist Wharf and away down the canal bank where the sheep scamper. Badgers crawled to earth, little lambs did their contortions, Shams-y-Coed's big black bull ran me over the fields regular on those spring mornings when

I poached down at Llanelen. Down to the Old Forge where the blacksmith changes the shoes of the gentry, and full of tales he is: of how his forebears heard the great Howell Harris preach; of another who shoed a horse back to front to save a preacher chased for sedition. But the anvil was quiet, the blacksmith was sleeping as I ran over the bridge and past the board that says *no fishing*. Panting, I lay on the bank of moss with the music of the river flowing over me. Weeds waved, stones shimmered, insects droned. This is the way to fish—with the fingers. I would not give houseroom to rods and deceitful baits. Crawl through the reeds and over the boulders to the big pools where the great trout sleep. Over the last rock. Steady, peep.

Quiet he lies in shade, all two pounds of him shimmering in his fishy world of peace.

Nearer, nearer, quiet as a cobra. Two Pounds waves and leers at the bubbles spinning up in the light-flood, dreaming of fat bugs and flies—spits and rolls his eye at a water beetle . . . dozing and swaying with lazy delight.

Slide over the boulder, in with the hand. Touch mud and send up a smokescreen, for this fish looks clever. Your hand is near him when the water clears and light darts and veers in the depths as the sun comes red and raging over the peaks. Narrow the eyes and reach deeper; bite back the gasp as the river comes flooding over your armpit. Two Pounds flaps his tail six inches from your fingers, shivering with joy at the approaching warmth. For two million years he has been frozen, little wonder that he paddles to meet you. Stretch and push and reach him. Tickle, and watch him grin. There is a daft old fish—old enough to know better. Wriggling like a bride in a feather bed he yawns and spits, rubbing his tail against the palm of your hand. Smooth his belly, stroke him round the privates, tickle him under the gills. Cup your hand and watch him roll into it while everything else with sense is flying for shelter. Count his breathing, open, close, open— act when he yawns and gain an advantage. The river swirls, the foam tumbles, the wind sighs. Two Pounds rolls and eddies, paralysed with pleasure.

Crook the fingers, heave up, throw him wide. Too late he remembers what his old mam told him. Gasping, flapping, he leaps against the green, a silver crescent of sunlight and terror. Getting up I put an end to his capers and stowed him high in a tree away from otters. With a good look round for bailiffs, I whistled downriver to the deeper pools.

The blackthorn was a shower of white blossom here and the chestnut trees and alders grew in profusion along the banks where the deep green moss framed the fumbling rush of the river. High above me, revelling in the growing heat of the sun, a lark nicked and dived, its song crystal clear in the white and blue. Resting now, with my head against the bank, I dozed in the glory of the solitude, watching the heat-flies dancing in early columns at the edge of the river that changed its colour with each fresh rush of the sun. There is a peace that comes into you on the banks of water; peace in the movement of small things that scratch and crawl, in the eternal rush and foaming. And you begin to think of the legions of men who have rested in such a place, weary after battle, sleeping after labour, or stretching out their arms for lovers. The peace is holier, I think, on Sundays, when the bells are ringing in the valley. What a land it is, this Wales! And of all its villages Llanelen is surely the best. The river is milk here, the country is honey, the mountains are crisp brown loaves hot from the baker's oven one moment and green or golden glory the next. Beauty lies here by the singing river where the otters bark and the salmon leap, and I wish to God the English had stayed in England and ripped their own fields and burst their own mountains.

I did not doze for long because a salmon was jumping downriver near the sandy bend, making enough palaver for a man diving. Rising, I pulled aside the branches and watched him. There is a salmon for you—five feet long if he is an inch, and well over a hundred pounds—a hen-salmon, by the look of it—standing on its tail in three feet of water, throwing its white arms about and combing out its long, black hair.

Lovely is a woman naked, bathing in a river.

Visiting the house of Grandfer Shams-y-Coed once I saw a

painting of a woman in water; one of the Greeks, she was, with enough breast and backside on her for three women. I have never understood the old painters, unless their women were different to mine. Once I saw Morfydd dressing for an outing. The old artists would have been hard put to give her a behind like they hang on some of their women, a belly like a drunkard and breasts like a sixteen-stone Irish labourer.

It was the same with this salmon. She could not have been behind the door when things were handed out, for a trimmer figure I have never seen in or out of a set of stays, with long slim legs and as narrow as a boy in the hips and thighs, but plenty in the right places, like Morfydd. I lay among the branches, hot to go on fire, calling myself every swine in creation and breaking my neck for another look. There she was, naked—in the shallows one moment, in the deep the next; splashing about like a mad woman, flinging her hair out and combing it clean, sending the spray misting coloured in sunlight. For minutes I watched her. She dived and swam closer. Nearer, nearer she came. Now, opposite my position on the bank, she stood upright and swept the water from her face, then, with arms held out for balance, she waded in to the shore. With my hands spread to move, I froze. Just beyond my feet, lying on the stones, were clothes. I sank back. Wishing myself to the devil I shut my eyes and listened to the stones turning as she tiptoed to the hiding place. I heard her singing; humming in a minor key between gasps. She was so close now that I could have touched her wet body through the leaves. Her hands were running in sunlight. They paused, then flew to her breasts. She gasped, staring. I stared back. It was so quiet that I heard fish sipping.

"Good morning," I said, sitting up. "There's strange where you came from."

She did not reply. With wild eyes she stooped, snatched up her dress, waved her arms into it and stumbled backwards, her hands pressed to her face.

"I was asleep," I said. "You are lighter on the feet than most, for the slightest sound wakes me. If you have come down to bathe then I will go from here sharp."

She was smaller with the dress on, a ragged dress ripped at the hem and I watched her tying it at the waist with rope. Fear was in her eyes, her face was pale, her fingers fumbling with the knot.

"Do not be afraid," I said. "I have sisters myself and often come down here to bathe with them naked. Look, I will turn my back while you put on the rest of your clothes."

I turned, staring over the meadow and heard her gasping haste behind me. So far she had not spoken a word.

"Where you from?" I asked, not turning, for I was struggling to remember where I had seen her before.

"Newport," said she.

"On your bare feet?"

"Aye. I had shoes when I started but they came to holes at Pontypool and at Llanover they dropped off."

"Newport hirings, is it?" I asked, half turning.

"Yes," said she, calmer, and I remembered. She was the girl the farmer had bought after little Dewi Lewis on the day of the annual outing at Newport Fair.

"And you ran?" I asked, facing her.

She was tying her hair back with faded ribbon and smoothing the wet strands from her face. She was beautiful as an Irish girl, her eyes large and dark, her lips red.

"Aye," she said, her eyes low. "Working like a slave and sleeping in a pig cot, and the farmer tried free with me, so I ran to follow the iron where money is paid for good women."

"For work?" I asked.

"Aye," said she. "What else, for God's sake?"

"Are you hungry?"

"Aye," she said. "Starved, but it is work I am after." She raised her feet. Blood was on them. "I have had berries but too sore in the feet to go much farther."

"Stomach first," I said. "We will see to feet after. Have you a fancy for trout cooked on a spit?"

She was weighing me up for something lunatic. "Plenty here," she replied, "but no way of catching them."

I grinned. "Come with me. Some of the stupid ones climb trees," and I led the way to the upriver pools.

Wonderful to see her face when I threw the trout from the branches, gutted him on a stone with my knife, skewered him and set him over a fire on sticks. Not a word, not a move from her as I rubbed for a flame, but I saw the spit wet upon her lips as I toasted him both sides and laid him flat for eating.

"There," I said. "Now I will disappear while you put him down as best you can," and I gave her the knife.

I might have been something in a grain sack for all the notice she took of me then, for her eyes were on the boulder where Two Pounds lay as brown as any out of a frying pan. And I went from her to a quiet place of bushes and took off my shirt and tore out the arms. When I came back the trout was down without even the head or tail to show which way he went.

"Sit you down," I said. "Now for the feet," and I knelt with the sleeves ready. She was mine now, I felt. Leave her to wander and she would end in an Irish hovel, giving herself to a rich master by day and a poor one at night.

She began to cry then, her eyes flooding and the tears splashing down the sack dress, her fist pressed into her mouth.

"Hell," I said. "Do not start that. Down on your backside with you and let me have the feet, then I will take you up the mountain where my mother will feed you like a dandy."

I bandaged her, and the blood grew in wide stains on Mam's white washing.

"What is your name?" she asked when I had done one.

"Iestyn Mortymer. What is yours?"

"Mari Dirion," she answered.

"There is Welsh in that, but you speak like a north country."

"My father was English and my mother Swansea," said she, "but both are dead. I was on my way south when I starved and went for the Newport hirings."

I nodded, not interested. It was close to chapel time and the river bailiff would be round. Tying the last knot I pulled her up. "Come," I said, helping her up the bank into the meadow.

Up the mountain we went, hand in hand, over the canal, over the top and down into town with the doors coming open and the curtains going back and look what Iestyn Mortymer has got, good God. People on street corners whispered behind their hands but the men knocked their caps and the women dropped a knee at the stranger, all very friendly and polite, and I was proud of my town.

Snell's trap was waiting outside our house. My father was bellowing to Jethro to make haste and Edwina was flouncing about in ribbons and lace when I took Mari Dirion up to the back gate. My mother came through it, her eyes like saucers.

"Good heavens!" said she. "Did you catch this fishing?" which made Mari smile. "A stranger, is it? A friend of yours, Iestyn?"

Not a glance from my mother at the ragged dress, the bandaged feet.

"Her name is Mari Dirion," I explained. "She has run from the Newport hirings, and she is starving."

"O, Mam!" cried Edwina, clutching her Bible. "Church is ringing already and if we wait to take you to Chapel we will be late!"

"Minutes late," said Snell, his feet itching on the road.

"Away with you, then, and give the devil a basting," said Mam, her arms waving. "A child is starving. The God I pray to will last another few hours. Hywel, out to the back with you and knock up another bed. Iestyn, away and tell Tomos Traherne we have a little visitor in need of help from the hirings, and are we within the law to keep her?"

"Aye," I said, and went like a maniac.

"Come, my child," said my father, and led Mari Dirion within.

# CHAPTER TEN

TROUBLE WAS coming. It was running in the air, breathed out in tap-rooms, shrieked at the stormy mountain meetings. Merthyr was seething under Crawshay; Risca, Tredegar, Dowlais and Nantyglo were whispering, and my town was little better. The men were taking hours over jobs that could be done in seconds and spent their time in drawing up protests that never reached the masters because of the people in between.

My father had forbidden me to visit Nantyglo now that Morfydd had settled there, for news that she was living in sin with Richard Bennet was quick to get around. Perhaps that was why there was no mention of Morfydd in the house, not even when her birthday came round. Strange are parents to forbid talk of a loved one and lay her place at table; to forbid a visit to her and yet keep flowers in her room.

Morfydd had been gone from home months now. She had stayed with us during the strike, scrubbing at Gilwern to bring home money, but she left the moment it was settled, and best for everybody, too, for she and my father were at each other's throats over politics. The fortnight Mari stayed at home helped to take away the loss of Morfydd, but the house was upside down again on the day Tomos Traherne called to take Mari over to Nantyglo, where he had found work for her with the wife of Solly Widdle Jew, the furniture man.

Living in sin, was Morfydd, it was whispered. No member of a decent family sets foot in Nantyglo, said my father.

Monday afternoon, on with my best trews and jacket, with creases to cut your shins; hair flattened down with water, shoes to shave in, and a buttonhole as big as a bride's bouquet.

In love, me. To hell with rules and regulations.

In love with Mari Dirion of Carmarthen, where her grandfather was born, and to hell with her English relations also.

Trembling, I went from our house that day and climbed the Coity in a riot of early summer flowers, with the heather coming alive and the ferns swinging flat in straight lines to the wind coming over from the Beacons. Larks were singing when I reached the top, and there was a gladness and purity about that Sunday that has stayed with me years. Soft was the wind that day, for he is usually in a terrible way with him up there, bringing up sulphur and cinders from the furnaces at Nantyglo and stripping the trees before their season—hitting them down one way, waiting for them to get up and then hitting them down the other. Like ironmasters, I thought, burning and starving people right and left and paying just enough in wages to guarantee the new generation and treat it just the same.

Tomos Traherne I found on the top of the Coity—of all places for a preacher. On his knees and well down to it, was Tomos, with the sun shining bright on his bald patch and the wind making ringlets in his beard.

"Good afternoon, Tomos," I said. "What are you doing up here?"

"Giving hell to ironmasters," said he, "from the Crawshays of Cyfarthfa to the Guests of Dowlais via the Baileys of Nantyglo and back return journey."

"I will join you in that," I said.

"Eh dear no," he replied, "though I go hot to burn when I see the Hollow of the Scab from the top of the Coity—Nantyglo that was once beautiful being burned out by one English devil after another. No, Iestyn," and he rose to face me and the goodness lay fresh and clear in his lined face. "Just for a walk, I am, and now giving thanks for the glory of the day and the goodness of the Lord to our town."

"Aye," I said. "Thank God we are not Cyfarthfa, with Crawshay starving them and the Redcoats shooting them down, and hangings."

I saw his face in profile then, granite in its strength and purpose. Generations were upon him standing there with his eyes narrowed against the sun and the smoke of Nantyglo flying across the frame of the sky; a second Moses with the

Book in his hands; a giant with the broken tablets of stone at his feet because of the wickedness of the people.

"Will you join me in asking for His justice upon the persecutors?" he asked.

"Aye, if you think it will help," I said.

"Kneel," said he, and we knelt. The wind swept about us, fanning the heather to life and blowing sweetness. "O Lord our God," cried Tomos, very fierce, "do You hearken unto two of Thy children who do call upon Thee for the justice written in the Book of Habakkuk, Thy holy Word. Chapter two, Iestyn, at random; you first, and give it glory."

I let the wind take the pages, and read:

" 'Woe to him that buildeth a town with blood, and stablisheth a city by iniquity. . . .' "

"Yea!" cried Tomos, swept away. " 'Because he transgresseth, by wine, he is a proud man, neither keepeth at home, who enlargeth his desire as hell, and is as death, and cannot be satisfied, but gathereth unto him all nations, and heapeth unto him all people!' "

"Verse seven!" I said fiercely. " 'Shall they not rise up suddenly that shall bite thee, and awake that shall vex thee, and thou shalt be for booties unto them?' "

" 'Because thou hast spoiled many nations,' " shouted Tomos, " 'all the remnant of the people shall spoil thee; because of men's blood, and for the violence of the land, of the city, and all that dwell therein.' "

We fell to silence. The wind sighed.

"O do Thou hear Thy Word, Lord," whispered Tomos, trembling, "and deliver Thy suffering people from the hands of the greedy and iniquitous, even as Thy Son did deliver the peoples of the earth!"

"Amen," I said, and helped him to his feet and we stood there with the sun hot upon us.

"Look you," said he, deep. "See the scab of Nanty, the blackened hollow that was once my home, Iestyn. The day is coming, mark me, when this town and every other iron town on the mountains will take revenge. Torches will flare, pulpits tremble, the rich flee the land and the crown of England quake before the onslaught of the burned and maimed. What has happened in France can happen here. Men stand so much, no more. Swords will unsheath, muskets fly, blood run. . . ."

"Negotiation is the principle of the Union," I said sharp.

"Aye?" and he looked at me very old-fashioned. "And who mentioned Unions? Do not lecture me about the principles of unionism for I am too old in the tooth. Men working under the lash are not stirred by organisations, boy, but ideals, and the Union is another name for Rabble, a dispute within itself. You shout about negotiation, but you need two for a negotiation and you will not find a master on The Top to sit the other side of a table to bandy words with the Unwashed. So what is left to us—force—force backed by ideals. How else will you win justice when the whip is backed by the bullets of garrisons and the laws of the land are perverted? Aye, Iestyn, blood. Black will be the day of reckoning, with much weeping and the crying of children over the graves of their fathers, and I hope to God I am crumbling when it comes."

His words shocked me.

"Look," said he. "A town tying up its loins for war—see the Hollow of the Scab. See Cwm Crachen!"

I looked down at Nanty. I saw the stunted trees, their blackened arms flaring skyward; the starved grass and bushes —ragged and charred as the lives of men are charred by oppression. And from the tall brick chimneys where the fireshot smoke poured there came a whisper in a lull of the wind; a whisper that grew into a great noise like the sobbing of a multitude. In hot flushes the sobbing grew, sweeping over the mountain that was trembling to the drop-hammers as to the explosion of cannon. I saw the little stone cottages flatten as the earth heaved and the long lines of coloured washing stripped clean, and women were weeping and begging to men with bright swords in their hands. The fields tore open and mountainous flame and smoke spewed out. Horses reared, wheels revolved into blurs of light, and balls of fire descended into the valley, exploding and maiming. And in my blindness I saw the town of Nantyglo shimmer like the coals of a forge before shattering into nothingness and brilliant light.

And from the heat of the vision came the shape of Tomos beside me. The grip of his hand turned me and his voice echoed from the pit I had created in my dream.

"*Iestyn!*"

I stared at him. Large in the eye he was, and ghostly, and sweat was upon his face. Gasping, I shook away his hand and turned and ran down the mountain with fearful looks at his squat body on the top. For what I had seen was real to me, brought about by the picture he conjured, and I knew the wizardry in him—knowing that all he had related I would see in my generation, when he was safe and dead, leaving me to suffer it.

A drunk I found in Nantyglo, rolling like a barrel on legs, with his cap on the back of his head and a posy in his button-hole big enough to bury him.

"Good God," said he, eyeing me. "Is it Morfydd Mortymer you'll be wanting, man?"

"Aye." I knew him for drunken Irish and was in no mood for humour.

"Is it a politician you are then?" he asked, staggering.

"No odds to that," I said. "Are you telling me or not?"

"No offence meant," and he put his finger up. "I am only asking, see, since this Mortymer woman is a witch for political speeches, and when she is not drawing up Union Charters she is rousing the rabble in Merthyr." He belched and patted his belly. "Old Guy Fawkes is a monk compared with her, man. She would have the Parliament sky-high while he was still mixing gunpowder. . . ."

"For Heaven's sake," I said. "Where does she live?"

"Go you," he gasped, leaning on me. "The last house to Coalbrookvale, she lives, near the chapel, and if deacons are there for the love of God do not mention the name of Barney Kerrigan."

Crowds of men and women thronged the doorways in Nantyglo, whispering and nodding as I passed—puddlers, most of the men, their faces blistered and hands bandaged and heavy in the legs, which is a drying of the joints by heat. Some were nearly blind, and their red eyes blinked away tears for a better look at the stranger. Little ragged children were playing *Diawl bach y ffenest* and screaming with delight, but scores of men were sitting on their hunkers farther down the street, many short of an arm or leg, others on crutches or in splints with grimed bandages. This was the refuse of the Bailey Empire, the price paid in blisters and maiming, when the spit of a cauldron or the fly of a winch brought discharge and starvation. And high above the roof-tops, dulling the sun, rolled the smoke and sulphur of Cwm Crachen, hanging in a pall over the house of Bailey with its round battlements of stone. Beautiful was the garden, a splash of colour in a wilderness, facing square to the hovels of the labourers and the thunder of the works.

At the door of the last house, I knocked.

The door opened and I smiled for Morfydd, but Mari Dirion stood there, and I do not know who was most surprised.

"Good God," she said. "Iestyn Mortymer, is it?"

"Aye. Is Morfydd here?"

"Eh dear, no!" she whispered. "Two days ago Morfydd and Richard Bennet went to Merthyr, and not back yet," and had she said China I would not have raised an eye, for the barrier of shyness was between us, built by absence.

I stood on the doorstep screwing my cap. The room behind her was small but tidy, with a smell of candles and warmth and people about it, and the cloth laid for tea was white.

"Come you in," she said. "Half the windows in town are open and the neighbours cracking their necks."

"It is not decent," I said. "Nobody but you in by there, and the deacons will have us."

"And Morfydd will have the deacons," said she, "and their children down to the fourth generation. This is her house now the widow woman is dead. A cup of tea for you and welcome?"

In with me quick before she changed her mind.

She was beautiful indeed, smiling at me now with something like tears as she closed the door and leaned against it. There was no sound but the hiss of the kettle and the distant thunder of the hammers.

"I did not expect you here," I said. "Tomos Traherne said he had got you with Solly Widdle Jew, and no mention of Morfydd."

"Sit you down," she whispered, and we sat down looking, but mostly at the floor. Pretty little things were hanging near the fire and she got up and snatched them down as if they were burning.

Tall and straight was this new Mari Dirion, narrow in the waist and pointed in the chest, and with a dignity I had not noticed down at the river.

"Are you still with Solly Widdle?" I asked.

"No. Down at Blaina scrubbing," said she. "Start at six in the Agent's office, then to his house to help his wife, but I am home here by evening to cook for Morfydd and Richard before the night meetings."

"Tomos brought you straight here, then?"

"Aye," said she with a giggle. "To make it decent, for the word was round that Morfydd and Richard were living in sin. So three in the bed now, it is, with me in the middle."

"The truth?" I said, frowning.

"Good Heavens, they are backward in your town! O, Iestyn! Can you imagine Morfydd sharing her man with anyone? *Diawl!* But you have to give something to the neighbours."

She laughed and hooked the kettle from the hob and the pot hissed and sighed. It was like home sitting there with the rustle of her dress about me; like a marriage, it was, with the cups tinkling and the firelight flickering on the drawn curtains which kept out the neighbours. A devil of a place for gossip was Nanty, Mari said. Faces six deep over the window-sill very often, she explained, with the one in the middle shouting what was happening to the crowd at the back, and cheers every time he took another piece of cherry cake or she poured another cup of tea—and the whole town knew if the lamp blew out.

Better than a man for telling a tale, she was; her face lighting up and her hands waving.

"Have you given a thought to me, Mari?"

This brought the light from her face.

"Tell me," I said like a man.

She smiled again. "There is nothing wrong with the old feet now," she said, "nor the stomach, come to that. Could I forget the one who fed and bandaged me and took me home?"

"You remember me because of those things?"

"Because of other things, too," she said, wistful. "When walking on the bank of the Afon-Llwyd and watching the colliers bring out the trout, or standing on the Llangattock tram road and hearing the rumbling and jingle of the harness, as I heard in your town."

"Only by those things?"

"It is enough for a start," she said, dimpling.

"Then we will do it again," I cried. "We will leave this dirty old place next Sunday and I will sleep by the river again and you will bathe, then I will catch a fine trout for you and roast him on a spit, be damn!"

"Never tasted the like since," said she, laughing. "Next Sunday, then, and teach me how to bring them out with my fingers, is it?"

"O, Mari!" I said, for she was upon her feet for the kettle and close enough to catch her waist. And before she knew it she was in my arms and hard against me, leaning back with the force of my lips on her mouth.

"Upon my soul," said she, gasping and pushing.

"Are you angry?" I asked.

She stood there with her fingers twisting together and her dark eyes rising and lowering, spreading the lashes wide over her cheeks.

"Mari, I love you," I said. "From the first moment . . . down at Llanelen, my precious."

Smiling, she caught my hand and pressed it against her breast. "Iestyn, not here, boy. Not in Morfydd's house. Next Sunday would be better. Down at Llanelen, I will meet you there to bathe. O, Iestyn, do you love me truly?"

"I love you," I said. "Mari Dirion, I do love you, my sweet."

"Then I shall be yours next Sunday," she answered, whispering, "for I love you, too, and would take a spoon and be your girl. But not here, Iestyn. Not in Morfydd's house."

A quick courtship even by Welsh standards, this one. I went over the Coity late that night before Richard and Morfydd got back from Merthyr, and the moon was a grinning pumpkin sitting on the mountain; grinning at me, perhaps, stepping so light in hobnails that I did not touch the heather.

But I was uneasy in my mind as I took my first tram down the Govilon Incline three days from then. The dawn had been up two hours. The Valley of the Usk lay misted and golden under the rising sun and the air was as crisp as frosted wine. Away to the west the pasture lands rolled to the Brecon Beacons, their peaks mist-shrouded and purple with threats, and below me as I rounded the breast of the mountain the thatched roofs of the Abergavenny wool weavers flashed like sovereigns in the happiness of the morning.

But Idris Foreman was not happy. I reined Elot to a halt, for he was sitting on the tramway with a straw between his teeth, staring into the valley. I spragged my tram and went round to him.

"Sit you down," said he. "Your father is coming for a bit of a conference," and he nodded to a tram coming down fast. Owen Howells bolted up and my father jumped down from the tram with Griff after him.

"You sent for us, Idris?" My father had little time for the foreman of Garndyrus, because of his politics.

Idris Foreman got up. "I have just heard from Merthyr," he said. "Richard Bennet, your daughter's man, has been killed in a riot."

A strange emotion is fear. The arrows of words plunge deep. Rooted, you stand as a furnace bolt screwed tight by men with shoulders, and voices are unheeded sounds that beat on the ears in stupid repetition.

"Two balls in his chest," said Idris. "Tonight his Union

brothers are bringing him home for a decent burial, as he requested."

"And Morfydd?" asked my father, his eyes closed.

"According to Gwallter's brother-in-law who brought the news, she is safe in Nantyglo. She left Merthyr last night after a meeting. The disturbances began after she left and the Redcoats were called out again. Bennet was captured and held for shouting the mob to violence. He was shot trying to escape this morning."

"You sent him," I said. "A set of bloody fanatics, the lot of you, except that some sit at home and others go out to fight."

"Aye," replied Idris smoothly. "The brains for the planning and brawn for violence. One Bennet more or less does not matter, remember it. And I got my position by distinctive service, so remember that, too. Ask them in London who disarmed the Swansea cavalry during the Merthyr riots and sent Major Penrice back to his depot on foot. We have all taken our risks for the likes of the Mortymers who sit and watch which way the wind blows before they act, so do not talk to me of sitting at home."

"What do you want with us?" asked my father, cold.

"Five men," replied Idris. "You four and me, to give a man a decent burial. Gwallter will be waiting in Llanfoist tunnel at midnight. Redcoats are all over the mountains between here and Merthyr and visiting towns in search of arms. Be up here by midnight, all of us, with picks and shovels to meet the tram bringing him up."

"What about the coffin?" asked Dada.

"A shroud is handier, mind," put in Owen Howells. "Griff and I have been sharing a penny a week for Ifor Sheddick our father-in-law, but the way he is chirping. . . ."

"Bring it," said Idris.

"A bit short it will be," whispered Griff. "Old Ifor never topped five feet, see, and no disrespect, Mr Mortymer, but your daughter's chap is damned near a foot taller, though we could tie it like a collar, eh, Owen?"

"A shroud is a shroud—never mind a tailor's fitting," said Idris. "The Mortymers will bring picks and the rest of us shovels, and up here by midnight. Back to work now before the Agent becomes suspicious."

"Eh, dear!" said my father beside me.

The early heat was rising in mists and he narrowed his eyes and looked towards Crickhowell, where the shadows of the trees were shortening and blackening as the sun came flaring red and hot with him over the ridges.

"Eh dear," he said again in a voice of tears. "Empty, empty my girl will be without him."

"Iestyn!" whispered my father.

My dream was peaceful when his hand tightened upon my shoulder; a dream of burial parties and Redcoats and musket volleys. I struggled up.

"Eleven o'clock," said my father. "Out to the back with you and fetch the picks."

The night was black with him and there was frost in the wind as I went into the hen-house near Dai Two's sty at the bottom of the garden.

Queer old things are hens on the roost when they are disturbed; grumbling balls of feather, knocking each other about and complaining to the rooster and making enough noise to raise the neighbourhood. A good rooster we had, too, with a chest on him like the prow of a battleship, tail feathers like a prize peacock and a crow that sent hens broody for miles. And now he was on the haft of the pick, making swipes at me to protect his furnishings.

"Get you over, you swine," I said, but he raved and got me twice on the knuckles, so I clenched my fist and got him with a right that knocked him flat. One pick out. I was reaching for the other when he came at me like a mad thing and no wonder they put spurs on the devils.

"What are you doing in there, laying eggs?" asked my father, frowning in with a lighted match.

"It is this bloody old cockerel," I said.

"For God's sake," said he. "Making enough noise to wake St Peter, the pair of you." And he pushed me aside, brought his fist in and hit the thing out for a week. "Get the pick and let us get on with it. It is a secret burial we are attending, not Newport Fair poultry."

With the pick heads wrapped for clanks, we took the mountain road to The Top, with me growing colder every step at the thought of approaching death. It was a cold black witch of a night with the moon watching us from a tear in the clouds and crooked shadows and little things screaming, for stoats were hunting—right music for a burial party. Up Turnpike, past the Garndyrus Inn and down to the Llanfoist Cable-House we went, and the men waiting there were ghosts of silence with mist for breath, their eyes shining from their corpse faces, the undertakers.

"All quiet up by here?" asked Idris Foreman, coming up.

"Like the grave," said Owen. "But Redcoats are guarding the road by the Puddler's Arms and searching people for weapons."

"And is it clear at Llanfoist?"

"Not a soul at the Wharf, thank God, except Gwallter, who is waiting for the hearse," and he chuckled deep.

"Treat it with respect," said Idris. "You may lie beside Bennet before the night is out."

"Aye aye," said Owen, his face turned up, "but this do strike me as damned stupid, Idris. *Diawch!* Six of us risking a roasting for a bit of dead meat that prefers a hole on a mountain to one in a valley, it do not make sense."

"Leave the sense of it to your betters," said Idris, "and put your ear to that cableway for the tram will be up any minute."

The mountain was shuddering to the forge-hammers of Garndyrus, and faintly on the wind came the plaintive singing of the Irish haulers. Llanfoist farms were sleeping in the pit-blackness below, their blind windows winking at the stars, and Abergavenny was a town of dead, strangled by the ribbon of the Usk that gleamed and flashed in the scudding moonlight. All that afternoon the Redcoats had been in town, questioning and looking for arms by order of the Lord Lieutenant of the county, my father said in whispers. The ironmasters were forming their volunteer units from loyal employees, new Redcoats had arrived at Brecon Garrison. Trouble was coming, God help us, said Griff. He did not know which was quicker, being hung by the rabble or shot by the Military, and what with Unions and Scotch Cattle and Charters it might be safer to vote for George the Fourth or whoever was sitting on the throne of England now. Had we heard of the Spanish arms that were coming in carts from Newport? asked Owen. Down in town the rumours were the same, said Idris, the Redcoats questioning at doors and searching. The Irish, with shot under their floorboards, were as dumb as usual, he said; arms folded on their shovels, watching every move, spitting on the doorsteps when the gold was shown. Dic Shon Ffyrnig, who would blab his soul to the devil in drink, had been refused drink at every beer-house in town. And poor Mrs Jeremiah Jones, the mad woman, had been carried to the cottage of Griff Howells, which was more an arsenal than a cottage these days, said Owen. With a pillow under her vest and a midwife either side of her saying her time was nigh, her screams shifted the Lieutenant sharper than a monkey, said Griff, and all credit to his wife for thinking of it.

"Hisht, you!" whispered Idris. "A tram is coming."

"Midnight," said my father. "He is a better timekeeper dead than alive, if it is Bennet."

In the horror of the mountain stillness I listened to the dead coming up from the valley. Strange that a thing alive is acceptable and when dead horrible. I knew the terror of the singing cable ropes, the pinched faces of the watchers, the loaded tram going down, the mist of the tram making shape, the arm that dangled over the side, the dead fist that thumped the iron, in death defiant; a white arm, clad in silk still bright with Morfydd's washing, thumping its dull blows as the tram lurched and swivelled to the cable stop. My father was instantly upon the tram, spragging it to a halt, and from its black inside the head and shoulders of Mr Gwallter rose up like a bear feasting.

"Is it quiet down at Llanfoist?" asked Idris.

"Like a tomb," replied Gwallter, climbing out. "Those

English brothers are loyal. They brought him up from the church, dodging Redcoats every yard. We could do with a few of their kind in town, by God," and he shivered. "A cold ride, Idris, with his dead eyes watching me all the way. Come on, boys, give a hand."

Gwallter, still weak from his flogging, grunted and pulled, and my father leaped to help him. "Come," he said to me. "There is nothing in death, man. Only sleeping and cold with the blanket slipped off."

I nodded, shivering.

"A light, for pity's sake," whispered Owen. "It is black as a pit by here and I do not know if I have an arm or a leg."

I had an arm.

Cold.

Cold as ice; an arm frozen; helpless in its stupid twisting and slapping as my father turned him. I heaved, lifting nothing.

"Up your end, Iestyn; the boy is head down. Put the arm around your neck, man; the dead do not strangle. Up!"

In Richard's embrace I stumbled forward, sweating.

We carried him up to the tram road. No sound but the sighing wind and the grunting men and my own heart thumping. We took him through the heather, in darkness one moment, in moonlight the next, and I saw his face and throat spotted with blood from the smack of the ball and his bared chest starched with blood under his torn, silken shirt. Under the crest of the mountain we laid him, this thing Morfydd had loved.

"Down by here," gasped Idris, wiping sweat. "We will rest for a bit, then dig deep. Young Mortymer—away with you to the tram road and watch for soldiers. Give us half an hour and we will have him down, but any sign of lanterns hurry and tell us or we will finish in Monmouth. Who has the shroud?"

"By here," whispered Owen, "and tidy, for our mam has stitched on the extra foot."

"Right, then," said Idris, grasping a pick. "You and I will take first dig, Owen," and as I left them the picks struck.

133

Down on the tram road I watched the toll-gate.

Vain things are tears. I fought mine down, listening to the sounds of the diggers. It was like a harmony of voices; the chinking of the picks, the deep thrusts of the shovels were like the piping of a woman and a man's grumbling responses, with a bit of a child butting in between.

And then the light at the toll-gate went out and a new, brighter light came swinging down the tram road from Garndyrus. Scrambling up, I ran back to the burial party.

"Out of it!" I cried. "The light is out at the Puddler's and another is coming down the tram road."

"Away," said Idris, collecting shovels. "Listen, young Mortymer. We are going over the crest. If the lamp passes, then up to the ridge to fetch us, is it?"

"Go," I said.

As the last of their footsteps thumped the heather I bent, turned out their dim lantern and knelt, watching for the light. Over the crest it came; nearer, nearer, straight, as if guided, for the shallow grave where Richard was lying, his face and shoulders in sharp outline against the sky. My heart was hiting away against my shirt as the light came on. Rabbits scampered from the feet of the wanderer, partridge clattered in terror from the waving circle of light, and the moon, findnig a rent, lit the mountain with blueness before pulling down her skirts and covering him with darkness.

Tall and straight was the woman carrying the lantern, and her skirt was billowing and her hair waving behind her as she held it high. Her face was white, her eyes wild as she drew nearer. And seeing Bennet in the grave she knelt and lowered the lantern. For seconds she stared at him, and then she made claws of her fingers and put them in her hair and turned her face to the sky and screamed. Three times she screamed, her breast going up, her eyes shut tight, her mouth gaping, but no sound came forth. Not a sound, not a whisper she made with those screams. And she flung herself down over the body of Bennet and gripped it, sobbing.

"Morfydd," I said, touching her.

She drew from him like a tiger from prey.

134

"Dead, is he?" she said at nothing.

"Aye, Morfydd. Aye. They told you in Nanty?"

The wind hit between us, sighing.

"No," she said, "I did not know. Tonight he was coming from Hereford. Cyfarthfa first, you understand, then Hereford to speak with Lovett, and was lifting back home along the limestone tram road. When he goes to Hereford I meet him at the cable house, but tonight I saw a lantern and came by here."

There was just the two of us in the world then.

I clenched my hands and shut my eyes, my head bowed. When I opened my eyes Morfydd was staring.

"Away," she said. "What is it now, then—peeping?"

The tone of her drove me back. I went into the deeper heather, for there was a strangeness about her that was fearful.

"O my love, my precious," she said. "Late you are tonight, but still time for loving before we go back. Kiss me now, for nobody is watching. Why, there is cold you are, boy, and no wonder with no coat. Take me quick, for I am warm, Richard. Still as brazen as the hussies in London, is it? But you are in love with me, your pretty little Welsh. Wicked enough for three I am, for you," and she kissed his lips in wildness and passion, her hands caressing his face.

I could bear it no longer. Leaping up, I dashed upon her, seized her shoulders and dragged her away. Her bodice tore in my hands. Crying out, I snatched at her waist, locked my fingers and flung myself backwards, but she rolled on top and clawed my face to the mouth. She was screaming now. Her face was with madness and her hair flying across it while she spat and bit like a cat. Sobbing, I fought her off, gasping and pleading, but she was blind in her lust to be back to Bennet. Kicking, scratching, she rolled from my arms and flung herself over the grave. Her hair was down, her breast bare and her skirt ripped to the waist. Like a guardian dog, on all fours, she faced me.

"Back home," she whispered, panting. "*Away!* Touch a hair of his head again and I will have you in bits and swinging from hooks."

I got to my feet.

"Morfydd, for the love of God leave him!"

"Eh dear!" she said, and laughed, her voice shrill. "If it's not parents it's brothers—nobody like the Welsh for busy-bodies, mind. To hell, Iestyn, you should know better! Keep to your own business and leave me to mine. Eh, dear! There is a life, Richard! Back to Nanty, is it? Mari is waiting with supper. Come now."

I saw the kick of her legs as she twisted her shoulders under his chest. She heaved, grunting, and crawled, dragging him after her.

"Morfydd," I whispered, and she looked from under the load with his arms swinging before her.

Kneeling, I brought up my fist.

The blow would have angered a man. Morfydd sighed and dropped flat. I hauled Bennet from her, straightened her clothes, and, sobbing, ran to the ridge for my father.

# CHAPTER ELEVEN

For weeks after we put Bennet down our house was like a tomb, everybody talking in whispers. Night after night it was the same; into the bath, out of it, empty it, up to supper, and face my father across the table after shift. Edwina did her embroidery, Mam her spinning, and the old black clock ticked our lives away with nothing but the clatter of plates or the whirring wheel to break the silence.

And up in the best bedroom sits Morfydd. No trouble bringing her back from Nanty, for we carried her; too big a sickness for Mari Dirion, who had gone to work full time for the Agent, Mr Hart.

"Have you finished, boy?" asked my mother.

"Aye."

The wheel spun from light to shape, her hands came down from the shuttle. Opening the oven door my mother put the plate of oatmeal on the table and looked at my father.

"Two mouthfuls a night, Hywel. She is starving to death."

"Only the soul can starve to death with food about," said he. "She will come to it. Take it up, Iestyn."

Up the stairs with it now, open the bedroom door. Jethro is asleep in the bed, Morfydd sits beside it. Still as a cat she sits, watching the window; watching the sun dip behind the mountain where her man lies buried. For three weeks she has sat like this dressed in her Sunday best, dead but breathing, waiting for Richard's knock. Beautiful, she looks, more lovely than when running in the wind with her cheeks bitten scarlet with frost and her hair tangled; lovelier than in summer and dressed in bright colours, swinging her hips through the heather with one or another. Now, in the silence of this grief, her beauty would tempt a saint. The brow is high and pale, the hair brushed back into plaits upon her head, streaked with

white at the temples. Her cheeks are stretched tight and with
deep shadows, her eyes in repose, sick of weeping. A new
Morfydd. No challenge left, no fight. As if the flood had
quenched the fierce heat of her, with her hands in her lap, she
sits.

"Have you seen Richard today, Iestyn?"

"Never mind about courting, girl—eat this oatmeal."

"What did he say?"

I took a deep breath. "Get some of this down and I will tell
you."

"Now," said she, swallowing a spoonful as if swallowing
chaff.

"Tonight Richard is going to Coalbrookvale," I said.

"To Zephaniah Williams at the Royal Oak?"

"To a meeting there, more fool him," I said sharp.

"The Charter it will be at the finish, mind," she said quick.
"You can say what you like about Benefits and Unions, but
the pair of them can be bought for pints. It is ideals the people
will follow, the Charter. God, but my boy is climbing!"

"In the wrong direction, if you ask me," I said, for she eats
better during an argument. "A pig is this Zephaniah man, and
a drunken atheist into the bargain."

"No proof of atheism, mind," she said sharp, "only gutter
talk." She had the spoon full in the pan and I helped it up to
her mouth and pushed it in. "Educated, is Zephaniah," she
spluttered, "even the young Bailey says that. These are the
men we want for leaders, not gutter rats and watchmakers,
and then we will get the Four Points of the Union's new
Charter from Parliament with the help of God or not."

"Four Points, Four Points!" I said. "If it is double-dutch
to me, how the devil can the masses understand it?" I got the
spoon in again.

"Listen, stupid," said she. "William Lovett, who has
formed the London Union of Workers, has drawn up a demand
from Parliament which asks four things—the right of every
man to vote; a secret vote; a new Parliament every year; and
Members of our choice whether they own land or not. And
when the people get this there will be no need of Unions. Put

the king in a mansion, says Richard, and away with his palaces. Away with dukes and knighthoods, earls and viscounts! This is the new generation pledged to break the grip of the aristocracy who rule our lives. This is the rise of the common people to new heights of liberty when the tyranny of Crown and Church shall be brought to ashes and goodness and equality exist among all men. . . ."

"Morfydd, hush," I said.

"O, God!" she whispered.

I held her hard against me.

"O, God!" she cried. "There's empty I am without my boy, Iestyn. Empty . . .!"

Downstairs with the plate now.

"Heaven be praised," said my mother.

"Clean as a bone," said my father.

"Funny she will eat for Iestyn," said Edwina; "she will not take a bite for me."

Through the madness of the make-believe Morfydd lived, dead inside.

And on the third month after Richard's death she came large in the waist with her and with sickness every morning, being in child.

A terrible thing is the scandal.

Those who live among filth are the first to throw it.

Like Mrs Pantrych and Mrs Ffyrnig and a few more I could mention.

Hands deep in my pockets I whistled my way home after shift at Garndyrus; as important as the accident trolley to Mrs Pantrych and Mrs Ffyrnig. Gabble gabble, gobble gobble. Their hair hangs low, darkness is in their faces. They lean on their gates with their breasts shoved up and split deep; soiled women, dirty in the mind and mouth; a pair of turkeys with noises to match.

"Hisht, Mrs Pantrych! Here is her brother."

"Do not hisht me, Mrs Ffyrnig. If a thing is indecent I be not afraid to say so—let him take it back to the family."

"Ten to one it is Iolo Milk. Twice I saw her up on the Coity with her skirt past her middle."

"Aye, woman, but not lately. Bennet is the second name, take it from me."

"Eh, hush you! Here is Iestyn."

"And he is not much better, mind. Mad for it are the Mortymers."

Whistle louder, go to walk past.

"Good evening, Iestyn Mortimer." The pair of them in chorus and with bows. Gentry now, their lips slobbering as tap-bar spittoons.

"Good evening, Mrs Pantrych. How are all the children?"

"Fine, fine, boy. How is your mam?"

"Happy as a skylark. How is Dic Shon, Mrs Ffyrnig? Still as round in the belly with the funds of the Benefit?"

This sets them looking.

And once they are running you kick their backsides.

"How is your husband, Mrs Pantrych? Well, I hope?" Eight she has now and expectations of ten by the stretch of her apron, and not a father between them.

I gave them scandal at first, but I was running in the end.


"You can always find somebody worse off than yourself, mind," said Morfydd. "Mrs Gwallter and Willie, for instance."

I was with Gwallter when he took the iron. Like Will Tafarn he took it, only worse.

Number Two Furnace was ready for tapping when the Agent brought three visitors round. English, by the look of them, up for the shooting, being August; dandies by the cut of them, proved as dandies later.

Everything was wrong for Gwallter when the Agent called for a tap of Number Two so the visitors could watch the molten iron coming out. Afel Hughes, who kept the furnace, was down in town with the Owner. Idris Foreman was lining a tram road over the Tumble, and Will Blaenavon, who knew Number Two like his hand, was down in Abergavenny for tools.

"Come on, come on!" said the Agent.

A bitch was Number Two. She made good iron but she boiled high and was always losing her bung, so Afel held her with a stone in the clay to keep her tight. But only Afel knew.

"Tell him to go to hell," whispered my father. "I would not touch that furnace with a hundred-foot rod unless I knew her."

But Gwallter, being Gwallter, only grinned and took the firing-iron and stooped and knocked out the stone and the liquid iron spat under blast in a shaft of white fire that took him in the face, and he screamed and fell and it sprayed him over the chest and set it on fire. He bit off the tips of his fingers when they pulled him clear, and died. Four bodies they laid out on the tumps, the other three being the dandies. And when they sprinkled water over their faces to bring them round, they sprinkled some on Gwallter, who had no face, which put the Irish into stitches.

"Thank God he went easy," said Morfydd now.

We sat quiet, thinking about the Gwallters.

"Are you telling Dada soon?" I asked her.

"About the baby? It would kill him."

"He will have to know some time," I said. "If Mam or the neighbours do not tell him he will see for himself."

She stood by the window looking at the mountain. "Do not worry," she said, "I am going from here soon."

"To where?"

"To London, perhaps."

"They are starving to death there according to Lovett, without you adding to it."

"One more will make no difference, then," said she. "If you think I am staying here as fun for deacons you are mistaken. This is Richard's boy and as Richard's boy I will raise him. I will sell myself to raise him, for in him lies the greatness that was his father's, the greatness that will sway his generation as Richard has swayed ours." She put her hands over her face.

"All right, all right," I said. "London it is, then—anywhere you like, but let's have an end to it."

I was half way down the stairs when knocking came on the back.

"Well, here's a surprise!" I heard my mother say. "Dafydd Phillips come to visit. Morfydd, Morfydd!"

From the bottom of the stairs, looking through the kitchen, I saw him. Very smart, looked Dafydd, very prosperous, with his nose back to brown and dressed to kill with button-holes either side.

"Just come to give my respects to Morfydd, Mrs Morty-mer," said he. "A sad time for her this, no mistake, and she will need her friends about her."

Aye, I thought, but you are a little late, and I was right.

Not a whisper had come from Morfydd about her trouble, not a word from me since she confessed it, but a town of neighbours is excellent at guessing. And strange it is, how often a town is right.

A gale of words swept through the rowdies now. Slander flew around corners, expelled in belches, bubbled through beer, undressing the man, raping the woman, but always keeping clear of the family. And from the moment of Dafydd's visit the slander grew.

"It is a wonder Tomos Traherne puts up with it after the way he ran Dathyl Jenkins and Gwen Lewis up the mountain."

And not one of them with proof that Morfydd was in child.

"Ought to have his head examined, did Dafydd—played second fiddle to that Englishman for years!"

Then the Irish got hold of it and said it was time Morfydd had one out. Mervyn Jones Counter put it round the Company Shop, smiling his rhubarb smile and giving short weight in the commotion.

Dafydd Phillips called again and again. He and Morfydd walked out together, unaware of the stares, and if Tomos Traherne knew of it he made no mention. I could bear it no longer. Edwina was down at Abergavenny with Snell, Jethro, my mother and father out for a Reading. Morfydd was dressing for Chapel, Dafydd was due.

"Morfydd," I said, in without knocking. "What is happening?"

"He knows," said she, tying her bows.

"Dafydd knows—you have told him about the baby?"

"He wants to wed me," she said.

"Is he in his right mind?"

Morfydd turned, lowering her hands. "Listen," she said. "I do not care. I am carrying Richard's child and I want a name for it. I have been wife to Richard a hundred times and more—he knows that, too, and still he wants me. Marrying Dafydd Phillips is better for my child, better for Dada."

"You will regret it," I said.

"No doubt," she replied, "but I am not thinking of myself."

"Nor are you thinking of Dafydd," I replied sharp. "No good will come of it, mark me, Morfydd. A marriage like this can be hell."

"Dafydd is willing; it is all that matters," she said. "It takes two to make a hell of marriage, and in return I will treat him decent, clean and cook, and be a wife."

"And loving Bennet every minute."

Morfydd sighed. "Too much store is put on this business of loving," she said. "If I was a man looking for a wife I would marry a girl full if it suited me. But I would kill her if one had his way with her after."

"That is one view," I replied. "Think hard and you will find another to suit you better. One month, two, might be all right. But after that Dafydd will grind you for what you have done to him and hate the sight of you and your child."

"Right, you," she said. "You have had your say. Out."

Things happened quickly after that.

First Harry Ostler, all fifteen stone of him, was found with his jaw smashed, propped against the walls of Ostler Row.

Big in the mouth was Harry and handy with a quart.

143

"Harry Ostler has been found with his jaw smashed and eyes he will not see from for weeks," I told my father.

We were in the shed, making a new trough for Dai Two.

"There's a pity," said he, staring at his hammer.

"And nobody can think who has done it."

"Really now."

"No," I said. "People are saying that three got him in the dark."

Very interesting was that hammer, it appeared.

"Show me your hands, Iestyn," said he, raising his eyes to mine. I did so, and he turned them over and hit the knuckles. "Shame on you that they are not cut to pieces," said he. "Do you know that grown men are writing things on walls?"

"Yes," I said, looking down.

"About one of your sisters?"

I nodded.

"Then cut your hands and quick," said he, "for men like Harry Ostler are a waste of time to me and should be yours," and he went from me to the door of the shed and put his hands to his face. He said, broken:

"You are close to Morfydd, Iestyn. Tell me, boy, and cut no words about it. Are these things true?"

I stood in silence.

He swung round, his face white, the fury in him striking me a blow. "The truth, Iestyn, or by God I will cripple you. Me, the father, and I am the last to know!"

"She is full, if that is what you want!" I cried. "By Bennet, and no amount of deacon palaver will alter it, and she will still be full though you cast her from Chapel and send her from home."

He stood as still as an image, eyes closed, hands clenched by his sides.

"She loved him," I said.

"Go from me, Iestyn."

I went past him to the door. "Dada," I said, "their love was great and beautiful. You could search the world over...."

"Go," he said.

And I went from him into the kitchen, and there, by the sink, I listened to him sobbing.

It was different up with Morfydd.

Straight to her room I went to tell her, for there was a madness in my father that had made me afraid.

She was kneeling in her stays, pawing the bedroom floor like a mare with a load on, the strings tied to the bed-rail.

Pretty enough to take the breath, this one, with her long, slim legs and her breast white and high-curved above the petticoats she had rolled to her waist.

"For God's sake," said she. "Two inches less and not a soul in the congregation will be the wiser."

"What are you up to?" I asked, gaping.

"Getting into my wedding dress. Now you are here you can help, man. Against the bed with you and your foot in my back and we will pull together, is it?"

"You will have it on the altar steps the way you are going," I said.

"Do not be vulgar, Iestyn."

"It is you who is vulgar for treating it so lightly!"

"It is done," she said, spreading her hands. "Nothing will undo it. Face facts, boy. Like a preacher you are, Church of England at that. Come now, another two inches, for the dress is going at the seams."

Blindly, I helped her. She kissed me as if I was the groom, danced to the middle of the floor and whirled out the measuring tape. "Twenty inches," she said with pride. "How is that for the family honour? Throw me the dress, boy."

I said, facing her:

"Morfydd, it is out. Dada knows."

Her expression changed from happiness to horror and she clapped her hands to her mouth.

"Aye," I said. "He knows. Perhaps for a day or two he has known."

"O God!" she said, and sank down by the bed with the dress crushed to her face and her fist thumping the blankets. "O God!"

To lose myself I went out.

But I did not lose myself, and when I came back down the mountain Snell's trap was outside our house, which meant that Mother, Edwina and Jethro had returned from Abergavenny. I went in my usual way, vaulting the gate. But when I got to the back door it was open and Tomos Traherne was standing there in black and fury, facing my family, who had their eyes cast down. Morfydd, in her wedding dress, pale and proud, had her face up.

"And so," went on Tomos, deep and fine, "as a fit punishment for the sin of fornication you will appear before the deacons tonight and be cast out. For never, as long as I am alive, will you be granted the sanctity of marriage in Chapel."

He had said this before, of course, and there had been weeping and pleading and God help me and God let me die.

Morfydd said, her eyes flashing, "Amen. A man of God you call yourself? The likes of you, Tomos Traherne, and the rest of your deacons will fry on the grids of hell at the Judgment for cruelty to the unborn. Now get from here sharp, you psalm-singing swine, before I take my nails to your face and act like the bitch you make me."

Very fast went Tomos, but bitter were the tears he left behind him.

# CHAPTER TWELVE

NEW TINTS were on the trees when Morfydd married Dafydd Phillips in Coalbrookvale, within sneezing distance of the Royal Oak Inn, the Chartist meeting-house, which was a sign of things to come, said Will Blaenavon.

All our family went to the wedding, which was a relief, said my mother, and it was well attended by people from our town, which was to be expected, said Morfydd, for it is unusual to have a bride in child. Dando looked Dafydd in his best suit and his white buttonhole of mock carnations, boots to shave in, a collar high enough to cut his throat and enough airs about him to grace a pack of gentry. Beautiful was Morfydd with her long, defiant stare around the congregation; looking for trouble, said my father, even at the moment of betrothal. But she need not have bothered, for she was loved and respected in Nanty and the people were there in force with bugles going and guns sounding and enough ropes tied across the chapel entrance to hold a troop of cavalry. My father was in a holy quiet all through the service but the demonstration of the people of Nanty impressed him, I think. My mother and Edwina were in tears, of course, which is the custom for the women, and Mari and I sat together with Jethro, waiting for our chance to get on the mountain. Big Rhys Jenkins and Mo were there, Afel Hughes and the Roberts family, with Sara all ribbons and lace and looking daggers at Mari. Mr and Mrs Twm-y-Beddau came in Snell's trap and Idris Foreman and the Howells boys, who brought half the revolutionaries in Monmouthshire. People I had never seen before were present, all friends of Morfydd, I heard; gentlemen, some of them, with good cuts to their suits and dignity about them. And when we got to Market Road the neighbours were waiting with their tables loaded and the children coming and going with their arms full of late summer flowers.

Very impressed with Nantyglo, I told Mari, although I could not get away from the reception and up the mountain quick enough. The sun was shining brilliantly as we walked into the shadows of trees and lay down there, hand in hand, each tense with the magic of the loneliness.

On my elbow, I looked at Mari. Her hair was tied in a black ribbon behind her head and her arms were bare to the shoulders. She looked golden, steeped in sun, the patterned shadows of the branches giving a rich, dark texture to her skin.

There was no need for words lying there. Below us lay the Cwm, about us was the mountain with his changing colours of sun. The stillness of the day brought tranquillity, a drowsiness that seemed part of loving. She was in my arms now. I caught a fleeting glimpse of her eyes, large and startled, as I kissed her. She was as grown from the summer, lithe, soft, resisting; part of the mountain moving beneath me as I kissed her again, and there were no sounds for us but the breathing of the wind and the rustling of the branches that sheltered us. The hammers of Coalbrookvale and the mills of Nanty were silent in that lovemaking, obliterated by the quickening surge of our blood as we lay together lips against lips. There is a searing of the blood when the breathing quickens, a heat and a madness, with the mouth crushing and the hands seeking soft places.

"No," whispered Mari.

And the sound of her brought me back to life, to the trees above us, to the mountain beneath us.

"Eh dear!" I said. "Yes for a change, is it?"

"Not in daylight," she said with business.

"In darkness, then?" I held her, kissing her throat.

"You are wicked to hell," said she, struggling up. "I am from here sharp before I am in trouble." Laughing, I pulled her to her feet and kissed her again, the length of her against me.

"O, Mari!" I said.

"No bathing with you down at Llanelen," she cried, "for you are grown up. Last one down to Cwm Crachen is brain-

148

less," and she lifted high her dress and ran like the wind with me after her and shrieking to her to stop. Morfydd and Dafydd we found there, standing in the kitchen of their Number Five, hand in hand, with all the guests gone.

"Five o'clock," said Morfydd. "Mam waited for as long as she could but the men had to get back for the killing."

It was then that I remembered. Murder was being committed that evening, murder by men of one of their fellows. The crime was to have been carried out before the wedding so Morfydd and Dafydd could have had a ham to cut at, but Billy Handy, the murderer, was drunk, so my father would not let him near Dai Two.

In the shock of remembering what was to happen I took my leave of Mari in a dream, bowed to Dafydd and Morfydd and left, leaving the three of them staring.

And back I went up the mountain.

A pig, I think, should die in darkness, so a man cannot see the shame of his neighbour's face. For what kind of man is it who can take the blood of his fellow over his hands with a smile? A pig is a very intelligent animal. There is much of a man in a pig and more of a swine in a man, and who are we to pass sentence over one who eats from soil while we have teeth and nails to tear with? Hypocrites, all of us, especially people like Billy Handy, professional stickers.

The sun was going down as I crested the Coity and I stood there on the top, seeking a movement in the scarred valley, listening for a scream. And then I sat in the heather remembering that I had been making love while poor little Dai was being penned for execution. For an hour I sat there, watching the sun go down, thinking of many clocks striking and cockerels three times crowing and Dai Two looking for me in his terror.

And at six o'clock, Judas, believing the betrayal complete, rose, and went down into the valley.

Mr Snell's trap and mare were outside our house when I got there, with Edwina sitting up in front, waiting. Hearing me coming she turned, up with her skirts and down into the road.

"O, Iestyn! Go from here!" she cried in panic.

"Why?" I asked.

"Because the killing is starting when Billy Handy gets here."

"But the killing is over," I said in wonder.

"No. Not started, see? Billy Handy was drunk again and Dada sent him back home to get sober," and her eyes, like saucers, threatened to drop from her face.

"Good God," I said, empty.

"So away with you, quick," said she, sweeping me up with her skirts.

There was a smell of death in the house, with people bustling about in new bonnets and trews after the wedding, and Mam, peeping round the doorpost to see if Billy Handy was coming, stared straight into my face.

"Good God," said she. "You are in Nanty."

"Do not tell me you have come," said Dada.

I groaned.

"To help in this crime?" He levelled his pipe at me and lowered his voice. "Now listen," said he, "no trouble, remember. There will be enough palaver sticking the thing without Billy Handy losing gallons of blood as well. Look now, Snell is taking Jethro and the women for a trot, so why not slip along?"

"Come with your old mam," said my mother, very damp. "I am nearly in tears myself and the sight of your old pig dying will affect you for weeks, Iestyn."

"Let him go and I will stay," said Jethro, coming up jaunty. "A good pig-sticker I am, says Billy Handy, for I have helped him tie sacks round their snouts to save worrying neighbours."

"Get the little savage from here," said my father.

"A fine future he has," I said. "Foreman at the Panty knacker yard," and I left them all and went down the garden path to make my peace with the criminal. Henry Snell was coming from the shed at the bottom, doing up his flies, something that should be done inside.

"Good evening, Iestyn," said he, pleasant. "A fine evening to be sure."

"Away to hell," I said, "and take that saintly lot with you before I cut a throat or two myself."

I had no time for Snell. Simpering hypocrisy, false religion were in his mouth, the Bible in one hand, the begging box in the other, and to this day I do not know why my father allowed him in the house. Dai Two was cleaner, and I stood by his sty scratching his shoulder until the hooves of Snell's mare faded down the road to Varteg, then I went back to the kitchen.

"I have no stomach for this," said my father, changing into old trews.

"No stomach? I would rather cut the throat of Edwina. For years I have had this pig as a pet and I think more of him than a dog."

"Do not make it harder, Iestyn," he replied. "Do you think I have no heart? And not my old pig either, mind. But big as a house he is getting and eating enough for a regiment of guards—even the pig could see the sense of it."

Tap, tap, tap on the window. The face of Twm-y-Beddau was on the glass.

"For God's sake what does he want?" said my father.

"For God's sake what do you want?" I said, shooting it up.

"It is this old pig, see?" said Twm, jerking his thumb.

"What of him?" asked Dada, lacing boots.

Pale around the mouth was Twm, and sweating. Twenty years he and his woman lived next door to us and not a word of complaint right or left. "Well," said Twm, "it is not so much the pig as my woman, see. Big in the stomach she is, as Mrs Mortymer knows, and most considerate, thank God, but the squealing of a pig could easily bring her on three days from her time. Will he die quiet?"

"If I have a hand in it," said Dada. "So back to your wife with you and tell her there are pigs dying all over the county."

"Thank you, Mr Mortymer, and do not mind my asking?"

"I do not," said Dada. "Now go to hell from here."

Down with the window. Bang bang on the back. "Good grief," said my father, "I am in rags. That will be Billy Handy and the Jenkins—let them in, Iestyn."

"Good afternoon, gentlemen," said Billy Handy, bowing low. "Does a little pig called Dai Two live by here?"

"If you are sober," replied my father, severe.

"Sober as a judge, Mr Mortymer, for I never kill intoxicated for fear of cutting the wrong throat. Tea, is it?" said he, sniffing sad.

"A cup for you, boy?" said my father to Big Rhys coming in.

"Something a little stronger, Hywel," replied Rhys, "for the presence of this man Handy is fair turning my stomach."

"But stomach enough for a slice of decent ham," said Billy, sharpening knives with a leer. "And there is tasty is a cut from the belly after a thick night at the Benefit, Rhys Jenkins. A mug of that very fine beer for me, too, please, Mr Mortymer." He drank deep and gasped. "Well, if it is hating live pigs that makes me a criminal, then you are right. But I am the same as the rest of you when it comes to eating, mind. It is the head of a home-fed pig I do like—slit down the nose and boiled with spice and onions, and the head belongs to the killer, Mr Mortymer, do not forget it. Another mug of this very fine beer again, if you please, and I will have my shilling before we begin, is it?"

"Here," said my father, dropping the silver. "And mind you take it gently with this pig for he is practically a member of the family."

"God help me," said Billy. "Another related pig. Lead the way, gentlemen," and led by my father we all went down the garden. Dai Two came grinning to the bars, happy at this sudden attention from humans.

"Good evening, Dai Two," said Billy, dangling a loop. "Get your snout into this and it will be easier for all of us," and he whipped the loop in and pulled the rope tight.

Captive.

The indecision was in Dai's little red eyes. Then he set his buttocks square and squealed as Billy heaved. The sty door came open, Big Rhys and Mo got on the rope. And as messages from his executed ancestors flashed into his brain, Dai screamed and screamed fit to be heard in Nanty.

Hot and cold, me.

"A very vocal pig this, Mr Mortymer," said Billy, pulling. "A good tenor for the Oratorio, think you? Fetch me a bloody sack, somebody, for I cannot kill during a commotion."

"Never mind sacks, he must die clean!" shouted my father. "This pig will not be tortured, so get him to the board, Billy Handy, and quick."

Up the garden path with us, Billy and Big Rhys heaving on the rope and Mo putting his knees into Dai's backside, and the noise of him was like a thousand babies under torture.

"For God's sake shut that pig!" shouted Twm-y-Beddau, his face over the garden wall.

"Come over that wall and I'll bloody shut you," cried Billy.

"With my woman near dropping her second, it is indecent," yelled Twm, very hot with him.

"If she makes as much noise with her second as she did with her first you will not hear this pig," said Billy, and brought his boot around Dai Two's rear to help him on a yard.

"Easy, easy with the boots!" cried my father between yells.

"It is trying to move him I am," gasped Billy. "And better employed you would be booting than criticising, man."

"Devil take me!" exclaimed Dada. "If you are a pig-sticker, then I am the bishop. Away out of it," and he stooped and hooked his arm under Dai's belly and carried him to the board like a baby.

"A set of cruel swines you are!" shouted Twm above the bedlam. "For years you have been stroking that animal and it would serve you right if he stuck in your throats."

"Hold him steady!" cried Billy. "By heaven, I will settle this palaver," and he reached for his knife and measured the distance to the gullet.

"Never in my life will I touch bacon again," wailed Twm-y-Beddau. "God forgive you, Billy Handy, but you will roast

153

on white-hot grids in hell for what you are doing to that poor defenceless animal!"

"Satan take me!" breathed Billy, resting on the knife and sweating. "How the hell can a man draw blood with people making remarks like that?"

"And my woman in here praying for it to stop," cried Twm. "It is enough to cripple the child having to put up with it."

"Silence!" roared Billy. "Or I will be in there and cut the throats of the three of you!" He groaned then. "Never have I heard the like of this, Mr Mortymer. What with the four of you in tears and half the neighbours in childbirth, it is enough to break the heart of a Carmarthen slaughterer. Do you want this bloody pig slit or not?"

"If there was a law in this town I would have it on you!" yelled Twm, up on the garden wall now and weeping. "A hard man I am in all conscience, Mortymer, but I have grown fond of little Dai and I will pay you double price to save my woman a child with two heads, and hark to her wailing."

And even Dai Two stopped his squealing to listen, I think.

Going very high was Mrs Twm-y-Beddau, howling to raise the churchyard. Easy births and strong in the vocal chords was her trouble, said Mam.

My father took a deep breath now. "Put that knife away and help this pig down, Billy Handy," said he, very firm. "I am decided against it."

"Well!" whispered Billy, gaping. "I will go to my death."

"You are no pig-sticker, see," I said sharp, "or you would have had him from hooks instead of arguing the toss, and now we have changed our minds, eh, Mo?"

"Right," said Mo, cutting his knuckles. "After this show of pig-sticking I would not employ Billy Handy skinning rabbits."

"God help me," said Billy, sitting on the killing board and fanning, and Dai Two took the chance to dive from the board and down the garden path like a hare coursing and nobody saw him for days.

"See what has happened?" said Rhys, looking ugly. "The

pig has left us. Ashamed of yourself you should be, Billy Handy, ashamed, that is the word."

Billy got up. Very pale he looked. "Goodbye," he said. "I have had enough of the Mortymers for one day and their pig in particular, so with all your permissions I am away back to Garndyrus and knock out a bung and lay me under a barrel."

"And welcome," I cried.

"God bless you!" shouted Twm, and ran back to the labour.

# CHAPTER THIRTEEN

Two months Morfydd was married before Mam talked my father into visiting them. Very firm upon this point of visiting was he, saying that young married ones should be left to themselves, which was only an excuse, we knew. Quiet he went when Morfydd's name was mentioned, filling his pipe as if to change the subject, and a narrowing of the eyes. Strong for his Chapel, was Dada, with fornication a long way down the list, said Tomos. And this business of Morfydd on heather instead of a mattress had played hell with him, said Big Rhys Jenkins.

But on the eve of Morfydd's twenty-sixth birthday, being a Saturday, my mother got him in the bedroom and rolled up her sleeves and gave it out sharp. And next morning my father shaved extra close, put on his Sunday best and shouted for Snell's trap and for Jethro and me to make ready. Here was a commotion, for I was only just back from furnace shift and Jethro was as black as a cotton slave, but no matter. Everything happened at once when my father made up his mind. Edwina went flying down the Abergavenny road for Snell, I went into the bath and dragged Jethro in after me, and Mam flapped about in silk and finery giving everybody hell. Out with my best suit and fit up the creases, borrow one of Dada's best Chapel collars and away to the mirror for a clean, white parting.

Off to Nanty to visit the lovers, said Jethro.

A word about Jethro while on the subject.

Dark handsome, he was, and knew it; broad in the shoulders and thick in the arms and hair on his belly at the age of ten. He was like my father in his every move and action, with the same feline grace that is born in the man handy with fists. Quiet was Jethro, speaking with his eyes, which were large and dark and filled with shadow. His teeth were square and white above the thick set of his chin. Hanging on the girls' pigtails to the age of eight, flicking up their skirts to hear them scream, and anything male from ten to fifteen was frightened to death of him.

"Men will be the end of me," said Mam, breathless. "Look at it—three in long trews now."

"Am I tidy?" asked Jethro, coming in.

Eh, tidy he looked, to bring a sigh to Satan, for there is something of sadness when the bony knees of a brother disappear and long trews come in their place. He stood there with his fists on his hips, a miniature Hywel Mortymer. Grief, I thought—with looks like that you will have every girl in town in a bother when you are six years older.

"You would pass in a crowd," I said. "What is that in your buttonhole?"

"Old man's beard," said he. "Morfydd's favourite."

"Visit Nanty with buttonholes and they will down your trews and check you for inches," I said. "Take it off. Flowers are for women, not men."

"Snell wears buttonholes," grumbled Jethro.

"Snell is not a man," I said. "Being dressed like a man does not make you one, either."

"Agreed," said my father, coming in, "there are a few in town who ought to be in skirts, but no names mentioned, mind. If that Dic Shon Ffyrnig calls on me again for contributions to Benefits or Unions, I am losing my temper and hitting him flat."

"Like I am doing to Snell if he calls for Readings," said Jethro, "for I am sick of him. Bloody flat I shall hit him."

"Who is hitting who flat?" asked Mam, coming in with ostrich feathers; "I will not stand for bad language in the house, remember it."

"Not a foul word from any of us yet," said Dada, "but if I start I will take the shine from cassocks."

"What about this old hitting, then?" She looked at us all very severe.

"Our business," said Dada. "And I am in a mood to begin on the nearest, so mind, woman."

"Listen you," said my mother, her finger up. "Listen all three of you—you too, long trews. One threat to poor Dafydd, let alone a hit at him, and I will have you out in the street, do you hear me?"

"Yes," said my father. "Eh dear! Hark at her!"

"Aye, hark," said she. "This is a peaceful visit after a kind invitation and I will make it warm for bruisers who are out to make bedlam."

"And who wants to hit out poor old Dafydd?" asked Dada, innocent.

"Never you mind," replied Mam. "We will have no more of it. Mr Snell's mare is clopping outside and it is time we were moving."

"Snell!" sniffed my father, winking. "No need to travel to Nanty to hit out a son-in-law—there is one I fancy clean on the doorstep."

"One son-in-law at a time," said Mam. "Nanty."

I had forgotten that Nantyglo was on strike again, although Coalbrookvale was going full blast by the sound of her. Down in the valley the furnaces were deserted and the chimneys stood red and derelict against the green. Men sat on their hunkers or were sprawled on the tips. Little groups of children played quietly around the Company Shop where the women were standing with their babies in shawl cradles.

Morfydd's neighbours were squatting around their back doors, but they got up very respectable and dropped a knee or knocked a cap as we went up the garden. Morfydd came to my father's rap. Pretty she looked standing there in the doorway with her hair over her shoulders, except for the eye.

Some good ones I have seen from bare-knuckle stuff, but never an eye like this. Shut tight, it was, and black; swollen like an egg, with cuts top and bottom and blood.

"Good God, girl," whispered Mam. "Whatever have you been doing?"

"A long story," said Morfydd with a laugh. "Come in and hear it and do not stand there gaping, the four of you."

It was a tiny room, with not much in the way of furniture

except boxes; but pretty with late autumn flowers she had picked especially for the occasion. No fire in the grate, no kettle singing; a floor of earth, no spinning-wheel. And cold as a Spanish prison.

"It is not much to ask you to," said Morfydd.

"But better than when we first started, eh, Hywel?" said Mam.

"Heavens, girl, do not expect too much when you are beginning. Silver plate she will be wanting next, like Crawshay Bailey," but I knew she was speaking with her tongue and not her heart. Her face was pale. The mess of Morfydd's eye held her like the rest of us.

"A little palace, girl," Mam went on, after the happy birthdays. "Good grief, what are you asking so soon? Better than seventeen to a room as in town. Find me a little house furnished like this one and I would move tomorrow, Hywel boy."

"And Jethro in long trews, is it?" Morfydd threw up her arms and pulled him against her. "Growing, too. After the women now is he, Iestyn?"

"A terror," I said.

"You have no cause to pass judgment from what I hear dropped occasionally," said Mam, severe. "He is over here most of his spare time, Morfydd, and not to visit his sister, I vow."

"Never you mind, Iestyn," whispered Morfydd, winking her good eye. "A pretty little thing is Mari Dirion. She is working full time down with Hart the Agent, so I do not see much of her now. How is Edwina?"

"Where is Dafydd?" said Dada. It was the way he said it that put an end to the stupid makeweight of a conversation.

"Over at the Lodge but back any minute," answered Morfydd. "Wait a bit while I get this old kettle hot. There is a regulation against gathering coal from the tips, so neighbours are sharing the boiling. It is the dirty old strike, see?"

"How long this time?" asked Mam, empty.

"Two weeks, but it will break us. It is the food he puts in the windows of the Shop that does it."

"What are you after?" asked my father.

"A rise of a shilling in the pound for everyone to bring us in line with Dowlais. Dafydd a pit overman drawing nineteen shillings for working the Balance, but there are women underground at the Garn drawing eight shillings and less. Six and seven children to keep." Morfydd's voice rose. "What the hell can a woman do with eight shillings and six children, tell me, Dada?"

"It is scandalous," said he quietly.

"It is criminal!" This was the old Morfydd. Her fist hit the nearest box. "The strike goes on. Children are starving to death, and the clerk can pass a three-foot coffin on his way to the office without a lift of his hat. Aye, Dafydd is strong for the strike and I am strong for Dafydd for once."

"That is how it should be," said my father.

"Wait now while I get this boiled," said she, "and I will be back," and she went through the door with the black kettle.

The four of us sitting in a circle now and finding the floor very interesting.

"Where is the furniture?" asked Jethro.

"*Hisht, you!* Bad boy!" hissed Mam, while we all looked daggers at him.

In silence we waited for Morfydd to come back.

"Come with me upstairs, Mam," she cried, running in. "It is pretty upstairs and every stick made by Dafydd."

"Wonderful to have a handy man," said my mother, rising. "Lucky to be wed to a craftsman while I am left with bruisers," and with her black skirt held like a tent she swept upstairs, chattering. Their feet were heavy overhead. My father sat like black stone, his eyes moving around the room.

"Is Dafydd strong for the Union?" I asked softly. "His mam was dead against it, remember?"

"There are no blacklegs in Nanty," he replied. "This town has suffered."

"Then their furniture has gone to feed them?"

"Either that or over the bar of The Bush."

"This is not like Dafydd," I said. "With Morfydd by him he would not go back to drinking?"

"Then did she grow that bruise on her face?" He rose, doubling his hands. "By God, Iestyn, if a fist has shut that eye I will make her a widow before I leave tonight."

"*Jawch!*" I scolded. "What an old fighting-cock you are. Dear me! Hit it on the door she has and not given a thought to mention it."

"O aye?" piped Jethro. "Mrs Tafarn got one like it last pay night and that was put with boots."

"Shut it!" I said. "Nobody is talking to you." I turned to my father. "Now keep your temper under your shirt until Morfydd tells you to lose it."

He obeyed, but it was anguish to him. In came my mother behind one of her best smiles. "A sweet little house, to be sure, Hywel," said she. "The upstairs is just like Evan ap Bethell next door but one in Cyfarthfa, remember?"

"Aye, a grand upstairs, that," said Dada.

"Just needs a bit of furnishing down by here," said Morfydd.

Tap tap on the back and a ghost of hunger aged ninety is there with the boiling kettle. Morfydd took it and paid the halfpenny as if it was solid gold.

"Now then, a cup of tea, is it? Dying of thirst you are," and she flung cups and saucers about just as at home. "How is Mrs Pantrych, Mam—still delivering?"

"Ninth coming, she is safer than a calendar."

"And Mrs Gwallter?"

"Sad with her man gone, but Tomos is good to her and Willie is starting at Garndyrus this week. Both the Edwards boys are courting, I hear. . . ."

They had denied it, but anything would do. Pitiful, it is, when loved ones meet behind the armour of pride, when nothing they say is true or with meaning; a conversation of strangers, unimportant, unloved. I sensed the mounting tension, knowing that soon the words would steam dry into silence. In desperation, I said:

"There is a fine old eye you have collected, girl—better than the one I had from Mo Jenkins, remember?"

Morfydd threw back her head and laughed like the old one.

"There now!" said she. "I had forgotten it. Is it that poorly, *bach*. Down at the Shop yesterday I met Mrs Eli Cohen, the Jew girl from London. 'Morfydd Mortymer!' said she. 'Is that Dafydd already knocking you about? For shame, I will take my fists to him, say.'" Morfydd leaned on the table, adding secretly, "And nothing more true, so I could not deny it, and that Cohen girl a terror with the tongue. Dafydd and me chopping sticks, see? A piece flew up from his axe and caught me by here," and she fingered the spot tenderly.

"What was he chopping—trees?" asked my father.

"It is easily done, mind," said Mam like lightning. "Back home a good bit of steak would have brought down the swelling, but no matter, Morfydd *fach*, it will soon be better. Now fill this old cup again, girl, for I am thirstier than a desert."

"How is Dafydd?" I asked, aware that until now he had not been considered much.

"As happy as a man on strike can be," said Morfydd, "but time is heavy. We were doing nicely until he came out. Now he is on Bailey's black list. Strong for the Union is Dafydd, a leader of a lodge, see, and the Agent found out. God knows what will become of us for we are straight from here the moment we cannot find the rent." She raised her head, her hand flying to her mouth.

Dafydd, shadow silent, was standing in the doorway.

Easy to tell when a man has been drinking quarts.

There is the first stage of one or two when the eyes dance; the second stage of three or four when the colour is high. The third is a blueness of the face, eyes half closed, and the manner dangerous. I flashed a look at Morfydd. She was frozen, her hands rigid in her lap.

"Well, well," said Dafydd, and grinned.

"Dafydd," said Morfydd like something wounded. "Mam and Dad have come to visit. . . ."

"Indeed?" he said, lumbering in. "Have I no eyes? Now tell the four of them to go to hell before I bloody shift them, is it?"

"Dafydd!" The shame was such in her face that I could have wept.

"Eh dear! Gentry, now? Not so long ago the Mortymers told me and my mam to go to hell, remember? But a very different story now, eh? What is a little going to hell between relations matter, anyway . . .?"

"Dafydd, my father is here, so mind."

"Aye, I see him. He is too big to miss. How are you, Mr Mortymer? Is it well with you?"

"It will be when you clean your mouth," said Dada.

"Will you please tell us why we are not welcome here?" asked Mam.

"Because you are nosey devils at the best of times, and only because of the old strike you have come, isn't it? Dafydd is drinking again, they told you, eh? It is enough to send any man on the drink to have a vixen of a wife and Four Points of a Workers' Charter for breakfast, dinner and tea."

"It is the meetings," said Morfydd wearily. "He is for the Union like me, but he does not agree with the Charter."

"And I should think not," said Mam sharp.

"O, to hell!" said Dafydd. "It is not only meetings and politics. It is the neighbours waving and pointing and bloody old whispering that does it."

"You knew Morfydd was in child," said my father. "I told you, Tomos told you. It was you who were strong for this marriage, not me."

"Aye," said Dafydd with a belch. "Begged for it, I did, and now I have got it."

"You would be better off without the beer, too," said my father. "A man who drinks in strike-time and blames his wife is not worth visiting."

"Drinking is the trouble, is it?" said Dafydd. "Wait you, I am not standing here to be insulted, Hywel Mortymer. Father-in-law or not, you will go straight through the window before I take orders from you, mind," and he roamed around the room like a dog hackled for fighting, thumping his fist into his palm.

"O, sit you down, Dafydd boy!" said Morfydd, dragging at him.

"And money it is now, I suppose," said he, glaring. "How do I get my money for drinking, is it? Well, that is my business too, Hywel Mortymer, so do not forget it."

"But how you use my daughter is mine," said Dada. He rose. "Drink The Bush dry, boy—join every Union from here to Cyfarthfa, sell every stick of furniture. Send her home if you do not want her, but put your hands on her again and I will be up by here to see you sharp."

"Hywel," whispered Mam, broken.

But Dafydd wheeled quick, ducked, came up and brought over a hook, good for a drunk. Dada slipped it, stepped in and hit up short. Off balance, Dafydd took it in the face, and dropped.

All in a flash; a good family quarrel one moment, fighting the next. Here is a palaver. Women up and rushing with skirts flying, bowls and bandages, and is he all right now, and half the neighbourhood looking through the windows, jawing left and right as to how he deserved it for laying into Morfydd or cursing flashes at interfering in-laws.

"Shame, shame on you!" cried Mam, stamping her foot at Dada, and him not giving a damn, but sitting there frowning and stroking his knuckles. Flat on his back was Dafydd with the egg over the same eye as Morfydd's getting bigger every minute, and breathing for a man embalmed. My father got up, cleared away the women with one arm, bent, and threw water into Dafydd's face. Dafydd groaned and opened his eyes, staring.

"Listen," said my father. "I am going now, but I will be back soon to look for hidings. Everything you give you get, man, but double. Do you understand?"

"Get out!" whispered Dafydd.

"Aye," said my father. "Double."

Not a very successful visit to a bride and groom, that.

I lay in the back of the trap listening to Snell's mare clip-clopping down the Brynmawr Road and my mother giving it to Dada proper. Not a word he said, but I knew what he was thinking. No man could have done more to stop this wedding than him. He sat with his big shoulders hunched and the reins loose in his fingers, and listened, and did not speak.

The autumn nights were drawing in and dusk and bats were dropping around us. Behind us was the red glow, before us the hills shone and sparked, with men working like demons against the glare, and as we came nearer town the night-shift going up Turnpike was whispering in the wind.

Good to be home and away from poor Nanty all weary with strike and fists in the faces of people you love.

Snell and Edwina were in the house together, sitting by the fire too far apart for innocence. They were not supposed to be in the rooms unattended, and I saw my father give Snell a queer old look and a sigh. But a silly view that, I had always thought. If they wanted to be under skirts there was plenty of room in the heather; no need to risk neighbours steaming through keyholes.

"Thank heaven that is over," said Mam, taking off her bonnet. "A decent cup of tea for God's sake."

"How did you find her, Mam?" asked Edwina.

"Happy as a fiddler," said my mother.

"Is Dafydd treating her well?"

"Wonderful."

"A good man is Dafydd Phillips," said Snell, beaming.

"The best," said Dada, "if a woman does not mind a little knocking about."

"Hywel!" said Mam. "Our business, please," and she began to lay the tea.

Snell got up. "I will go now," said he. "At a time like this the family should be alone, not with strangers."

Good for him that he did.

We all went to bed early that night.

Lying there with Jethro asleep beside me I thought of the days when Morfydd and I were children and Jethro a baby and the house full of our gay wickedness. I would have given my soul just then to have such times back. It was black outside and the wind was getting up to tricks, howling in secret places, sighing like cats and hitting gates to bring them from hinges. At times he came to an unholy quiet, as if tired of playing and getting serious. Growing into shape, Tomos once called it.

I like the wind when he is blustering along the cobbles and blowing up the women's skirts, taking the washing from lines and generally playing hell. But in the mood of shape he is different; an animal in shadows crouching to spring, and with claws. And the country he has been thrashing to death all day lies quiet and shivering, awaiting the blow.

That is the wind-silence of fear.

Terrible is this silence, this threat. It comes through cracks and sits by the fire with you, haggard and fearful, snatching at unuttered words, pressing cold fingers around hearts. You cannot see it, but it is there in the lull of the wind; a scent of danger caught on forest air after the world was ice. The stink of the festering claws of the tiger that flies to the nostrils of the trapped hunter.

Jethro stirred in the bed beside me.

"What was that?"

"Lie still," I whispered. "I am going down."

Down the stairs I went like a wraith of silence. The wind was buffeting again, the roof creaking. Landing in the kitchen I crept to the back door. I listened. A footstep scraped the flags outside. Bracing myself, I flung the door wide. And I saw, in a flash of the driving moon, the face of a man terrified, his eyes wide and shining. Something clattered as I struck blindly. Leaping at him I hit a bucket, tripped and fell, cursing. Lying, I listened to the thump of his retreating footsteps, heard the crash of the gate as he flung it back and his hobnails sparking down the cobbled hill.

By the time I had got to my feet my father was in the doorway swinging the lantern.

"Look," I said, and he held the lantern high.

The Mark of the Scab, the Sign of the Blackleg, was painted in red on the door, the bull's head of the Scotch Cattle.

# CHAPTER FOURTEEN

GOING ON shift next day was more like a military parade, and the three of us were on early morning at that, which meant half the town was risen at first light.

"Dear me," said Mam, cutting sandwiches. "If ever a man was begging for a hammering it is mine. Hywel, have sense! With the three of you on the books at Nantyglo the Cattle will be here by dark if you spend an hour on shift."

"And plenty of workers here to throw them back where they came from," said my father, easing into his boots.

"Is there going to be trouble?" begged Edwina, her eyes going big.

"If there is you will not be in it," said Jethro. "We will give him Dai Probert Scotch Cattle, mind, and you can tell them that in Nanty."

My father grinned as he sat at table. Jethro was his image, fearless, years before his time for manhood.

Courage was all right, but often, when women are about, there is not enough to go round. The case to me was clear. We were men employed by Crawshay Bailey. We were on the books of Nantyglo, paid by the Nantyglo paymasters but lent to Garndyrus. If Nantyglo was on strike then we should be on strike, according to the Union. The Scotch Cattle, born and bred in Nanty, were getting bolder. Even Crawshay Bailey had doubled the strength of his 'Workmen Volunteers' and strengthened the walls of his defence roundhouses. For the crime of scab or blackleg men were being dragged out for floggings, furniture was being burned. Legs were being broken in Blackwood for the sin of working when the Union said stop. And Dai Probert, the giant Bull of the Nantyglo Scotch Cattle, was a pig when it came to forcing the Union. Nantyglo had been out two weeks—she had been out for shorter times before and my father and I had worked on at Garndyrus. But now the warning had been given.

And the town rose early to see if we had the courage.

"Dai Probert will take some stopping, Dada," I said at table.

"It is time he was stopped," said he, chewing.

"By who—the three of us?"

"Not in front of your mother, if you please, Iestyn."

"Eh? And why not, may I ask?" said she.

"Ears like bats, but sharper. Get on with the bread, woman, and leave men's business to men." He sighed.

"Aye aye?" she replied, the knife a point at him. "But I am in this, too, mind, if there is trouble, and Edwina. Dai Probert do not come all the way from Nanty to paint doors unless they are special ones." She flung down the knife. "The Mortymers—it is always the Mortymers to set the examples and do the spouting, and when it comes to the end of it less notice is taken than if we were Twm-y-Beddau or the Ffyrnigs."

The walk to Garndyrus was worth seeing that morning.

Every light in The Square was on; people very busy hanging out washing when it was too dark to see pegs. Men who should have been abed were smoking in doorways, and the coming and going up and down garden paths was enough for Fair Day. All up North Street it was the same. Two windows out of the whole of the Row were in darkness. Even Polly Morgan was standing outside the door of the Drum and Monkey, and people were clustered in the yards of Shop Row, talking fifteen to the dozen.

Jethro walked between my father and me. He was working in the Garndyrus Forge with Roberts—I was glad he was not out on the tramways, where an attack could be made to look an accident. I was not worried about my mother or Edwina. Probert had not flogged a woman yet, with or without a Union card.

"If they come it will be tonight," said my father, voicing my thoughts.

"Aye," I said.

"And I will see to it my way, Iestyn, do you understand?"

"By hitting the first one flat? That is the way they tried it in Blackwood. One good leg between four of them they had after Probert was finished." I trudged on, my eyes closed to the pale light of the morning stars.

"And how would you handle Probert?" There was a smile in his words.

"By the three of us buying Union Cards and signing off midday," I replied. "I am good for a fight if there is a chance, but the Cattle are roving in sixties."

"The town will stand by us," said he.

"Aye?" It was Jethro this time, his face upturned. "Twm-y-Beddau next door said to hell with the Mortymers when it comes to Scotch Cattle, and straight over the mountain with him at the first sight of Dai Probert."

"Twm-y-Beddau does not represent the people of this town, thank God," said my father. "The town will stand by us."

"And why should it?" I asked sharp. "We are paid by Crawshay Bailey."

"Look you, stupid," he replied, getting short. "We are paid here in the end. It is only a money transaction in the books, see; only an entry, man. It is this owner we work for."

"God help us," I said. "When Dai Probert hits down the door tonight you can explain the money part of it to him for he cannot count up to five."

"Let him come!" shouted Jethro, fists up, striking at nothing. "Over into Twm-y-Beddau's garden I will hit him and bury him in the Baptist churchyard."

"You cannot see or you will not see," said my father, his eyes on me, his face taut.

"I see all right," I said, "but will Probert? It is him handing out the floggings."

"God help him when I am done with him, mind," said Jethro, still sparring.

"I wonder where your sense is, too," I said, eyeing him.

"And I am wondering which son I would rather have," said

my father. "Ten years back you would have been sparring for a fight, like Jethro. Now you are whining about striking and Union cards. What the devil is wrong with this generation?"

I did not reply. I dare not. The injustice was burning me. His obstinacy against the Union was a stupidity that involved not only us but our women. He despised my generation for its refusal to grovel to authority as he had grovelled and his father before him. Theirs was the blind loyalty that had brought about the need for Unions when, if the profits were shared, there was plenty for everybody. I saw my father in a new light that morning: a man of clay; one ready to tug the forelock as the squire went by. He was set against any form of resistance to the masters who were bleeding us; against the Union, which demanded the right to put a standard upon its labour; against the Benefit Clubs, which existed to feed the starving; and against the coming Charter, which was the new standard of decency forged by men of learning and courage, men like Lovett and O'Connor, the heroes of my generation.

We walked on into the gathering light of the morning. There might have been other blacklegs—men who would pay for their courage—but it seemed to me as we walked down the tram road to the Garndyrus furnaces that we were the only scabs in the county.

The shift was changing and the iron was coming out, and I saw hate in the faces of the men around us. Idris Foreman was standing at Number Two, hitching at his belt.

"You are asking for trouble this time," said he. "More sense you should have, Mortymer, with Probert loose and two women at home."

The puddlers were tapping and the iron was streaming and firing in the sand moulds. Eyes on the Mortymers from all directions; the Mortymers who were on the books of Nantyglo and breaking the Nantyglo strike.

My father did not answer.

"For God's sake!" whispered Will Blaenavon to me. "What the hell are you up to, man? And you with a Union card, too!"

"I do what my father does," I said.

"But it is madness. Have sense! Tomorrow or the day after Garndyrus might be out, too."

They were coming in from the mountain: the mule drovers, the miners, the limestone cutters, the sprag-men, to end the old shift. And while we waited in the heat of the furnaces for the manager to check us in, they eyed us. Leaning on shovels or ladles, with their backs against their trams or lying on the slag, they eyed us. Owen Howells came up with Griff, hands in the waist of his trews, his grin wide.

"Look where you like, deacon," he said, "you will never find such stupidity in the Book, and you have told me to look there once or twice. Probert will take the pair of you and draw bones from your back."

All that day not another man spoke to us, not even to Jethro.

So much for neighbours, I said to my father, and nobody can blame them.

We went back home in daylight, watched the same as on the way out. Dusk came, then darkness. We ate our tea in silence. My mother's face was calm, but her eyes strained. Fear was in Edwina's face, in her trembling hands. Earlier there had been talk of sending her down to Snell at Abergavenny, but my father decided against it. When the family runs the house dies, he said. So we cleared away the things and sat round the fire, Mam spinning, as usual, Edwina well into the Old Testament but not reading a word, and the rest of us listening to the wind. At nine o'clock I went down the garden path to look at the night. The town was dead under the bright stars and the roofs shone black and silver in the frosty air. Not a sound the town made. It crouched in its shadows, holding its breath, amazed at the stupidity of the Mortymers, who had broken the Nantyglo strike and told Dai Probert to go to hell.

And then I heard it.

Faintly on the wind came the lowing of the Cattle, and the sound grew in fury. Like a madness, it was, this faint bellowing. Grown men dressed in the skins of beasts, bellowing in grief for the ones to be flogged. They were coming from the

Coity. Sparks from their torches sailed up against the clouds. All up North Street keys were being turned, bolts thrust over, windows pegged down. The lowing of the Cattle grew nearer. Light shot over the garden as my father opened the door of the back.

"Iestyn."

I went to him.

"Listen," he said. "This is the end of Probert, not us. Do not fight. I will do the talking, you will stay with Mam. When I go with Probert send Jethro to bring Rhys Jenkins and Mo. You run for Mr Traherne and fetch as many men as you can to guard the house and save a burning. There is a military troop waiting for Probert and his Cattle on the road to Nantyglo, waiting to catch him with a prisoner. This was arranged weeks back by the owners. You have your Union card?"

And me thinking he did not know . . .

"Yes," I said, ashamed.

"Show it when they ask—they will not touch Jethro. Probert takes me out for a flogging and lands in the arms of the military. It is time his scum was cleared from the mountains—a good thing for the Union, the workers and the owners, all in one, eh?"

"Yes, Dada," I said.

"For what a man believes in he must fight for, remember. In to the women now, Edwina is taking it hard."

They came in minutes, bellowing, but they went silent when they reached our gate and clustered together, grumbling deep, like cattle nosing an empty manger. Edwina was whimpering in my mother's arms. Our door was unlocked, to save them the trouble of breaking it down. Whispers now as they came over the gate. Silence as they huddled together by the window. My father flung open the door. Six deep they stood, their blackened faces streaming sweat from the running and bellowing. Some were in skins, others in rags, with naked chests and shoulders scarred with the weals of old burns. The light from our kitchen flung the shadows into their eyes, and their sunken, starved faces stared into the room.

Silence, but for their breathing, Edwina's sighing, and the ticking of the clock.

"Well?" said my father. "You come with enough noise. Is there nobody with a tongue?" He stood with his fists on his hips like a giant before them.

"Dai Probert will do the talking," said one in a soft Irish accent.

"Then fetch your bull, for at least he is Welsh. I am not talking to Irish."

"Dai Probert coming now," said another, a gnome of a man with a bandaged face. "And take it from me, Mortymer, you will not know Welsh from Irish before we have finished."

He came with a whip, swinging his comrades aside with his wide shoulders. He was dressed as all Scotch Cattle bulls, in ragged skins that left his chest bare. His face was blackened for night beating but his cheeks were criss-crossed with the vicious ridges of a furnace blow-back, and the wounds were white. The red horns of a cow were strapped to his head with a bandage. He was filthy, and the stink of him crept about us. Inches taller than my father, he outweighed him by stones.

"Hywel Mortymer?" he asked in Welsh.

My father nodded.

"And your son—both on the books of Nantyglo?"

"We work for Hill of Garndyrus."

"To hell with where you work, man—you are paid by Bailey?"

"On behalf of Mr Hill," said my father.

"Aye," and he looked very old fashioned at his Irish. "Nantyglo or Garndyrus, let us see your Union cards or the colour of your money. Your names are on the books of Bailey, and no swine of a blackleg starves our children."

"I have no card," replied my father. "And I do not join anything under the threat of a whip, so away, before I kick you and your Irish back to Nanty."

"Dear me, listen to it!" said Probert. "There is too much talk here for my liking. Moc, boy!" he called. "Have this

173

bastard out into the street for a flogging. Pitch out the women, take the food next door and leave me to the furniture."

A brutal-faced man in skins moved through the crowd at the door. Probert turned to me. "Where is your card?"

"Here," and I offered it, but my father snatched it and flung it away.

"Be clear about this, Probert," he said. "One in a family is a member to you but a scab to me, and he has just resigned." Seeing Probert's changed expression, I looked down. My father held a flintlock pistol. "Now out!" he cried. "Or I will blow your stomach into the legs of the man behind you. Fetch me for a flogging now, man, do not run. To hell with you and your Union that is backed by the whips of bastard Welshmen," and he drove forward into them, the pistol in one hand, hitting out with the other. They flooded before him, tripping over the smashed gate, crying warnings to their comrades on the road.

"Rush him!" roared Probert.

"Aye, rush," cried my father, "for I am tired of playing bloody fancy with scum. Scotch Cattle you call yourselves? Unionists, are you? God forbid that I ever drop a penny a week to the likes of you. Rush and be damned to you," and he walked through them, striking them down, working closer to Probert, who was afraid of the gun. I could not see Dada for the crowd now, but I heard his voice from the road:

"Iestyn! Back in with the women while I drive this rabble back to Nanty where they belong!"

And those were the last words I heard as the Cattle rose about him and struck him down. Baying, lowing, they dragged him to the Brynmawr Road. I watched them take him, sick with despair. And the thing shining in the gutter was a little flintlock pistol. With this he had shifted fifty Scotch Cattle.

I went back to the kitchen. Jethro was there with his arm about my mother. Edwina was crying alone.

"He has moved them from the house, Mam," I said. "He is taking them to the military, who are waiting for Probert."

"God help him," she said at nothing.

"He is working it for the owners, understand?" I shook her. "He is the bait through which the military will catch Probert. It is all arranged. No harm will come to him."

My mother rose. Little and old she looked then, as if ten years had come with the mob and touched her. "Believe that and you are a larger fool than I took you for," she said. "He is too big a man to be a bait for the English against the Welsh—even Scotch Cattle Welsh. He has told you that to keep you safe." Bending, she picked up my Union card and tore it to pieces. "Jethro," she said, "Run down to Mr Rhys Jenkins' house and tell him to come with all the men he can collect. Iestyn," and she turned to me, "go and fetch Tomos Traherne, then away to your father and share what he is having. We will watch the house so you have a roof to come back to, and nothing on your conscience."

In a panic at the thought of dishonour, I ran.

Over the tumps to River Row I went, and screamed it at Tomos, then on to the mountain, sick inside that I had let Dada go without lifting a finger. It began to rain and the night was coming down black and with a nip of winter frost in the wind, and the Coity was blue and misted against a sodden moon. The rain came harder, blinding me in the open country and driving in waves over the heather. A madness seized me then and drove me on down the slope of the mountain. For half an hour I searched before I saw three torches smoking in the rain and another four taking a path to distant Nantyglo, waved in the hands of men. Three more blazed steadily, in a triangle, and I knew that the mob had delivered its justice. The undergrowth thickened in the valley and I tore a path through thorn and bramble towards the three points of light. The scent of burning wood was in the air, changing to the tang of melted tar as I drew nearer. I crashed on, flinging aside the branches towards a far clearing that I saw reflected in red light. Sobbing for breath, I stumbled to the edge of the clearing and a man's shape rose up clearly outlined. I saw the curve of his jaw and the swing of his shoulders as he leaped to face me. With my last strength I hooked a blow at the jaw and felt the jarring pain in my elbow as my fist caught him square. He fell, tumbling sideways against me, and I held him off with one hand and smashed him to the ground with the other. He lay down with a sigh, and I tripped over his body into the clearing.

They were cutting my father free. Rhys Jenkins and the Howells boys were kneeling beside him, and blood was on their hands. Nearby lay Mo Jenkins, his chin upturned against the light and his chest heaving like a dying man. I knelt by my father.

"Better late than never, man," said Big Rhys with bile in his voice. "Will your friends always have to do your fighting?"

My father was lying as the Cattle had left him, face down, arms and legs outstretched, but cut free of the pegs. He was bare to the waist and his shirt had been flogged into bloody shreds over his trews. His back, from the bulge of his biceps to his hips, was stripped of skin, and the weals of the whips were as proud as fingers on his flesh.

"Dada," I said.

Not my father, this one. Slits for eyes, this one, with cuts running across each other and the mouth split top and bottom; suffused with blood, this face, from the booting of the mob.

I wept.

Big Rhys stirred his feet in the soaked grass beside me.

"Do not bother him," he said. "And do not mind his face —it is not so bad as it looks. I have had worse in my time from hobnails, but his back is down to the bone."

"Not whips, see," said Owen Howells. "Willow sticks, the swines. Two of them at him, and Probert dancing mad because he would not give a groan."

"And he still has not signed for the Union," said Griff. He peered at me. "Where the hell did you get to, boyo?"

I told them about the Military.

"Where is your sense?" Rhys asked him. "A man has to save his furniture, and why should two wage-earners take a

176

flogging and miss shifts when one will do? Even Probert would see the sense of that." He grinned at me. "Your flogging will come with the Union card. That will be a pretty one to answer."

"He knew," I said. "He knew all the time I was in the Union." I stood up. "What is wrong with Mo by there?"

"Just a stone on the nut, nothing to bother," said Rhys. "We were coming out of the Lamb Row public when we heard the palaver, see? So me and Mo followed the Cattle to here. Owen and Griff waded in minutes before, but the Cattle pinned them down to watch the flogging. But Mo put Probert on his back and took a stone on the nut from behind. Very handy are these hooligans with hitting from behind."

"Mo is breathing now," said Owen, kneeling.

"Good," said Rhys beside my father. "Rattle him under the chops—no need for him to make a meal of it."

My father spoke then. Bloody froth was on his lips.

"Iestyn?"

"Yes, Dada."

"Away with this old coat and let the rain on my back. I am not going home in this state." He clutched the grass and buried his face in it.

I lifted my coat from his back and watched the rain wash him clean.

"There is cool," he said. "God, there is cool!"

"Look you, Hywel—are you there, boy?" called Rhys from the darkness.

"Aye, here, Rhys," said my father.

"Do not disturb yourself, mind, but hearken to me. This son of mine by here. There is a good old stone he took on the nut. Only a relation of the great Dai Benyon Champion could expose his brains and live to see them."

"That is the first brains I have heard of in the Jenkins family," said my father, tearing at grass. "Tell him not to overdo it—he will get worse from Knocker Daniels at Carmarthen a week next Friday."

"Ready, is it, Hywel?"

"Aye, ready, man," said my father.

"Up then!" said Rhys. "Home with the invalids. Come on, Mo, step lively!", and he rattled poor Mo under the chin to straighten him. "Home quick, or the women will have chest troubles to deal with as well as split heads and backs. And me to rub salad oil into my hands, for they are stiff to hell with hitting out hooligans."

"Is it all right with Mam and Edwina, Iestyn?" asked Dada.

"Aye," I said.

"The furniture is safe?"

"Yes, Dada."

"Good, my son." He turned on his side. "Rise me now, and easy with you on my poor old back, eh?"

"Look, Dada, I will run for old Snell's trap and we will do it in style. . . ."

"To the devil with Snell's trap," said Rhys, coming up. "You cannot drive a man home from a flogging. He will fit snug across my back."

"Nor is he frogmarched," said my father. "He walks. Iestyn, rise me."

Owen came on the other side and we lifted him while Big Rhys snorted in disgust.

"Now leave me," said my father, and Owen and I stood aside, leaving him bowed and swaying. And if my mother had come in search of him she would have passed him by, not knowing.

"Mo is ready," called Griff. "And what is more he remembers the one who stoned him, so his brains are undamaged. It was Moc Evans, a spare time Scotch Cattle, one who did the flogging."

"Then he can write his will," said Rhys. "I got the other flogger, mind. I had him with my boot when he had finished and put him down in the heather by here, but the swine crawled off."

"And I put him down again coming in by that path," I said.

"God be praised," exclaimed Owen. "The devil may still be with us," and he ran to the edge of the clearing and kicked aside the heather.

He was there.

We ringed him as he climbed to his feet. With Griff holding a torch high we pulled him out and blood was on his hands and the willow stick with which he had flogged my father was near him. Down he went again now, grovelling, pleading, reaching for our boots.

It was Dafydd Phillips.

"Aye," said Rhys to me. "There's a surprise. Very friendly are the relations in your family by the look of it." He bent and handed me the willow stick. "Peg him, flog him fifty and kick him back to his criminals in Nanty. Owen, you will help Iestyn. Griff, you will help me get the invalids back to town. We will go slow, Iestyn, and meet you on the Brynmawr Corner."

I saw Dafydd's face as he raised it to the light, streaked with rain and sweat, one eye still shut tight. He opened his mouth to shout for my father but Big Rhys shut it with the toe of his boot.

"Give it him," he said, "before I start it myself."

It was the law.

Owen and I waited until Big Rhys and Griff had got my father clear, then we pegged him and I tore back his shirt and flogged him fifty with the same stick he had taken to my father.

And when I had finished and his howls were over, we booted him across the grass to the Brynmawr Road, and left him.

Big Rhys and Griff were resting Mo and my father on the Brynmawr Corner. There we formed up and went into town. Down North Street we went, past the people huddled on the doorsteps of the Row, and I knew in an instant something was wrong, for the women were wringing their hands and weeping. The crowd parted as we reached it, and my father, soaked with blood and rain, walked through it to our front door. Twm-y-Beddau was there beside my mother. Edwina and Jethro stood nearby. There was a smell of burning in the air and ashes were hot under the feet.

"They came back, Hywel," said Twm-y-Beddau. "They flogged you first to be sure of it, they said. My woman has your food. Dai Pig is alive, although they looked at him twice, mind."

This was the law of the Scotch Cattle. Every stick of furniture was burned, every possession except the clothes we stood in, Edwina's Bible, food and money.

# CHAPTER FIFTEEN

For ten days my father lay on straw with bandages over his face and back, groaning at times, but mostly playing hell because I had left the house unguarded.

But heroes overnight, the Mortymers.

"Mind," said Tomos Traherne on one of his visits to us, "you are popular for handing back a flogging, for that is a rare thing to happen to Scotch Cattle. But it is not forgotten that you were scabs, either here or in Nanty."

That was right, too, as we found out later.

The whispering grew into thunder when Mr Hart, the Nantyglo agent, came to visit us. Neighbours were hanging on the garden walls like beans when his pony and trap came up to The Square all burnished and jingling.

Very toothy, this Mr Hart, handy from the waist down, I heard, every inch of him bowing and scraping on the threshold, for he knew how the Welsh loved an ironmaster's agent. Six feet of skin and bone, this one, with an onion for a head sitting in the bowl of his high starched collar; wringing his hands and blessing us for our courage and wishing to God there was more like us.

My mother wished him to hell privately. A visit from an Agent often meant one from the ironmaster, she said, and not even the Mortymers deserved that.

Ten shillings he brought as a gift towards the furniture we had lost, but better were the gifts that came from neighbours.

A scrubbing brush and broom from Mrs Roberts, Sara's mam. Mrs Tossach up at Cae White sent us two blankets, and Willie Gwallter brought down three pictures of country scenes and a ram dying in snow. The Howells boys made up a chair and Rhys and Mo trundled down a settle. The Stafford men landed us with pots and pans, the Garndyrus Irish came loaded with two tables and a chest of drawers. By the time everybody was finished we were only short of beds, and that went round like fire. But nothing could replace the things we had lost, not even the kindness of neighbours.

But there are neighbours and neighbours, and there were some who hated us. Mrs Dic Shon Ffyrnig, for instance.

I was knocking in nails, making a bed for my father when Mrs Ffyrnig called with something to go under it; a two gallon china one by the size of it. Mrs Pantrych, full again by the look of her, was there beside her, grinning on the doorstep.

"Good morning, Mrs Mortymer," they said in tune.

Here to bring the Mortymers down a peg. Sin and mischief was in their faces.

"Good morning," said my mother, enough to freeze.

"Just called with the good wishes of the Benefit, Elianor," said Mrs Ffyrnig. "And Dic Shon do say what a terrible thing it is mixing labour with politics."

"I have been telling your husband that for years," said Mam.

"Aye, but the Benefit might have saved him, girl. All your good things burned, and some were good quality, too, as I was telling Mrs Pantrych when Mr Moc Evans brought them out."

"Especially in the bedding line, if I might say," said Mrs Pantrych. "How is your poor man now?"

"Healthier than before he was flogged," said Mam, "and life is easier for the family."

"Eh no! Fighting for his life, they told us."

"Ten days from now it will be Dai Probert Scotch Cattle fighting for his," replied my mother. "He will give them Scotch Cattle and Probert in particular, or I was not born in Cyfarthfa. Thankful I am for seeing you, good morning to you, now."

"On behalf of the Benefit, please accept this token of our respect," said Mrs Ffyrnig. "A special collection was made last night and this brought from Pontypool," and from behind her she brought out the china, not even wrapped. "Something to go under the bed when you get it, girl," and they threw back their heads and cackled like hens.

Very fast down that path went Mrs Ffyrnig and Mrs Pantrych with the special collection after them, and Mam slammed the door to warm its hinges.

"There is a pair of old bitches," she said.

"Do not mind them, Mam," I replied, starting my sawing.

"They came to laugh and gloat, not in charity like the others." Twisting her fingers now and walking about. "Special collection, indeed. I would not have their old china if it was silver-plated, but it is all you can expect from people not Chapel."

"Easy," I said. "It was a gift, Mam, though it was stupid of them to giggle. Church or Chapel makes no difference, dear."

Suddenly, without warning, she began to cry in gasps, her fingers forming a cage over her mouth, stifling the indignity.

"Hush you," I said. "Dada has not given a sigh."

"O, my poor Hywel, sad I am! Sad for you and my home, and all my pretty little things from Cyfarthfa. Not a bed between us, and all because of politics like the old bitch said."

"Dada flogged for a principle, not politics."

"Principle or politics, it is all the same," said she, sniffing and wiping. "There is a mess for you. His back torn to shreds and his face booted in. And it is not finished yet, mark me. I know that one upstairs."

"It is finished, we have won," I said, my arms around her. "The town is with us to the end, now. Next time Probert shows his nose will be the last. Every worker from here to Garndyrus will be after him since Dada made his stand. And as for furniture, you will have a houseful when I get this old saw going smooth."

"God bless you, Iestyn," she whispered. "But it is a bed I am after first, see? This old cot you are making can come later, boy. It is a bed I need to raise my man from straw."

"One coming tonight," I said, and went on sawing.

"Have sense," said she, drying up. "Where from, may I ask?"

"Never mind where from," I said. "A good strong iron bed with a mattress is due this evening, and do not say it is any the worse for belonging to Iolo Milk."

Up on her feet now and blazing. "Do I hear right?" she cried. "Iolo Milk, is it? And his bed at that? Listen, you! Unconscious I will be when I place my body on a bed belonging to that one, and do you hear me? We are poor in all truth, but I would rather sleep with the devil than on a bed of fornication." Pale and shocked she looked. "An old hair mattress too, I suppose."

"Feather," I replied. "But what does it matter if you will not have it?"

"Indeed not. I am not having the couch of the Devil in the house and it was shameful of you to suggest it."

I sighed, and went on sawing.

"Do you hear me? Shameful!"

"Yes, Mother."

"Then do you mind me," and she went round the room looking daggers and twisting at her fingers.

"I hope I have made myself clear," said she after a bit.

I was hitting in nails now. "Clear on what?" I asked, the hammer up.

"This old bed. Over my dead body it comes through that door, you understand?"

"All right, all right. *Dammo di!* I will tell Iolo Milk to kick it to China and back so long as we have some peace."

"Double, is it?" she asked then.

I put down the hammer. "Listen," I said. "The thing will sleep four in comfort, not that you are interested. It is solid iron with brass balls, a spring under a feather mattress and rollers on its feet, and Iolo Milk said he can bounce his backside six feet high and it doesn't give a groan, which is more than can be said for the ones Probert burned."

"No need to be vulgar," she replied sharp. "Anyway, we would never get it through the door."

"It comes to bits," I said, "but I am sorry I mentioned it."

"Well then, I will give it some thought," she answered. "Kick it to China and back, indeed! There is good in everybody and I am not having Iolo Milk insulted. So you get this bed up to Dada the moment it comes or you will never hear the end of it."

"Good God," I said.

With her mouth a little red button and her nose up, she left me.

As long as I live I will remember the coming of Iolo's iron bed.

Jethro saw it first and came in whooping like an Indian and pointing. Up the hill laboured Enid Donkey with the bed over her back and steadied either side by Iolo's Irish friends. And up to the door came Iolo, dressed in his Sunday best with the mock carnation he wore especially for women-killing and his white teeth flashing.

"Good afternoon, Mrs Mortymer," said he. "Here is a good strong bed fit to hold a fighter for the community," and he swept off his cap into the gutter with a nobility and grace that would have brought joy to the Young Queen.

"God bless you, Iolo," said Mam, all blushes.

"And the same to you, girl," he replied. "I am having a better welcome this time than last, remember? Flat down by here your man hit me, and I came with the same honourable intentions as now, mind."

"But he was not himself that day, boy. Eh dear! There is a strong iron bed," said she, patting it.

"Very comfortable the pair of you will be, Mrs Mortymer, for I have spent enjoyable hours on this feather mattress. And with a woman of your proportions a man would be a fool not to follow my example, no offence intended."

"O, Iolo!" giggled Mam.

"In with it," I said to him, "no need for details," for the neighbours were gathering and whispering. Giggles, too, for everybody knew that Iolo used his beds for anything but sleeping in.

"How now?" asked Iolo, when it was set up for examination.

"Wonderful," said Mam, and everybody nodded, for the window was up and the door open and half the neighbours were in or coming.

"Then up with a broom to scatter the crowd," shouted

Iolo, "for we need a bit of privacy. There is a history to this four-poster, Mrs Mortymer, and I am just in the mood to tell it."

"Hush, you!" I said, elbowing him while the neighbours roared and my mother went scarlet.

"*Diawl!*" he cried. "Here is an example of false modesty. With little Iestyn scarcely out of his woollens it is understandable, woman, but for the likes of you and me, girl, we could teach this old bed a thing or two, look you. *Dammo!* Do not look so grieved, Elianor. A very fine friend is a bed, with blankets over it in cold and nothing at all in hot, and every other page of the Good Book talking about courtings, deaths, and births between four posts. And look you how soft!" Up with him then and down on it and bounced three feet. "Now settle yourself here with me, Elianor, and we will christen the thing, for to lie full length with a milkman in the sight of neighbours is going half way to a fortune."

"O, Iolo!" giggled Mam. "Hell and damnation on you for such a suggestion, and me married!" And she peeped and wriggled like a maid. "True, is it?"

"*Mam!*" I said.

"Whoo, there!" cried Iolo, getting ferocious. "Here is sixpence to clear the neighbours while I tell your mam the story of this very fine bed, Iestyn."

"Good afternoon," I said. "We have had enough of you."

"Enough? And with your little mam here just coming girlish? I would harm her, you think? In the same house as her man who has taken a flogging? Cleanse your mind, my boy. When the great call comes I will be there in the Upper Palace under the hand of St Peter while you brew tea in the coals of hell. Eh dear, Mrs Mortymer, forgive the rising generation who do turn a little harmless fun into an improper suggestion."

"Do not heed him, Iolo," she replied, keen now. "What about the history of this bed?"

"It is a pleasant history in truth," said Iolo, sighing. "Megan and me were two years married and childless when this bed came to us—through the family, you understand, after knowing nothing but happy lovers and easy births. My grandfather from Carmarthen bought it in London from a travelling tinker who was in tears at parting with it, for his three wives had rested their fair limbs in it, cleaving in joy before dying in peace on it. Fifteen children had that tinker, all on this bed, mind, and two wives had my grandfather and each brought forth six. And since we are four now and Megan waiting for the fifth you cannot but respect an article that bore half the population of Carmarthen before coming to Monmouthshire to start all over again."

"Wonderful!" everybody cried.

"Aye," said Iolo, "so you can have it with my blessing, for with Megan full again I would rather she slept on heather than this old mattress. Out with the old thing, Megan said, and take it down to Hywel Mortymer, who has less chance of being caught turning than me."

Which put everybody double, of course.

"And proper, too," said my mother, crimson again "for some beds are suspicious things indeed, but my man will sleep soft upon it. A cup of tea before you go, Iolo?"

"Something stronger, woman," said he. "I am away to the Drum and Monkey to fortify my soul, for I was hoping to find you alone. I am a wicked man indeed, but I know I am beaten when faced with such virtue and a six-foot son within kicking distance."

"O, go on with you!" said Mam, very pretty with her.

And he took her hand and kissed it, bowing low, which put the neighbours on tiptoe and screaming with laughter.

"This way out," I said, showing him the door, but Edwina came flying through it with her basket waving and her white hair blowing over her face.

"I will have that cup of tea now, Mrs Mortymer," said Iolo at once, eyeing Edwina. "Two of a kind are always more enjoyable than one."

"Indeed you will not!" cried Edwina. "You will away outside and clear that Enid Donkey from the gate for there is a visitor with a coach and pair prancing outside and postillions grinding their teeth with rage."

"Who is it?" I asked, for the neighbours were vanishing.

"A man in a cape," she gasped, "and blue in the face with him and get to hell out of it with that damned old donkey."

"O, hisht, Edwina," breathed Mam.

"A coach and pair, you say. What like was he?"

"Thick and black, with a riding crop and boots."

"And postillions, you say?" whispered Iolo.

"Two, and two white mares," said Edwina.

"Coming in here? God help us!" said Iolo. "Crawshay Bailey!" and he was straight through the door and over Twm-y-Beddau's hedge without touching a leaf while the rest of the neighbours scattered.

"Crawshay Bailey!" whispered my mother, going white.

"Aye, and what of it!" I asked, but she swung from me. "Edwina," she said, "upstairs to the children's bedroom quick, and not a sound from you till I say come out."

"But why, Mam?"

"Away!" And she drove Edwina before her with her apron, locked the bedroom door, and dropped its key down the neck of her bodice, all in seconds. Trembling, she came back to me, her hands to her face.

"Easy with you," I said. "He has two legs, two arms and one head, and he is not the King of England."

"But damned near it," she said. "Crawshay Bailey coming and that old Enid Donkey and Iolo Milk dropping the tone of the place," and she went around the bare room demented with a duster.

No time for more. He was in.

No knocking from this one who owned a town, its people and his iron empire. He stood on the threshold with his cape thrown back, showing the fine cut of his black frock coat. Lace was at his wrists and throat. This was the iron master who looked like a country squire, the man notorious in commerce, hated equally by workers and unions; disdaining aristocratic gestures, this one, brother to Joseph, the tramping boy, who took a donkey to Cyfarthfa and borrowed a thousand pounds to crucify Nantyglo. Feet astride he bent his riding crop over his belly and peered at us.

"Mistress Mortymer?"

Mam bobbed a curtsey, speechless, her hands shaking her skirt.

"And you?" His florid, baby face swung to me.

"Iestyn, the son," I said.

"The son of the man who was flogged."

"Aye, sir."

He walked in, owning the place, and the authority crept out of him and owned us, too.

"My sympathy on the loss of your furniture, ma'am," he said. "But it is happening every week between here and Blackwood, the Welsh breaking the limbs of their fellows and destroying the homes of the Welsh. We are doing all we can to stop it."

"Thank you, sir," said my mother.

"Irish workers, mostly," I said, "and from Nanty."

His eyes flicked to me. "Is Probert Irish?"

"For every Probert there are fifty Irish."

"Interesting," said he. "I will note it. What trade are you?"

"Spragger," I said.

"What do I pay you?"

"Six shilling a week."

"Remember it. Speak when I bid you or you will find yourself on the blacklist." He turned to my mother. "You were here when the furniture was burned, woman?"

"Aye, sir," she said faintly.

"Then you recognised the man Probert?"

"Yes, sir."

"Could you identify others if called upon?"

"Only Probert, sir. . . ."

"God," said he, and groaned, turning.

"It was night," whispered my mother. "Both my men had gone when the Cattle came back and drove me out and pulled out the furniture. Their faces were blackened. . . ."

"And where were you?" he turned to me.

"One for the flogging, one to earn, or the family starves," I said. "My father ordered me to stay here when they took him."

His expression changed and he nodded at the sense of it.

"But I flogged one back," I said. "I flogged him fifty to mark him."

"You knew this man?"

"No."

"But you would recognise him?"

"It was dark," I said. "I did not see his face."

There was no sound but the steady tap of his crop against his high leather boots, then he said, "And that is the end of it. There is no law, no recognition of authority. One is flogged, his son flogs back. At a time when the transportation hulks are filling their holds with hooligans you flog a man with a whip, a nameless man." Walking to the window he stared out. "I pay taxes for military protection, but not a single worker can pick Scotch Cattle from the identity parades." He lowered his voice. "Your memory appears better than your son's, Mrs Mortymer. If Probert is caught I will depend upon you to identify him, remember it."

"She will not," I said quickly. "My father would never allow it. It is asking for death to name one of the Cattle."

"Name a few, hang a few, and we will soon be rid of them," he replied.

Blindly, I went on, in dread of the blacklist but forced to answer him. "Hanging a few will not sweep them from the mountains," I said. "The Cattle are with us because of the blacklist, and the blacklist is with us because of the Irish you import as ballast to undercut the wages of the Welsh. You will never sweep away Scotch Cattle. As the Union grows stronger they will multiply to force the hand of the workers against the wages and conditions of labour."

He fixed me with his eyes.

"You are trying to help but doing it backwards," I said. "You bring the Irish in barrels, put them in the bridge arches and pay them in iron coins, with fat old prices in your Company Shops and cheap beer for them in The Bush. You expect us to be the same but we will never be, because we are Welsh."

"O, Iestyn!" whimpered my mother, eyes wide.

"Shut it, woman," I said. "He can starve us but he cannot hang us, so to hell with him and anything to do with iron."

"Well said," replied Bailey. "Pray continue."

"Aye, and welcome," I said, desperately. "My father belongs to no Benefit or Union. He has taught me that it is loyalty to the master that counts, but I am changing my mind, for it is a stink to work on the books of a man who treats his workers like trash, drives them to the mountains as outlaws and expects their countrymen to betray them."

"Are you finished?" he asked, calm.

"Just about," I said. "Get rid of the Irish, negotiate with the Union, close the Tommy Shops and raise wages all round. That will get rid of the Cattle. Leave the rest to the workers and you will send more iron to Newport than Dowlais and Merthyr put together."

The room tinkled with silence. From his waistcoat pocket he drew out a little book and pencil.

"Name?" he said.

"I have told you. Iestyn Mortymer."

"Good," said he, and wrote it down. He snapped the book shut and put it back into his pocket. "Raise your voice to me again and I will bring this family to its sense, but flog a few more Cattle and I will raise your pay." He turned to my mother. "Pack what you have left, Mrs Mortymer, for you are coming to live in Nantyglo, but keep a guard on this boy's tongue for he is too young to know the length of it. Now take me to your husband. I can do with men like yours to speak with honesty and break strikes and flog Scotch Cattle."

Not much wrong with Crawshay on the day he came to town.

# CHAPTER SIXTEEN

AND SO, on a cold day in mid-October, we cleared from home and set off for Nanty, and it was sad.

Good people are neighbours in time of trouble, and anyone moving to Nantyglo at a time like this was in for plenty, said Tomos Traherne behind my mother's back. For news from Nantyglo was bad. Special arrangements were being made to receive us, it was said, with bands of strikers waiting on the roadside to welcome the blacklegs and give them hell.

But worst of all, Dafydd Phillips had left Morfydd and taken to the mountains with Dai Probert Scotch Cattle, which meant transportation if he was caught, or worse, said my father.

"The Redcoats are after arrests and convictions," said Owen Howells, "but the Volunteer squads will shoot on sight with a set of cow horns for proof."

It was more like a wake than a moving out, for the Irish came up from the valley and packed ten deep on the road outside to sing their songs of home to the Welsh. The children brought leaves and winter flowers to decorate the rooms, and everybody was dressed in best Sunday black to mourn the parting neighbours.

Straight inside for the last sweep-up, me, as the Irish began their songs to the Welsh, which is enough to start a fight any Benefit night. For the terrible thing about Irish is that they think they can sing. But how can voices that bear a grudge give joy? All the Irish can sing about is how wicked it is in Ireland under the English and how cruel the rest of the world is to the Irish, but we will straighten our backs and put up with it all for the sake of Killarney.

No offence to the Irish, says my father, but he would rather listen to the Welsh.

On that morning of parting no instruments made sweeter

sounds than the voices of our neighbours in full harmony. I stood at the top of the stairs and leaned on the broom and listened to the pure altos, the soaring tenors and the sweet sopranos sitting on a foundation of rough bass. From the window I saw the people packed in the square. Big Rhys and Mo Jenkins were there shoulder to shoulder with the Howells boys, Will Blaenavon, Afel Hughes and Mr Roberts, all the men of Garndyrus. Mrs Gwallter was leading the sopranos; Mrs Pantrych and Mrs Ffyrnig, respectable for once, were letting it fly, Dathyl Jenkins and Gwen Lewis were singing to the sky, and round them were ringed the neighbours of the Rows, and people come from as far afield as Cae White.

And there in front was Tomos Traherne, double bass, beating time.

Give me a hymn to a good Welsh tune to bring out pride of race and love of country. The key is minor and the very breath of Wales. I thought of the mountains and valleys; of the great names of the north filled with magic; of Plynlymon, Snowdon and Cader Idris, the mountain chair of the clouds, and the great flat tracts where the Roman legions formed; of ancient Brecon that still echoes the clash of alien swords; of Senny, and the Little England beyond Wales. I saw a vision of ancients long dead whose bones have kindled the fire of greatness; of Howell Harris and William Williams, great with the Word. I thought of my river, the Afon-Lwydd, that my father had fished in youth, with rod and line for the leaping salmon under the drooping alders. The alders, he said, that fringed the banks ten deep, planted by the wind of the mountains. But no salmon leap in the river now, for it is black with furnace washings and slag, and the great silver fish have been beaten back to the sea or gasped out their lives on sands of coal. No alders stand now for they have been chopped as fuel for the cold blast. Even the mountains are shells, groaning in their hollows of emptiness, trembling to the arrows of the pit-props in their sides, bellowing down the old workings that collapse in unseen dust five hundred feet below.

Plundered is my country, violated, *raped.*

On goes the hymn. The wind was playing tricks with hair

and bonnet streamers, sniffing at the dewdrop on Willie Gwallter's nose, picking up the hem of Polly Morgan's skirt, bringing Owen's eyes down. From the window I saw it all, and could have wept.

I knew then that I loved my town, my people, my country. The room faced me, the room where Mam delivered Jethro. What is there in a house that lodges so deeply in the heart? Here is the little square window that faces the mountain, always red with furnace glare, here is the board with the knot shaped like a little brown mouse, here is the stair that creaks, the banister for sliding down, the big black ball at the end that was dangerous to boys, Mam said.

"Iestyn!"

"Aye," I called back. "Coming."

"For God's sake," said my father. "We are off directly."

I knew, then, how the miner feels when he strikes the Farewell Rock. The hymn had finished. Snell's mare was clattering on the cobbles. Everybody was embracing and backslapping and kissing, with the women letting it go into their handkerchiefs. What little we possessed was loaded on the cart of Shant-y-Brain the undertaker and the back of Enid Donkey. Up we went to the Brynmawr Corner. Over my shoulder I saw Mr and Mrs Roberts and Sara moving in without enough furniture to fill a sty. I was glad the house had gone to Sara. Driving Dai Two before me I followed Snell's trap carrying the rest of the family, and behind me came Shant-y-Brain's cart and Enid Donkey.

And I would have given my soul to turn and run back to the house in the Square.

Nantyglo was still a dead town with the blacklist strikers sitting on their heels, their starved faces pinched in the weak sun of the cold October morning. Redcoats marched in pairs from Brynmawr to Coalbrookvale to keep the peace, and I was thankful to see them for once, although there was no signs of a reception committee. Morfydd was waiting for us at the end of Chapel Road, strong and healthy by the look of her, carrying enough milk to satisfy six, by the size of her. Snell's mare nearly went up when she stepped on the back of the trap, but I got her in somehow, and away we went past Cwm Crachen to Market Road and the house Crawshay had laid for us. Up went the windows and out came the heads and doors came open and washing went aside to size up the new tenants. Solly Widdle Jew was outside the door of Number Six bargaining with the tenant for the furniture he was moving out.

"What is happening here?" asked my mother.

"Shanco Mathews and his family turning out," said Morfydd. "He is up to his neck in debt at The Bush and the Company Shop and last week he was in a row with the Agent for taking part in a demonstration. Crawshay listed him, so now he is out."

"To make room for us, by the look of it," said my father.

"Aye, but it is chiefly the demonstration."

"No home at all now, then?" said Mam, her eyes on Mrs Mathews and three children sitting on the furniture where Shanco and Solly Widdle were bargaining.

"They are going to the old ironworks," said Morfydd. "Their friends are up there now bricking a space. It is the demonstration, see—none of us agree with them. It is branding us all as hooligans for a few, and people in Nanty are respectable." Very happy she looked standing there, waiting for us to move in next door to her; and beautiful, too, as most women are when carrying, with her hair over her shoulders, bright in the eyes and rosy in the cheeks.

I got in front of my father as Shanco Mathews came up from the bargaining. He was middle-aged, quite as tall as me but great in the shoulders and with the look of a mountain fighter. His nose was flattened, both ears screwed to balls. Loose-limbed and free he came over the slag towards us and stood there, hands on hips.

"How are you?" said he, and his voice was as light as a girl's through too many throat punches.

I nodded, sizing his chin for a right.

"Morfydd's relations, is it?" he asked. "The strike-breakers, they tell me."

"Now, now!" said Mam, sharp. "Who are you?"

"Blackbird Shanco Mathews," said he, "and do not say now now to me, ma'am, or I will hit your two men flat. A little stiff I am in the head from fighting men two stone larger, but I am still good for boys, so do not get free with them."

"We have had enough fighting to last us a lifetime," said my father. "Speak your business and go, man."

"Goodness me," said Shanco. "There is a large mistake. And they told me I would have trouble from the Mortymers. Caradoc Owen Foreman told me to get free with them, but I am addled in the brain from head punching or I would have had Solly Widdle Jew flat down here before now, the bastard."

"Why?" I asked.

"Four pounds he is offering for my furniture, and me and my woman paid nine for it not twelve months back in the city of Carmarthen."

"Do not mind us," said my father. "Flat on his back he should be for making profit out of misfortune, but please mind your language in front of my women."

"Forgive me, ma'am," said Shanco, and he bowed and swept his cap in the slag at my mother's feet, "but it makes life hard when one is surrounded by ironmasters, Irish and Israelites."

"Five it is worth from this distance," said Dada. "Take us closer and we may offer you more, for we have Scotch Cattle furniture."

"Dear me," replied Mathews. "You are sent by the grace of God," and he elbowed me aside. "Shift you over, boy. Do not stand on guard or I will be damned fretful with you. Me and your dad are full of years. Away!"

And from then I heard no more. High on the tram road Mari was waving, and she ran down into the hollow, calling me. Without being seen I got away to meet her, and we ran into the shadows of the furnaces. There, I twisted her into my arms and kissed her lips.

"You are here!" she cried.

"But God knows for how long," I replied. "I can smell trouble—we got in too easy. It will be harder getting out."

"Caradoc Owen is the enemy," she said. "He will leave you alone unless you try to break the strike, so Hart says. The owner is waiting to see what happens when you and your father go in with tools."

"One thing at a time," I said. "At last I am here with you, in the same town."

"In the same house for today," Mari whispered. "I have the day free from Mr Hart to help with the scrubbing, for with Morfydd full and Edwina lazy it will all fall on your mother."

"Come, and I will find you a bucket," I said.

My father bought Shanco's furniture and we got it in and lost ourselves in labour, with Mam giving it to everybody about the state of the house. With Dafydd gone from next door Morfydd moved in with us. By darkness the rooms were clean and furnished after a fashion. Mari and Edwina were upstairs making beds when I met Morfydd out in the garden. She came down the path to me while I was building a roof for Dai Two. There was talk from the neighbours that furnace ashes sprayed white-hot from the chimneys, and I did not want him blistered. Morfydd came quietly and leaned against the shed and gave me a wink.

"Aye aye?" she said. "At it again, eh?"

"At what?" I said, hammering.

"Poor Mari. She do not dream what is coming to her."

"Do not be evil," I said.

"Manna from heaven," said she. "*Duw!* No wonder he wanted to come to Nanty. Hell support us. If I were her dada I would not sleep a wink with a mad Mortymer after her, poor girl."

"She is English," I said. "She will not get a second look," for it was asking for a life of hell to tell Morfydd your business.

"Half English, perhaps, but a dear little girl. High in the breast and narrow in the waist, she is, and the English things under her dress are just as pretty as Welsh, for I have seen them, dear me!"

"Away back to your scrubbing; it is all you are fit for," I said.

"Treat me civil," she answered, "or you will regret it. Do

197

you think she would be interested to hear the scandal of Polly-Without-Trews?"

"Go to hell," I said, grinning.

"Do not love her more than me, then," said she, "for I am jealous," and she kissed me on the cheek.

"Away," I said. "I am trying to get this roof up."

It was twilight now and I saw her profile against the rising moon, still beautiful, young, and her eyes were happy.

I said, "Morfydd, where is Dafydd?"

"Lord!" she exclaimed. "My business now, is it?"

"Gone, has he?"

She laughed. "Out on his neck," she said. "Do you expect me to lie with a man who flogs my father?"

"You know, then?"

"Not much misses me," she answered. "He came in crying for bandages and breathing fire over the Mortymers for the flogging you gave him. I called for the Chartists and they threw him out. Now he has taken to the mountains with Probert, they tell me."

"He is dangerous," I said. "I am glad you are living with us."

"Perhaps you would be safer without me," she replied.

My father called us and we went in together and sat down at table. It was as if the years had rolled back and made us one again, but with the joyful difference of Mari's eyes, rising and lowering above her plate opposite, where Morfydd used to be.

We were seven in family now, my mother said, counting Mari Dirion who worked down the road at Coalbrookvale.

Report to Furnace Five, said the Agent next morning, and my father and I went out and worked it, lighting it from cold while the Nantyglo puddlers stood at the entrance and watched. We lit it and brought it to blast and coaled it and tipped in ore, and by night we had tapped it and filled the sand moulds with iron. Alone we did this, watched by half the strikers of Nanty. They made no move to stop us, they spoke not a word. On the second day we did the same, and by midday eight men had joined us despite the warnings

198

pinned up overnight by the Scotch Cattle. We tapped earlier that day, and when nineteen men had returned to work we decided on a night shift and ran it to two tons of iron. By the fourth day the strike was broken. Ninety men were back and more flooding in every hour.

And with them came Caradoc Owen.

Here was a sample of a man; a trouble maker famed for striking, a foreman Bailey could not do without. What Owen could not drive with his tongue he drove with his fist or the nearest thing handy. Men feared him, women despised him, children ran from him. He had his wife down in Shant-y-Brain's shippon carting dung when she was full, and one Christmas he had lit a furnace with a Roman Catholic crucifix.

"So the strike-breakers are here, I see," said he, coming into Furnace Five. My father was stoking when Caradoc Owen tapped him. Coming in with the nose-bag Morfydd had cut for us I saw my father turn and face the foreman. Dada was full six inches taller but Owen was a foot the wider, deep-chested, hairy. Other workers crowded in, Owen's men, silent, threatening.

"Aye," said my father, throwing down the irons. "When the children begin to die the strike has been on long enough, or don't you see the sense of it?"

"Marked by the Cattle, too, God be praised," said Owen, touching Dada's back where the stripes were still raised and red. "Some people never learn, it seems. Not enough scabs in Nanty so Bailey brings his pets from Garndyrus, eh?"

I pushed my way through the men and tossed the bundle and my father caught it. "Nose-bag," I said, "and tell him to go to hell before we shift him," and I picked up irons and carried on stoking.

"Blacklegs and bruisers, is it?" said Owen, cool as ice. "Out, Mortymer, and take this cheeky swine with you. I am in charge here."

"Good grief," said Dada to me. "What is the use of signing the pledge?" He turned to Owen. "We stay. If you want to shift us, take your pick—the Agent, or make a ring and the best man is in?"

Owen spat, grinning. His men murmured. I saw their faces in the glare of the firebox. Many had the scars of fighting over their eyes, their faces streaked with sweat and lined deep with hunger. Half of them in touch with Scotch Cattle by the look of them, standing very quiet for men with hobnails, but all were with honour when it came to a ring.

I had never seen my father fight; only heard of him from men like Big Rhys, who said he was a terror, more afraid of his woman than any man on the mountains. But he was still weak from the flogging, and his back was still crusted and split deep. Already the workers were out, making a circle in front of the Company Shop in full view of the office, and from all directions the townspeople came running, as they always did for a fight. The news spread like a furnace blow-back, and before a blow had been struck the tap-rooms had emptied and' the cinder-pit in front of the furnaces was solid with people. I watched my father as he pulled off his coat. The old casual air had come upon him that I had seen before in time of trouble, but his face was pale as he drew on to his fingers the thin leather gloves he wore for stoking. He squinted into the sun and looked towards our house. I knew he was thankful that my mother was down at Abergavenny for market.

Caradoc Owen, ten years the younger, rose from his haunches at the edge of the crowd.

"Ready?" he called.

My father nodded. Left hand out, he circled, frowning over his clenched fist, and Owen followed round, giving time for the laying of bets, as was the custom. A Hercules, this one; broad as an ox across the shoulders through years of breaking pig at Dowlais. The muscles bulged and swelled along his thick arms, his movements were ponderous, drunk with strength. He moved flat-footed, swaying from the waist, his black-maned head thrust forward, inviting a blow. Round, round the circle they went, Owen bunched and tense, my father lithe, the long slim muscles of his fine body shining with furnace sweat, and I heard women gasp at his bright red weals.

"Bets laid!" cried a man, and Owen grunted, spat over his

shoulder and rushed, hooking. Dada stepped aside. Owen went sprawling into the crowd and rose, kicking them away for room. Steadier now, he walked in, chin upon his jutting chest, his thick arms working in widening swings, but he took a left like a whiplash that stopped him dead and a dig to the midriff that doubled him. Opening his fingers, Owen clutched and ran, seeking a hold, and the blow that felled him hooked between his arms flush to the point of his chin. His head snapped back, his shoulders followed, his heels lifted and he landed with a crash on the slag. Dust rose. The crowd gasped. There was no sound but the wind and the simmer of Furnace Five. And Caradoc Owen, who had never been on a knee before, turned upon his side and rested, shaking his great head. Blood and froth bubbled from his mouth and ran down his hairy chest. I glanced at my father. He was looking at the mountain, deep in thought, it seemed, eyes narrowed. Owen got on all fours and rose. Swaying, his legs wide, he walked in again, hitting with tremendous blows that swept the air as they were neatly parried or guarded. There was no expression upon my father's face as he retreated. Swaying easily from the waist, swerving, riding the chopping fists, he paused only to smash single, vicious blows into the face of the man before him; blows launched on the twist that cut and blinded the bull-like Owen. Grunting, cursing, Owen lumbered to his doom, his senses numbed by the first terrible blow that had felled him; lumbered into a poetry of hooks and smashes that brought the blood pouring over his chest from a dozen facial cuts. And he reeled and moaned under the precision of the hands that lashed him, cried aloud when the cutting lefts stopped his forward plunge, doubled and gasped at the uppercuts that sank deep into his body. His breathing came in sobs as he flung out his arms for holds that missed by yards. Battered, peering through his puffed slits of eyes, he walked into the avalanche, taking everything, succeeding in nothing. And when, bewildered and in agony, he cried aloud in rage and dropped his hands, my father took his first step forward. With the brutal Owen staggering on bowed legs before him, he began to cut him to pieces. The crowd gaped, held its breath as the artist steadied himself. The last blow came. Owen's head snapped back and he took the following crude swing full in the throat. He fell, face down, full length at my father's feet, his big white body shuddering to the gasping intakes of his breath.

Not a soul moved except my father. He flung his shirt up and waved his arms into it, took a breath and tucked the flaps under his belt. With his coat trailing, he walked back to the entrance of Furnace Five, raised his face and looked for me among the crowd. Thrusting men and women aside I ran to him.

Sad he looked, standing there, his head low.

"Well done, Dada," I said. "That is the last of Caradoc Owen for one."

"Poor man, but it was the only way, God forgive me," he said.

"Look who is coming, Mr Mortymer," said a man nearby.

The crowd was shuffling and swaying near the road by the Company Shop. My mother walked through the press of men and into the narrowing ring. Her face was white and pinched with anger. The wind took her hair and flung it about as she knelt beside Caradoc Owen. With her hand upon his naked shoulder she looked up at my father. In Welsh, she said:

"This is the last time, Hywel, do you understand? The last time, or by God I will leave you."

A man called, "A fair fight, mind. Clean as a nut."

"Bloody old Caradoc do ask for it, woman!" shouted another.

My mother rose and faced them. "A fair fight, you call it? Look at him!" She pointed down. "You have set this one up for slaughter, not a fight." Her voice rose to a shout. "Not any ten men here could pull my man down, and if you doubt me then go to Carmarthen and ask what happened to Dai Benyon Pugilist in his prime. Champion of Wales, is he not? Aye, the champion, until he quarrelled with my man for easy money and went home over the back of a pony. And any man alive would have the same as this one if he tried booting my

Hywel from his furnace. Who began this fight? Ask it fair, now. Not the Mortymers, I am bound, but Nanty. For the few days we have been here we have been ignored and insulted because we choose to work instead of strike. You call us scabs and blacklegs. You string my husband up and flog him raw because he has no Union card; did you see his poor back just now? You shout about Benefits, but you have no benefits for the funds are drunk away by the organisers. You shout about the Union but you have no Union. All you have got is a disorganised rabble that is better at beer than seeking fair negotiation of complaints. Do you expect me to starve my children for that kind of Union?" She was striding among them now, shouting into their faces. "Do you? Starve if you like, the little ones, too, but mine will still be eating, for my family will work where they like and on masters' terms, for better or worse until it gets decent representation. It was that in Garndyrus, it will be the same here in Nanty, mark me. Aye, and I can fight too, so try me, any woman here, and my boys are handy with them, so watch out. And for every flogging and insult we will give twenty back for we are here to stay in Nantyglo whether you like us or not. Iestyn!"

I went to her through the men.

"Lift this man and take him home for repair," said she. "Edwina! Down to Mr Owen's house with you and bring his woman here sharp before he dies on us."

Edwina, frail and trembling, hurried away.

Ten minutes to thrash Caradoc Owen, two minutes to thrash a town. The eyes of everyone was on her as she led the way home for the bandaging. Hooking Owen's arm around my neck I dragged him after her. Like the Queen of Sheba she went, her dress held as a tent before her, her nose high, back to her kitchen.

It was pleasant living in Nantyglo for a while after that, with the men knocking up their caps to my mother and some of the women even dropping a knee, for it soon got round that the Mortymers had broken the strike four days after landing. Special invitations came from the chapels and women dropped in for cups of tea and chats, for women hate strikes whatever they say to their men. Little else happened that first Christmas, except that Morfydd had her baby.

Trust Morfydd to be inconvenient, starting her pains with the house empty for one reason or another, and having it on the floor of the bedroom like a Kentucky labourer. Eleven pounds after two hours, said my mother, and not so much as a whisper from Morfydd according to the next-door neighbours. And when my father and I came in at the end of day shift Morfydd had him on the breast.

Richard, she called him. A miniature Richard, too, lusty, and as hungry after Morfydd as Jethro had been for Mam.

Eight of us now, with Mari practically living in the place; two rooms up, one down. The men slept in one bedroom, the women and Richard in the other, but nobody got much sleep with the baby screaming.

On the first night of full working I laid on my back beside Jethro and watched the room change from moonlight to red as Furnace One grew into blast. By midnight it was shrieking and the house trembled to the thudding drop-hammers and the new rolling mill whined like something from the pit of Hell. Plaster flaked and drifted down from the ceiling, light ran in red tongues over the window as the thunder grew and the night caught alight. Jethro and my father were on their backs, sleeping through it. Throwing aside the blanket I went to the window and looked out. The side of the mountain had dissolved into a single fire; a maze of individual furnaces that blended their flames into an orbit, and along the flaming rim of the cauldron the stone cottages of the workers withered and shrank into strange shapes. This was the Bailey empire where the iron bubbles into a thousand moulds. Sweat pours here, beer is taken by the gallon, men die in mutilation, children are old at ten. Eyes are put out here, sleeves are tied with string. The turrets of the ironmaster's house were stark black against the glow, the windows glinting, his defence towers threatening any challenge. From Cwm Crachen to Coalbrookvale was a river of fire. Ash drifted past the window, settling like snow. As the night went on the clamour grew and the sky flashed red as the bungs were tapped and cauldrons stirred. And next door, beyond the thin partition, Richard cried on Morfydd's breast; the new generation to be charred by Bailey's son.

I longed for my town on that first night of full blast in Nantyglo. I longed for it more on a night of early spring when my mother came to my father for comfort, and I was a witness.

It was a Sunday, after chapel, with the darkness of many a winter's night between me and Garndyrus. The hoar frost had gone from the hedges and the early buds were green and the Coity thinking of changing colour. Those were the nights when the moon was full and rolling along the Coity and the nightingales left alive were calling to lovers.

On such a night, when the furnaces were simmering, my mother came.

"Hywel!" she whispered from the door.

Pretty she looked in the moonlight with her knitted white shawl over her shoulders and her nightdress beneath; like a young girl, I thought, ready for her lover. The door of our bedroom rasped as she opened it wider and she came, her hand out as if in sleep, and called again:

"Hywel!"

I heard my father rise in the bed by the window.

"Elianor," he whispered back.

Over the boards she went on tiptoe, the shawl brushing my hand. Her face, in the moonlight, was shadowed. He opened his arms to her and gathered her to him, his lips against her mouth. They were lovers, and I the watcher. Trapped, I laid there.

"Elianor, not here, my sweet," he said. "Tomorrow, girl. I will meet you up on the mountain, not here. . . ."

"The boys are sleeping, Hywel," she said back. "Is there nothing for us then except eating and sleeping? And work? O, Hywel, take me; the boys will not hear."

Fathers slept with daughters, mothers with sons, brothers with sisters in the hovels of Nanty. Sixteen to a room in Coalbrookvale, four to a bed.

Now I heard the springs go down as she got in beside him.

I heard the quickening heat of their breathing change to low sobbing. Anger and sickness I knew, and pity.

The night went on, the pattern of moonlight crossed the floor, and I saw by the curve of the blanket that covered them that they were one; lost, unmindful of sounds.

They did not stir as I went from the room, down to the kitchen and through the door to the mountain. There, I watched the dawn come up, a flaring streak of red out of the blackness. And with the dawn the mystery vanished, the sickness in me passed. The beauty of it came and brought me peace as the stars paled and faded from sight. There was no sound from the cwm; nothing but the song of the mountain streams as I sat there praying that Jethro would not wake, until their loving was finished.

# CHAPTER SEVENTEEN

I cut a spoon for Mari in springtime.

It was still cold and there was a stillness over the land as if the sap was breathless with waiting. And it was dark on the night of our meeting. We met most nights, of course, but this was special; necessary, too, for very strict about herself was Mari, wriggling and slapping, and not a decent kiss she would part with unless things were done properly, she said.

Which meant a spoon, of course, although I could hardly expect her to ask for one. So I cut a spoon for her, being full of ambition to lie with her, and so far getting nowhere.

Out in the yard I looked up at the mountain. Away over the dim jag of the Coity Pleiades, brilliant in silver, ran before the wind, Orion was flashing gold and green and Venus was making her sign of the Cross, the old ones say. Up to meet her, me—straight up the long green slope, and I sat in the crisp heather with the blaze of Nanty below me. There, with fingers of ice, I fashioned the little spoon.

I had planned a small one; something Mari could wear on a trinket chain in the divide of her breast. From cedar I cut it, out of a piece I chopped down at Llanelen last summer.

There are spoons and spoons, of course. Morfydd had quite a few in her workbasket, some as trinkets, others for wearing, and one from a Carmarthen farm boy big enough to fork manure. The one from Dafydd Phillips had *Cariad anwyl* carved upon the handle, for trust Dafydd not to think of anything unusual. She had no spoon from Bennet, he being English. But the biggest spoon I have ever heard of was the one Will Tafarn carved for Martha, his wife. It stood on the hillside between Nanty and Varteg, and was ten feet high from the roots with 'Those whom God hast joined together let no man put asunder' cut on its trunk in six-inch letters. But it has sprouted branches and leaves, they tell me, as if God has done what He can to hide it, for Will beats Martha every pay night now.

So with this in mind I did a little spoon for Mari, whittling it free of wanes and shakes. It was slender and curved in the handle and holed for the trinket chain, and due to be finished by half past eight. I had just fixed the chain when I saw Mari coming up the slope, so I got it away and hid out of the moonlight behind a rock.

"Oi!" said she, peering. "Iestyn, are you there?"

"Scotch Cattle, God help you!" I said, and caught her by the waist and swung her down among the leaves. Panting, she put her hand between our lips.

"Is it finished?" she asked, breathless.

"Aye, but still doubtful if you will get it. Six weeks I have been carving the thing and there is nothing on the end of it."

"Do not be too sure," said she. "It depends if it is a good one."

"One kiss for a start?" But she shook her head, sending her hair flying, and wriggled off. I was after her, drawing her against me, and her body was warm under my coat. I tried to kiss her but she nipped me and turned her face away, smiling, her teeth white and her cheeks patterned by the moonlight through leaves.

"Not until I get the spoon," she said with business.

A dog fox barked from the valley and the vixen answered away to the east, and the sounds were like wine on the still, cold air. All the beauty of the night was about us, the rushing of streams, the low chord of the wind in dark places, buffeting the heather, shivering round our clothes, sighing down the mountain to the black roofs of Nanty that glistened with frost under the lanterned sky.

"No," whispered Mari.

Down on the Brynmawr Road the lights of a trap winked in blackness and the clatter of hooves came crystal clear, bringing to us a deeper remoteness, a warmer nearness.

"No," whispered Mari, slapping.

"Eh dear," I said. "There's a woman for no's. Yes for a change, is it?"

"Give me the spoon," she said against my throat.

I fumbled with fingers of ice, found it, and held it clear.

"Answer truly, then, or descend to the grids of hell with Satan. Who do you love, Mari Dirion?"

"A boy from Garndyrus," said she.

"Tell his name, then."

"Iestyn Mortymer."

"Do you swear to that love?"

"On the Bible black," she said. "Three times I swear."

And I kissed her once on the lips, longer than the rules allowed, which was only a peck. Gasping, we laid close, our breath steaming in the frost.

"Who do you love, Iestyn Mortymer, and answer truly or descend to the grids of hell."

"A girl from Carmarthen," I said.

"Tell her name, then."

"Mari Dirion."

"Will you swear to that love, boy?"

"On the black Bible," I replied, "three times. Will you take my spoon and be my love, Mari Dirion?"

"Aye," she answered, and she kissed me on the mouth.

So I took the thing out and fastened the trinket chain around her neck and opened the top of her dress and dropped it down, but it stuck half way because we were lying.

Beautiful she looked then, her face turned away and the redness flying into her cheeks.

"The old thing will not go down," I said. "Sit you up and give it a shake, girl."

But she did not move. I felt her trembling, though, and her trembling crept into me and flew to my thighs, and I was ashamed.

White and smooth was her throat. Soft was her breast under fingers that were brittle with cold, and the shock of my hand took her breath. I had never before touched a woman's breast. There was wonder in it, and longing, and a desire to press secret places. There was no winter with us then. The cold vanished and warmth came with our kisses, and there was no sound in the world but our sobbing as we lay together.

"Am I sinful?" she asked in a whisper.

"Sinful enough to bring deacons from pews," I said, "but I do not care. O, Mari!"

She smiled, her teeth white against the dark curves of her lips as she whispered, "The deacons are on furnace shift or loving their wives in bed," and she kissed me with a new fierceness. "Iestyn, boy, take me up to The Top?"

I knew what she meant by instinct, for there was a wildness about her that caught me up, making me a part of her passion that was mysterious and strange after her coldness of past months. It was as a chord singing between us, growing in increasing beauty and power, strident and clear as a clarion call; a chord that took a swing at the senses, forging us into one as the red iron is forged, in heat and shape, together.

The moon had gone now and the sky was alight with silver clouds and owls were hooting east of the Coity. Other sounds echoed; the wind-sigh of the heather, the clattering panic of a disturbed bird as we rose to our feet. All Nature seemed to call us with relentless strength. The flood-gates of longing had been opened by a single touch. I kissed her again and again, lost in the magic, all reason obliterated by the rushing urge to possess her.

"Do you know what will happen if we go up there?" I asked.

"Yes," said Mari. "And I do not care. We are one now, in honour. I have wanted you long enough, Iestyn. Take me."

"Come," I said, and I led her to a path.

Beautiful is the woman a man is to mate with, in moonlight.

We walked up through the heather in silence, hand in hand. The night was strangely quiet now, for the wind had dropped and the air was warmer with a threat of rain. Up in the blackness thunder boomed faintly and lightning flashed over Coldbrook. We had reached the crest of the Coity with the glow of Garndyrus in sight when the first rain pattered on the heather.

"Dammo!" said Mari. "The pair of us will catch our deaths."

"Can you run?" I asked her, dragging at her hand.

"Aye, but not back to Nanty!"

"Down to Shant-y-Brain's," I cried. "Over the tumps and into his barn. It will be warm in the hay—look, the light down by there, see it?"

"Satan fry the one behind," said she, and she was away and leaping over the boulders with her dress up round her thighs and her bare legs twinkling. After her I went like something demented, shouting to her to stop. Down, down we went as the storm broke about us, cracking over the sky and brushing sweeps of water over the dark country. Lightning split the clouds in blue flashes, the rain sheeted down in an explosion after the calm. Catching Mari, I caught her hand and dragged her on. Her shawl was gone, her hair was wet and flying. Laughing, breathless, we staggered and slipped down the slope to Shant-y-Brain's shippon, scrambled over his gate and ran to the barn where last year's harvest was streaking out in the wind. Scrambling up the ladder we flung ourselves down in the hay with the roof bible-black a foot from our faces. Our hearts were beating wildly, but not with running, as I turned in the bed and heaved over into the warmth of her.

"Quiet now, mind," I whispered, "or Shant-y-Brain will have us out with pitchforks. No giggling, no shouting for help, or he will put it over the county. Is it wet with you?"

"Soaked, man. I will chatter to bring him out if I stay in this wet old dress; the only dry thing on me is the spoon."

"Do not mind me," I said. "I have seen you wearing less."

"Heaven bless me," she giggled, "there's a big mistake if you think I am stripping for you in March. That was nearer June."

"Lie quiet, then, and let the hay dry you out."

The storm blew like a mad thing over the moontain, hammering everything in thunder and wind and away as quick as he came. The night was bright again with moonlight, the stars were washed clean.

"There's a handy old storm," I said, "getting you in this barn with me and no chance of you getting out."

Quiet, she was, her breathing steady.

"Mari," I whispered, up on an elbow.

"Hush you, go to sleep," she said.

"Sleep? Be human. Do you think I am risking Shant-y-Brain for sleep? I can do that in bed back home."

"Sleep," said she, "for I have changed my mind. Put a finger on me and I will howl like ten thousand cats and rise every deacon for miles."

"Too late," I answered, finding her lips. "The deacons are on furnace shift or loving their wives in bed, as I am loving you."

And her arms went about me as I kissed her, pulling me down.

Strange and wonderful is the first loving.

The blood runs hot with the kiss, hammering on the heart with quickening beats, forging muscles to steel in a riot of manhood as yet undiscovered. Trembling are the fingers that twist and seek, searching warm places blindly in darkness, and, finding, grip to hurt. There is no pity for the captive then. The pain is deep under a rush of breathing as the lancing steel is poised. Pennants fly, forests rise and swords go reaping in satanic joy. The back is bent in the bowman's hands and the arrows fly, plunging to wound, rending, as befits a conqueror. The tongue is noble then, the breathing is a sigh.

All in hours, all in seconds.

"Iestyn," she said.

Her hair was wet in my hands, lying in thick strands over her breasts, and hay was upon her shoulders. We lay together, listening to the sounds of the night growing out of the wildness and silence: the cattle lowing from the farm, the swish of the rain over the heather, the distant thuds of Garndyrus making iron. I looked at Mari. Her eyes were wide and moving over my face, large and glittering in the faint, blue light.

"Eh dear," she whispered. "You loved me, Iestyn."

"Aye," I said.

She giggled then, which was shameful, but wonderful.

"O," said she, "there's wicked I am, and you for doing it. This time next year I will be walking twins round town."

"They will beat you up the mountain with Bibles and sticks months before that," I said, kissing her.

"Well," said she, "I will be caught for two as happily as one. Love me again, my precious," and she reached up and pulled my face down, kissing.

So I loved her again.

"You will catch your death in this soaked dress," I said, and raised her and pulled it over her shoulders.

"Whee!" she whispered. "Now I must strip to please it, eh? Here I lie as a hoyden, naked in a barn with Iestyn Mortymer. There is a handy old storm for the boys of Garndyrus."

I did not answer, being a man.

Warm were her lips, and her trembling was not with cold.

# CHAPTER EIGHTEEN

ALL THAT spring the Chartists gathered and workers from towns as far apart as Hirwaun and Blaenafon flooded up the mountain to the torchlight meetings. The movement grew. As the Benefit Clubs were the springboards of the workers' Union, so the Union was the backbone of the new Charter. Speakers for Chartism were travelling from London and Birmingham: men like Henry Vincent, who could sway a thousand men with a phrase and change the politics of women with a song. Pamphlets were being distributed at the furnaces and pinned on the lodge gates of the owners, and sermons of sedition were preached against the young Queen. Chartism was the promise of freedom, and the workers seized at it. The Chartists met openly in defiance of the Military, and the Benefit Clubs and Unions flocked to the meetings and sent their invitation to attend to the owners. Even the men of Garndyrus came over the mountain. Just as Big Rhys and Mo and the old crowd did on the night I first heard the words of Zephaniah Williams of Coalbrookvale.

"A pig of a man if ever there was one," said my mother at table, and she smoothed Richard's black hair. "If the likes of little ones such as these are dependent upon him, then God help them, I say."

"Have you met him, then?" asked Morfydd, innocent. Richard was at her breast, her voice was gentle, but her eyes burned with the old fire.

"No," retorted Mam, "and not likely to. Hearing about him is enough."

"From the gossip in town?" asked Morfydd.

"From what I read in *The Merlin*."

"If you want the truth you must read the pamphlets, Mam. But there are none so stupid as those who will not try to understand. Have you heard about William Lovett's new Six Point Charter for the workers, even?"

"Leave it, Morfydd," said my father, glancing up.

"Stupid, is it?" flashed my mother. "Is it stupid to know the truth now? Charters, indeed!"

"It is stupid to reject it," replied Morfydd, shifting the baby on to the other.

Very pretty were Morfydd's breasts when she was feeding Richard, and although she was my sister I could not help a peep when her eyes were turned away. Mari's breasts were round and firm, pink-tipped, each small enough to be cupped in my hand, but Morfydd's were melon-shaped, standing straight out from her shoulders, and Richard's tiny fingers were red against them as he buried his face in their smoothness, his slobbering rosebud of a mouth running with milk.

"Get on with your dinner," said Dada.

"Yes," I said.

"And an atheist into the bargain," said my mother. "If this landlord of the Royal Oak Inn is a sample of a Chartist, then thank God the military are in Brecon Garrison and the Volunteers on a five minute tap."

"Do you think we could have a little less of the politics?" asked my father, polite. "We have it from morning to night now, which would not be so bad if either of you knew what you were talking about."

"He keeps a picture of Our Lord in his room," said Edwina bitterly, "with the words underneath, 'This is the man who stole the ass'. It is blasphemy that, not politics."

"Well said," answered Mam. "None shall stand who deride Him, and neither will Zephaniah Williams, mark me, for God will take revenge, and hell hath enlarged herself and opened her mouth without measure, and men like Williams will ascend into it with all his pomp and glory."

"Descend," said my father, reading now.

"Ascend," said my mother.

"Look," said Dada. "How the devil can anyone ascend into hell, woman?"

"Ascend or descend, it is all the same to me so long as he finishes up there," said Mam, "which he surely will."

"Where does his glory come in?" asked Edwina. "There is not much glory in an atheist, mind."

"And not much pomp in an unpaid Chartist," said Morfydd.

"Good God," said Mam, fanning. "You open your mouth in this house and six are down it, and all of you together have less sense than me."

"Then use it," said Dada. "Isaiah Five, verse fourteen. Look it up, for I cannot stick a wrong quotation. Or pamphlets or *Merlins*, come to that. The newspapers roar at us like lions, telling us what they would have us believe," and he got up and took Richard in his arms, and cooed and bounced to make him chuckle while Morfydd, eyes lowered, tucked away her beautiful, full breasts.

Not much interest in Chartists, my father.

I had just finished helping Edwina wash the dishes when the kitchen door came open to a boot and several faces peered around it, grinning, which brought my father to his feet in joy.

"In with you all!" he cried, giving Richard to Morfydd, and he pulled them in—Big Rhys and Mo, Afel Hughes and Mr Roberts, and the Howells boys and Will Blaenavon pushing up behind until the room was full and Mam tipped on the end of her chair and cursing flashes. Pretty full, too, by the look of them, and noisy enough for rowdies, with Mo sporting head bandages from cuts he had taken prize fighting on the Blorenge. Hard and strong was Mo these days, a grown man, with fifty guineas of a gentry's purse to back him against the best in Wales.

"Look you, boys, what we have here!" he roared, kissing my mother and ducking her slap. "The best cook in Garndyrus and the prettiest mother in Nanty," and he bowed low to Morfydd, who closed a fist and threatened to straighten him. Very pretty she looked then, smiling and sparring.

"Clear in the eyes she is and strong, see?" said Owen Howells. "And they talk of the Carmarthen girls. Firm in the legs and good in the milk by the size of her, look you!"

and he feinted and pinched but took a swing from Morfydd that sent him staggering.

"Out of it, all of you!" shouted Mam, giggling. "With all these decent chapel people in town, Hywel, you have to fill the house with indecent bruisers from Garndyrus. Out, out!" and she flapped at them with her apron, delighted, while Will behind her was on his knees handing out her cakes from the oven with oh's and ah's from the invaders as they bit them steaming hot. Good it was to have them and all their commotion and cheek.

"Let us have some sense in this," pleaded Dada. "What is the reason for the visit?"

"The meeting at Coalbrookvale tonight," spluttered Rhys, wiping his mouth. "Do not say you are not going, man!"

"Have you never heard of Zephaniah Williams, then?" asked Mo.

"*Duw!* Not again," said Dada, suffering. "Stuffed and cooked he is, and we have him for breakfast, dinner and supper in here."

"Then you will come with us to hear him?" asked Owen.

"Not if he is talking Charters, Benefits or Unions, for you know my views upon them, and so will he if I am fool enough to go."

"Charters it is tonight, man, and it will be lively, for Henry Vincent is coming over from Pontypool, they say."

"Zephaniah is explaining the new Six Points in Welsh and Vincent is driving it in English, see?"

"Where to?" asked Mam.

"Good God," said Big Rhys, while Morfydd giggled. "It is rules and regulations, do you understand—six points that the workers are driving into the gentry to get a fair deal from Parliament."

"Parliament now, is it?" said she. "There is a funny old place to drive anything to, least of all six rules and regulations. You would be handier employed getting better conditions and lower prices in the Shops."

"I am getting from here," laughed Rhys, "for one is bewitched and the other noodled. Iestyn?"

"Aye, I am coming," I said.

"Morfydd?"

"The Devil take me!" cried Morfydd. "Coming, indeed? And I helped organise it. Away, before I take boots to you all."

"Where is Jethro?"

"On shift," I said. "We do not want him with us, Mam. Keep him here when he comes off."

Down to Coalbrookvale we went, all eight of us, with Afel Hughes giving Nanty the trumpet to let it know who was in town, and more than once we ducked slops from a window. The Royal Oak Inn was crowded to the door, and with Mo leading we pushed a path to the bar and hammered it for beer while men whispered behind their hands at the sight of Mo and God help Dai Benyon Champion when this big boy got his hooks on him, for Mo's fame with his fists was spreading like a fire. Zephaniah Williams was out speaking, they told us, so we polished our quarts and went out to the tumps.

It was a strident, witch-ridden night, with the full moon throwing the shadows of the stricken trees like hunchbacks on the grass, and the rocks of the mountain were squat and evil in the light where torches flared. Hundreds were standing there in the wind: men from the valleys of Gwent, their faces still black from shift; women, shawled and shivering, with babies on their backs, and little barefooted children crying on the tips.

For the first time I saw the Chartist, Zephaniah Williams; the man of destiny standing high on a rock, wonderful in oratory, ominous in silence. So will I remember him all the days of my life, then, in the greatness of his power, not chained in the working gang under a pitiless sun and with an overseer's lash to drive him. Fine he looked on that rock with his arms outstretched.

"Look," whispered Mo. "There is Henry Vincent, and William Jones Watchmaker beside him," and he pointed.

"To the sword, then!" Williams cried in Welsh. "To powder and shot, then, if it is forced upon us, for how else

218

can we negotiate if they will not come to table? And even if we got them to table can mere words sway the likes of Guest of Dowlais and Crawshay of Cyfarthfa, these dogs of masters? Has Parliament any interest in petition when it is run by these aristocrats of wealth who rule our lives? What kind of freedom is it when we are driven to the polls to vote for Whig or Tory under threat of the blacklist? Where is a recognised anti-Truck Bill or a Bill for stabilised prices? You have none, and you will never have one, for Parliament is run by men who own the Shops and fix the prices that starve us—not by the will of the people, mark me, but by the law of birth and wealth, and so it will be until we dislodge them!"

The crowd howled at this and showed their fists.

"We are men of peace and threaten nobody!" shouted Zephaniah. "But if it is blood they are after they shall have it, for the time is past when they can ride roughshod and break up meetings with crops. So if Crawshay Bailey has ideas about breaking this one let him come with his Volunteers and try it, for we will meet him with muskets."

"Damned near sedition," whispered Afel Hughes to me. "Soon he will be baiting Victoria."

"Aye!" roared Zephaniah, as if he had heard. "The Gentlemen Cavalry, booted and spurred, straight from the hunt to flog the Unwashed. Do you want the truth of them—these men of idleness who sit in their Company Parks and make profit from your misery and watch your children die—protected by the laws they alter to suit their pockets, hiding under the skirt of the Queen they use as a puppet, God bless her," and he winked while the crowd yelled. "To hell with them and to hell with Parliament, and God help our Virgin Queen, I say, for if words cannot shift the iniquitous laws of England that bind her hands, then the cannon of the people must, and blow into oblivion her enemies, the parasites of her crown and the wanglers of the Pension List!"

Bedlam.

"Sedition now," cried Afel. "To the devil with Zephaniah Williams, boy—give me Lovett, for I would rather have a sea trip to Botany Bay than hang my head on a spike in London and the rest of me in strips."

"That is because there is no stomach to you, Afel," cried Rhys. "I am all for Zephaniah; it is all or nothing now, man."

The crowd was thick about us, swaying, with lanterns on sticks and flares flaming madly. "A bit of room by here!" shouted Mo, widening his shoulders and shoving, and fists went up as a mad stampede nearly overturned us. For another figure mounted the rock as Zephaniah leaped down, and stood there, serene and smiling.

"Henry Vincent, is it?" bawled Rhys. "Dock me in the stomach and tie me in skirts. Soon they will be sending us women for agitators. Do you sing, too, lad?"

"Not so loud," said Will. "In Carmarthen they are fair bandy over him, so give him a hearing, for I heard him speak by Picton's Column on the night Mo here flattened Knocker Daniels."

Fine and handsome Henry Vincent looked, the English Chartist who was reckless in his criticism of the aristocracy, Church and Throne. "Do not heed him," he cried, jerking his thumb at Zephaniah Williams. "Even the truth is sickening if you hear it too often. Let us take another course for a lark. Who is with me for a visit to Mr Crawshay Bailey?"

Roars of laughter greeted this and hoots of delight.

"A little walk to Nantyglo with a bottle of brandy to entice him out, eh? And call the place to strike if he cannot show a Union card?"

"A tidy old boy, this Vincent," said Mo, nudging me, "but I am wondering where he will land us all."

"On a gibbet," replied Big Rhys, "or picking oakum in a poorhouse, but I am following the lad for courage, tenor or not."

So we worked our way to the head of the column with Mo and Big Rhys pitching out the rowdies right and left. Hundreds strong now and growing every minute, we took the track back to Chapel Road, singing and shouting with the torches a fiery stream right down to Blaina. Windows went up, doors came open, and women and children were dancing in the street as we roared our way towards the home of Bailey. But then, above the tumult, I heard Mari's voice and saw her running beside the column with men pushing her off when she tried to break through to me. In seconds I was beside her.

"For God's sake!" she cried. "Home quick, Iestyn. Jethro has been splashed!"

My mother and father were with Jethro.

He lay on the floor where the accident men had put him down, his eyes clenched tight, his jaw set. His right sleeve was rolled up, and I saw the cuff charred and the knuckles of his hand, wrist and forearm burned to the bone in a bright red weal where the molten splash had laid its finger. But the iron was cool now, tucked down and rigid, and the swollen skin was heaped high above it where the blood had boiled.

"Up with his head, Iestyn," whispered Dada, and we got the whisky flask between his teeth. He took a full mug before his eyes opened and rolled at us, and he screamed once and went out again, which is usual for a bad burn, the old puddlers say.

My mother was sobbing, her hands over her face.

"O God!" she whispered.

"Away upstairs if you cannot stomach it," said Dada. "Iestyn, fetch me a knife."

I did so, and gave it to him and gripped Jethro's good hand and bowed my head, and hatred, deeper and stronger than I had ever known it, ran riot in me. Mari was standing by the window, shivering in her shawl, and beyond her I saw the torches smoking at the gates of Bailey's house. The murmur of the mob entered the room, gushing into sound as the door came open, snapping to a whisper as it slammed shut. Morfydd stood there, her face white, her eyes large.

"Jethro," I said to her. "Caught by a splash."

"I know," said she. "Barney Kerrigan it was, and he is ladling drunk on Caradoc Owen's shift at Number Five."

I looked at my father. He was levering with the knife and

221

the iron came clear, long and jagged as it dropped on the boards. Jethro tensed and sighed.

"I will bandage him," said Morfydd, and took the roll and ointment, kissing him first.

"Somebody will pay for this," she said through her teeth.

"Who ordered him into the furnace shed?" asked Dada, cold.

"Bailey's agent, they say. Most of the men had thrown their tools to go to the Coalbrookvale meeting. Furnace Five had just been tapped," she said. "Jethro was coming in from Llangattock, and the Agent saw him and sent him with Kerrigan to ladle."

"Was Owen there?" he asked, frowning.

"Aye, I have just left him."

"Dada," I said, rising, "leave it now. The harm is done. See to Jethro now and leave trouble till morning."

"Aye," he said.

The women got the bed ready and we carried him up and covered him, deep in the sleep of whisky. Mari, Morfydd and I came down, leaving the others with him, and thank God Edwina was out with Snell that night, said Morfydd.

"A child, and he is splashed by iron," said Mari, walking about, pressing her hands.

"Know them by their children who labour in dark places, to be burned and maimed," said Morfydd. She went to the window and flung it open. The mob was chanting for Bailey at the lower lodge, and waving its torches. "Thank God for men like Vincent," she added. "With him and Frost and the Charter we will change it all."

"I am changing it now," said Dada, coming in. "I am having the skin from every man in Furnace Five and the bloody Agent when I land on him." And he reached for his coat, pulling Morfydd from the door.

I was quick and turned the lock. "For God's sake," I said. "If you start trouble at a time like this Bailey will blame you for violence with the mob."

"Out of my way," he said. "Nobody splashes my son with iron."

"Kerrigan is nearly blind with furnace glare," I said, "and find me the Irishman who ladles sober," and I pushed him back.

"Do not blame the drunken Irish," said Morfydd. "And remember this. Lay a finger on that precious Agent at a time like this, and Bailey will blacklist the house."

"So be it," said he. Reaching out he flung me headlong, unbolted the door and ran into the cwm.

# CHAPTER NINETEEN

ACCORDING TO Shanco Mathews, who was grubbing for coal on the night Jethro was splashed, he had never seen the like of it. A swinging boot blew the near-blind Kerrigan out of harm's way, a right uppercut dropped Caradoc Owen for dead, Mr Hart, the Agent, had every tooth rattled loose and his face smacked black and blue, and two puddlers from Furnace Two who came running with ladles had never been heard of since.

Very businesslike was the Agent, very just. Dada was suspended for a month for unprovoked violence, Jethro with him for being implicated, and me for two weeks for being a relation.

The only breadwinner left was Mari, and Mrs Hart saw to her.

"Now perhaps you are satisfied," said Mam.

"I am," said my father. "The owners have seen the last of my loyalty."

"Thank God," said Mam, cutting him. "Now we will eat. Can you tell me how I manage with nothing coming in and two pounds left of our savings?"

"The Lord will provide," whispered Edwina.

"Amen," said Mam, "but there are people already starving in Nanty and He will see to them first. Can anyone tell me what happens in the meantime?"

"We share," said my father.

"God help me," said Mam. "I was born in a manse on black cloth, and ever since I can remember I have been mixing with bruisers who cannot keep their hands to themselves. The two pounds will keep us for a month, but before you begin hitting Agents about again, remember we will starve."

"Do not worry," said Dada, and got up.

"And where are you going now, pray, with the supper on the boil?"

"To Coalbrookvale," said he.

"And what for, may I ask?"

"To a meeting of the Chartists, with Idris Foreman, Garndyrus," said he, "and never get mixed with politics for views can change overnight, I find."

"Good God!" breathed Morfydd, putting down her sewing.

"Upon my soul," whispered Mam. "Suspended now, we will all be hung or transported next. O, Hywel, do not drive me mad. Are you from your senses?"

"I have never been saner," said he. "At Garndyrus there was little need for a Charter. Under Bailey, in this town, it is a necessity for he shows no justice."

"Amazing what an iron-splash can do," said Morfydd. "One moment cursing Chartists, the next moment joining them, and me hitting the principle of the thing for the last ten years. Next he will be standing for Mayor."

Dada did not answer, except for his look, but he did not slam the door behind him.

"*Dammo di!*" said my mother. "What a life it is! Charters and Unions, torchlight processions, Benefit Clubs and secret meetings. Down to Abergavenny with me, I think, and join the Quakers or wear sackcloth and ashes, and to hell with the damned old cooking."

"Very beautiful you would look in sackcloth and ashes, too," said Mari, kissing her. "Do not worry, Mam, he will take care."

The month of my father's suspension pulled us down, and with three weeks of it gone Crawshay Bailey cut wages by a seventh and put up his Tommy Shop prices an eighth, thinking that it was cheaper for the workers to live during summer.

And cheaper for masters, too, said the workers, so the town came out. Every man and boy from rollers to Irish labourers, greasers, furnace men, and ballers came out, taking the women and children. The cauldron began to boil at last. Pikes were under beds, powder and shot were being stored in the mountains, muskets stolen from sentries, swords and pistols from the gentry's private collections. Government spies came from London and some never went back. The pamphlets, bolder every week, screamed the cause of Chartism at the workers and openly criticised the aristocracy as puppets of the Crown. The gentry struck back. Harry Vincent, the first to see the strength of the masters, was thrown into Monmouth Gaol. John Frost, at the head of the snowball, was open in his contempt of Church and Throne. Twelve grooms of the bedchamber had the young Queen, said he, and each one of them drawing a thousand pounds a year while the workers starved. And what the poor girl was doing with twelve grooms was beyond his understanding, he said. For if he had a groom he would give him a horse to polish, and his pay would be ten pounds a year, not a thousand. So would somebody please tell him what the Queen was doing with twelve at a cost of twelve thousand?

"Very dangerous, all this," said my father.

"It is about time it was told," flashed Morfydd.

"She is like any other girl," said Mam. "She does as she is told. Twelve grooms in a bedchamber, indeed, I do not believe it. And if one of them smelled like those in Cyfarthfa stables she has my sympathy."

It was a joy having my mother in the house when things went political, but it was not as bad as the old days with my father and Morfydd at each other's throats, one waving the Union Jack, the other giving lectures on Feargy O'Connor. My father had changed since his loyalty was destroyed by the master who could have strengthened it, but he was not an extremist. It was justice he was after, not blood; negotiation, not violence.

I was with him on this. I wanted Lovett's new Six Points of the Workers' Charter as much as any man on the mountains, but I was against the torchlight meetings, the inflamed speeches, the mouthings and cruelties of men who would bawl anything for a laugh from the mob. And I was sorry for the Queen. She was about my own age then, alone, unaided.

Over the length and breadth of the country her crown was being used by men in authority to increase their personal fortunes. A pretty little thing was Victoria; one bound by the chains of the community, said Tomos Traherne; educated since her birth to put her signature where grasping ministers put their thumbs. So Frost went a bit small to me when he criticised her, and smaller still when he was taxed with it and denied it, saying he was misquoted. Not misquoted at all. I was in Blackwood that night and heard him.

"Twelve grooms or one," said Morfydd now, "we cannot afford her. And whether she agrees with her ministers or not, whether she has a tongue of her own or not, she is head of the State and responsible to the people."

"She is a child, a child," said my father, sick of it.

"I do not care if she is in arms," answered Morfydd. "She is put there by the people who expect something back. Give her a groom if you like, give her a palace, but not twenty, for the God she prays to never owned a palace in His life. No grooms for Him Who had nothing but a rag around His middle. No bishops and convocations and three-cornered hats and mitres and five thousand a year pension in the name of God. For the ministers of her church are better than the politicians for squeezing pennies out of the poor every Lady Day and Michaelmas."

"We were discussing Victoria," said Dada wearily. "How the hell we have got to three-cornered hats and Michaelmas I do not know."

"One and the same," said Morfydd. "When we tip her we will tip her gently, but there will be a clatter when the gentry and clergy come down with her, with their silver plate, decorations and money bags."

"Do you tip her with boots?" I asked.

Morfydd sniffed.

"With tumbrils and guillotines, then?"

"Jethro," said my mother, "into the bath and quick."

"Not in front of Mari," said he, for she sat in a corner, her eyes down, as she always did during the politics.

"Into the bath," said my father, pointing.

Morfydd said earnestly, "It matters little how we do it, but it must be done, by force if necessary. We plead for negotiation, and where does it lead us—deeper in iron, deeper into the pits. Unwashed, they call us, but if they blind themselves to our power they will regret it."

"Aye," said Mam. "Unwashed is the word, and if Jethro is not down in that bath in under five seconds I will hit him sideways, iron-splashes and all."

"What is for supper?" asked my father, changing the subject.

"Nothing," said Mam, "the same as last night, unless somebody can spare a shilling for the Shop?"

"What is the debt there?" I asked.

"Thirty-two shillings, and likely to go higher now the strike is on again. Upon my soul, what a state for a country! I pray for little Victoria, but I am hungry enough to eat her."

"Do not waste your breath," said Morfydd. "The bishops pray better, and there is nothing in the Convocation of Canterbury to stop you going hungry."

"What is this old Convocation thing now?" asked Mam. "There are new words cropping up every minute."

"The laws of the Church," replied Morfydd, "and God bless the Queen every two minutes. I could write them a Convocation that would leave them breathless and take the robes from every bishop between here and Glasgow."

"No doubt," said Dada.

"Charters for the last two years, now Convocations," said Mam, pulling down Jethro's trews while he hopped and covered his front with his good hand. "*Diawl!*" she said. "A tail back or front is much the same, and Mari is not interested. God help us. Soon it will be John Frost in Nantyglo House and Crawshay puddling iron," and she belted Jethro to steady him.

"One devil in exchange for another," said Mari, tossing over a towel.

This sent eyebrows up—the first time Mari had wasted a word on politics. My father smiled. "Some views at last, eh? These spots are catching. Air them, girl."

Mari shrugged. "A still tongue is wiser, Mr Mortymer. The house is split from top to bottom already, but I say this— a little more love of God, and the world would be happier, for it is greed you are discussing, not politics. And until greed is taken from the hearts of men you will always have masters and poor, and which way round it is matters little. I am much more interested in my wedding."

"Well spoken," said my mother, swabbing at Jethro's back. "Births and deaths, too, if you like—anything but the politics." Sweating, she brushed stray hairs from her eyes. "Chapel is it?"

"Church of England," I said. "You have known it since a week last Sunday, for I told you."

The expression on her face was enough to freeze us, but she knew I was acting to rules. Mari was Church for three genera- tions, she said, but she left it to me nevertheless. My mother stood up, hooking Jethro out with her arm and he stood there dripping and shivering.

"With respect to Mari," she said, "we have been Chapel since the start of time, never mind about three generations and rules to suit people who cannot agree to something reasonable. Not much to ask, is it?"

There was no sound but Jethro chattering.

"Eh dear!" said she.

"Mam, it is not important," said Morfydd.

"Not important, you say? Only the difference between the Upper Palace and Damnation. *Diawl!* I do not know what the modern generation is coming to." She pointed at Dada. "And it is your fault for encouraging them, mind!"

"Upon my soul," said he, removing his pipe. "I have not breathed a word."

"Then it is high time you did," said she, getting it up her apron. "If you had taught the children the difference between pagan rites and Christian behaviour we would never have been within a mile of a Church of England." Stamping about now, looks to kill, flapping the cloth and throwing cups at the table. "God forgive me if ever I stand before a gilded altar."

"No need for an altar, come to that," said Morfydd. "Just

229

an old man in black spouting to make it legal and two and sixpence please and out with you quick to make room for the next. A waste of good money is weddings and burials. Like Owen ap Bethell's daughter, for instance. The Bishop himself wedded her; in white lace, she was, with train-bearers and bugles and half the gentry in the county, but where did she land them? Found in bed three nights after with a red-headed preacher from Ponty and cast out by her dada by the end of the week, and they talk about the working classes."

"Found in bed with red-headed preachers is nothing to do with Church or Chapel," said Mam, "and kindly mind your words before Jethro."

"Taken in adultery, nevertheless," said Morfydd, "and that was Church of England. If you want some examples of Chapel marriages I will start now and we will stay up late."

"What is adultery, Mam?" asked Jethro, scratching.

"See now?" said my mother. "Ashamed you should be, Morfydd! A wicked thing it is, Jethro, and terrible to have a loose-mouthed sister in the house."

"Loose-mouthed when it comes to the clergy," said Morfydd. "When the Devil opens his gates the men in black will be first in and the gentry pushing up their shoulderblades."

"Politics again," sighed my father. "Give it a rest, girl." He turned to me. "Church or Chapel, no odds, boy. Please yourself, for I have been trying to please your mother for the last twenty years and I haven't managed it yet," and he took his handkerchief from his pocket and pressed it against his eyes. It was Furnace Five, they told me; she was a bitch for glare. Thank God for the suspension, in one way, said my mother. At least it gave his old eyes a rest.

He rested all right, so did everyone else in town. The only people working were the women in childbirth. The spring went on. The pits were idle, the furnaces cold and the people starved, the children dying first, with the old ones hard on their heels in the long black columns going to the chapels. For the first time since I could remember it was hungry in our house, for there was eight to feed and not a penny coming in, and Morfydd had gone very pale and stately while Mari's waist was so slender that I could nearly span it with my hands.

The mountain was bright in the sun as Mari and I came down hand in hand on the last day of the striking. The valley below us was misted, the dusty air rising in billows as the carts went by. Over the road to Brynmawr had passed cattle for slaughter at Shant-y-Brain's, and the white dust was criss-crossed with saliva trickles from their mouths. Later we saw them, froth on their necks as white as snow, standing together in the furnace heat, bellowing for water. And above us the Coity, great and golden, reared into the sun, her rocks reflecting strickening light, not caring whether anybody lived or not.

But for all the desolation of that afternoon the strike was broken, and out of it came hope of life. Back on workers' terms, too, the first victory.

And before spring was out Mari and I had planned our marriage.

To celebrate the coming event, said my father, we will take Dai Two Pig down to Shant-y-Brain's for mating.

"Wait, I am coming!" cried Jethro.

"Back here, you," said Mam. "You are staying for cutting down."

A devil of a palaver this cutting down, with Jethro up on the table near to tears and Mam, Edwina and Mari pushing and shoving him, the trews going on and coming off him like lightning, and are they too tight or too slack, with the baby crying and everybody shouting directions.

It was always the same for Jethro when Dada or me moved out on a pair, for money was short.

"Let us go," said my father. "The boy will be amputated the way they are going," for scissors were cheeping right and left and pins were going in and coming out.

"Aye," I said, "there are enough here to stop the bleeding."

I will always remember Jethro standing there on the table with tears in his eyes surrounded by women with needles and knives. Mari looked longingly at me, but I did not spare her a look extra. The mating of an animal is a very delicate thing and not for the eyes of women.

Out in the yard came Dai Two, very happy and snorting to get going for his wedding, and along Market Road went the three of us with my father raising his cap to the women and Dai Two grunting his pleasure.

"You are sure of the time, now?" asked my father.

"Aye. Seven sharp," said I.

"Is the boar tame? I am not having a maniac, mind, and I know that Mo Jenkins."

"Big Rhys has seen the thing, Dada. A Hereford boar, it is, sawn in the tusks and short in the privates, he said, and like a cat for eating from a human hand."

"Heaven help the pair of them if it is wild," said Dada. "A family pig like Dai Two is not likely to take to a bruiser and a virgin pig is always tight, mind."

Very fond of Dai Two was my father since the day we saved him from Billy Handy, years back, it seemed. But he saw the sense of my argument squarely. An easy life had Dai Two up to date, rooting the years away, eating his head off. Work days, strike days, they were all the same to Dai, while every other pig on the mountains had a heart attack when the men came out. It was past time he did something with his life, said Mam, so I arranged a date with Mo's new Hereford boar for a furrowing.

Down the mountain to Shant-y-Brain's we went now, the three of us, which was a convenient place for the mating.

All was quiet when we reached the shippon, but people were about, for the manure had just been stacked for spreading and it steamed like a volcano in the fenced yard.

"Ho, there!" I shouted. "Anybody home?" and out of the farm came Mo and Big Rhys, roaring and sparring up at the sight of us.

"Well, man?" began Rhys. "Very happy the three of you are looking for people half starved in Nanty. How are the rest at home?"

"Healthy enough," said my father, eyeing them, for Mo was doing a giggle and there was a bit of boot tapping and

O, aye's and dear me's between the pair of them that was unnatural.

"And your good neighbours? Well with them, is it?" asked Mo.

"Never mind our neighbours," I said sharp. "We are here for a furrowing."

"And a quick one," said Dada, "so I can get back home to supper. Where is the boar?"

"Eh dear!" whispered Mo, "have patience, please. Just like you Mortymers to bring a pig and loose her to the boar. Have you any experience with pig mating?"

"No," we said, feeling small.

"Well, then, leave it to your betters," said Rhys. "If you think it is in with him and out with him and pick up your pig and back home in five minutes you are mistaken, eh, Mo?"

"Indeed," said Mo, grinning.

"For a very romantic business it is, and done tidy, so do not flurry us into speed or the boar will get his temper up and be into the three of you, for standing by here I see little to choose between you and the pig."

"No offence intended, mind," said Mo.

My father rubbed his chin, grinning. "Eh, now!" said he. "I can smell trouble. May I remind you that we are here for a furrowing? And if anything goes wrong with the deal somebody will be bedridden for weeks. Out with your boar now, and get it over and done with."

"The two shillings first, then," said Mo, his hand out.

"One and sixpence!" I cried, indignant. "It was agreed."

"Two shillings now. True Hereford blood is this boar, and he charges sixpence for walking from Garndyrus," and he spat.

"Take it or leave it," said Rhys.

"Damned highway robbery it is," said Dada.

"Put it on the price of the litter," replied Mo. "Sixpence extra is little enough to pay for an aristocrat, and the pig he is serving is nothing but an insult—all ears and backside she is.'

"An ordinary boar would not give her a second look," said Rhys. "Two and sixpence would be fairer, Mo."

"Pay him quick, Dada," I said.

"That is better," said Mo, spitting on the silver, and they walked off, grinning.

"I do not trust them," said my father. "Something is afoot or I am not Hywel Mortymer."

With Dai Two standing between us we watched them walk back to the farm, nudging each other and giggling like Sunday school girls instead of grown pugilists. At the door of the out-house Big Rhys turned and cupped his hands to his mouth. "There is nothing in the contract against an audience, mind. A few of your old friends have come as witnesses all the way from Garndyrus, Hywel, so treat them tidy," and he hooted and yelled like an Indian.

Out they came—Owen and Griff Howells, Afel Hughes, Iolo Milk, Twm-y-Beddau, Will Blaenavon and half a dozen others, blowing on hunting horns and bugles and enough drum beating to send any boar raving mad. Dai Two cocked an ear, took one look and was off with his nose cord flying. Round the manure heap he went like a whippet, while I cursed his ancestors and flung handfuls of manure at him to head him back to the rails.

"Look out!" yelled Dada, but his warning was wasted. I was over the fence and out of the yard like lightning. For through the gate came Mo's boar, roaring and furious; a full twenty stones of him, grizzled and hackled, driving everything before him with tusks like a rhino. Little Dai skidded to a stop, looked, screamed, and cleared the manure by a foot.

"Good God," said Dada.

Round and round the heap went Dai with the bruiser after him, while the Garndyrus criminals whooped with unholy joy. Into the manure now, to come out streaming, with the old boar looking for short cuts to head him off, and the grunting and screaming could be heard in Nanty. Will Blaenavon was helpless on the ground, clutching his stomach and choking with laughter, Big Rhys was hanging on the rails, fisting the air and roaring, and the rest of them were shrieking like women. Mo was rolling his backside along the gate, sagging at the knees, his eyes streaming, shouting encouragement to his boar between breaths. Poor little Dai was tiring, but I dare not go to his aid. It was a mad boar now, his red eyes gleaming above his whiskered snout, and galloping scarcely a yard behind poor Dai, who was bellowing his last as he leaped high and laid there shivering. On top of the manure the bruiser had him. I could bear it no longer and covered my eyes. And when I looked again little Dai was disappearing into the muck with nothing but the boar's backside to tell which way he was going. No pity in Mo, as if his triumph was incomplete, for he lined up the Garndyrus buglers for unison blasts as the boar's tail came up and drum beats and rolls every time it went down.

"Somebody will pay for this," said my father.

"Aye!" whimpered Mo, agonised. "Two shillings, is it?" and he rolled away, his ribs shaking.

Not much of a palaver about boars when they are down to business. This one was off in half a minute and rooting and grunting like a spring lamb, but no sign of little Dai, and my father and I were two feet into the muck, throwing out armfuls of kale before we came across him. It took an hour to get him clean, and we were still at it with the pump long after the Garndyrus hooligans had whooped and blasted their way down the mountains to home.

"One we owe them," said my father, severe.

"Two," I said, "if this pig is not in litter."

And then he chuckled and began to laugh, and my father's laugh would drown the basso profundos of the Italian opera. Just the pair of us there in the middle of Shant-y-Brain's shippon, opposite the barn where I had made love to Mari. I will always remember it, the way we laughed, him and I, while Dai Two winked and snorted at the stupid humans.

Very happy was Dai Two, we noticed; most contented, and with good reason.

Later, my mother sat with him by lamplight, and he brought forth twelve, two for each week of strike, they said in Nanty.

# CHAPTER TWENTY

APRIL WAS the month of my wedding to Mari.

I awoke early, went to the window and looked beyond the ash tips to where the mountains met the sky, wondering at the changing colours of the heather as the sun took charge of the day. The night shift was coming off, whooping and quarrelling in the valley, nearly drowning the clatter from the bedroom next door where Morfydd and my mother, clucking like layers, were stitching the white dress around Mari. A great business it had been for weeks now, this dress on borrowed money: special material bought from Abergavenny, full of frills and laces and ribbons of colour. Take it in here, let it out there, down to her ankles, up to her knees, and for God's sake keep if off the ground at sevenpence a yard. Glory to marriage, I thought, to its frills, lace, pins and fittings; glory to all that is written in the Old Book about the joining of one to the other in body and spirit. I can see Mari now as I opened the door in mistake. Beautiful she looked in her white petticoat, her shoulders naked, her long slim arms held high as the women measured. Aye, glory to love and desire! For while the mountain is vast and full of secret places, there can surely be no sweetness like possessing the one you want within the warmth and quiet of walls, away from chance eyes. With Jethro still snoring I was first down the stairs and into the tub outside. The dew was sparkling upon every leaf as I splashed into the icy water and rubbed myself for a glow.

"Hurry!" called my father, coming down. "Mam wants us out of the house before eight, remember."

"What the devil is happening?" she cried then from the landing. "The pair of you due at Shant-y-Brain's at a quarter past and you are creeping for a funeral. Move!"

"What is all the hurry?" I asked. "The wedding is not until two o'clock. Am I going to sleep on the mountain?"

"To hell out of it," said Morfydd half through the window, "or do you want me to come down with boots?"

Claps and cheers from the window now as Dada and I moved off. The women were at the doors, chattering and happy at the prospect of a new bride, and they shouted good wishes as we went by. Very fine I felt walking up Market Road that morning; dressed in my Sunday black, brushed up and pulled in and polished in the boots to shave in and my starched collar killing me. My father, as usual, was perfectly turned out, and still a fine figure despite the slight swell of his stomach. His collar was snow white and his black satin stock beneath it arched proudly under the square cut of his chin. Only his eyes saddened him. The glare had taken them proper now, and they were red and slow to move, as if dying in his face. Dada knew, we all knew, what was coming, for nine puddlers in ten were half blind, but we never spoke of it. Side by side we went up the mountain now, and over the crest down to Shant-y-Brain's for the trap, and the ferns were a dazzling green as we turned our faces to the valley.

"It is a long time since we walked like this together, boy," he said after a silence. "Do you remember how I once talked of women and marriage?"

I laughed. "Aye, but it was so long ago that I have forgotten. Is it something you are doubtful about now?"

"No sniggers," he said, "or I will have you flat, big as you are."

"Yes, I remember," I said. "I remember, too, how I wished you to the devil and back."

"Wait now," said he, sitting on a hillock. "Down here beside me, my son, for I would speak to you again. Come, Iestyn, it is important to Mari."

Until that moment I had not realised the limit to his sight. For weeks now he had not read the pamphlets, and I had seen the failure of his eyes in small things—the outstretched hands, the fixed stare of the pupils, unblinking to the white-hot swing of the firebox. Now, in bright sunlight, I saw them clearly; their light blue strangely opaque and filmed,

237

and his left hand went up to me as I flung myself down to his right.

"What the hell," I said, swallowing my grief. "Is she marrying a bruiser, then?"

He said into the sun, "You will treat this girl with tenderness, Iestyn. Times are hard and likely to get harder, especially for women who bear the children and work to make the money spin. A man in his full strength can torture. The woman beneath him is as clay to be honoured or crushed as he wills, and by the way he treats her she will remember him. Go gently."

"Yes, Dada," I said.

"Save your strength for the men, where you will need it. Do not pour your goodness into the bed. A woman is not an animal to be filled every night out of habit, remember, nor did God ordain that she is loaded with child every year to be kept in milk. She is your wife, mother, your sister if you like. Do you heed me?"

"Yes, Dada."

He went on, his face turned down, "Do not rebel too much. A rebel is all right in his place—there is a place for all kinds of men, but do not defy every law and authority, Iestyn, or you will suffer. Do not hate—not even your masters. Ironmasters may seem born of the devil, but they are not without character, nor are they short of their troubles. They represent the class and system we hate, but they dominate us, and they will not be easily brought down. They suffer as we suffer, remember, so be charitable to them, and be loyal to your Queen."

"Yes," I said.

"But I did not intend to mouth politics, boy. I wanted to speak of the holy bond of marriage, the gift of God. Keep it holy always. Its sanctity is above any system and government, so do not defile it whatever else you see go down, or you will defile the law of the Maker."

He went quiet, so I chanced a look at him. A sudden weariness seemed upon him, a premature age. He had been working in iron for over twenty years now, only three years less than Barney Kerrigan, the blind puddler. Many good men had given their sight to the firebox and gone into the Quakers' Home, those blessed people who were giving back to my country what the ironmasters were taking out of it. Others, like Grandfer Shams-y-Coed who could not see his nose now, had taken to the farms again, which was their birthright. I looked again at my father and saw his face suddenly lined where the sun searched it, the heaviness of the jowls that sagged over his stiff collar. It was a shock to know that he could age; that the muscles of his neck and throat could wither and his great shoulders sag. He had not been the same since Probert had flogged him, and the torchlight meetings of the Chartists, their heat and plans for power through force, seemed to have sapped him of strength. In a morning he was old, for the sun was pitiless.

"Now away," he said, twisting up. "Are we sitting here all day?"

When we reached Shant-y-Brain's farm the wedding trap and mare were ready, together with my old mare Elot, whom Griff Howells had brought over from Garndyrus the previous night. The trap gleamed in the sun and the lively little mare flashed her burnished brass and danced along merrily under the reins while I rode Elot behind. A good judge of nature was Shant-y-Brain, with his wedding trap jaunty and gay and shining red and white and the wheels a golden yellow. Like a bride herself was that little black mare, too, so polished and willing and laden with flowers. But his funeral carts were bible-black, and to get good squeaks he never greased the wheels; pulled by the oldest nags he could find, with soot well rubbed into their hides to add a little more misery, and special flower beds he kept behind his shippon for lilies of the valley. Aye, when it came to business Shant-y-Brain was a mile in front of Evans the Death, who used the same cart for every occasion. And there should be a difference between a funeral and a wedding, although Morfydd says there is nothing to choose between the two. Like the time when Twm-y-Beddau our next-door neighbour married. Evans did the business then, and Twm and his bride went to Chapel sitting on the coffin of Butcher Harris, who burst. Killing two birds with one stone, said Evans, and a cut rate it would be at the settlement. But not much of a wedding with the bride fainting away when Twm lifted the seat, for there was Butcher Harris with flowers in his hand and not even screwed. Refused to pay, did Twm, and the parson backed him, but Evans carved a twin coffin on the wedding night and put Twm's name on one lid and *Jane, Beloved Wife*, on the other, and carted it up to the bedroom window, and Twm paid full price to have the inscription removed.

Not undertaking that, but plain deceit, and people took note of it. No, not a patch on Shant-y-Brain was Evans when it came to business, and the way Shant-y-Brain was going— with the Mortymers, for instance —he would soon be burying gentry.

"Right, you," said Dada now. "Away out of it anywhere you like. At one o'clock sharp we will leave Nantyglo, and if you get to Church late you will never hear the end of it," and he waved his whip above his head and was off in the trap back to Nanty.

A beautiful day for marriage to a bride like Mari. The mountain swelled up either side of us as Elot trotted. The stillness of the trees, the blue loveliness of the sky brought me to tranquillity. Mari Dirion! How lovely was her name! I said it aloud again and again, delighting in its beauty, saying it to the sky, to the rhythm of Elot's hoofbeats on the mountain turf. Spurring her, we made a gallop, entering a line of firs standing bright green and misted in the growing heat, then we swung across the mountain to the Whistle Inn.

A pint to settle the dust, a pail of spring water for Elot and a sleep beneath a tree. It was past one o'clock when the landlord woke me, pointing. And there, on the Brynmawr road was the long line of the Nantyglo guests, the women on the right, the men on the left, following the trap that carried Mari, Mam and Morfydd, and Snell's trap with Jethro, Edwina and Dada coming up behind.

Bread and cheese then and another pint for courage, and I was away. Short of the Corner I dismounted, tethered the

mare and lay in the grass by the roadside watching the larks
nicking and diving against a sky of unbroken blue, then I re-
mounted and took the short cut down into town, and was
waiting at the lych gate as the wedding traps came up.

I saw Mari first, of course, radiant in her long white dress
with frills and laces and her face flushed and beautiful under
her big summer hat.

"All right," said Tomos. "Take her and God bless the pair
of you, church wedding or not."

"God bless you, too," said my mother, tearful, a sure sign
she was enjoying things.

The bells were ringing joyfully, the sun blazed down. It was
a happy, golden wedding day.

The church was crowded, even the balcony was filled, and
the tall hats of the women came round as we walked in and up
the long, red carpet to the altar while Mrs Gwallter played
'And He Shall Feed his Flock' on the organ, and trust
Gwallter to make a damned mess of things for the Mortymers,
said Mam. The altar was beautiful, heavy with flowers, and
the sun shafted through the stained glass in golden pools of
light in which the dust of well-hung clothes hung suspended
and glittering. Together we knelt, Mari and I. Behind us the
congregation was tuning up for the singing, shuffling and
coughing until the minister appeared. I looked at Mari. Her
face was pale and her eyes cast down. And I wondered, with
the black shine of the Book between us, if she was thinking of
home, being in loneliness because there was nobody to give
her away. But she said her vows with a smile, her head uplifted. Yes, glory to marriage, I thought then, to a home, a
woman and her children. Then, with the ring on, came the
prayers and the flapping of the pages as the congregation got
ready; a clearing of throats and an elbowing for room, and
when Mrs Gwallter gave the note for the chanting every soul
in the place let fly. I heard my mother's deep contralto, my
father's bass above the heavy swell of sound, the sweet soaring
of the tenors, and the church timbers trembled as they reached
for the high ones. Even Mo was singing, mostly out of
tune, with Big Rhys making faces and nudging him. Fine

and strong looked Mo then with his chest up and his coat seams giving to the great width of his shoulders. I watched Mari's profile under her straw hat; her teeth were even and white, her lips red and faintly smiling as she sang, the voice of youth and beauty. She is far away now, my Mari, but as I saw her that day I will remember her, my wife.

Out into the sun after the signing, and if every soul in town was there I am not mistaken, for the rattle they made with their muskets and whistles has never been heard since, said Tomos afterwards. Good, it was, to own a woman like Mari, to eat and walk with, to take to bed in love. These things I thought with her hand in mine and the wedding ring clutched tight, loving her amid all the commotion.

"Into the trap and away!" shouted my father, so I handed Mari up and got in beside her while Morfydd and the others scrambled for seats, with everybody laughing and shouting and taking deep breaths for room. Like herrings in a barrel now, and Morfydd took the chance to slip her hand up Mari's leg and screamed with joy when I caught one and was told to behave since the pastor was watching. The crowd pressed around the trap, hooting and whistling as we moved off and guns were popping to set the mare into a trot. Other traps followed for the return trip to Nanty, fifty yards long, said Jethro after, and everybody in town hanging from the windows shouting good luck and congratulations to the mad Mortymers. The clamour died as we reached the Brynmawr Corner and the mare took into a run along the rutted road. The sun blazed down, slanting in reflected brilliance off the green slope of the mountain. The swaying of the trap, the clopping of the hooves were a drug to the senses, and Mari was against me, whispering love one moment, pulling at Morfydd's bonnet streamers, chattering and laughing and giving herself to me with secret glances. At Garn-yrirw cottages the neighbours were out in force, waving and cheering, and the top of Market Road was lined with people welcoming us back. The little mare was sweating and frothing as we ran down into the hollow, and whoops of joy went up at the sight that met us, for the women had got their chairs and tables out and made a collection of food; enough to feed Brecon Redcoats, said Mam, and to run them all short for the month. Even Billy Handy had sent a two-gallon cask as a present from the Garndyrus Benefit, and Mo was carrying it above his head to our doorstep. Out came the mugs and the beer was soon flowing, and when all the traps got in from the mountain the whole street was thronged with people.

"Look you!" shouted Owen Howells, running up to us. "It is not a wedding this but a political meeting," and he pointed.

"It is Zephaniah," said Morfydd, breathless.

"Talking to the parson, too," whispered Edwina.

"And about time, from what I hear," said Mam.

"Plenty of room for them," cried Griff, "especially Chartists, but if I had my way I would kick the little one out. It is more pigs and less parsons we are needing, for I am sick to death of collars back to front bowing and scraping over hungry children."

"Steady, Griff," I said, seeing him flushed with drink already.

"Oh dear," whispered Mari. "It is politics already? Can't they forget the old Charter for a minute?" Turning, she ran through the crowd into the house. Following, I caught her in my arms, kissing her lips.

"Tantrums already, is it?" I cried.

"O, I am sick, sick to death of the politics!" she gasped.

"Easy!" I said. "Why pick on it now, of all times?"

"Because it is even at my wedding," said she. "Will we never get peace and quiet from it? Even now, at this time, do you see? Do you understand, Iestyn?"

"Only that I love you," I said.

"And I love you, my precious," and she clung to me, her body shaking. "But promise me this is the end of it, Unions, Charters, meetings and the Six Points being driven to God knows where—promise me you are finished with it, boy?"

"All this because Zephaniah Williams arrives and talks to a parson, Mari? There is much more to it than that."

"Promise, Iestyn! No more demonstrations or mountain meetings or threats of fighting?"

"Aye," I said, kissing her, "we will talk about it later."

"We will talk about it now," said she, cool. "Promise."

Strange are women. No man knows their secrets. Within an hour of her wedding she stood before me, face pale, hands clenched, chaining me to a decision.

I said, smiling, "Enough I do's in the church to fill a coal-tram less than an hour back, Mari. But the kind of promise you are asking for now is best got before the ring, not after. You keep the house. I will take care of the politics."

She turned to the window and stood there watching the people dancing. Mo Jenkins was going it very gay with Mrs Twm-y-Beddau, who was lifting her skirts in the ring and showing her black stockings and stamping to raise dust. Dathyl Jenkins and Gwen Lewis were there, and other people from Garndyrus whom I had not seen for months. My father was filling the mugs and Jethro was carrying them round and Snell and Edwina handing out food. Harps were down on the cobbles and Irish fiddles were going and skirts rising and falling and coloured scarves waving in a medley of movement and joy. I looked at Mari. Her eyes were bright, her hands trembling.

"I am afraid, Iestyn," she said.

"For God's sake!" I said sharp. "Do you have to choose a time like this for it?"

Open came the door then and Morfydd was there, her hair tangled, her face flushed with happiness. "*Duw mawr!*" said she. "Everybody is shouting for the bride and groom and the pair of them at it before dark? What is happening?"

"It is Griff Howells has upset her," I said, "talking politics about more pigs and less parsons, she says."

"I did not," said Mari.

"And why not?" asked Morfydd. "Griff Howells is a moral force Chartist, I am physical force, so listen. Cut the throat of every parson in the country, I say, and put all the pigs in collars and pulpits and the nation would be saved overnight. Is that upsetting, girl?" She pulled me aside and brought the flat

244

of her hand across Mari's rump. "Outside into the dancing the pair of you, while I get the beds made up."

Taking Mari's hand I pulled her into the crowd. As simple as a child she was then, laughing, gay in a moment as the young men crowded up to kiss her and whirl her away.

Until dusk the celebrations went on. One by one the chairs and tables were collected by the neighbours and the hollow began to empty. It was getting dark, but Zephaniah Williams was still talking to my father with the friends he had brought down from Coalbrookvale Royal Oak. The traps moved off. The hollow was nearly silent as Mari and I went hand in hand together up the mountain.

"To give them time to get settled and abed," I told her.

"And time to be sound asleep," said Mari, giggling.

And I shivered in the moonlight as I kissed her, knowing what she meant.

Her body was trembling. A moonlight to remember, that, standing with my wife, knowing her longing was as great as my own.

"Together, at last," I whispered.

"Not a stitch between us," she said, and giggled again.

"Do not be vulgar," I whispered. "Down into the bed with you and we will see what you are made of, for you are a devil of a girl for promises."

"Promises?" she said, and kissed me with a fierceness that sent my blood racing. "You will see," she added through her teeth, "and be lucky if you are alive in the morning."

There is only one place for a woman who talks like that, so I seized her hand and we ran down the mountain to the hollow, down to the house whose windows were glinting in the moonlight, and the moon, who had seen it all before, was as round as a pumpkin, rolling on the ridge of the roof.

For a day before the wedding the furnaces had been cold for cleaning, but now the wood was crackling in the Aames as the fireman got going on them all, making ready for the dawn shift. The house was dark and dead as we crept up the stairs hand in hand to the room set aside for us. A little spray of primroses my mother had pinned on the door, and I have them still, pressed in the leaves of a book. The room was in darkness save for a chink of moonlight through the drawn curtains, and the tassled blanket Mam had brought from Cyfarthfa was cut by a sword of light.

There is much to be said for mountain lovemaking when two meet in a room with the same thing in mind. All Nature is in love on a mountain; the kiss of water is in the wind, birds give their song, leaves and branches their movement. There is no embarrassment in nakedness then, no shock in new learning, no hiding of faces. There is a laughter in mountain loving that cannot enter a room which has a place in the middle to lie on and another for laying the heads, and you stand here and undress while I do it there.

It is one thing dreaming of love between walls, but now we had come to it I longed for the mountain places.

Outside in the blue the firer was singing to himself as we undressed, Mari on one side, me on the other, both disappointed, both on the hot side after our run, and I, for one, was dying to giggle. Taking my time over my boots I watched her. No shame in Mari ever since Llanelen; just secret smiles as she took the things off. Down on the bed for the high-buttoned boots, put them tidy; up with the dress, shake the hair free, start on the stockings. Off with two petticoats, the last one flannel, and she is there in her stays. Down with the stockings, roll them for shape, down with the lace-trimmed drawers, off with the stays and she stands in her vest.

"Good God," I said. "How much more?"

"Pull that old curtain," said she, "for now I am shy."

Very strange are women, I thought then. They are lovely with everything on and provoking with everything off. But when they stand before you half on and half off they are maddening, as Mari was that wedding night, in shadows with the dim white bed beyond her.

"Iestyn!" she said, gasping to breathe.

I was with her at the start of time, kissing her in love and fierceness, losing her lips and finding them as she twisted away for breath, fighting her strength, defeating her, clasping

246

her to the hoarse strains of the firer's song. No sound but that song, not a whisper.

"For God's sake," she said. "Would you eat me? Bread and cheese now, is it?"

"I am sorry," I said.

"Not me," said she. "I enjoyed it. Into bed I am now. O, I am a hoyden and you are one worse! To hell with the pair of us," and threw back her head and shrieked with laughter.

"*Hisht!*" I whispered. "You will have Morfydd in."

"Three in here now! *Whee!* There is an ocean of a bed— have you ever seen the like? One finger on me and I am round it and you will not see me all night."

Glory to marriage when the moon rides high and the world is sleeping and lovers are awake. We stood like statues in that beam of moonlight, kissing, naked, unashamed.

"Cold for April," said she. "Away to go I am before I catch my death," and she was out of my arms and dived full length. She bounced once, did Mari, and rolled over and sat, her jaw dropping, her eyes transfixed as the old thing crashed and shrieked and twanged with enough bell-ringing to wake Nanty.

"Good God," I said, going cold.

"*Jawch!*" whispered Mari. "Harps are tied to it," and she rolled over for a look underneath, bringing it to fresh peals.

"Keep still!" I whispered, and she lay like a dead thing while I ran my hands over the big brass balls above her head.

"Just as I thought," I said. "That Morfydd is a damned bitch, mind. This is Iolo Milk's bed changed with Mam's especially to ruin the first night."

This set Mari off again and she hugged herself and rolled up and over the thing, giggling, and the springs clanged louder and brought me out in a sweat.

"Lie still!" I commanded. "It is fine fun now but different at breakfast with the family knowing we have been up to capers."

Nothing funny in that as far as I could see, but it set her off double, holding her stomach and blue in the face with her, while the tears streamed down, and spluttering.

Five spring bells I got from that bed, bells like the gentry have in kitchens, wired on solid, while Mari lay like a mouse above me, her face buried in the pillow and pressing in her sides to stop her explosions.

"Wait for the morning," I said, working under it. "I am stripping that damned Morfydd and hang for murder."

No sleep for either of us now; not in the mood for love-making, for I was never one to turn it on and off like a tap, as I explained. Back into my nightshirt, me; back into her vest and drawers went Mari, and both pretty civil about it, too. We were getting the Cyfarthfa blanket straight when Mari went to the door.

"Damme, how did that get there?" she asked, pulling down a note. "From Morfydd, it is," she said, taking it to the light.

"We missed it coming in," I said. "Read it loud," and she read, saying, "Have the house to yourselves for once and make the old bed happy, for the family are staying at Garn-dyrus."

And Mari smiled and kissed me. "Back into bed with me now, is it?"

So I kissed her, forgetting my sulking, and we put the blankets back and the sheets tidy, and crept in. And had Lucifer been under us with fiddles and gongs, we would not have heard him. For sounds vanish with lovemaking when there is no fear of a listener. A man is great then, with the petal smoothness of a woman's body under his hands and the rushing sweetness of her breathing in his ears. Tired, we watched the moon lifting her skirts over the Coity, flooding the earth and paling the stars with her brilliance. The fade of the moon meant sleeping, each awakening a dawn of new loving, until the clouds dropped their curtains and brought us to darkness, and the furnaces quickened and shrieked into blast.

Honour to woman and her secret haven where the lancing steel goes deep, wounding in love and fierceness.

Honour to Mari now the first heat is past.

Honour to all things that breathe; to this land that powders the bones of its conquerors, honour to my father's strength, to Jethro in youth, to Morfydd's sad beauty and Edwina's new faith. And to the people of the earth, rich or poor, give the joy of this dividing, O God, until the darkness fades and reality breaks and the lights come flaring over the mountain. Glory to St Peter and the One Who united us, to the ring of gold that binds us, to the rivers, the stars above us. Glory to Wales and the men who will lead us—*Gogoniant i fywyd, i gariad, i wreigiaeth, i Mari, gyda mi'n Un!*

# CHAPTER TWENTY-ONE

AND SO passed the summer, in loving. Autumn came in cold and brown, and Mari and I got the house that Morfydd had next door, being on the list, at one and threepence a week, enough to break us. But it was best to be on our own, said my mother, for two women in a kitchen can be hell and four were in ours.

It was the Sunday that Tomos Traherne called that will stay for ever in my mind.

The early darkness was upon us, a sadness of twilight between summer and winter, and The Top was wreathed in perpetual mist, a blanket to the drilling of the Chartists and the torchlight meetings of the Union. Music, brittle and high, came from the stripped hedgerows, and the corn scythed from the old farms stood in long stooks of shadow when my father, Jethro and I came off shift. The moon and stars held a new brilliance, blue on the blackberry cobwebs in the frosty mornings as I went into the outside tub, and the road to Blaenafon stood out sharp and cold against the dull country.

It was such an evening that brought Tomos over from Garndyrus; wheezing after his five-mile walk and the weight of his Book, the old fool, which was enough to cripple a donkey. My mother was spinning, as usual, Morfydd sewing and Mari making pretty little things and giving me secret looks across the table. Dada, dozing by the fire, was snoring and waking in fumbles.

It was the first time Tomos had visited since the birth of Richard and it took Morfydd all her time to give him a glance. But it was so much like the old days when Tomos came for a Reading; ducking his head under the sill, arms out to my mother and kissed her, his hand, the size of a ham, out to me and Dada. Here is a commotion! Back with the chairs, poke up the fire, everybody chattering and congratulations on the new baby, which put Morfydd very dull, and they pulled the little thing from his cot and Tomos kissed and blessed him, which set Richard howling. One moment peace, the next bedlam; a very different tune this to the one Tomos sang when he threatened to have the pair of them for casting out; illegitimate and sinful then, heartiest congratulations now. The one thing the Lord left from His Bible was a Commandment on the ways of His preachers, said Morfydd. She was cool now, and little wonder.

"Excuse me, please," she said, and took Richard up to bed again and did not come down.

"Where is Edwina?" asked Tomos, taking her place by the fire.

"Over with Mr Snell in Abergavenny," said my mother, flapping on the tablecloth.

"Is that business still strong?" he guffawed.

"It is," said my father, cool on purpose.

"Another marriage into the Church, I suppose? What with Iestyn's wedding and Edwina's crucifix you will soon have enough converts to open a theological school, Hywel. Is it true you are taking the cloth, too?"

"See now," said my mother. "I am not alone when I uphold Chapel, it appears," and she looked most satisfied and waved things about.

"I wonder I did not meet her on the Brynmawr road," said Tomos, changing the subject.

"She went across the mountain," I said.

"Eh now! In darkness? Alone?"

"It was light when she went," said Mari. "Mr Snell is bringing her home by trap from the service at St Mary's."

"Is that safe with Probert and his Cattle loose on the tracks?" Tomos turned his head to the stairs and lowered his voice. "Wise, is it, with men as mad as Dafydd Phillips running riot over The Top? Seen in Blackwood last week, they tell me, breaking legs."

"No!" whispered Mam fearfully. "Whee, hisht you man!" and she turned her eyes upwards.

"Aye," said Tomos. "And fifty pounds upon his head

now, the same as Probert. It is sorry for his mother I am, Hywel, for a good little woman is Mrs Phillips and she do not deserve it."

"Blaming the Mortymers, though, I'll be bound," said Mam. "Everyone do blame the Mortymers, poor souls, and not a word of blame for Dafydd throwing himself at Morfydd's head and blacking her eyes after he was sure of her. Breaking legs now, is it? Let him come down by here and try it."

"Hark at the old fighting cock," said Dada.

"Aye, I can fight when my children are involved, mind."

"Are you for the Chartists or the Union when the time comes?" asked Tomos, winking.

"There is no politics about my fighting, thank you," said Mam. "One side is as bad as the other."

"Maybe," replied Tomos, "but one is more dangerous."

"The aims of the Charter and the aims of the Union are indivisible," I said sharp.

"Well now," replied Tomos, swinging. "The babies are from their long clothes at last. Did you read that in *The Vindicator*?"

"The aims are the same," I said. "Freedom."

"Unionism," said Tomos sedately, "is the bonding together of the workers for the purpose of negotiation of complaints. Chartism is the banner of revolt against Queen and State. They blacklist you for one and hang you for the other, so be warned, for the time is nigh. There will not be enough chains in England to fetter us if men like Frost and Vincent have their way."

"That is the chance we take."

"You see what I have to put up with?" said Mari.

"I see that you are bound for trouble," said Tomos. "What do you think, Hywel? Peaceful negotiation is our only hope, not arms, for one volley from the Military and every Chartist in sight would go flying, leaving the brave to swing."

"I am with Iestyn," said Dada, sitting everybody up except Tomos. "The owners will not negotiate and we have been sitting tight too long. It is war if they insist on it. It has taken me twenty years of loyalty to learn that they make profits out of peace."

"Sense at last," said Tomos, grinning.

"Tomos, you old fox!" I exclaimed.

"And where does God come in on all this?" asked Mam. "You agree with violence and killing, man?"

"Not with killing," replied Tomos, "for the Commandments stand firm in my faith, but with violence, yes—as He showed them in the Temple, the men of greed."

My mother said, coming near, "If this old Charter thing means drunkenness and insulting Bailey on his doorstep, then we are best off without it, so go, Tomos."

"Hush, Elianor," said Dada.

"Hush, indeed!" she cried. "Are the men and a pixilated daughter the only ones to count in the house, then? And now we are getting violence condoned by preachers and deacons. Politics every moment of the day, it sickens. Four Points here, Six Points there—paid members of Parliament when we can get them free. Secret voting, and women are not entitled to a vote, Whig or Tory. Leave us in peace, Tomos Traherne. Working in iron is misery enough for a woman without ending up a widow as well." Close to tears she looked then.

"Listen, Elianor," said Tomos, "you have children—you have grandchildren. This violence is the risk we must take—not for this burned out generation, but for the next. Or are you satisfied with conditions that will make them perpetual slaves, as we are? For the Negro children of the Kentucky plantations do not labour as ours. Freedom has been fought for down the ages, with tooth and sword and fire. Listen, you! To everything there is a season, and a time to every purpose under Heaven. Remember, girl? A time to be born, and a time to die; a time to plant, and a time to pluck up that which is planted; a time to kill, even, and a time to heal; a time to break down, and a time to build up."

"A time to weep, and a time to laugh," whispered Mari by my side, and the shock of her voice turned us all. "A time to mourn, and a time to dance. To love, hate, make war and make peace, Mr Traherne, and to them I could add a hundred of equal virtue, every one telling of love, not hatred, peace, not war," Mari rose to her feet. "How will the men of God stand in this at the Judgment?"

"Thou knowest the Book," replied Tomos, "and the purpose of the Word. By thy obedience to it shalt thou be judged, I also. But there is nothing in the Commandments that instructs men of honour to hide behind a woman's fear while the young and old are starved and maimed for the price of bread. There also lies a duty to the oppressed, a raising up of those cast down. And we will sweep the oppressors from the land, even as Moses sent the tribes to war against the Midianites, Numbers, chapter thirty-one, to slay even as the kings of Midian were slain; namely Evi and Rekem, and Zur, Hur and Reba, and Balaam the son of Beor. So shall we sweep them away, slaying if they oppose us."

"I am off from here," said Mari. "As you found a chapter for casting out Morfydd, so you will find one to suit your every argument. It is wicked when men like Iestyn turn to revenge and killing, but there is no hope for us when men of the chapels come to incite them," and the door went back on its hinges and she was away.

She was half way up the Coity before I caught her, and turned her to my lips. Gasping, leaning upon each other, we laughed a little and then walked on, hand in hand.

"I told him," said she at length. "The damned old God-botherer he is, and not a streak of the Christian in him."

"Oh, he is not so bad," I said.

"No indeed, he is not—he is wicked. A lot of old soaking about the benefits of Chapel over Church and then biblical quotations and a preaching of blood and killing to make the Devil dance. Iestyn, I am afraid."

"Do not heed him," I said.

"I will not," said she. "But will you? All the old ones are the same now, telling the young ones to get set for the battle, but you will not find an old one in sight when the Redcoats come out. O, Iestyn, where will you land us if you follow the Chartists? Keep by me, boy. Leave it to the old ones."

"To hell with the Chartists," I said. "Do not tell me you ran me up here just to talk the politics."

The leaves of past autumns were piled here, a softer bed than any made by man. Her breath was warm and sweet, and beyond the curve of her cheek I saw the mountain sweeping away in blueness down to the red fires of the Garn. The wind breathed about us, twanging the branches like harp strings and hissing softly through the grass. Mari slipped to my feet and the sight of her lying there brought the old dryness and trembling back from the days of courting. Long and slim she looked, a part of the dusk in her loveliness. Kneeling, I kissed her, and she turned away her face as I unbuttoned the high neck of her dress, and her heart throbbed wildly under my hand.

"There is stupid," she whispered, "with a good strong bed back home and sheets."

"But beautiful, Mari. Will you have me here?"

Wildly she kissed me then and her arms went about me hard and strong, and her hands moved over my body, making me the loved and her the lover. The stifled sobbing of her breath against my mouth became a whisper as she held me closer.

The moon, respectful, hid while I loved her, pulling down black dresses over her brightness, covering us with night and a temple of silence. Warm and quick was Mari beneath me, responding in wildness and a murmuring joy as I divided her body, and the lightning of youth flashed between us. And then, spent and near sleeping, we laid together, kissing, while the world of wind and water crept back with all its sounds.

A cry I heard then, a scream like an animal trapped. Far below in the valley it was and the wind took it and whirled it over the peaks into the night.

Mari stiffened. "What was that?"

Again the scream. Not the scream of anything human but that of something unknown, fearsome in its terror.

"For God's sake what was that?" whispered Mari, sitting up. Strange how I can remember the beauty of her naked legs, long and slim against the leaves, and the way her dress, flaring from her waist, stained them like a crescent pool, and the frantic working of her fingers as she pulled it down.

"It is a woman," she said then, and clasped me, and from beauty grew horror for the woman screamed again, long and clear from the valley, and the scream faded into mutterings and guttural cries of suffering, and silence.

"O God, there is terrible," said Mari, trembling. "From the Brynmawr road, is it?"

"Down at the Garn by the sound of it," I replied. "One of the Irish beating his wife, perhaps?"

"She is dying, then. He is beating her to death."

"The neighbours will see to it," I said, sweating. "There are good men down at the Garn, and it is too far away for us to help. Home now, is it? Mari, you are shivering."

Tomos was in the middle of a Reading by the look of things, so we did not go back in for supper. Lying together in the bed next door we listened to the drone of his bass voice, my mother's treble replies, the scrape of my father's chair from the hearth. By midnight I was asleep, but the crying of Richard awakened me, and Morfydd's soothing voice was clear in every word as she comforted him, for the wall between us was thin. And that was the last sound I remember before Snell's mare and trap came down the slope of Market Road, the hoofbeats ringing. Getting out, I went to the window and looked down. The trap was deserted in the moonlight, the flanks of the little mare steaming, and her jaws and bridle were white with froth.

And then came Morfydd's voice, broken with fear, calling my name, and a hammering on our door.

"Edwina left Snell for home at eight o'clock after the service at St Mary's. She is missing somewhere on the mountain," she cried. "Dada has gone to search already."

"Good God!" I whispered.

"The fool to let her come back alone!" Mari whispered behind me.

"We will sort out the fools afterwards," I said, and called, "Where is Snell now?"

"In with Mam crying his eyes out."

"Free the mare from the trap," I said. "Keep Snell here. I will be down in a minute," and I ran upstairs and pulled on my clothes. I was lacing my boots when Mari came in. She said, her eyes wide:

"The screams. Do you remember them? Leaving Snell at eight o'clock it would give her an hour to get to the Garn, on foot."

"Mari, for Heaven's sake!" I said, sweating.

"It was her," she went on, weeping. "O, holy God, we are cursed!"

"Shut it!" I said. "Worse than Snell you are. Pull yourself together and go down and comfort Mam."

"We are cursed," said she, thumping her hands together. "Cursed we are, because of the politics."

"Away out of it," I said. Morfydd held the mare steady and I took her bareback into the night, across the tracks, galloping.

The moon was like a platter on the back of the mountain, and I saw the thorn spiked and black against its light, and the tops of the hedgerows streaked past me all white and smoking as if on fire. She was a good little mare at the best of times, this one, and now she was free of the trap she excelled herself. To the quickening clatter of her hooves we took over the mountain, leaping the boulders, flattening down over streams. Away to my left burned the lamps of Garn-yrirw cottages, and doors were opening, for yellow light was flashing against the mist. I wheeled the mare towards them, struck the road and slackened to a trot, for men with lanterns were gathering outside the rank and spilling over the slope, and I heard shouting and a voice raised in command.

"What is happening?" I cried, reining in.

Lanterns went up, shadowed faces were thrust into the light.

"A search party going out for the Nanty girl," said one, thick and bearded. "Where you from, boy?"

"The girl is my sister," I said. "One of the Mortymers. Has my father been up by here?"

"Now just, with Traherne the preacher," came the cry.

"But he is on the mountain now going up to Waunavon with Garndyrus men, and God help any man loose tonight if she is harmed. Raving is Hywel Mortymer, and Rhys Jenkins with him sweating blood."

"Look you!" shouted another. "There are the torches."

A mile away, on the foothills of the Coity, the torches burned in the mist. Rain began to fall then, and the men about me turned up their collars, blinking the wet from their eyes as they waited for their search leaders. A sickness rose in my throat, stifling my breathing, and an anger greater than anything I had known spewed up in me. I thought of my father's agony, of my mother comforting the useless Snell while her heart was breaking, and the stupidity of the man in allowing Edwina to return home alone with mad Scotch Cattle loose and baying. Reining the mare I turned her, and she brought up her forelegs, neighing, and galloped over the tumps toward the distant torches.

Mo Jenkins I found standing in a hollow of mist, with Will Blaenavon and Phil Benjamin, soaked, all three, and looking murderous.

"Have the others found a trace?" asked Mo.

"None of the men at Garn-yrirw," I said. "What the devil is my father and the others doing so far off the track?"

"Searching the slopes up to Waunavon. We have been over here every inch. The Whistle Inn landlord saw her on the road near the Garn at nine o'clock, but no sign of her since, not even from Betsy Garn-yrirw who was sitting outside waiting for her man. Only the screams Betsy heard."

"Screams?" I said, going colder, remembering.

"You know Betsy ap Fynn," said Phil. "If she heard no screams she would bloody soon invent some. Do not look so ghostly, boy. If this sister is anything like the rest of the Mortymers, she is tucked up safe and sound in a quarry and screaming because he is slow."

"Easy," said Mo, elbowing him. He wiped rain from his face. "Up to Waunavon with you, Iestyn, and tell Rhys we will meet him at the Whistle for a pint going back, is it?"

"Aye," I said.

"And sharp," said Will, smacking the mare's flank. "By the time you get there Edwina will be safely home. You will work yourself into ten murders sitting here doing nothing. Away!"

It was raining sheets now, the water running in icy trickles down my chest and back. The heather was loaded, and each brush of the mare's chest sent the spray high. The track was narrower here, the ground rising sharply to the Coity foothills. Before me, ascending the ridge, was the red line of torches where my father and Big Rhys were searching with the Garndyrus men, and their hoarse shouts came faintly on the wind. To my left burned a single torch, a lonely searcher who was bending into the heather. Wheeling towards him, the mare slipped on flints, nearly unseating me. Dismounting, I led her, picking my way cautiously. I had not gone ten yards before the man held high his torch and whistled shrilly. Throwing aside the mare's bridle, I ran, shouting, but the man's frantic whistling had already turned the torches on the ridge and I saw the sparks flying as the men came down. I dashed on, tearing through undergrowth, leaping high over the flooded streams, shouting to ease the growing panic within me. From all directions the men were coming now, even from the Garn where the night-shift miners were thronging in on their ponies. And only one man was still, the man in the heather, standing upright, his fingers in his teeth, blowing his shrill whistles of terror. I was the first to reach him. Shanco Mathews it was, wild in the face and hair, and his clothes soaked with rain. The smoke of the torch had blackened him as with the smoke of hell itself, and beneath him, half naked, arms and legs flung out, lay Edwina. With my hands pressed to my face I stood there in horror while Shanco blew his whistles beside me. A man joined me, then another, and soon a ring was made with others pressing in closer. In the red light of their uplifted torches I saw their faces, sweating and horrified, and the burning stares of their eyes. I was upon my knees with Edwina's hand in mine when my father burst into the ring and went down and flung his arms around her, calling her name.

"She is dead," I said.

Squatting, he lifted her across his lap and the men sighed and moaned as he kissed her and held her fast against him.

"Hywel, she is dead, man," said Rhys.

Aye, dead.

Her hair was stained red in the torchlight but black where the mud and leaves had caught it, and her face and breast were white, too, except where smeared with blood. All white, she was, except for this; nearly naked, for shreds of her dress had been ripped from her body by the claws of Beast and lay scattered about her on the sodden grass. But my father saw none of these things, it seemed. Like a lover he sat there with his arms about her, kissing her face and whispering. My bowels were shrinking tight, my heart pulsating in the agony. Clenching my fists I lowered my face from the sight.

"Iestyn," said my father.

The torches went up and I saw his face. His eyes were the eyes of a man crucified, brilliant from their shadows of a face stark white and old.

"Find him, Iestyn," he said then.

"Find him we will, Mr Mortymer," said Shanco Mathews. "If it takes all winter we will find him and kill him with red irons."

"Home to Elianor, Hywel," said Big Rhys, kneeling.

"Leave me," said my father.

"For God's sake, man," said Rhys, pulling at his hands. "She is dead, look you, you cannot kiss her back. Come now, she is bare, let us make her decent."

"Her crucifix is gone," said Mo, pulling his coat up to her throat. "O Christ, I will kill, kill! Bloody murder I will do for this!"

"Away," said my father. "Leave us," and his eyes, sightless, looked past us towards the flare of Nanty. But Rhys knelt and gripped Edwina and tore her from his arms and flung him back.

And my father went full length, face down in the place where Beast had raped her, and clutched the grass, and wept.

# CHAPTER TWENTY-TWO

CHURCH OF England for everything now, said my mother, weeping.

No need to tell of the grief. No need to tell of the miles we searched. From Cwm Crachen to Ebbw Vale we searched in our hundreds, and the time off was paid by Bailey, to his credit. With pitchforks and cudgels we went, night and day, carrying our food, sleeping in quarries. Even the Irish came, hitting the heather flat with one hand and telling their beads with the other. Strangers were taken and laid out. Down with their trews, up with their shirts for bloodstains. Beards were pulled aside, faces peered at in the light of lanterns. God help the man who cut himself shaving, said Mo. God help the man if we find him, said my father.

But we did not find him.

As one goes out another comes in, said Tomos.

Mari was coming full with her by September. And very pretty she was, red in the cheeks and full in the breast, and Morfydd and my mother pushing and prodding and slitting up the seams of her skirts where the hollows of her stays used to be.

There is beauty in the body of a woman with child, when she carries as primly as Mari. She walked with dignity, lifting the men's caps in every direction and dropping the women in bows. It is strange how some fall to bits when they are caught, like Mrs Twm-y-Beddau and Mrs Pantrych. Very objectionable, says my mother, with their hair tied with string like the poor Irish, and their breasts half bare and skirts pulled up short in front with ropes to carry their stomachs while labouring. And they are loud in their chatter, too, as I heard one night from Mo Jenkins' sister, who ought to have known better. Putting the Shop into fits, was Dathyl, saying how she would never turn her back to her man after a Benefit Night, and always slept with her chastity belt on, for he was a madman and whooping after ten quarts unless she had a stick handy to cool him. Yes, it is amazing how low some women sink when they get into corners, and they are the first to play hell about jokes when the men get hold of it. Thank God women like Mari are above such discussion, as Afron Madoc, the Swansea deacon, and Caradoc Owen discovered.

"Look you," said Mari in bed, balancing the tea cup upon her stomach. "Whee! There is an old kicker you have coming, man; he is worse than a Staffordshire mule."

And she folded her hands behind her head and giggled and shook, balancing the cup to the kicking within her. "Whoops!" she cried as the tea splashed into the saucer. "O, Iestyn, look!"

"A boy it will be, with hobnails," I said, dressing. "If it is a girl then heaven help you," and I kissed her.

It was still dark, five o'clock in the morning, and the early frosts were into us, lying white over the country. My father was on night shift and I was due to follow him at six. Morfydd and Mari were working underground now, pulling trams —Mari due there an hour later because she was pregnant, which was very kind of the Agent, said my mother.

"Aye," said Morfydd. "Special treatment because she worked for him once. Very special treatment I would hand to Agents who work expectant mothers, and they talk of the Spanish Inquisition. Boiling lead is too good for him."

"Why?" asked Jethro, at breakfast now.

I said, "You should know better than to shout in front of children, Morfydd."

"Aye?" she answered. "Then let me say this. Six shillings a week she earns on the trams like an animal, too big round the waist for the towing belt. In less than four months she will drop it in coal dust. It is time she worked here with Mam."

"There is stupid," said my mother. "She is good for weeks."

"She is signing off this morning," I said. "An hour ago the child moved, and she is not delivering underground like the Irish."

"Thank God for sense," said Morfydd.

"Eh dear," sighed Mam. "Times are changing indeed. Half the population of Wales is born underground these days, and they are none the worse for it."

"None the better for it, either," said Morfydd. "A good boy you are, Iestyn, for stopping Mari's shift."

"She is full and the child is kicking to be out, is it?" asked Jethro, chewing.

"Get on with your breakfast," I said.

And Furnace Five split under blast.

With a shudder and a roar it split further, and we sat crouching at the table as fire leaped at the window and iron rattled in drips on the roof. Transfixed, we sat, and Mari's feet drummed on the stairs and the door burst open and she stood there, shocked white and trembling.

"In the name of God what was that?" she whispered.

"A split," I cried, and ran from the house, pulling my coat over my shoulders.

The hollow was a beehive, with men running and others coming in from the tram roads, and crowds were already pressing around Furnace Five where my father was on shift. Women and children were screaming, men shouting commands, and a pump was already manned and buckets of water being passed down the line. Shanco Mathews came face to face with me, his hair smoking.

"Where is my father?" I cried.

"Three men are in the puddling shed," he shouted. "For God's sake fetch the Agent."

"Away out of it!" I pulled him aside, but he tripped me, sending me sprawling. Up then, and I had two others down before I barged headlong through the men.

"Come back, you fool!" shouted Caradoc Owen. "She is split and will topple any minute."

Free of them, I stripped off my coat and wound it around

my head and shoulders and stumbled into the heat of the furnace. It was going like a pillar of fire, burning in quick, noisy flares that licked at the base of the cylinder and puffed up in balls of flames to the lip of the flue. Smoke was exploding in mushrooms from the wrecked puddling-house, weaving around the shattered roof and condensing in shafts of steam. Splintered timbers projected from the ruins where the roof slanted drunkenly, and beneath the roof a man was screaming, his voice as shrill as a child's, in short staccato cries, catching his breath to the torture of the scalding. The sand moulds were overflowing and the molten iron was running in little rivers of flame. The choked furnace was under pressure again, bellowing at the blocked shaft. Leaping past it I jumped the moulds and reached the door of the puddling house. The charred wood, slammed shut by the blast of the split, went down like paper as I charged it, and I fell flat, gasping. It was strangely cool here away from the furnace, but the timber in the walls was coming alight as the glowing fingers of iron moved in. The man was no longer screaming, for the water in the steaming pits had dried, but I heard a low sighing that came from the overturned cauldrons where the metal was cooling on the floor. In darkness I stumbled forward, hands groping. Tripping over fallen beams and scattered ladles I lurched towards the sighing, and my path was lighted by the burning walls as the iron took them into a bonfire.

"Dada!" I cried.

No answer, and the piled wreckage about me made shape in redness.

The centre wall was down and with it the puddling flues, and the cauldrons that tapped from the furnace direct were on their sides or upside down. Ladles and tools were lying as the men had flung them, coats and gloves and eye-shades were scattered about. Looking through the torn roof I saw the stars and racing white clouds sweeping over the moon.

"Dada!" I cried, sobbing. Iron was dull black on the floor and every footstep was agony.

"Three men are in there!" shouted the Agent from the door. "Can you see them?"

"Dada!" I called. "Dada!"

"Are the basins upright, Mortymer?" bawled Mr Hart.

"Where are you, Iestyn?" Shanco Mathews this time.

"Over by here," I called. "Bring a torch, for God's sake, and watch your feet, the basins are over."

In he came. No Agent this, hanging back by the door. With the flaring torch held high he came, hopping to the heat of the floor, and I kicked at a ladle to give him direction. On came Shanco, cursing, and reaching me he raised the torch and I saw his eyes widen.

A man's face I saw then, in profile at my feet, burned black; a face of marble, drawn clean against the sooted walls of the house, and I knelt, touching it. The flesh of the cheekbone was hot on one side. The other side was melted into streams and the tips of my fingers touched jaw and teeth. Dead, this man, by iron scalding, but the ladle was still in his hand, gripped like a shepherd's crook. Dead, with his legs and hips in the puddling cauldron, rigid to the waist where the forty gallons had caught him in its arms of molten iron, and cooling, gripped him.

"Blood of Christ," said Shanco. "Barney Kerrigan," and he turned away his face.

Sickened, I raised myself, wondering what I would find for a father.

The walls were well alight now, and the wind was sucking out the smoke in gusts through the roof.

"Over here," cried Shanco, hopping.

"Iestyn," said my father.

Under the arch of the furnace we found him; one leg and one arm thrusting out from the heaped bricks of the firebox lining, and the rest of him buried but safe from the iron.

"Iestyn," he said, and his voice echoed strong in his tomb.

"Dada!" I cried, and we went to our knees and heaved the beams and bricks aside as men came flooding through the entrance.

"Faster!" I called to Shanco.

"Watch the wall!" cried the Agent, but I saw no wall. Only my father I saw, his buttocks arching as the weight of the wall was raised, and I heard no sounds but his gasping. A dozen men were working now, spitting, coughing, cursing in the smoke. The walls were roaring with flame as we pulled the last beam up and dragged him clear.

"Easy, for Christ's sake!" I whispered, but I knew we were too late.

His face was wealed with furnace burns, and the black iron splashes were rigid in his cheeks and across his chest, and he sighed as a man in death and moved his lips.

"Iestyn," he said.

"Still breathing, though," whispered Shanco. "Down to Abergavenny with him and quick, or bring the doctor here. . . ."

"Leave him," I said, and caught my father's hand and gripped it.

"Stand aside, Mortymer," said a voice.

"Dada," I whispered, and he opened one eye, but he did not see me, though he smiled.

"For God's sake, Mortymer," said Shanco in a panic. "It is Mr Hart ordering you and Crawshay is coming behind him."

"Out of the way, Mortymer," said the Agent then.

"Let him die in peace," I said, swinging a fist at his legs.

"Is that the son?" said another voice. "Out of the way, young man, or you will regret it."

"Dada," I said, weeping.

"Watch for your mam and Jethro, Iestyn. Take them back to the farms. . . ." Clear, every word clear, despite the iron that was taking over his soul.

Whispers behind me, shuffling feet, and men pecking at my coat and plucking at my sleeves. "I give you one last warning, Mortymer," said the Agent, pulling me.

"By God," I said, and gripped a ladle. "Away to hell out of it or I will have you down with this iron, you and Bailey, so bloody leave him!"

"Elianor," said my father.

"Good little man," I said, and kissed him.

"Eh, dear."

I got up then, blinded, pushing them all aside. Steam was

rising and the walls were smoking under the buckets. Through an avenue of men I walked, seeing nothing, until I came to the entrance where the women were waiting. My mother was before me suddenly, with Mari and Morfydd standing either side, and women were sobbing, but no sound came from mine. I raised my face.

"Finished, is he, Iestyn?"

"Aye, Mama," I said.

"In peace now, my boy?" Her fingers screwed at her apron.

I nodded, choking.

The wind whispered between us then, bringing smoke. My mother lowered her face and clenched her hands, and weeping, said:

"O, Hywel, my dearest one, my precious."

I went from them, shivering, cold.

Jethro I met on the doorstep. His hair was ragged, his eyes wild. I saw in his face the face of my father, then; square, strong, unravaged.

"Dada, is it?" he said.

"Aye, man," I replied.

Three times he called to me as I walked towards the mountain.

Cursed, we are.

Cursed, said Mari, cursed by Nanty.

Two in six weeks.

# CHAPTER TWENTY-THREE

Two IN six weeks, we said; Edwina, Dada.

But you can starve to death grieving, said Morfydd. We must live for the living, if Bailey will let us.

Not even gunpowder will shift me from Nanty, said my mother.

"Mari is coming very big in the stomach still," said Jethro out on the tram road where Hart had sent us.

"Yes," I said.

"Waiting for her sign, is it?" he asked, frowning.

"Yes," I said, jerking at the reins.

"Is it bad, then?" he asked, squinting.

"What now?" I was miles away just then.

"Mari's stomach coming big these days. Bitten by a worm, she is, a boy said."

"She is with child, you know that," I replied, furious.

I looked at him. Beautiful was his face, the features noble and clear, yet strong with a man's strength. A lone boy was Jethro, one removed from the font of knowledge, the whispers of the dark quarries. At thirteen he was more the man than many ten years older, and his virtue must have delighted the saints.

"She is with a baby, Jethro," I said then. "Which is a cleaner way to speak of a girl like Mari."

The morning was cold with early frost on the hedges, and the country of Llanwennarth Citra was mist-covered except for the church tower. We had become closer, Jethro and I, since my father died, and when Hart reduced my rates and kicked me back to the tram road he kicked Jethro too, which suited me.

We took the tram round to Llangattock and the cutters loaded it with limestone. On the way back to Nanty the tram horse was straining and his flanks steaming. Side by side on the limestone we sat now, Jethro and me.

"About Mari again," he said, his dark eyes slanting over the rails. "A boy, is it?"

I was tiring of the stupid conversation, but then I remembered my father and the pains he took with me. Jethro's ignorance was stupidity, but it was like that with some children of the mountains. Too much Chapel was at fault, perhaps, with deacons dancing along the pews and hush this and hush that and pushing everything into corners.

"Look you," I said, taking a breath. "Mari is with child. When we were married I took her to bed and loved her, and now the child is growing within her. Like an apple it grows, see, but takes nine months, which is up next January, and we do not know if it is a boy or girl until it is out."

"Good God," he said.

"Until the women deliver it, do you understand?"

"Aye," said he. "Dada told me a bit."

So sad he looked then that I fisted his chin, bringing him to a smile.

The horse was walking easily between the rails, his harness jingling, and the frosted peaks around the Lonely Shepherd were bright with a sudden warmth that shone through a rent in the clouds and struck us like furnace glow.

"Anyway," said Jethro moodily. "I am pleased that you are the father." Sober serious, he was, not a muscle in his face moving as I glanced his way.

"Not more than I am," I said, trying to be calm.

"Then it is not true that Hart jumped her, eh?"

I closed my eyes. "Where did you hear that?"

Jethro squinted into the weak sunlight. "Whee! If I tell you that you will be as wise as me, boy. But I will hit him, mind, I will hit him to bounce six feet, the swine."

"Who?" I asked, boiling.

"Eh! There is an old long-nose! It is not your business anyway, it is Mari's. Jumped by Hart, indeed—just because she worked for him and the date comes right." He sighed. "But old Hart is the trouble, mind. He always do have the single girls who come in scrubbing, with a register for the single births and another for the twins, like the Bad Old Man of Cyfarthfa."

"Do not believe all you hear," I said. "And do not believe such things of Mari, who is pure, and would not allow the likes of Hart within a yard of her."

"Aye, aye?" said Jethro, and whistled at the sun.

I sat there in growing anger. Rumours were flooding and Jethro was a parrot repeating slander he did not understand. The incline steepened. Foam was on the bridle as I reined in the tram horse for a rest before beginning the climb.

"Good," said Jethro as I pulled up the sprag. He was looking over his shoulder, grinning, the sudden image of my father. "Now we shall see."

"See what?" I asked, turning. Caradoc Owen and his driver were coming up behind.

Caradoc Owen had been begging me for trouble since the day my father died, in hope of revenge, perhaps, for what Dada gave him. And since the fight he had fallen from grace, like me, being sent on the road as mate to Afron Madoc.

A handful was this Afron Madoc, and new to Nanty. Swansea born and Swansea temper, a man quick with his fists and wicked with his tongue. Ambitious at work, too. He was hitting it up for tram-road foreman and tipped his whips with wire and blackthorn for an extra journey a day. Now, jumping down from the load, I spragged my tram, and the horse eased back, snorting for breath. Round the curve behind me came Owen and Madoc, flogging their mare to death. She came at a gallop, drenched with sweat and reared as she saw the line blocked, and Afron cursed her and spragged and up he went to the top of his load.

"What the devil!" he cried. "Half a dozen more like the Mortymers and Bailey would go out of business. Shift that old tram along so busy men can earn their money."

"I am resting the horse," I shouted back.

"Then shift you off the line!" roared Caradoc, getting hot.

"You come and bloody shift us," said Jethro.

"Hush you!" I whispered, slapping his ear.

"What was that?" roared Afron. Black and broad, this

270

one, though not much taller than Jethro, and hackled for a fight to prove his worth.

"Five minutes rest at the incline is the Agent's rule!" shouted Jethro. "So down on your knees, Afron, and five minutes prayers while you wait, is it?"

"I am coming!" roared Afron, scrambling down.

"Thank God," cried Jethro, "and bring along old Caradoc for my brother. Eh dear!" he sighed. "Manna from heaven. For weeks now I have been waiting for Afron Madoc and for months to see you dust old Caradoc."

"Listen," I said, swinging him round. "This is your fight, for you have made it. I am sick to death of quarrelling. So your fight, mind—Afron Madoc first and Caradoc Owen after —I am not raising a finger to help."

"Good grief," said he, his eyes like saucers. "I can handle Madoc but Caradoc will coffin me, Caradoc is grown."

"I know," I said. "I will pray for you."

Up came Caradoc Owen, off with his coat, up with his sleeves. "Right you, Mortymer," said he, but I ducked his swing and got behind the tram, watching for Jethro, who was taking his first man, Madoc, ten years older. Madoc came raging. Jethro tripped him, sending him skidding on chest and elbows. Up got Madoc, shouting mad, and leaped. But the fist that caught him knocked him spinning, a glorious hook. Up again, and Jethro, cool, stepped in with a cross. Down went Madoc, howling with rage, to rise immediately, fists white, ready for murder. But under his guard went Jethro, flatfooted, ducking, weaving, the image of my father as he squinted up. One in the stomach brought Madoc's head down, up came a knee to bring his head up, for Jethro was never particular, a vicious right-hander sent Madoc staggering and a swinging left put him flat.

"That for my sister-in-law," said Jethro, walking away.

And even Caradoc Owen stared at the speed of things. Afron Madoc pulled himself up.

"A harlot, she is!" he shouted, choking with anger. "Mari Mortymer is a harlot, and I am putting it over the county!"

And Jethro, walking back, put him flat again.

The horror of it struck me dumb. Sick, I stared at Owen. He smiled, his teeth white in his square brown face, and clicked his tongue. "Dear me," he said, "the Mortymers are fighters, indeed to goodness. But out of the mouth of Madoc has come the truth, mind, and before a man is punished he should be judged as to whether he speaks falsely. Surely now, it is two whores we are dealing with, not one. For your sister Morfydd was jumped by an Englishman as well, I hear, and that was years before yours worked for Hart."

I stared.

"When will you Mortymers learn you are not wanted in Nanty?" he asked. "Away sharp, now, before I tip you from the road."

My first blind punch spun him like a top. My next checked him and flattened him against the tram. As his knees went I straightened him, and his cheekbone cracked under my knuckles. With his bloodstained face swaying before me I hooked and swung, hitting to go through him, until Jethro dived at my legs and brought me down.

Missed fourteen shifts, did Caradoc Owen; worse than from Dada.

Afron Madoc missed eight, with teeth.

Suspended for fighting, me. Nobody would believe that Jethro had a hand in it.

"For a month," said the Agent. "You Mortymers are nothing but a pest and I shall be glad to see the back of you. Were it not for the distressing circumstances of this case, I would certainly have put you on the blacklist."

"A fine state of affairs," said my mother. "As if things are not bad enough. *Jawch!* Talk about the bruising Mortymers. Tongues are the trouble in most women's families, fists in this. And a disgusting thing to fight about, too, it seems, without the grace of a word to explain it," and she stared at the ceiling.

We were at the table. Morfydd with Richard asleep in her arms, Jethro reading the pamphlets. Mari's eyes, bright with unshed tears, were lifting at me in sorrow and understanding.

"For God's sake," said Morfydd. "You must have had a reason?"

I stirred my tea.

"Why did you fight?" asked my mother.

I drank, blowing at the steam.

"Jethro," she said, swinging to him, "I demand to know."

"Leave him alone," I said.

"Oh, dear me!" Her hands were on her hips now. "Head of the house, is it?" She thumped the table. "And since when, may I ask—since suspension and everybody going to rags since Dada died?"

"Iestyn," whispered Mari, her eyes warm.

"Do not appeal to him," said my mother. "All he can think of is hitting holes in Mr Afron Madoc. It is a wonder the poor man is alive, they tell me."

"We know who hit hardest, see," said Morfydd, very sober, "for I have just seen the poor soul, thank God."

"You keep from this, Morfydd," shouted Mam, rounding on her. "A man of peace is Afron Madoc, a deacon with the Word in his mouth, as God is my witness."

"*Dammo di!*" exclaimed Morfydd, "there is ignorance for you! For my part I am happy about you hitting deacons out, too. But why Afron Madoc?"

"He was the biggest and handiest," said Jethro, ducking my mother's swipe, and he was away through the door, leaving the rest of us sulking.

"I will be back before supper," I said, getting up.

"If there is any supper," said my mother.

It was cold in the wind of the mountain, and the cattle were bellowing for milking down at Shant-y-Brain's where the night mist was steaming in the heather. Nanty was roaring in blast like something demented; the new rail consignment for Spain ringing and clanging like bells during loading, and the hoarse commands of the foremen came up to me on the road. Cold as ice I stood there waiting for Mari. She came as I had expected, muffled against the wind.

"Do not heed her, Iestyn. Sick and sad she is for Dada."

"How much have we in the box?"

"Four shillings," said she. "The debt at the Shop is six."

"Pay it," I said, giving her two shillings. "It is better to start square on the starve. Take it quick, here is Morfydd."

"The chinking of money always brings me," said Morfydd. "Count it well, for we will need every penny. Hart came in as you went out. He has been thinking things over, he said, and is going to teach the Mortymers a lesson for life. The month's suspension applies to everybody, which means that Jethro and I are out, too."

"Good God," I said, going colder.

"And any more trouble and we go on the blacklist."

Her face was white and strained against the outline of her shawl.

"It was Dada they wanted, not us," I said.

Morfydd laughed. "Has it taken you so long to work it out? It is the first time a man has been suspended for a sober fight." She put her arm around Mari's waist and led her away.

"Is the credit still good?" I called.

"We are in trouble if it is not," said Morfydd.

When they had gone into the house I went back to the hollow. The light of the Company Shop shone bright despite the glare, and at the end of Market Road I saw Bailey's paymasters and clerks bending over their books. A few Irish women were standing outside as usual with their babies in shawls. I have never met anyone like the Irish for eating through glass, standing with their lips frosting the loaves and cheeses. The Irish were expert in starving in Nanty, especially the women, who gave their share to the children.

"The credit is dead, too," said Shanco Mathews, coming out of the shadows, "so do not lower yourself. Who the hell do you think you are, man, under suspension and expecting credit?"

Cold, cold I felt, with the faces of Mari and Morfydd before me, Jethro, my mother, and Richard, the baby. And soon my own child would come, making seven. If a strike came after the suspension it would be the end of us. Sick, I felt.

"Damned lucky not to be turned out, mind," said Shanco. "Bailey had no truck with me and mine, and all for a ten-minute demonstration—bloody out, it was, over to the old ironworks, remember, boy?"

"Aye," I said, scarcely hearing.

"Away from the light where people can see us," said Shanco. "There is always a friend for a man suspended," and he pulled me away. A man was standing under the wall of the Shop. Tall and broad, he was.

"Iestyn Mortymer?" said he.

"Aye," I said.

"Blacklist or suspension, what is it?" he asked.

"Suspended," I said. "What is it to you?"

"My name is Abraham Thomas of Coalbrookvale. Do you stand for the Union?"

"Aye," I said.

"Show your card, then," whispered Shanco, nudging me. "It is a Union representative."

I did so. The man peered at it and gave it back.

"You will be welcome down at the Royal Oak as your father was before you," said he. "Good, staunch, independent brothers are needed for the Chartist army under Zephaniah Williams. Deacons are needed to take charge of sections. The men of the Six Point Charter are asking for your name."

"It is money I am after, not politics. I have mouths to feed," I said.

"You will have no money while we have such politics," said Thomas. "You will have suspension, blacklist, hangings and transportations all the time we have men like Bailey for masters. The people are rising, one for all, all for one. Give your loyalty to the people and the people will feed you and yours, none shall go hungry."

"Through this suspension?" I asked. "Four weeks?"

"Four months if needs be, though we will have the Charter long before then and none shall go hungry again. Shall I mark you for a Deacon?"

"Down with his name," whispered Shanco. "He will serve."

"You say my father was down at the Royal Oak?" I asked.

"He joined for an iron splash upon his boy," said Thomas.

"Zephaniah himself took your father's name. He attended the torchlight meetings, he drilled, he handled arms, and took the oath of allegiance to fight and bleed for the Charter."

Very educated, this one, for a man working in iron.

"How will you get the Charter?" I asked him.

"For Heaven's sake," whispered Shanco, "leave things like that to your betters, Mortymer."

"If I am going to bleed for it I have a right to know," I said. "For a start I cannot see us shifting the Church without a struggle, and men like Lord John Russell, Melbourne, and the Duke of Wellington will nail the crown to Victoria's head before she loses it."

"Where did you learn such things?" asked Abraham Thomas, peering. "You are better informed than most, by God!"

"Is the mass of the people behind this fight," I said, ignoring his surprise, "or is it a few hotheads like Jones, Frost and Williams?"

"The masses are with us!" cried he, recovering himself. "The executions of Bristol and Nottingham are not forgotten. The Chartists are everywhere. Through the length and breadth of the land the people are waiting to force evil from their midst." His voice rose. "Peaceful negotiation is out of date. Physical force will be met with force. Down with the tyrants who rule us, away with the Crown and its landed estates!"

"Hisht!" I said. "You will get us all hung with your shouting. Thank God we are not all like you, Abraham Thomas. Cool men may win, but Wellington will cut the fanatics to pieces, as he did the French. What would you have me do?"

He straightened. "Sign for shot-making, on Chartist pay. Over at Mynydd Llangynidr you will be paid puddler's rates for a fair day's work."

"And hang in Parliament Square if I am caught, eh?"

"Better than starving on the blacklist," said Shanco.

"Sign my name," I said.

The three of us went to the Royal Oak Inn, through the back entrance to a room set aside from the tap-room where the men were putting it down and singing. A man called Edwards, a black-maned giant with a fist like a ham, took my oath of loyalty to the Charter. "Perish the privileged orders, death to the aristocracy," said he. "These are the words of our beloved Henry Vincent, the Englishman. If these words are uttered by Englishmen they should be good enough for the Welsh, you think?"

"Good enough for me," I replied, and repeated them.

"Do you know the Points of the Charter?" he rumbled.

"By heart," and I said them.

"We are wasting our time with this one," said Edwards. "He should have been enrolled years back. Puddler's rates down at Mynydd Llangynidr at once, and pay him over his suspension. Bring in the next."

I lied to them all except Morfydd.

"There is money on the end of it," I said. "If I do not earn we will starve."

"If you are not careful you will hang up at Mynydd Llangynidr," said she. "Making arms for rebels is a bigger crime than firing them, and if a stray patrol of Redcoats puts its nose into the caves the ones inside are caught like rats, they tell me. There is no back way out."

"It is a chance I must take."

"What are you telling the others?"

"That I am working with a farmer over the suspension."

"With Llewelyn Jones of Llangattock, then. Have a name ready, for God's sake, you know what Mam is, and at least it is in the right direction."

"God bless you, Morfydd," I said.

"God help me," said she. "God help us all in this forsaken country. O, that my Richard were here!"

"It will tide us over," said my mother next day. "At last we are back to the farms. Make good there, Iestyn. Who knows, it may be the end of us in iron. I curse the day we ever came into it."

"You will come and see us often?" begged Mari.

"Every hour I can get away."

"An easy journey, mind," said Jethro. "If it is Llangattock you can lift there and back by tram road."

"Not now Afron Madoc is hitting up for road foreman," I replied, to put him off.

"Get on with your supper," said Morfydd, nudging him.

"To hell," he said, his eyes big. "Leave on the night tram and back on the dawn one, Iestyn. You could sleep at home every night and save the expense of the lodging."

"O, could you?" whispered Mari, her hands clasped.

"Have sense, man," I said to Jethro. "You know what farmers are. Half the value of having a milking drover is having him live in with the cattle."

"How did you find this position?" asked my mother, sewing.

"Through Shanco Mathews," said Morfydd.

My mother frowned up at her and her eyes were old and weak in the light of the lamp. "Has he no tongue to speak for himself, then?"

"It was Shanco Mathews," I said. "When he was suspended for the demonstration he worked for Llewelyn Jones of Llangattock."

"I see," said she, and I sighed with relief when she said, "I remember how Dada used to long for the old days back—the days of the farms. Eh dear! You children did not know our generation. Quiet and full it was, with nothing happening except milking time and meal times and three times to Chapel on Sunday. No ironmasters then to pull us from our beds for killing and maiming, no roaring furnaces, no fighting, no Charters, and it was a different kind of gentry to the Baileys and Crawshays." She smiled at her needle. "Aye," she said, "the days were sweet, with weddings and biddings coming in for miles, and if a finger was slammed in a gate it was known all over the county. Beautiful, it was, until the ironmasters came and destroyed it. No lies, no deceit we had then, with the family one in love and truth." She raised her eyes to mine.

"As with this family," said Mari.

If my mother knew that most men on the blacklist or suspension were earning their money at Llangynidr, she never mentioned it. That night I kissed Mari goodbye and rode with Abraham Thomas on a Chartist horse over the mountains to the wild desolate range of Mynydd Llangynidr. It was midnight when we struck the tram road near Llangattock, and the trams were rumbling under a misty moon, limestone on top, muskets underneath, and one in every six carrying powder and shot. Down the line of trams we went to the cave entrance where a man was standing guard. Big and broad he was in the shadows, with the smoke of his clay curling up in the still air.

"Good grief," I said, reining in.

He peered from beneath his cap. "Heaven preserve us," he whispered, then slapped his thigh and shouted, "Mo! Come out here, man. The Mortymers are with us."

"Not so loud," hushed Abraham Thomas, flapping at him.

"To hell with you," said Big Rhys. "Now that Garndyrus men are running arms you can call out Brecon Garrison." He gripped my hand. "What has happened, boy?"

"Suspension for fighting a deacon," I said. "What brought you and Mo up here?"

"*Diawl!*" exclaimed Mo, running up. "It is like old times, eh? Six of us here from town, Iestyn—Dada and me, Will Blaenavon, Afel Hughes, and the Howells boys, and Idris Foreman and Iolo Milk coming up tomorrow, whatever!"

"Have you struck, then—it is half Garndyrus!"

"It was the Union," explained Big Rhys. "What the devil is the use of a Parliamentary Bill permitting the Union if the owner is going to suspend a man for being a member? Where is the sense of it? asked Idris Foreman, and he took it up official, so here we are working for Chartists."

"Get inside and chatter, do not do it here," said Thomas.

"Shade down the light!" shouted Rhys, and pulled aside an entrance board. I tethered my horse and followed him in. It was a cavern inside, a fissure cut through solid limestone by the rushing waters of a world melting from ice a hundred million years ago; a weird place of grotesque shadows and chilling echoes where the only light was flung by lanterns. Deeper into the mountain we went, through cavern after cavern where men sat at tables pouching shot and filling powder horns. Deeper still, crouching at times, we reached the gunsmiths' rooms where skilled men fitted barrels to stocks of pistols and muskets. On, into the bowels of the mountain of Mynydd Llangynidr, and into the pit of hell itself. Here were the blacksmiths, stripped and sweating, and the air was ringing to the beat of hammers. Here red iron was hammered into steel. Here, in neat rows, were the pikeheads and spears that were to wrest power from the aristocracy and give it to the people. I saw men armed, coming and going with missions of importance. And on the tram road outside the arms were being loaded and transported to all the valleys of Gwent. Men from Risca and Pontypool, Blackwood and Dowlais were working here, said Rhys.

"Blacksmiths from Newport smithies," added Abraham Thomas. "Gunsmiths from London, powder mixers from as far north as Lancashire, Chartists all, men prepared to die if needs be, to force the Six Points."

"Where do I work?" I asked.

"On the tram road for the time being," he replied. "At puddler's rates less food, like all the rest here. Jenkins, see to him."

"Come," said Big Rhys now. "I will show you to a bed."

Two weeks passed, every hour a fever to be back with Mari. I spent the days working at the forges in the ventilated caves with Owen and Griff Howells, stripped to the waist, with the encrusting soot in layers on my sweating body. From daylight to dusk we laboured on casting. And at night, like moles, we crept down to the mist-laden valley and the brooks that sang and splashed their way to Llangattock. There we bathed naked with the Llangynidr mountain sharp and clear against the stars and the owls hooting their heads off in the thickets.

On such a night, when the moon lay white and cold over the country, I walked down the bank of the stream towards Llangattock and saw the lights of the village winking like eyes from the darkness. The track, beaten flat by countless hooves, lay like a grey ribbon through the heather. Above me came the clatter of the Chartist patrols, below me the rushing music of the brook. And before me flared Nanty, making strange shapes of red beauty against the clouds, flashing white now as the iron poured in strickening brilliance, and the air was cool after the incinerating heat of the caves.

I burned for Mari, for the sight and sound of her. I longed for her with a power that caught me up and guided me towards the red glow that shone as a beacon. The patrols passed on the high ground. Llangattock came nearer, and I heard the rumble of the night-shift trams and the cracking of whips as the spraggers urged their horses to the loads. Lamps burned along the face of Llangattock mountain and burnished iron flashed as the cutters filled the trams. Cutting away from the track I went across country, leaping through the heather to the foot of the mountain. The trams were rumbling above me as I climbed, impelled upward by the same strange power that had no reason. Hand over hand I climbed until I reached the tram road. Lying motionless in the heather I waited until a line of trams passed, then ran to the checking point at the end of the line.

Shanco Mathews I found there, as expected, sitting hunched in a cutting, warming his hands over a glowing brazier.

"God alive," he whispered, leaping up.

"Hisht!" I said. "Are you alone, Shanco?"

"Aye," he replied, wiping away sweat, "but it will not be for long with Chartist sentries coming one way and Redcoat patrols coming the other. Have you a pass for this far, man?"

"Never mind the pass," I said. "Have you news of my people?"

"Dear me," and he groaned. "I mind Iowerth Morgan last month when he left Llangynidr without permission. Rags and bloody bones he was by the time his Chartist brothers had done with him—hit his old knee-caps up, they did; crippled his descendants for a century, poor soul. And right and fair, mind. We cannot have damned lankies streaming right and left away from an arsenal."

"For God's sake, Shanco, quiet! How is Mari?"

And Shanco sighed and spat and just looked at me.

"Answer me!" I took him by the coat and shook him to rattle.

"Right you," he said. "In labour, they tell me. Now then." My hands dropped from him.

"You are lying. She is only seven months gone."

"You should know," said he at the stars. "But three days she has been at it, so my woman tells me last pay night, and that is two days back. And there is nothing like a bellyful of trouble to bring production down, mind, for half the Irishwomen are holding their stomachs and having it with her, but God knows, if she is only seven months it is bound to be a little one, but she is making enough fuss for breech-birth twins."

I stared at him.

"Never you mind," said he. "And do not bother with dirty old Shanco, boy. If she loses this one the next will be that much sweeter. And now I had better tell you all. Jethro came. Three nights back he came, for Hart has tipped them into the Old Works."

I closed my eyes, seeing a vision of the disused works where the debtors and the infirm lived, the place where was tipped the human refuse, the diseased, with cholera in the heaped garbage. Leaping to the rock face I climbed up and was away into the darkness high above the road. Reaching the top I buttoned my coat and turned my face towards Garndyrus.

I took the road to Abergavenny and wealth by running, not daring to use the Blorenge Incline for fear of being recognised. The clocks were striking one o'clock as I entered Abergavenny through the Western Gate, going like a ghost up Byfield Lane, soaked to the waist and shivering with wading Llanfoist ford. Redcoats were in the town I had heard; brought in to put down a wage disturbance at a Govilon forge, it was said, but that was only the excuse for bigger things. A pair of them passed the top of Tidder Street as I approached the old gate. Standing in the shadows, I watched them out of sight. Fine and proud they looked, these men of the English counties, their coats purple in the moonlight, their burnished brass flashing—Chartists every one, from what I had heard at Llangynidr—men enduring an oppression from their gentry officers worse than we were getting from ironmasters; men of the working classes like us, it was said, waiting, like us, for the signal to rise.

But we know better now.

It was as black as a witch's gown in Tidder Street, and Nevill Street was cast in shadows, asleep behind its shuttered windows, but beams of light shafted the cobbles under the windows of the gentry. Distantly on the still air came the music of a minuet. I went towards it and found myself opposite a window where ladies and gentlemen were dancing to a spinnet. Beautiful they looked under the flash of the chandeliers, the men with lace at their wrists and throats, the women in satin gowns down to the floor and hawking enough bosom for harlots in gin. All was beautiful in colour and symmetry, all was grace, and the whole glittering chorus of wealth and music and chatter came through the window.

The passage that led to the stables echoed to my boots, but I reached the yard without being seen. The music of the minuet came clearly as I raised myself to the stable roof and reached for the sill of the nearest window. The horses rustled uneasily beneath me, scenting an intruder. The stable yard below me was white in the moonlight, so I waited until it sank again into blackness. The dance below ended. In the surge of applause I elbowed the window. Glass tinkled faintly on to the thick pile of the carpet within. Hooking my arm through the hole I slipped the catch and slid the sash up. Swinging myself into the bedroom I listened, staring at the open door, the scarlet stair carpet of the landing with its rich mahogany handrail, the hanging lamp bowl as lovely as mother-of-pearl. Nothing stirred. The music vibrated gently against my feet. Turning, I began to search. It was a man's room. Loose change in silver and copper lay in a stream across the dressing-table. I gathered it silently, brushing aside jewelled studs and cufflinks, a silver snuff-box. Crossing the room I searched a wardrobe. Almost immediately I found a purse heavy with sovereigns, and another smaller one in the pocket of a frock-coat. I was still behind the door of the wardrobe when I heard footsteps ascending the stairs. Time only to push the door of the wardrobe shut and leap towards the window. I stood behind the heavy velvet curtains of the window and waited, holding my breath. The room tingled with silence, and the sweat started to my forehead and trickled down my face. Somebody had entered, making no sound, and then I heard the faint turn of a lock. A girl's voice then, a whispered protest, a man's soft laugh, a kiss. No more sounds they made in that lovemaking save the swift inrush of their breathing and their endearments. Minutes passed in kisses and faint sobbing from the rustling coverlet of the bed.

"I must go," she whispered.

"I will light the lamp," he said.

"No, please," she answered, and I heard her dressing in the darkness scarcely a yard from where I stood. The lock turned.

"Do not be long," she said. The door clicked shut behind her. The man grunted and sighed and swung himself from the bed. I tensed myself as he approached the window. As he flung the curtains back I struck, seeing a glimpse of the white silk shirt open to the waist and the square set of his chin above a stocky neck. Crying out, he staggered back, hit the dressing-table and overturned it with a crash of splintering wood and glass. Legs waving, jammed between the table and the bed, he screamed like a woman. Through the window, me. Landing on the cobbled yard fifteen feet below I rolled once, scrambled up, flattened an ostler coming from the stables and raced up the narrow passage into the street with cries of pursuit growing every second. At the head of Tidder Street I turned left and ran swiftly to the freedom of the Meadows. Down to the river I went and swam it opposite the Castle, not daring to cross at Llanfoist for fear of Redcoats. Soaked, shivering, I made my way to the foot of the Blorenge and climbed into the safety of its woods. Wading the canal I climbed upward past Keeper's Pond and down Turnpike to the Brynmawr road and the open ground of the Coity. The stars were still bright in the sky as I came down into Nanty. There, as at Garndyrus, the furnaces were flashing to the night shift and the little bloomeries all along the Garn were pinned with lights.

But below me, near the pit of Cwm Crachen, there shone no light. The hollow was wreathed in mist, and the ragged walls and chimneys of the disused works rose up like wounds in the blanket of white. Sitting on a tump I buried the two purses and counted the money; thirty-eight sovereigns and loose change, more than I had seen in my life. Tying it in my muffler I went down the slope, into a stink of garbage. A baby was crying from the broken walls. Dogs drifted like ghosts from the refuse piles, eyes gleamed from corners. The whispers of living beings came through shattered windows, voices crucified by battens. Smoke from makeshift chimneys stood in grey columns in the windless air, and firelight flickered from the makeshift rooms where the aged and ill, the useless and the maimed slept amid the rubble of furnaces they had once worked. Shattered engines, rusted through, stood guardians of the misery; wire ropes coiled fitfully over the littered floors. Like a tomb the relics of the town breathed in the November mist, its breath steaming up in the strange, dejected silence. Here lived the debtors who owed no debt: the old who had built the iron empire and become worked out, the men of strength whose joints were dried, the women whose breasts had vanished in the muscles of underground hauling, the blind, the diseased, the dying. Here lived the blacklist men because of a difference with master or agent; here lived their children, the skeletons of the tumps who spent their lives begging and playing on slag.

I found my mother standing in a doorway, bareheaded, her shawl low over her shoulders, her face pale, her eyes hollows of shadow.

"Iestyn," she said, as one aged.

I went past her to the smashed flagging of the old forge room with its twisted girders rising from the baseplates; grotesque arms that caught the moon and stars of the shattered vents in the grip of an octopus. The candle that flickered in the draught cast shadows among the piled bricks and furnace slag, and in its light I saw them: Jethro clutching at the floor in sleep; Morfydd propped against the sooted walls with Richard snuffling in her arms, awake, her eyes brilliant and strange. Mari I saw then, lying with the blankets heaped on her stomach, her face wet with sweat, her hair tangled. And as I knelt the pain bloomed within her and she clenched her hands and bit at them, whimpering.

My tongue cleaved against my teeth. Her eyes opened and she gripped me.

"Mari!"

"Steady," said Morfydd, rising.

"For God's sake, what is wrong with her?"

"It is a seven month child, and it turned," said Morfydd. "She is coming to her time now, boy. Away out of it if you cannot stomach it, like Dada says."

I left them, seeking oblivion in the yard, away from the noisy intakes of Mari's breathing and her bright explosions of pain. Shivering, I ran to a wall and leaned against it. The mist had risen from the cwm and the moon was high over the Coity, bringing the ruins into deeper shadows. I do not know how long I stood there. My mother came once, I think, for I heard her whispering, but Morfydd drew her away, and there was no sound but Mari's sobbing and a little hammering of the dawn wind.

Footsteps then, and Mrs Shanco Mathews went past with a bowl and flannel; Old Meg, they called her, as fat as Mrs Twym-y-Beddau and as dirty as Mrs Ffyrnig; rolled to the elbows, she was, important in her business.

"Right, you," said she, passing. "Do not look so jaggerty, boy, Old Meg will soon have it out. This is the trouble with the Mortymers, mind—the men putting in twelve-pounders and the women with hips for fairies," and she threw back her head and cackled with laughter.

Number Four over the road went into blast then. With a mushroom of smoke and flame it blew from its simmering for the dawn shift and screamed like a thing demented. Soot and sparks shot up, white ash swirled in the frosty air and red light played on Cwm Crachen, glinting on the windows of the forge room as I gripped the sill, looking in.

And in the hours that brought the dawn in golden light over the Coity, I grew to manhood.

"They have got it!" shouted Jethro, skidding into the icy yard. "Eh, by God, there is a business!" He clattered to the door, and skidded back. "And a boy, mind, the spit and image of Dada, Mam says!"

"Away!" said Morfydd, clipping him. "Inside for your son, Iestyn; I will come, too."

"He goes in alone," said Mrs Shanco Mathews, coming with a shawl. "Out of it, everybody," and she put the baby into my arms, a screaming bundle of life against my chest.

"Steady, man," said Morfydd. "You are squeezing the stomach from him. In to Mari quick now, she is asking for you."

And I went within and knelt on the floor beside my girl.

"Iestyn," she said.

I was with her at the start of time, kneeling there; kissing her in love. I was down at Llanelen, binding her feet. Under the summer moons of the Coity I was with her, in Shant-y-Brain's shippon, or carving her spoon from cedar. Her face was wet against my lips, her eyes bright and dancing in the red light.

"Jonathan, is it?" she said then, but I heard no sound.

I heard no sound but the sudden screech of the mill and the clanging beats of iron bellowing under the hammers as the dawn shifts got going. Whips were cracking as the tram roads came lively, horses stamped, curses and commands filled the bitter air.

I looked around the forge room, at the heaped debris beyond the door, at the shattered place where my son was born; slowly, never to forget it.

"Aye," I said. "Jonathan."

# CHAPTER TWENTY-FOUR

"The Lord giveth," said Tomos. "The Lord taketh away. May the Lord shine the light of His countenance upon you, and bring you peace."

And he closed the Book.

His voice, clear and deep, the scene in his little room, will stay for ever in my mind. Big, black and severe was Tomos that early November day when we left the hospitality of his house, after Cwm Crachen. I can see it through the mist of years; my mother in the best black I had bought her, smaller and greyer; Morfydd, beautiful still, and Mari beside her, pale but smiling. And Jethro—how well I remember Jethro—the square cut of him inches past my shoulder, and his eyes so childlike in his man's brown face; Jonathan, my son, was asleep on a chair.

So clearly I can see them, as if it was yesterday.

And with good reason, for it was the day that the men of Blaenau Gwent sickened of the yoke and gathered for the march; the day when every furnace between Hirwaun and Risca, Pontypool and Blaenavon was blown out. The pot that had simmered for fifty years boiled over. Colliers and miners, furnacemen and tram-road labourers were flooding down the valleys to the Chartist rendezvous; men from Dowlais under the Guests, Cyfarthfa under the Crawshays, Nantyglo under Bailey and a thousand forges and bloomeries in the hills; men of the farming Welsh, the Staffordshire specialists and the labouring Irish were taking to arms. The Chartists were rising in the towns and cities of England, too, from every line of the compass, but the Welsh were chosen to spearhead the attack on the old aristocracy and the newer, profit-seeking classes.

Faintly, into the quiet room, came the tramp of their marching.

"Eh dear," said Tomos now, "black it will be. Torches will flare and pulpits tremble, and the very crown of England quake before the onslaught. And there will be no victory, I tell you. To win will be to lose, for government by physical force will be worse than a government of kings, as France has learned, for we are not yet ready to rise." Deeply he sighed while we stood in respectful silence, and turned to face us. "Would you have them back, then? Are those who have gone from us not happier standing in the light of the Father, Elianor, as your man is, and his daughter? Aye! Think on this and bring yourself comfort, or be of greed and wish them back to the spiritual poverty that we in this room will share. Do you hear me?"

"Aye," we said.

"Then do you mind me, for I have little time for grief, which is nothing but self-pity when you boil it down. Let there be no tears when loved ones die in this hell, my people; save your tears for the day they are born."

Faint light from the overcast sky shafted the room, falling on my mother's black gown, and her hands, thin and worn, were as yellow as old parchment. Dust from our new Abergavenny clothes, bought in Flannel Street with the stolen money, danced in the beam of silence.

"God rest you, Elianor," said Tomos to my mother. "You are wise to take Iestyn's advice. Back to the Carmarthen farms with you, and put a lifetime between yourself and iron that will scar you to the third generation of sons. Indeed, I wish to God that I could go, but my place is here with my people."

"You are welcome, mind," whispered my mother. "As in the old days when my Hywel lived, remember? Just as welcome, remember, Monmouthshire or Carmarthen town, we will always find a bed for one like you, Tomos."

"Bless you, Elianor," and he raised his eyes to Morfydd, lowering them to the frowning challenge that greeted him, as usual, and he drew sharp his breath.

"And you, Jethro. What do you plan?"

"To work for Mam," said Jethro, a light in his face. "On the farms, see, with milking and fleecing and crowstarving like old Granfer Shams-y-Coed down Llanelen way, and I will see to it pretty, for I have always wanted for a farmer."

"Iestyn?" Tomos turned to me.

"The coach is here," I said, rising. "She is beating over at River Row by the sound of her. Are you ready, Mari?"

Out with the little travelling-bundles now. Morfydd and Mari gathered the sleeping children, and Tomos went outside with Mam and Jethro to await the coach.

"Wait you," I said to Morfydd at the door.

The wind had frost in him all night from the Coity, but the sun of midday had melted it and the rain came now in spears of light at the window, sweeping in gusts over the dull country, drowning the distant clatter of the marching men.

"I am not coming," I said after Mari had gone.

She looked at me, disbelief in her eyes.

"What is this nonsense?" she said.

"I am not coming," I repeated. "I have work to do here."

She stood looking at me, beautiful still, but with the besetting matron of iron touching at her face for entry. Suddenly older, she was, in the light of the window, the fullness of her lips looking forward to thirty, until she smiled, and then she was Morfydd.

"Take this," I said, and I gave her the rest of the money, twenty sovereigns left over from buying the clothes.

"I had been wondering," she said, her eyes lowered. "Lucky for you that Mam and Mari think well of you. Stolen, is it?"

"Stolen from us in the first place," I replied, "so do not play the virgin. It is eat or be eaten, kill or be killed. Twenty in gold will settle them in Carmarthen for weeks, until I come to you. Take it."

"Mam would die of shame, Iestyn."

"Aye? Then more fool her, for this is a stink of a country. From now I am having the things that are mine."

The coach and pair came streaming in the rain and pulled to a halt outside the window.

"Iestyn, Morfydd!" shouted Jethro.

"Into it and away quick," I said. "I am not saying goodbye.

Tell them I am doing what Dada would have done, I am fighting for the Charter."

"Because of Dada?" she said.

"Because of Jonathan, because men like Frost and Vincent are right, because of Cwm Crachen; to change things, as Richard said, and make them decent. If foreigners like Richard are prepared to die, then the least we can do is to fight. Quick now, or Mari will be back."

"Fight, then, and God bless you," and she kissed me and turned away her face. "Goodbye, my boy," she said.

I did not wait for Tomos. He shouted once as I went into his kitchen, but I did not answer. Through the back I went and down his garden and through the gate, climbing the hill that led to Turnpike. Standing there I listened to Mari calling me, my mother's voice raised in argument and Morfydd's commanding replies. The door of the coach slammed shut, a whip cracked, and the hooves of the horses clattered. Mari called again, her voice breaking. I waited in the teeming rain and saw the coach up Turnpike. I stayed until it was outlined against the sky over Garndyrus; saw it slowly disappear over the crest to Abergavenny.

"Goodbye," I said then, and I turned my face towards the mountain.

"*Mae'r Siartwyr yn dod!*" was the cry. "The Chartists are coming!"

Dic Shon Ffyrnig I saw in the street near Heol ust twi, rolling drunk as usual, and Sunday at that.

"For God's sake, Mortymer," he gibbered. "Have you heard the news? *Mae'r Siartwyr yn dod!* It is the end of us!"

"The end of drunken Benefits," I said. "The end of men like you and Billy Handy who have drunk away the funds of honest men."

"Have pity!" he wailed. "Never in my life have I breathed a word against the Mortymers. Tidy people, all of you, and ready to forgive a few mistakes, for none of us are perfect, mind."

Up he came and running beside me, pulling at my hands.

291

"Oh, for God's sake do you speak for me, Mortymer!"

"Aye," I said, and threw him off, and he went to his knees, the spittle dripping from his chin in threads. "Aye, Dic Shon Ffyrnig, I will speak for you, and Billy Handy, too. Away now and lock yourself in until the Chartists do come for you. Red-hot pokers, it is, for drunken Benefit chairmen who have thieved the funds, and I will be doing the poking."

"Wait!" His terror brought faces to the blind windows, but I pushed him down.

Gibbering, biting at his hands, he went like the wind to the Drum and Monkey, Gwennie Lewis told me, to kill a few more pints.

"Good morning, Iestyn Mortymer," said Gwennie, shooting up her window.

Very pretty and prosperous looks Gwennie, with the room behind her neat and tidy, and not a child in sight.

"Going like the Devil with a saint behind him," said Gwennie. "A terrible thing it must be to have a conscience, and Billy Handy gone to a shadow, too, they tell me. Eh dear! there is a life; one moment up, next moment down like Polly Morgan's petticoats. She is the red woman now, you know, for I am respectable."

"Indeed," I said.

"Married to Iolo Milk; have you not heard?" and she patted her hair and tidied her shawl. "Well, not married exactly, but I have expectations, mind. He has left his old Megan now, and no wonder. There is a slut for you, that Megan, living in filth and cannot boil water, and at least I am clean, says Iolo. So Mrs Pantrych has taken Meg's children, making fourteen, for she lost one of her own last strike."

"And yours?" I asked her.

"Gone with the cholera," she said. "What time is it?"

"Iestyn Mortymer!" cried Gwennie now. "What the hell is wrong?"

In a corner, out of the rain, I cleaned my father's pistol.

"Well! Good grief!" said Willie Gwallter nearby, "if

292

you did not expect to be kissed you should stay in the light."

I saw him through the glass of Mrs Tossach's shop; tall, straight, fifteen, but gangling—narrow in the face like his hatchet-faced mam, but great in the shoulders like his elephant of a father these years dead.

"O Willie, do not be wicked," came the answer.

"Wicked, is it!" said Willie. "Wait you, Sara Roberts, I have not started yet. I am grown up now, remember."

"Dear me! Listen to it," said Sara, bored.

Stamping and heaving is Willie Gwallter, his eyes on sticks, his breath frosting the glass.

"I will fetch you one in the chops, mind," said Sara. "So stop it this minute, Willie Gwallter."

Strange about Sara Roberts of the Garndyrus cave; always short of a man, said Morfydd once—there for the boys to learn on, and Willie is big for fifteen.

"First thing in the morning, too," said Sara with business. "Like a mad bull and roaring you must be at night. Loose me."

But Willie fights on, losing his battle of growing up. Now he whispers.

"No, indeed!" said she. "Down by here? In the middle of the town? With preachers loose and Mrs Tossach due back any minute, to say nothing of Chartists with swords and muskets? Have sense, boy; I am not Gwennie Lewis."

The wind howls down the mountain, rain is streaming on the glass; darkening the doorway of the Tossach shop, and the drowning cobbles of the town are flying in sheets to the river. Kissing they are now, with Willie subsiding, and about time, too, says Sara. Above them flashes the Tossach sign, groaning in the wind. Above it is the window and the curtains blowing out. Mrs Tossach's hair is flying, too; her eyes are burning in her puddle of a face as she lifts her bucket.

No time to warn them as the bucket goes up, only time for a shriek as the bucket tips. Very handy is Mrs Tossach with a bucket of slops.

"Put that skirt down," said Sara, the last words she spoke as the Tossach slops hit her.

"And pull your trews up, Willie Gwallter," said Mrs Tossach, shaking out the drops. "I will tell your mama. Fornication on a Sunday and on my doorstep at that."

Down by River Row I met Mrs Phillips, Dafydd's mam, God help her. Weak in the head was Mrs Phillips now, said Tomos; pining for Dafydd who had ambitions for the Church, once. Pining to death for him, her only love.

"Good afternoon, Iestyn Mortymer," said she now, standing beside the Avon Lwydd that was roaring in flood.

"Good afternoon, Mrs Phillips," I said.

"Now then, have you seen my Dafydd lately, boy?" she asked, and I saw the madness of her face shine under her black Quaker bonnet.

"Not lately," I answered, wondering if he was caught for leg-breaking with Dai Probert Scotch Caattle.

"And you living in Nanty, they tell me? Where are your eyes, boy, with my Dafydd head deacon of the Ebenezer!"

My mother was strong for the Ebenezer, but she had never mentioned Dafydd.

"My mother has often heard him preach there," I lied.

"Then she is privileged. Aye, strong for the Lord is Dafydd. Taking after his English father, but he was Church, mind. Eh! Hitting the old pulpit about is Dafydd, from Swansea to right up north, and the like of him has not been heard since Howell Harris hit the devil flat at Talgarth, they tell me. Do you hear me, boy?"

"Yes, Mrs Phillips."

"Got on, has my Dafydd. A different tale to the day he wed your bitch of a sister and lent his name to a bastard, eh? Do you hear that, too, Iestyn Mortymer, or are your ears gone loose?"

I did not answer. She came nearer, leaning on her staff, needing only a brush to make her a witch, saying, "A curse is on her. Cursed was your father from the day he laid hands on my son, cursed was Edwina and your wife Mari, and I do know, for I did the cursing," and she laughed with her face to the rain and clutched at her hands.

I looked at her, at the lonely fields about us, the shining roofs of River Row drowning, and I looked at the river beside me.

"Black be your house, Mortymer," she said, coming within reach. "Black be the Mortymers from the youngest to the oldest; from the cradle to the grave down to the third generation do I put my stain. Even on the soul of Richard Bennet and on the body of his living son, black, black!"

The river foamed in torment beside us, crying for her, throwing up its white arms, begging for her.

"And cursed are you, Iestyn Mortymer," she said, "before three days are out."

Blindly, I left her, to save me the sin of murder. And the wind caught up her shrieks and flung them after me along the road that led to Nanty.

# CHAPTER TWENTY-FIVE

ON THE track to Pen-y-Carn the mountain was drowning under skies leaden with rain and the brooks were roaring in flood through the heather.

But the wilderness was alive with men I knew; men from the valleys of Blaenau Gwent, deacons, sidesmen, drunkards, fighters, all were flocking to the tumps. Men from Garndyrus and Blaenavon, Coalbrookvale and Abertillery, Brynmawr and Nantyglo; wild men, starving men, soldiers with military bearing were on the march to freedom. I saw them bending into the rain, marching to Pen-y-Garn and Zephaniah Williams, the leader. They came armed, with pitchforks, mandrills, swords and muskets, they came with powder and shot. Every ironworks on The Top from Hirwaun to Blaenafon was on strike, every furnace blown out, and owners who challenged were kicked aside or beaten. In the rain we gathered, lawless, leaderless, seeking Zephaniah Williams. We were the men of the valleys three thousand strong, it was said. Over at Abersychan the men of the Llwyd Valley were marching under William Jones the watchmaker, and they were twice as many, while John Frost himself was gathering an army at the Coach and Horses, Blackwood.

At Pen-y-Garn we found the great Zephaniah, his fists raised and his voice like thunder.

"This is the day of reckoning!" he cried. "This is the day of revolt when Welshmen band together in the name of justice and equality to seek the banners of freedom. Listen, you!"

And we listened, lifting our arms and cheering.

"As our brothers in France have gained victory over tyranny, so we will gain ours. This is the end of the yoke, the end of the insults. To the march! Frost is driving from Blackwood with an army, and William Jones is leading the Eastern Valley. Who knows the password, boys?"

"Beanswell!" roared the men of Nanty.

"Aye, Beanswell. Last verse by Ernest Jones, then, and roar it, lads! 'Then rouse, my boys. . . .' "

> "Then rouse my boys, and fight the foe,
> Your weapons are truth and reason,
> We will let the Whigs and Tories know,
> That thinking is not treason.
> Ye lords oppose us if you can,
> Your own doom you seek after;
> With or without you we will stand
> Until we gain the Charter!"

I looked at the mob. Wild men, mad men were there, their faces blackened and streaked with rain, soaked bundles of rags with their arms held high at the leader; unkempt, bearded, as ferocious as the Frenchmen who stormed the Bastille.

"So we will take a turn as far as Newport!" cried Zephaniah. "We have nothing to fear, I pledge it. Even the Redcoats are Chartists waiting for the signal to rise. Even their captains are in sympathy with our cause!"

Cheers to split the heavens at this, with boys on the edge of the crowd turning cartwheels in joy.

"Second verse of the Charter Song!" cried Zephaniah.

> "The labourer toils and strives the more
> While tyrants are carousing.
> But hark! I hear the lions roar,
> The British youths are rousing.
> The rich are liable to pain,
> The poor man feel the smart, sir.
> But let us break the despot's chain,
> We soon will have the Charter!"

"Well sung by good Welsh voices!" roared Zephaniah. "Now listen again. Our comrade Henry Vincent, beloved and respected by all men who fight for justice, is languishing in Monmouth gaol. Starved and beaten, he lies there on lying charges, this man, the English martyr. Will we let him die?"

"No!" roared the mob.

"Will we let die the spirit of Dic Penderyn that has brought us this far? Will we let go all that we hold dear—wives, children, homes? For we are committed already, mark me! God help us if we turn back now. And the same can be said of every city in England where the workers are waiting for the Welshmen's lead. We are the spearhead, remember! Upon what we achieve tomorrow depend the liberty and happiness of Britons for countless generations. From London to Newcastle the Chartists are ready for rebellion, from Sunderland to Birmingham our comrades are under arms!"

The rain beat down, the wind swept like a mad thing over Pen-y-Garn, drowning the drunken cheering. They pressed about me, maddened men inflamed by beer and Zephaniah's oratory.

"One question," called a man from the crowd, King Crispian, the Brynmawr shoemaker. "If we are going to release Vincent from Monmouth gaol, why the hell are we going to Newport?"

"Good Heavens!" cried Zephaniah, shocked. "Would you have me splash the plan over the county? But out of the goodness of my heart I will tell you, and take the risk of Government agents among us. We are going to Newport to take the town and seize the schemer Prothero, then on to Monmouth to release Vincent. Are we ready now?"

"Aye!"

"Then forward. We will take the road to Llanhilleth."

Cheering, waving arms, the men of Gwent began the march; gathering strength with every mile; pulling laggards from their houses and kicking them into line, threatening women who protested, pushing aside screaming children. The rain teemed down. The wind lashed the long black columns sweeping down from the mountains. Through Llanhilleth we went, shouting and wailing, putting the gentry under beds and deacons under pulpits. All that day we marched, with food from looted bakeries being handed down the line; like a column of locusts, drinking the beer houses

298

dry, shouting the poems of our defiant Ernest Jones. Into the darkness of the cold November night we marched, shivering, hungry but relentless. Through Newbridge and Abercarne we roared; and on the tram road leading to Risca, we rested under the stormy moon of midnight. Huddled against the downpour I walked the tram road in search of the men of Nanty.

Deacons and Captains were arguing nearby and sending scouts in search of Zephaniah Williams, who had not been seen since we left Llanhilleth. There, in the darkness, I heard the voice of Abraham Thomas shouting commands, so I sat by the roadside and watched the mob rise and march past me. A man was lying near, too drunk to stand, and singing and groaning in sickness. He was old and wasted and lying in a brook with the water foaming over his bearded face. I pulled him clear and dragged him to a tump. I was wiping rain from his face when he opened his eyes, and I saw in the light of the torches that he was blind; a puddler, this one; near to death by the look of him, and as sober as me.

"You feel young," said he. "O Christ, to be young at a time like this! Are you Cyfarthfa?"

"No, old man. I am Garndyrus," I said.

"Do they make good iron there, boy?"

"Better than at Cyfarthfa," I said, to humour him, but it only angered him.

"Have you seen the iron of Cyfarthfa, then?" he asked, struggling up. "Have you even heard of Merthyr that is dying under Crawshay? Have you heard of Crawshay, even?"

"Yes," I said.

"Yes, indeed! You cheeky hobbledehoy! And Bacon the Pig before the Crawshays? God alive, we thought him bad enough. What right have you to march for freedom, Garndyrus, if you have not worked the firebox under Bacon and Crawshay? Tell me, have you seen Cyfarthfa by night even?"

"From the belly of my mother," I said, talking the old language to please him. "She was born in Cyfarthfa before Bacon puddled a furnace."

"Well!" said he.

"Can you walk?" I asked him.

"I have walked from Merthyr hand in hand with Saint Tydfil," he said. "I have been splashed eight times and blinded, but the saint led me across The Top to the great Zephaniah Williams, for I put no trust in our mad Dr Price. I put my trust in no man but Williams, whom I once saw spit at the feet of Robert Crawshay, who starved us."

The column was thinning, the marching song of the Chartists growing weaker.

"He will starve you no more," I said. "Can you stand, old man?"

But he was still. Quite still he lay in the fading light of the torches, and his hands were frozen to the musket he held.

Through the night we marched, down to the Welsh Oak and Ty'n-y-Cwm Farm, and in the first faint flushes of a watery dawn I saw an army of men resting along the tram road. These were the men of Blackwood, Caerphilly and Pengam; the men of the Western Valley under John Frost, the leader, who had preceded us from Newbridge according to plan. I saw him for the second time in my life, short, square and dominant; wearing a heavy greatcoat and a red neck-scarf, dwarfed by his bodyguard of gigantic Blackwood colliers. I saw him again in daylight, sitting at a table in Ty'n-y-Cwm Farm shippon while two men of Pontypool, Brough the Brewer and Watkins the Currier, were brought as prisoners from Croes-y-Ceiliog. And I saw him set them free, in anger, demanding that William Jones the watchmaker, the leader of the Eastern men, be brought instead, for lingering.

And among the men who brought the prisoners in were Mo Jenkins and his father Rhys.

"Great God!" whispered Mo, peering. "Is it Iestyn Mortymer?"

"It is," said Rhys, gripping my hand. "Where is your Mam, Mari, and the children?"

I told them.

"And safest, too, for this business stinks," whispered Mo. "If there are two thousand here I am surprised, and they

300

promised us twenty. Out of his mind is Frost for trusting the Eastern Valley to the blabbering watchmaker—going like a snail, he is."

"Where is he now?" I asked.

"At Llantarnam Abbey when we left him," replied Rhys, "and playing the devil with the Member of Parliament there. Too much shouting and too little marching is William Jones's trouble, and enough Eastern Valley men with him to eat Newport, if he ever gets there. Will Blaenavon is kicking his feet off to get forward, and Caradoc Owen and Dafydd Phillips are saying they will be lucky to get as far as Cwrt-y-Bela."

"Those two are together, eh?" I sniffed. "With Scotch Cattle floggers among them Jones will be lucky if he gets to Allt-yr-Yn. There are Redcoats in Newport, have you heard?"

"Aye," said Mo. "With my little pistol here and my right knuckles sound I am good for two hundred."

"Perhaps," I said, "but look at the rest of us. Half of us drowned and the rest of us drunk. The Redcoats have got discipline, we are a rabble."

"A rabble that outnumbers them fifty to one, though," said Big Rhys. "And it will take a day to gallop artillery from Brecon. Frost is no fool."

"And the Redcoats are Chartists, anyway," added Mo.

"I hope to God that is right," said Rhys. "Scores of muskets they handed out from the Bristol Beerhouse at Ponty, but the powder was liquid in the pouches and the ball rusted. Can you imagine that happening under Wellington? Aye, it is discipline we need, as you say, Iestyn. Taking Newport and releasing Vincent from Monmouth is one thing, but resisting the Royal Army is another, and I will not believe the army is Chartist until I see the white flag over Brecon Barracks."

"That is a fine musket you have got," said Mo, taking it. "Have you ball and powder for it?"

"Aye," I said, and told how I took it from the dying puddler of Cyfarthfa.

"But it looks too big on you to be comfortable," said he.

"Will you change it with this good little pistol made at Llangynidr by a craftsman?"

"Change your arms and you change your luck," said Rhys, chuckling. "Here I am with two sound fists and good enough for anyone, including Tom Phillips the Mayor and his friend Mr. Prothero."

"Protheros I cannot hit holes through I will blow holes through," said Mo, handling the musket, "and this will blow a bigger hole than a pistol."

"Change, then," I said, "you bloodthirsty swine, but do not blame me if you swing over Parliament Square for carrying it. Have you heard they are having us for treason already?"

"On what grounds?" asked Rhys.

"For carrying arms in defiance of the Queen."

"When I go duck-shooting every Sunday over the mountain?"

"Be fair, Rhys," said Jack Lovell, coming up. "You are not marching down Stow Hill looking forducks."

A good-looking man was Jack Lovell, one of the captains, square and strong, with the face of a soldier and breeding in his voice. I will remember Lovell as I saw him then, matching Big Rhys for size and strength, not as I saw him three hours later, shrieking on the corner of Skinner Street, spilling his blood on the cobbles.

"Aye, then," answered Rhys, "treason it is, but I will swing in pretty good company. When do we move, Jack?"

"When William Jones arrives, which is not until he has drunk Y Ty Gwyrdd dry at Llantarnum, from what I hear. Are you three armed?"

"Aye," said Mo.

"Forward with me in the vanguard, then. Firearms will be carried in front, pikes next and mandrills in the rear. Move, boys."

Zephaniah Williams came then, striding through the crowd into Ty'n-y-Cwm Farm. Weary and sick he looked, drenched to the skin and cursing as he swung the men aside. I was near when he met Frost later.

"There is no sign of Jones, I understand," he cried. "And him playing the trooper captain on horseback. Riding, if you please, while I have marched every inch of the way."

Which is a lie, said Big Rhys quietly, for I have seen you dozing in a tram down the valley.

"He will come," said Frost.

"He had better," shouted Zephaniah. "I am in no mood for traitors." He turned his face to the sky, to the black clouds tinging red with dawn. The rain poured down, splashing over his breast, running in streams from the brim of his broad felt hat. Great and powerful looked Zephaniah standing there; a god among Chartists, a man of war who was bringing to the masses the freedom others had promised; the man of destiny for whom we had prayed. Thus will I remember Zephaniah Williams. Not as the man of clay, who ran before the wind in search of his freedom, leaving captivity to his comrades and his cowardice to his relations.

We moved down the tram road from the Welsh Oak at break of day with John Frost leading and the Deacons urging us to follow. Jack Lovell marched behind Frost with his lieutenants, about a score all told. And behind them came Big Rhys, Mo and me, and William Griffiths, the man from Merthyr who died, was on my right. The gale that had raged all night fiercened with daylight, rising into a frenzy of howling, and the bitter rain cut our faces. For hours the icy water had been chilling my body. My boots were ragged with marching, my limbs heavy. Up and down the line of thousands of soaked, dispirited men came sounds of anger, at the forced march. Muskets were fired to test the dryness of powder, for at Llanhilleth I had seen powder flasks filled with rain and shot-firing packets soaked to destruction, while at New Inn Croes-y-Ceiliog, said Big Rhys, desperate men had dried powder in a housewife's oven. No Charter Song echoed now. There was nothing but the wind-silence that foretold the horror to come. I looked at Mo Jenkins. His face was stained red in the torchlight, split with the white grin of determination he had worn since a boy, and his eyes were shining with hope of a fight. No weariness in this one, my friend since childhood, since the night of the swinging lamp over the Keeper's Pond signpost when I ducked the swing of his right boot and ran into the left. Good it was, to have Mo beside me at a time like this, marching to take a town; marching for the good of women like Mari, men like my father, and the ghost of Richard Bennet. These things I thought as we went down to Pye Corner and forward the two miles to Cwrt-y-Bela, where we rested for the last time before Newport.

"Why are you fighting?" said a man to me at Cwrt-y-Bela.
"It is a funny thing to ask," I replied. "Why are you?"
"For my children," said he, "to get them out of iron."
"Where you from?" I asked, and he smiled.
"From Nanty," said he, "same place as you, for everyone in Nanty, Welsh or foreign, knows the Mortymers. But nobody is likely to notice Isaac Thomas at five-feet-two, the limestone cutter on Afron Madoc's shift, Llangattock." He grinned through the rain, and spat. "You did him pretty well, old Afron—remember?"
"Aye," I said.
"Two of his teeth my mate Joseph picked up and wore them on his watch-chain, threaded, thank God. A pig is Afron Madoc, and Caradoc Owen is one worse."
"Aye, but Owen is here today, they tell me—back with Jones the watchmaker, give him credit, though you will never find Afron Madoc."
"Never again," said Isaac Thomas, "for he is down six feet, and I put him. I put him before I left, you understand? An eye for an eye, says the Book, and I had him for killing my girl. Ten years old, she was, and pretty, until he took her underground at the Garn—working at the face—at ten—on Afron's recommendation, filling trams, and the roof came down and took her legs to the thigh."
I pitied him.
"But I had all of Madoc."
"Do not talk too loud," I said, glancing around.
"Do not worry yourself, man," said Isaac. "I am not that

stupid. I had him legitimate, under ten tons at Llangattock quarry, but he died too quick for decency."

"And now?" I asked.

"Now I am fighting for the others, for my wife bore me nine. Three of them are working under the Coity as colliers and four of the others are in Crawshay Bailey's iron. It is a stink and it must stop, says my wife, with a four-pound debt at the Shop in the bargain. It is dying, this, says my wife, not living, and we are decent Chapel people, mind."

The wind wailed about us and we shivered as the rain flooded into us with a new fury.

"Why are you fighting, then?" asked Isaac Thomas.

"For my son and against Cwm Crachen," I told him. "Do not ask more, leave it at that."

Through the head they got Isaac Thomas. He was the first to die, they say, when the shutters of the Westgate Inn went back and showed us muskets. For the Redcoats took us low with their first volley, and Isaac was five-feet-two.

# CHAPTER TWENTY-SIX

It was broad daylight when Frost and Rees the Fifer got us moving again, and David Jones the Tinker and men like Lovell took the word to arm right down the line. The rain had stopped as we left the tram road and climbed the hill past the Friars and St Woolos Church to the crest of Stow Hill. With Frost·at the head we waved and cheered at the Redcoats crowding in the entrance of the workhouse.

"You see!" cried Lovell near me. "Chartists to a man. Not a musket raised to stop us."

"Aye?" replied Big Rhys above the din of cheering and the clatter of shots. "Very funny that they did not wave back, then."

Down Stow Hill we went, calling to the people staring in terror from their windows. Down to the high footway where the townsfolk were clustered, waving and firing into the air we went, our hopes soaring with every step, drunk with power, top dogs at last, as Lovell said. But God knows where we were going, said Mo marching beside me, and God knows what we do when we get there, said Big Rhys.

"To the Westgate!" shouted Frost then, throwing up his arms.

At the bottom of Stow Hill little groups of watchers were pressed against the buildings, frightened faces peeped from shop windows, children peered from behind half closed doors and shutters. Singing the songs of Ernest Jones, shouting at the top of our lungs, we swept to the entrance of the Westgate yard, following Lovell's command, but the gateway was chained and locked.

"Show yourselves at the front, then!" shouted Frost. "Chartist prisoners have been taken. Demand their release or let them take the consequences!"

We left Frost at the stable-yard gateway. With Jack Lovell

leading, the column wheeled right in front of the Westgate Inn.

"Look you!" roared Rees the Fifer, pointing up. "The old swine himself is up at a window!" and he pointed his musket high just as Mayor Phillips ducked down.

A sudden silence came over the men about me. With Lovell leading, a column of men pressed up the Westgate steps towards the open doorway. And in that silence my mind flew back across the years to my last visit to Newport; to the hiring fair where I first laid eyes on Mari; to the hand of John Frost who raised me from the cobbles, to the sixpence he gave me that I still carried in my pocket, and these same steps that later he had climbed with mayoral dignity. I looked for Frost now, but the mob was thick as it packed down from the Hill, and sticks and mandrills were raised like a forest.

"Surrender your prisoners!" shouted Lovell in the doorway.

"Never!" cried a constable.

Muskets and pikes went up, voices were raised in protest, a shot rang out and the inn door slammed shut. The mob about me swayed and roared. I saw Lovell fight himself free of the press of men; saw his fist shake at the door.

"In, my men!" he yelled, and I forced myself forward with Mo and Rhys either side of me as the hatchets went into the big door. The men about me were screaming to get forward, many roaring the Charter Song, others discharging pistols and muskets at the high windows of the Westgate. Before me, between the swaying heads, I saw the hatchets rising and falling and the polished wood splintering white as the panels went down.

"In, in!" It was Lovell's voice again, pulling the men against him with his fire. Muskets were crashing, the air filled with the bitter smell of powder. Glass tinkled from the windows as the shots went home. Mo was using his fists now, and heads disappeared as he chopped them down. Driving onward, he tripped on the bottom steps of the inn and fell with me on top of him. Cursing, we staggered upright. A hatchet-shaft hissed past my head. Ducking, I caught at Mo and dragged him forward, and the door went down and Lovell was in with fifteen or more falling headlong after him on to the polished floor. I was on my back now, levelled by the mad rush of the men behind me, and Mo was beside me, pinned by the tramping feet. We were kicked down as we tried to rise, an army passing over us, forced on by the maddened rush from the square where thousands were heaving hundreds forward. As the rush subsided and we clambered up, we were forced out of the entrance and headlong down the steps by men retreating. Explosions were shattering the hall. Men were screaming in pain, their voices falsetto. Lying on the steps, enduring the hammering boots that crashed against my head and shoulders, I struggled for consciousness. Blood streamed into my eyes from a cut on my forehead and I dashed it away with my arm, rolling down the steps in an effort to escape the entangling forest of legs, the boots that trampled me, thudding into my face, crushing my hands on the cobbles. I rolled sideways to escape a fresh rush of the mob. I saw them coming, yelling their battle cries, shoulder to shoulder, their mandrills and pitchforks swinging before them, their pistols and muskets exploding in shafts of fire. This was the second mad charge, and I escaped it by rolling to the wall, under the very windows of the ground floor as their shutters went back with a crash, exposing Redcoats. The mob swept straight to the windows, firing wildly, flinging stones. Staves came showering against the windows as men streamed from the hall; staggering, crawling some of them, most of them clutching at wounds. And then the Redcoats fired. Flame and white smoke burst from the public-room windows in a volley of death. I saw the mob shudder as the balls went home into the packed ranks. They dropped like wheat to the scythe, these men, in long fingers through the mob, and to my death bed will I remember their cries. Yet above the bedlam, the explosions, the shrieks of wounded and dying, I heard Jack Lovell's voice from the hall, and turned. Wiping the blood from my eyes I crawled up the steps.

The Westgate entrance was a shambles of blood and arms, with dead and wounded entangled in grotesque attitudes over the floor. Commands from soldiers and Chartists cut across the cries of the wounded. Muskets were detonating in the confined space, and the air swirling with smoke and fumes.

"Charge down the door, my hearties!" yelled Lovell. "Down with the door and we gain the day!" and I followed his cry, leaping over sprawling bodies. The passage turned here and I collided with a wall of men. This led to the public room that housed the Redcoats. Once inside and our numbers would tell. I saw the hatchets going up again, the splinters flying.

"In, in!" screamed Lovell, but his voice was lost in the bedlam of battle cries. I heaved at the back. Other men from the square joined me and we set our shoulders and thrust our weight at the backs of the men before us. But the door held. And then I saw Mo Jenkins with Big Rhys behind him. Mo had a hatchet and was going at the door, driving its head deep into the solid oak, tearing aside the panels that sheltered the Redcoats.

"Give him room!" shouted Lovell, and flung himself back. Again the hatchet went deep with all Mo's brute strength behind it. He was wrenching the steel clear and preparing for a swing when the door flew back, opened from within. Five Redcoats were kneeling, others standing above them, muskets levelled, bayonets fixed. They fired, and the volley raked us. Hit in the shoulder, I spun, and I saw my blood spray high on the gilded walls as I fell. Mo was down, the hatchet twisted under him, Big Rhys on all fours, his arms thrown over his son. Lovell was down, but crawling, blood gushing from his mouth. I writhed. The pain in my arm was excruciating, but I lay still. Above and behind me men were cursing and groping in the smoke-wreathed graveyard of a passage, blinded instantly by the flash of the volley. The door of the public room slammed shut. The lock grated. Another concussion shook the building as the soldiers sent a fusillade through the windows into the packed mob outside.

"Iestyn! For God's sake!" cried Rhys like a child.

Throwing aside the weight of a body, I dragged myself up and fell on my knees beside him.

"Mo, my son!" cried Rhys, weeping. "O holy Christ, do you save him, my son!"

"Quick," I whispered with a glance at the door. "Quick with us and we will get him out of this hell. Are you hurt, man?"

"If that door comes open again they will bloody carve you," gasped Mo. "I am dying, can you see straight? Leave me."

"Here, catch hold," I whispered, panting with fear, and I hooked my good arm under his. "Up, Rhys, for God's sake, before they swing the door."

The passage was empty except for the dead, and one named Shell. He stood in an alcove, his pike held tight against him, his young face white, his lips trembling.

"To hell out of it, boy!" I whispered as we dragged Mo past him into the hall. And even as we reached the entrance I had to heave Mo aside, for the mob was coming again for another attack and pouring through the hall into the passage, whooping and cheering to its death. Back went the public-room door again and the vicious volleys of the Redcoats raked them, cutting them down, knocking flat the ones who sought to rise. I caught a glimpse of George Shell running, on tiptoe, leaping lightly over the packed bodies; I saw his pike go up and the startled cry of Phillips the mayor pierced the commotion. But a musket flashed and Shell staggered, to spin and fall flat, the pike shattering beneath him. The door slammed shut.

It was the end. I saw it at the entrance steps. Caught in the open by trained men under cover, the Chartists were breaking. The square was emptying, littered with writhing men, and arms; groans and cries rose from the smoke. Big Rhys and me, with the dying Mo held between us, crouched in the door-way of the Westgate, the only three in the world, it seemed. Under the portico of the mayor's house at the bottom of Stow Hill a man was dying—Abraham Thomas, men said later, Abraham who had sent me to Llangynidr. And he called for the Charter now, his voice vibrant, a contrast to Jack Lovell. Lovell died in screams, as a woman being mutilated, writhing on the corner of Skinner Street, beating his hands against the cobbles. Before me in the road lay Isaac Five-feet-two of Afron Madoc's shift; hit in the face by the look of him, because he was short, but he went in peace, not like his girl. Like a tomb it was, crouching there; hell itself said Big Rhys later. Behind us the Chartists were dead or wounded, before us they lay under the scorching fire of the Redcoats. Only one fired back now, a man with one leg, the last broken hero of the Chartist cause.

Idris Foreman died, they told me; in a field near Pye Corner, in the arms of the Howells twins. Always handy with shovels, Owen and Griff had him three feet down still warm while the special constables and troops from Newport Workhouse were beating the hedges nearby. Will Blaenavon, too, according to reports, and Dathyl Jenkins, his unwedded wife, put laurels on the Chartist graves in St Woolas Yard on the Palm Sunday following, though they never found his body. Some say he took the chance to die and puddled for ten years over at Risca, just to lose Dathyl, but I never had the proof of it. Dai Probert Scotch Cattle died, they said, deep in the mountains near Waunavon, with a ball in his chest, among his men; and so did Caradoc Owen—of drink to drown his cowardice, at the bar of the Drum and Monkey. Many died that were not recorded, in fields, under the hedges and in barns and ditches from Malpas to Pontypool, Newbridge to Blackwood. Some died in days, some years after, in foreign lands or the starving prisons under foreign gaolers. Most died with friends about them, in the hall of the Westgate or its bloodstained yard.

But Mo died alone.

"Get up," said the constable, and swung his boot to hasten me.

"My friend is dying," I said, kneeling. "Let me stay."

"Get up!" and he brought out his bayonet.

I rose, but Rhys was quicker, and stretched him flat with a right to the throat. They were round us then like locusts, Redcoats mostly, kicking us away, levelling their muskets.

"My boy is dying," said Rhys. "Let me to him."

"Aye?" said one. "You should have thought of that before."

"Take him gently, Dada," said Mo, grinning, as they backed us away to a wall.

Ten Redcoats came through from the public room; fine men, good soldiers, give them credit. They brought out the mayor next, short of an arm by the way it was bleeding, and another wound in the thigh, playing hell with Welshmen from Newport to Cyfarthfa. A lieutenant followed him, swarthy and confident, this one, and get these damned ruffians out of here quick.

"Officer," said Big Rhys, begging with his hands. "My son is over by there and dying. For God's sake let me to him."

"Take him out with the rest," said the officer. "Let nobody near him. Keep the people away from the wounded, let the dead lie where they have fallen. Nobody near them, do you understand? By God, we will teach these bloody Welsh a lesson."

"O, *fy mab*," said Rhys, "*fy machgen, fy macghen bach dewr!*"

They took Mo down and spread him on the cobbles, and he moved but once to wipe sweat from his face. And Big Rhys, with a Redcoat bayonet against his stomach, watched him die.

They took us to the stable yard, the first prisoners of the Westgate, and they herded the rest in after us. Hour after hour they were brought in from tram roads as far as Pye Corner; broken, dejected men and boys, soaked and weary, many of them wounded; silent, unprotesting under the musket butts of the Redcoats. I saw in their grey faces of defeat the tragedy of my generation. They came from the iron towns of Beaufort and Tredegar, Merthyr and Dowlais, from the employ of men like Robert Thomas Crawshay who ruled them from the hated battlements of his Cyfarthfa Castle; or the Baileys who used starvation wages to beat them into submission. Was there no end to the persecution? Or was this misery a birthright handed down through generations of men oppressed by men of power?

"Where is Frost?" was the whisper.

"Going like a rabbit for Tredegar Park," came an answer. "Dodging the keepers and playing touch-me-not. Thank God for such a leader. No wonder he is English."

"English? Do not blame the bloody nationality, man, or is Zephaniah Williams not Welsh? Watch your tongue. We are big enough fools as it is."

"And what of William Jones Watchmaker and his five thousand terrors from Ponty, look you! Aye, terrors indeed, for the swines never got nearer than Cefn, while we were out with the hatchets."

Another spat. "Every Redcoat a Chartist, eh? Every man ready for the march on London, is it? God help us now, our wives and our little ones. Starving and beating Vincent to death in Monmouth, are they? Vincent is lucky. They will give us bloody Chartists, with burning too good for us."

"And Dr Price of Merthyr, eh? Where the hell did he get to with his thousands starving under Crawshay? There is a hot one for a Welsh nationalist—racing round Merthyr with his bardic sword and goat cart. What with this one and that one I am ashamed of being bloody Welsh."

They pushed, they quarrelled, they cursed; comrades one moment, enemies the next.

"Iestyn," said Rhys. "Little Mo is dead. Dead, do you hear me?"

They fought one another, bitterly. Some wept, some prayed. They fought the Westgate over again, taking it in the rear this time, pulling cannon down Commercial Street, flinging firebrands through its windows.

"The organisation was wrong, see? Men like Frost and Zephaniah could not lead a pack of women, let alone men. Leaders, you call them? They have not the sense to be good politicians. By God, if I get my hands on William Jones Watchmaker!"

"What the hell is wrong with you, Boxer?" said one, passing.

In a corner of the yard Big Rhys was weeping.

"What is wrong with him?" they asked me, nudging.

"His son is dead," I told them.

"Eh, dear! It is too late for snivelling now, bach."

"O, God," sighed Rhys, biting at his knuckles.

"Steady," I said.

"Dear me," shouted one in passing. "What will my old woman say when they string me? She hit me black and blue about coming on this caper with Frost."

"Thank God the debt is still good at the Shop, man. If Lord John Russell transports me, Crawshay will have to sing for it!"

"Does Bailey pay pensions to widows, you say?"

They joked, they bantered, they laid wagers on their lot, and some wept.

"Mo Jenkins was your boy, eh, man?" one asked Rhys. "Eh, now! The boy who was chasing Dai Benyon Champion? Good grief! Call him lucky, and weep for the living, do not weep for the dead. For they will burn us alive now, these English, with burning too good for us. They will bring back the stake to tame us and put other rebellions down. They will hit the country so hard that she will not stand straight for a hundred years, mark me."

"My son is dead," said Rhys to me, not listening. "O, Christ, pity me."

And he beat his fists together, weeping.

Is my friend dead? Is Mo Jenkins gone, the boy of the Garndyrus cave, of the fight up on Turnpike. He who sang when I was wedded to Mari, great in his strength, fearless before the might of the terrible Dai Benyon; is he gone for eternity on the rush of his father's tears?

Is Idris Foreman gone, and Afel Hughes to his burned wife and his girl Ceinie? Is Richard Bennet in the Great Palace, entering in his youth the portals of the dead when all his life he had fought for a heaven of the living? He whom Morfydd loved, is he with us this day of defeat, this tumult of a day that has beaten down all he strove for?

Is Edwina gone, the sister I never understood? Does she sleep under the yew trees in St Mary's, her frail, white beauty going to dust? Is my father gone, he so great in strength? Is my country dead, this beloved land that has powdered the bones of other conquerors and trampled their pennants into dust? O, this Land of the Ancients that has echoed to the feet of Rome and known the laurels of victory; who has snatched her soul from the fire of her persecutors and held high her honour in the face of shame! I can see from here the black outline of The Top. I see the white streams tumbling from the Afon Lwydd through the heather of Waunavon. I see the mountains green again in the lazy heat of summer, and cold and black under the frozen moons of winter. Is the hay still flying from the barn down at Shant-y-Brain's? Is the canal still swimming through the alders from Brecon to Ponty?

The Redcoats came to search us, clearing a path with musket butts, knocking up our elbows, slapping at our pockets.

"You swines! There are enough arms among this lot to fit out Brecon Garrison."

"You—your name?"

"Iestyn Mortymer."

"A Chartist, eh? We will give you Chartist. You will dance for eighteen bloody months when we get you to Monmouth."

Aye, I thought, *if* you get me to Monmouth.

"You are wounded," said a sergeant.

"This man's arm is broken. Hey, you! Drop that musket and break me a pike for splints."

His hands were rough, but he served me well. He spoke Lancashire while he bandaged, but I did not heed him.

For I was up at Garndyrus watching the iron coming out.

I was away down the Garn hunting for Edwina. I was walking with my father over Llangynidr Mountain, and kissing Mari in the heather after Chapel on Easter Sunday.

"Right! Into the carts!"

They kicked us out of the stable yard and into carts for Monmouth, standing too tight to fall out. The Redcoats marched beside us, muskets primed, bayonets fixed, and we went like the tumbrils of France.

"By God," said a man beside me, "they are doing us fine, eh? We are going like the aristocracy. Take it proudly, Welshmen; and last verse of the old Charter Song to guide the way for others," and we sang:

"For ages deep wrongs have been hopelessly borne;
Despair shall no longer our spirits dismay,
Nor wither the arm when upraised for the fray;
The conflict for freedom is gathering nigh.
We live to secure it, or gloriously die!"

Book Two

HOSTS OF REBECCA

For Georgina

. . . I retain my belief in the nobility and excellence of the human. I believe that spiritual sweetness and unselfishness will conquer the gross gluttony of today. And last of all, my faith is in the working class. As some Frenchman has said, 'The stairway of time is ever echoing with the wooden shoe going up, the polished boot descending.'

Jack London

# CHAPTER 1

## 1839

A PEBBLE HIT the window, bringing me upright.
 In the sea of Grandfer's fourposter bed I sat, staring into
the nothingness between sleeping and waking, shivering in the
pindrop silence.

A handful of gravel at the glass now, spraying as thunder.
Out of bed head-first then, scrambling over the boards. Nightshirt billowing, I raised the sash.

"Hush you for God's sake," I said. "You will have Morfydd
out."

"Then move your backside," said Joey in the frost below.
"It is damned near midnight."

Twelve years old, this one – a year and a bit younger than
me, with corn-coloured hair and the face of a churchyard
ghost, starved at that. A criminal was Tramping Boy Joey, the
son of a Shropshire sin-eater; raised in a poorhouse, thumped
by life into skin and bone, but the best poaching man in the
county of Carmarthenshire. Our bailiff had fits with his legs up
when Joey was loose, for he poached every meal. You keep from
that Joey, said Morfydd, my sister – you can always stoop to
pick up trash.

I dressed like a madman in the stinging silence of December
with the window throwing icicles into the room, for it was a
winter to freeze dewdrops, and the moon was shivering in the
sky that night, rolling over the rim of the mountain. Ice hung
from down-spouts, water butts creaked solid and the white
plains were hammered into silence. Black was the river where
the hen coots were skating, and the whole rolling country from
Narberth to Carmarthen city was dying for the warmth and
tumble of spring.

"You got a woman up there or something?" whispered
Joey, blowing on his fingers and steaming.

I flapped him into silence.

A house of ghosts, this one; ruined and turreted, where the creak of a board was clatter. I listened. No sound but Grandfer's hop-reeking snores from the kitchen below. A hell of a Grandfer I had – back teeth awash every night regular, head sunk on his chest and bellowing in the place like a man demented, legs thrust out before the fire. Had to get past him somehow. A peep and a listen at the bedroom door and I crept back. Under the bed now, fish out the china, wrap it in a bedsheet and lay it snug, with a pillow below it for the curve of the body. Enemies right and left when you are thirteen. Back to the window with me like lightning.

"Right, you," I said.

"About time, too," said Joey, stroking his ferret.

With my boots in my hand I crept down the stairs, pausing outside Morfydd's door, for she was the true enemy. Thunderbolts could fall and nobody stir but Morfydd, my sister, for when my mam hit the bed she died. But Morfydd's sleep was the sleep of a conscience, breathing as something embalmed but one eye open for saints. And the step of a mouse would bring her out with hatchets, a wraith on tiptoe that peeped round doors and bent over beds.

Down to the kitchen now with its smells of last night's supper. A shadow moved from under the table, a crescent of whining joy that encircled my legs. Ever wakeful was Tara, like all Welsh terriers, and already hearing the stamp of the rabbit.

"Quiet!" I breathed, gathering her up. With my hand over her muzzle I tiptoed past Grandfer. Flat out in the armchair was Grandfer, his snores spouting up from his belted belly, his goat beard trembling in the thunder of his dreaming. The big lock grated its betrayal, but I got out somehow and clicked the door shut.

"Look!" whispered Joey, pointing. "Rebecca is at it again," and the name snatched at my breath. For bonfires were simmering and flashing on the white hills and a rocket arced in a trail of fire and drooped, spluttering into stars.

"Rebecca rioters, is it?" I whispered.

8

"Come," said Joey. "While Waldo Bailiff is out chasing rioters he is not trapping poachers. You got the towser?"

"Under my arm," I said.

"You scared of mantraps, Jethro Mortymer?"

Just looked at him, and spat.

"Right, us. Away!" whispered Joey. "We will give him Waldo."

As ragged heathens we ran down to Tarn, to the white-bouldered world of skulls and skinny sheep – to the burrows of the rabbits that riddled Squire's Reach, leaping frozen streams, plunging through undergrowth and wallowing in the marsh track till we came to the fence of Waldo Bailiff. Gasping, we rested here, steaming, flat on our backs. Tara and the ferret were running in circles about us, playing as children in bounds and squeaks, working up a joy for the coming hunt.

"Easy now," said Joey, sitting up. "Under the fence and follow me, and watch for mantraps."

This was Joey's world and he knew it backwards. Wild as a gipsy, this one, his bed under the moon in summer, seeking warmth on the rim of the limekiln fires in winter. He had lived alone since Cassie, his mam, hoofed it out of the county two years back – wanted by the military for caravan stealing. Joey baked his hedgehogs in balls of clay; was a better cook than Morfydd when it came to a rabbit, roasting them on spits or stirring them in stews.

"Mantraps are against the law," I said.

"O, aye?" said he, old-fashioned. "And who do say so?"

"My grandfer."

Joey jerked up the wire for me to crawl through. "Mantraps with spikes is against the law," said he. "Waldo's are legal, for they only break the leg. You watch for spikes, though – the spikes I fear for they rip and tear – like little Dai Shenkins down at New Inn – you heard about Dai?"

"No," I replied.

"Night before last, it was. Addled was Dai, poaching without a moon, for the moon shows mantraps, never mind bailiffs. Over at Simmons place he caught it, did Dai."

"Bad?"

9

"Rest another minute," said he. "Jethro Mortymer, d'you think much of me?"

"Pretty tidy." Strange was his face turned up to the moon. "What about Dai Shenkins, then?"

"Never mind him, you think about me." He sighed. "Look, these old nights are shivery, and you got a henhouse back home at your grandfer's. Hens are warm old things in nights of frost. Could you get me in?"

"A booting, mind, if Grandfer do find you."

"Aye, a stinkifying grandfer that one," said he, vicious.

"Could try, if you sleep quiet. You slept with hens before?"

"O, eh! Often," and deep he sighed, his face pale and shadowed in the blue light and his eyes all mystery and brightness. "You ever stopped to think, Jethro Mortymer, hens are better'n humans. Humans be thumpers and hens gentle old women. Sorry I am for hens, too, being done down for eggs all their lives and finishing up between knees. But I do not love cockerels, mind – there's lust in them cockerels, says Cassie, my mam – always leapfrogging and crowing to tell the neighbourhood. You eat a cockerel every Christmas for the rest of your life and you will eat more sin than me eventually."

"You eaten sin?"

"Aye, and why not? Folks got to eat something, says Cassie, my mam, so we did the funerals – swallowing the sins of the dear departed, taking the blackness off the poor soul going down, or up – case may be."

"Good God."

"You know Clun?"

I shook my head.

"Eight years old, me, when we did Clungunford – first time at sin-eating, for me. We knew we were into something pretty shocking when we got a spring chicken and wine to wash it down. And us that hungry we'd have stained our souls with child-killing for a piece of poorhouse bread, said Cassie. And the dear departed a clergy, at that."

"Chapel?"

"Church of England, but we sent him up clean as a washday. Eh, dear me, I reckon I be loaded black. Who started all this?"

"Hens," I said.

"Right, then – you fix me in your henhouse?"

"Out at first light, is it?"

"And not an egg missing. God bless you, Jethro Mortymer." He rose and stretched. "Right you, Waldo," he said. "Just look out."

"Come easy or she'll spring."

On tiptoe I came, peering.

"Throw me that stick. Watch the towser," said Joey.

I saw the steel jaws of the mantrap, gaping, smothered in leaves, and the spring steel curved tight and ready for the footstep.

"Eh, Waldo, you swine of a bailiff," said Joey, and swung the stick and the jaws leaped and slammed shut. "But not as bad as some – all legal. You seen Dai's leg?"

"Dai Shenkins?"

"Neither has Dai. Spikes, see? Took it off neat at the knee. And the Simmons bailiff found it next morning and followed the blood right up to New Inn. They'd have had little Dai, but he died. Died to spite them, his old mam said – hopping his way to his Maker for a rabbit, you can keep your old Botany Bay – she's a regular cheek is Dai's old mam. You got the towser?"

"Aye."

"Right," said Joey, and fished in his rags for his ferret, parted bushes and stuffed it down a hole. "Put the towser by the hole near that tree. Ready?"

I nodded, and set Tara down. And out came the rabbits in a stream.

I have seen dogs at rabbits but never one like Tara, my little bitch, for she threw them up as soon as they showed their eyes – two in the air at a time, hitting the frost as dead as doornails.

"Some terrier!" cried Joey, delighted.

Five rabbits came from the burrow and then came Joey's ferret, nose up, sniffing for more, and Tara got him square, for the light was bad that minute. Six feet up went that ferret, dying in flight, and Tara ran round him, sniffing delighted.

Good God.

"You black-faced bitch!" yelled Joey, and aimed his boot, but I caught his ankle and brought him down flat. With the mantrap between us we faced each other, sitting, and the silence grew in the shivering yard between us with Tara going round us in circles of joy, counting the dead.

"Here, Tara!" I said, and she leaped into my arms, licking and grinning.

He wept then, did Joey, with the tears leaving tracks on his grimed face.

"I am sorry," I said.

No sound he made in that sobbing, and he reached for the ferret and put it against his face; just sitting there with the wind stirring the branches above him, wisping up his bright hair.

Minutes I stood there kicking at leaves, for words are useless things in the presence of injured friendship, then I gathered up the rabbits and put them tidy at his feet, but he made no sign that he noticed.

"Rebecca is about," I said. "You heard they carried Sam Williams on the pole for blowing up that serving-maid down in Plasy? And the hayricks of the gentry are blazing something beautiful. Look, Joey boy, you can see them from here."

But he just went on weeping and kissing the ferret.

"Look, now," I said, short. "There is more than one ferret. That old thing was a rabbit-feeder, anyway. I will buy you another and train him rigid. Heisht you, is it?"

"Go to hell," he said, and his eyes were as fire.

"It is only a ferret, Joey – let us be friends."

Up with him then and blazing. "Out you get, Mortymer – you and that black-faced towser!" he shrieked. "You be bastards the pair of you, you and the bitch!"

With Tara held against me I watched as he turned and climbed the fence, bending to the hill on his way to his lime-kiln sleep.

"I will slip up the catch in the henhouse, Joey!" I called.

Not even a look. Just me left, and moonlight.

Nothing to do but go back home, taking the short cut this

time along the road to Carmarthen, but I dived into a ditch pretty sharp as the cavalry came galloping. Helmeted, spurred, they rounded the bend, thundering hooves, jingling and clanking, flashing to the moon, their big mares sweating and snorting smoke. Trouble in St Clears by the look of it; twelve dragoons this time of night.

I stopped near the shippon of home and unlatched the henhouse to give Joey a welcome, and the feathered old things grumbled, fearing the fox. In the back now, put Tara under the table; tiptoe past Grandfer who was snoring in shouts, up the stairs as a wraith and I got to my room. Up to the bed, throwing off my clothes. Shivering in the nightshirt I reached for the china; touched Morfydd's face and nearly hit the ceiling.

"Right, you," said she, rising up like the Day of Reckoning. "Poaching again with Tramping Boy Joey. Account for yourself, and quick."

Black hair over her shoulders, eyes narrowed with sleep, face as a madonna and looks like daggers. Beautiful, she was, to anyone but a brother.

"Quick," she said, thumping the blanket. "And no lies!"

A saint of a mother I had, but a tidy old bitch of a sister.

## CHAPTER 2

JUST A couple of months me and my women had been at Cae White, Grandfer's house – Morfydd, my sister; my mother, and Mari my sister-in-law – running to Carmarthenshire from Monmouthshire iron; from the flash and glare of the Top Town furnaces where my father had died to the pasturelands of the west. Quiet and sweet it was here, a change from starving and sweating; far from the bellowing industry, as the opening of a Bible after a bedlam of labour.

Hitting it up for fourteen I was at this time, and coming a little hot with me about women. There are women and women, said Morfydd my sister, who was no better than she ought to be, but my mam, as I say, was a saint. Even the neighbours admitted she was a cut above the rest of them, with Good morning to you, Mr Waldo Bailiff, and Good afternoon to you, Mr Tom Griffiths, and God help even a seller of coloured Bibles who put his foot in the door without her permission.

"Rebecca was burning the hayricks last night," I said at breakfast, aware of slanting eyes.

"And how do you know when you were in bed and asleep?" asked Grandfer.

Five feet exactly, this one – every inch of him pickled in hops. The villagers said he was Quaker blood that had slipped off the black shine of the Book, though some said he was gipsy. But whatever his blood he soused himself regular five nights a week on the profits of the farm – ten jugs on a Tuesday when the drovers came down; with a crag for a settle and the moon for a blanket, snoring in icicles out in the mist, singing his bawdies in the company of goblins. Reckon Mari, my sister-in-law, was ashamed of her Grandfer Zephaniah.

"Big fires, though," said my mam. "Looked like tollgates – saw them myself."

"Read your history," said Grandfer. "Hayricks. Rebecca rioters – eight barns went up last night – and the dragoons came out from Carmarthen. I would give them rioters if I got my hands on them."

I chewed the black bread, watching Morfydd. Flushed and angry she looked, spooning up the oatmeal broth.

"Eh," sighed Mam. "We run from Monmouthshire iron for a bit of peace and we bump into riots all over again. Isn't just, is it?"

"You will always have riots while we bear such injustices," said Morfydd, eyes snapping up.

"Now, now!" said Mam, finger up. "Not our house, remember."

"I would burn the damned gentry, never mind their ricks," said Morfydd, and she swept back her hair. Excellent at rebellion and speeches, this one, especially when it came to hanging the Queen. Beautiful, but a woman of fire; an agitator in the Top Towns, married to an agitator once but no ring to

14

prove it, and God knows where she would land us if she started tricks here, for we got out of Monmouthshire by the skin of our teeth.

"Let her speak," said Grandfer. "Let her be. Does she also write poetry?"

"Aye," said Morfydd, and fixed him with her eyes. "The centuries of Time echo to the tread of the clog going up the stairs and the buckle coming down. Burning hayricks – chopping down tollgates? A barrel of gunpowder would bring this county alive."

I looked at my mother. Her face was agonized. For this was the old Morfydd sparring for a fight, and we were here by the grace of Grandfer. But he smiled, to his credit, and stirred his tea.

"Speak, child, speak," said he. "You know your Bible? Genesis twenty-four, verse sixty. Let us draw your teeth." And Morfydd raised her dark eyes to his, saying, " 'And they blessed Rebekah, and said unto her, thou art our sister. Be thou the mother of thousands of millions, and let thy seed possess the gate of those which hate them.' "

"Amen," said Grandfer, eyes closed, and turned to my mother. "God help me, woman. Retired, I am, and I have opened the house to a nest of Welsh agitators." He swung to Morfydd. "The first tollgate burned, young woman?"

"Efail-wen, just this year," said she.

"When?"

"May the thirteenth – by Thomas Rees of Carnabwth. Burned twice since, thank God – June the sixth and July the seventeenth. Tollgates!" Morfydd sniffed. "Back home in my county we fought it out with redcoats."

"Remarkable," said Grandfer, quizzy.

"Aye, remarkable," said Morfydd. "If your people had half the spunk of the Welsh I come from you'd have taken to arms and marched on Carmarthen. Look at the place! The people are either starving or pinched to the bone, your workhouses are filling up daily – they transport you here for poaching rabbits," and here she looked at me, "and all you can do is burn a tollgate when you ought to be hauling up cannon. Good God!"

Sweating now, the beads bright on her face, and she sighed and wiped it into her hair.

"You see what I have to put up with?" asked Mam, hands empty to Grandfer. "She lost her own man to the riots in Monmouthshire, and I lost mine to the iron. You see what I have for a daughter?"

"I see that you are harbouring a vixen," said Grandfer. "But the goals are the same north or west." Down came his fist and he thumped the table. "Keep a grip on that tongue, young woman – I have no use for it here."

And Morfydd rose, shaking off crumbs. "And I have no use for yours. Thank God for starving, thank God for kicks. If the damned house burned down you'd be too frit to fetch water," and she slammed back her chair, looking knives. As she reached the door her son came through it – Richard, her beloved, aged three, and she stooped and snatched him up and held him against her. "Come, boy," said she. "There is no place for us here."

That is what it was like in those early days at Cae White Farm; my mam the sandwich between Grandfer's dislike and my sister's fire, but it settled down after a bit, thank God. To hell with Morfydd, I used to think; to heaven with my mother, she being all gentleness in the face of rebellion. Eh, did I love my mam! If I had to die on the breast of a woman I would die on my mother's – Morfydd's next, though hers was mainly occupied. But where my mother went, I went; touching the things she touched, smoothing her place at table. Sometimes I wondered who was the more beautiful, Morfydd or Mam, who could give her twenty years, for Morfydd was lifting up the latch for thirty. Smooth in the face was my mother, carrying herself with dignity; pretty with her bonnet streamers tied under her chin, five feet of black mourning that turned every set in whiskers in the county. The basses went a semitone flat in the Horeb when she was present, but there beside me, singing like an angel, she didn't spare the men a look. A smile for everyone, her contralto greeting, she was alive and dancing outside. Inside she was dead, in the same grave as my father. My father had joined the Man in the Big Pew over twelve months now but he still lived with us, I reckoned. For sometimes, when the house was sleeping, I would hear my mam talking to him in a voice of tears. And next morning at breakfast the redness was in her eyes and her mouth was trembling to her smile, as if it had just been kissed.

"Somebody slept in the henhouse last night," said Grandfer now.

I got some more barley bread and packed it well in.

"Not rioters?" whispered Mam.

"Boys," said he, eyeing me. "Same thing. And anyone this applies to can listen. If Tramping Boy Joey shows his backside round Cae White I will kick the thing over to St Clears, understand? Poachers and thieves, stinking of the gutter – I will not have him near!"

Chewing, me, eyes on the ceiling.

"Did you see anything of that Joey last night, Jethro?" asked Mam.

"How could he have seen him?" asked Morfydd from the door with Richard in her arms. "He was in well before dark and he slept with me. Come, Jethro, *bach*, it is cleaner outside."

A bitch one moment, sister the next.

Two months of hell, it was, living with Grandfer.

Yet I remember with joy the early spring days in the new county, especially the Sundays in the pews of the Horeb. Mam one side of me, Morfydd on the other, she with an eye for every pair of trews in sight, until she caught my mother's glance which set her back miles. Proud I felt, the only man in the family now; well soaped up and my hair combed to a quiff, singing quiet according to instructions, because my voice was breaking, but dying to let things rip. Little Meg Benyon was hitting it up on the harmonium, eyes on sticks, feet going, tongue peeping out between her white teeth, one missing; with Dai Alltwen Preacher beating time and the tenors soaring and basses grovelling. Deep and beautiful was Mam's voice in the descant, and Morfydd with her elbow in my ribs.

" 'All hail the power of Jesu's name . . .!' " Tenor, me,

threatening to crack, hanging on to Mam's contralto. Double bass now, with the crack turning heads and bringing me out into a sweat. And the hymn of Shrubsole flooded over us in glory and Dai Preacher lifted his eyes to the vaults of Heaven.

" 'Crown Him, Crown Him, *Crown Him . . .!*' " Top E, and me hitting soprano.

"For God's sake!" whispered Morfydd as I hung on the note.

"Leave him be," said Mam with her soft, sad smile.

"I will be doing some crowning when I get you back home," and I get the elbow.

"Mam," I said, "look at this Morfydd!"

*"Hush!"*

Aye, good it was, those spring Sundays, with the smell of Sunday clothes and lavender about us, and peacock feathers waving and watch chains drooping over stomachs begging for Sunday dinner, and the farmers had twenty quart ones in this county. There is Hettie Winetree in front of me done up in white silk and black stockings, all peeps and wriggles around her little black hymn book – second prize for missing a Sunday School attendance, presented by Tom the Faith – fancies herself, does Hettie Winetree. Behind me sits Dilly Morgan, tall, cool, and fair for Welsh, her tonic-solfa beating hot on my neck. Down comes Meg Benyon's little fat behind as she thumps the keyboard for the Amen and Dai Alltwen Preacher is up in the pulpit before you can say Carmarthen, leaping around the mahogany, working up his *hwyl*, handing hell to sinners from Genesis to Jonah. Motionless, we Mortymers, though other eyes may roam and other throats may clear. For a speck of dust do show like a whitewash stain on strangers wearing the black, says Mam.

Sunlit were those mornings after Chapel and the fields were alight with greenness and river-flash from the estuary where the Tywi ran. This was the time for talking, and the women lost no chance, giving birth to some, burying others while the men, in funeral black, talked bass about ploughing and harvest. Waldo Bailiff was always to the front, the devil, handsome and bearded, little hands folded on his silver-topped cane and his nose a dewdrop. Very sanctimonious was Waldo, loving his neighbour, and a hit over the backside for anyone breathing near Squire's salmon steps, never mind poaching. A big fish in a little puddle, said Morfydd, and when his dewdrop falls Waldo will fall like the leaning tree of Carmarthen. I never got the hang of how that dewdrop stayed with him; stitched on, I reckon, for when a gale took every other dewdrop in the county Waldo's was still present. But Welsh to his fingertips, give him credit, as Welsh as Owain Glyndwr but no credit to Wales, and more Sunday quarts died in Waldo than Glyndwr could boast dead English. But he drew me as a magnet because of Tessa, the daughter of Squire Lloyd Parry.

A lonely half hour, this, waiting for Sunday dinner, and grown-ups chattering. Lean against the chapel gate and watch them. Crows are shouting in the tops of the elms for you, half boy, half man. Yellow beaks gape in the scarecrowed pattern of branches. And you think of the lichened bark of Tessa's tree as being velvet to the touch, and the cowslip path to the river that is crumpled gold. There we would stand in my dreams, me and Tessa Lloyd Parry, watching the river, eyes drooping to brightness while the reed music of spring flooded over us.

"You dreaming, Jethro Mortymer?"

Do you see her framed by leaves, wide-eyed, restless always – as leaf-movement and the foaming roar of the river under wind; never still was Tessa – all life and quickness with words, snatching at every precious second. Small and dark was she, with the face of a child and the body of a woman, and often I would dream of kissing her. A week next Sunday if I plucked up courage. But Tessa flies in the movement of men. Waldo wipes his whiskers in expectation of a quart in Black Boar tavern. The men drift away, the women chatter on.

Here comes Polly Scandal now, black beads and crepe, donkey ears wagging in her fluffy tufts of hair. Straighten now, hands from pockets. Buzzing around the women, she is, getting a word from here, a word from there, and saving it up for weekdays. She will have them over the county by Monday with a death before the croak and a pain before conception. My turn now. Flouncing, hips swaying, she comes to the gate; three sets of teeth.

"Good morning, Jethro Mortymer."

Nod.

"Very happy you are looking, if I may say. Courting, is it?"

"No."

"Tessa Lloyd Parry, eh? And her the daughter of Squire! There is gentry you are now, boy."

"O, aye?"

"Aye, good grief! Marrying you will be before long, I vow. Whee, terrible, you new Mortymers, and such beautiful women! True your big sister Morfydd's moonlighting with Osian Hughes Bayleaves?"

"First I've heard of it," I answered, rumbling for dinner.

"Couldn't do better, mind. Prospects has Osian Hughes with fifty acres in the family and his dada starting death rattles. Eh, close you are, but Polly do know, mind – can't deceive Polly. And that mam of yours too pretty for singles, too. Waldo Bailiff off his ale because of her and Tom the Faith laying a shilling to nothing he has her altared before summer. You heard?" Up with her skirts then. "Eh, got to go. Goodbye, Jethro Mortymer, give my love to Tessa."

And here comes Hettie Winetree with her little black hymn book, brown hair drooping, a hole in each heel of her mam's black stockings.

"Good morning, Jethro Mortymer," flushing to a strawberry.

The trees wave in perpendicular light, the wind sighs.

"Enjoy the service, Mr Mortymer?" Screwing the back from her hymn book now, eyes peeping, dying inside at the shame of her harlotry. Anxious was Hettie for the facts of life, according to her mam, said Morfydd.

"No," I said.

"O, God forgive you," says she, pale. "Hell and Damnation for you if Dai Alltwen do hear you, mind."

"And to hell with Dai Alltwen via Carmarthen," I said.

This sets her scampering and I mooched over to Morfydd, digging her. "Damned starved, I am," I said. "You coming?"

But she, like the rest, are into it proper now. Nineteen to the dozen they go it after Chapel; hands waving, tongues wagging; dear me's and good grief's left and right, shocked and shamed and shrieking in chorus; the crescent jaw of the crone with her champing, the double chin creases of the matron and the quick, shadowed cheek of the maiden, all lifting in bedlam to a chorus of harmony, hitting Top C. And God put Eve under the belly of the serpent.

"Good God," whispered Morfydd. "Look what is coming!"

Osian Hughes Bayleaves, six-foot-six of him, with a waist like Hettie's and a chest as Hercules, white teeth shining in the leather of his face. Low he bows, jerked into beetroot by his high, starched collar.

"Good morning, Miss Mortymer," he murmurs.

Down they go, all eight of them. Pretty it looks, mind.

"My mam have sent me to ask you to tea, Miss Mortymer."

"Eh, there's a pity," says Morfydd to me. "Today of all days, and we have company, eh, Jethro?"

"First I've heard of it." Gave her a wink. For beauty as Morfydd's must duck its own trouble.

"Damned swine," she whispers, smiling innocently. "Some other time, Mr Hughes, and thank your mam kindly." And away she goes in a swirl of skirts, giving honey to Osian and daggers to me.

"But Osian Hughes has prospects, remember," says Mam on the way home.

"You are not bedding me with prospects," says Morfydd. "Give me a man a foot lower and fire in him, not milky rice pudding. Pathetic is that one," and she sniffed. "A body made for throwing bullocks pumped into passion by the heart of a rabbit."

"Time you was settled, nevertheless," and Mam sighs.

"I don't do so bad, mind," said Morfydd, and I saw Mam's dig.

We had put up with all this before, of course. I wandered beside them kicking at stones in visions of the lips of Tessa Lloyd Parry, dying for manhood that I might honour her. The wind whispered as we laboured up the hill, and it was perfumed.

"You cannot live in the past," said Mam to Morfydd.

No answer from Morfydd, but her eyes were bright.

"You must think of your Richard. Soon he will ask for a dada."

Out came a handkerchief.

"Now, now!" said my mother, sharp.

"O, God," said Morfydd.

It was the Richard that did it, the name of her son and the lover who sired him three years back.

"Hush, love her," whispered Mam, holding her. "Jethro, walk on." But a bit of sniffing and wiping and we were back to normal and Cae White grew before us ruined and turreted, blazing in the sun, with Mari, my sister-in-law, waiting in the doorway with Jonathon, her baby, asleep in her shawl.

O, this Mari!


# CHAPTER 3

STRANGE THAT I knew Cae White was mine the moment I set foot in it; that I would shoulder the burden that Mari's grandfather had carried for life, and mate with it, and bring it to flower. Beautiful was this old Welsh gentry place gone to ruin, standing in its thirty acres with pride of nobility, shunning lesser neighbours. No time for it, said Morfydd – too damned proud – and how the hell Grandfer got hold of it I will never understand. Cheap, mind, at a pound a week rent, land included. Fishy. For places half the size Squire Lloyd Parry was charging double and he was not a man to lose sight of a pound. Most of the villagers worked for Squire, but not Grandfer, and Cae White was stuck in the middle of Squire's acres as a ship in full sail. Left and right the little farmers were being pushed out by rising rents and the gentry were forcing out their land enclosures faster than a wizard mouths spells, but nobody shifted Grandfer who had the power of the Devil in him, some said. Others said that Squire was pixilated and had never set eyes on Cae White though he passed it most days of the week. And I had seen him and Grandfer walk within feet and neither offer the other a glance while grown men were tugging out forelocks and their wives draping the ground. Indecent, said Morfydd, there are secrets at Cae White.

Things were happening in Carmarthenshire just now. The gentry were forming Trusts for road repairs and setting up toll-gates to pay for the labour, but drawing fat profits for the money invested by charging the earth for tolls. Left and right the gates were going up now, placed to trap the small farmers. Graft, too, as usual, for some gentlemen's carriages passed the tollgates free and bridges were being built to serve the needs of big houses. Men were flocking away from the land, queueing for the workhouses, and at the beginning of spring whole families were starving. And I was starving for Tessa Lloyd Parry.

"You keep from that one," said Morfydd. "Hobnails mating with lace."

"Leave him be," said Mam, sewing up to the light, squint-ing.

"To make a fool of the lot of us? Listen, you!" And Morfydd peered at me. "Gentry are running this county same as back home. You heard of Regan Killarney?"

"South of Ireland," I said to shift her.

"Transportation for twenty salmon – dished out by a clergy-man magistrate yesterday – getting his protection for the water he owned. While men like Killarney stink in the hulks for Botany Bay you'd best keep away from gentry Welsh lest the working Welsh call you traitor. You listening?"

"Half the county's listening," said Mam, stitching, sighing.

"Too damned young to be courting, anyway," said Morfydd, pale.

"Too damned old, you," I said, ducking her swipe.

Wandering about now, hands pressed together. Gunpowder, this one, dangerous to a flame. "The Devil take me," said she. "When I was his age I was spinning six days a week and hymning in Sunday School the seventh. . . ."

"O, aye?" said Mam, pins in her mouth.

23

"And here he is cooing and sweeting on gentry lawns with the people who starve us!" Dead and buried, me, with her looks.

"Not much starved you look from here, mind," said Mam.

"Not yet," said Morfydd. "But give them time. A tollgate went up on Flannigan's road last week and another's going up on the road to Kidwelly. Wait till lime-carting time – cost more for the tolls than the lime."

"Eh, agitators," said Mam. "God save me."

"And it is long past time somebody agitated. For where does the money go? On road repairs? Aye, on road repairs after it has paid a nice fat profit – on the backs of gentry or buying new plate for Church." She jerked her thumb at me. "And here is a worker playing silk purses and sows' ears and snobbing with people who are bleeding the county."

"Please do not refer to Jethro as sows' ears or I will be having a hand in it," said Mam.

"Trouble is coming," whispered Morfydd, tightlipped.

"If it doesn't you'll soon fetch some," I whispered, but Mam did not hear. She lowered the new backside she was putting on to Richard.

"Too old I am for fighting, Morfydd, too tired to get hot. Been flogged enough, I reckon. I have a man in a grave and a son in transportation. The gentry have the whip and they use it. Leave it, there's a good girl."

"This county is a bitch to nothing," said Morfydd, rising again. "My brother gets seven years transportation for a rebellion against Queen and State but Killarney is joining him for poaching."

"Hush you when Grandfer gets in, mind," said Mam. "And the rivers are owned by the gentry."

"The rivers are owned by God," shouted Morfydd, swinging to her. "And by God we will have our share. Salmon are so thick at the Reach that Lloyd Parry can't cast a fly in season, and the children of Killarney will grow legs like beansticks."

"Do not remind me," whispered Mam.

"O, Morfydd, shut it," I said.

"Shut it, eh?" She leaned, peering. "You ever seen a child die of hunger?"

"Saw them back home," said Mam. "No need to travel for that."

"With their bellies as balloons and the bread whooping up as fast as you push it down?" Morfydd straightened, and I saw tears in her eyes. "God, I have seen them – six died the week I came here and another three at Whitland a week after that – on the poor rate, mind – two shillings a week, with reverend fathers rooting round the sty for the last little chicken and hauling down the last scratch of bacon to pay Church tithes." Colder now, her voice breaking. "God, I would give them God if I were God Almighty. Too much jolting on the knees has driven the Church loopy, the ministers in the pay of the gentry and the gentry in the prayers of the ministers – walking into the City of Judah seven days a week while helpless children starve. Eh!" Deep she sighed. "The trouble with hassock-bumpers is that they forget the poor and needy, but God's people will remember them. Wait and see."

"Talking about chickens and bacon you'd better get the potato soup back on," said my mother. "Grandfer and Mari will be in directly."

"God forgive you, Mam," said Morfydd, eyes closed.

"God grant me peace," said my mother. "I cannot feed the county, I can only cast it from my mind." Rising, she kissed my sister. "O," she said, "afire was my womb when it brought forth you. Please God you find peace, like me."

And the door came open and Mari came in.

"There is a miserable set of old faces," she cried, smiling. "Tollgates again, is it?" And she danced in with her basket.

"It is Jethro courting little Tessa and Morfydd handing hell to hassock-bumpers in the name of the poor and needy," said Mam. "Come you in, girl – got anything decent?"

And she looked at me and smiled, did Mari, bringing low my eyes.

This was my sister-in-law, wife to Iestyn my brother in seven years transportation. Months he had been gone now, leaving her with Jonathon, her son. To this day I cannot explain the sweetness her presence brought me. Church of England, was Mari, from hooded bishops to gilded altars, and Christian. She blunted the edge of Morfydd's fire, forgiving trespasses in her every word and glance. Four years the younger, I had once shared her kisses, till I grew a head the taller and too high for her lips. Now she winked.

"At last we know why the boy's off his food." Eyes dancing, with her baby cradled against her now, and Mam reached up, taking him on her knee.

"No laughing matter, Mari," said Morfydd at the window.

"O, come," said Mari, hooking the door shut. "Do a little boy's courting put the house untidy when there's three grown women by here and not a man in sight save Grandfer?"

"Daughter of a squire," said Morfydd, gentle. In love with Mari, like me.

"And crumbs on her mouth from her tea. O, girl, they are children!"

"And not so much of the children," said Morfydd. "Nigh twelve stone is that thing and hair on its chest. Before we know it we'll be washing gentry napkins and I'm full to the stomach with gentry."

"And my stomach is empty and howling for supper," said Mari. "Where's my Grandfer?"

"Black Boar tavern, as usual," said Morfydd. "Drowning his sorrows – the house is plagued with drunkards and lovers."

"Morfydd!" said Mam sharp, but Mari only smiled.

"Strange he should drink at a time like this," said she.

"He drinks because of a time like this," answered Morfydd. "The man has lived alone for over half a century and we hit him up with six women and kids," and she turned from the window as a shadow went by it. "God, here it comes."

Loaded was Grandfer, with only his staff to keep him upright; as a leathery little goat complete with beard and his little pot of a waistcoat tearing at its seams above his bandy, gaitered legs. Bald as an egg, toothless, he had been good in his time, said Waldo Bailiff, but cooled after sixty, and the more virgins he had around him now the holier he felt, something we were short of at Cae White.

"Grandfer!" cried Mari, ducking his stick.

Belching, drooling, the senility blundered in, taking breath to keep its quarts down, glazed in the eye, dragging its feet. Hobnails clattering it leaned on the table, wagging its head in grief.

"Knowest thou the biblical? Ah, me!" said he. "Woe is Grandfer! The house is filled to the brim with suckling children and female Nonconformists." He belched deep, begging our pardons. "Knowest thou the murmurings of the Israelites through the speeches of Moses? 'Have I conceived all these people – have I begotten them that thou should sayest unto me, carry them in thy bosom as a nursing father beareth a suckling child?' Eh, dear me! 'I am not able to bear all these people alone because it is too heavy for me. Kill me, I pray you, out of hand, let me not see my wretchedness.' "

"Amen," said Morfydd.

"A fine one to talk of the biblical!" said Mari, shocked. "He is not himself today, forgive him."

"Old and feeble, he is," whispered Mam. "Do not take it hard, girl. A smell of the Black Boar pints and he is standing on his head."

"Not true," I said. "He can sink twenty without breathing."

"You will speak when you are spoken to," said Mam, eyes wide and flashing.

"Leave Grandfer to me," said Morfydd, taking his arm. "I can handle grandfers."

"Twenty years back you wouldn't," said he, leering into her smile. "Look upon her now, this vision of beauty!" Swinging wide, he fell into Morfydd's arms. "The only woman among you with the spunk of a man. Rebecca and Chartist, a fighter for the rights of men – Venus reborn! Clear the house of infidels and varmints, especially God-forsaken poachers – may they soil themselves in their pits of iniquity, but save me Morfydd. Still got an eye for a pretty woman, mind, and I like them rebellious."

"Take him up to bed," said Mari in disgust.

"Will you take me up to bed, Morfydd Mortymer?" Evil was his eye.

"As far as the landing," said she. "You are not as old as I thought. Come, Grandfer."

Bride and groom left for the bedchamber.

"O, he is disgraceful," whispered Mari, red and ashamed.

"When the ale is in the wits are out," said Mam, soothing. "But I know the truth of it, we should not be here. Too much to ask," and she followed Morfydd to see fair play, leaving me and Mari alone.

Tragic is the one who is meat in the sandwich. Oblivious of me she paced the room, her teeth on her lips, holding back tears. But more tragic still is the one to whom love flies and the longing to give comfort, but words are useless things between boy and married woman. I sat and longed and found no words. At the window now she picked up her baby Jonathon, hugging him against her.

"I am sorry, Mari," I said.

A brush at her eyes, a flash of a smile.

"With his tongue submerged he can still use it," she said. "O, God, if only my Iestyn were here."

"He will come back," I said.

As stabbed she stopped pacing and swung to me. "O, do not take on so, Jethro!" Fingers at her wedding ring now, twisting. She did this when the talk was of Iestyn. "I see him in your face, your smile. Jethro!" She wept, turning.

Up like lightning and she was in my arms. No ring, no Iestyn. Back even quicker to Morfydd's clatter on the stairs. Strange the guilt.

"Now, that is over," said Morfydd, coming in. "A cup of decent tea, for God's sake. Fought like a demon when I put him in his nightshirt – like the rest of the men, he is – all promises. Supper, is it?" She kissed Mari in passing.

Nothing like a table for taking away gloom. And I think a house is happy with its table dressed in its white, starched apron and its spoons tinkling as people go past. Come from a gentry house, Grandfer's table, serving rye bread and buttermilk now, but dreaming its past of silver plate and feasts; of crinoline gowns and fingers touching secretly in its curtained darkness. And pretty was the kitchen at Cae White with its great Welsh dresser standing in polished dignity on the flag-stones, heavy with its scores of jugs and their sighs of a thousand cows. My women were beggars for the polishing, like most – flicking the dust from one corner to another, burnishing the brass trinkets for shaving in. The low ships' timbers bore down upon us, the sea murmuring in their splits; faded wall-paper where the bed-warming pan flashed copper light; a painting called *Lost* was above the mantel, where a man of icicles groped in a blizzard. *God Bless Our Home* hung in laurel leaves next to the portrait of Victoria whom Morfydd had managed to crack. But best of all was that table made for a company of Guards. Grandfer, now absent, always sat at the top with Mari on his right and Mam and Morfydd on his left, with Richard aged three beside me and Jonathon in Mari's lap. And at the end sat the ghosts – four empty places that my mother always laid – for my father and sister who had died up in Monmouthshire; Richard, Morfydd's man who was shot by redcoats, and Iestyn my brother who was in Botany Bay. Only Morfydd railed at this palaver – let the dead lie in peace, she said, but Mam still laid the places. Strange are women who treasure the dust of memories, eating at table with dead men, sleeping with them in the beds. Strange was Cae White with its three longing women, their make-believe love-making, their intercourse of ghosts. And upstairs was Grandfer, hop-soaked to drown other memories, it seemed, puggled with his past.

Me of the lot of them the only one normal.


## CHAPTER 4

VERY STITCHED up are the Welsh when it comes to neigh-bours, till they know you. Most prim was everyone, bowing very formal when we went out for Chapel or market, and, being strangers, we were doing our best to make a good impression, though we were at a disadvantage with my sister Morfydd in the house. For it was not only rebellion that stirred in Morfydd's breast, said Mam; at thirty she is old enough to know better. Most fanciful for the men, was Morfydd, with the lips and eyes that drove the chaps demented. I know that the loss of her man was unstitched within her but she still had an eye for trews. And it soon got round the village about the beautiful women at Cae White, one prim, the other improper. Very alike were Mari and Morfydd – could be taken for sisters being both dark and curled, lithe in the step and with dignity. Long-waisted, high-breasted, they swirled around Cae White, and the men were hanging on the gate like string beans for a sight of them, which shocked my mam, put Mari dull, and painted up Morfydd's cheeks with expectation.

"Willie O'Hara again," said she, lifting the curtain. "Must be keen, see, in four degrees of frost."

"Shameful," said Mam. "Down with that curtain this minute."

"And Elias the Shop all the way from Kidwelly. There's a compliment. Did you invite him, Mam?"

"No fool like an old fool," Mam replied. "If my Hywel was alive he'd soon clear them."

"O, look now!" cried Morfydd. "Old Uncle Silas from the Burrows – coming very jaunty, too – life in the old dog yet."

"Let's have a look, girl," I said, getting up.

"Back you," cried Mam. "Objectionable, it is."

Pretty wrinkled was Uncle Silas; buried two wives and looking for a third, said Grandfer, and his eye was on Morfydd, strange enough. Every Sunday regular after Chapel he was pacing the end of our shippon with his starched collar round his ears and his bunch of winter flowers. Queer are old men looking for wives, for ten minutes with Morfydd my sister and anything under five-foot-ten went out boots first, I had heard. But Willie O'Hara, now here was a difference. Topped six feet, did Willie, big in the shoulders and sinewy, with mop-gold hair on him, strange for Welsh Irish. Come down from the industries, it was said, but not long enough in iron to be branded. And he leaned on the gate now, broad back turned, settling for a fortnight's wait by the look of him.

Lucky for me having my woman inside.

The old log fire flamed red and cosy in the kitchen that night near Christmas. Sitting crosslegged before it I would watch Mari's hands; long, tapering fingers white against the black braid of her dress, with her needle flashing through my dreams.

"There now, that's you," and she flung me the socks.

They landed in my lap but I did not really notice, for her eyes were staring past me into the fire and she took a breath and sighed, telling of her longing for my brother.

"Irish potatoes, is it?" said she. "I know some good round Welsh ones. Easy on the socks, Jethro, you will wear me out." She smiled at the window where Morfydd was standing. "Still at it, are they? Do not blame me, Mam, I do not give them the eye."

"No need to tell me who does that," said Mam, treadling at the wheel. "Damned criminal, it is, when you have no intentions, and Dai Alltwen Preacher swimming the river Jordan every night down in the Horeb. God help you, Morfydd, if Dai finds out."

"Can't let Willie starve," said Morfydd, lifting her bonnet. "Solid ice he will be in another ten minutes. I will not be late, Mam."

"At this time of night? Morfydd, it is indecent!"

"Now what is indecent in a bit of a walk?"

"Nothing," said Mam. It was the way she looked.

"I am thirty years old," said Morfydd, eyes lighting up. "Do I have to account to you for every minute?"

"Every second while you live here," replied Mam, sleeves going up.

"At thirty I am past those damned silly capers!"

"Count yourself lucky," said Mam. "When I was thirty I wasn't."

"Don't do as I do but do as I say, is it?"

"Morfydd, hush!" whispered Mari.

"Do not be rude to our mam," I said.

"Quiet, you, or I'll clip that damned ear," said Morfydd, swinging to me.

"And I will clip the other one," said Mam. "But a boy, you are, and you will keep from this conversation. You will be back at eight o'clock, Morfydd, understand? Nine o'clock otherwise, but I do not stand for rudeness."

"Yes, Mother."

"And you keep walking with that Willie O'Hara, understand?"

"O, Mam," said Mari. "She would not breathe on Willie O'Hara."

Under judgement stands Morfydd and I gave her a wink.

"You may kiss me," said my mother, taking the wish for granted.

Kisses all round except for me, and off Morfydd went under her black poke bonnet. I waited till she had gone then stretched and sighed.

"And where are you off to, pray?" asked Mam.

"Not in front of Mari, please," I said.

"I am sorry," said my mother. "But do not bait your sister, remember."

Cold round the back with the stars all Venuses and the Milky Way dripping with cream in the frost. I whistled, and Morfydd paused, a black witch against the stars, and came back.

"And what do you want, little pig?"

"Back home at eight, remember," I said. "Eh, there's delightful, and Mam don't know. Do not make a meal of it – tin drawers it is with Willie O'Hara, so watch it or he'll have you."

"One word from you . . ." she whispered, her finger going over her throat.

"Get on, get on," I said. "He'll be no good to you freezing."

She laughed then, head back, and ran to the gate. I stood there as she took Willie's hand and he swung her down the road to Ferry.

The wildness of her made me afraid, but I would not have changed her for any woman in Carmarthen, save perhaps one.

Never in my life will I forget that first Christmas at Cae White; the service at Chapel with Dai Alltwen roasting the Devil up in the front pews, then back home, Grandfer leading, for he always reckoned on Chapel for Christmas Day. Back home now and I hit out a poor little chicken from the henhouse and plucked him and handed him to Mari who was cook at Cae White, and the smell of him was all over the house, with Jonathon crowing and Richard toddling around the kitchen for peeps at him on the spit. Blistering and browning he turns above the fire and the fat drips and flares. Up at Squire's Reach they had a little dog to do it, says Morfydd; climbing the circle of the stepped wheel, panting in the heat, tongue hanging out, coat singed, shrinking to a prune for the lusts of humans. Wonder what the baby Jesus would say if he saw that little dog, I wondered, for I was sweating for two in the glow, with Mari dashing around with her spoons and pans, working herself to death for that Christmas dinner, our first meat since we came to Carmarthenshire. Boiled potatoes and cabbage and gallons of gravy, and she always made pints because she knew I loved it. If a woman can make gravy it is enough to ask of a wife, I think, and anything she has after that is only grist to the mill. The seven of us at table now, Grandfer going at the chicken and tongues wagging and the boys banging spoons, with Mari scooping up the vegetables and handing down the plates, me last, though she fixed me with a leg while nobody was looking. Into it now, smiles all round, and isn't it delicious and thank God for Grandfer who was enjoying himself for once. And there is nothing like a plate when a dinner is finished, I think, and you get the bread in a putty and wipe it round, making the old thing shine. Polished is a plate by the time I have finished with it, saving the washing-up if I had my way, but doing it under the eagle eye for I always sat next to Morfydd.

"O, look, Mam," said she. "Tell him to behave."

"Leave him be," said Mari. "He is enjoying it."

"I will not have beastly eating," said Mam, her fork up. "There's plenty of room for that in sties. Jethro!"

Another bit of bread, with your eye on Morfydd's gravy, she being finished and glaring. Couldn't get enough those days – eat her, too, if she slipped on the plate.

"O, God," says she, disgusted.

"Stop it this minute!" shouted Mam, hitting the table and bouncing forks.

"You have raised it, woman," said Grandfer. "It is you who should stop it."

Eyes cast down at this.

"More?" whispers Mari from the top of the table.

"There now, you can start again," says Mam. "And knife and fork like the rest of us, no need for piglets."

So I gave the thing to Morfydd to pass up.

"I am off," says she. "I can get this in barnyards, no point in coming to table."

"You stay till the rest of us are finished, Morfydd!"

Grandfer at the top, whiskers drooping, getting well into it, and everyone else pretty busy, so I gave Morfydd one with the hobnails as she passed the plate down with looks to kill at me.

"Eh, you bloody little devil!"

"*Morfydd!*" Mam now, pale and shocked, glancing at Grandfer who didn't bat an eyelid.

Everything in the county from bishops to lay preachers, cassocks flying, up and rushing.

"I beg your pardon," said Mam.

"Mam, he booted me."

"Never touched her," I said. "Hell and Damnation she will have for that, mind, straight to Hell's sulphur."

"And hush you, too!" Mam shouting now, flushed and ashamed, for a bloody or two could be mortal sin on a Sunday, never mind Christmas Day. I gave Morfydd a glance in the pinging silence, for even Grandfer had raised his head now. In disgrace, poor soul. Head low she sat, face pale, sending me threats from the corners of her eyes.

"And where did you learn such language, pray?" asked Mam, solid ice. "Not in this house, I vow. Thirty years old, is it? Old enough to give an example, especially to the children. You will keep a clean mouth, do you understand?"

"Bloody, bloody, bloody," cried Richard, hitting his plate.

"Do you hear that?" asked Mam, and Mari clouted Richard and he opened his mouth and howled.

34

"Go to your room this minute," said Mam. "Christmas dinner or not I will make an example of you."

No reply from Morfydd and I was into the gravy again.

"Do you hear me! Stop eating this minute, Jethro – leave the table!"

"Me?" I asked.

"Away this minute, and do not come down till I tell you."

"She did the swearing, mind."

"And you the booting to make her swear. Up this instant or I will take a stick to you, big as you are."

"Go quick, Jethro," whispered Mari, agitated.

Left the plate with half an inch of gravy, and Morfydd jerking her thumb at me under cover of the tablecloth. Could have killed her. One word from me about her and Willie O'Hara and Mam would have roped her for razors. I got up and went to the door.

"Now you," said Mam, and Morfydd rose, which sent me a bit faster for the lock on my bedroom door. Twelve months back she got into me and I wasn't having it again, for she swung and hooked like a man and I couldn't hit back because of the chest.

"I apologize for my children," said Mam sorrowful as I climbed the stairs with Morfydd following. "God knows I have done my best to bring them up decent. A grown woman, but she acts like a child, and the other. *Well* . . ."

Into the bedroom now, swing the key, and the handle goes round as Morfydd tries it. Nothing but the black of her dress the other side of the keyhole.

Silence, then:

"Jethro," she croons.

"Aye, girl?"

"I will have you, mind. If I wait six months I will have you for that."

But I know she will not because of Willie O'Hara.

# CHAPTER 5

CHRISTMAS NIGHT!

The family circle now, all trespasses forgiven, sitting round the fire with the lamp turned low, the windows rimed with frost and the snow falling vertically as big as rose petals against the white dresses of the mountain. All was silent save for Mari's voice as she shivered us to the marrow with ghost stories from way back in history, then a bit of a prayer for the Christmas dinner and a Reading from Grandfer, all very holy. Must have been nine o'clock, for Richard and Jonathon were abed, I remember, and I was thinking of Tessa and spring when the tap on the door brought us all upright.

"For Heaven's sake," said Mam. "This time of night?"

And then it began!

*Sanctus.* Full harmony from the back. In glorious song came the old Welsh hymn flung by soaring sopranos, blasted by bass, with the tenors doing a descant over the top, and the sudden glory of the sound froze us into wonder and we got to our feet as with cramp and stared at the back door.

> 'Round the Lord in glory seated, Cherubim and Seraphim
> Filled His temple, and repeated each to each the alternate hymn . . . !
> Lord, Thy glory fills the heaven, earth is with its fullness stored;
> Unto Thee be glory given, Holy, Holy, Holy Lord!'

And my mother cried out in joy and flung open the door to the great choir of neighbours and we formed up before them and joined in the hymn that breathes of my country. Last verse now, with my mother's rich contralto in my ears, Grandfer's squeaky tenor and Mari and Morfydd going like angels. O, good it was to be accepted by neighbours at last with this, their seal of friendship. Biddy Flannigan front rank with her son Abel a foot above her; Tom the Faith grunting and growling

36

and Dilly Morgan and Hettie Winetree holding hands and singing to the stars. Pleased to see Dilly there for she was heading for a haystack midsummer though she didn't know it. Osian Hughes and his mam back row; Toby Benyon and missus, Dai Alltwen Preacher, Adam Funeral, gaunt and black, come for measuring up; Willie O'Hara, his eye on Morfydd; Justin Slaughterer with his eye on Mari, and I hated him. Thick and strong and handsome, this one – cutting throats spare time to labouring and enjoying every minute, and he'd had his peeps on Mari from the second we'd come to Cae White. Cut a throat or two myself if this continued: waylaying her from Chapel and happy I am to know you, girl – Mari first name, isn't it? Justin be mine. Permission to call would be very tidy, Mari Mortymer, me being friends with Grandfer. Thank God she sent him about his business, her a decent married woman. He could even sing well, the swine, booming bass, and I closed my hand as he winked at her now. Last chord to strip the whitewash, and the crowd suddenly parted, cowering back in mock horror, for the terrifying *Mari Lwyd* was shoving a path through them. Now it stood on the threshold, its lower jaw champing, glass eyes flashing. This, the horrifying *Mari Lwyd* – a man clad in a white bedsheet wearing the skeleton of a horse's head where his own head should be.

"God save us," whispered Mam.

Glass eyeballs on this one, its skeleton head covered with gay rosettes, and its coloured rein streamers were flying in the wind. Jawbone champing like the bell of doom, it surveyed us, gaze sweeping right and left – fixing on Morfydd now, bringing her hands to her face. Then, in a shrill falsetto, the horse began to sing, though I knew it was Waldo Bailiff by the size of its boots. Enough to frighten decent folk to death.

"O, *Mari Lwyd* so jolly has come all the way from Kidwelly," sang he. "So will you invite us to sing, good people. And if we are not welcome then please let us know with your singing," and he flung up his skeleton head and neighed like a soul in torment. "O, please let us know with some singing."

Dead silence.

"For God's sake give it a penny and shift it," whispered

Morfydd, but Grandfer, grinning, faced the apparition, flung his arms wide to it and replied in his squeaky tenor:

"O, *Mari Lwyd* so jolly, come all the way from Kidwelly to visit friendly neighbours. If you are friendly too, then welcome to this house."

"Friends and neighbours indeed!" bawled the *Mari Lwyd*, tossing and neighing. "And we beg entry, mam – is it in or out?"

And Grandfer bowed low and touched Mam's arm, leaving it to her. Would have died scalded for Grandfer at that moment.

"Open to friends and neighbours!" cried Mam, going damp, and she flung her arms wide. "Come in, people, do not starve to death in the cold!"

A hell of a thing it is to be accepted, mind.

And in they came, the *Mari Lwyd* leading, snapping and snarling left and right at the men and bowing to the women. Waldo Bailiff in his element, holding the stage, and Mari and Morfydd were dashing round shouting for cups and plates and digging out the larder for the Christmas cake which was damned near finished. But they need not have worried for the neighbours brought things with them, specially cooked for the surprise, they said, and soon the table was groaning.

"Greetings to the Mortymers!" cried Waldo through bared teeth. "Welcome to the county, I say – the prettiest women in Wales, not counting fat little Biddy Flannigan by here!"

"O, go on with you, Waldo," said Biddy, all creases and blushes. "There's terrible he is, now, and in front of strangers."

"Strangers no more!" roared Abel her brawny son. "For I have a little barrel of good stuff from Betsi Ramrod's place but I am needing a woman to roll it in, doing the custom. Any volunteers?"

"I will go," said Morfydd, rolling her sleeves, and the look she gave Abel Flannigan sent up my blood, never mind his.

"A kiss from the beer-roller, remember," called Mari. "Mind what you are taking on, Morfydd!"

"Dark out there!" I cried, while everyone roared.

"Darker the better," shouted Morfydd. "Bring him back in one piece, is it?"

"Morfydd, behave!" called Mam, looking worried. Cheers and shrieks as Morfydd rolled the little barrel in and Abel came staggering after her on rubber legs, and I saw Osian Hughes Bayleaves send Abel a filthy look from his corner where he sat with his mam. Ring-dancing now, singing and laughing, back-slapping and a bit of spare kissing going on, with the young men rushing round with jugs of the foaming ale and Mari dashed past me for the boys who were bellowing upstairs. Caught the eye of Dilly Morgan through the surge of the crowd.

"*Phist!*" I said.

Ambitions for this one, me, for Tessa was up at Squire's Reach and every woman has a separate appeal.

"Me?" she mouthed back, eyebrows up, thumbing herself.

I jerked my head and went through the door of the back and I heard the rustle of her behind me.

"What you want, Jethro Mortymer?" Knew damned well what I wanted.

"Plenty of old kissing going on, Dilly Morgan," I said. "You fancy kissing me?"

"And me fourteen? Eh, there's indecent!"

"Got to start some time," I said. "Look up by there, girl – you seen Venus?" and I got my arm around her waist.

"Don't you start tricks, now. I have heard about you, Jethro Mortymer. Sixpenny Jane down at Betsi's place do say you're a grown man the way you're behaving. Loose me this moment."

But I had her, though she was thrusting, and her lips were as wine in the frosted air. Pushed me off and caught me square, the bitch. "Tell my mam, I will," said she, and up with her skirts and away through the door.

Not much doing when you are fourteen, but I waited a bit for I knew Hettie would come. Beggars are women when they think they are missing something. Pretty she looked, though, in the light from the door, skirt held up between fingers and thumbs, and she bowed with a nod.

"Happy Christmas," said she. "Didn't expect to find you

out here, Jethro Mortymer," and she nearly fainted for the shame of it.

"Same to you," I said. "You come for kissing?"

"Just passing," said she. "Looking for Dilly."

No slaps from this one. Soft were her lips, unprotesting; been at it all her life on this performance. Got a future, Hettie, but I'd much rather had Dilly. Just getting her set up again and the door came open and Morfydd peered.

"What is happening out there?" she asked.

"Looking at Venus," I said.

"O, aye? You can see it through glass, then. Want your head read sharing darkness with that thing of a brother, Hettie Winetree. In, in!" And she whirled behind us and brushed us in with her skirts. Probably for the good for I was coming a little hot with me, and I saw a few guests give us the eye as we came into the light. Betsi Ramrod followed us in, five-feet-ten of ramrod mourning, and Gipsy May her assistant from Black Boar tavern followed her rolling a barrel, and I heard Dai Alltwen Preacher give them a sigh, for their tavern had a name in the county. Waldo up on a barrel now, hoofs beating time to a roar of singing, and then, quite suddenly, the bedlam died. People were turning towards the door, and Mari shrieked in joy.

Black-frocked, enormous, he stood in the doorway, hands clasped on his stomach, beaming down. As a sentinel of Fate Tomos Traherne stood there, smiling around the room; full twenty stone of him, spade beard snowflecked, his broad felt hat under his arm. And my mother turned from the table and saw him.

"Tomos!" And she ran straight into his arms.

There's awkward.

Half a dozen possible suitors in here already and in comes a stranger and she greets him like a lover; a fine one for examples, said Morfydd after.

But it was better than that, though the locals did not know it.

Everyone going formal now, backing to the wall, trying to look uninterested – very interested in boots, nudging their neighbours, and when Mam's handkerchief came out the women started whispering. Didn't blame them. Couldn't expect them to understand.

For this was our Tomos from back home in Monmouthshire; the giant of the Faith; fearful to the iniquitous, the persecutor of harlots, but a broth of a man when it came to the hungry. Fat, ungainly, his belly belt was worn bright on the backsides of children late for Sunday School, and he could hit wickedness from South Wales to North in a single swipe. Friend of my dead father, this; the protector of my mother in the agony of her grief. Mari at him now, hanging on to the other arm. A foot the taller, he stood quite still, then turned to face the room. A bit of sniffing from my mother, and then she spoke.

"Dai Alltwen and friends," said she, taking local preacher first. "This is our friend, my husband's beloved friend, come down from Monmouthshire Top Towns to visit us. I ask all here to give him a welcome."

This didn't do Dai Alltwen much good but he bowed proper and the man-mountain bowed back, catching my eye and winking as he came upright.

"Any news of Iestyn, Tomos?" asked Mari, and I saw the pain fly into her face as he pressed her hand for answer. Round he went in the circle now, bowing to the women, breaking the hands of the men, until he came to Morfydd. With her illegitimate son held against her she faced him and her voice was cold and clear.

"Good evening, Mr Traherne."

History here. Cast out from Chapel by Tomos when she brought forth Richard.

But not as easy as that, for Tomos bent and kissed her face, and then her son, and took him from her arms and carried him round the circle, and Morfydd lowered her arms, her eyes cast down. But nobody really noticed Morfydd for all eyes were on the gigantic minister. The introductions completed he raised his hand and roars and cheers as it hit the ceiling, and his voice as thunder boomed around the room.

"Good people, God's people," said he, double bass. "You of this county are as the Welsh of my county – faithful in labour, generous to neighbours – true Welsh, I see, by all the saints!

41

As a Welshman I greet you and bring you God's blessing. As the adopted father of this beloved family I give you thanks from the bottom of my heart that you should show them such kindness. And here I vow . . . !" and he raised his fist, "that whatever trust you put in them they will not be found wanting. Look the world over and you will find no better neighbours with whom to share this Christmas. And may the good Lord, Whose eternal Spirit guides the hearts and minds of decent men and women, cover you with the mantle of His blessing, and keep you pure and free from harm. Amen."

And we stood in respectful silence, conscious of his greatness, trembling to his *hwyl*. Vibrant, fervent, his voice rolled on:

"And listen! Do not mistake the kiss of this lady, for she has kissed me often when her man was alive, and he never raised an eye! Shall I tell you of this family, of its father who stood for the things that are good and clean in life ? Shall I tell you of the son who languishes in far off Van Diemen's Land because he fought, prepared to die, for the things that are decent – against the tyranny of foreign masters in a revolt against the State ? Let there be no sin in opposing evil wherever it is found. And Richard Bennet, Morfydd's man, do you know that he died in this fight and left her alone to raise her son ? I can see that you do not know these things, for the Mortymers were never ones for speeches, so I tell you now with pride. Let there be no secrets between such neighbours as you. Let it be known that the Mortymers, too, have their place among you, that they have earned the respect you pay them, with their lives."

Clapping and cheers at this, and I must admit I felt a thrill of pride that brought the water stinging to my eyes as I thought of my father and Iestyn, my brother. My women were standing rigid, their heads low, and my mother was weeping, her face wet, with no attempt to wipe the tears. I looked hard at Mari. White faced, she stood by Tomos, and I pitied her. For I had heard in her first shriek of joy at the sight of him that she was hoping for news of my brother. Nothing for her save confirmation of Botany Bay, with visions of the chained labourers and the blood-soaked ground of the triangles. But Tomos was speaking on:

"And as I laboured along the road from Carmarthen town I rested by the wayside to catch my breath. There, in the frost, I listened to *Sanctus* – to the sound of your voices, and beautiful it was to the weary traveller who has walked nigh eighty miles. The sound of your hymn ennobled me, and I knelt in the snow and gave prayers for you, receiving in turn renewed strength for the journey." His voice rose higher. "And so now, before I take leave of you to find rest – last verse of *Sanctus* again. Lift the roof with it – ring it out to Monmouthshire. Full chorus now, full harmony, to the beautiful words of your Richard Mant. Ready, ready . . . ?" And his arm swept up and down, and we sang. God, how we sang! Deafening to the ears, this time, rising to such beauty and power that it caught at my soul and snatched it upwards in the last, glorious line.

"Holy, Holy, Holy Lord!"

And in the ringing silence Tomos caught my eye again.

"Jethro!"

"Tomos!"

I ran into his arms.


# CHAPTER 6

BITTER OLD winter, this first one at Cae White, with the coots slipping on their backsides well into March and the hedges iced like gentry wedding cakes. The trees rattled as moody skeletons in the salt-tang of the estuary and the peat bogs rammed themselves into glass. No longer the otters barked along the banks of the Tywi, with the curlews too nipped to shout at dawn. Gaunt and forbidding was the country still, biting at fingers, twisting at noses, and the whole rolling country of mountains and pastures from Llandeilo to Haverfordwest was hammered into frost by the thumps of winter.

Out at first light, me, back with the curtains. I dressed quickly with mist billowing against the window, trying to get down before Morfydd for once. Snatching my towel I went on the landing and Mari stood there, her eyes dazed through the loss of another night.

"You all right, girl?"

She nodded, smiling faintly.

"Heard you last night, tossing and turning," I said.

"Too tired for sleep," she said. "It will pass."

"Do not come down," I said. "Morfydd and me will get ourselves off."

Morfydd at the bottom of the stairs then, peering up. "Mari," she whispered. "Go back to bed – do you think we need nursing?"

"But you must have some breakfast," she replied.

"God alive, woman, can't we get that ourselves? Back and try to sleep, there's a good girl. Mam says she will have Jonathon and Richard."

Haggard in the eyes, Mari turned without a word.

Slower now, thoughtful, I went down to the kitchen. Morfydd was already boiling the oatmeal broth. Nearly retched. Sick of the name of it, the smell of it, stomach-heaving at the taste of it, for things were coming shrimpy with us now our savings were gone. And though Grandfer gave us house room he couldn't be expected to feed us, though most of what Cae White brought in was put against the walls of the taverns. Rye bread, oatmeal broth, potato soup, a bit of fried bread, no meat, a cabbage or two and buttermilk when we could get it. Reckon I could have eaten a mattress of fat bacon. In the Monmouthshire iron they laboured us to death, but at least we fed except in strike times. I joined Morfydd at the hob in the kitchen.

"That girl's going under," said she.

Haggard in the eyes and sleepless, was Mari, since Tomos Traherne had visited three months back. Pleased enough to see him, true, but God knows what he had brought with him that Christmas, for Mari was a different girl since. No tears, no sadness one could see; just sleepless and wandering as if dazed.

"Happy enough until Tomos came," I said. "You noticed?"

She shook her head. "I wondered that, but I doubt it. Only just occurred to her, I think, that she'll wait years for Iestyn.

44

You be gentle to her, Jethro, you could not have a better relation, and she needs a boy like you – you being his brother."

"Now what have I done wrong now, for God's sake?"

This turned her, spoon up. "Nothing, or you'd never hear the end of it. Just be gentle, that's all. Poor little Mari."

Nothing angered me more than this sister-in-law stuff that Morfydd was always turning out. Indecent to have a relative nigh a head shorter but only four years older than you. Facing Morfydd I got the bread down somehow and spooned up the dirty old oatmeal.

"We will try Ponty," said she.

I just sighed.

"Well, don't look so ghostly – something's got to be done. We will work the only way we know – in coal."

"It is spring, damned near. I could try my hand at farming, for the place is going to the dogs under Grandfer."

"Grandfer's privilege – his farm. Best stick to what you know." She sighed herself then. "Queer, isn't it – just as Mam says – we run from iron for a bit of peace and land in dirty old coal. *Diawch!*"

I had worked coal in Nanty, like Morfydd, the rest of my family being in iron, except Mari, who had taken her share of hauling trams one time. I hated coal – sixteen hour shifts six days a week, a shilling a day if the seam held out, nothing if it ceased. Black trash were colliers, these days. I had seen the battered heads of the Top Town colliers, the smashed hands of the hewing poor. Furnace work I do like if you can keep clear of the scald, but coal is a trap with no back door out. I cannot stand the galleries and the creak of the splintering prop. Drop the pick, go sideways, watch the slow lengthening of the wane of the pole. Upward it spreads to the pitch, widening: ten million tons of mountain moving, perched on the tip of a four inch prop, and you hold your breath in the seconds of eternity while the county yawns and stretches in sunlight. For you, the microbe, work in the belly, raking at entrails, tunnelling in bowels, and the mountain groans as a child with an ache and its guts rumble thunder. It howls then as the wind breaks and seeks relief by changing position, then bucks to a bright

45

explosion of pain, seeking the balm of its underground rivers. A hit in the stomach as its floor comes up; you squirm for protection as the roof comes down; grip, wait, ready for the crush. Dai Skewen caught it in Number Five, two others walled up.

"What is wrong with you, now?" asked Morfydd.

"Nothing, but I would like iron."

"Who wouldn't. Is this Ponty pit a winder?"

"Ladder. And the foreman Job Gower is blessed double with bastards, I heard say, but he is dying for labour."

"Hush your bad language," said she. "But I will give him, bastards if he proves a thumper. We go on Top Town rates mind." Rising, she swung off the kettle and screamed the teapot. "Skilled rates or nothing, or I will tell him what he does with his Ponty – ladders and all."

I sipped the tea, blowing steam. "We look like staying, then, for he don't like barristers."

"Skilled labour," said she. "Different." She chewed at the window.

"Skilled or unskilled, all the same rate. Sixpence a pound for a dead pig – shilling a week for a live serving-maid."

"There is a dainty expression – where did you learn it?"

"Tramping Boy Joey – he had it off his mam. Two-pounds-ten a year she drew as a scrubbing-girl, all in, keep included."

"O, aye," said she. "Everything counts."

"But happy enough was Cassie Scarlet, mind, while she was scrubbing."

"Pity," said Morfydd. "If the two-pounds-ten includes being bedded you might as well enjoy it."

Bitter, she was, and I chanced a look at her. Grey streaks at the temples now, the high bones of her face flinging shadow into her cheeks. Black-eyed, gipsy-slanted; and beautiful was her mouth so full and red when not twisted as now. Dress her in lace and she'd rock the county.

"Morfydd."

She didn't hear three feet away.

"Morfydd, listen," I said.

She sighed, eyes closed, her lashes spread wide on her cheeks.

"No lectures, Jethro."

"Just this, then," and I took her hand. "Treat Ponty respectful and bring home money, is it? Just for a little while. In a month or two I'll be into farming, then no more coal."

"Yes," she said.

She gripped my hand then and my fingers cracked, and in the ringing silence between us came the grumble of the bed as Mam turned over and the dribbling tune of Richard at the china and his call to Mari to waken and help. Morfydd rose and kicked back her chair. "I will work," she said. "But no lash will drive me now, for I am past those damned capers. Labour, nothing more, for I have heard of this Job Gower, too – women's language that you do not understand. Sixpence a pound for dead pigs, is it? Twopence a stone for a dead Ponty foreman if he tries his tricks on me. There's advantage in being born with the looks of a sow." She pointed. "And you keep clear. I take care of myself."

Got up and kissed her, couldn't think why, and the look she gave me froze me standing.

The windows winked with light from the blackness as we took the road to coal.

It was a two mile walk along the river to Ponty and the mountain behind us frowned blue with the promise of dawn. Over Fox Brow we went, leaping the puddled places, tiptoeing over the iced peat with our hair riming in the frost and the wind from the estuary tearing into us. Near Treforris the track narrowed and the woods of the hollow rose up sharp and clear as the sun ripped at the veil of night with a hatchet of fire. As scarecrows stood the trees, their boles gleaming white with frost, branches flaring and all over dripping as long suddy fingers from the weekly wash. An eye out for corpse candles, me, though Morfydd seemed at peace, whistling quietly under her shawl. I have never been afraid of things on four legs or two, but Will o' the Wisps and Buggy Bo Goblins do give me the creeps when trees are standing as tombstones and the thick pile of a thousand autumns sigh beneath the feet. Grandfer reckoned he saw a corpse candle once; red and evil, it was,

47

topped with yellow and dancing over the peat – sure sign of
death for someone, and God knows what is happening fifty
feet down where Buggy Bo lives with his blistered victims.
Sweating, me; nearly died when Morfydd gripped me and
drew me behind a tree.

"Down!" she hissed.

She pulled me closer and I saw the sudden white of her face
smudged with shadows.

"Look," she breathed.

"Buggy Bo," I whispered.

"Buggy Bo to hell," said she. "Look, *Rebecca*!"

A Rebeccaite was standing in a clearing before us, dressed
in white from head to feet and the wind caught at his gown,
billowing the hem as he raised his hands as if in a signal. Leaves
rustled, branches snapped. A company of men came from the
woods and made a ring in the clearing, all dressed in women's
petticoats, their faces blackened. A horseman came next. Tall
and broad in the saddle was this Rebecca, his petticoat streaming over the horse's flanks, and he entered the ring of his
daughters and the horse reared, forelegs pawing as he checked
on the rein. On his head was a turban as of silk, bejewelled and
flashing in the shafts of dawn and the golden locks of his wig
reached to his waist.

"Bring Luke Talog!" he cried.

"A judgement," Morfydd whispered. "Look, a prisoner."

"Heisht!" I whispered back, "or they will have us, too."

Two men came from the tree-fringe, dragging between them
a naked man, and I saw his face upturned in terror as he
drooped before the horseman.

"Luke Talog, is this your name?"

And the naked man sank to his knees, biting at his hands.

"Luke Talog," cried Rebecca, "by us will you be judged.
For you have crossed a serving-maid in the house of your wife,
and filled her, and cast her out into hunger, which is against the
law of God. Dost know the Word, Luke Talog – Deuteronomy
twenty-two, which saith, 'If a man finds a damsel that is a
virgin, which is not betrothed, and lay hold on her, and lie with
her, and they shall be found . . . then the man that lay with her

48

shall give unto the damsel's father fifty shekels of silver, and she shall be his wife: because he hath humbled her, he may not put her away all his days.' Right now, Luke, will you marry the damsel?"

And the prisoner trembled and shook his head.

"Aye, Luke boy, that is the trouble, eh? Already married, isn't it?"

The palaver that followed raised me a foot. A weeping of mock tears at this news, and a beating of breasts, with the tormentors in white gowns sobbing on each other's shoulders in grief. Rebecca rose up in his stirrups, shouting:

"See the grief you are causing my daughters, Luke Talog – what about the poor bloody damsel's. Ashamed you should be. Now bring forth the father of the poor girl who was wronged!"

A stooping, white-haired old labourer was pushed into the clearing.

"Thou art the father of the maid," said Rebecca. "Take thou these fifty shekels of silver that have been wrung from the pockets of Luke Talog, being the payment exacted under the law of God," and the shillings were counted into the old man's hands.

"The law of God has been fulfilled, O, Mother!" called a follower. "But what of the law of Rebecca. What is the price of virginity?"

"Can you prove it?" shouted another, and laughter echoed.

"Was she worth it, Luke?"

"Should he not be cast into a pit?"

"A pit of spikes?"

"Or be hanged by the neck?"

"For Luke Talog has worshipped the phallus, and the price of that is death!"

The naked man screamed as they laid hands on him and dragged him upright for the judgement, and the man Rebecca raised his hand as if in blessing, bringing all to silence.

"*Listen!*" whispered Morfydd.

"Hearken ye, my daughters!" Rebecca cried. "The judgement is given. A man who worships his body and defiles that of a child must endure the shame of his own obscenity. Luke

Talog shall have his obscenity exposed by the shame of the *ceffyl pren*."

"The wooden horse," Morfydd whispered. "O, God!"

Hustle, bustle now, with white gowns dashing demented, tripping in leaves, scrambling, and where the hell is the pole of shame and who had it last, for God's sake. This, the miming, part of the punishment. Couldn't find it. Up came a wraith and bowed low to the leader.

"A little pole or a big pole, Mother?"

"Was it a big pole or a little pole he used on the maid?"

"A little stick or a big stick to quieten her?"

"He is not being judged for thrashings," cried Rebecca. "Hasten! The dawn is up and the dragoons are out from St Clears – do you think we have all day?"

Comedy now, the sentence given. They jostled each other, measuring poles for length, testing them for strength while Luke Talog on his knees stared at them in terror.

"What will his poor wife say when we carry him through the parish?"

"What will the neighbours say when Luke goes through on the pole?"

"With his backside turned to the sky and the wind taking a whistle at his poor little troubles."

"Chair him," said Rebecca. "He can put on his coat. Up on the wooden horse. Up, up!"

And I could not drag away my eyes.

To business now, the fun over. Up with him, down with him flat in leaves; squirming, screaming, mudstained – blood-stained when they hit him quiet. Pitiless these men of Rebecca, as their own oppressors. And they roped Luke Talog across two poles and hoisted him up, with the ends of the poles resting on two horses. Head lolling, he drooped, pot-bellied, obscene, cradled.

"Pretty brisky for spring, mind. The poor soul will catch his death. O, Mother, have pity – it is a four mile march to his parish."

Rebecca wheeled his horse, bridle chinking, white shroud streaming.

"Down to his parish with him," he cried. "Spare your pity. From magistrates to adulterers we will carry them on poles – clergy, even, if the crime deserves it, and show them the fury of the people. For the bars of Hell are crammed with Luke Talogs and the gates of Heaven are thronged with the helpless. Time it was changed and by God we will change it, and cleanse the fair name of our beloved county. Away!"

In single file they went, Rebecca leading, the wooden horse next, and then the Daughters, as ghosts of silence till the clearing was empty.

## CHAPTER 7

WE SPOKE little the rest of the way, shocked into silence by the punishment of Luke Talog. The wooden horse was everywhere these days, although only one tollgate had so far been burned. Rebecca, more powerful every minute, was now fighting to put right the social wrongs, setting herself up as judge of social morals. Horsewhipping for the minor crimes, burning in effigy most nights now, threatening letters to magistrates for unfair sentences, rumours of attacks on the workhouses which were springing up like mushrooms under the new Poor Law. Rebecca was everywhere, especially in Pembrokeshire, but our county was getting its share. Daren't kiss your girl without a glance over your shoulder, and thinking of girls brought me back to Mari. Sweet, sad Mari.

Strange it was Mari who was sending me back to coal. . . .

The lights of Gower's mine winked through the mist as we climbed the last hillock to Ponty. This, a green land ten years back, was now outraged. For the new industry of coal was treading on the skirts of iron and the black diamond wealth of my country was making fortunes for men who had never set foot in Wales. When a shaft struck a black seam the merchants were killed in the rush for profit. Ironmasters, greedy for better investment, came running, and their capital was doubled by our cheap Welsh labour, for taxes and tithes and tolls were lowering our power of bargaining. Slave-owners, fresh from their auctions of the Black Trash of Africa, came surging in shoulder to shoulder with the new Welsh gentry who hated their brothers for the sin of their poverty. These, our great benefactors, came flying – from the slave buying of Bristol to the counting houses of Mother London – to negotiate and quarrel on the body of my country, and the scars of their greed will stand for everlasting.

Across the blackened tips went Morfydd and me to the rag-tailed, heaving labourers staggering under their baskets of coal and mine – women and children, mostly, cheaper labour than men. Little ones bent under loads, their stoops a perpetual deformity that jackknifed them over the eating tables and doubled them in their beds; black-faced, white-teethed; spewed from the womb of a deeper world, chanting to the labour of the stamping trot; a tuneless breath of a song that kept them to the rhythm, this, the night shift ending in exhaustion. Eyes peeped at the strangers, heads turned under baskets, but the labour never faltered, and the shale trembled to hobnail stamping. And we stood in the misted air, me and Morfydd, and watched the ants; watched them building the anthill; chanting, scurrying, one eye wide for Foreman – building up the monuments that future generations will despise, sweating and dying for their ninepence a day.

"Worse than bloody Nanty this," I said, and fisted Foreman's door.

Never seen the like of this Job Gower for size. Ducking under the frame he grinned at Morfydd, ham-hands on hips, stripped to the waist in frost. Deep-chested, hairy, the bull of his family; out of a Welsh womb by a Donegal slaughterer, according to Grandfer; tore his mam to pieces, sixteen pounds.

"You wanting labour?" asked Morfydd, hands on hips, too.

"*Well*, now!" Double bass, flat as that.

"Good labour. Skilled," I said, but he never even heard; just strolling around Morfydd inspecting fresh cattle.

52

"Brecon coal, Top Town iron," said she at nothing, "and we work on rates."

He rubbed his bristled chin, grinning.

"Monmouthshire rates for skilled labour," I said. "Trams or basketing, ladders or winding – towing if you like."

"Coal face hewing and he works to chalk," said Morfydd.

The bedlam rose to a shout about us, the tempo surging at the sight of Foreman. The pigmies scurried, these the brothers; brother to the black-skinned slave of the cotton lands, the ear-nicked trash of the branding iron, whip-scarred, mutilated.

"There is a beauty," said Job.

"Till you put a hand on her," said Morfydd. "Then she's a bitch."

Didn't stop grinning, to his credit.

"Bargaining, eh?" He turned to me. "Coal face, you – with Liam Muldooney on Number Two. He's driving me to hell, let's see what he'll do for you. The woman goes towing, no skilled women."

"Monmouthshire rates. Penny a basket," said Morfydd.

"Trams, too – halfpenny a basket – twenty a day," he replied.

"Ladders thrown in?" I asked, innocent.

He grunted.

"And what height is this pit?" asked Morfydd.

"A hundred feet – you can damned near jump it."

"Then jump," said she. "A penny a basket is Top Town rates and we weren't born yesterday."

"I can see that," said he, looking her over. "Take it or leave it."

"Come, Jethro," said Morfydd. "Work to death by all means, but not starving too. Come."

"Penny a basket," said Job Gower. "But keep it to yourself."

"Thank God for the Unions," said Morfydd.

"Plenty of tongue for strangers," said he. "We will see how you do. If not, you're out, the two of you."

Twenty shillings a week between us, six day week. Not bad, I thought, but I was afraid of the ladders for Morfydd.

A hundred feet down is a platform of light and the two

53

ladders are snakes that reach to the bottom, baskets coming up one side, baskets going down the other.

"You first," said Morfydd, and I saw the sweat suddenly bright on her face, for she had never done ladders before, and I wondered at her head for heights. Job Gower was behind us as I swung myself into space and gripped the rungs, and I saw the shadow of Morfydd's leg come over above me as I went down hand over hand. Twenty feet down I stopped, for a woman was climbing against the platform of light, and her gasps were preceding her on the swaying rungs.

"Down with you," roared Job from the top. "Don't mind old Towey, plenty of room to pass."

Down, down, hand over hand, with the ladder bucking and the coal dust flying up, sucked upwards by the draught. Looked up at the light above me and the morning clouds and saw Morfydd coming after me, her fingers peaked white on the rungs, skirts and petticoats billowing indecent, and I knew she was fearing the drop. Began to wonder how I could break her if she came, hang on and elbow her against the shaft, foot against the up-ladder, but I knew she'd take me if she came from a height. So I waited a bit till her feet were above me.

Down fifty feet and I met Mrs Towey. Swing over to the right as she comes labouring up, for her basket is lopsided and her body is swaying.

"Good morning, Mrs Towey," I said to cheer her.

"O, Christ," said she. "Do you give me a hand."

Sixty if she's a day, this one, eyes upturned, breathing in gasps; sweat-streamed, shuddering, clinging to the rungs, with the coal from her basket spilling down and dancing as gnats against the square of light. Thank God nobody was following her.

"O, God," said Towey.

"Shift you over, woman," I said. "I will come on your ladder," and steadied her basket.

"O, man," said she. "Let me keep my coal."

"Easy with it, then," and I jacked the thing up with my knee. "Rest," I said, gripping her skirts. The two of us there with Morfydd above me, and I looked up past her to the sky and

Gower's face was peering down with clouds doing halos above his head.

"What the hell is happening down there, Towey?" he roared.

"Come down and see," I roared back. "Little old Towey it is, and I am giving her a spell. Damned scandal, it is."

"Aye? She'll have you basketing for her before you are finished."

"Strangers, is it?" asked Towey, eyes closed, forehead sweating against a rung.

"Aye," I said. "Rest yourself, girl."

"Kind, you are, boy. This old ladder will be the death of me, mind. Twenty times I have been up it since last night. Is it light up by Job, or darkness?"

"Morning," I said. "The end of the shift."

"Thank God for His mercies," said she. "For there is fire in my chest and I couldn't climb again" and she opened her eyes and looked at me with a wrinkled grandmother of a smile. "Eh, now, young you are, man. But a baby."

"Nigh fourteen," I replied. "Do not talk."

So we rested, Towey and me, with Job shouting his head off at the top till Morfydd started some lip and he went off disgusted.

"Will you climb now, old woman?" I asked.

"Eh, aye! Got my breath back now. Mind, fit as a horse I am most times, see, but poorly lately, not up to standard. You Chapel?"

"For God's sake," I said, heaving back to my ladder.

"O, a curse on the first woman who ever climbed this ladder," said she, "and rot her soul in everlasting Hell. Dying this, not living, and I have a husband to keep – you heard about Tom Towey?"

"For grief's sake," said Morfydd above us. "Are we serving up tea?"

"Go now, Towey," I said. "It is only fifty feet."

Up with her then, basket creaking and her coal spilling down, clouting on the head and naked shoulders of a woman coming after her. Irish by the sound of her, sending up Irish curses. Legs as sticks has Mrs Towey, the rags about them fluttering, and Morfydd gave her an elbow as she went up past her to Job hands on hips at the top.

Welsh and Irish waiting at the bottom; waiting for their turn with their baskets at their feet. Waiting for Towey to get clear being the truth of it, for a six inch coal nut takes some heading.

"Good morning," they said in chorus. "Who you after, man?"

"Liam Muldooney."

"Down on Number Two, girl."

"Eh, there's lucky. Biblical, mind, but a dear little man, old Liam."

"Hewing, then?" asks one, stumps of teeth champing – Towey's mam by the look of this one.

"Hewing for him," said Morfydd. "I am for towing."

"You got the pads, girl? 'Tis terrible rocky. Plays the devil with your poor old knees."

"I have pads," says another, and Morfydd catches them.

"Strangers, is it?"

"Aye."

"Brother and sister?"

"Don't be daft, girl – look, spit and image."

"Dear God, anna she pretty!"

"Church of England, is it?"

"Chapel," I said.

"Eh, Chapel! Oi, Meg Benyon by there – strangers are Chapel, you heard? Nothing like Chapel, mind, real Christian, and a fine little minister we have in our Horeb, very good to the children, bless him, too."

"We are Horeb," I said to please her.

"Speak for yourself," whispered Morfydd.

"Now, where's that Meg Benyon? Anyone seen Meg Benyon?"

"Passed just now, Crid – gone back to Muldooney."

"Well, there's a pity, for she is with Muldooney. Horeb, eh? What a coincidence. Where you from, boyo?"

"Nantyglo."

"Where the hell's that, man?"

Morfydd told her.

"Other end of the earth, eh? O, well, got to get going."

"Is that old Towey up?" She looked Towey's grandmer till she bent to the basket and it flew up under her hands. Must have been forty, no more.

"Shake your legs, woman."

"Up a dando, then – give a bunk on this old basket. Take care of the strangers, mind. Liam Muldooney they are after, see?"

On.

Hand in hand now, me and Morfydd; along the galleries where the trams are thundering, with the tallow lamps flaring in crevices of rock, on to the switch road where the nightshift lies hewing, naked as babies, these men, flat on their backs. And the tallow lamps flash on their postures of love-making, rolling, frowning up to the black seam, picking, chinking as they head the new gallery. A snake of women now, bending to their baskets, headed by a Welsh girl, broad as a man, stripped to the waist and shining with sweat.

"Right for Number Two, Liam Muldooney?" I asked her.

"Next gallery, boy. You just come down?"

"Aye," said Morfydd.

"The props are going on Six – has Gower heard?"

"Never mentioned it," said I.

"Give it an hour and the roof will be in." She turned, cupping her hands, shouting above the picks. "Gower don't know, Mark. Send Foreman down, is it?"

"Head first if you can, followed by the owner," came a whisper from darkness.

The Welsh girl nudged me sideways.

"That your sister, man?"

"Aye."

"Watch, then. A swine for a face as pretty as that, is Job Gower. Eh, *hark* at that Bronwen!"

Bronwen is howling by the draught door of the gallery that heads Number Six. Important is Bronwen, shilling a week;

opening and closing the draught doors so men can breathe.

"Now, now," said Morfydd, kneeling. "What you crying for, you pretty little thing?"

Cats.

"Cats, is it?" asks Morfydd, cooing.

"Took the bread from my fingers," says Bron, and her arms went out, but Morfydd folded them back. Frowning up, she said, "Bait bag, Jethro," and I gave it to her. "There now," says Morfydd, "we will give you more bread. Damned old thievers, them cats. You have this, Bron."

"Stand clear," cries a voice, and Bron opens the draught door.

Meg Benyon, this time, the Meg we missed farther back. On all fours is Meg Benyon, shod as a donkey, kneepads, handpads, with a belt round her middle and a chain over her flanks, and up on her haunches she goes, smoothing her black hair from her face.

"Well now, good morning. Just come to see Bronwen I have, and bump into strangers. Welsh, is it?"

I gave her some and she slapped her thigh, joyful. "Well, there's a pleasure – all in the family. Two in three are foreigners these days, undercutting wages. Chapel, too, is it?"

"Horeb," I said, getting used to it.

"*Well!* And I called you strangers! O, hush your moaning, Bronwen, *fach*. You still weeping? Still the old cats, is it? Now you leave them to Benyon, I will give them a belting." She looked as us, eyes flat. "A scandal, isn't it?"

I nodded.

"No child of mine would come down the pits. Die first. You towing, girl?"

"Over with Muldooney."

"And I am hewing there," I said.

"Same face as me. There's fine. A caution is Liam, mind – good job you're Chapel, though he's Irish as the shamrock. Lay preacher spare time, too – very kind to my mam, Mrs Towey – taking her from ladders a week next Monday. Never been the same since she lost our dad. You see her coming down?"

"Saw her going up," I said.

"Six at home she had, see? Me being eldest, and I am going up soon, says Muldooney, being in child. Three months more, have it in summer. You be gentry, says old Liam Muldooney, you have it in comfort up in daylight, leave the pit-births to donkeys though they carried our Lord. Eh, God bless our Liam – second saviour, I reckon, treats you respectful, not like that Gower. Ah, well, got to get going. Straight down, now, follow your noses."

Mane flying in the draught, hooves scraping, harness chinking, Mrs Benyon goes through with the coal tram after her, ducking her head to the two foot roof – the tunnel that leads to the waiting carts.

Liam Muldooney is fetching out coal, trews on, thank heavens, lying in the pit props. Long and gaunt, with the face of a grandfather, was Liam, though I guessed him right at under fifty. Away with his pick and he scrambled out.

"Be damned," said he. "There's a neat little woman for me – Irish, is it?"

"Welsh," I said. "Are you Liam Muldooney?"

"Sure as I'm Irish – you sent by Gower?"

We told him. "Trams and hewing, when do we start?"

"God be praised for a spirit, now," said he, and down on a rock with him and out with a pipe. "It's a rest I am needing and you have come the right time, for I have a few minutes to give praise to my Lord." From a little box beside him he pulled out a Bible. "Do you know this little Book, now, me darlin's?"

"We are Welsh," I said.

"Eh, and I forgot. The harder they hit us the deeper we go, isn't it, and there's fine feathers up in London town who'd have difficulty spelling the great name Samuel, and you and me know it off by heart. Lucky you are, mind, best face in the county, this – best vein and easiest pickings since shamrock land, or I'm not Liam Muldooney, though me real name's foreign, now! Settle you down the pair of you for a talk with Liam," and he patted the rock. I looked at Morfydd and saw pity in her face.

And I looked at Muldooney; at the battered head bumped by

coal, the red-rimmed eyes of the lifelong collier. Men like Muldooney were as thousands in the upland counties, most with the look of the mountain fighter, though many had not seen a fist closed in anger. Flattened noses; screwball ears, as little bits of brain battered out of their skulls, by falls and clouts, not fists, and their speech came slow.

"Have you heard of the man of Kabzeel who did the fine acts, now?"

"Kabzeel," I said, searching Samuel.

"Make it short, Benaiah," said Morfydd.

"Well, there's a woman – got me right first time, for sure. Just giving a little test, I am, for your knowledge of the Scriptures – necessary for people like us working within three foot of the Devil. And no offence, little maiden. Benaiah is my name, speak now."

Morfydd was smiling, ever a soft spot for the Irish.

"Samuel twenty-three," said she, "but you've hit me for the verse. Book two."

"Good enough. I am working with christian brother and sister – I can see that a mile. Verse twenty, for your information. Jchoiada was me dad, you see; slaughtering up the men of Moab – hitting up the Philistines right and left in spare time as I do every Sunday from pulpits in the name of Jesus the Lord. And down into a pit comes Benaiah to slay a lion in time of snow. You see the connection?"

"No," I said.

"And you in a pit a hundred feet down?"

"Go on," said Morfydd, happy with him.

"And in the depth of winter, and all!" He flared his pipe and the flame lit the forest of props about us and the tram line shimmering down the tunnel. Strange place to find a man with a Bible, least of all a prowling lion.

"Ah, me, little lady," said Liam, and took Morfydd's hand and kissed it. "No offence, you understand, for being shamrock I always kiss me friends, and I will not ask more, alone or not. Fallen among thieves, the pair of you, taking work with that pig Job Gower, but you will work at peace with Liam Muldooney who is a slayer when it comes to women-snatching foremen. And now it is winter and a time of snow, so hip and bloody thigh I will strike him if he pesters my women, begging the pardon of the Lord for the language, for with Jchoiada for a dad I couldn't do otherwise. You listening?"

"God bless you, Mr Muldooney," said Morfydd.

"So you come hewing, little man, and you go towing, little woman, with never a backward look for Gower, and I prefer my women covered in the breast, you understand?"

"Yes," said Morfydd.

"And my men with trews, you see."

"Of course," I said.

"Now then, you seen my little Meg Benyon go by just now?"

"We passed her coming in," I said.

"Aye, well I sent her up the switch to see to my Bronwen, for the tears of a child is the grief of angels. Right now, do not sit around. Kneepads, handpads, pick – down and get towing, girl, or we will not enjoy the Sundays."

Stripping to the waist I joined him in the props. Morfydd waited till Meg Benyon got back with her empty tram, and she harnessed up to the one I was filling. Down on all fours she went between the rails, heaving.

"Good little tower, though," said Liam, eyeing her. "She done it before?"

"Yes," I said.

"She conceived?"

"She is single," I said.

"Safe she will be on Muldooney's shift though, and she is safer on towing than them dirty old ladders, so shift you over and do not be fidgety. Would you hear again about my dad?"

So we started in coal, Morfydd and me, at Ponty.

# CHAPTER 8

FOR A year me and Morfydd had laboured with Muldooney for the first summer had been drenching and most harvests failing, and Grandfer was not keen to have me in the farming, though he did precious little of it himself.

But this spring had been glorious, with the countryside melting early in the quickening sun, and even the weeping willows on the banks of the Tywi were laughing and the lanes from Cae White fluttering white with blossom. Hedgehog Grandfer, yawning and stretching from his hop-winter sleep, rose up in April, and belted and buckled he fair bounced round the place. Even Mam came from mourning, dainty with lace from the money coming in. Mari had grown new smiles again, singing and tickling her baby Jonathon, growing lovelier with every day's passing, and I was fishing for kissing terms with Tessa Lloyd Parry.

Eh, were I a poet I would write a song to Tessa up at Squire's Reach, telling of the beauty of the daughters of the gentry. Seeing quite a bit of her lately, though I kept it secret, and sharp after Sunday dinners I would go through Waldo's preserves to Squire's Reach and a once-a-week loving. Held her hand Sunday before last. Kissing this week if I plucked up the courage.

There is kissing and kissing, of course. You can have one for a penny from Sixpenny Jane, though I'd never tried it, and I could have had one a minute from Hettie Winetree, though Dilly Morgan was sharp with backhanders, her dad being strict. But the kissing of gentry is a very different thing, and practice is needed to get the thing perfect.

Morfydd's mirror. Into her bedroom for a good clean parting, polished up and pulled in, hair flat with water.

"Tessa!"

I would have given my soul to be gentry just then; cool, calm, sure of myself. And then I remembered a painting Mam had once, of a poor chap grovelling, all wigs and laces, beseeching a bone from a lady disdainful.

"*Tessa!*"

Try one knee, for both looks like begging, giving it to her with a voice like a tombstone, and Morfydd comes in. Took one look, the bitch, and sat down rocking. Just sat there holding her stays, beetroot in the face to burst blood vessels, making no sound.

Up scalded me.

62

"A damned sneak you are!" I shouted.

"Aye? Then whose damned mirror, whose damned bed-room? Cross my palm with silver or it is going over the county," and she reeled away to the bed and went flat on it, thumping.

"What is the trouble, what is the commotion?" Mam now, feathers waving, just come from Chapel. "And bad language, too – I will not stand for it, Sunday at that!"

But Morfydd just shrieked, thumping the pillow.

Away, me. Downstairs like a bullet, skidded through the kitchen and out the back, upending Grandfer coming in for dinner.

Sunday afternoon.

Along the spring lanes, me; full of beef undercut and Mari's plum pudding, for we were eating better these days; whistling to lose my front ones, hands in pockets, special combed and fluffed up like a hen coming broody. Quite determined, now. One day, I knew, I would marry Tessa Lloyd Parry and bring some gentry into the Mortymer blood and knock some of the pugilism out of it. One day from Tessa I would bring forth my kind, though just then I couldn't imagine her bringing anything forth save a little silver slipper. Dainty, she was; Welsh dark, only up to my shoulder, but educated. Fifteen today, too, with Greek verses and Homers on her table at tea: raised in a hammock between two cherry trees, eating honeybread to pass the time while I was into oatmeal soup and crawling under the county. Queer old pair we made, come to think of it.

Some nights, when we first came to Cae White, I would walk in the darkness of her home at Squire's Reach and watch the comings and goings behind the lace-covered windows. There, dying for a peep at Tessa, I would see the gentry; the men, elegant in their frock coats bowing to carpets; slim men, tall, the pick of the English officers, some billeted there to put down Rebecca. And lovely were the women, with waists for dog-collars and their high-pushed breasts curved white under the chandeliers. Minuet now, the hand-drooping dances, with harpists brought in for the price of a dinner. I am partial to music myself, being Welsh; preferring a good solid choir with

63

plenty of brass under it to a milky minuet. And colour and dignity I like, too, seeing them sometimes in a woman off to Chapel or the sight of a big man hewing in strength. But the bowing and scraping of lords and ladies I could never bear, especially in the men. For the fingers of Man were made for clenching and handclasp, not for waving lace, and I would rather stink of honest cow muck than despoil my manhood with perfume.

Beautiful was Squire's mansion up on the Reach, with the flowering clematis and creeper of centuries drooping in profusion over its entrance, while behind the marble columns all the pride and wealth of the county danced and curtseyed to the bowed good evenings. And sometimes, in the glitter of the room, I would see my Tessa staying up late for a special occasion, being delicate. In her high cane chair she would sit with the beaux of the county dancing her attention. About my own age, some of these, and I longed to get among them three at a time. Bitter, unequal, I would watch from the shadows of the drive, born the wrong side of the blanket, listening for the gardener and his get to hell out of it. But sustained within by the truth of it – that Tessa Lloyd Parry didn't give a damn for the gentry sons while I was loose – me, Jethro Mortymer, torn coat and hobnails.

We met first on Waldo Bailiff's afternoon off. Up on the Reach I was, looking for suicide salmon, Mam being partial to it, though it damned near choked her with the speed she got it down. But a salmon has a right to die as anyone else, I reckon, being sick of the parasites and weary of the journeyings. So down on the bank you go, slip in a stick with a wire noose on the end. For hours you might lie till the poor creature comes, jaded, unhappy, seeking an end to it. In goes his head, pull the noose tight, out on the bank with him and a crack with a boulder, and you slip him back in the river to float past Cae White where Morfydd, by chance, happens to be waiting. Salmon, I think, are much like humans. Like Jess Williams, Grandfer's neighbour about thirty years back – dying to meet his Maker, was Jess, and down he comes in his nightshirt, a rope in one hand, a bucket in the other, with Moc, his twin brother, waiting in their barn. Up on the bucket went Jess with the rope over a beam, and Moc kicked the bucket away at a given signal. Helpful, I call that; brotherly love. Murder they called it in Carmarthen, and they hanged Moc in public.

"Die hard, Moc Williams," called his mam from the crowd. "Die hard like our Jess," and Moc did so, for he loved his mam.

Wrong, this, for if a man is begging for St Peter he should be assisted.

I helped my first salmon out of it soon after arriving. This summer I was waiting for my fifteenth; dozing on the banks of the Reach in the bee-loud silence, watching the waving of the water-lilies and the caress of bindweed where the quicksilver fins flashed bright in the depths. Ring-doves were shouting from the fringes of Cae White, rising as diamonds in the windless air. Sweating, I dozed, but a splash brought me upright. More fishermen – splashing along in a welter of foam, mam leading, dad following and three babies after him swimming demented. Whiskered noses swept the river, black eyes gleamed in sunlight – throwing a live trout from snout to snout, an arc of silver, wriggling, diving. Whistling, plunging, the otters played, and I never heard a footstep.

"Good afternoon," said Tessa.

Up like lightning, fists clenched, looking for a bailiff's chin, and the stick and noose slipped into the river and drifted down to Cae White. Through a pattern of branches Tessa made shape.

Am I supposed to tell of her with only words to use?

Pale was her face, lips stained red; thin and dark, a hand would have snapped her. Her long, summer dress was white and dainty with lace, her long hair black against it. And she held aside her pink parasol and smiled, her eyes coming alive in her face. Always known her behind glass before, never met officially.

"How are you?" I said. Just sat, awaiting sentence. Caught poaching on her dada's river, and in daylight. And how the hell she got there was anyone's guess just then.

"Jethro Mortymer, is it?"

65

Amazing what gentry know. Hooking at my collar, me.

"How is your mother, Jethro Mortymer?"

"Very pleasant."

"Did you see the otters?"

"O, aye."

"Beggars for the poaching, though. Listen to that, now," said she, for the belly-flops of a salmon pursued came up the river and the otters were whistling and plunging as madmen. "O, that sound drives Waldo Bailiff demented. Do you come here often?"

"First time."

"To poach salmon?"

"Upon my soul!" I said, shocked.

She laughed then, face turned up.

"There's a pity, for one salmon more or less don't make much difference," which is not the way she said it but the only way I can tell it. "Especially when the otters kill for sport. You heard them at night?"

Nearer she leaned, her voice coming secret. "O, there is a wildness and freedom about otters, I do think, and a good full moon will always start them capering. Some nights, when the vapours are billowing, I pull back the curtains and listen till dawn. And old Grandfer Badger down in Bully Hole Bottom grunting and singing at the moon. Killed four fox hounds last fall – you seen him?"

"Never," I answered, for he had his hole in Waldo's preserves and I had sprung four gins to save him last spring. "Never seen a badger in my life."

"You seen herons down on the estuary?"

"No," I said, for the estuary was near the rabbit warren.

"Old Bill Stork on the mere?"

I knew him like a brother; shook my head.

"Backward, you, for a farming boy," said she, peeved. "Hen coots you know of, I expect?"

"O, aye, seen tons of coots."

"And heard the Reach curlews calling at dawn?"

"Then I be sleeping."

"Good grief," said she, and straightened herself tidy.

"Reckon if Grandfer Zephaniah wants Cae White ploughing this year he must do it himself again."

"Ploughed," I said.

"But not by you, I vow.'

"Indeed?" I said, cool.

"Indeed," said she, cooler, and we sat there just looking, knives chiefly.

I glanced at the sky for the sun had pulled up his trews again and the air of the river blew sudden cold, though a mite warmer than Tessa who had one shoulder turned.

"How old are you, Jethro Mortymer?" Duchess now.

"Hitting it up for fourteen."

She eyed me sideways. "Is it true you've got a brother?"

I nodded, coming warmer, for this was Iestyn my god.

"In transportation, isn't he?"

"Seven years he got at Monmouth," I replied.

Her chin an inch higher now, untouchable.

"A criminal he is, says Waldo Bailiff. That true?"

"Seven years," I said, hot. "For fighting against gentry like you and scum like Waldo Bailiff, to make things decent for people starving. And we are waiting for him, me and the family, keeping Cae White until he comes back."

Eyes like saucers now with me standing over her.

"And when he comes back he will build the place up," I said, hotter. "He'll build Cae White as big as Squire's Reach, and we will buy up the river and fish our own salmon, for he'd dust any ten round here with Waldo Bailiff to fill in time, so tell him watch out."

Pretty worked up. Always the same when I spoke of Iestyn. She was staring at me, her eyes ringed with their sleepless nights of shadow, and as we were looking it rained.

No warning, just pelted; hitting the river into life in a sudden sweep of the wind.

"O, dear!" said Tessa, and up with her parasol. "Ben, Ben!"

"Who's Ben?" I asked, standing over her with the flaps of my coat trying to keep her dry.

"My servant. Ben!"

Squinted through the trees, but no sign of him.

67

"O, my dress – just *look* at my dress!" She turned her face to mine, rain-splashed, appealing, and I thought she would cry.

"Up a dando," I said, and knelt, lifting her, running like a demon to the veranda of the big house. There I set her in a cane chair, and turned, skidding down the steps from the holy portals of Squire to the teeming white of the river. Awkward questions to be answered if I hung round there. Away then, back to Cae White, reaching home just as Morfydd was fishing the stick and noose from the river and yelling to Mam that Jethro was drowned.

Damned near it.

I leaned against the shed at the back and looked up the Reach, thinking of Tessa. Wet was my face, and not all the wetness rain. For the cripples of Carmarthen city are as Tessa Lloyd Parry, I thought; knobbled knees on their winter pavements, the drumstick wavings of their starving children, the ragged droop of their twisted crones.

From a lopsided womb had come Tessa, spewed, not delivered, and she had not walked since birth. Strange you can pass the cripples of the poor without a second look while the sight of crippled gentry brings you to tears. Strange is Man's pity. The cripple in rags is revolting but pity is flung at the cripple in silk.

Cutting hearts in oak trees now, entwined, pierced, dripping with blood.

We met in secret, of course, with a tongue-pie for Tessa and a belting for me if her dad, the Squire, got hold of it, and if old Ben, the servant, knew of our meetings he kept it pretty well buttoned. Special, this Sunday – Tessa's birthday, being June, and a cameo brooch for presentation from me – thieved by moonlight from Morfydd's room. Death by fire for the thief if she found him.

O, that Sunday!

Larks were singing in the unbroken blue and just enough heat in the air to evaporate Waldo's dewdrop. White-sailed schooners ploughed the estuary and the mountains were fleeced with the splashing brooks as the bath plug came out of spring. Bedsheet clouds were billowing round Gabriel who was sorting them out for weddings and shrouds, and the old sun, catching alight to the flame of summer, flung golden swords over the bright green country. O, wonderful is summer! Crescent wing on bubbling air, the eaves-chattering sparrows, with a million hearts leaping to the wooing every square mile, including me. Singing, face turned up to the sun, my heart was pounding with every step nearer to Tessa. Down from Cae White to the woods of the Reach, leaping the gates, diving over the hedges to Tessa's red lips and a once-a-week loving – through Waldo's game preserves now, into Squire's field where his rams were grazing. Clovenhooved swines, these, with the faces of Satan and enough lust in their matings to satisfy Nick himself. Never took to rams much, preferring their wives and their children with their thumb-sucking daintiness. So over the gate with me and I landed on one's back, gripping his horns, heeling his sides, and away across the field we went as things insane with the other ram following and baa-ing blue murder. Nothing like a ride on a ram, says Joey; an art in itself, says he, for if you can stay on a ram in June you'll ride most things. Through the lambs we went and over his backside went me, with his mate catching me square as I presented the target, the devil, bowling me somersaults. I fled with rams after me and belly-dived the fence into Bully Hole Bottom. Duck Waldo's fence again and the mantrap faces you; try it with your toe for the fun of it, risking your foot for the joy of it, and the game birds rise to the shattering crash. Wait, steady. Stand stock still, for the woods have eyes, one pair especially. Over by there, a bit to the left. Motionless he stands, old Grandfer Badger, carved in stone, every nerve trembling, for he knows what is coming if I get within reach of him. Nose down to leaves he stands, hoping to be missed in the forest stillness of branch and leaf. Hands in pockets, I started whistling, wandering towards him, kicking at stones, not the least bit interested in badgers. Then leap the last yards. Shoulders screwing he dives for his earth, frantic, for the earth is a fox hole and not designed for badgers. In! Kneeling, I stared into darkness, then cursed his soul, for he kicked with his hind feet and shot out pebbles to blind me. Down flat for revenge then, one arm down the hole. Legs waving, I reached for him, fingers prodding till I touched his backside, then walked my fingers to the stump of his tail, gripped it and heaved; and the earth is rumbling to the thunder of his indignity. Red in the face, he is, bracing his forelegs, scraping his hindlegs, for that swine Jethro Mortymer's got hold of my tail. Heave. Grandfer heaves back. Seen and unseen we grunt and strain, but he is a grandfer and I am younger, and out he comes bellowing. Roaring, he comes, stumps of teeth bared, wheeling for the conflict, snapping, snarling. Away, me, followed by Grandfer, leaping the boulders, putting up pheasants. But wait!

Little Mam Pheasant is lying in leaves, and her beak is red and her chest is heaving, for Waldo and his gun have passed her in flight, and she turns up her head to the tickle of my finger. Dad Pheasant now, head on one side, inquiring; cannot make out why she's broody in June. Soft was her neck in the twist of my fingers and the wind did a sigh as her little soul flew upward. Up in a branch with her, for Mam has a fancy for pheasants; up beyond the reach of thieving badgers, and on to the river. Running now, hobnails thumping for the last quarter mile. Breasting a rise I raced down the hollow and along the bank where Tessa sits waiting.

"Tessa!"

Sitting as I left her last Sunday. But different this time, sweetened by the year of our parting. Breathless, I reached her, and knelt.

"Tessa," I said, gasping.

The way she looked, perhaps, the narrowing of eyes. No need for mirrors. I kissed her. And I heard the quick inrush of her breath as I put my arms about her and kissed her again and her yellow straw hat fell off to her shoulders and her hair tumbled down to the force and fire. Great was the strength in me, sudden, unpitying, and she turned away her face and twisted in my arms, and there was a trembling within her that leaped to my fingers. Soft was her breast. . . .

"Jethro!" she said, sharp. "*Jethro!*"

Didn't mean to do it, sorry now; but I'd do it again if she so much as looked. Sat back then and watched her in profile, seeing the flash of the river behind her, and her eyes were all mystery and brightness. Gave me a glance then, the glance of a woman, and I reckoned she knew what I had in mind, for she put on her straw hat and set it tidy, very prim, tying the bows again, looking away.

"If you don't mind," she said.

"Many happy returns," I said.

"Thank you," said she. "But my birthday. Not yours, remember."

O, beautiful, she looked just then.

"I am sorry," I said.

Silence, save for the wind and the splash-plops of the river, and gurgling.

"But a child you are, Jethro," she said then. "Do not make it hard."

Poor Tessa. Just wanted to hold her then and soothe and kiss her, but I did not dare. Had to say something.

"Look," I said. "Old Grandfer Badger is down in Bully Hole Bottom, girl. Roaring and raging, he is, for I've just had him out by the tail. You ever seen Grandfer?"

"No," she said. Eyes low now, threatening tears, fingers ripping at her little lace handkerchief.

"Not interested?"

She shook her head, lips trembling.

"O, Jethro," she whispered, and wept.

I held her. All the heat gone, I held her, and her old hat fell off again and her hair went down again. Just the two of us in the world then.

"Thought I'd forgotten?" I asked, holding her away. "See now, here is a valuable. Your birthday, and I've been saving up for months. Tessa, don't cry. Look, look!" and I fished out the brooch. Wonderful was her face as she blinked away tears and her eyes opened wide at the sight of it. God knows what would happen if Morfydd saw it on her.

"Jethro, you shouldn't have done it!"

"Cost a small fortune," I said, but I know it cost twopence

for I watched Morfydd buy it from the tinker. "Got it down in Whitland," I said. "Fair day."

"O, it is lovely!"

"Shall I pin it on, girl?"

Eyes up at this. "I can manage myself, thank you."

"Tessa!"

"Eh?"

"Will you be my girl now and stick to me, is it?"

"Not much chance of me running," she answered. "Look, boy – is it tidy?"

"There's an old wacko you are," I said. "Pretty it do look on you," and I leaned forward as she reached for my lips.

"Pretty for you," she said.

"Till death do us part and down in wooden suits," I said. "You are my girl now, you promise?"

"Yes."

"Dry up, then," I said. "Do not look so mournful. Down to Bully Hole Bottom with us, is it?"

"How can I walk to Bully Hole Bottom? Jethro, have sense!"

"On my back," I cried. "I could carry an elephant. Look, if we hurry grandfer will still be there and I will fetch him out again for you. Come on!"

"O, stay!" she replied, and just looked. And the way she looked.

"To the devil with badgers," she said. "Jethro!"

The lips so curved are dying for kisses, and her eyes closed to the sun as I drew her against me, and saw, in a rift of her hair the distant roof of the mansion and the poplars of the Big Field misted in sunlight and the silver ribbon river winding to the hills.

Cool is the kiss at the beginning, then growing to warmth as the kiss is longer, steaming dry to fire as the breaths come quicker, till the kissed is a quarry that seeks escape from the circling iron of the capturing arm and she sighs and faints in the greater strength. O, mad is that strength!

"Jethro!"

I did not answer and she clung to me, and I saw the faint

72

white scratches of my chin on her face, that would later turn red.

"Jethro, do not touch me, not again!"

"Tessa," I said, and was ashamed.

"Just . . . kiss me. So I can remember?"

## CHAPTER 9

NOW I STOOD in a universe of nights and days boiling in the inch between boyhood and manhood, and listened to the call of the scythe. The wind sighed through the grasses and the corn of Grandfer's acres were as gold. Coo-doves called from the woods, herons from the Tywi where the salmon swirled up for their act of creation and Tessa's otters barked in moonlight.

Waking early that morning I pulled on my boots and went down to the kitchen to the back, listening to the tinkling splashes from the mere as the hencoots got busy among beaks where the bulrushes stood in shimmering silence. There came to me a song then, not the song of Ponty, sweating and grimed, but the windy sighing of corn falling obliquely to the scythe, its razor edge flashing and stained with clover flowers that clung to the wetted shine of boots. I saw, in my sleep-gummed eyes, the line of the reapers, waist-deep in the corn, their naked backs sweating in midday heat, and the swing of their blades made sunfire in the gold. Earth smells came; the scent of burned pine; sour stinks from the rotted dumps of kale, the perfumed wind of overflowing barns. Great was Cae White then, as a ship at sea with billowing mists sailing in her turrets.

The women were stirring in the bedrooms now, curtains swishing to let in sunlight; pot-clanking, bed-squeaks as Morfydd got out and her son's thin protest at the sudden bedlam. She awoke like a man, this one, with all the palaver of a man, and what damned time do you call this and get to hell out of it. She washed as a man, too, stripped to the waist in frost.

"*Diawl!*" she said at the door now. "Somebody's got a conscience. Have you put her in trouble?"

Venus, complete with arms, towel dangling, hair on her shoulders.

"Don't worry about me," I said. "Just come naked."

She smiled at this and came to the water butt beside me and flung back her hair and tied it with red ribbon, and I turned away as she hit the tub with all the corkings and bubblings of a man from shift.

"Well, now," said she, rubbing for a glow. "And what is it thinking?"

"My business."

"O, aye? Then it do happen to be mine also. D'you know what time Grandfer got in last night?"

"I go to bed to sleep," I said.

"Not much option round these parts, mind," and she winked and held the towel against her. "Coo-dove time, an hour or so back. Belted with quarts, he was, climbing up one stair and belly-sliding ten – making enough commotion to raise the damned rent. Reckon you must die if you didn't hear Grandfer. Drunk? Three nights running now." She jerked her head at the standing corn. "The place won't get a shave this side of Christmas the way he's going. Time those fields was down."

"Where he gets the money from puzzles me," I said.

"Grandfer's business – not yours, or mine. Neither is scything my business. What I know about farming can be written on a toenail, but I reckon to eat next winter."

"And I know less than you," I said.

"Time somebody learned, then, time somebody moved. I'm a different shape in the chest to you but I'd have a try if there wasn't a man around."

"What about Ponty? Do I hew with Muldooney and farm, too?"

"I'll handle Ponty."

"Twenty acres of corn," I said. "Abel Flannigan might help."

She was tapping her foot now, eyes narrowed.

74

"Or Osian Hughes," I said.

I had made a note of Osian. With Morfydd's suitors tiptoeing around Cae White thicker than fleas in workhouse bedding, Osian was the handiest. She had only to wink her eye and he'd have lowered our corn in fifteen minutes.

"Listen, you," said she. "If we take scissors to these fields we will cut them alone, for our men have never gone crying yet. Grandfer's finished, understood? Give him six months and he'll be boxed in cedar and brass handles. When a man slips on quarts he slides to the devil. Do you want your Squire Parry to take the place over? For he'll damned soon do it if the corn isn't lowered."

"He will not do that," I said.

"Gratifying. Influence, is it? You'll get some influence if he catches you with Tessa." She turned to the door. "You heard what happened at the Reach last night?"

I nodded.

"And how your Parry is roaring and threatening to put out his tenants?"

With good reason, I thought.

For his river had been emptied between Tarn and the Reach; near four hundred salmon littering the banks, brought out by the poachers and left to rot. This was Rebecca again, dishing out punishment because Squire had lent money to a turnpike trust. By night she visited the Tywi with flares and cudgels and the fish were harpooned and dragged out to die; scores being spitted on the railings of the mansion, flung over his steps and lawns, thrown through his windows, tied to his knockers. There is no law to say that Squire is sole owner, of roads or salmon, said Rebecca in her note. With hungry men in gaol for poaching the temptation must be removed, said Rebecca, and Squire Lloyd Parry must have the lot. As his gates will be burned when he puts them up.

"And tonight we are eating like fighting cocks," said Morfydd, "for I fetched in a fresh one at midnight."

"That is asking for trouble," I replied sharp. "Waldo Bailiff has a nose for boiling salmon."

"Boiled," said she. "And if he shows his dewdrop in here he

will breathe his last. I will handle Waldo – you handle that corn. I am going alone to Ponty."

Cups and saucers were tinkling from the kitchen as I came in from the tub. Smoke curled from the twisted chimney, chairs scraped on flagstones, and I thought of the days when we first came to Cae White. Grandfer was in charge then. Seven of us down to supper at night and not a whisper while we fed; just belches and pardons from Grandfer at the top and wallowings from Richard and Jonathon, while the big black clock on the mantel ticked time to the pork crackling, with hands reaching for bread or grasping pewter for cider gulps. Money in plenty those days, too, and Grandfer was a giant of a man for five feet odd, very much in charge; beating his breast with one little hand, thumbing up the Testaments with the other, and every Grace was the same – a whine about some poor soul at a feast who was told to get shifting and who up and said that even curs were due for crumbs, Amen, and slap went the Book and into things went Grandfer, for the head of the house had to be fed with a regiment of in-laws to keep. Different now. Grandfer was finished with Cae White. So with my first harvest waiting I went into the kitchen, and the table, I saw, was laid for one. Husbandman first, said Mari, smiling. Farming stock for generations and proud of it.

I sat down, watching her as she sweated over the hob.

"Men first, Jethro, women later," she said, smiling wider, and I knew then that the women had been planning, with Morfydd having the first go at me and Mam coming after. Fat bacon was sizzling in the pan, God knows where they got it; the kettle singing his lovesong to the pot; buttermilk, bread whiter than usual, and the cloth was as snow. Most important now, Jethro Mortymer, with the head man gone lazy and pickled in hops.

"Sit you down, *bach*," said Mari, smoothing and patting, and I looked at her.

Expectation was in her, evident in her trembling hands, and I saw the ring of gold that bound her to my brother, and smelled the lavender sweetness that was Mari's from the day

76

Iestyn brought her home to Blaenafon. Bright were her eyes, meeting mine but once, flicking away with the colour reddening her cheeks. Jonathon, Mari's baby, was two years old now, but she still had him on the breast. We saved the easy work for her for she was still making up for her breech-birth labour; couldn't pull round on oatmeal soup, said Mam. But satisfying Jonathon was harder than kitchen work with his cooings and bubblings and reaching for her breast. Strange that I was jealous of Jonathon. His whimpering offended me because she was slave to him, leaping to serve his first strangled cry. His pear-shaped bottom was vulgarity to me – something that was smoothed with oils in public, reflected in mirrors, even kissed. The body of a girl child to me is a thing of beauty, and the body of a baby boy atrocious. For one paints its picture of the fountain of life, and is fruitful. But the body of a boy is all cherubs and cupids, the lie to manhood with its belly-rolls and wrist bangles.

Sometimes, from my chair in the corner, I would watch Mari with Jonathon; one eye on the *Cambrian,* the other on his suspended animation, frenzied in his fight for freedom while she gripped his fat ankles between fingers and thumb. Head dangling, upside down, he would catch my eye and bubble his smiles, exposing his nakedness without a blush and his shocking maleness with pride. And Mari, pins in mouth, would be ardent to do best by him in sweating concentration; wiping stray hairs from her eyes, forearm on his chest, tiptoeing her knees up in case he rolled off. And fighting to get the rag round him he streams his indecency down to her ankles.

"O, Duw! O, there's a horrid boy, Jonathon. O, Jethro, look now, drenched, I am drenched!"

Up with the newspaper, pretend not to look, and he crows his delight in shouts and gurgles. Hand up, she threatens, but never brings it down.

"I will smack you next time, mind, or call Uncle Jethro, for he is handy with smackings. Dirty old boy!"

"Taking after his uncle, though," says Morfydd, sewing, needle held up to the light. "Remember, Mam – a soaking baby if ever there was one, that Jethro."

77

"Whoever was nearest, girl. You, me or the Bishop of Bangor."

Up with the *Cambrian*.

"And the time he drowned old Tomos back home, remember?" Morfydd again. In her element, the bitch. "And Tomos dressed for speechifying. Aye, aye, and the Sunday trews his speciality, too." She winks at Mari. "But take a tip, girl – contented was Jethro. Two and a half and still on the breast – never got a fork into solids till he was nigh on three, and what we lost in the soakings we saved on the stomach gripe, eh, Mam?"

"And the belly band – remember the belly band." Mam now, treadling away.

"O, aye, girl. Never without it. It do cut the wind for certain do the belly band."

And there was Mari's eyes sober serious, meeting mine over the top of the *Cambrian* with her sweet, sad smile; not knowing of the torment, pure in heart.

Too pure in heart to realize that the inch of her breast was curved in whiteness, switching my eyes.

Eh, this business of growing to manhood.


Now she stood beside me to serve my plate in the kitchen, with something of love in her face.

"Jethro," she said.

"Aye?" I turned away, breaking bread.

"Jethro, you will reap the corn for me? Never mind the old coaling down in Ponty – it can wait, and with Morfydd labouring it is enough for a family. Ashamed, I am, with Grandfer sleeping drunk, but already the fields are turning. For a field of blackened corn is as sad as a funeral cloth, and everyone has their barns stacked save us." Back at the hob now, she turned. "I will cook and mend for you, as I did for my Iestyn. O, but a boy you are, but there is life in Cae White and you must not let it die."

"I am a furnace man and collier," I said. "I know nothing of farming."

"But you will try?"

78

Just went on chewing, wanting to hear her voice.

"Mam and me will work, too, and Richard will come for the gleanings. To build Cae White for Iestyn, Jethro – for when he comes back."

"Long years yet, Mari."

"But they will pass. O, I have been waiting, waiting, and you have made no move."

"All right, all right," I said.

Her face was radiant. "Today?"

Strange the glory in seeing her pleading.

"Yes," I said. "Now send Mam in, it is her turn now."

"I am here," said Mam. "Do not worry."

"Jethro," said Morfydd from behind her. "Mam do want to speak to you, official."

"Away the lot of you," I answered. "I am entitled to breakfast."

"He is reaping, he is reaping!" cried Mari, dancing.

"Should be worth seeing," said Morfydd, in now. "Two feet shorter by the time he comes in tonight. And the point of a scythe can get into funny old places, so mind."

I just ignored it, feeling superior. Never before was I so wanted; walked out and left them, in search of the scythe.

I have seen white beards waving over the snathes of sythes, and arms no thicker than my wrist that have swung from dawn to dusk; the sinewy bodies of grandfathers too old to die, the pendulum bellies of drunkards that have swayed to the sigh of the whetted ground. Spitting on my hands I gripped the splits, and swung, and sunfire flashed on the edge of the blade as it hissed for my ankles. Leaping high, I fell, with the thing pitchforking as something alive.

Gently, this time, the point held low, I cut a few stalks at a time, feeling for the balance, for the touch of a gorse-fly's wing is enough to send the point diving. An hour of practice and I was revelling in the singing cut of the steel, though I knew it would take a lifetime of learning; left foot forward swing, and the corn lies down; the backward swing, then forward in the rhythm of Nature. The sun, flushing after his heavy meal of summer, was strickening in brilliance. Left foot forward, swing

79

and back. I smelled the mowing smells of bruised corn, a dryness crept to my throat, but the song of the scythe was an exultation within me, and I disdained the pain of my already blistered hands. On, on, the blade flatter now, a bow of steel encircling my legs. The ache of my loins crept to my back, spreading fingers of fire to my shoulders, but still I worked on. Sweat ran in streams over my face. On, on, left foot forward, swing, and back. Sickening now, but I was still at it strongly, scything in a fashion, getting the damned stuff down. Great I felt then, tied at the knees and belted. Above me in the incinerating blue a lark nicked and dived, his body a diamond of light, and his joy drove me on, eyes narrowed to midday glare now, teeth gritted to the cramping agony in a world of gold that shimmered and swayed. An hour later the sun was hottest, the poplars of Cae White alight and glittering. Heat reflected on my naked shoulders, but I plunged on blindly. Gasping now, longing for the cold draughts of the colliery shafts, the pain was a ring of steel about me, and the last swing came with an indrawn breath. The point hit a stone. The sky somersaulted as the scythe heeled again. I fell, seeking oblivion in the earth and the waving ears above me. Panting, I opened my hands. Claws for fingers, cramped and red, and the sudden gush of tears splashed and stung them, running in salt veins, mingling with blood. Knew I was beaten. Shutting my eyes to the sunglare I let the fire and sweat run over me.

An ant was crawling on the snathe of the scythe, just an inch from my nose. Brushing away tears, I watched; the posturing daintiness, the nibbling, acrobatic dancing, seeking everything, finding nothing in a world of exploration. Up the handle with you, down again in whiskered concentration; wipe your face, clean your teeth, then round you go in a circle, bright you flash in sunlight. I watched and dreamed. Sleep lazed my eyes again in the metallic burnishing of the sun. Reed-music whispered to the scent of bruised corn, and I awoke again with visions dancing and the stalks above me rippled in an oven of heat, for steepled ears had risen beside me; a harelip snitched not a foot from mine. Face to face, we were, the beaten and the hunted, and the wheat went flat to the brown streak's passing.

Next came the stoat, black, relentless, lithe body swerving in the jungle of corn, but I clenched my hand and hit him flat. Smooth was his coat to the touch of my fingers and the corn stalks waved to the terror of the rabbit. The corn hummed into silence. Nothing remained but the molten pour of the sun. In nothingness, with the stoat in my hand, I slept.

Give me a pick and a colliery face if I have to labour. Leave the scything to grandfers.

## CHAPTER 10

IN BED for two days, with Morfydd and Mari dashing round with flannels, giving me hell.

Eight days it took me, but I scythed Cae White, with Morfydd on her knees spare time swiping with a reaping hook and Mam, Mari and Richard coming for the gleanings, and we stacked the barn high. If Grandfer saw it happen he did not make mention. Didn't see much of him these days at all, with him lying in bed all the morning and teetering bowlegged down to Black Boar tavern on his ploughing corns and not a glance for anyone. Going to the devil fast, was Grandfer, not even an eye for Randy, his horse.

A black-faced towser of a horse, this one, and he'd seen better times, having once served apprenticeship as a travelling stallion, and he couldn't forget his past. Grandfer loved him as life itself, but he didn't work him often, and now I had him in the shafts for the harvest. Very pugnacious, this one, with the kick of an elephant, and every ploughing regular he sent Grandfer ears over backside along the shippon, but I was used to four legs, having worked them in iron. I let him belt the plough to bits and then I belted him, but he never forgave me for it, I knew. Along the ruts with a load we would go with the old traces slapping in a jingle of harness and horse and man friendship, but I knew he was watching by the roll of his eye. Cruel, I suppose, being a horse when you have once been a stallion – a hell of a time with the women one moment and cut off without an option the next, but he came pretty useful later, did Randy.

Tired to death that night, I sat in a chair with Richard on my knee. Four years old was Morfydd's boy now, light-faced and fair, with gold curls to his neck and as pretty as a girl, save for the square of his jaw and his deepset eyes – a throw-back from the dark Mortymers.

"The white line is in us," Mam used to say. "As a white-breasted blackbird, he is, as my little girl Edwina."

For Edwina, my sister who died up in Monmouthshire, was albino, and the strain had come out in Morfydd's son, though her lover, like Morfydd, was as dark as a gipsy. A dear little boy, this Richard; quiet about the house in his comings and goings, busy with his labour of tying stooks now harvest had come, and lessons in English from Mari when she had spare time. There was no school near save the keeper of the new tollgate near Flannigan's farm, and he is not being taught by traitors, said Morfydd.

"You joining Rebecca, Uncle Jethro?" said he now.

"Not while he lives in this house," said Mam, pottering. "Just farming for us now, no need to look for trouble."

"That right, Uncle Jethro?"

I was giving a bit of thought to tollgates and Rebecca about this time, for big Trusts were being formed by the gentry who were investing money in them for the erection of tollgates which were supposed to earn money for the road repairs, and the gates were going up like mushrooms. Rebecca who burned gates once was now sending threatening letters to Trusts and tollgate keepers. Humble men and women, these keepers – the Welsh bleeding the Welsh, said Morfydd. The levying of the tolls was unjust, too, for some gentlemen's carriages passed free, because they were gentlemen; the charge for a horse and cart with broad wheels was fourpence while a cart with narrow wheels cost sixpence, so the richer the farmer the cheaper the toll. Time was when the Kidwelly Turnpike Trust let lime through free, but new gates were springing up round the kilns now. Osian Hughes Bayleaves was a business man, though Morfydd gave him no credit for gumption. Thought nothing of a five mile detour, did Osian, to avoid a tollgate, sometimes ending in gentry fields. When building his new barn he brought in his bricks under a layer of manure, which passed through free. Aye, no fool was Osian till we all started trying it, and then he got caught and fined three pounds, enough to set him back weeks. Every night, lying in bed, I could hear the tollgate carpenters knocking them up, and the noise made me sweat with seven people to keep and a harvest to sell, for to try to get into Carmarthen or St Clears was like trying to enter a besieged city.

I could see us starving at the height of winter. Sweated blood at the thought of it.

"We will work it out," said Mari.

The house was quiet that night for Morfydd, exhausted by a late Ponty day shift, had gone to bed with Richard and Jonathon. Grandfer was drowning his back teeth down at Black Boar tavern, but Mari and me were not alone, Mam saw to that. Sitting in Grandfer's rocking-chair she was dozing and waking in snuffles. Keeping things decent, she said, you understand, you two, no offence meant, mind, she said.

"None taken," replied Mari, but I saw the hurt in her eyes.

"Gone dark, see," said Mam. "A young married woman ought to be escorted after nine o'clock at night, never know who might be looking through a window."

"My sister-in-law," I said.

"Never mind," said Mam.

"Iestyn's wife, then."

Fingers up now. "Look," said she. "I am not accusing anyone of capers. It is only the custom, and customs die hard. Old fashioned, perhaps, but I think it safer."

"You are making too much of it, Mam," I said.

"Jethro, I am only thinking of Iestyn. So hush!"

"I am doing that night and day," said Mari, and I saw her eyes go bright.

"Fetch the accounts," I said. "We will see how we stand. And enter a sixpence for Mam standing guard."

Up with her then. "No cheek, Jethro, I will not stand for it. Still your mam, I am, and I will take a stick to you, big as you are. Now then."

Gave her a sigh, fluttered an eye at Mari. So we had Mam's company when we worked the accounts, adding up rent and church tithes, coal rates and toll payment, with Mam going soprano in snoring, keeping it decent. Full length on the mat and she wouldn't have known it.

"Rent, rates and tithes," said Mari. "Eighty pounds outlay, and wear and tear."

"And with decent harvests like this last one, a hundred and thirty pounds income – fifty to live on and seven to keep."

"Pretty shrimpy," I said, thinking of the tolls.

"But that is not counting Morfydd, mind – ten shillings a week, remember. How much is that a year?"

"Take us all night to work it out," I said. "And she will not earn it for ever. You noticed Morfydd lately?"

"Time she came from coal."

"Long past," I said. "Nothing for it. I will have to go back to Ponty and part-time farming." Sick, I went to the door.

"Where you going, Jethro?"

"Black Boar tavern."

"Got money?"

I rattled it, grinning. "Enough for a quart."

"At this time of night?"

I shrugged. "Early for Betsi. She don't close at all these days."

I pulled on my coat and Tara, my terrier, came wriggling to my heels.

"Jethro."

"Aye?"

Pale was her face. "We will manage, mind. A bit shrimpy it will be, but we will manage. You keep from Betsi's place, boy."

"Listen. If Grandfer can souse himself on his savings every night the least I am entitled to is a quart."

After me now, her hand on mine. "It is not the old drinking, Jethro, it is where you drink that matters. Drink quarts, if you like, but at the Miner's Arms, is it – somewhere decent."

Over her shoulder I saw Mam's eyes open, watching. Give her a broomstick just then and she'd have been round chimneys.

"Jethro," said Mari, begging, "you keep from Rebecca. For me, boy? Wicked, it is, carrying poor men on the *ceffyl pren* and slaughtering salmon and burning ricks."

"More wicked to build the gates that cripple us."

"Then leave it to others – remember my Iestyn."

This turned me. "I am doing that. There will be no Cae White for my brother to come back to unless the gates come down."

"O, God," she said, empty.

"Go to bed, Mari. Here, Tara!" and the terrier scrambled into my arms.

But Mari did not move. It was as if I had struck her. Motionless, she stood, shocked pale; always the same these days when her husband's name was mentioned, and I pitied her. Helpless, I touched her hand. "Bed," I said.

"What is happening out by there?" Mam now, peering, spectacles on the end of her nose.

"Me and Mari kissing," I said, hot. "For God's sake go back to your snoring."

I heard Mam's voice raised in protest as I slammed the door to show her my anger. Getting sick of things at Cae White lately, with Morfydd coming snappy with overwork, Mari mooning about Iestyn and Grandfer stupified. Enough to think of without having to put up with guardians of virginities, and it infuriated me that Mam, of all people, should go under skirts with thoughts of Mari who was pure and beautiful, for a thought like that brings canker into a house and we had given her no reason for it. But with every day's passing now Mari was more substantial, less of a relation. This working together, the sweet intimacy of her presence, had brought me joy, obliterating something of Tessa, the girl. I loved her, of course.

Cursed myself for it under the stars.

The moon was hanging doomed in a friendless sky as I went down to Tarn.

The sheep track from Cae White leads to Black Boar tavern, a track that carries the refuse of the north; the Midland drovers with their stinks, ghosts of the transportation hulks and prison, the fire-scarred puddlers of the Monmouthshire iron – not a pint of good Welsh blood in a thousand; all come flocking to the coal industry of Carmarthenshire and to Betsi's place, the strongest ale in the county. Light and smoke hit me as I shouldered the door.

Betsi Ramrod is serving the jugs, dark eyes flashing in her hatchet of a face, swabbing up her counter now, scooping up her pennies. Irish as Killarney is Betsi Ramrod – the Welsh had a name for her – man-hating, man-loving but fearful of conceiving, straighter than a fir tree and twice as prickly. She hoofed it out of Ireland ten years back, it was said, her black shawl scragging her domed head, her stockinged sticks of legs plastered with the mud of her barren country – running from the rumbling bellies of a potato famine, one hand gripping her twopenny fare, the other waving the last crust in Ireland: running for Rosslare Wharf and Freedom's schooner, a walking ballast journey of no return alive. A hundred thousand Irish crossed the sea about then, most to neat Welsh graves, but Betsi was one who did well out of it. From the ballooning stomachs of her country to the best cellar in Carmarthen county via the bed of a travelling tinker, she gave short change over the counter if you dared to bat an eye.

A few of my neighbours were drinking when I got in there – Osian Hughes Bayleaves for one, shivering in his corner to draw my attention, mortifying for Morfydd still, scared of her reception, for she'd split his skull with the nearest thing handy if he tried it on, and he knew it. Hairy Abel Flannigan sat opposite him, one hand gripping a jug, the other a bottle, stupefied, trying to forget tollgates, and God help him if Biddy his mam finds out, for she is still serving him beltings. Job Gower, of all people, Morfydd's Ponty boss; up at the counter, dwarfing every man in sight, his eyes still black-ringed from the day shift and roving for good labour. And the sawdust was jammed with farmers and drovers, with the foreigners of iron quarrelling and bellowing, spilling out their wages; ragged

86

men, beggars, hoydens and hags, two per cent Welsh, thank God. A cock-fight in a corner now, bloodstained, wine-stained, elegant with dandies; a man-fight in another – two north country drovers, their blue chins jutting with lip from Lancashire, fists bristling, eyes glaring, dying for each other and the meaty thuds of the slug it out, with dark Gipsy May thrusting between them to take the first thump, hands spread on their chests, her white teeth shining as she laughs at the lamp.

"Trouble, Betsi, trouble! Grandfer Zephaniah, up by here and give me a hand with some muscle!"

"Settle your own business," says Grandfer, steering up his quart.

Not seen me yet.

"Oi! Osian Hughes Bayleaves – six-foot-six of you for God's sake. Part these two pugilists for your poor little gipsy, eh?"

And Osian trembles and goes deeper into his mug. From the table rises Abel Flannigan and shoulders through the crowd, undoing his coat: a north country drover every week for supper, this one.

"Now, now!" shrieks Betsi Ramrod, and up on the counter she goes, landing in the sawdust with a flurry of drawers. "Sit you down, Abel boy, Betsi will handle it." She shoves the drovers out of it. "This is a respectable establishment, me boyo, anyone fighting will pay for the damages, a penny for every mug broken, twopence for a jug. By all the saints suffering, God what a life. Fighting, fighting! Good evening, Jethro Mortymer, most unhappy you are looking for somebody courting the gentry. How is Tessa Lloyd Parry?"

"She does not come in here," I answered, and shouldered drovers aside for the counter.

"No offence, mind, only asking. Heard she was poorly again, that's all."

"Right poorly," said Gipsy May, joining me. Strange about this gipsy. Coffee-coloured, blowsy, half a yard of breast showing and bangle-earrings, was Gipsy, the daughter of Liza Heron of a Cardigan tribe; a woman in love with things that screeched and as tame as a meat-fed tiger, but mother-gentle when it came to Tessa. I lifted the mug and blew off the froth with Grandfer's eyes boring holes in my shoulders. First time we had shared Black Boar.

"You heard what ails her, Jethro Mortymer?"

I had heard but I would not say in there. Weak in the chest, was Tessa, and coughing with her the last time I saw her, eyes as bright as stones in her fever, and I had called old Ben, her servant, and he had carried her back to the house in tears. Three Sundays running I had walked to the Reach, letting Grandfer Badger off with a caution, feeling dull, and Tessa had not been there. Called at the house once and fished out old Ben, but he had turned up his nose at the garbage.

Sixpenny Jane in the corner by there, buxom, dark, pretty as a picture, giggling, posturing, her head flung back, kissing the air with her lips at a drover, driving him daft. Down on the Burrows lives Jane with her dad; a terror for the men, the curse of the women, but as clean as a new pin, and quiet. Strange how she resembled Mari with her inborn daintiness; cast in the same mould, the woman and the harlot. I cursed her soul as I saw her coming over for Grandfer's little eyes were peeping over his quart.

"You loose tonight, Jethro Mortymer?"

I looked at her, at the smoothness of her, the whiteness of her throat, and she smiled then and her lips were red and curved above the shine of her teeth.

"Don't judge by yourself," I said.

"O, hoity toity, eh? Respectable, is it? Gentry, is it?" Eyes closed to the light, she laughed, tinkling above the bedlam. Saw the curve of her waist, the dress taut across the upward sweep of her breasts. Pity I felt, and longing. But up leaped Flannigan, and shouldered her out of it.

"Leave her," he said. "There's quicker ways of dying," and he grinned and back-handed his bristling chin. "You heard, Mortymer? I've got a gate."

"You're lucky," I said. "Tom Rhayader's got two."

"Bullin's men. Sassenachs, not even Welsh. God, what a country. Another's going up in front of the kilns – that will catch the lot of us."

I drank, watching him. Dangerous, this one. I reckoned I

could take most there that night, including Gower, but not Abel Flannigan. Deep-chested, he topped six feet, and his hobby was bull-taming. When bulls went mad they always called for Abel. "Bull gone mad down at Morgan's place, Abel me son," Biddy would shout, "slip down and see to him, there's a good boy," and Abel would kill a quart or two to liven him up and cut a yew branch for the taming. Slippery on his feet for a big man, he would vault the gate and get the bull's tail and hang on relentless to the kicking and bucking, and every time the thing turned its head Abel would cut him on the nose with the yew. Bulls around our parts tossed and turned in their dreams of Abel.

"Something's got to be done, hear me? I'm burning ricks now but I'm heading for tollgates."

I jerked my head and lifted my mug as Osian Hughes got to his feet. Towering above us, he was biting at his fingers, his looks girlish, his face as white as a fish belly.

"O, God," said Abel. "Don't tell me," and turned.

"I've got a gate," said Osian, soprano.

"And what are you doing about it?"

Osian wrung his fingers.

"Look what we're up against," said Abel. "No guts, no fight, no nothing. Go to hell, girl, find yourself a drover."

"My mam says pay," whispered Osian. "We can't fight the Trusts."

"We can't fight with the likes of you to fight with," said Flannigan. "Thank God I was born with an Irish surname if yours is Welsh. But my mam Biddy is proper Welsh, and Biddy says fight. Look, Mortymer," he turned to me. "I have reckoned it up. If I take a cart to the kilns for a three-and-six-penny load it'll cost me one-and-a-penny to get it through. Three gates stand between me and the lime now, and full price tolls, mind, not halves."

"That's the gatekeepers," I said. "More fool you."

"But the notice is up there – full price tolls!"

"And you can't read and they know it."

"By heaven, I will have those keepers," he whispered, fist in his hand.

"And they are planning for another – Kidwelly to St Clears," said Osian.

I nodded. I had heard, but did not say, not with Flannigan in this mood.

"Bastards," said Flannigan. "You thought how many of us will use that one?"

"Nigh twenty," replied Osian, "counting me."

"Nobody's counting you," said Flannigan. His eyes narrowed and he prodded me. "More like fifty, I say – counting the upland people – folks like Tom Rhayader, and the upland boys like a fight for the fun of it. What you say?"

The cockfight grew to a shriek about us and feathers flew in a flash of spurs. Blood spattered the boards where a cock lay dying and money chinked from hand to hand. Men were shouting, shoving to the counter but giving the three of us a wide berth, eyeing Flannigan.

"Rebecca, eh?" I grinned at him.

"O, dear God!" whispered Osian, sweating.

"You get to hell out of it," said Flannigan. "Get yourself weaned," and brought up his elbow. He frowned around the room then, his eyes on Gower.

"Mind your tongue," he said soft. "There is more than one Judas."

"Just counted another," I replied, for Grandfer's eyes were unwinking from his corner, his little nose shining over the top of his quart. "And leave Gower be," I added.

"Just thinking," said he. "Best treat him respectable. Six months of this and we will all be at Ponty. How's that Morfydd of yours sticking it?"

"Don't mention her in here," I said.

"Outside, then. We will stick to Rebecca." He looked at me. "Bloody fool to talk in front of Osian. If they closed a fist at him he'd blab to the devil."

The June night was warm and alive with candle-flame stars, with a fat, kind moon. We leaned against Betsi's fence.

"You in with us or out, boy?"

"In," I replied. "Those gates come down."

90

"Which gates?"

"Kidwelly to St Clears."

"Give me strength, but a kid you are for all your size. The bloody things aren't up yet. Gates in general, I mean – round these parts."

"I'm with you."

"Right, you." He fisted my chin, knocking me sideways. "It's fixed. We are meeting next Wednesday, midnight. Up on the mountain in Tom Rhayader's barn."

"First meeting, Rebecca? Damned near Squire's Reach, mind."

"Poetic justice, boy. It was Squire Lloyd Parry who started the Trust and he is taking his profits from Lewis, the toll-contractor. Have his mansion next, like we had his salmon."

"You?" I had suspected it was Flannigan.

"Me and six others – Tom Rhayader leading. You heard about this Rhayader?"

"Seen him, that's all."

"We couldn't have a better Rebecca. He was there at Efailwen with Twm Carnabwth when they burned the gate. Chapel pugilist. I wouldn't tangle with him."

"Some man," I said.

"And a brain. Dangerous, mind – he will not stand non-sense."

"I will be there," I said.

"God help us," said he. "Goodnight."

I watched the stars for a bit, thinking of Mari, not knowing why, and turned to go back into Betsi's tavern and found myself facing Grandfer.

"Nice night, Jethro."

I nodded, sick of him.

"You mind your company, boy."

"You mind your business."

He chuckled then, tapping with his stick, his bald head scarcely up to my shoulder.

"How old are you, Jethro?"

"Hitting sixteen."

"Big boy – you look like gone twenty. And you mate with Abel Flannigan near twice your age?"

"I mate with whom I like," I said.

"Take you to the Devil, mind."

"Then I'll be in good company."

He looked up then and I saw the pouches of his red-rimmed eyes, his pickled walnut of a face, his jagged smile.

"Pretty stinky you think me, is it?"

I did not reply. Half a man is better than nothing and with this one living on ale and sawdust for no good reason I had worked myself stupid to harvest Cae White. Time was I owed him something. Not now.

"You make no allowance for age?"

"Uncle Silas is damned near eighty and still farming." I turned away.

"You know how old I be?"

"No more'n seventy."

And he grunted and cackled and stamped with his stick on my boot. "Don't know my age myself," said he. "Old enough to be born twice, I reckon," and he sighed deep and gripped my arm. "I've fought and drunk with most round here, young lusties – last fifty year – and they've all been called by St Peter 'cept me. You know my christian name. Zephaniah. Zephaniah, there's a mouthful. You know something more? Could be that a man with a name like that comes at the end of the cloud alphabet – could be St Peter's got his thumb on my name when he turns the pages of Paradise. Keeps passing me over, see? Me, poor old Grandfer, longing to die. You like the women, Jethro?"

"Old devil, you are, worrying Mari to death," I said.

"I asked you a question – you fancy the women?"

"Sick of women," I said. "Got too many back home."

"And poor little Sixpenny Jane back in there coming fidgety for turfing – there's a waste." He tapped with his stick and rocked with laughter. "Bless me, she'd get what she wanted from Grandfer forty years back – most did, forgive me soul." He belched and pardoned, staggering against me and I held him off, for there is nothing so vulgar as age and its conquests.

"Aye," he added, "a century back, it do seem. All honey and fire, I was chasing the skirts. But I've worn pretty well, mind, everything considered."

"For God's sake come home," I said, but he set back his shoulders and pulled up his shirt and his chest was white in its parchment of age. "Look now," he cried. "There's beautiful for eighty and some – very gratifying, life in the old dog yet, and I've laid my mark on the women of this county, don't you worry; many being privileged to say nothing of thankful. Now, that Morfydd sister of yours, there is a woman for favours to keep a man awake – with the face of an Irish and hair from Spain, and a temper on her like a boar coming frisky. You like my Mari?"

This turned me. Wicked was his eye, mouth grinning, beard trembling, knowing of the shaft. I sighed, bored.

"Oi, oi! Strikes a chord, do it? But no offence intended, mind – it was the same for me when I was your age."

"I am going home," I said, but he hooked me with his stick and looked up at the moon.

"Hush, you," he said. "Give me a minute, Jethro. All for your good."

I waited, disquieted, and listened as his voice came low and sad.

"A long time ago I knew a woman like our Mari. Bronwen was her name. In a shroud of night is our Mari, dark, dark, but this Bronwen girl came opposite – a white, blossomy piece as a hawthorn bush in spring blow and the face of a madonna – never seen the like of her since for beautifying." He looked at me and his eyes were different. "And gentry, too – remember that – gentry. All crinoline and ribbons, she was, and with perfume, and riding habit regular, she being keen on the hunt. She lived up by Laugharne with her dad, Sir Robert, her mam being dead. And I was her stable boy – ostler, you gather me?"

I nodded.

"And every evening on Sundays she would gallop her mare along the banks of the Taf River to Milton – to the long grasses where I lay waiting." He sucked his teeth, eyes narrowed to the memory. "And up she would come with her mare fairly lathered, wild as a gipsy, dying for me – me, Zephaniah, the ostler."

He looked at me. "You want more because you won't bloody like it."

"Go on," I said.

"Well, we met first when harvest was on us and the barn hay flying all golden and windy – in secret, remember, because of her dad. Eh, beautiful in summer are the crags and whirlpools of the Taf, with the herons crying doleful over the marshes, but terrible it is in winter when the snows are melting and the river is rushing in anger, spraying arms. But even in winter she came to me – for lovering."

"How old were you this time?"

"Stripling – same age as you, thereabouts, dying for garters. And after the lovering we would part pretty formal – Bron going back to her gentry feathers and me to my stable straw. 'Yes, ma'am, and no, ma'am,' it was, of course, with her folks growing ears, but every Sunday regular we would make love red-headed, my Bron and me, with naked bathing in the Taf pools and frolics on the river bank after with nobody watching but herons. You get much practice at that, boy?"

He was coming to a point now. I did not trust him. "I am going," I said, but he barred the way.

"Wait, you," he said. "Nothing personal, mind, lest you run a conscience."

"Wicked old devil," I said.

"Ah, so! But so was this Bronwen, remember – showed me the way, she did – near twice as wicked as me. You know Dai Education, the new tollkeeper up at the kilns near the Reach?"

"What's he to do with it?"

"Just wondered. Reckon little Dai might give us the answer, him being a scholar – as to why a beauty like Bron was interested in a chap like me. You fancy a quart, Jethro? Your Grandfer's gone dry."

"Just had a quart."

"But you want the rest of it, eh?"

I had to know the rest of it.

"Well, well! A wicked old tale it is for a chit of a boy like

94

you," and he gave a long shroud of a sigh. "Listen, then. Welsh gentry was my Bronwen – Welsh to her fingertips, as her name do tell, and Welsh-speaking, like me – which is proper Welshness, none of the foreign old English stuff you bring down here. County's changed, boy. Fifty years back you'd be straining your ears for an English damn, but the place is going to the bloodies just now. Mind, Dai Education do say it's the industry, these furnace men and collier chaps coming in, staining the land with their foreign ideas . . ."

"For God's sake," I said. "What about this woman?"

"And me with a throat like the bottom of a bird cage – parrots at that."

"Just one, then we're back out."

"Sharper than billhooks, boy – promise."

So we went back into Black Boar tavern.

I passed over the twopence and Grandfer went up for the quarts, slapping down the money, bawling for attention, helloing to strangers – one in particular, a tiny wizened shrew of a man who was cranked and blue. Jackknifed, hobbling on his ploughing corns, he was carrying and slopping his ale to a table. Back came Grandfer wobbling the quarts and we sat down opposite.

Grandfer jerked his head. "You notice Ezekiel?"

I nodded. Bald as an egg was this Ezekiel, whiskers drooping, and his face and hands were as blue as a blackberry, and I pitied him.

"Reckoned Ezekiel would be in just now. That's why I came back."

"Why?" I asked.

Grandfer drank deep and wiped with his cuff. "Powerful is the Man in the Big Pew, and fearful when He is denied. Terrible is He to His misbehaving children." He waved his mug at the room. "And there's one or two in by here due for His wrath pretty soon, boy. You mind you don't join them. Have a look at Ezekiel."

"What about your Bronwen?"

"Bronwen can wait. You see Ezekiel there? You know how

he got so cranked? Well, thirty years back it would be when Ezekiel was courting Biddy Flannigan, Abel's mam. Down in the Big Wheatfield, it was, all of a summer's day. Tall and straight was Ezekiel then, forking a harvest as high as the next. You listening?"

I sighed.

"Well, coming pretty hot with him was Ezekiel, and poor little Biddy was all legs and petticoats and hollering for her mam, for the boy was that determined. Not a cloud in the sky, remember – harvest time, remember. But the Big Man was watching and His sky came dark – nobody near to give Biddy a hand. So down came the lightning and caught Ezekiel square – smack in the middle of the back, and Biddy Flannigan not even singed."

"O, aye?" I cocked an eye at him.

"The truth. Just for fulfilling a normal function. And that is the first example. Now for the second, the lesson of wrath." He lowered his mug and stared at nothing. "In child, was Bronwen. In child by me, you understand?"

The bellowing of the room died between us.

"And the child was born, Jethro. The child was Mari's mother, which makes our Mari gentry blood." He turned to me, eyes fixed to mine. "Down from Laugharne came her dad with his whip, and I had it. God, I had it naked – damned near killed me. But he left me Bronwen – cast her out as the gentry do a wayward hound. He left me Bronwen and Cae White to go with her for a pound a week rent for the rest of my life. Now listen," and he gripped my wrist. "Payable on his death to his son, Squire Lloyd Parry. You following me?"

I was gaping now, knowing the secrets of Cae White, knowing of Mari.

"Aye, Cae White is mine, and Parry can't turn me out of it, and it is Mari's after I am gone. . . ."

"And your Bronwen?" I whispered in a lull.

"If I go on the hops it is because of my Bronwen, boy. For she bore my child and then she vanished, went down to the river for the shame of it, in the place where we loved. And they found her three weeks later on the reaches of Laugharne – on

96

the night of Whitland Fair, it was, with mud in her mouth and her eyes taken by gulls. Reckon she walks Cae White by night. You heard her?"

Terrible was his face in that grief.

"God help you, Grandfer," I said, and he raised his face, his eyes swimming.

"God help me, is it?" he said. "God help you for mating with gentry, Mortymer, d'you hear me?"

I rose, staring down at him. "You cranked little devil," I whispered. "Me and Tessa Lloyd Parry's been nothing but decent!"

"Sit down!" and he got me sharp with his stick. "Do I fear the wrath of the likes of you when I have faced the wrath of God? Who's talking about Tessa Lloyd Parry? The girl is a cripple and couldn't mate with a butterfly, her body dead from the waist down. Is she the only gentry girl who is taking the rove of your eye?"

I clenched my hands.

"Be warned, Mortymer," said he. "Grandfer has been watching. With Cae White as your Eden and your brother's wife for a lover, the fingers of Cain shall reach up from the dust, and seek you. Be gone!"

Light chopped the hedge as I opened the door. The gables of Kidwelly were gaunt in the distance, a steeple a pine-needle of silver in moonlight. With Tara against me I walked back home. Sick, sick I felt, of life.

## CHAPTER 11

*September!*

I AWOKE ON the Feast Day Sunday to a dazzling, jewel-blue morning, and the air through my window was sparkling and heady with its scents of coming autumn and the fields below me swam in vivid light, every bough tipped with hoar frost and dripping diamonds as the sun kicked Jack Frost out of it. Rebecca meetings, threats of action, notes to magistrates, but not a suggestion from Tom Rhayader that we should get down to the business of tollgates, and I was getting sick of it. To hell with Rebecca, I said, and to hell with Grandfer, too, including his gentry Bronwen.

To hell with farming, too, for this was the Feast Day.

Plenty of activity downstairs, with women up and rushing with pots and pans clattering, everyone singing and laughing in anticipation of the joys to come.

Up and doing, me – dashing down the stairs with the towel waving, gave Morfydd one with it as I skidded through the kitchen, and out to the water butt to plunge my head down. Splashing, ducking, I didn't hear them come up behind me, and Mari got one leg and Morfydd the other and I was in head first and drowning till Mam ran out swiping with a dishcloth and hauling me out while the boys were leaping around as things possessed. O, great was the joy of that September morning, all cares forgotten, the house tinkling with laughter, and even Grandfer allowed himself a chuckle, his warnings washed away in the Black Boar jugs. Best clothes, me; smarming my hair down with Mari's goose fat which she used for chests; getting the hair flat to the head; clean shirt, belted up to strangle; nip into Grandfer's room for his funeral stock, and I stood before Morfydd's mirror all shines and creases, a sight fit to turn the head of a countess. Downstairs to make an impression, for a man who is handsome and six feet is a fool not to make the best of it, but everyone seemed too busy to take notice, for Mam and Morfydd were dressed for prize bantams and Mari came down all ribbons and lace, slim and willowy in the new black dress she had made. Richard, too, very smart in the suit Mam had stitched for him, and Jonathon with an old one of Richard's cut down. Eh, there's handsome are little boys dressed for Feast Days, all curls and podges, their little faces alight with teary excitement.

"Precious baby!" cried Morfydd, throwing up Jonathon and kissing him and Richard climbed up me with Tara trying to nip him out of it, and in the middle of the commotion in comes Grandfer.

"*Whee*, there's an old wacko!" cried Morfydd. "Look, Mam, look! O, love him!"

Funeral suit for Grandfer; bald head polished for glass; breeches and knee gaiters, frock coat and buttonholes either side and a gold-knobbed cane, proper gentry. And the women got him in a ring and danced around him shrieking and laughing, with Mam soothing and patting him, telling what a good boy he was not to let the family down, and Morfydd even kissed his cheek. No damned notice of me, anyone. Set the room tidy, a last brush of clothes, looking for stray hairs on the black dresses and Mam saying her stays were killing her, and then the form up. Hushing for quiet then, fingers to lips, behave to the children, and out of the front we went very sedate and along the road to Osian Hughes Bayleaves' field where the Fair was set; Mam and Grandfer leading, Morfydd and Mari next, then the boys, and me at the behind to keep them in order. And my heart thumped with pride as we entered the field. Not a glance right or left, keeping our dignity, for there is nothing neighbours like better than a good impression, so we gave them proud Mortymers. Knew their places, too, for the women were dropping curtseys and the men thumbing their hats. Can't beat the Welsh for politeness in the morning, mind, even if it comes to free fights at night. O, that Fair Day! We came a bit late, of course, which we thought proper, and hundreds were there lining the field, all green and sunshine and colour, with scarves waving and skirts swirling, and some of the couples pairing off already. Saw Sixpenny Jane as we walked in, very pretty, very swelling above the waist, thank God, and the look of adoration she gave me lasted a lifetime. Biddy Flannigan next, wheezing and panting, with Abel, her son, beside her, his brow dark with his plans for burnings.

"Good morning, Mam Mortymer and family. Good morning, Grandfer!"

"Good morning, Mrs Flannigan," said Mam, inclining her hat, though any other time she'd have gone rings round Biddy. But stepping it out on Grandfer's arm now – taking the obeisance like a French aristocrat. Saw Osian Hughes by the gate, too, fish face lighting up at the sight of Morfydd.

"A very handsome family, if I might say, Mrs Mortymer," said Mrs Toby Maudlin scarecrowed in black, her stays creaking for ship's timbers as she made her bow, hitting her Toby with an elbow till he lifted his hat. On, on, to the middle of the field, turning every head in the place, with the labourers pausing at the field ovens for eyefuls of Mari and Morfydd, easy the loveliest women in the place. Saw Hettie Winetree near the cider barrels with something under her apron, feet itching, hands screwing for a sight of me, then found she was looking at some other chap, could have killed him. Nobody taking a blind bit of notice of me so far, except Sixpenny, and she was man-mad. And then, O, joy! I saw Tessa watching me from Squire's party in the middle of the field. Pale and thin she sat in her wheelchair, scarfed and rugged against the wind while old Ben, her servant, bowed and grey, stood behind her, watching every move. On, the procession – straight up to Squire Lloyd Parry, and full marks to Squire despite his Trusts. Surrounded by gentry on all sides, he came out and waited – didn't give Grandfer a glance, but he bowed back low to Mam as she stepped aside and held her skirt wide to her headdown curtsy. Don't like scraping, mind, but I like good manners between man and maid, and so pretty it looks when they bow to one's mother. Morfydd next after Mari went down. Stipped naked she would have faced tigers before lowering a knee to a man, least of all Squire, but she inclined her head, and I saw a few gentry ladies whispering behind fans. Ten thousand pounds for a face like Morfydd's, this, the hauler of gentry trams. Harps and singers were rolling up now, Irish fiddles being tuned, drums beaten, horses neighing and a roar from the crowd as a dead pig was hauled up. Could have wept, for I thought of poor Dai Two back home in Nanty going to his ancestors like a saint. Did it myself, too, God forgive me, had to eat something. A little sucking pig came next, first prize by Squire for the wrestling contest, and I saw Justin Slaughterer smack his backside to send him screaming and then wipe the spit from his chops in anticipation, for he was reckoning to win it.

"Is he getting away with that?" asked Morfydd after the reception.

"Who, now?"

"That Justin Carver, wrestling."

"Never wrestled in my life," I said.

"O, aye? What was that look from Sixpenny Jane, then?"

"*Heisht!*" I said, for Mari was in earshot.

"Big and stupid enough, mind," said Morfydd. "All backside he is. If you fetch him low enough he'd never get up, and I would like that pig. You see to him later or you'll never hear the end of it."

"Justin would cripple me," I said, weighing him.

"Doesn't matter what he does to you, just get me that pig. Hey, look now!"

"Where by?"

"Over by there, man, you are getting the eye. Mind you don't waste it."

"And what is this about wrestling and sucking pigs?" asked Mam, tapping.

Asses ears, this one, whispers being shouts to her.

"Eh, nothing," said Morfydd.

"And you the instigator? Being watched today, so I will not have violence. Wrestling, indeed!"

"Do you think I would throw him to Justin Slaughterer?" asked Morfydd. "For the sake of a sucking-pig? And me in love with the family?"

"I am happy I misheard, then," said Mam. "Sorry."

"You get me that pig, mind," said Morfydd, moving away, "or I might drop a word out of place."

"A lady is waving to you, Jethro," said Mam, coming back, and her face was flushed with pleasure.

"Tessa!" I whispered, straightening my stock.

Gentry now, a rise in social standards, with the ladies and gentlemen all looking our way and Mam nodding and bowing and he won't be a minute he's just coming over.

"Squire is asking for you, Jethro," said Mari, running breathless.

"Away," said Morfydd, "and don't make a pig of yourself."

"Mind your manners, mind," said Mam, flushing with

pleasure. "Pleases and thank you's if you are offered anything, remember."

"And straight back, too," whispered Morfydd. "None of your Sixpenny Janes."

"There's a good boy," said Mari, brushing at me. "Try to make a good impression. O, there's an honour for the Morty-mers, that proud I am!"

Over the fifty yards or so to where the gentry were standing, with glasses going up and fans coming down and look at that fine young man, good God. As a man to gallows, me, with me going one way and my suit another and my feet all hobnails, red as a lobster, for a hell of a thing it is to be called over to gentry. Nearer they came, grouped and dignified, the ladies on one side of Tessa, gentlemen on the other, all polished bellies and chins and gold-topped canes, and lovely were their women haughty and drooping under their lace-fringed parasoles, sweeping the grass with their long, white dresses. Heard Morfydd's giggle as I stopped short, and I put my hand to my breast and bowed to Tessa, and the men bowed back.

"Good day, young Mortymer." Squire now, his voice bass music.

"Good day, sir," I said.

O, what is it that bites and tears in the breast when you feel unequal? I fought it down in Tessa's radiant smile, and then my world was made.

"Handsome boy," whispered Squire to a lady. "And from a handsome line, I would say. Have you noticed his sister? Most respectable people, also."

"And Tessa appears interested, I can see," and the fan came up to hide the kind smile.

"Jethro!" Hand out, was Tessa, her eyes burning in her thin, grey face.

"Good day, Miss Lloyd Parry," I said, going down again. Up and down like a bloody ninepin me, that Fair Day, but it had its compensations, for every eye in the field was on me and Mam coming a bit damp with her and dabbing with pride, no doubt.

"Well mannered, most collected, d'you notice?" whispered a man.

If I looked collected I didn't feel it for my belt had stopped my breathing minutes back and my new oiled boots were killing me.

"How is your mother, Jethro?" Poor Tessa, a whisper for a voice.

"Most pleasant, I may say, Miss Lloyd Parry. I trust you are better?"

This put a couple of them sideways. Give hobnails a chance and they soon match gentry.

"I have never felt better," Tessa replied, clutching at her handkerchief. "O, Jethro, what a beautiful day!"

Searing is the sadness that hits you in the face of such courage; when words are empty, useless things. Sick to death she looked at that moment, but with a spirit that would have taken her twenty rounds and stripped to the waist with Justin Slaughterer. She smiled then, her red lips fevered against the paper whiteness of her cheeks and her fingers brushed old Ben's knee. He drifted away, as did the gentry. Saw Squire move then, pressing his fingers to his forehead, his face turned down.

"There now!" I said, and sat down beside her.

Her hand sought for mine and found it, gripping, unashamed.

"Jethro, when are you coming again to the Reach?"

"Been up six times," I said. "No sign of you, girl."

This sat her up. "God bless you," she said. "O, Jethro, I do love you so. I have been off colour a bit lately, but I will be there again now, for they say I am better."

"Truly better?"

"And this is the best day of all. Wonderful I feel today, every scent, every breath . . ."

God help her.

"Jethro."

"Yes, girl?"

"You . . . will come to me again?"

"Every Sunday. I promise."

"And you will wait for me there – no other girls?"

"Just you," I said.

"O, I am terrible," she whispered. "Jethro, I am ashamed!"

I thought she was going to cry and longed to hold her.

"Tessa, people are watching."

"I do not care. Jethro, you are still my boy? There is nobody else? Sometimes when a girl is away . . ."

"Still for you, Tessa," I said.

She laughed then, and I saw her father give us a queer old look and a smile.

Strange are gentry. Boiling oil for me twelve months back.

"Before the autumn goes I will meet you," she said. "I will come down to the river again with Ben, and you will kiss me again as you did in summer?"

"Hush, you are making me wicked," I said. The woman leaped into her face at this and she clutched at my fingers and closed her eyes, gusty in breathing.

"Jethro."

"Yes?"

She turned away her face.

"Nothing," she said, but I knew what she was thinking. Then:

"One day I will love you, Jethro. Truly. One day . . ."

"Aye," I replied. People were watching us now. Didn't give a damn for them, except for Tessa. Gentry eyes were switching, hats coming round.

"One day you will touch me, I promise," she whispered.

"Tessa, I must go."

"Yes. Goodbye, my darling."

I do not remember going back to my family, but I know I went without pride, and Morfydd touched my hand when I got back, and smiled.

"Good boy, you are," she said. "He can have his old pig. Poor little Tessa."

Dancing now, in the midst of joy, for the wind had blown up sudden and cold and Tessa went home with a waved goodbye. Just couldn't have danced with Tessa there.

Dancing to the Irish fiddles now, with the bright red stockings going up in a thrill of lace petticoats, Biddy Flannigan in the middle beating the time, and the leather-jacketed men turning in circles, hands on hips, poaching caps at jaunty angles, linking arms with the maidens, breathless, singing.

"Come on in!" cried Morfydd, whirling me into it, dragging at Mari, and the three of us went into the *Gower Reel*, taking partners, backwards and forwards, and I noticed Justin Slaughterer prancing away opposite Mari and Abel Flannigan bowing to Morfydd and handing her round. Fiddles were soaring, harps twanging and the drums beating in a medley of joy and movement. The crowd surged round us, laughing and clapping to time. Little Meg Benyon, up with her skirts, handing on to Osian Hughes; Toby and Mrs Maudlin, Gipsy May and Betsi, even Grandfer and Mam now, skirts swirling, boots tapping, O, joyful is the dance! The longer it runs to the rhythmic beat the wilder and wilder it comes, throbbing at the heart, swinging at the senses, and the last, breathless chord comes when you kiss your partner. Biddy Flannigan nearest, so I grabbed her, fighting another man off, and a good old smacker I gave Biddy, bringing down her bun and making her scream, and then I saw Mari. Justin had her – kissed her once and pulling at her again while she fought him off, shrieking and laughing. But her laughter died in the crush of his lips as he hooked her against him when everyone had finished. As a bear he had her then, laughing, his hair ragged while she pushed at his chest and yelled for Morfydd. Fun, of course.

"Oi, Oi, Oi!" shouted Morfydd, coming up, tapping him.

"Oi, Oi," said Justin over his shoulder and bent to Mari again.

Fun no longer. In a stride I was at him and yanked him away from her.

"No, Jethro, no!" screamed Mari. Too late, for I had him; seeing the swing of his hands as he turned to face me and the square of his jaw. He fell against me, scraping down the front of me, landing at my feet. Just stood there, aware of eyes, and silence, and the searing pain of my hand, for Justin was cast iron. Whispers now. Men bending to pull him off; lay him out tidy, snoring happily. Strange how a man unconscious snores. Stranger his face, alive one moment, lifeless the next. Caught him right – everything right for me, a three inch hook and him running on to it. Didn't know what hit him, just dropped. Then Mam came up and swung me round, her face blazing, her arm pointing.

"Home," she said. "Home this minute!"

"Mam," said Morfydd, her hands out, and I saw Mari weeping.

"Home!" My mother brushed Morfydd aside; tongue-tied, white with fury.

"Mrs Mortymer," said Biddy Flannigan. "You cannot blame the boy."

"That is no kind of kissing," said another. "And she a young married woman. Isn't decent."

"And it is not decent to resort to fists. Jethro, I said *home*!"

"Count me, then," said Morfydd. "I go with him."

"Go, then. O, I am ashamed, ashamed," whispered Mam.

People crowding round her now, sympathizing, women chiefly, but Dai Alltwen gave me a look to kill, though out of the corner of my eye I saw Abel Flannigan nodding and smiling as he bent above Justin who was coming round now, and Abel winked. Soon fixed the Feast Day, put an end to the dancing. Everyone very dull now and thank God Squire had left, might have frightened little Tessa to death, poor soul, and isn't it a shame having to mix with pugilists, battering each others brains out, you heard about these Mortymers – the same up in Monmouthshire, you heard? The father being the worst, and what can you expect of people not Church, to say nothing of Horeb.

"Pretty good hook that, though," said Morfydd, going home.

"Shut it," I said.

"He'd have got worse, mind, if I'd been three feet nearer, the beast."

Too ashamed to talk, me. Grandfer was standing at the gate, I noticed.

"It'll be a day or two before he gets his chops into beef," said Morfydd. "Justin Slaughterer, is it? Justin just slaughtered. Eh, pretty good that. Look out, here is trouble."

Grandfer barring the way from the field, smiling, his hand up to stop us.

"Do not take it badly, Jethro," said he. "Your mam will come round."

"You on our side, Grandfer?" asked Morfydd.

"Who else, girl? Does he stand and watch her ravished?"

"The filthy swine," I said, trembling. "It will teach him to keep his dirty hands off her. Filthy, filthy . . .!" The anger was coming to me now, strangely, and I saw Morfydd's glance.

"Just what her husband would have done, Jethro," said Grandfer, leering. "Rest you in peace, do not have a conscience."

But I did not really hear his words until I got home. I knew what he meant, and hated him.

"Better go up," said Morfydd. "You know what Mam is."

"She wouldn't dare!" I said.

"I have had it, remember – she can hand out beltings, little as she is. And she don't know her strength with a three foot willow."

"I am not being thrashed like a child!"

Morfydd jerked her thumb. "Up, boy, you've got to bloody have it. Thumpers and pugilists have got to be brought into line – reckon you'd better fold up the *Cambrian*. She raised lumps on me last time she belted, and you'll be lucky with trews on and good sound packing, I was drawers off."

Fussy walk coming down the path now, Mam meaning business, with Mari running beside her dragging at her and the boys tearing after them for a look at the slaughter.

"Up," said Morfydd, "lest you have it down by here."

"Jethro!" Mari at the bottom of the stairs now, weeping, clutching her dress. "O, Jethro, I am sorry."

I winked, grinning at her. "What Mam gives me now I will give back to Justin, do not worry, girl."

Mam now, just found the stick after rummaging, working herself into a fury, blocked at the bottom of the stairs with Morfydd and Mari pushing and shoving her and begging her to be reasonable. Don't know what hit me then but I had to laugh. I threw back my head and rocked with laughter, ran to my room and went full length on the bed. Just hit out flat a fifteen stone slaughterer and running from a five foot mam with a stick. I laughed till I cried and the first stroke hit me. Round the room we went, Mam swinging, me ducking, but she cornered me at last.

She should have been in the Navy with her mainmast floggings.

# CHAPTER 12

TROUBLE WAS coming.

The wooden horse was stalking the Carmarthenshire hills most nights now, catching the spots from Pembrokeshire. In every town Rebecca was springing up, and this, a movement that began with the small farmers, was now bringing in farm labourers and even quite rich farmers – both ends of the social scale. No gates were burned since Efail-wen, but hayricks were going up nightly, fewer threatening letters sent to the magistrates, more action instead. Floggings were frequent for those who dished out floggings, but Rebecca was best with the moral wrongs. Chiefly a Nonconformist movement, the laws of God were invoked as reason for the punishments. A man could not even beat his wife without a warning or worse; flog a child and be flogged; bastard babies were delivered at night to callous fathers who had cast off their mothers. A guardian of public morals was Rebecca, thank God, said Morfydd, who was a fine one to talk, said Mam, the way she had carried on in Monmouthshire and now trying the same antics here.

September died into the mists of late autumn. Prices were going up, the cost of living leaping weekly, but the price of corn was coming down – blame the damned speculators, said Flannigan, though he couldn't spell the name – blame the rapacious men of industry who were discharging labour in order to keep their bulbous profits. Blame the swindlers who were jacking up food prices without official control at a time when people were starving and prepared to work for a loaf. One thing to grow your corn these days, quite another thing to sell it, and what slender profit you managed to get was swallowed by the iniquitous road tolls. So I threshed our corn that year, paid in kind to the miller for its grinding, and used the flour for our bread – living off the land in every sense, but I knew this would not last for long. I was paying the pound a week rent now, not Grandfer, and our savings were again nearly gone; Morfydd alone kept us from the workhouse, and I knew I would have to join her at Ponty soon again, although I had grown to love farming.

"Potatoes, potatoes," said Morfydd, "that is the county's trouble.

"The county would starve without them, though," said Mam.

"Work it out," replied Morfydd, hot as usual. "Potatoes and biddings are the root of starvation, and this is how it works. A couple in love want to marry, and can't – they can't because they haven't twopence to bless themselves with. So they have a bidding and their friends subscribe, and they rake up a few pounds to start a home. Then come the kids, one every year, with the couple forking out their shilling a week for their friends who want to marry – returning the bidding money. This brings them low, so they drop to potatoes – once a day for a start – three times a day later, and that is starvation."

"Nothing wrong with a mess of potatoes, though," said Mam. "God knows what we'd do without the old spud."

"God knows," I said, "until you eat them every meal."

"And if the crop fails, you starve," said Morfydd, "like Ireland. Potatoes, undernourishment; more potatoes, illness; no potatoes, death. And if you doubt me ask them in Dublin. Same with this country. A north country farm labourer is cheaper to employ at fifteen shillings a week than a Welsh labourer on half the money, for the Welshman has been reared on your precious spuds and his output is a third of the man from the north. If you flog him to work, he dies – worked out at thirty – open your church registers."

"Happy little soul, you are," said Mam. "Talking about death. Do you think we could talk about living for a change."

"Give me something to live for and I'll try," replied Morfydd.

I chanced a look at her. Still beautiful, still vital, I could see her changing with every month at Ponty. For a tram-tower she was living on borrowed time; should have passed on years back.

"Something will have to be done," continued Morfydd. "Wherever you look the coffins are out and doing, but few bishops die, except from overeating, arriving at the throne room with a chicken leg in each hand, side by side with the workhouse poor. One consolation, questions will be asked. The gentry the same – go to Carmarthen for the gilded carriages with their damned postillions whipping for a path. Eh, God alive! Banquets and feasts on the smallest excuse while we get by on oatmeal broth. Few gentry die, except from port."

"How is Tessa these days?" asked Mari.

This as always, the discreet, the gentle; changing the subject, blunting the edge of Morfydd's knife; God, I loved her, and flung my thoughts back to Tessa.

"I have not heard," I said.

"Do you think it would be too much trouble to find out?" asked Morfydd.

"I have been to the Reach waiting every Sunday for months."

"If I loved a man who was dying I would not knock at the door. I would be in there quick, and hook him out. You could have called, Jethro." She looked at me.

"Leave it," said Mam, frowning.

"Seconds back you were shouting about gentry," I said, bitter.

Morfydd glanced up. "Gentry living and gentry dying are two different things. Poor little soul."

"You cannot expect him to knock at the door," said Mari. "Morfydd, they would only throw him out."

"He is a Mortymer," said Morfydd. "He does the throwing."

"Better go up, boy," said Mam. "For once Morfydd is right."

Morfydd rose and went to the fire, hands spread to the peat blaze. "You don't have to worry, they are sending for you tonight."

"Who?" I asked.

"Squire. Don't ask me more, I don't know any more – heard it in the village. Tessa is nearing the end. . . ."

"God," I said, and got up, wandering, gripping things.

"And Squire is sending down for Jethro?" whispered Mari.

There was a meeting that night up on the mountain, but I could not go now. Rising, I went out the back and looked at the sky. I was watching for rain about then, having in mind an early ploughing. Leaned against the back, dreaming. The fields were coming ghostly under the moon and he was as big as a cheese with him and rolling over the mountains. A nip of frost was in the air and a scent of peat fires, and I saw for the first time quite clearly the mud and wattle houses squatting on the foothills as little bullfrogs, their blind windows glinting for eyes. Went back into the house, cold away from the fire. And Mari was reading from the Book.

" 'By night on my bed I sought him whom my soul loveth: I sought him, but I found him not. I will rise now, and go about the city in the streets, and in the broad ways. I will seek him whom my soul loveth: I sought him, but found him not. The watchmen that go about the city found me; to whom I said, Saw ye him whom my soul loveth . . . ?' "

Sitting down, I watched Mari's face. No grief there, save for the brightness of her eyes, which could have been because of the beauty, then I looked at my mother. Stitching away like mad, she was, too busy for innocence, and Morfydd nodded at them a queer old look and a sigh. I knew what she was thinking.

"Can't you find something happier, Mari?" I asked, sitting down.

"It is what Mam wants," said Mari.

"Great is the Lord and with humour," said Morfydd. "Heaven knows why we clad Him in sackcloth and misery, as if He never smiled."

"My Reading," said Mam. "There are other rooms in the house. Go on, Mari."

And Mari read:

" 'It was but a little while that I passed from them, but I found him whom my soul loveth; I held him, and would not

III

let him go, until I had brought him into my mother's house, and into the chamber of her that conceived me . . .' "

My mother was weeping softly, stitching away.

"Mam, for God's sake," I said, and she raised her eyes at me, lowering them with a gesture of helplessness.

"No good hunting for tears, Mam," said Morfydd. "There is enough to go round for the lot of us."

Something was into me that night. I said, "A damned grave this is, not a house. Is it right to bleed yourself about Dada one minute and sing the glories of meeting in Heaven the next?"

"Jethro," Mam whispered, helpless.

"You mind, now!" said Morfydd in panic.

"Weepings and Readings will not bring him back!" I said. "God, if he could see you sometimes. Ghosts walk this house, not people – Richard; my father, and Iestyn – even Grandfer has his own pet ghost. Is it courage, is it living?"

"One day you will lose somebody, Jethro," said Mari.

"I am losing somebody now. And when once she is gone nothing will be gained by weeping and moaning."

It is bitter to see someone you care for making no fight of it. My mother had courage once, when she fought Nanty; when she scraped night and day to keep her family alive. Arrogant was her grief when she lost Edwina, as if she had made a fist of sorrow and brandished it in faces. No patience in me for this milksop weeping, singing the Song of Solomon, twisting herself to tears.

"You finished?" asked Morfydd, cold.

I turned away.

"Good," said she, "now let me have a say. It do so happen that I have lost a man, too, and though I may not show it his loss turns like a knife, and we do not need the likes of you to tell us how to bear it lest you tell us with your fist in the fire till the sinews stretch and snap. Women have tears and men mind their business. Damned cruel, you are, to our little mam."

"I am going," I said, and got up.

"And damned good riddance, forgive me, Mam."

"Wait," said Mari. "Somebody is coming."

"Hearing things," I said.

I was not heartless, just bitter that my mother should torture herself, and I knew why. The visions of my father returned with greater power, she had said, since Morfydd had started coaling in Ponty; as if the grime of the washing-sink had re-stained her; the galleries of Nantyglo making echo in the dust of Morfydd's hair and her coal-rimmed eyes. *Bitter*. I could have taken the name of my father just then and hurled it over towns, over the smoke-grimed roofs of Nanty where he died, battered it on the walls of mansions. Bitter, bitter, and I spit at grief. I got up, swinging on my coat, knowing a morgue better than this one, Black Boar tavern.

"I said somebody was coming," said Mari. "Listen," and a footstep scraped on the flags outside and a fist came on the door. I opened it.

Ben, Tessa's servant, come down from the Reach.

"You Jethro Mortymer?"

"Know damned well I am."

"Squire wants you up there, it's important," and he wept.

I closed my eyes and turned, looking into the room, and there came to me a song that was mine, the song of Tessa.

Left them alone with their Song of Solomon.

Queer is life and its sweet, sad music.


Never been up to the mansion before save for kisses and poaching, strange going up as a guest. And I went in the front way to Lloyd Parry's credit, old Ben standing aside. Parry was awaiting me in the hall, the hall I had seen so often through windows. Narrow waisted, six feet odd, handsome in his black frock coat and cravat, he was waiting.

"Tessa is calling for you, Mortymer," he said, and gripped my shoulder.

This was the ogre of the Trusts, a man broken, grey with grief. This was the one they had over every night in the taverns now, roasting him alive, drawing his name in ale. A fine as soon as he looks at you, they said, six months gaol for the leg of a rabbit. If his mantraps don't get you Squire Parry will. Land in prison for sure if you stand before his bench; enter his Reach and you don't come out alive.

"O, Jethro," he said, and gripped me, sobbing against me.
Just two men now. I held him, giving the nod to Ben over his
shoulder.

"All I've got," he said.

Just held him, nothing more I could do. Then he straightened, bracing himself and his head went up, bringing out the
breeding.

"Tessa is dying," he said.

Words come like fists swung in anger and you cannot ride or
duck them, but stand square to the smack, as rooted.

He ran his fingers through his hair, lost, and I pitied him.

"For some time she has been asking, it seems, but we could
not make it out till old Ben listened."

"Yes," I said.

"You will see her?"

"Yes, sir."

"You will be good to her."

I nodded, screwing at my hat.

"Come," he said, "I will take you up," and turned to the
great white staircase and its thick, crimson carpet. I followed
him up the stairs to the landing where peak-faced servants
rustled to a great white door as the gateway of Heaven. Silently,
he opened it.

"I will leave you alone with her," he whispered.

The room was musty, every window shut tight against the
chance of draught, with a smell of burned tallow. A great log
fire burned in the hearth, leaping, spluttering. An ocean of a
bed with a silk panelled head and blue counterpane, and the
ship of its sea was Tessa's face; stark white that face, her black
hair flung over the pillows. Tiptoed in and stood beside her,
looking down. Beautiful. Her skin was transparent in the light
of the bedside candles; one hand on the silk, as wax; and the
long, slim fingers were moving, seeking. Kneeling, I pressed
them.

"Tessa," I said, but she made no sign.

Just knelt there beside her, watching, remembering summer,
and I bowed my head. When I looked again her eyes were open
and she smiled, but not with her lips.

"Tessa." I bent nearer. "Jethro, it is. You asking, girl?"

An otter barked down on the Reach and its mate replied with a whistle and I saw her eyes move to the window.

"You hear the otters, Tess?"

She nodded. No sound then but the sparking of the candles and her gusty breathing. The barking came again and she moved her eyes, listening. I leaned closer.

"You hear them?" I whispered. "Them old poachers still at it – going like demons for the salmon near the steps. God, there is big ones this year, coming up for spawning. Thirty pounds or more, I reckon, you should see them leaping!"

It breathed new life into her and she gripped my hand.

"And Bill Stork is still on one leg, down on the estuary – old Grandfer Badger's rooting round Bully Hole Bottom – remember Grandfer? Had him out by the tail again last Sunday when I come up. And the curlews are crying from here to Kidwelly – you heard them?"

She smiled then, her eyes coming alive. Excited, I drove on.

"And the hayricks are burning right down to Tarn – remember Rebecca? Rockets most nights, too, but beautiful are the fires, as glow-worms, just as you said. Rebecca like I told you, done up in petticoats, looking for bad men to carry on poles. O, Tess, when you get better I will take you down to the Taf, and I will kiss you and you will weave a rush hat for me just like you did last spring, remember?"

But she was not really listening now, though her eyes were full on my face.

"O, God," I said, and wept.

Just once she spoke, scarcely heard it:

"Jethro," and she took my hand and held it against her breast.

Wearing the birthday brooch, too, just seen it.

Soft her breast on the tips of my fingers, cold her lips in that autumn of fire.

I kissed her.

Dear little woman.

# CHAPTER 13

THE TIME for lovering is spring but they do things different round our way. The blood heats up in November, it seems, and thins itself down for May, though Morfydd reckoned the sport was all the year round.

One or two going daft in our village. Tom the Faith for one – dying for our mam, pitiful to see him, and Waldo Rees Bailiff likewise, the pair of them losing weight. Very rarely apart, these two, which is strange for chalk and cheese, with only one thing in common – the Black Boar tavern ale, though Tom the Faith went there for pints and Waldo for Gipsy May.

A maligned man was Tom Griffiths the Faith, with a wedded-all-over look since my mother came to Cae White. He lived on the banks of the Tywi in a cottage old enough for savages. Grandfer's height but big in the stomach, Tom's pipe was his only friend; his music the clatter of his dead wife's teacups, his memories the swish of her shuttle when spinning. Sitting by his winter fires with the rushes of the river tapping his window, Tom's short life with Martha was the past, present and future in the hands of the Lord. For Tom the Faith knew it all, from Genesis to Revelation and back return journey, and every Sunday at dawn he would stand up to his neck in the river for an hour to atone for the sins of the village. Cherubim and Seraphim mated, was Tom, till he sighed at our mam and went on the hops.

Different was Waldo Rees Bailiff; most sure of himself, this one, with the spiked moustache and fob watch and all the things that go to make up gentry save gentility. Virgin pure, too, saving himself for the right lady, he said, though Morfydd reckoned she was safer with Grandfer's stallion than trusting herself to Waldo, who spent a shilling a week on Gipsy May.

Tom Griffiths first. Did things properly, give him credit; very spruced up and collared was Tom, fortified well by the smell of his breath. And he stood at the door in splendour, did Tom, bowing double, his hat sweeping the doorstep.

"What the hell does he want?" asked Grandfer, peeping over the top of the *Cambrian*.

"It is only a social visit, mind," said Tom, and the heels of his boots were hitting like clappers.

"Wants our mam," said Morfydd.

"Good God," said Grandfer. "Honey and Hornets. Grant me release. This is a house of virgins, Tom Griffiths, and I will not have it otherwise. I know you biblicals."

"Never mind Grandfer," said Morfydd, "come you in, Tom Griffiths," she having a sneaking regard for Tom because he worked among the poor.

"I will not come in, never mind," said Tom, crimson. "Just passing, I was, and hoping for an appointment with Mrs Mortymer, no offence, she being a widow lady."

"God help us," said Grandfer. "I will be sheltering four generations. Make no mistake, Tom Griffiths, you are not living here."

"O, Tom!" cried Mari coming in, and she hooked Morfydd out of it. "In with you, *bach*, and welcome. Is it Mrs Mortymer you are after, man?"

"Just passing, I was, and . . ."

"For an appointment, is it? O, yes, now." Finger under her chin, working things out. "Let me see. She is out tomorrow, down at Chapel. Thursday she is visiting Dai Alltwen Preacher, being he has people coming. Friday she is down with Mrs Tom Rhayader, the baby expected, you understand . . ."

"Eh, grief," said Tom, "she is a very busy woman. Saturday, is it?"

"Saturday she is bathing me," said Grandfer.

"Do not notice him," said Mari. "Saturday would be convenient, say half past seven?"

" 'Tis private, you understand," said he, mystic.

Private all right now Grandfer had it.

"And . . . and you will tell her I visited, mind. Expect you guess the reason?"

"Got a fair idea, Tom Griffiths, you leave her to me."

"God bless you, Mari, girl. Goodnight, now."

And Morfydd exploded as the door closed.

"Enough of that," said Mari, severe. "The man is entitled to a hearing."

"About all he will get," I said.

"Mam's business, please. A good little man is Tom Griffiths. I could think of a few worse, I expect," and she shot Grandfer a look that brought up his *Cambrian*.

"Hey, you know about this!" said Morfydd, giggling. "Matchmaking, is it?"

"Ask your mother. I am nothing to do with it," replied Mari.

I had often wondered if my mother would marry again, too good a woman to stay single with decent men in loneliness. And I was partial to Tom the Faith. Barge poles would not have touched her when she first came to Cae White, but time and tears were making her mellow and she had come from black some time now, looking lovely in her lace and dainty little hats. She may not have forgiven me for protesting about her grief, but at least she had listened, being different lately.

The house was close and silent that night, with nothing but the rustle of Grandfer's newspaper, and I wished him to the devil with his champings and grunts. Tessa was with me, too; strange I could not lose Tessa. Every bark of an otter brought me her face. About then I was losing myself with the mountain meetings where the talk was now growing like a flame to the burning of gates. A gate that would catch me square was going up on the road to Kidwelly, so I got up and left Grandfer to it.

Spring air is like wine, autumn air as old casked ale, with a smell of centuries about it. Night birds were doing themselves proud in the elms that night, late for November, and I stood for a bit on the road outside Cae White and listened to their chirping; their beaks uplifted against the moon and the saliva bubbles from their throats sailing upward in the windless air. Screeches came from Waldo's woods where things were dying, for owls were hunting with beak and claw. A screech time is late autumn, I think; of round eyes glowing from shadows, as if the winged things have starved themselves with song-making all summer and now squaring up their stomachs for the torrent of winter. But I do like autumn and her glories; the blood-stained edges of the beech leaves, the boles of the alders painted silver. Aye, autumn to me is best, as a perfumed gentle old matron, while winter I think of as a crone, toothless, shivering, nose-jewelled and with frost on her lashes. Summer could be Mari swinging out on the road for Chapel; spring is like Tessa dancing naked on lawns.

Drinking pretty hard these days, Squire; fist to his head, legs thrust out, hammering for bottles according to reports. Never been outside the Reach since Tessa died, grief being as sharp for beggar or gentry. I gave him a thought as I passed the mansion, muffled against the wind. Thought of Tessa then, for the stars were as little moons above Kidwelly and the wind had promises to freeze in his shrieks, buffeting down on the foaming river. Heard the door of Cae White come open in a lull and a sword of light shafted the shippon far below me, with Grandfer stumbling in the hilt of it. This moved me faster and I turned by the bend of Osian's place and bumped into Waldo Rees Bailiff.

"Well, good evening. Jethro Mortymer, is it." He peered up into my face.

"Good evening, Waldo Bailiff," I said.

Carrying twins by the look of him, most expansive, thumbs in his waistcoat holes, fingers wagging.

"Is it well with you, Mortymer?"

"Not since that gate went up."

"Gate, gate? O, come now, do not be so peevish. You use the roads you must face the tolls, is it? And a trifling amount is sixpence a load."

"My sister hauls trams for a shilling a day," I said.

"Mind you," and he looked at the moon, going secret, dew-drop swinging. "It do seem unjust for some, those just starting. But there is plenty of fair men in the county, remember – and many have influence. So how is your dear little mam?"

"Very clever," I replied. "You know the tollkeeper?"

"A word in the right place, boy – leave it to Waldo. Come from black, I notice?"

"Who, the tollkeeper?"

"No, you bloody fool, your mam. Setting them alight in Chapel last Sunday, did you hear? Pretty as a picture, too, laughing and chattering, quite at home with Waldo. Mind you, I am choosey about the women, not like some I could mention. Respectability do count every time."

"Whiskers, too – I give you the tip," I said.

"Aye?" And he twirled them delighted, sharp as rose thorns, hooked at the end.

Gripped my arm. "Do you think I have a chance, boy?"

"Same as any other," I said. "You seen Tom the Faith lately?"

"Great God, why mention him? Would she choose a worn-out widower before a man in his prime and lusty?" And he thumped his chest as a barrel. "Three in a bed, it would be, with his dead wife Martha in shrouds down the middle. At least I have never been wedded – single as the day, I am, and free for loving!"

"And never been bedded, counts a lot, for virginity comes uppermost with a lady as my mam. You fix that gatekeeper and I will put in a word for you, but watch that Tom the Faith for he has a deceitful nature. Goodnight, Waldo Bailiff."

"But wait, wait!"

"Go to hell," I said, and was away along the road and singing, happy in my soul at the knowledge of his misery, for he knew he had no chance. And round the corner now in the floodlight of the moon I thought of my father, the giant of strength; fervent in love, demanding in purpose, with Waldo Rees in one hand and Tom Griffiths in the other, holding them high to Mam, shaking them in a thunder of laughter, that they should presume to desire her, she whom his body had worshipped and given his kisses of gentleness. I saw my father on that walk in the moonlight. Wide of the shoulders, he was, lithe of step, bright-eyed, quick with words, noble in features, sullen in anger. And these, the dead fish of a county's manhood were quarrelling and whining over her body. Tom the Faith; well, not so bad. Waldo Rees Bailiff . . . ?

Standing in the road, I listened to his galloping. Waldo of the mantraps, the virgin of the bedposts, running to the arms of Gipsy May; tearing her skirt in the hayloft, despoiling her womanhood, degrading his manhood. Obese, despicable, soiled, *obscene*.

See my mam dead first.

## CHAPTER 14

MEMORIES FADE on most things with the passage of the years, but never will I forget the day Tom the Faith called to ask for Mam's hand, bringing references with him ranging from Squire Lloyd Parry, who thought he was honest to his marriage lines, and his Martha's death certificate entered as natural causes.

"It is what Dada would have wanted, Mam," I said.

"Perhaps," said she, "but I do not intend to be rushed."

"Rushed?" said Morfydd. "The chap has been at you two years."

"And another two if I will it," replied my mother. "Taking a bit for granted, he is, coming a bit previous," and she bustled about the kitchen.

"Look," said Morfydd. "It is all right starting that business now, but you must have given him the eye, Mam."

"And I did no such thing. Heaven forgive me if I have given any man just reason . . ."

"Do not heed her, Mam," I said. "A lonely old life it is being a widow and you are entitled to company, so give it careful thought – a nice little man is Tom Griffiths, as long as it isn't that Waldo Bailiff."

"Eh, that thing? Wouldn't be seen dead with that."

Morfydd said, eyes slanting, "But still rivers run deep, girl – not such a fool as he looks, old Tom – might expect more than your company, mind."

"O, Morfydd, hush!" whispered Mari.

Blushes and looks at boots at this. Devil, that Morfydd.

"Are you raising them in singles, Mam, or settling for twins?" said she.

"Not very considerate the way you are behaving, I must say, Morfydd."

Had to giggle myself with Mam trying not to laugh. In front of the mirror now, pushing and patting her hair, straightening her neck lace. "Indeed, I do not know what the present generation is coming to – no respect for parents, is there? Only just turned fifty I am, remember. In oak and brass knobs you would have me half a chance."

"And very beautiful you are, too," said Mari, kissing her. "Do not mind old Morfydd, Mam. An old torment, she is, and jealous. Can't find a man for herself and determined you won't have one," and she clipped at Morfydd's ear going past.

"Two minutes to go," I said.

"Lace on the head, is it?" asked Mari.

"I will stick to my bonnet," said Mam. "Now listen, listen all of you. This proposal of marriage do not mean I am going to accept Tom Griffiths, understand? I am giving him a hearing out of politeness, but nobody is sewing me in bridal sheets before I am ready, so I want no interference, especially from you, Morfydd Mortymer."

"Heaven forbid!"

"Aye, well don't look so damned innocent. Very embarrassing it will be for Mr Griffiths with me pushing him out and you pushing him in, and you will have me to contend with afterwards, remember. Get the old pot on the go, Mari girl, parched I am at the thought of it."

"Half a minute late," I said, looking at the clock.

"Left at the altar, Mam – probably changed his mind. Quick now, first impressions count most. Line up, all of us, quick. I can hear him coming."

And the door burst open and through it came Grandfer, a bunch of flowers held high, whooping and cackling.

"A damned fine proposal of marriage this will be," cried Mam. "Mari, get the old varmint out of it."

This even shifted me and the four of us were pushing and flapping at him but he rose up like a dog hackled and threw us off. "Am I not the head of the house?" he roared. "Am I to be rushed to bed because of a chit of a man coming courting?"

"Grandfer," begged Mari. "It is not decent. Away now!"

"Now rest your hearts my pretties," said he. "Just a little seat at the back to watch the capers, I promise to sit quiet. Tom the Faith, is it? God, there's a selection."

"He is coming," I said. "Quick, the tableau," and we all formed up opposite the door to give good impressions to the suitor.

Tap tap at the door like the brush of a butterfly's wing.

"Come on in," called Mari, and in came Tom the Faith, all five feet of him with a stook of flowers up to his ears and his little bald head shining above his high starched collar; funeral black proposal clothes, very gallant, and down with him, then, bald head gleaming, very elegant, and Grandfer lifted a knee and swung his face to the wall, slapping it and howling.

"O, God," said Tom, white as a bedsheet. "Not Grandfer!"

"Do not mind him, Tom Griffiths," said Morfydd. "In with you now and welcome, he is just off to bed, anyway," and she took the flowers and swept him in.

"Most welcome, if I might say," said Mam, looking rosy. Young and happy she looked standing there with the flowers now. Pleasant to know she was wanted, I expect. Official introductions then, though everybody knew everybody else, and the chairs were brought up to the fire while Mari dragged Grandfer to bed shrieking. We all sat down when Mari came back; backs like ramrods, most formal, expectant, for it was up to Tom to make the first move, he being suitor. And never in my life have I seen an Adam's apple like Tom's for travelling, creeping up under his chin one moment then diving out of sight, but to his credit he rose and spoke.

"Mam Mortymer," said he. "Nigh sixty years I am, living the last ten of them alone, and the loneliness is upon me, having lost my Martha. God-fearing I have always been, strict Chapel, and if I take a couple at times it is only for the company, you understand. Childless I am, too, with no fine children like yours to bring me company. I have little money, but I am industrious and will work for you and keep you in gentleness if you decide to treat this offer kindly. Mam Mortymer, I do come to offer you marriage, making the offer in the company of your children, according to custom, you being widowed, that they may advise you after I am left here."

And down he went, Adam's apple leaping.

Damned good, I thought. Must have rehearsed it for months, word perfect.

Up got Morfydd then, she being eldest. At Sunday School she was, fingers entwined, eyes cast up, shoulders rocking.

"Mr Tom Griffiths," said she. "Me being eldest it is up to me to reply. Of all the men of this village I do like you most. Industrious you are, for I have been inside your house and seen it. Clean as a new pin, if I may say," and here she bowed to him, "although there is no woman about yet," and she smiled down at Mam who was coming pretty hot, I noticed. "And when you are left here, Tom Griffiths, I will advise my mother that she do think of you kindly, and more, because you are good to the needy and speak the true word of God."

Down with Morfydd and I noticed Mari was a bit bright in the eye with a secret sniffing and wiping, for it is touching when older people present themselves in this fashion, I think; being sincere and humble, with little thoughts of marriage beds and the breathless kisses of midnight. So we sat in silence now and there was no awkwardness in us, no shame at this counselling, for the purity of it had filled us, and made us at peace.

But that was all he had coming just then, of course, for a woman cannot make up her mind on the spot, so we just sat a few minutes in quiet with the wind doing his falsetto in the eaves and buffeting in the chimney, till Mam gave Mari the eye.

"I will read from the Book," said Mari, and rose, drifting across the room, her black skirts held between fingers and thumbs, and she sat down in rustles and opened the Book of the King, and read:

" 'I am come into my garden, my sister, my spouse: I have gathered my myrrh with my spices; I have eaten my honey-

comb with my honey: I have drunk my wine with my milk: eat,
O friends; drink, yea, drink abundantly, O beloved. I sleep,
but my heart waketh: it is the voice of my beloved that
knocketh, saying, Open to me, my sister, my love, my dove,
my undefiled: for my head is filled with dew, and my locks with
the drops of the night . . .' " and she closed the Book.

"Amen," we all said.

Usually made me pretty hungry, this one, but the others
found it touching, with handkerchiefs turning out and dabbings
from the women and a good strong trumpet from Tom.

"Now to food," said Morfydd, recovering. "Starved, I am,
and the body must be fortified as well as the soul. A good little
man you are, Tom Griffiths, with speeches like that last one
you ought to be in the Parliament."

Out with the cups and saucers then, cups of tea and bread
and a two pound cheese that had set me back a fortnight, and
we chattered and feasted, and Mari fetched Grandfer down in
his nightshirt for his supper and congratulations all round.
Well after ten o'clock before Tom left, jaunty and confident,
bowing himself out, but I didn't give a lot for his chances by
the look in Mam's eyes. Bit of a comedown, mind, when you've
been used to two yards of a man and drop overnight to a bald
five feet. Morfydd and me got into the crockery. The house was
quiet save for Grandfer's snoring, and there was a silence in
Morfydd as she handed them from the sink. I knew she had
something under her apron.

She handed me a cup.

"Jethro, boy, you keep from Abel Flannigan."

I grunted, wiping.

"This county's going on fire soon, and Abel is doing the
kindling in this part of the world – he will lead you to trouble,
mark me."

"Do you think Mam will take Tom Griffiths?" I asked.

"Not for a moment; we were talking about Flannigan."

"So what do we do – sit down and whine?"

This turned her. "The Mortymers haven't whined yet,
Jethro, and not likely to start now, but this Rebecca business
fair stinks of danger."

Unlike Morfydd this. Even six months back it was go to the foot of the scaffold rather than bow to injustice. Now she was swilling the cups and saucers and smacking them down on the board. We did not speak for a bit, then:

"You keep out of it – leave it to the county men, it is their county. I do not like this Rebecca movement."

"Six months from now you won't get a cart to Carmarthen market," I said. "County people or not, we still have to live here. Move or starve, just as you like."

"Who builds the gates, Jethro?"

"Gentry – landowners, squires, squireens."

"Who else?"

"I do not know what you mean," I said.

"I will tell you – magistrates. The people who build the gates fork out the sentences to those who burn them. So expect no mercy if you are caught in white petticoats and happen to be a foreigner – they will make an example of the foreigners because of the bad blood coming in." She looked at me. "Special, you are, so watch it. And talking of petticoats, I have missed one. When did you take it?"

Worn out, ragged old thing. God, she didn't miss much.

"Night before last," I said.

"My property, Jethro. I will have it back, if you please."

"Slit over the shoulders now," I said. "The thing wouldn't fit me."

She flung the rag into the sink, dried her hands and turned to the dying fire. The lamp was low, flinging soot into her eyes as she sat down. "Eh, Jethro, come to me."

I went, standing before her.

"Down by here, boy," and she patted. "Now, listen. Time was when I was as you – full of the injustices, mixing gunpowder, and where has it landed me? Alone with my son and not a thing gained, save bitterness. Where did it land the Chartists – even your brother Iestyn?" She shook her head. "They are too big for us, too many. Power is always slipping from the many to the few because the few are more vigilant. In my time I have fought to raise the poor, but do they want to be raised? Nothing but defeat on the end of this Rebecca business, boy, believe me – the poor are the mass but they are not behind you – too afraid to help, and too weak."

"You are a fine one to talk," I replied. "Fight and be damned, it was, less than six months back."

"We are doing all right!" said she, thumping the chair. "We are making a living, What else do you want?"

"What living we have you are making. If you came from Ponty we would start starving tomorrow for there is nothing in farming. Every yard I move now swallows the profits."

"Then let the farm rot – come back to Ponty."

"Any day now," I said, "but there is more to it than that now. You may be beaten, but I am not. Whole families are starving between here and Pembroke, bled to death by grasping landlords. The magistrates are corrupt, the workhouses spilling from the windows – whole families are queueing at the doors – children torn from parents, husbands from wives, living like animals on scraps, working their fingers to blood on the oakum. Is it decent for men to sit down under this?"

"And you will fight for them, is it?"

She looked at me steady. The fire blazed suddenly, lighting her face, and she never moved her eyes from mine.

"Are you sure you are fighting for the poor?"

"For the lot of us – for you, Mam, the children – even for Grandfer."

"But not for Mari?"

Still those eyes. Uncertain, I moved away. She was watching me. The clock ticked in the sudden silence.

"A bitch of a sister, isn't it?" she said.

"For . . . Mari, too," I said, sullen.

"Thank God she's mentioned. You love her, don't you?"

"Not in the way you think."

Damned women. They take a lever to the soul and prise and peep.

"Think again, Jethro."

This swung me. "I do not love her as you call love!"

"All right, all right. You are not selling pigs. I only asked."

A moth flapped over the lamp, creeping from his rot-corner,

thinking it was summer, and the shadow of him was as big as a bat on the wall as he pecked at the glass.

"Singe your wings," said Morfydd.

"I do not love Mari!"

"Half dead if you didn't. If I were a man I would want her lying. Couldn't help myself. I would want all of her, soul and body."

"You and me think different," I said to wound her.

"Much obliged. We think the same, but I am more honest."

"She is Iestyn's wife!"

"Thanks for reminding me." Very smooth now, possessed, smiling. She rose. "Listen, you. You are hitting seventeen now – big enough for double your age – big enough to be talked to straight. The way you love Mari is the way you love me, Jethro. And any other kind of love you can save for Sixpenny Jane down at Betsi's place, though the way she looked at you Fair Day I reckon you could get her free."

"You don't understand," I said, furious.

"About men?" She laughed soft and low. "*Duw!* If you know of one wild enough you can send him down to Morfydd for taming, just to keep my hand in. If you throw enough buckets you quench the fire but the sister still burns bright, thank God. Aye, I know most about men and you in particular, including the birth mark somewhere special . . ."

"Please don't be vulgar."

"Right, then, but hear this, Jethro. To love Mari wrong is to love her vulgar, and I will not have it, not while Iestyn breathes."

Gave her a glance and wandered about. Witch-black she sat, hands folded in her lap, her eyes following my every move.

"You do her no credit, Morfydd," I said, but I could have struck her.

"And I do you less, boy, but I know I am right. Poor Jethro." She cornered me by the fire and her arms went round me. "Do not be ashamed," she whispered. "To love her is dangerous. It will grow and grow inside lest you knife it quick. O, the little shrew, she is, being so beautiful, being Mari.

Jethro, come back to Ponty. I will help you, I will make it easy."

"I . . . I would not touch her, you understand?"

"Yes," she said.

"Not . . . not even give her a look."

She nodded, kissing me although I twisted away. She caught my hand then and we stood together. Strange the heaping love I felt for her then.

"If you must fight for Mari, then do it careful, Jethro. Look now, there is soot on your collar." She ringed it with her finger showing the black.

"Those are the mistakes," she whispered, "sometimes the difference between life and death. When you blacken your face for the night meetings tuck a rag round your collar first. Has Flannigan mentioned that?"

I shook my head.

"Saw it last night," she said. "Now look at the fire. Do you see the grooves of your fingers scratching on the chimney? Take it with your palm, boy, not the tips of the fingers, for the first thing they looked for in Twm Carnabwth's house was the marks of his fingers on the back of the fire. None there, and as white as snow was his collar. They knew who broke the Efail-wen gate, but no one could prove it. Another thing."

I listened.

"Watch for informers – the prissy men like Osian Hughes, the evil men like Waldo Rees Bailiff, though he will never join Rebecca. But a man like Hughes would not stand for two minutes with his hands tied behind him and a dragoon booting him in the belly. You can trust your Flannigans for all their Irish names – real Welshmen, see. But men like Osian are an abomination – with a name as Welsh as Mynydd Sylen but ashamed of his ancestry." She narrowed her eyes at the fire, sitting down. "Strange is my country – the people are either afire – harp-Welsh people and dying to prove it, or Welsh to their toes and dying to forget it; slipping and sliding and whispering about being English – Irish, Scottish – anything will do. Lucky those people are few, but we've got them. And

God knows what Wales has done to have to put up with them."

Never seen her in this mood before. Leaning against the wall, I listened.

"And people write books – wish I could write. For I would write a book that would stand for a century – a book telling of my people and how they fought to live; telling of their music, their courage, their forbearance, their love of things beautiful, their fire, their God. And I would write of the money-beggars who suck them, the magistrates, squireens, the gentry who live on them, the gaols, the transportations, the unfair trials, and of those who spit on our language." Her voice rose. "And what the hell am I talking English for now? With centuries of Welsh behind me I am speaking in a foreign tongue, which shows the job we are making of it." Empty, she looked, fingers spread. "And if my book was printed they would call it fairy tales, revolutionary, a pack of damned lies, for people believe only what they are told to believe, and anything contrary to the preachings of Church and State is rejected. People are strange – no intelligence, no compassion. Aye, muckraking they would call it in a hundred years time, because they did not know my generation that died for the things they will enjoy." She sighed, and the blaze in her died with her sad, sweet smile. "Well, fight if you must, but fight for Wales, nothing else, remember, for the land of your fathers. Your blood is of Wales, every drop – your heart is of Wales, for she created you – the breath you draw is of the mountains of my country. O, God, to be part of this country, to love her as I do! And listen. Make it vicious – no half measures – for the people who oppose you are clever and vicious. Hit the big man, easy with the small man, do not take advantage. Burn your gates not singly but in hundreds, and when they go up again burn them down again. Fire your hayricks, massacre your salmon, walk with the *ceffyl pren* against the moral injustices – put the wrongs right! 'Woe of the bloody city! it is full of lies and robbery; the prey departeth not; the noise of the whip . . . the horseman lifteth up the bright sword and the glittering spear . . . and there is none end of their corpses . . . Nineveh is laid waste!' " She put her hands over her face, whispering now. "Fight to the death if needs be, for the land is despoiled. Better to destroy the Wales we love than stand to see her degraded."

I nodded, commanded by her, unable to reply. She rose, trembling.

"Got to be up early tomorrow," she said. "Dawn; deep shift with Liam Muldooney, bless him. God, there is Welsh Irish, good little man. Agitators, is it? Crawling round on all fours harnessed like a bloody donkey, fine job we've made of it." She came and kissed me. "Fight, but be careful – remember Iestyn. I will not stand idle if I lose you, too."

"I am not afraid," I said.

"Aye, of course not." She shrugged, looking helpless. "Do not mind old Morfydd – an old frump she is getting. All embers now, no fire. Goodnight."

"Goodnight," I said.

## CHAPTER 15

As a moth on a pin Tom the Faith fluttered, and a month went by and my mother made no move to stem the bleeding heart. Then Waldo Rees Bailiff tried her, and Morfydd slipped with a bucket of water, half drowning him, though what she was doing with a bucket on a window sill was anyone's guess. Terrible to see poor Tom, though – mooning around the lanes, hand-wringing on the doorstep, never within yards of Black Boar tavern, hangdog, drooping with lovelight in December.

These were the mornings of the frozen water butt; of ice-cold water freezing teeth in their sockets when you washed every morning in the grip of the frosted land. The snows came in beauty and the flaring bare arms of winter were all over dripping with icicles. The rivers were shouting again after the drought of summer, their music a thunder that bellowed at Cae White, and with Christmas upon us I thought of Him Who was born for us. I am not much one for religion but I believe in the Man, though I could never accept Him from the brushes of painters; soft-faced, doe-eyed, gentle as a baby. For great are His works, and wonderful. So the God I see is a man of strength, with a chest as a ship's prow and ten feet tall. Seaweed for hair has He, seven fathoms deep are His eyes as green as the waves in anger, with a voice as the thunder.

I gave Him more thought as I went up to Tom Rhayader's place that night for my third proper Rebecca meeting. The sky was lanterned over the crest of the hill where Toby Maudlin lived. Not very bright, was little Toby, but a good man with a vixen of a wife from Cardie, sharp as a needle and a tongue as a razor, and she raised lumps on Toby every Monday night regular when he went to Black Boar for his weekly pint. Light kissed the snow from his door as I passed, and I saw him creep out with his boots in his hand.

"Good evening, Toby Maudlin."

"Good evening, Jethro Mortymer. Where you bound for?"

"Same place as you by the look of it. You joining?"

"Got a gate," said Toby, lacing his boots.

"Damned lucky. I've got three and more every week."

"Same up at Tom Rhayader's place – you heard? Four if he works to St Clears. But he can still work to Carmarthen if he adds six miles though he'll be paying out more for boots. Eh, these Trusts! The county's gone mad."

"Not as mad as you think, Toby. Speculation is the same whatever road it takes. They know what they're doing."

"There's a queer old word. Speculation, is it? New words cropping up every minute. Is the toll money likely to go on road repairs, for instance – I've got Moses' tablets on mine."

"That is the excuse," I answered. "But most of the money is for paying out the investors and we don't get a pothole filled till the rich get their cut, and there isn't much left after Bullin takes his share and we build new bridges near the houses of the gentry."

"Good God," said he, "there's education for you. Speculation and investors, is it, bridges and Bullins and gentry. Explain it, please."

"The money is being stolen, or just about."

"Good enough for me," said Toby. "Thieves and vagabonds, is it. Count me in, man – you know the password?"

"Genesis for us. You brought a petticoat, and soot?"

"The soot I have here," replied Toby. "Got me old girl's nightshirt under me waistcoat. Hunted high and low for it, she did, then hopped in naked. Hope she bloody freezes. You know what she hit me with a week last Monday?"

"Hush, you," I said. "Rhayader don't like bellowing."

"Better get garmented, lad. We're here."

Ghostly he looked in the moonlight with his little round face blackened and shrouded in white, nightdress trailing, for his wife was a head the taller. I raised my fist to hit the barn door.

"Wait, you," said Toby. "Somebody's coming."

A lanky wraith now, mooching against the snow.

Tramping Boy Joey.

I had not seen Joey for months. Last time I heard of him he was cowman over at Kidwelly with a Cardie farmer and I'd heard he had done a stretch in Carmarthen workhouse in between. Now he was poaching Waldo again, sleeping at the lime kilns where we went for our lime. Not much time for me, Joey – couldn't forget his ferret, though he must have had fifty through the passage of the years. Strange, I thought, that Joey should stand for Rebecca when a labourer, for the movement was backed mostly by farmers.

"There's a stranger," I said.

"That makes two of us," said Joey, looking evil.

Abel Flannigan opened the door.

Fifty or so Rebecca's daughters were squatting in Rhayader's barn, mostly smocked, but some dressed normal like me. Powder-guns, I noticed, were stacked near the door; axes, hatchets, scythes were piled in a corner. Looked like business. The place reeked with smoke, pipes glowed in the darkness.

"Right, Jethro," said Flannigan, and I was in. "Who's this?"

"I've got a gate, mind," chirped Toby.

"Through," said Flannigan. "And watch that tongue. Who's this one?"

"Joey Scarlet," said Joey, eyes shining in Flannigan's lamp.

133

"You a farmer?"

"Workhouse boy, mind," said a voice. Got a shock when I saw the speaker – Tom the Faith. "He's entitled."

"To what?" grunted Flannigan.

"More to it than gates," said another. "The first thing Rebecca did, damned near, was to burn Narberth workhouse. What workhouse, son?"

"Carmarthen," said Joey.

"In," said Flannigan. "And get here on time – midnight. The Sunday school's next door, not here." He turned and hung the lamp. "Two new members, eh? Let me make something clear. Rebecca has a knife and a fancy for tongues, so we brought in Justin Slaughterer to oblige. You can take the oath afterwards. Right, Rhayader."

And Tom Rhayader rose from his box in the corner; small, lithe, nothing like a leader save for his eyes. On fire were those eyes, bright in his strong, square face. He had kept to himself till now, coming down from the north with his wife and daughter a year or so back, and Mam had delivered his second. He had never seen the counter of Black Boar tavern; was a bit of a lay preacher and three times to Chapel every Sunday, Baptist. Easy was Rhayader, fists on hips, an inch higher than Flannigan's shoulder, but he had the thin scars of fighting over his eyes. I would have backed him against Flannigan there on the spot.

"First," he began, "I have a message from Rebecca who governs West Wales, our leader. Listen," and he read from a paper, " 'The masses to a man throughout the three counties of Carmarthen, Cardigan and Pembroke are with me. O, yes, they are all my children. When I meet the lime-men on the road covered with sweat and dust, I know they are Rebeccaites. When I see the coalmen coming to town clothed in rags, hard worked and hard fed, I know they are mine, these are Rebecca's children. When I see the farmers' wives carrying loaded baskets to market, bending under the weight, I know well that these are my daughters. If I turn into a farmer's house and see them eating barley bread and drinking whey, surely, say I, these are the members of my family, these are the oppressed sons and daughters of Rebecca.' "

134

Rhayader lowered the letter. "The message is unsigned," said he. "And if the message were signed it would rock the magistrates of the county, for we are led by a man of high birth and responsibility. May his name never be mentioned lest someone die for it. May he be respected and shown honour by all the daughters of Rebecca, this man who works for justice and against the oppressions that bring us together this night."

Very cool, very calm, and the men nudged each other and murmured. I glanced at Joey. Mushrooms for eyes had Joey, staring hypnotized, and Justin Slaughterer beside him, his broad chin cupped in his hairy hands, intent.

"So let us pray that we are together tonight," went on Rhayader, "for this is a meeting of war. The time has come for this village, too, to take its part in the fight against oppression and we are the better equipped because we are men of God. Yes, we will burn the tollgates, we will smash tollhouses, and carry the fight to the very seat of authority, but have this clear in your minds. Do not encompass your minds with mere bars and chains, for the barred road that exacts the unfair toll is only the symbol of the resentment we suffer. The mud-walled cottages must be razed to the ground, the rat-infested hovels of the starving poor swept away and new dwellings built to house a fair people. Our men and women must be fed well, not on rye bread and potato soup; be clothed in wool, not in rags. Our women must come from the fields and carry their children with dignity, not labour as oxen at the plough from dawn to darkness, barefooted, ill-fed, treated as animals. Skeleton children must be fattened and taken from straw when in fever. North and west of us the gentry are merging their farms into holdings, their rents going higher to turn small farmers out. From Llandovery to Pembroke the workhouses are crowded by people who have lived in dread of the workhouses which are leaping up under the new Poor Law, dividing whole families, making it a sin for a man to honour his wife." Rhayader paused, his dark eyes drifting over us. Powerful in oratory, this one, with the *hwyl* of the good minister. No need to raise his voice.

"With the gates flying up and the tolls going higher the price of producing is rocketing. The Corn Law levy is ruining us.

Wheat at sixty-two shillings, is dropping; barley at six shillings a bushel, is plunging lower. Butter, which we cannot afford for our hungry children is at sevenpence a pound, half its price. The upland farmers like me are throwing away their stock, too dear to feed them, for we must raise corn to live. But worse lies ahead, for the country is being invaded by the colliers and iron-workers of Monmouthshire, where pits are being closed and furnaces blown out since the fall of the Chartists. And where are the authorities who guide our destinies? I will tell you – roystering in the London taverns!" His voice rose to a shout of sudden anger. "The squireen landlords are bleeding the counties to death – drawing incomes of thousands in rents for farms they see once a year, if that. But they depute their responsibilities, mind, O, yes, they depute – to the crooked little Napoleons you find in every corner of Wales – and not only English, remember – Welsh, too – by God, we've got them, for easy pickings bring up the dregs of a country. So we are dominated by the little landowners who have the power of life and death over us – the crooked little magistrates. Heaven help you speaking Welsh at the hands of their interpreters – pleading guilty before you go in. God help you more if you have deducted a single penny from their profits. And some are Church clergy! Is it the function of men of God to send their neighbours to prison or transportation, even death?" His fist came down on the box and he glared around us. Pretty worked up now. He stopped for breath.

"Listen," he ended. "We cannot burn investments or bonds or tithes or Corn Laws or Poor Laws, but we can burn the things that stand as other injustices – the gates! We cannot feed the starving in their thousands or succour our poor, but we can fight the moral wrongs, break down the workhouses that shame our country and carry the transgressors on the wooden horse – from squireen to clergy we will carry them and bring them to ridicule, because they dishonour us and the law of God. 'And they blessed Rebekah, and said unto her, Thou art our sister, be thou the mother of thousands of millions, and let thy seed possess the gate of those which hate them.' Amen."

"Amen," came the grumble of voices.

He spoke again.

"Flannigan – the first gate?"

"Two, sir – the bar and gate, Kidwelly to Carmarthen. And while we are in that district I know a couple of ricks for tinder – the Reverend John Jenkins, for unfair gathering of tithes."

"His crime?" asked Rhayader.

"Sold a labourer's Bible, being a shilling short of his tithe."

"Good God, forgive him," said Rhayader. "We will not. Have his ricks, then, every one in sight. Give the labourer a Bible, present from Rebecca."

"I will see to that, sir," came a voice from the back. "My old Gran's got two and she's pretty well blind."

"Good. Enough for one night," said Rhayader. "Back here in half an hour, every man. Bring horses those who have them, for the way is long – hooves covered with grain sacks, reins tied against chinking. The dragoons are out near Kidwelly, remember."

"Dragoons moved to St Clears, maister – night 'fore last."

"Good."

"What about snow, Tom Rhayader? Making fair tracks, mind!"

"God will smooth us out."

"Isn't the dragoons scaring me, mind. Case my old woman do follow us!"

Roars at this, with Flannigan hushing at us for silence. Rhayader said:

"Those who have powder-guns, carry them, but God help the man I find with shot. Bring hatchets, axes, pikes and levers – saws and scythes. And hearken. We do not fight unless cornered. We drift back into the night where we came from. If we become divided then make your way home separately, not in parties. The man who returns to this barn gets my gun – with shot." Laughter at this. "If you are taken tie up your tongue – you cannot even spell Rebecca – or Justin Slaughterer will have it out the day you are loosed. No man knows his brother, his Rebecca sister, his daughters, and, by God, no man knows me. The informer dies. Right, away! Fifty-three strong we start from here for the march on Kidwelly. But we will gather them from the villages in hundreds. God bless us as God-fearing men. And may God help us. Back in half an hour. Away!"

Flannigan doused the lamp and we filed out into the snow.

Back home I went for Randy, for it was some way to the gates beyond Kidwelly and I did not fancy the walk. Besides, he was always looking for trouble and here was his chance for some; so far spent the winter eating his head off and dreaming of straw and women. Cae White was iced as I crept into the shippon and slipped up the peg on the stable door, and the smoke from the kitchen chimney was standing as a bar in the still, frosty air. Randy wagged at me as I went round his hind legs, snorting and looking ugly as I hooked up the saddle, so I gave him one in the chops to quieten him and he lifted up his hooves as a lamb while I tied them with corn sacks. Strap down the reins now to stop them jingling and Tara was whining at the kitchen door, knowing I was there. Crept to the door and opened it and she came out sideways with wriggling, then leaped into my arms. Had to laugh at the thought of it – it would have shortened Grandfer's span had he seen me just then – a shrouded ghost with a blackened face, creeping over the shippon with Tara in its arms. I thought I'd got away with it but a window grated as I led Randy out.

Morfydd was standing by the landing window, face white, diamonds for eyes, and her hair black against the crusted sill.

"Jethro, for God's sake take care!"

I nodded and climbed into the saddle, leaned down and hooked up Tara. And together we went up to Rhayader's barn.

I didn't look back, but I knew she was there.

## CHAPTER 16

OVER FIFTY strong, we started, about thirteen horses between us, some two up, but most on foot. But we gathered them in scores on the road to Kidwelly where groups of the daughters were standing in the woods. Powder-guns shouldered, pikes swaying as a forest, we moved through the woods single file just short of the town; Tom Rhayader leading, sitting proud on his mare. Excitement mingled with awe within me as we drifted on in the misted silence; could not drag my eyes from Rhayader, my first Rebecca. His head was turbanned with silk, the back-knot flowing over his long, white shroud. Erect he sat as born to a horse, peacock feathers waving high, glass earrings flashing in moonlight. In his right hand he held a sword, wielding it for direction. Behind the magnificent leader came the gigantic Abel Flannigan. Drooping in the saddle was Flannigan, long legs trailing the snowladen undergrowth, confident, dark with anger. Good to have Flannigan about for he was spawned in these parts and knew every track as the hairs of his hands, every escape road home. Behind him came Justin Slaughterer, a barrel with legs, bowing his horse to the weight of him, bareheaded, his new-grown spade beard flecked with snow. Tramping Boy Joey was walking alongside Justin, gripping his stirrup. This disturbed me. Just plain mischief had brought Joey Scarlet, for he had no gates, and there was a roll in his eye I distrusted. Joey hated people; magistrates, bailiffs and Rebecca alike; come to destroy, nothing else. Only an inch of tongue was needed to send us all to the hulks, and Joey had yards of it, and I could not make out why Flannigan had sworn him. On, on, silent, dozing to the muffled clops and the stuttering crunch of boots in snow. A curse here and there as a man slipped flat and the crack of a twig was enough to send Rhayader swinging in the saddle. Keep clear of the roads now; whispered consultation as we lost direction in the depths of the woods with Joey whipping up from Flannigan to point out the way. A hand gripped my stirrup and I gave him a glance. Stranger to me, this one, with a sallow, pinched face and the big dull eyes of hunger. Just a boy by his looks, and he brushed snow from his wheat-coloured hair and smiled, his face coming alive.

"You weary, boy?"

"After my bedtime," said he.

"Kidwelly you belong, is it?"

"Pembrey."

"What is your name?" I asked.

"Matthew Luke John, last being the surname – the whole New Testament."

"Heavens," I said. "You got gates down in Pembrey?"

"Not me personal but my dada has plenty, back home in bed."

"Then rake him out of it. Anyone can lie in bed."

"Different, man. The old bull got him," he answered. "Last spring, it was – ripped him something cruel. And there's only me working – me and my mam. Five kids to keep, see, the youngest six weeks. O, it's a bastard. You got kids?" He wiped snow from his eyes, peering up.

"Sort of," I answered.

"And these damned old gates, see – cannot get moving. Couldn't bring in the lime last carting season, hadn't got the toll money. Poor harvest this year because of it."

"Aye," I said.

It was snowing harder now, riming his lashes, painting up his hair, changing his sex. Lovely he looked just then but he grinned of a sudden and spat like a man.

"Eh," he said, "my mam's an old witch. Comes pretty hard on her – working her fingers to the bone with the old man lying stitched – and one on the breast, did I tell you? Our Glyn – rare little savage, he is, always at her, but you don't make milk on potato soup. You get those gates down, Matthew Luke John, says she, being Welsh. You Welsh?"

I gave him some, pretty rough, and he answered me back, delighted, though I thought his accent was Cardie.

"Up here in the saddle, boy," I said. "We'll give you a spell."

"Whee, bloody jakes!" he said and took hold of Tara while I dragged him, and Randy turned with hate in his eye. "Easy on the cloth, Rebecca," he added. "Sackcloth and ashes if I tear the old girl's petticoat. Eh, there's delightful!" and he fingered the lace of Morfydd's nightshirt. "That come from a real woman, never mind my mam, is she better with it off?"

"Hush, you," I said, for Flannigan was trotting towards us, face thunderous.

"What the hell is this?" he demanded – "a Rebecca burning or an Irish Wedding? Shut your chops or I'll damned soon shut them, the pair of you!"

"God, he's a brute. Who's he, then, the Spanish torturer?" said Matthew Luke John. "Send him back home for a week with my mam, she'd damned soon settle him."

"Abel is right," I said. "Hush."

On, on, plodding, drooping; feeling like death at that time of the morning after a hard day of it farming. The boy drooped on Randy and I drooped on him; eyes wide open I caught myself snoring.

Big country now, rolling and jagged, the limestone outcrops of a shattered world painted into artistry with the hand of snow. The woods stood loaded in sombre silence and the stars were as fire above the stark outline of Kidwelly; dear little town, this, hit sideways by the Trusts. Dead and gaunt it looked now to my drooping eyes; flat and dreary, strangled into silence by the garrot of the moon. A dog barked, yelping, as frightened by its shadow, for nothing moved in Kidwelly save the sick, denied sleep by weariness; and babies seeking food and fisting at ribbons for the sleeping breast, for one cried plaintive. We straggled past, and I thought of the town and its low, thatched roofs quilting the sleepers; the sharp-nosed widow lying flat on her back; jaw-sunk, eye-sunk, snoring for a grampus with widow weeds behind the door, the high-laced boots with their toe-kissing postures, laces dangling beneath the iron bed. Brass knobs on this one, with clover-leaf railings, romantic one time, holding up lovers, now creaking its sadness at feather-bedding widows. Grey-haired, she sleeps, hands entwined on stomach, third finger left hand being ringed with gold. Sam Lent was his name, girl, thirty years dead, girl, what a waste of loving – knew he was for it the moment they brought him in, girl; knew he was past it when they laid him on the bed. Half past two from the house, girl – knew it the second I saw him – never strong in the ticker, mind, just like his dad, God rest him. Went the same way, girl, didn't know what hit him, expired without a word. Looked lovely in his box, mind – did him a world of good that week down at Tenby, bless him.

Had him done in medium oak, him being in the timber business. God grant him peace, girl, he is happier dead.

*Creep on, drooping, snuffling, plodding.*

Silent he sleeps, smooth-faced, and mottled, his blood-pressure up with that little tot of brandy, hands as if in prayer flat beneath his head. Smiling, he sleeps, and with every breath exhaling the little bit of pillow-down leans over gracefully, struggling upright as he draws back in. Shiny black coat is hanging on the hanger, trews with seat to shave in are under the bed – creases, see – sharper for pulpit next Sunday, for the matron in the front row gets the best view. Black Book, black cassock, me – very Church of England; John chapter eleven for my sermon next Sunday, got to get it off by heart, the raising of the dead. For Lazarus is my name, and that is my sermon. O, there's a lovely story of our Jesus of Nazareth! Parson of Kidwelly, me; trying to be decent, but would to Heaven people would give more love to neighbours. Nothing wrong with this town, mind, O, grant the world be like it! Welsh as me this town, but full of Nonconformists – like that little serving-maid living down the way – will have to win her round one way or the other. O, God, she is pretty, that little Rhiannon – not a patch on her is that front pew matron. Wonder if she'd have me if I tried her quiet – married to a maiden as sweet as my Rhiannon! Ten years older, but I still keep my figure . . . a bit flabby in places though she doesn't seem to notice. In a little ring of gold I circle my Rhiannon . . . and Jesus my Master and His raising of Lazarus.

*On, on, harness creaking, on . . .*

Parson Lazarus Frolic is lying on my pillow. Dear little man, he is, gentle as a baby. Wonder if he'll speak to me a week next Sunday? Strange how he's always strolling past the old chapel. . . .

Smiling, she lies, arms by her sides, eyes half open in her dreaming sleep, and her nightie is sideways and her breast is mother-of-pearl in moonlight, the leaded lights are prison bars black on her face. Red lips half open, she pouts and dreams: little serving-maid, second parlourmaid; Cook is a bitch, mind, but Butler most considerate. Black cotton dress is hanging on the wardrobe, wrist-lace on the marble slab gravestone to the china, hairpins on the floor, stays on the window sill crumpled at the waist – nineteen inches round, and the laces are swinging in the draught from the window. Bright red garters on the handle of the door. That old black suit he wears, now there is a scandal! I think he sleeps on it the way it is creased. Rhiannon and her flat iron would do something about it; little Parson Frolic, will you never bring it down? And that chap down at hotel stables coming very hot for winter . . . find it most upsetting. O, dear little parson, won't you save my soul for Heaven? For the boys of the village are wicked and the men are even worse, save in Kidwelly where they come pretty tidy. . . .

Think I'll turn over, and she pouts and dreams.

And that Church of England matron who eyes you every Sunday, smiling at your sermon with her ear inclined – you'd be shocked about that matron if I cared to open my mouth. Too mean for words, she is, lived next door for life, she has, and nothing on her washing-line in nineteen years. Mam says it isn't decent – not even a pair of drawers, mind – perhaps she doesn't wear them, shouldn't be surprised. . . . O, why was my dad born an old Nonconformist when you know the path that will carry me to Heaven? And talking of trews, boy, yours are quite indecent – spit on that iron, girl, send up steam. O, little Parson Lazarus Frolic, don't you ever dream . . . ?

And the first slashing finger of dawn rose up behind Kidwelly and the cocks yelled like demons as we hit the tollgate.

I awoke from the swaying slush of my visions as Tom Rhayader hit the tollhouse, and the top window came open and out came a face; terrified that face above its nightshirt, sleeping-cap slipping sideways, bobble swinging.

"What the hell is happening, have you all gone raving?"

"Out, out!" and Rhayader's sword was slashing, ripping at the tollhouse door. "Out this minute or we burn you alive. Out!"

"And me with wife and children, man? Six children, last one hardly weaned?"

"*Out!*" cried Rebecca, his horse wheeling. Sword lowered, he clattered about while men and horses pressed about him.

"For God's sake, pity!" yelled the face.

Flannigan said, "A tinder to that thatch would damned soon shift him, Tom."

"He has two minutes," said Rhayader.

"Two minutes could cost us our lives," grumbled Justin.

"The chance we take. I am not burning people."

The door burst open and the wife came out, hair in curlers, eyes stuck with sleep. One look at the wraiths and back she went, hand to her heart, moaning. A tot at the door now, barefooted, terrified. A girl was screaming inside; grunts and cries now as the keeper booted them awake.

"You, you," said Rhayader, pointing. "Inside quick and give him a hand. Bring out his blankets, clothes, furniture – everything you can save and work like devils, every second counts," and two men leaped to his command.

"But where will we go?" The woman now, recovering; down on her knees pleading, pulling at Rhayader's gown. "For God's sake, man, have mercy! Six children in here and the depth of winter – where will we lie?"

"You should have thought of that before," said Flannigan, pushing her off. "You damned keepers are the scum of the Welsh!"

"But my daughter – sixteen years old? O, God!" Her wild eyes looked round our blackened faces.

"She is safe with us, woman – go fetch her out. Mortymer, where the hell's Mortymer?" he turned in the saddle.

"Here," I said.

"Bring out the girl, Mortymer, you've got a good handsome eye, and treat her as a sister or I bring you to account." Damned fool, I thought, for mentioning my name, but I flung a man aside and entered the tollhouse.

"There's a farm down the road!" roared Flannigan then. "Two of you fetch a cart."

`Bedlam inside the tollhouse; children wailing, the baby screaming and the girl in a corner screeching with fear. Ducking the furniture I slipped along the wall beside her.

144

Tables were going up, bedding being dragged out, china from the dresser smashing on the floor as I reached her.

"Hush," I said, "nobody will harm you, hush!"

You can see a man's fist coming but women strike like cats. Caught me square, the bitch; uncovering her eyes and striking with talons, ripping me from forehead to chin. I gripped her wrists.

"For God's sake, girl, you only have to walk. Would you rather stay to fry?"

The blood of my face seemed to quieten her. Hands lowered, she stared, then rolled her eyes and slipped down at my feet. Sickened, I stooped and gathered her up. I had not bargained on war against children. Her head lolling, hair streaming down, I kicked my way through the room, giving a special boot to Joey Scarlet who was already into it, swinging an axe like a man seeking freedom, roaring with triumph.

"First blood to the tollgates," said Rhayader as I got to the door. "Next time you search them for bread knives, Jethro."

"Fainted," I said.

"Right, find a blanket and cover her. Get her on the cart when the boys come back." He wheeled. "Where the devil's that cart, are they building it?"

"Are you going to burn us, sir?" A blue-eyed youngster of six eyed Flannigan.

"Not you, son, but your house. To the ground, and the gate with it – you can warm yourself to the blaze." Flannigan cupped his hands. "Out everybody, out!"

"I'm the last one," cried Tramping Boy Joey at the door, and he swung his axe at the window, shattering it. "Where's the tinder?"

"The gate first," said Rebecca. He raised his hand. "Silence, silence!"

And the roars and cheering died. This, our first gate, was due for the opening ceremony. Tom Rhayader dismounted and walked towards it, hands groping blindly, eyes closed, touching it, feeling it; wandering along it seeking to pass.

Dead silence now save for the weeping of the keeper's wife

and the chattering of the children. Strange how a mob is silenced by ceremony.

"My daughters," said Rhayader, turning. "I can go no further. There is something here that impedes me and I cannot pass. What is it, my daughters?"

"Why, there's a strange thing, Mother," boomed Flannigan, touching it. "'Tis an old wooden gate across the road. *Well!*"

"But what is it doing here, my daughters?" asked Rhayader, groping. "My old eyes are not too good, see – the thing wasn't here last time I went to Carmarthen."

"O, aye, Mother," said Flannigan. "Just remembered. It is one of them old tollgate things built by the Trusts. Hundreds and hundreds are going up in the county." He turned to us. "That right, sisters?"

"Hundreds and hundreds," we cried.

"But the gate must come down, my daughters," said Rhayader. "We cannot have gates on the roads of Wales – for how will we get to the city of Carmarthen? How will I take my goods to market?" And he turned then and faced us. "This is the first, my daughters. Smash it to matchwood, burn it to ashes – the tollhouse, too. By God, we will give them tollgates – down with it, down with it! Hatchets! Tinder! Down, down!"

A roar of cheering now. The powder-guns were going, pinning the moonlight with shafts of fire. Tarred brushwood was lit for flares and flung through the windows, tossed on the thatch. Flames billowed and swept along the eaves. The thatch caught, spluttering, flashing. Flannigan and Justin, Joey and a dozen others were chopping at the gate, their axes rising and falling and glinting red in the flames. Guns were exploding, men cheering as demons, dancing against the fire, drunk with success. Kneeling beside the unconscious girl, I watched. Pretty little thing she looked with the redness on her face and her black hair down. Opened her eyes then and the fear sprang back.

"Easy," I said. "It is only the old tollgate, easy," and turned. "Mam Keeper," I cried. "Your girl's come round. Mam Keeper!"

"Here comes the cart," someone bellowed. It came galloping, skidding, scattering the men. Bending, I raised the girl.

"Can you walk now?"

And she spat in my face.

"Get the family into it," said Rhayader. "Eh, there's a sight, boy," and he grinned at me. "A cat you've got there, spitting and scratching – give her one on the backside if she doesn't behave. Come on, come on! Pile them in – the children first, then the furniture – blankets, bedding, throw it all in, and watch this vixen of a girl by here if you fancy your eyes. Hurry, hurry!"

The bile was rising to my throat. I spat, turning away, wiping blood from my face. She had done me pretty well for her age; nails like cut-throat razors by the feel of my face. Felt sick as they flung the belongings into the cart and hustled the people in after them: thought of my mother and what she would say. The gate was flat now. Joey was flinging the smashed timbers on to the tollhouse blaze which was going like Hades and setting the night alight, with flames roaring up and ammunition exploding inside. I looked towards the cart again. It was ready for off, with the keeper's family hunched among the furniture. The girl was sitting motionless in her blanket, watching me, I noticed, with her great brown eyes.

"Rhayader," I said. "What happens to these people?"

And Justin Slaughterer shouldered his axe and turned from the fire.

"Aw, shut it, man! Rebecca, is it? Your petticoats suit you," and he spat. "Dancing and dabbing at women and kids – get back to your gentry!"

Suddenly enraged, I leaped and hooked him but he ducked and brought up the axe and Rhayader was instantly between us, one fist for Justin and the other for me, like lightning, and I staggered against the cart, tripped and rolled between its wheels.

"Abel Flannigan, my hearty!" laughed Rhayader. "Come and settle these two slaughterers," and he caught Abel by the shoulder as he lumbered over. "No, leave it, man – no time now. Private fights after. Come on, lads, do not look pitiful.

Just the same as Efail-wen, we are bound to get tempers. It's a dirty old business, mind, the boy is right."

"But what about these people?" I was up now, gripping him.

He smacked my hands away. "All arranged," and he turned, shouting:

"Down to Kidwelly, lads – down to the squire. He has a snug little barn he is going to hand over or risk a visit from Mother Rebecca – she will see people housed. Away now, the gate is down!"

The flames were dying as we mounted the horses. Randy took a belt at me as I caught his bridle but I did not fight back – too weary, too sickened by the violence and savagery of men.

"You give me a lift again?" Matthew Luke John, standing below me and I leaned and hooked him up. Jogging on the horses now, eyes drooping for sleep, we marched on Kidwelly itself and the house of the squire; smashing the bar at the village entrance, going right up his drive. He dared not come out but I saw him at a window, face parched in moonlight. Very tidy was his barn by the time we had finished with it, and we put the tollkeeper and his family in warm and snug with a notice on the door daring anyone to evict them. Off again under the eyes of the peakfaced servants to the farm of the Reverend John Jenkins two miles east. A tinder to his ricks and we left them blazing, worth at least a thousand Bibles, and a Bible was left on the doorstep of the labourer, not even waking him.

Home now came the wraiths, soot-stained, weary; little bands leaving us as we passed the villages, and we dispersed a mile or so short of Tom Rhayader's place.

Strange that Matthew Luke John should kiss me goodbye, disappearing into the frozen woods without a wave.

The house was dead silent when I got in. I stabled Randy silently, stripped to the waist and washed myself clean. To bed now, watched every board for a creak, and I slipped into the blankets and laid there staring at the flush of dawn. Nearly daylight. With the nails of the vixen throbbing on my face, I dreamed. And the last thing I saw was the door coming open inches and Morfydd's face peeping to see if I was in. Heard her sigh.

I slept.

## CHAPTER 17

WENT BACK to Ponty a week after this, for the bottom had come out of farming and we were only keeping alive by the skin of our fingers. No trouble with Job Gower, though he grinned a knowing grin: labour would be easy the way things were going, skilled men especially. And I went back to Liam Muldooney in his two foot seam. Good to be with Morfydd again. We were closer than ever now on the morning walks to the pit. Good to be relieved of the strain of pinching, too, for our combined wages were now nineteen shillings. Good to be away from Mari, hell to be away from Mari.

Came Christmas with its white dresses and glaciers, its red log fires and goodwill to neighbours though we were still burning ricks and gates. I was out most weeks with Rhayader now, save when on night shift and somehow or other Mam did not get wind of it though she had played the devil about the state of my face, with a pinch round her mouth and her suspicions of Sixpenny Jane who had marked more than one in the village.

Sweet were the nights when the neighbours called to sit in a circle for Readings of Him. Most religious, our friends, chiefly Nonconformists, though we sported a few Church of England, making allowances for the misguided, being Christmas. Matrons I do love to call at the house best, for they are of the world and with kindness, women like Biddy Flannigan with breasts for weeping on, Abel's mam, though she'd have given him Abel if she'd known he was burning gates.

"Well, well! Biddy Flannigan!" Mam would cry. "Come you in, *fach*, get warm by the fire!" And in she would come, black as a tomb with her bulges and wheezings as a mother should be. She sits in fat comfort, then, the sweat lying bright in the folds

149

of her chins, black bun, black brooch with its picture of Victoria, God bless her. Living to satisfy the appetite of Abel, this one; going to grease in the heat of her oven. But she had another at home besides Abel – the idiot offspring of a churchyard digger, second husband, now deceased. Head lolling, spit dribbling, her idiot floundered and grunted, wallowing at table, screaming in bed. My cross, said Biddy, every woman's got one, if it isn't the womb it's the offspring, and Cain is mine, God help him. Strange is the body of Woman, delivering a man one year and spewing a devil the next, though with Abel and Cain in the house it was hard to find the devil.

Christmas dinner eaten now and Black Boar tavern was going like something out of Hades, for the men of the northern industries were sweeping in proper, coming like an army, ragged, starving, desperate; running from the closed pits and blown-out furnaces of the industry. Men who had not seen Carmarthen for years came home, dragging themselves along the highways, sleeping in snow with their little scrags of women and children dragging behind them. But a few had money that Christmas, single ones mostly, and they crowded the taverns from morning till night, quarrelling and drinking to drown their desperation. In his element was Grandfer now, of course; beer-swilled, tub-thumping, laying down the law, and night after night I heard him stumble to his room with Mari's gentle voice to guide him. Amazing to me that he'd lasted so long – still more amazing where he got his money from for the drinking – must have salted a tidy bit away before the gates sprang up. And the second day after Christmas it lasted no longer.

The county blew up as Grandfer blew up.

The wooden horse was marching day and night now and the hatreds were rising in bitterness and threats. Burning hayricks dotted the countryside, the tollgates were blazing from Llandeilo to Pembroke, and as fast as we burned them they were rebuilt by Bullin, the price of the damage put on the tolls, and burned again. Windows were smashed nightly, gentry salmon weirs blown up, magistrates burned in effigy, people ridiculed in public. The whole teeming countryside from coast to coast brawled and rioted into open revolution. Special constables were sworn in to protect the gates, special constables were dragged out and horsewhipped by the Rebeccas. The dragoons and marines were dashing around arresting people, the magistrates had special sittings, with public warnings and transportations; the prisons were crammed to their doors, workhouses bulging. From Whitland to Laugharne, Saundersfoot to Carmarthen, the yeoman farmers armed for the fight. The poor became poorer, the poorest starved under the new Poor Law. Spindle-legged children were wandering the villages and dying of fever on beds of straw. Mass meetings were held on Mynydd Sylen and the torchlight processions around Picton's Column, Carmarthen, became bolder and bolder. From the first Rebecca – Tom Rees of Efail-wen – there sprang up a host of new Rebeccas, men of education and most with deep religious beliefs, and the gates went down in scores. But the gates, as Rhayader had told us, were only the outward symbol of oppression. The reasons of discontent reached out to the very throne of England. One bitter complaint was the workhouse test, and people were starving rather than accept it. An evil exchange, Rebecca said; better auction the poor to the highest bidder as in the old days than drive them to the workhouse to be torn apart from their families and starved. Unmarried mothers were another indignity. The new Poor Law sent them straight to the workhouse, for the task of proving paternity was now placed on the woman, and the man usually got off scotfree. Good women, many of these unmarried mothers, said Rebecca – violated by deceit and the promise of marriage, and the Poor Law violated them again. To starve was a crime and thousands were starving rather than enter the workhouses. The industrial depression of the east had hooked our county flat, and the ironworkers poured in with their tales of poverty and dying – thirteen hundred deaths from cholera in a year in Merthyr and Dowlais alone. People were banding together and emigrating – single fare to America the land of justice – four pounds a head steerage. Better to die in steerage than starve in this winter of hell, they said. And in the turmoil of a land where there was plenty for all Rebecca stacked her barrels of gunpowder high, cupping her hands to the tinder, watchful, waiting for the chance of a bloody revolution. And in the new year the tinder struck. The flash of the explosion detonated into thunder.

And in the blaze of Rebecca, Grandfer died.

In the kitchen now, two days after Christmas, all the guests gone.

"What you say his name is?" asked Mam, spinning.

"Hugh Williams," I said.

"There's a lovely Welsh name," said Mari, smiling at her sewing.

"Aye," said Mam. "I know a good English one that led us to hell in Monmouthshire. John Frost, is it?"

"Frost had no chance," I said. "We shifted him before he was ready," and I gave Morfydd a glance.

"Should have had Vincent for the march on Newport. No Queen on the throne now if we'd had Vincent," said she.

"O, aye?" said Mam. "A finger on her and I would have a hand in it."

Spectacles on the end of her nose, she was, spinning away. Revolts came and went but Mam just went on spinning. "And what does he do for a living?" she asked.

"Hugh Williams?"

"That's who I'm after."

"Solicitor," I said.

"History repeating itself," said Mam. "Another with a tongue, it seems."

"Frost was a draper," said Morfydd.

"A cloth-cutter," I said. "Hugh Williams is a leader."

And Morfydd turned her eyes from the fire. "Like a damned parrot," said she. "Repeating the rumours. Where did you learn such nonsense?"

"Never mind," I said.

"Aye, never mind!" Disdainful now, she rose. "Half chit revolutionaries, the lot of them – they wouldn't have lived with Frost. But no discredit to Mr Hugh Williams, mind. Mam is right. He is a solicitor, nothing more. There is no single Rebecca, nor could there be one for he would dare not show his

152

face in defiance of the law. Williams might defend Rebecca at the Assizes, but it ends at that – too much has happened to men like Frost – a life sentence in Van Diemen's Land, so don't talk nonsense."

I did not reply. Expert, Morfydd.

"Now that we've had a revolution do you think I might have a cup of tea," said Mam. "I've been promised one six times an hour back."

"I will get it, Mam," said Mari.

Mam sniffed. "Pray God the world could be governed by women," she said. "Women like that."

"Damned fine state we'd be in then," I said.

"And a damned fine job you've made of it to date," replied Morfydd.

"But not so much greed, mind," said Mari, fetching the kettle.

"Tongue-pie in Parliament," I said. "Morning till night."

With the kettle on the hook Mari went back to her needling and Richard, Morfydd's boy, climbed up on her knee, knowing it was bedtime. She kissed him and bent again to her darning. Socks most nights for Mari, very calm, serene, smiling over the potato holes, mine chiefly, fingers spread, examining her art.

"Prancing round Parliament with the latest in hats," I said.

"The country could only starve, though," replied Mam. "And the country is doing that now, God bless the Members. Hey, you," she stirred Richard with her foot. "Time for bed, nippy," and he clung to Mari.

"Up," said Morfydd, jerking her thumb at him.

"Before you start shooting Members of Parliament – we shouldn't be talking like this in front of the children," said Mam. "Bed."

"This minute," said Morfydd.

"Is somebody coming up?" Great were his eyes in his little man's face; six years old now, handsome, strong, and I loved him.

"O, God," said Morfydd. "No peace for the wicked, is there?"

"Them old ghosties be roaming, Mam," he said. "They are

153

always out and doing about Christmas. Another five minutes?"

We wavered.

"Not much control, is there," said Mam, treadling. "Feet first they went in my day, mind – no argument."

"I will take you," said Mari, kissing him.

"Give him here," I said. "I am going up, anyway. Come on, Dick boy, we will give them old ghosties," and I hooked my arm under him and turned him in a circle for kissing.

"Richard, if you please," said Morfydd. "There are no Dicks here."

In the bed beside Jonathon I put him down and covered him.

"Uncle Jethro?"

"Aye, Dick?"

"Where do the old moons go when they sink over Carmarthen?"

"Chopped up into stars and put over Tenby," I said at the window.

"O, aye?" He fell to silence.

I stood looking through the window. The country was white and misted and the snow caps of the hills were spearing at the moon like hunters. Away to the east the clouds flashed in strickening brilliance and I heard the faint plopping of the powder-guns of Rebecca.

"Uncle Jethro?"

I grunted.

"You out again tonight, Uncle Jethro?"

"Never go out," I answered. "Too cold to be roaming."

"There's strange," said he. "I see you out there most time, for the slightest sound do wake me. A secret, is it?"

"Sort of," I said. "Will you tell on me?"

"Swear honest," said he. "Wait now before you tell me while I fetch out the china or I will wake my mam later and then there will be a palaver."

"Right," I said, "but hurry."

Down with him, under with him, heaving it out, kneeling now, nightshirt held up, eyeing me excited.

"Please turn away," I said. "It is not a public exhibition, Dick."

"To the wall, turn round, is it?"

I nodded.

At the wall he said, "You courting then, Uncle Jethro?"

"Aye, a lady, but keep it secret, remember."

"Cross my heart, man," and I toed the thing under as he climbed into bed.

"What lady, Uncle Jethro?" His eyes were as jewels in that light.

"You never tell the lady's name," I replied.

"Sixpenny Jane?"

"Who said that?" This turned me.

"Is she indecent, then?" He played with his fingers. "Old Grandfer said it – that telling? All you are worth, he said."

"Aye?"

"And my mam do tell him to shut his mouth, eh, the wicked old bastard."

"Do not say bastard," I answered. "Least of all about Grandfer."

Nodding now, the blankets up to his chin. "Do all men wear petticoats when they do the courting, man?"

Just looked at him.

"I see'd you, remember – night after night – sitting on old Randy, wearing the petticoat, and I told my mam and she said hairpins in the bed next, poor old Jethro."

"Mistaken," I said. "Pretty snowy lately, Dick. When I go courting with the lady I come back covered. It wasn't a petticoat."

"O, aye?"

I examined his eyes for disbelief, finding none. O, for the eyes of children – innocent, trustful, read as a book. I had settled him, but not myself.

Coming sick of it, fearful of the danger. God knows what would happen to them here if the dragoons tailed me one night. More than once I had galloped Randy to shake off the military, for the new Colonel just come in had a nose for Rebecca. Only last week I had laid in a hedge a hundred yards from Cae White waiting for a patrol to move off. Very interested in the house, it appeared, and I had sweated. Rhayader said somebody was informing – somebody among us but he did not know who. So we watched each other at the meetings now; took breaths while eyes switched, the sentences stopped half way. And now a child was tracking me – little hope if the dragoons got onto him, aged six. God help him if I find that tongue, said Justin Slaughterer. I will have the thing out bloody and dripping.

Terrible to be harbouring the ears of a Judas.

"Sleep now, Dick," I said. "Don't forget your prayers."

"Our Father, is it?"

"He will listen. Just pray. Good night, boy."

I was going down the stairs when Morfydd met me halfway.

"Is Grandfer in?" she asked.

Opening his bedroom door I looked in; shook my head.

"Little devil," said she. "We thought he was abed. He is worrying that girl into her grave."

"Leave the back door," I said. "I am off to bed."

"Early tonight?"

"Yes," I said, "I am tired to death."

She smiled. "You won't serve Job Gower and Rebecca, too, man. Bed with you. At least I will sleep tonight." She came up the stairs and kissed me.

"Goodnight."

The problems multiply in darkness, pressing in heat and sweat. Yet when morning comes, fortified, you wake and face the molehills that were mountains last night. But even this remembering does not bring you peace, and you toss and hump about, knees up one minute, six feet down in the bed the next. Distantly that night I heard the thumps and clanks of the dragoons and waited with pent breathing till their galloping drifted into silence, and sleep came, fitfully, with visions of Tramping Boy Joey parting the hedges for a journey to St Clears and the special constables. It was close to dawn when the door of my room rasped and I rose up in the bed.

Mari stood there in her nightdress, hair down over her shoulders, holding a candle like a wandering saint.

"Jethro!"

She came towards me, drifting. "Grandfer," she said. "I have been waiting and it is nearly dawn. He has rarely been as late as this."

I sank back, sweating, cruelly relieved. "He will come in soon."

"Jethro . . ." now she was standing above me, her face pale, her eyes moving in anguish. "I am worried."

"For God's sake go back to bed," I said. "Does he give a thought for you ?"

She sat on the bed then, shifting my knees. Beautiful she looked. Her clenched hand was lying an inch from mine, and my fingers itched to be upon it. I looked at her, closed my eyes as the magnet drew me, gripping myself in the bed as I flew against her, cursing myself.

"Jethro, please," she said.

"Away, then, let me get up."

She gripped my hand at this, her eyes narrowing with some kind of love and her touch brought fire to me, with a longing greater than I had ever known before, to hold her, to be one with her.

"Poor old Jethro," she said, smiling down. "Loaded with women and kids and drunkards, worrying day and night, trying to make ends meet, pestered with women like me."

God, the stupidity of women. She was leaning above me. The white smoothness of her breast, I saw, neck and throat. And her womanhood flashed between us in the instant I moved towards her, and she drew away sharp, eyes startled. Unblinking, we looked, in the year of that second as the understanding flew into her, and she caught her breath, her fingers pulling together the neck of her nightdress.

"Damned woman," I whispered. "Do you think I am stone ?"

"I . . . I did not know, Jethro," she said, and lowered her face.

"Now . . . now get out before it's two in the bed."

Faltering, she stood, eyes closed.

"Go on, get out," I said, and turned away from her.

I did not hear the door shut but knew she was still there, and turned. She was standing with the candle, a look of infinite kindness on her face, and pity.

I dressed in a daze to go out looking for Grandfer, and crossing the snow-covered shippon I looked back at the house. Mari was standing by the window of the landing where Morfydd had stood when I first went out with Rebecca; holding the candle, misty in white, beautiful, looking as a soul in search of God. She waved.

I did not wave back but ran, taking the track to Tarn.

Raw cold are the peat bogs when they dress themselves in shrouds. I kept to the track through the peat, knowing the way Grandfer took on his stumbling journeys home. An unholy place this, billowy and wraithy in the hour before dawn; a world of tinkling icicles shivering in sweeps of the wind, with the branches bare-black against the moon. Bending, I examined the new sprinkling of snow and found footsteps, Grandfer's most likely, but leading one way – to the tavern. There was no sound but faint wind-sigh and the creaking of trees. All yesterday a thaw had been upon us with the rivers running wild again and the little brooks shouting down to the Tywi. But at night had come frost, fisting them into silence, and they stood as glass now, ready for the footstep and the wallowing plunge. Nothing moved in the stink of the peat. Wiping sweat from my eyes, I turned. The mere at the end of the track was black, its rushes as spears, and beyond lay the pine end of Black Boar tavern with its mud and wattle chimney stark against the sky. Took a step towards it, and sank. Twisting sideways, I threw myself flat and the peat bog bubbled in splinters of ice as I rolled back to the track. Panic hit me then, for the bog was fishing for sober men now, never mind drunkards.

"Grandfer!" I called, and the woods flung it back.

On again, cursing myself for bringing no lantern.

And the hiss came from behind me, swinging me round.

In the place where I had fallen the Corpse Candle was rising, with the peat bog hissing and sighing. And the flame of it struck then, glowing into a brilliance. Gripping a tree I watched. Now the blaze died, leaving one straight candle, three feet high from the goblin of the peat. Red-topped, evil, it danced and swayed; yellow now, leaping high into incandescent fire, and I felt the warmth of it. Then it moved, rushing past me along the track, thrusting me back, hands to my face.

For I had seen him.

Grandfer, not two yards from the track, ten feet from me, frozen, and in the light of the Corpse Candle I saw his face, eyes bulging, jaw dropped for the scream.

Flat on my belly now, wriggling towards him, grasping the tuft-grasses, the hair of the peat bog, and I reached him in pistol shots of cracking ice.

"Grandfer!" I cried, but he gave no answer. Not a sound he made standing there to his waist in bog, with one hand gripping a bottle and the other hand pointing to Tarn.

The fingers I clutched were frozen solid.

Preserved all right was Grandfer but not in hops as he'd planned it.

Preserved by peat for Cae White's generations.

As I snatched at his belt he slipped from my sight and his soul flew up to Bronwen, his lover.

And the peat bog sighed and sucked in hunger.


## CHAPTER 18

AMAZING HOW many friends one has when it comes to weddings and funerals. Reckon half the county was in Mam's kitchen, come to pay respects to Grandfer, although we had lost the body, with people sitting around bowed under the weight of the loss. Respectful, kind, generous, but I prefer the habits of the Irish, for a man is grown up when he understands that death is a joke. For instance, a whale of a time Biddy Flannigan gave Dick Churchyard, her man, when he went down, according to reports. Called in his Irish friends from ten miles round, did Biddy, and they boxed old Dick and set him up in a corner with a quart mug of ale in his hand and the feasting went on till dawn. Everyone to their beliefs, said Biddy Flannigan – the Welsh have their black funerals, the Shropshire's their sin-eating, the Indians their burnings and the Irish their Wakes. Gave my Dick what he requested, face down burial, too – no conscience.

"Buried face down?" whispered Morfydd. "Why?"

"Well, being a gravedigger my Dick wanted something out of the ordinary," said Biddy. "For he'd put down hundreds proper way up, see?"

"*Well!*" said my mother.

"But I might just as well have saved myself trouble," said Biddy, "for a variable man was my Dick and bound to change his mind. Just back home I was, tired to death, for wearing old things be funerals, and then he started. First he hit up the chimney in Dai Alltwen Preacher's place, then he rattled the pots and pans in by here, which was clever, for a haunted man was Grandfer at the best of times. . . ."

"Good grief," whispered Mam.

"And when gravel sprayed my window near midnight I knew it was Dick playing up, see. 'Abel Flannigan,' I shouted down. 'Turn out of bed this minute, your stepfather's changed his mind again,' and up got Abel cursing. Pouring cats, it was – I stayed in, mind. It was a four mile walk and a two hour dig to turn my Dick face up. But worth it, eh, son?"

"Aye," grunted Abel. "Good man was Dick."

"Lucky in some ways, Mrs Mortymer, if I might say," added Biddy, "having no body."

"And Grandfer that variable, too," said Morfydd. "Anything could happen."

"Hush," I said. "Mari is coming."

Prayers now, but wasting their time in respect of Grandfer. I sat, listening, my heart aching for the living, not the dead. Poor Mari.

"We are gathered here to pay our last respects to our friend," said Tom the Faith. "Grandfer Zephaniah, rest his soul."

"Amen," said Justin Slaughterer beside me. Close as twin nuts was Justin and Grandfer in ale, but I was surprised to see Justin there next to me.

"For a good man knoweth the light of Heaven, and his face shall shine," said Tom the Faith, and we clasped our hands and bowed our heads, doing our best for Grandfer who was about ten to one on my betting.

And Justin beside me wept for Grandfer's soul. One sob only, and the silence rang.

"Good God," said a calf in the terror of that silence. "Just look what Justin Slaughterer is doing to Joe."

And Justin wept louder while Mari sat dry-eyed. If I'd had my way I'd have straightened him with a right, for I could smell his hops from here.

"Amen," we intoned.

"Good grief," whispered the calf in my ear, high-pitched. "Just look at Justin Slaughterer weeping."

For getting it proper was little Joe Calf the last time I called on Justin Slaughterer – getting it good to Justin's song; a bawling blackguard of a song that spouted from the end of his bloodstained pipe and battered on the slaughterhouse walls. O's and Ah's from his friends as Joe Calf went down. Shivering is in them at the blood on Justin's hands, gasps as the belly hide rips to the upward casual stroke, calf one moment, dinner the next. "And I am next," whispers another as Justin reaches to drag. Powerful on his knees is Justin Slaughterer, bass in the chanting, right on the note, loving his God, grieving for his neighbour. Come to pay respects to Grandfer, newly slaughtered.

"And may the Lord have mercy on his soul," ends Tom the Faith in deep reverence.

"Amen," we said.

"Amen," boomed Justin Slaughterer, dabbing, snuffling.

"Amen," said Joe Calf, treble from the fields.

I clenched my hands and rose; went out into air.

Couldn't bloody stick it. The brother of hypocrisy is the blubbering of drunkards.

Biddy Flannigan, every time. Death is a joke.

Much better are the memories of my last spring at Cae White. The wind blew cool from the south, the country flowered, joyful with birdsong, with the blackbirds singing around our door and the young woodpeckers laughing and twittering in the alders of the Tywi. Sometimes I went down to watch them in their mating, thinking of Tessa, listening to the harsh shrilling of their lovers' quarrelling, following the tossing and tumbling of the peewits and their bright diamond flutterings in sunlight against a cloudless blue. Pale green were the buds of the willows, shy and waving in the winds of spring, breathless as children before adventure, the bursting ecstasy of their flowering. Foxes stole from lairs among the ripening heather, eyes slanting to the scent of hounds, nose high for the stamping panic of the rabbit. Old Grandfer Badger rolled from his earth down in Bully Hole Bottom and lumbered around the mantraps of Waldo's preserves, nose twitching for the stink of Jethro Mortymer the man. And at night the young, fresh moon made the circle of her eternal fullness, waning before the invisible Lord. Bill Stork was down on the estuary, one-legged in white purity, monumental against the patterned branches of yew where Hesperus watched. The corncrakes were crying masterful, the herons were singing doleful from Kidwelly. Feather and fur, leaf and branch, man and maiden were reaching up fingers, vital, reborn, for the tumbling, shouting torrent of spring.

Eighteen now, me; feeling the surge of manhood. Six-feet-one in socks, every inch alive, every pound bothering, feeling the rise of the sap in me, with the flicker of an eye for an incautious maiden, longing for Woman.

Tessa was but a dream now, as eggshell china standing behind glass. Even Mari faded in these spring-heat days; something apart and unattainable that washed and mended in her nunlike purity, dedicated to another. So enough of Tessa, I thought, enough of Mari.

Dilly Morgan, me.

Dilly Morgan aged seventeen, lately come from carrots for hair and one tooth missing. God help her since she crossed my path.

Come beautiful all of a sudden, had Dilly; tall and willowy, black-haired and with a beckoning eye and lashes slanted low with a spring come-hither; narrow in the waist and hips, most pleasant in other places to say the least of it. From childhood to womanhood I had watched this Dilly bud, flower and bloom. It is strange to me how the little scrags of females grow to such beauty – the muddy sticks of legs that lengthen to stately grace, the dribble-stained pinafores that peak to curved beauty, the tight-scragged tufted hair that flowers to grace the Helen; discoloured, aching teeth change to pearls and the cracked lips of winter come cupid bows for kissing. From little dumps of shapelessness grows Woman; desirable, desiring, the perfect animal for the mating of Man. And as such grew Dilly Morgan or very damned near it.

Met her one Sunday, resting that Sunday from underground at Ponty. I was wandering down the lanes near Ferry with the Devil sitting on my shoulder looking for idle hands. Bright was the sun, and the world in love with the newborn spring and the hedges all leafy and the azalea bushes golden.

"Good afternoon, Jethro Mortymer," said Dilly, looking glorious.

"Good afternoon, Dilly Morgan."

She was picking primroses, fingers dainty and plucking, showing a yard of black-stockinged leg as she leaned to the hedges, so I plucked a posy for her.

"For me?" said she delighted.

"For you," I said, and pinned it on her breast.

"O, my," said she. "Hell and damnation for us if that Polly Scandal do see us. Loose me quick, Jethro Mortymer."

"One kiss first?"

"There is damned forward."

"Just one for spring, Dilly."

Soft were her lips.

"Another for summer?"

"Good grief, man, you'll have me in the heather. One for summer, then, and no more seasons."

Wind whisper.

"Eh," she said. "Grown up lately, is it?"

"One for autumn," I said, "don't waste time."

"Damned brutal, you are," said she, pushing and shoving.

163

"Eh, and none of that here, Jethro Mortymer! Stop it this minute!" And she fetched me a swing with a fist that I just ducked in time.

"Right, you!" said she, furious. "Now you've done it. Tell me dad, I will. Front row chapel, mind, strict deacon. Virtue has its own reward and it don't include that. He'll be up to see your mam in under five minutes."

I went like something scalded.

Hettie Winetree next. Second best choice was Hettie, hardly the figure for courting, but you can't be choosey in spring. Where Hettie went out Dilly went in, but her mam was having trouble with her still, it seemed, yearning for the facts of life. Sitting on a barrel was Hettie Winetree with a straw in her mouth, dressed more for farming than Sunday, with a lace cap on her little black curls and her sleeves rolled to the elbow.

"Good afternoon, Hettie Winetree."

"O, God," said she, going crimson.

"Haven't seen much of you lately," I said. "You free for a walk?"

"Welcome, I must say," which was a step in the right direction, but she went pretty frigid when we got to the woods. Just peeps and shivers at this the target of her visions, this the torment of her dreams.

"Down by here," I said, patting grass.

"O, my," said she.

"Come on, come on," I said.

"And what will happen then, Jethro Mortymer?"

"One guess is as good as another, girl."

"You heard about Beth Shenkins?"

"No," I replied.

"Little Beth Shenkins sat on grass and she hasn't been the same girl since."

I eyed her.

"Down by here came poor little Beth – courting that Ianto Powell from Cefn, thought it was for kissing, see? But she came home at midnight short of a garment, was in child by that

Ianto three months later, beaten by her mam, cast out by her dad, all in under a week." She stopped for breath.

"Go on," I said.

"Ended in the workhouse, caught a chill scrubbing, child died at birth and her dead three days later, poor Beth Shenkins. Just thinking the same thing could happen to me. That likely?"

"More than likely," I said.

Skirts up and running, with looks over her shoulder to see if I was following.

Pretty good spring so far, but probably for the best, for I couldn't help thinking of Dilly.

Black Boar tavern now, leaning over a quart. All the men were strangers save Ezekiel Marner who eyed me, blue-faced, red-eyed, cranked over his mug. I grinned at my thoughts. Could be that special punishments were being handed out for spring fulfilments. And up came Sixpenny Jane, smiling, and leaned her arms on the counter opposite.

"What is your pleasure, Jethro Mortymer?"

"A mug," I said, looking away.

"Eh, hoity-toity tonight, is it?"

"No, just drinking."

"You seen Justin Slaughterer?"

I shook my head.

"Looking for you, mind," she said. She pushed the ale towards me and I blew off the froth and drank.

"Aye?"

"Breathing fire and brimstone, too. Drunk as a coot on ice, he is. Squaring accounts, he said. You mind."

Didn't really hear her. Strange is ale with strong light above it, the image of the face: the bulbous nose, the slits of eyes, the heaped cheekbones; all refracting and shimmering in the amber haze; the hop-flecked mouth, the mad dog froth of the lips, the sabre teeth of the tiger, all is flung back, warping the vision as it warps the wits.

"You listening, Jethro. Raging is Justin, out for blood."

"O, aye?"

And ale is like life, I thought, the gentry froth at the top, puffed up and pompous, the dregs of beggars at the bottom.

Lower the mug and leave the dregs. Fighting, fighting, I thought, and for what? For another master, a dreg of a master; beggar or gentry they are tuned to greed. One pig in exchange for another one uneducated. I looked past Jane, thinking.

"Gone down to your house just now, you see him?"

"Who, now?" I asked.

"Justin Slaughterer. What the devil is wrong with you tonight?"

"Morfydd's back home. She will give him slaughterer. Another mug." I tossed her a penny. "One for you," I said.

"You'll be drinking in good company," said Jane. "You heard about Betsi?"

"No."

"Courting strong, Waldo Bailiff."

"Good match," I said.

"Turned over a new leaf, has Betsi, mind. And when Betsi turns we both turn, Gipsy May and me. A house of virgins this, all we lack is lamps. Taking the cloth, the three of us, sackcloth and ashes henceforth. Respectable now, says Betsi, convents don't come into it. But my time is my own after closing, of course." She dimpled and smirked and fluffed her hair. "You free tonight, Jethro Mortymer?"

I looked at her. The youth of her was reaching over the counter; skidding over the wet teak between us as a clarion sail on a sea of ale. I blinked away the fumes, unused to drinking. She smiled, head on one side.

"Have to make your mind up quick," she said. "Here comes Justin."

The shouting of the room died to silence as I turned. The door slammed as Justin heeled it. Men muttered, their eyes switching from Justin to me. North country colliers, mostly; massive men, hardened to iron by the tools of their trade, sensing the vendetta.

"Away," whispered Jane, gripping the counter.

I turned on my elbow and faced him.

I knew Justin Slaughterer in this mood; the trash of manhood, this one – six fights a week and a woman thrown in. I may have had an inch on him but he was a full two stone the heavier, deep-chested, with black hair sprouting round the ring of his collar. He smiled then, his white teeth showing in the tan of his face. Handsome devil.

"Right you, Mortymer," he said, and slipped off his coat.

"Better outside, Justin."

"Outside last time, boy. Better in here." Hands on hips he wandered towards me. Thought he was drunk at first, but his feet were steady; as sober as me. Jane came round the counter, elbowing aside the audience.

"This is Betsi's night off, Justin," said she. "Outside now, we want no fighting in here."

Justin swept her behind him with one arm, grinning.

"Rebecca, is it, Mortymer? Handy enough with fifty behind you."

"You fool, shut your mouth," I said.

"I am here to shut yours," said Justin, and leaped.

I got him with the ale as he blundered past me, worth the price of the quart, and he tripped in his plunge and went over a table, smashing it to matchwood. A man laughed, the men lined the walls. Justin knelt, wiped the beer from his eyes, and rose.

It was strange that I knew no fear. Not a nerve moved in me as he planted his feet for swinging. Calmness is the key to it when handling bruisers, my father had taught me; the watchful eye more important than the fist: left knee turned in to ward off kicks, up on tiptoe and ready to drop, never stand square to the swing. The eye switches to the handy bottle, to the broken table where the wooden spears stick up white; the eye sticks on Justin's chin – thick and bristled that chin, begging for the cross. The smack hit to stop, the slanted hit to cut. And the swing came wide as Justin rushed. Stepping inside it I hooked him square like Fair Day, and his chin went up as he closed and gripped me, and he went to one knee and lifted me high. Locked, I went over with him on top of me. Legs sprawling, we fought, and I rose first.

"Mind the furnishings!" Jane now, screaming. "Every stick you break you pay for, remember!"

Had to keep away from him, I knew, for he was twice as

strong as me. I took the middle of the floor now, tried to side-step him but hit the counter, and he wheeled and gripped me but I slung him off and stopped him dead with a left, and crossed him again as he roared back in. I thought of Mari as I fought, trying to anger myself into greater strength. Up against the counter again now with the thudding impact of his fifteen stone against me, my back arched over the rail as he fought for my throat. Slipping away I tried to cross him, missed and fell into his arms again. Again the counter; sliding along it now, hitting short. I got him away somehow but he rushed again, keeping close quarters while I wanted him away. And every time he rushed I caught him square. Like hitting trees, for his onward rush bore me backwards. Sickening the smack of that rail in my back. Panic came then, for my strength was ebbing. I saw his face flushed and brutal, eyes gleaming, mouth gaping, gasping at breath, and I swung for the first time and slammed the mouth shut, but still he came on, and I saw the fist rushing up as the counter stopped me. Big as a tub that fist as I tried to ride it, but it took me square in the body, doubling me up. The lamp reeled over the ceiling as he hit me left and right full strength, and I slid along the rail seeking escape, but still he thudded them home. Weary, in agony, I sought a hold, but he flung me off and hit out again. Through slits of eyes I saw Justin now. His face was bleeding, his hair on end, but he was calm as he held me with one hand and measured for the blow. I tried to duck it but it caught me flush, spinning me sideways. The lamplight exploded, and I sank down, gripping his legs. Just peace then, lying at his feet, with the lace of his hobnails in the corner of my eye. I tried to climb up him they said later, but he hit me down, thumping, thumping.

I remember nothing more till I woke in the arms of Jane.
"Eh, there's a damned mess," she whispered, and held me.
I blinked about me at the barn next to the tavern, at the oil lamp hanging on the gnarled beam above us, and the face of Jane smiled down. She was sitting in the hay with her back against a tub, and me across the legs of her, my head in her lap, and the flannel she was dabbing with was red. Pretty good, me.

Cuts over each eye, lips swollen as a Negro's, and split. Very handsome, said Jane, with my new humped cheekbones, one going black.

"Teeth?" said she, and her hair swept my face.

I tried them with my tongue. "All there," I said.

"I will have him, mind," she said then. "Bricks and bottles, but I will bloody have him," and I felt her body tense with its sudden fire. Thin, her dress.

"Leave him," I said. "At least he fought fair."

"With me hanging on to his hobnails and three men dragging him off?"

I didn't remember that.

"And opening the door and dumping you out like a sack?" Too sick just then to realize the indignity.

"Fair?" she exclaimed, indignant. "The men back in there told him you'd have killed him in the open. Half his weight and no room to move in! Eh, I will have him for this. Justin Slaughterer, is it? I will do him in dripping lumps and still carving."

Pretty good lying there with her flushed face above me for I had never been so close to wickedness before. And youth is good – awake now I could feel the strength sweeping back, but I was far too interested in Jane just then to have thoughts of Justin. Her fingers were soft on my face and I saw the high curve of her cheek shadowed and beautiful in the lamplight. Harlot one moment, mother the next. Many and varied are the characters of women I have found since, but all are mothers. I rose, unsteady, my hands to my face, waiting for strength to grip me then. When I uncovered my eyes Jane was kneeling at my feet, smiling up.

"Jethro," she said.

I looked down.

"Jethro, do not go," she said, and opened her arms.

But something in the night called and turned me.

"Not yet," I said.

It was cold in the wind outside the bar. The water butt was near and I plunged my head into it and let the trickles of freeze run down to my waist to shock me into sense and feeling, and I stood there looking at the stars, drawing great breaths. For many minutes I stood in growing anger: something from my father this, a blind obstinacy that forbade any movement save back into the tavern.

"I will take you home," said Jane behind me, but I scarcely heard her. Instead I heard the hoarse laughter of men, the guffaws of Justin, the high-pitched shrieks of Gipsy May who had taken the counter in place of Jane.

Couldn't go home, to be thumped by Justin every time he saw me.

I looked at the tavern door, at the bar of light beneath it. Mugs were thumping the counter, money chinking.

"No," whispered Jane, pulling at me. "Jethro, no!"

I shook her off, remembering my father. First time a Mortymer had been dumped outside, I reckoned.

"Jethro!"

I walked up the steps, slipped the catch and shouldered the door. The light was blinding as I went inside, kicked the door shut and leaned against it. All faces swung, and Justin's swung last, and never will I forget the look he gave; jaw dropped, frowning, mug half raised.

"Right, you, Justin," I said, and walked towards him. And he laughed as I reached him, smacking the counter, head flung back, roaring.

"Well, give you credit!" he shouted in the second before I hooked him, and his mug went up and he reeled away, his stool clattering. After him now, hitting to go through him as I turned him to the counter and he screamed as an injured child as the rail caught him, bouncing him on to the next one. Raging was Justin, and I was cool, with a brain snatched from the head of my father; cool as ice, measuring distance, calculating. The place was bedlam now, tables being cleared, chairs hooked aside and men flat against the walls, with Gipsy up on the counter fisting and screaming and threatening damages. A rush from Justin nearly upended her as I stepped aside, and I pulled him off her and crossed him solid, bringing him down. It should have killed him, but he got up slowly, spat blood and ran, clawing for a hold. Things reversed now as I turned him to the counter, snapping back his head with lefts, and I saw the boot coming and caught it, lifting high. Off-balance, he teetered on one foot, and I saw the curve of his chin and took my time. This staggered him. His eyes were glazed as he came off the counter and I swung with all my strength. The blow took him full and Gipsy screamed. Up on the counter went Justin, and me after him, pitiless, for to be beaten is one thing but dumped is another. Shoulders slipping, legs waving, he lay across the counter. A hand under his heel, I helped him over. Ten pounds damages by the sound of the glass, but not a sound from Justin. Wiping sweat from my eyes, I peeped. Sleeping like a baby, standing on his head, so I went round after him and pulled Gipsy out of it, getting my shoulder under him. Jane had opened the door and I carried Justin over and threw him out to the cheers of the men. Spreadeagled he fell and laid there, as he had spreadeagled a score of men, and I went back to the counter and drank what was left of his ale, doing the custom.

Stupid is fighting.

"You did him pretty well," said Jane.

With the tavern door shut behind me I turned to the sound of her voice, for fighting and women go together, handed down from the age of the club.

I did not reply. Just stood watching her. Tombstone blackness just then, but the night came brilliant in sudden majesty, bringing her to flesh and shape, and I went to the door of the barn. Ghostly she looked, her hairpins out, hair tumbling down, as if she would fade with the first touch.

"Never seen one done better," she said. "The boy can't complain."

Just stood watching; watching her eyes narrowed with their laughter; getting the scent of her, the curve of her. The lamp was glowing behind her and the barn was golden with hay, and warm.

"Dear me," she said. "Is it frightened? And you fight with grown men?" Dimpling now, posturing, her hands round her waist. "Only little I am, mind. Nobody will kill you in here, least of all Jane."

What is it that leaps, banishing pain, tensing the muscles, throbbing in the head? A vision of Mari flashed then, her fingers spread, examining her darning, her feet crossed before the fire, but the vision fled as Jane's hand reached out.

"Come, Jethro," she said, and drew me within.

"Come, Jethro," said Morfydd beside me, and I swung, hit into reality, the fire exploding as doused with buckets. But the shock of her voice died in shame.

"Eh, now, here's a pickle," said Morfydd. "I guessed you'd be here when Justin called. Just saw him again, going like the wind . . ." and she peered at my face and gripped me, turning me. "God, there's a mess. Did Justin do that, or Jane?" and she pushed me aside and turned. White as a sheet was Jane, I noticed, though she flushed a bit under Morfydd's smile.

"Not with Jethro, Jane," said Morfydd. "A pretty little girl you are, mind, and a man could do worse. But this thing's no good to you, it's only half grown." She turned to me. "Home, you. Or I will start slaughtering."

Head and shoulders above her I went, being prodded.

But I was not leaving it at that. Even more determined when the clock from the village struck midnight. Down the stairs with me, boots in hand, through the kitchen, hushing Tara quiet, and out of the back with owls hooting their heads off as I went down to Tarn.

Black Boar was silent and in darkness save for a chink of light. The world of night was silent here, the barn as black as gravestones at the entrance, but the lamp still burned dimly in the feeding bars below the rafters, and I went in on tiptoe, knowing that Jane was somewhere around, soon to come to her bed of straw. Dry in the throat I crept inside, peering, wondering what I would do when she came; cursing myself for the coming, wondering why I was there. Shivering, I laid myself down in the darkness, hands clenched, waiting, and my heart beat faster as the straw rustled to footsteps; moved over a bit as she laid herself down.

"Jane," I whispered.

"Gipsy," whispered Waldo Bailiff.

And we put out hands and gripped each other. Up scalded, me – skidded through the door and into the night with Waldo Bailiff howling.

A damned good spring, so far. Enjoying every minute.

## CHAPTER 19

QUEER PEOPLE were getting into the country just now – that is the trouble with a decent revolution, said Tom Rhayader. We take to arms with Genesis behind us, play fair, fight fair against oppression and for the word of God, and in comes scum. In comes the scum for easy pickings, the adventurers who fight for a shilling a time. Men like Dai'r Cantwr and Shoni Sgubor Fawr, there's a mouthful, said Rhayader.

Take the last one first, the polluted.

I first met Shoni the night after dusting Justin, and was resting with my feet up and watching people from slits, getting tender glances from Mari, digs from Morfydd and mouth from Mam, she being dead against pugilists.

"Shameful," she breathed, laying the table. "God knows I have done my best to bring you up decent, and the poor man is over at Bayleaves with the Hughes putting on beef to bring down his swellings."

"Two to make a fight, remember," said Morfydd, and whispered, "lucky I was there in time to stop another slaughter, too."

"Hush," I whispered back, my eyes on Mari who was stitching as usual.

"And you keep from this!" Mam swung to Morfydd. "Fight decent, then. Osian says someone has been into him with an axe. Damned mutilated, he is."

"Some of his own medicine," I said, rising. "And I am off from here."

"Somebody will be killed," said Mam. "That will be the end of it."

"A joyful death, mind," said Morfydd on one side.

I gave her a look to settle her. I had to go out with Morfydd talking in riddles. Mam might have been bad at hearing but Mari had ears like a bat.

"And where are you off to this time of night, pray?" asked Mam, hands full of cups. "Supper in ten minutes, trust you to be off."

"Back by supper time," I answered.

"Kiss her for me," said Morfydd, and I got her with my finger and thumb as I passed, pinching open her eyes.

"And keep from Black Boar tavern, mind," said Mam.

"And Jane's stable straw," murmured Morfydd, and I saw Mari glance up.

But the walk was an excuse for I'd heard something more above the chatter of the women. Never heard screech owls as near to our shippon before.

Toby Maudlin.

Toby Maudlin sure enough, standing clear of the light as I opened the door, with his hair on end and his eyes as saucers.

"What is wrong?" I asked him.

Gasping, he patted his chest. "Rhayader's been taken."

As the sickening bite of the bread knife.

"Taken," gasped Toby. "I am rounding them up – midnight up on the mountain. Flannigan's called a meeting. . . ."

"But Tom Rhayader!" I gripped him, and he was shivering.

"The St Clears dragoons," gasped Toby. "Six of them, and special constables. They came down to Tom's place at dusk, and took him. God, there's some wailing and gnashing of teeth down his place I can tell you, his woman's gone demented."

"But on what charge?"

"Burning Pwll-trap gate – papers they had, and signatures, all very official."

"And Tom just went?"

"Just as you please, they told him – come dead or alive. Got him coming from chapel."

"God," I breathed. "And we haven't been near Pwll-trap."

"But somebody has, that's what Flannigan says. And he says something more – an informer," and he shrank at the name.

174

"Who?"

"Don't ask me," said Toby. "That's for Flannigan to find out – midnight, at Pengam, to elect a new leader."

"Go," I said.

I stood against the wall as Toby scampered away. Cool to my face, that wall, for my head was thumping. It seemed impossible that Rhayader could be taken, and I bled for his wife. A pretty little thing was Mrs Rhayader, prim for chapel and with lovely children, and they worshipped Tom. I clenched my fist and hit the wall. Gates were one thing; dumb wooden things ready for tinder, but Tom was flesh and blood, and the tongue put a limit on the thumbscrew, the bawlings and kicks of drunken tormentors. Not the dragoons, for they were disciplined – not the serving constables under men like George Martin the Welsh-speaking Englishman. It was the special constables we feared, the hired thumpers; scum like Shoni Sgubor Fawr who would break a man's arm for the price of his silence. Yet deep in me I knew Tom would not talk. If they set him on fire he would spit in their faces. Tramping Boy Joey rose up like a vision. Joey would sell a man's soul for the price of a dinner, because Tom was leader, that was enough. I fisted the wall, wanting Morfydd. Lost, I wanted her. And she came as if called by the heat and sweat of me, slowly into the yard, peering into shadows.

"That you, Jethro?"

"Quick," I said, and she ran the last yards. "Tom Rhayader's been taken."

"O, God," she said, her hands to her face.

"Morfydd, go down to Mrs Rhayader."

"Now, directly. No. Supper first, or Mam will be suspicious. You too, boy – supper first." She paused, her eyes steady. "Who?" she said.

"Who informed? God knows. We are meeting tonight."

"Is Osian Hughes in this?"

I shook my head.

"Who do you think, then?"

"We've got Joey," I answered.

"Tramping Boy Joey?" she peered, horrified. "Give me

175

strength! Do not tell me you gave house room to Joey Scarlet!"

"Workhouse boy. Entitled. You try keeping him out."

She drew herself up. "Revolution, you call it, and you bring in Joey! Perhaps my revolt failed but at least we were organized – at least we had oaths and people tried and trusted. But you are throwing away your lives!" She snatched at my hand. "Jethro, do you know what this means? Joey's tongue is loose – a pint of ale it needs, no more. He will gabble Rebecca all over the county, to dragoons, constables, anyone handy. He is gabbling now, can you hear him? Spouting it in bars – Rhayader, Flannigan, Maudlin, Mortymer – shouting it in markets – little Joey Scarlet grown to six-feet-six. And he has spouted Tom Rhayader because he hates authority – Rebecca or magistrate, they are all in authority, so Joey brings them down, can't you see?"

"Flannigan brought Joey in, not me."

Morfydd sighed. Sweat was lying on her face and she wiped it into her hair.

"I am disgusted with Flannigan," she whispered. "He is begging for Botany Bay. Listen, Jethro. Find Joey Scarlet or you will not last the night."

"You seem damned sure it is him," I said.

"Lay my life on it," said she. "Find Joey Scarlet, quick."

"And Mrs Rhayader? You will go down?"

"I . . . I will wink at Mari and get Mam steered early to bed. Leave it to me." At the door she turned. "O, you fools," she said.

Dark was the night with a hint of sleet in him from rolling black clouds running before the bloom of spring. With Morfydd down with Mrs Rhayader I set out early for the mountain meeting in the disused quarry, but took the path through Waldo's preserves. Nothing stirred in the woods and beyond the Reach Squire's mansion stood gaunt and lonely, shuttered and barred. No gentry carriages came there now. Empty it stood save for Lloyd Parry and old Ben since Tessa died. Nothing stirred as I went past it to the lime kilns where the cauldron burned the builders' lime, and the bee-hive kilns were as camels' humps against a crescent moon. Beside the slaking-pit now I looked around. Here was Joey's bed of straw; a half eaten crust nearby, the peat scarred here by the thrust of a boot. No sound save the cry of a distant bird and the bubbling of the pit where steam wisped up. I stood alone, listening, then turned and ran down the bank to the trees that reared as hunchback skeletons, stripped bare by the Atlantic gales. Leaping the peaty places, handspringing boulders I got to the foothills of the mountain and began the climb. Far below me I saw a light in Rhayader's cottage and imagined Morfydd there with Mrs Rhayader. Strange it would be without Tom tonight. Flannigan was standing at the entrance to the quarry, a dog's leg entrance that obliterated light.

"You seen Toby?" he asked. Vicious looked Flannigan.

"Bringing in the men," I said.

"Don't be too sure, Mortymer, you can't trust your neighbour."

"Joey Scarlet here yet?" I asked.

"Get inside, we can all talk there."

Must have sworn a few in since I came last. Nigh two hundred there that night; squatting shoulder to shoulder, leaning against the rocks, and they were as statues, making no sound, their faces shadowed and intense in the moonlight, and they grumbled like cattle as Flannigan followed me in.

"Two missing," said Flannigan. "Maudlin and Scarlet. Now listen, all of you know that Rhayader's been taken. Somebody's played Judas and we reckon to find him. Who saw Joey Scarlet last?"

"Up in Carmarthen market this forenoon, Flannigan," said a man at the back.

"You are sure?"

"Saw him plain as my face."

"Who's that speaking?"

"Evan ap Rees. Saw him right enough."

"What doing?"

"Begging."

"Sober?"

"More sober'n me, then some," and the men laughed.

"What time did you see him?"

"Close on midday – walking round the horses, he was – telling the tale, hat in his hand – you know Joey."

"Do I?" asked Flannigan.

"Don't jump, don't jump, man," said someone at the front. "Just a kid he is and too bloody frightened to turn informer – what about losing his tongue to Justin – you there, Justin boy?"

"Right here with the knife," said Justin, and I saw him for the first time since our fight, his face humped and bruised like mine, but grinning.

"Somebody's been slaughtering you for a change, is it?" and men guffawed.

"And he got his share," said Justin, "eh, Jethro man?"

I grinned back. One thing about fighting; you do it with men, but I still did not trust him.

"You heard about the reward St Clears has put up?" asked Flannigan.

This put them quiet. Pipes came out and they shouldered and muttered.

"Fifty pounds a time for Rebeccas. A little bit more than they paid for the Lord. You heard they picked up four Rebeccas between here and Carmarthen at fifty pounds a time, Tom included?"

"A fortune to Joey, fifty pounds," said one.

"Could have been any one of us."

"Some queer old boys been coming in lately, remember."

"You think Rhayader will talk – he can hook the lot of us."

"Shut your mouth," I said.

"Or I will shut it," said Flannigan.

We sat then, uncertain, lacking a leader. Flannigan wavered. I watched him walking about, thumping his hands, and I longed for Rhayader.

"Where have they got Tom?" asked one.

"St Clears."

"What about fetching him out of it, then?"

"Talk sense," said Flannigan.

"Do we leave him to rot? He'll get transportation next assizes for sure."

"And him with a wife and little ones."

"It was the chance he took," said Flannigan.

"Wouldn't take a lot to winkle him out of it, you thought?"

"We are not having bloodshed," said Flannigan.

"Half past two for Sunday School, prompt, mind. What is this, an outing?"

"Just a little buckshot and a few little knives."

"Where's your stomach, man?"

"We are not going after Rhayader," shouted Flannigan. "That's final."

"Since when were you Rebecca, then?"

"Not even elected. I say Rhayader comes out."

And Flannigan wavered, walking about. This is the time when the new man is born, the leader to be clutched at, revered. Up he got. He was a stranger to me, and never have I seen the like of him for size and power.

"And you sit down, Shoni," said Flannigan, eyeing him.

"You try and sit me," said Shoni Sgubor Fawr, and he came to the front.

I drew my breath at the sight of his face. It was ravaged, with the flattened features of the mountain fighter. Bull-necked, mop-haired, grinning, this one, and his clothes were ragged, his shirt open to the waist despite the frosty night and his feet and legs were bare, his ragged gentry riding breeches tied at the knees. Shoni Sgubor Fawr. This was the trash that was hanging a stink on the name of Rebecca, the scum that gathers on the top of the brew. Emperor of China, this one – emperor of the hell's kitchen of Merthyr called China where huddled a pitiful humanity. Wanted by the police in more than one county, this man; a kick-fighter, gouge-fighter. The men murmured at the sight of him.

"We can do without this one," I said to Flannigan.

"You can't do without Shoni," replied the stranger. "Not now you lack a leader, and if you want the proof of me I will take any three men here." The smile left his face. "Informers, is it? And what are you doing about it – nothing. You've lost Rhayader, and you're leaving him to rot. I say find the informer and slit his throat, march on St Clears and release Rhayader.

Does the burning of the gates bring you respect – prancing round the countryside in turbans and petticoats? Where's the belly of the county, men? By God, you should come to Monmouthshire if you want rebellion – look at the Chartists!"

"Aye, look at them," I shouted back.

"At least they had the guts to fight it out. To arms, I say – take shot to your powder-guns, forge your pikes, build your cannon and blow the military off the face of the earth!"

"I am out for one," I said, shifting.

"Who follows little Shoni?" yelled Sgubor Fawr.

"Get out," said a man. "We work it Flannigan's way."

"And my way is Tom Rhayader's way," shouted Flannigan. "Which do you want?"

The men waved a forest of hands. "Flannigan, Flannigan!"

"Out," said Flannigan, and jerked his thumb at Shoni, "You will find ten Rebeccas between here and Pembroke and I wish you luck, you are not needed here."

"And your informer?" yelled Shoni.

"Yours if you can find him," replied Flannigan, laughing, and turned as Toby Maudlin ran in.

"Been searching for young Joey," gasped Toby. "High and low I have searched – no sign."

"You tried the lime kilns?" I asked, and could have bitten of my tongue.

"Why the kilns?" asked one.

"Just wondered," I said.

"Then wonder again," answered Flannigan.

"Starts sleeping there in spring, Abel," called Evan ap Rees. "Could be he's just started. Worth trying."

"You and young Joey were pretty thick one time, remember?" mumbled Justin.

All I felt was eyes.

"Years back," I swung to him. "And if Joey talks I go under same as you," I·said.

"Go there tonight," said Flannigan. "Any likely place must be searched, and if we find him he gets a fair trial."

"Like the other two hundred here," I said.

"You try the kilns and do less talking."

"What about the notice?" asked Justin, holding up a paper.
"O, aye, the notice," said Flannigan. "Now listen all! It was George Martin who pulled in Tom Rhayader, for he is behind the military, every move. We owe him one back and by God he'll get it. We are taking his gates next, but first he'll have notice – much more difficult to explain London. You with me?"

Good humour, now, with the men nudging and loving every minute.

"So hearken," shouted Flannigan. "Justin by here is good at writing, so Justin turned this out," which put the men into stitches for Justin was no scholar. "We will post this up to-night," and he read from the paper:

" ' Take Notice. I wish to give especial notice to those who have sworn to be constable in order to grasp 'Becca and her children, but I can assure you it will be too hard a matter for Bullin to finish the job that he began. . . .' "

His voice boomed on, telling of the gates that were soon to come down, and ended:

" 'As for the constables and the policemen Rebecca and her children heeds no more of them than the grasshoppers that fly in the summer, for the gates will be burned to the ground. Faithful to death with the county, Rebecca and her daughters.' "

Muffled cheers at this, especially for the poetic bits about grasshoppers and summer, and Flannigan shouted. "George Martin will lose some sleep now that Justin's started writing him love letters. Matthew Luke John – have this pinned up in the town before dawn light," and the boy I had met on my first burning sprang up to take it. "Next meeting Wednesday," said Flannigan. "Come armed and disguised, and we will burn every gate to do honour to Tom Rhayader, our old Rebecca. Right, meeting closed. Jethro!"
I went to him.
"You will search the kilns for Joey Scarlet?"
"Yes, Abel," I said, sickened.

The men crept out of the quarry and over the mountain to their homes.

I took the path home through Waldo's preserves again. A wet bitch of a night now for spring with the wind owl-screeching like a lost soul, right old music when searching for informers. Black and spooky was the wood now with the branches rattling for skeletons as I skidded down to the limekiln humps. I walked much slower as I came in sight of the kilns, for if Joey had blabbed about Rhayader his mood would now be murderous with conscience and fear. So I came on tiptoe the last few yards, going on all fours in the peat at the first tang of the kiln fires, wiped rain from my eyes and peered.

Joey was lying face down on the slaking-rim with a shroud of canvas pulled up to his ears, his body black against the glow of the fires.

"Joey!" Behind the bole of a tree, kneeling, I called.

This brought him upright.

"Who's there?"

"Mortymer," I shouted back.

"What you want with me, Mortymer?"

"Didn't see you at the meeting tonight," I shouted.

"To hell with the meeting and to hell with Rebecca."

"And Tom Rhayader in particular, Joey? You heard about Tom?"

This brought him to his feet, standing on the rim, white as a ghost in his dusting of lime. Hair plastered, rags fluttering, he peered for me, but I had already seen the gleam of his powder-gun and kept under cover.

"You alone?" he called.

"Aye."

"Then why don't you come out, man?"

"Not likely," I shouted. "Not considering what you did to Tom Rhayader."

Stiff he stood, then his hands went to his face.

"O, God," he said.

"You sold a Christian man, Joey Scarlet, God help you. You know what will happen if Justin lays hands on you?"

Kneeling now, he wept, crying as a child cries. "Mortymer! Drunk, I was, I swear it!" he shouted. "I'd never have done it sober. O, help me, Mortymer – pretty tidy you was to me in the old days, remember?" He was wringing his hands now, giving peeps for listeners, standing above the slaking-pit as something in the steam of hell, his face wet with tears and rain.

"Joey!" I shouted. "Are you listening? Up and away with you – hoof it out of the county. Put as much room as you can between you and Rebecca – and never mention the name of Rhayader again, for if Justin Slaughterer don't land you another slaughterer will. Where's your mam?"

"Shropshire county, sin-eating," he whimpered.

"Right then, move. Away with you quick, for if I get a sight of you round here again I'll do what Justin's aching to do – rid the world of another Judas. Away!"

Gibbering now, biting at his hands, God-blessing me, scampering around the wall of the pit, gathering up his possessions and bundling them into the canvas.

And I saw quite clearly the hand that rose from behind and pushed him.

Joey teetered on the edge of the slaking-pit, and screamed. Slowly he turned, snatching at air, his bundles flying, and he wheeled towards me as he fell face down, arms and legs spreadeagled, screaming once more as he hit the boiling lime, and the end of his scream was scalded into silence. In horror I leaped from my hiding place, racing up the mound to the rim of the pit, turning away from the stew that was Joey. The undergrowth was crashing to the passage of the murderer. Sickened, I turned.

"Joey," I said.

The slaking lime bubbled his answer, speaking for his soul for the next million years.

# CHAPTER 20

MAY WAS flooding into us now and the lanes were glorious with primroses and celandine. Golden my country now, the fields shimmering with buttercups and dandelions and the old burn was stoking up for a furnace of a summer. O, sweet is wet-a-bed days, with the taste of the gold in the milk and the chops of the cows all plastered with yellow petals as they peep through the hedges at strangers, grinning their joy of fat udders and milkmaids, dripping their beads of silver spit. And the whole rolling county was alive and shimmering breathless with the promise of a belly-full harvest by day and weeping in dew for the rusted ploughs at night. Few fields were ploughed near us for the levy on corn and the tolls were killing us. But up and down the country the gates were going up in flames, with scores of Rebeccas and hundreds of men riding every night, winning the race of building and burning. Magistrates were shivering in their beds, horses of the dragoons dropping dead in the fruitless gallops after Rebecca; lost in the maze of a country we knew backwards, redirected, misdirected, laughed to scorn, publicly insulted. The military heads were being recalled and replaced, the military stations were strengthened, all to no avail. Rebecca grew as an army in numbers. The Trusts were being defeated, and knew it.

I had been out burning most nights since Joey's death at the kilns. Down had come the special constables, of course; notebooks, pencils, all very official, but it was not worth risking to tell what had happened and a week or two after the inquiries ceased. We had hooked Joey out, what was left of him, and buried him decent in a pauper's grave, with Dai Alltwen embalming him with the biblical and talk of the All-Seeing Eye that watches the fall of the sparrow, and a day later Joey Scarlet had never existed. Reckon I know who got Joey but I never had the proof of it, for nobody was steadier than Justin Slaughterer on the day Joey went down in his wooden suit.

Tom Rhayader was still at St Clears awaiting justice and his woman and kids long gone to the workhouse, Carmarthen. Talk of a Rebecca attack on this workhouse was in the wind at the night meetings now, for our people were starving in it, said Flannigan. Something's got to be done, the Rebeccas said. How can we sleep while our kinfolk starve. Floggings were being talked about, too, though we had no proof of this. A pig of a Master at Carmarthen house especially, it was said. Starve to death or be beaten to death, were the rumours. Gather the evidence and we will raze the place, said Rebecca – we will burn it as we burned Narberth house, and bring out our people. Then for some floggings, we will show who is master.

The strain of the night meetings were taking toll of me – in just before dawn sometimes, going on shift with Morfydd at the pit after an hour of sleep. Coming pretty gaunt were most of the daughters of Rebecca, very severe this night courting on little growing maids, the men joked. I looked in the mirror one day and saw my face, lined, shadowed, and the haggard swellings beneath my eyes. Nigh eighteen, is it? said Morfydd, you look like forty, then some, there's a damned sight. Mam and Mari must have noticed this but they made no mention; just quick glances over the table with the buttoned-up air of women disapproving, Mam believing it was a misspent life. I often wonder if my mother knew the truth, for most women did. Even the parish was complaining about the drop in the birth rate, so the joke went, with the men out burning every night when they should have been back home loving. But things were coming a mite better, people said. Now the gates were coming less we were having whey and rye bread twice a day instead of once, thank God for mercy. But we were all right at Cae White with double money coming in from coaling though the farm had gone to pot. Do not mind me, said Morfydd – why should farming pay while I can crawl round Ponty like a bloody donkey, one eye cocked for Job Gower Foreman.

"It will not be for ever, Morfydd," I said.

"Damned right you are," said she. "Remember it. But do not hurry, man, I am loving every minute."

"Easy," I said. "It is not my fault."

"Perhaps not, but I am sick of it!"

I had been watching Morfydd lately. Touchy, to say the least of it; silent in our walks to Ponty, ready for the quarrel, eyebrows up, flushing over nothing. Change of life, said Mam. Treat her kindly, Jethro, or account for it to me.

"Be damned for a tale," I said. "She's only turned thirty."

"You are discussing something you do not understand," replied Mam. "Kindly cease this conversation directly."

"Change of life, indeed – she is good for years yet. There is Mrs Evan ap Rees over at Llansaint carrying for her sixth and she is over fifty."

"Mrs Evan ap Rees has not worked in the heat of iron," replied Mam "Neither has she towed trams, neither has she starved half her life by the size of her. Now cease, it is most embarrassing."

"She will have no more babies, is it?"

"If she does I will want to know why," said Mam. "Leave it now, I am coming to a flush again myself. Just treat her gentle."

"Just gently, Jethro," said Mari, smiling up from her corner. "It will pass."

Expect no kisses from the mouth of a vixen.


"How are you today now?" I asked, very pleasant.

"Go to the devil," said Morfydd.

"Asking after your health, I am. Anything wrong with that?"

"Ask about Towey's," she replied, staring. "Towey can't be bothered now."

We were alone in the kitchen that night – Mam out delivering somewhere, Mari with flowers down at church, the boys up in bed.

This set me quiet. I did not see Towey catch it, being down with Muldooney in Number Two gallery at the time, but I had heard of it from him. Tripped on the top ladder rungs, had Towey, and fallen the whole hundred feet, clothes round her ears, head-diving, with her basket of coal coming down after her, collecting the other carriers. And they followed Towey down, all five of them, with their coal pouring on top of them, giving them a decent burial. Two Welsh women, a couple of Irish, and a Spanish boy aged ten. A long way for a soul to travel to Spain. "These bloody old ladders," said Liam, the first time I had heard him swear in anger. "I will rig one on St Paul's for the aristocracy of England, though long before that it will be worn out by Welsh squireens."

"I am sorry about Towey," I said to Morfydd now.

"Missus, to you," said she, touchy.

"We will have you up from the pit directly."

"And scrape on your eleven shillings a week? You see to your own business and leave me to mine, Jethro. I was born to coal and I will die in coal – you just go on burning gates, the farm can go to hell, isn't it?"

"Morfydd, the farm will not pay. I tried it." She did not pull away when I took her from the sink and held her. "O, fach," I said. "What is wrong these days?"

And she bent her head, and wept.

"Old Mrs Towey, is it?"

"No, the boy. So little, he was. Got to love him. I saw his face when I lifted his chin, and thought of my Richard – could have been Richard, mind – only a few years older. O, God!" And she swung in my arms and gripped me. "Now, listen, Jethro, listen. I will kill someone if this farm goes flat and my boy goes into coal – I will hold you responsible." She lowered her hands. "Nothing left for me, I am finished – I am coal outside and in now; corns on my knees that do credit to a horse. Dyed in coal, I am, in my mouth, my chest, my heart," and she gripped her wrist making the veins stand out proud. "Look now, coal rivers I am, not normal flesh and blood, going to a prune with the towing, stinking of coal, coughing coal; dried of my womanhood and just over thirty. D'you hear me?" Her eyes were wide and strangely bright and I saw the lashes and brows still rimmed black after the washing.

"As a pillar of salt, I am," she said, "useless to a bed, and I have longed for more children – ten if I'd had my way. Now too late."

I turned to the window.

"Saw little Towey yesterday," she said. "I helped pull them off her and cart her out of it. God, there's a mess, and I am used to messes. It didn't worry me much, seeing Towey. But, O, God, that boy!" She covered her face.

Just useless standing there. I went to the window. The fields were ablaze beyond, all over golden with buttercups. Quietly, behind me, she began to cry again, and I went to her and touched her.

"Keep away from me," she said.

I longed for Mari to come in just then, for there are places in a woman not even a brother can invade.

"You are leaving the pit," I said. "Today."

"You starting farming again, then?" she asked. "Is Randy getting sick of it? Aye, I'll take on. One pair of shafts is as good as another and at least I'd be towing in daylight."

"That was cruel," I said.

I turned to her. Strange it did not seem like Morfydd standing there, and strange, too, that she was smiling. Terrible is coal, reaching out its fingers for those who carve it; drawing their souls into its seams, making them one with it though hating it; taking over the brain.

"Jethro."

I did not reply.

"I am sorry," she said, and went to the table and gripped the edge of it and bent, her eyes clenched. "Do not go, Jethro," she said as I reached the door, and she turned to me.

"Come here, boy."

I went to her and she straightened. "There now," said she. "It has passed. There is a swine of a sister for you, cursing and swearing, and not your fault. Don't tell Mam, is it?"

I shook my head.

"No living soul?"

"Nobody, but you are leaving the pit."

She did not hear me. "Jethro . . ." she whispered, smiling. "Hold me. Do not let me go."

I held her, and she was trembling.

"You listening, boy?" she whispered, and I nodded against her face.

"Jethro, I am going into coal – as Liam Muldooney, and Towey, and Gwallter – and Dada. . . ."

"O, for God's sake!" I said, and tried to throw her off but she clung as if sewn to me.

"I have seen the leaf," she said. "I saw it yesterday – down in Number Six, before old Towey came down with the others. O, clear as day was that leaf in every vein, with a million years engraved on the shine! You heard what the old ones say about Number Six? As the leaf is pressed in coal, so will I become part of coal. Terrible is that Number Six. Day after day the props go down, it will have us for sure. First leaf seen for ages, this one."

I held her off. "You will never see it again," I said. "Forget the leaf."

She smiled then, changed. Brilliant was that smile.

"Not bloody having me, is it?"

I looked at her.

"Not sharp enough by halves, eh?" And she whistled a note or two and snatched at her bonnet, tying the ribbons under her chin, turning her head at me, dimpling, changed. "You like this old hat, Jethro Mortymer?"

"Seen worse," I said. "You are leaving Gower today, understand?"

"Gracious, no. I am seeing out the year now I've started, I am having my wages. But never mind about Gower. What you say about this new bonnet?"

"Wonderful," I said to please her.

She put her hand to her waist and postured, swinging her hips. "Not bad for thirty-two, is it? Come on, boy, be honest. I still get the eye, mind, when I walk down the village. Very cosy, still drive the chaps demented. Reckon I might meet Willie O'Hara tonight; give the boy a treat, begging like a dog, poor soul."

"That is better," I said, relieved.

"Down on the Burrows. You ever gone courting on the Burrows down by the sea?"

"My business," I said.

"O, beautiful is summer! And the moon comes up over the sea very tidy, very romantic, and the air is warm and sweet. Gentleman is Willie O'Hara, remember. Don't let them tell you otherwise, Jethro. Might even marry little Willie, all two yards of him, you astonished?"

"No, Morfydd."

"Cowman over at Kidwelly, good job, and ambitious. Might do worse, come to think of it."

"Bring him home, then."

"Eh, steady," said she. "Mam would have him in bits. And I am trying him first, anyway, to see what stitches him together. Let you know later. Goodbye."

"Goodbye," I said.

"Give my love to Mam and Mari. Back before midnight, God willing."

As a young girl she went, bonnet tilted back, ribbons fluttering, and I stood by the door watching her as she went towards the Reach.

I covered my face.

As long as I live I will remember that May night, but not because of Morfydd. Strange it is how Fate strikes twice, sometimes within the hour; as if it brings its clenched fist to the face, crouched for the felling blow. With the house empty save for the boys asleep upstairs I was wandering about the kitchen lost, dying for Mam or Mari to come home, when a tap came on the door, and I opened it.

Effie Downpillow stood there.

Fresh from Monmouthshire was Effie; come back home to her county when the Top Town furnaces blew out, and scrubbing for Osian Hughes and his mam this past week, no more. Last Sunday at Chapel we all saw Effie, a little rag of a woman no older than Morfydd but belted by iron into skin and bone. She made spare money, she said, by selling her hair for wigs to gentry; sitting at home for weeks bald as a badger, rubbing in oils until the next harvest, but I never had the proof of it for she was pretty well shod when Osian took her in. Strange little woman this, and with dignity, though her legs and feet were bare. And at her first chapel Sunday I saw her eyeing me from the back pews, treating me important.

"You Jethro Mortymer?" she whispered now, hugging herself.

"Yes," I said.

"The man of the Mortymer family, is it?"

I nodded, wondering.

"You asking me in, man?"

"Aye, come on," I said.

Wandering in, hugging herself for winter, looking around with a vacant stare, and bags under her eyes like the fleshpots of Jerusalem.

"Over at Osian Hughes, I am," she said.

I nodded, watching.

"Sit down, is it?"

"Yes," I said. "Sit down." And she sat, perched as a bird, with her white hair hanging down either side of her face.

"You called to see my mam, Effie Downpillow?" I asked.

"Called to see you," she said, so I sat down opposite, wishing her to the devil. Her eyes drifted around the room.

"Used to scrub here once," she said. "For old Grandfer, before I took my two-room tumbledown up by Osian Hughes. Been away years, see – following the iron up to Monmouthshire, where you come from." And she smiled of a sudden, leaning towards me. "You heard about my man, Sam Miller – his dad being in flour?"

"No," I answered.

Strange, those eyes. In repose one moment, wild with their inner madness the next.

"Good grief, man. And my Sam foreman puddler over at Blaina – next place to yours – Nantyglo, isn't it?"

"Who told you that?" I asked, more interested.

"Never mind who told me. Strikes me I'm on the wrong chap – you've never seen the sky over Nanty and Blaina if you didn't know my Sam. Best puddler-man the county ever had, was Sam. Marched with the men of the Eastern Valley when they went to hit up Newport. Reckon you know Abel Flannigan, Biddy's boy?"

"Aye, I know Abel."

"There's bright. My Sam could give him a good two inches up and a foot sideways. Dear God, you never seen such a man for looks and fortifying. Aye! Topped six feet naked and as broad as a barrel, with a smell of caulking tar and tobacco about him, being of ships. Up Whitland way, you understand."

"Look, Miss Effie," I said. "I will tell my mam you called and you come back later, is it?"

"And me been waiting till the three women were out? Damned days I have waited. A monkey-tail had Sam, you see. Fine, fine, he looked – worked the big two-riggers down in Saundersfoot till he heard the iron call and made for Blaina. Eh, God!" She narrowed her eyes. "Shoulders on him like two bull heifers, eyes as black as coal and the grip of his arm could break a woman's back. You seen such a man, Jethro Mortymer?"

"Not lately," I said, pitying her. "You've been waiting till my women were out?"

"Never mind that now," she replied. "Will you hear about Sam?"

"Aye," I answered, eyeing her, and her voice went low and sweet:

"Well, outside my tumbledown I found him," said she. "Nigh six years back, could be more. Drunk as a coot, he was – his friends forced it on him, see – down in that stinky old Black Boar tavern. So I came out with my barrow and wheeled him in – never had a man under a roof before – and I stripped him and washed him clean. Like a baby he was in that washing, my Sam, but I covered him well, mind, keeping it decent."

"Go on," I said, kinder, for she was with purity.

"Well, then I got him in the sheets, hit out my last little hen, made him hot broth and fed him like a mother – bellowing all through it, of course – but I got it down him." She raised her face, screwing at her hands. "But there was only the one bed, see, and he was cold to shivering. So in with me quick beside him for thawing, it being winter. Was that improper?"

"No, Effie," I said.

"Slept without a snore, he did, by here," and she held her breast. "On here, you understand, where a man's head should be? You ever slept that way, boy?"

"Not yet."

A silence fell between us then and she lowered her head, picking at her ragged dress. I longed for my mother to come then. Thank God she did not.

"But . . . but men get drunk by night and come sober by morning," she whispered. "And in dawn light Sam woke and parted my hair and looked me in the face. Just one look, mind, then up with him screaming – one jump to the door and through it streaming bedsheets, hollering blue murder down the village. Can you explain such behaviour, Jethro Mortymer?"

I shook my head, and she smiled wistful, head on one side. "Scared of females, perhaps – him being of ships and with men all his years, for these sailor men don't know much about women, you see." She smiled, straightening. "But he did not go for good, remember. I still have my Sam for lovering, remember. And at night I do know the heat and strength of him and his childer leaping within me, down by here," and she held herself, smiling.

"Gone for good, then?" I asked.

"Good God, no. Do you think us women give up so easy? I tracked him. He sailed from Saundersfoot to Newport and un-loaded himself for the Monmouthshire iron and legged it down to Blaina. But he opened his mouth in Black Boar tavern before he went, and I followed him to Blaina on foot. Aye, to Blaina town I went – barefoot, and I nailed him. 'Sam Miller,' I said, 'you have shared a bed with this Effie. Would you put me to shame and leave me stranded? Make me decent, Sam Miller, lest you be judged for it.'" She grinned up at me with a naked mouth. "More than one way of hitting out hens, but it takes a woman to think of it. You interested?"

"And he married you?"

"Galloped to the altar, thinking me in child. Aye, decent! Damned good Welsh, that one; proud to lie with him. Pity such men die."

"He died?"

"Like a dog – going in the carts to Monmouth. He marched with the men of the Eastern Valley, to Newport. And they shot him down on the steps of the Westgate and tied him, and put him in the carts for Monmouth trials."

My heart was thumping now. Leaning, I gripped her wrist. "My brother was in those carts," I whispered.

"O, aye," said she. "That is why I am here. You got a sister-in-law here by the name of Mari?"

"Yes, yes!" I had hold of her now, drawing her up. "What of her?"

"And do you know a man called Idris Foreman, Blaenafon?"

"My father's foreman, my brother's friend. For God's sake, woman, what are you trying to tell me?"

"Just this," she said. "Iestyn, your brother, is dead."

I heard her but faintly, as through the veil of years.

"Aye, dead," she said. "He died with my Sam. Your brother, my Sam and Idris Foreman, Blaenafon. And a man called Shanco Mathews charged me to tell you. Four years I waited, starving in Nanty, and then the news came through, and Shanco told me. 'Go back home to your county, Effie girl,' he said. 'And if ever you happen on people called Mortymer, you tell Jethro, the son, that his brother is dead,' and he gave me two shillings to help on the journey. 'Tell Jethro the son, but keep it from his women, for all three will go mad. As mad as you, Effie Downpillow,' he said. You think me mad, Jethro Mortymer?"

"Sane as me," I said, weeping.

"And I happened by here and Osian Hughes took me in. Saw you last Sunday near Chapel – you and three women, and I asked who you were. It is the Mortymers, Osian told me, him being sweet on your Morfydd."

"Do you know how it happened?" I asked, broken.

"You know Griff and Owen Howells, the brothers?"

"Aye, I know them."

"Well, Griff died, too, though Owen got clear – over in transportation, mind, like I hoped for my Sam," and she sighed. "I knew the Howells boys – they were more than just twins –

they shared the same plate, sparked the same women, drew the same breath, hand in hand in the womb. . . ."

"Tell me," I said.

"Well, the redcoats crammed them in the carts for Monmouth, with Sam, your Iestyn and Idris in one and the Howells boys in the cart following – standing and singing along the road to Monmouth, but Griff Howells was silent, standing stone dead. It took half a mile of whispers and kisses, said Shanco, before Owen Howells screamed and went into bedlam for the death of his twin. Over the cart side he went, bringing down redcoats, and all twelve carts stopped because of the palaver, with muskets going and redcoats swiping at Owen who was mad losing Griff. And Idris Foreman slipped out in the commotion and dragged my Sam and your brother after him, and they dived like demons for the open country. But the soldiers came up and gave them a volley, and the only one who got clear was Shanco Mathews from a cart farther down."

"They killed him?"

"The three of them. Idris, my Sam, your brother Iestyn."

"And not so much as a word," I said, thumping the chair.

"O, God," said Effie. "Were they important?" She sighed. "If you happen on the Mortymers you tell the boy Jethro, said Shanco Mathews – leave it to young Jethro, for there's a woman in that three who will march on Victoria."

"Go now," I said.

"Eh, so early – with the evening to myself? Now, listen, little man – have you heard about Sam, my man, Sam Miller?"

I raised my eyes and she swam, distorting.

"Dear God," said she. "You've never seen a man like my Sam for looks. Topped six feet naked, he did, and as broad as a barrel, with a smell of caulking-tar about him, being of ships . . . Jethro Mortymer, you are not listening!"

Through the door I went, swinging it shut. I walked, walked, praying for Mari. And the world was dark in a blustering wind, not a glimmer of light.

# CHAPTER 21

BACK FROM Ponty, coal-grimed, sweaty, I broke it to Mari that night, and the face of Fate changed. For days I had gripped it to myself with love and duty tearing different ways. And I bided my time. Mam was over at Flannigan's place for a tongue-pie with Biddy, Morfydd was out courting with Willie O'Hara. Out every night now, Morfydd – snatching at life, grasping every second in false laughter, and I longed to get her from Ponty. And Willie O'Hara was another worry with Morfydd in this mood. She had fallen before and she might fall again, and we had enough to contend with. And this Willie not so simple as he looked, according to Abel Flannigan – stretching more aprons in the northern shires than gentry ham teas and come down west to start it again.

Hot from labour I came to the back and leaned against the shed, wiping with a sweat rag, cooling off in the shade when I heard Mari singing. She was flapping around the kitchen with her pots and pans and Richard and her son Jonathon were hammering something out at the front, shouting and playing. I listened. I am not one for singing, but being Welsh I am in love with the throat and its wondrous noises, and I stood there in sadness listening to Mari. Beautifully she sang in the minor key, tuning in to the great Welsh hymns. Is there a voice in the world more lovely than that of a woman working, unsuspecting? Thin is the note, plaintive, trembling wobbly to the lifting of pans and stoopings, snatching at breath. Closing my eyes I leaned and listened, and Mari's voice drifted out to me on the heat-laden air with its message of the moors and mountains of Mother Wales and her muted sadness. In the knowledge of God we sing, with words that spring from the Books of the Testaments; rising from the great believers, from the organ lofts of those who have clutched at glory, in praise of Him. The voices of sopranos are of the alders where streams are leaping, each silver leaf rimmed with the autumn stain. Welsh tenors, to me, are the tree's upper branches, but the bole beneath gnarled as a fist, clenched for the singer's hook of manhood. Bass comes as roots to me; of grovelling limbs sapbound in darkness, splitting forth in thunder from the belted bellies of men defiant.

The soul of Wales is the throat of its people.

Mari now. Had to tell her somehow. And her song stopped dead at the sight of my shadow, flung into crippledom over the flags. Heard her step then, saw her eyes.

"Mari," I said.

Beautiful, those eyes.

"You frightened me."

"I am sorry," I said.

Just stood there watching her, and she smiled and shrugged and turned to go.

"No, Mari, wait," I said, and reached out, taking her hand and drawing her closer. My throat was dust-dry, the lump rising, and I took a deep breath.

Out with it, no other way. Better do it quick as a smack in the face.

"Iestyn is dead."

She smiled faintly. "I know," she said.

The hammering of the boys drifted between us in Jonathon's treble shrieks of joy as Richard got a hammer to something, thudding away, thudding . . . and sunlight flashed from the green of the fields, and the wind was sudden cool to my face.

"I know," she repeated. "O, poor Jethro."

I waited disbelieving, but knowing the truth of it in her eyes. And she looked past me towards the field, lips moving, then lowered her face.

"How did you learn, Jethro?"

"From Effie Downpillow three days back – come back from Monmouthshire, and told by a friend to bring me the news. But you . . . ? Who told you?"

She clasped her hands, her face was in repose.

"Tomos Traherne," she said. "When he called at Christmas years back."

"Tomos?"

"Came special to break the news."

"But Mam and Morfydd – do they know, too?"

"To tell you is my duty, said Tomos Traherne, let them live in the paradise of hope. So much can happen in a seven year transportation, people can die. And the wound comes shallow with the passing of time. No, Jethro, they do not know."

"But Tomos's duty was to them, too – to me, his brother!"

"Four years of your life you have not mourned him dead," she replied. "Most of the men in the carts got seven years transportation – I will run your poor mother to six and a half, said Tomos – no point in taking all she has left." She turned to me. "Who is the Effie woman?"

"A little iron-rag – been down here a week – saw her in Chapel last Sunday evening? She is living over at Osian Hughes Bayleaves."

"O, aye," she said, remembering. "Has Effie a tongue?"

"Two feet of it, and addled in the head."

"But she called here with you alone?"

"Three days back while the rest of the family were out."

"Addled, perhaps," she replied, "but I doubt if she will talk – she was brainy enough to pick her time. Still, I will speak to her."

"And you know how he died."

"Yes, I know. And I am proud. Hitting it out in the carts for Monmouth, that is how he died, and best that way. For men like Iestyn were not born for the cage. No lash would drive him, no cruelties break him. Men like Iestyn are victors, not beggars – better he should stand in the light of the Father than scratch out a living in this pig of a place, as we. Can you imagine him landed with the troubles of Rebecca? 'Becca and her children, one to each village?" and she laughed deep in memory, her eyes alive. "He would rally them together for a march on London, and die there instead. No, Jethro, better this way."

"Perhaps," I said.

"Perhaps? I know it. Fighters are the Mortymers, and I am glad the blood is in my son. But it do not make for peace, Jethro. Remember it. It only breaks hearts. You stopping fighting one day?"

"Soon," I said.

She sighed deep. "Well, I am not begging you like I begged of my Iestyn. God help your woman, that is all I say." She walked to the end of the wall and leaned against it, her back towards me.

"Poor Jethro," she said, and reached out her hand. "A little pig, I am, forgetting you. Is it sad with you to tears, now you have lost your brother?"

I did not reply. Later, ashamed, I remembered only that she was near to me, that she was free, that she could be mine. For the wind hit between us then in a sweep from the fields and my arms reached out and caught her against me and my lips sought her lips in the yard between us. Empty that yard, could have been miles.

"You love him still, don't you, Mari," I whispered.

"Yes, I love him," and she turned to me again. "Still decent people about, isn't it – with you loving me?"

"Aye, I love you. You guessed?"

"Years back, Jethro. Years. . . ." Her eyes moved over my face.

No heat in me, as for Jane at Black Boar; no longing that springs from the surge of manhood, no aches, no fires I felt. Just empty for her as a cask is emptied of wine. Desolate as I turned away to the wall. Eyes closed, not trusting myself, I thought she had gone, but I heard her breathing beside me.

"Jethro, not yet," she said.

I kept the yard between us, because of her eyes, and she gripped my hand, smiled, and went from me, closing the kitchen door.

I do not know how long I stood there. The boys came scampering round the back and they gripped my legs, swinging themselves around me and Jonathon leaped against me till I lifted him, kissing his face, setting him quiet, for I had not kissed him before. A joy rose high in me when I should have been grieving, and I kissed him again. Great the strength in me as I reached down and hooked Richard up beside him, and stood there holding the pair of them, one in each arm to the wideflung door.

"Jethro!" said Mari.

# CHAPTER 22

TOMOS TRAHERNE came back to Cae White in June.

No Tom the Faith, this one, creeping in as a mouse. He came demanding, in a trap with a little brown pony, all polish and jingles, trotting down the road from Carmarthen, sending satans belly-sliding over the hedges at the sight of him sitting there with the reins in his hand and his big Bible beside him. Coffin black, enormous he sat, gowned and collared, his spade beard trembling in the fervour of his love, but not with the love of God. He came for the love of Mam.

"Tomos!"

Mam shoved pretty fast for the creaking joints of middle age – arms out, skirts billowing, thumping down the path to the trap and not even giving him time to get down. Up on the step she went and straight into his hug. And they sat, the pair of them, motionless in the clear summer air, and then he kissed her face.

"One less in the family or I'm mistaken," said Morfydd. "And her bouncing me about Willie O'Hara."

"God bless him for coming back," whispered Mari.

"She has always loved him – even when Dada was alive," I said.

"No doubt," said Morfydd. "This will settle Tom Griffiths and Waldo Bailiff. Hairpins falling, lovers calling – eh, just look at that!"

"Inside quick, it is not decent watching," said Mari, and swept us all in with her skirts. But I went to the window and watched them from there: speaking no words by the look of them, with Mam only up to his shoulder, gripping his arm down the path to the house, and Tomos smiling down. I will always remember how I saw them, walking down the path with the trap behind them, enwrapped in the love and respect that leaps from old friendship. We waited pent, the three of us, holding the boys steady from confusion as the door opened and they stood there hand in hand.

"He has come back," said Mam, her eyes bright. "The day he said he would, to the very hour."

"O, Tomos!" exclaimed Mari.

"To claim her," boomed Tomos. "Five minutes late for this one would make a man a fool."

"And not a word to the family, mind," I said. "Driving the men of the village demented, and pledged to another all the time!" I gripped his hand, drawing him in. "God bless you, Tomos. Mari, get the kettle on – Morfydd, lay the cloth. . . ."

"Eh, hark at the head of the family!"

"And am I not the head of the family – for who will give her away? Food first," I cried, "and then Mam will walk him twice round the village hand in hand to settle the suitors!"

"Suitors? What suitors?" rumbled Tomos, eyebrows bushing up.

"Now, hush!" cried Mam, going scarlet.

"Nothing to get bothered about, Tomos," said Morfydd, sitting him down. "Just a little trouble with the men, it is – always the same when attractive widows are loose, but we kept her on the right path."

"O, Morfydd, you vixen," said Mari.

And there was Mam beside him wriggling and blushing as a young girl, with protests, giggles and peeps at his face. It is at such times that you see the woman in the mother, I think, as an eye behind the white starched apron that prises at the secrets. And the heart you see is young again, beating fast; no longer a couch for your head, that breast, but soft to the touch of another, and the lips that have scolded and crooned at you are strange lips for kissing, and red. Strange is the bitterness; that another should lie in her bed, turning at midnight in the place I had moulded. So great her lover.

"Mind," said Tomos, getting the spirit of it. "If she has been tempted in my absence I will make inquiries, and heaven help her if she is found wanting. More than one suitor, is it?"

"Queueing at the door," I said.

"With flowers every Sunday," added Morfydd. "Wearing out knees with biddings and beggings. Another five minutes and you'd have been too damned late, man."

"Tomos, Tomos! Do not heed them!" begged Mari, pulling at him. "Indelicate, they are."

"Not very considerate to your mother, I must say," said Mam, sniffing.

"O, Mam!" we cried while Tomos guffawed.

"All very well," she answered, well into her dignity. "But anyone human is likely to take it wrong."

Up with us then, dancing around her, pulling at her and kissing her, with Mari taking swipes at us and the boys screaming with joy. And there was Tomos with his arms around her consoling and teasing her in turn till we got her back mellow. Tea then, everyone happy, sitting at the table well into dusk, with Tomos telling us of his journey down and the state of things back home in Nanty.

"And so," said he, "after these years I return to you, fulfilling the promise I made to your mother that, should she remain unwed, I would offer her marriage and a home. . . ." Deep and pure was his voice as we sat in respectful silence. "I come in humility," said he, "having little to offer save food and a bed, being of little money. Yet I offer her more than life itself if I offer her service in the way of the Lord. For did she not spring from the black cloth of the manse? And is it not true that service to His children is the true path to joy? Elianor . . ." and here he used her name the first time I had heard it since the days of my father. "Will you come back with me to Nantyglo, to the town you learned to hate because of your Hywel who died there, and give me the chance to teach you how to love it?"

I stayed just long enough to see her touch his hand. Golden, this tongue, deep and sincere his offer. I knew my mother would not refuse him, this friend of my father, though I could not bear to see her accept a continuation of the poverty she had borne so long. Tomos would set her soul in diamonds, leaving her body to fend with sackcloth, yet this, I knew, was the way she would prefer it; this was how she was raised; as a flower pressed in the leaves of the Book of God, ending her life on the arm of Tomos, loving my father in the bed of his friend.

Dusk and bats had dropped over Cae White as I stood there

at the back listening to the laughter of Morfydd inside, the excited chatter of Mari, the protests of Richard and Jonathon as they were hooked up to bed. Silence was about me save for wind-whisper and the flea-scratching of crickets. The hens were still loose in the shippon, walking the path in their spiked, measured tread, the cockerel standing in his petrified confusion, mouthing unholy thoughts. I remembered the old days of Blaenafon where I was born and the care my mother took over her chickens; as a young girl she was then with her unbridled laughter; her childlike joy at finding an egg, her tears when my father brought in the lifeless body of a hen knocked off for the pot. The business of living had ground out the joy now, leaving her empty. Only in her God would she find solace, and Tomos had plenty of God. Heard the door click behind me as I moved to pen the chickens against the fox, and I turned. The mountain of Tomos drew beside me, and he gripped my shoulder, smiling down.

"To you I come, Jethro, not to your sisters, for you are the man of the Mortymers now. To you I come for blessing."

"You have it in full," I answered.

"From your heart now?"

"From my heart," I said. "My father would have wanted it."

He leaned on the rail beside me, frowning into the dusk, and the rail creaked at him and I sensed the power of him, and some of the soul.

"You will be good to her, Tomos."

He nodded.

"And gentle, as my father was gentle."

"As my Father do hear me, I love her," he whispered. "As He is witness, I have loved her from the day we met, Jethro, never coveting that which was my friend's, but loving, nevertheless, and I seek no forgiveness since Man is twopenny clay. This I tell you now, as man to man, that I have not sought her with my body as I have sought other women in the days of my youth, and found them wanting. For I met her when the soul enmeshed the body, draining it of fire." He chuckled deep, and grunted. "Just now you left too early for decency, and your mother, I could see, wondered why. But there are looks between men that need no explanation, so I came to tell you something to remember. In the bed of our marriage your mother wil hold me when I am dispirited or fierce to the injustices. This and her presence is all I seek of her, asking nothing more, save that she keeps me fed. Aye, the fire has died, Jethro, and it is peaceful, and she is in love with your father."

"You know this, then?"

"She has never been short of a tongue. She made that clear four years back when I called at Christmas."

"Best you should know, Tomos."

"Aye." He sighed. "A man such as Hywel do take some shifting."

"We will miss her. Could you not live here?"

"No, my place is back with my people who need me. But there is a bed for any one of you, remember it. You will be welcome since I will be your father."

"Thank you," I said.

"Jethro." The tone of his voice turned me. "Jethro, another thing. Just now, on the stairs I spoke to Mari. You know about your brother?"

"Yes."

He nodded. "When I heard of Iestyn's death I hurried to tell Mari, for it was my duty. I owe the same duty to Morfydd and your mother, but I will not tell them. I stopped my mouth to them four years back, and I will not tell them now. Mari had to know because she was young and with her life before her, that is why I came that Christmas. But I will never tell your mother. Better for her to live in hope – already I have saved her years of grief. She believes he is in transportation for seven years. A lot can happen in three more years. You agree?"

I shrugged.

"And Mari?" he said.

"What of Mari?"

"She is in love with you, do you know?"

I swung to him, searching for his eyes shadowed under the bushy brows.

"She told you?" I whispered.

"Aye." He lit his pipe and played with the tinderbox. "Just now. And you love her, I hear it in your voice. Take her then, when you can afford it, but tread wary for youth is fire. Gently with her remember, until you are sure that Iestyn has gone. Hell it can be sitting in a kitchen with another man opposite."

I pitied him.

"Two in one boat," he said, grinning. "Though mine is but a ten year marriage, perhaps a little longer. Yours is for life."

He straightened then.

"I am going back in now," he said. "For women are as wary as cats at times like this. You coming?"

"Yes," I said. "But first I will lock the hens. Tomos. . . ."

He turned, black in the coming of night, smiling.

"Tomos, will you send Mari to me?"

"God bless the loyalty and love in this house," he said. "I will send her. She will help you catch the waywards hens, is it?"

I waited until he was back in the kitchen then went into the shippon and gathered the hens. There by the henhouse I waited. I saw the door come open again; heard Mari's footsteps.

"Over by here," I said, and she came.

"The old cockerel again, is it?" she asked, peering about her.

"They are all safe in bed," I answered. "Mari . . ." and I took her hand.

For the first time in my life I felt her near me.

"Mari, Mari!" I whispered, and drew her into my arms.

"Jethro!" she said as I kissed her.

And her arms went about me hard and strong as I bent above her, kissing her, kissing her, and I knew the trembling of her. Warm were her lips, snatching at breath.

"Jethro," she said, but I heard no sound, just saw her lips. As rock were we to the pressure of mountains; locked; beating as one, together.

Summer warm was the wind of the estuary, and the night was silver and rimming the clouds, the full moon shafting the sea with a broadsword of light. Wave-thunder came from the beach still heaped and despoiled from the low tide hunting of cockle-women, its forehead fringed with dark lines of weed. In my arbour of rocks above the beach I waited and great was the excitement within me, my heart thumping to the turn of the stones, waiting. Waiting for Mari at the end of the sheep track that led from Squire's Reach.

Eerie is the Burrows in moonlight, this place of rabbits and honeycombed with lairs; a refuge of steepled ears and screams: home of the fox, the bared teeth of vixens, the prancing death dances of stoats, the madbrained leapings of the March hares. And ghosts walk here, it is said. Here float the faces of murdered seamen, the souls of the sea, victims of plunder, walking out of the waves with seaweed for shrouds, in search of decent graves. Sitting alone I stared at the sea, seeing again the storm-tossed barques plunging to the swinging beacons of the criminal wreckers, wallowing, their decks awash, streaming to their doom on the outcrop rocks. And I saw again the falling cudgels, heard the screams of ancient crews as they staggered half drowned to the butchery of their brothers.

But this place of wraiths is the arbour of lovers, for ghosts are forgotten in the heat of kisses, and because of its name the Burrows were free of peepers. One pair of eyes was enough to have us round the village. So I waited, dry in the mouth and trembling, for Mari to come.

I fell to wondering, then, how many kisses had been given and taken in this haven clear of the sea, and new visions rose on the crested waves. Flying pennants I saw then; the curved bows of foreign invaders came driving in on the surf. Lance and mace flashed in fierce sunlight, swords were raised high. Invading banners I saw, strange tongues I heard, naked legs splashed to the shores as the horde drove in to lock in battle with the fur-clad ancients. Flung spears I saw, the skull-splitting hatchets, the new tide bloodstained to the wallowing dead. And then the conquest, the drunken goblets of the conquerors, the chained oars of the conquered creaking on the road to Rome.

But then I thought of lovers, the giving and taking of foreign kisses in this place where I was waiting to make love to Mari.

Roman warrior and Saxon maiden, conquering Greek and Celtic matron; mouth on mouth, breast against breast on this same sand while the same moon as mine, hooded and broody as a Benedictine monk, pulled up his skirts to shield his eyes as two became one. By here, just where I was sitting. Plaited hair I saw, the Nordic breast, the armour flung aside. I touched the rock beside me, feeling under my fingers its dumb eternity. O, that it had eyes and a mouth with which to speak that it might tell of my people from the time of the club; talk of the tears, the sighs, the laughter of children, the riven steel of the armour, the crumpled skirt. Here the invader, pining in his dreams of columned cities, has leaped to the arms of the humble cottager and buried his longing in the tumult of her breathing.

"Jethro!"
And the visions were banished in the shock of reality. Leaping up, I swung to her voice.
Mari, standing above me, her hands clasped, smiling down.
"You came!" I gasped.
"But not for long, mind – Mam will soon miss me."
Joyful that we were together I reached up and lifted her down beside me, and we stood clasped, shivering at the sudden nearness after the barren years of standing apart.
"Anyone see you?"
"Good grief, I saw to that. Came on all fours round the edge of the Reach!" Holding my hands she looked about her, then up at the moon, her eyes coming wide and bright as if startled. "O, Jethro, what a lovely place!"
"Secret," I whispered, holding her. I felt her heart thumping, thumping.
"And you behave," she whispered back.
"I've been doing that years," I said. "O, Mari!"
"Then another half an hour won't do you any harm," and she kissed my face. "What happens now?"
"Down by here," I said, squatting at her feet, patting sand.
"O, aye?"
The wind had her hair, whirling it about in a sudden warm gust from the sea, and she stood above me, tying it back,

patting it, smoothing it, with downward flashes of smile, knowing her mastery.

"Down here," I said, dragging at her skirt.

"Safer up standing. I know you Mortymers."

Gave her ten seconds to enjoy her mastery, then I rolled towards her snatching at her ankle and pulled her kneeling in a cry of laughter. Whirling like a sand-crab I was there beside her, and I lay there holding her helpless while she shivered and giggled. Young again, girlish again . . . the years of sitting and darning over, the barrier crumbling. I was just content to lie there holding her, my face above her, her lips an inch from mine, waiting. Waiting for the final crash of the barrier, the rolling dust of its storm to drift to the sea. And there was no sound but breathing and wavelap to the incoming tide. Eyes shut tight, her face was turned away; as Morfydd lying there; the same deep shadows of her cheek; black her lips in that misty light. Smoothing her hair, I lay, watching, contented at last, whole for the first time in my life, since she was near. Strange is love in these moments of quiet, this the proof of love; to lie without demanding. No jangle in this loving, no sweeping hands, no hotness then. I lowered my face to hers, and we lay, just breathing, listening to heartbeat, at peace. Wind-murmur was in the cave, and the sand beneath us thumping to the fist of the breakers, and I raised my head, seeing beyond the tangle of her hair an emblazoned sea of moonlight with the solitary sails of a lonely ship, three-masted, standing against a line of silver. And farther beyond were the wastes of the Atlantic, thousands of miles of nothingness to the seagull cries of the shores of Newfoundland, and farther still to Philadelphia where the ovens of iron flash at the sky. This my industry, the call of the iron; calling again as it forever called me. Strange the call at a time like this, crying to a man on the breast of a woman. *Pittsburgh!* The magic name where the molten stream flashes to a thousand moulds, and its red brick chimneys flame to the sky. Calling to the Welsh for its experts of iron, for the craftsmen who can set the curve of the furnace-arch, for the men who know the colour of the pilot flame before the cauldron is turned, the length of the firing-iron, the time to rake, to coal, the ore to burn, the grade of limestone and thickness of layer; for the men who are tuned to the clang of the bar and chalk the cross that guarantees perfection. In the stink of coal and tollgate farming the call leaped high to start a new life.

"What you thinking?" said Mari.

I stirred, suddenly aware of her, ringing her waist with my arm, drawing her against me.

"I am taking you away," I said.

"Aye?" she said.

"Because I love you. Because I am sick of fighting." I drew from her, and knelt, and she turned, cupping her chin on her elbow, following my finger.

"Nothing between us and America. Look. Nothing but sea and more sea, ships and gulls and sky. Go as an arrow and you crawl out on sand, Mari – to a new land, to a new life. Cae White is finished, Mari. There is nothing left here except hunger and labour; no chance for your Jonathon, no promise for my children," and I caught her hand, kissing it.

"Next Sunday," she said. "To travel costs money, sovereigns, mind, not shillings."

"Five pounds a head steerage, that is all," I answered.

"A fortune," she said.

"I will find it, somehow."

"What is this old steerage thing, then?" she asked.

"Working the passage, girl. Scrubbing and waiting, rope-coiling, tarring and labouring – cheaper steerage, see."

"Eh, more labour, is it? Whee, I would rather go cabins."

"Gentry, is it? Peacock feathers and parasols, is it? You be content with steerage."

"You go steerage, then. I will go cabins."

"Then near thirty pounds between us if we tie Jonathon to the yard-arm – where the hell do you think I am getting thirty pounds from, woman?"

"Got fifty," said she, "all but two shillings."

"How many toes has a pig got?"

"Take off your boots and count them," said she. "Fifty pounds be mine all but two shillings."

"O, aye? Not that much money in the county of Carmarthen. Addled, you."

"So addled that I will give you every penny, man, if you kiss me proper. O, *Jethro*! Do I come down here for the town of Philadelphia, or for loving?"

The way she looked, then, the way she smiled, her mouth reaching for kissing.

How can a man know the heart of a woman. Frigid to freeze one minute, the flash in the mould the next.

"Mari," I whispered.

As a mirage she was in the faint blue light, to be snatched at and lost in the parched desert of my longing. In the years of waiting I had been denied her, and now she was against me she still seemed a part of my dreaming; that the ghost of her would fade to the opening eyes. Yet the arms I held now were tensed and strong; no visions these arms; no mirage the eyes that lowered to the kiss, and her breathing no sighing of some distant wind. Sudden the tumult between us, as if the night had exploded in brilliance, leaving blackness that enveloped us, obliterating all save its gusty breath. Once she opened her eyes and looked at me with the look I have seen in the eyes of things trapped and shrinking to the grip of the iron jaw.

"Jethro!" she said, just once.

And I kissed her to silence, hearing nothing, reasoning nothing as the wall went down, thundering in the breast. Great is a man then with the shout of the Unborn thrusting within him, strident, demanding as the falcon's cry; leaping to heights of power and beauty, denying the kiss as breath snatches breath in a perfumed fire; this, the song of the honeyed middle, the quenchless song, the chord that leaps from the fountain of life, that chains the singer and sung as one, and, chaining, transcends them as one, in joy.

I kissed her, and her cheek was wet.

"Mari," I said.

A nightbird sang in the troubled light. Wave-thump I heard, the wind of the Burrows and blackness came as the moon fainted; gave him a glance above her head, and hated him. Generations of this and still he was virginal. But the stars still shone as if approving, with Orion beaming silver and Venus still waving at her latticed window her lamp that brought out Mars.

"Mari. . . ."

And she wept.

Something shrieked from the woods of the Reach and branches snapped in the clattering panic of wings, then all was stillness save for the sobbing restrictions of her breast, and she turned away her face as I bent to kiss her again. Three of us lying in sand, I knew; not one.

"Mari!" I said, and pulled her against me, forcing her to face me. "It is me, Jethro. It is Jethro who is loving you. Iestyn is dead."

She stared at me, then closed her eyes again and her lips trembled to the inward breath.

"My woman now," I said. "The past is past."

I knelt as she sat up, head turned away, fingers working in a frenzy, straightening, tidying: brush away sand, straighten the lace; then flew to her hair, smoothing, patting and there's a damned mess. Strange, these women.

"All over the place," I said.

"O, no! Is it?"

"Through a hedge backwards, then over the haystack," I said.

"And that Morfydd with eyes for a lynx," she said. "Hairpins, see. That is the trouble," and she went round on all fours, feeling and patting.

Never looked for hairpins in sand before. Please God I never do it again.

Like sea-urchins, the pair of us then; going in circles, holding up seaweed and shells, and excuse me, please, there's one behind you, sweeping and smoothing half an acre. We were yards apart when Mari smiled. As a prowling dog I saw that smile. Then she put her hands to her face and laughed. God was wise when He invented sense of humour. As baying hounds we knelt, laughing, pealing it to the sky, then I rose and leaped the distance between us and gripped her waist and bent, kissing her. Her hair was down now, waving to her waist. Beautiful the kiss, joyful the reunion.

"O, Jethro, I love you, love you!" she said.
I did not answer, having loved so long.
Two of us went home, and no Iestyn.

Should not tell of it really, too secret to tell; too hot the fire of that week when Tomos stayed at Cae White and kept Mam occupied. Night after night, come in from shift at Ponty, strip to the bare and wash the body clean, then down to the kitchen for the evening meal with secret glances over the table at Mari; the raised eyebrow of the evening question, the narrowed promise in her eyes for reply. Easy, too, with Morfydd out courting with Willie O'Hara; no prowling eyes, no listening ears.

"Think I'll go out, Mam."

Only too pleased to be rid of me, the pair of them, for it is only right that courting couples like Mam and Tomos wanted to be alone. And they made no complaints when Mari went for her summer night strolls, either ... summer night strolls down to the estuary where I lay waiting.

"Jethro, you there?"

And the sound of her voice set my heart leaping.

Too secret to tell of the summer lovering; of the unbridled passion of our kisses, lying in sand. Rebecca and her burnings were forgotten in the newfound fire of possession. No blaze of ricks or tollgates invaded this mating, no eyes save the eyes of ghosts watched our kisses snatched in the roll of the breakers. As primaeval beings we were, diving together from rocks into the warm sea of moonlight, splashing demented in the surf, laughing, joyful, naked and unashamed, echoing the laughter of distant lovers on this same sand a thousand years before. Beautiful this new Mari in the shroud of her long, dark hair, resisting no more: and I would have the tongue of those who call it hateful, denouncing as obscene the purity of our love-making, making that which is noble into a thing satanic; twisting the beauty of God's present to lovers by darkened minds and crippled words. Three days before Tomos was due to leave Cae White we lay together, Mari and me, in our haven of rocks.

212

"And Jonathon?" she said.

"Jonathon is mine," I answered.

"You will love him, too, Jethro?"

"As my own son," I said.

"Time was you were jealous, mind."

I laughed, remembering. "That time has passed, Mari. The three of us it is from now on. Nothing will come between us now, nothing," and even as I said it the face of Grandfer seemed to rise before me in some strange trick of moonlight. Clear as living that face, toothless, goat-bearded, grinning as he grinned on the night he told me of his Bronwen. I shut my eyes and lowered my head to the sand.

"Jethro," Mari whispered, but I scarcely heard her.

'With Cae White as your Eden and your brother's wife for a lover, the fingers of Cain shall reach up from the dust, and seek you . . .'

Years, it seemed, since Grandfer died yet I heard his words again like yesterday; saw the face of my brother then, square and strong, unravaged by the blood and screams of the Westgate, yet Iestyn was smiling.

"Jethro, is it sad with you?" Mari now, turning on her elbow, brushing the water from her face, smoothing back her wet hair.

"No," I said, and rose and left her, going to the outcorp of the haven where the sea was cresting silver to the breakers. Warm the night, but I was shivering.

'For she bore my child and then she vanished, went down to the river for the shame of it, in the place where we loved. And they found her three weeks later on the reaches of Laugharne . . . with mud in her mouth and her eyes taken by gulls . . .'

Grandfer now, whispering again, words I had long forgotten; whispering in the rocks, but a trumpet of sound. I swung as Mari approached, fearing she would hear it.

"Jethro, for God's sake, what is the matter?" she said, arms out.

Leaned against the rocks and looked. This, my brother's wife, naked as me; beautiful this woman, the wife of Iestyn.

"Mari!" I took her against me, kissing her face, but she

213

fought herself free and pushed me away, staring, eyes wild.

"Jethro, what is wrong?"

I could not face her.

"Iestyn, is it?" she said, cold.

I nodded.

Strange that the Father with His one great eye Who has in His face the weight of the moon can suffer His children to know contemplation; stopping the lover's words in the mouth, turning joy to fear by the cold light of Reason.

"Sorry now, is it?" she whispered, frightened. I held her, but the night was between us.

"Mari, you will never leave me?"

She shook her head. "Jethro, listen. Iestyn is dead. You told me that but for years I have known it. I loved him as you, mind, do not forget it. Dead. And even if he is alive we cannot go back. . . ."

"Now I will say it, Mari. Listen, you will hear me. Iestyn is dead – there is only the two of us, you and me, Mari and Jethro."

"And Jonathon," she said.

"Aye, and Jonathon. Dress now, quick, or Mam will have babies."

"Rather Mam than me," she said.

## CHAPTER 23

JUST THREE days more I had my mother before Tomos Traherne hooked her away.

Fully-fledged minister now, was Tomos, a man with his hand in God's and in love with His people, preaching His goodness; a man with a chapel of his own and a little stone manse. Rising in the world, we Mortymers, and I was proud. So pretty Mam looked as Tomos led her out to the trap that Sunday; as a young girl going for marriage; dressed in her chapel black with starched white frills at her wrists and throat and well pulled in at the waist; hair in a bun, the temples streaked with grey. Wished I was marrying her so she would not go away.

Half the county was out on the road; Biddy Flannigan to the front, as usual, wheezing and dabbing with a little lace handkerchief, for she loved my mam as a sister. Toby and Mrs Maudlin, the long and the short of it, the Parcybrains who were new neighbours down at Tarn; Tom the Faith, too, give him credit, though Waldo Bailiff was absent, and Polly Scandal knew why. I was out in the barn grooming Randy when Polly looked over the top of the door.

"There's a fine big man that Mr Traherne, isn't it?" said she, horse teeth shining. "Lucky, she is, mind, marrying the cloth, and Tom the Faith that miserable, you seen him, Jethro Mortymer?"

"Leave Tom be, Polly. At least he is here," and I went on brushing.

"But not Waldo Bailiff, I'll be bound."

I grunted.

"You heard about Waldo?"

I had heard but I was not telling Polly.

"Bound to happen sooner or later, mind – couldn't go on. And Tom the Faith standing up to his neck in the mere last night praying for his soul with the Lord slipping in ice-bags. Eh, it's a scandal!"

"No proof about Waldo Bailiff," I said. "You get on, Polly."

"No proof, is it? One arm round Gipsy May and another round Betsi, and poor little Gipsy outraged."

"Not before time."

"Waldo's child, nevertheless, and Waldo and Betsi have sent her on her way – back up to Cardie to her gipsy tribe, and crossed her palm with silver to shift her. Better things crawl from holes than that man Waldo Bailiff, says my mam."

"Your mam's right," I said.

"Isn't decent, mind. Isn't proper, not in a religious county. Leave him to Rebecca, is it? Leave him to the women, my mam says, they will see to him – they will give him Waldo Bailiff."

215

"Excuse me," I said, wiping away sweat, and pushed her aside as Mari ran up.

"Jethro, for heaven's sake!" she cried. "Tomos is ready for off."

"I have said goodbye once, Mari."

"And you will say it again. O, Jethro, you are not even dressed!" Pouting now, beautiful as summer, hands outspread as she eyed me. "Just come as you are, then, but come you must, for Mam is asking. Do not spoil her day."

I dreaded it, not trusting myself. I had hoped to hide and not be missed.

The trap was out on the road now with the crowd standing about it and Mam and Tomos already up in front and the little brown pony itching to get going. Backslapping and laughter from some, tears from others, though Morfydd, I noticed, was dry-eyed and pale, preferring her weeping at night. Willie O'Hara was standing beside her, fair-haired and handsome. Knew how to pick her men, this one, though I did not trust him. Old Uncle Silas was other side of her, teetering on his ploughing corns, wizened face turned up at her, begging for a smile. Abel Flannigan was there; Elias the Shop come down from Kidwelly; even Justin Slaughterer – eying Mari, I noticed. Got the size of Justin now; take him with one hand if he got within a foot of her, and he knew it. Everybody chattering and making conversation in that dreaded moment before the parting, and a silence fell upon us as my mother looked down.

"Jethro," she said.

Me, Jethro Mortymer, the last man left.

"Now, now," whispered Morfydd as I went slowly past her. I mounted the trap and Mam opened her arms to me.

Is there a face as beautiful as a mother's before her goodbye? The narrowing of the eyes before the kiss, the gasp before the miles divide. And the frail thing you hold in strength is the body from whence you sprung; the breast against you is the breast you fisted and suckled. No tongue will charm like this, or scold: she who gave life: one becoming two. I kissed her, screwing up my fist. Better this purity than two becoming one. . . .

"Watch for Morfydd, Jethro?"

I nodded against her.

"And Mari. Be a good boy, now. Decent, remember."

I closed my eyes. She knew.

"Yes, Mam."

And she, the stronger, pushed me off.

"Go now," she said.

I pushed a path through their forest of arms and shouldered my way to the rail behind the shippon. Head bowed, I gripped it, listening to the hooves of the pony beating on the road to Carmarthen.

## CHAPTER 24

WE DID the gates proud under the leadership of Flannigan; got two down and in flames and heading for the third. If Tom Rhayader had coolness Flannigan had dash and he led us headlong down the main street of the town, galloping wraiths with a thunder of hoofbeats – all sixty of us that night and mounted, more on foot. Caught a glimpse of wizened faces at windows, heard the screaming of a frightened child. Curtains were going over, doors being bolted, windows slamming to the galloping Rebeccas. Powder-guns raised we clattered down the cobbles past the Black Lion to the end of the town and wheeled, Randy sitting back on his haunches, pawing the air at the obstructing gate.

"Down with it, down with it!" roared Flannigan, dismounting, and men fell to the task with the hatchets going up and the powder-guns crashing. I saw Matthew Luke John again, well to the front, ramming his powder-gun, shouting with joy, and he swung it to the window of the tollhouse as I was spitting on my hands to swing an axe at the bar. A window came open and out popped a head, weeping, protesting, begging for life.

"Leave the house!" cried Flannigan. "No time for the house, get the gate – just heard the dragoons are two miles off. By God, we will finish the job we started."

"Out sentries!" yelled a man, and the outriders wheeled and galloped up the road. Men were working like things gone mad, cursing, bringing down the hatchets, splinters of timber flying in all directions. Spitting on my hands I took a fresh grip on my axe, bringing it down. Joyful it is to feel the bite of steel into something you hate. Over your head with the shaft, open the shoulders and hear it whistling, slide up the left hand to join the right and the muscles of the back arch and tighten to the biting thump, high rise the splinters. These the hateful things that represent government, these the bleeding things that starve.

"Down, down!" yelled Flannigan, up on his horse, petticoat streaming, the hooves prancing. "Down, down, my daughters, work like demons, every second counts. Splinter it, carve it. Up beacons! Who the hell has the tinder? Fire, man, fire!"

And the tinderman knelt and the torch came up, circling in the darkness before the wreckage caught alight. But I was looking past him to the road through the town where a single horseman in shrouds was coming headlong, hooves sparking, shouting, waving.

"Leave the tollhouse!" yelled Flannigan. "A few minutes are left – who says we try for Tom Rhayader? Who says we free the old Rebecca? He must be somewhere in the town!" Bellows and cheers at this with Toby Maudlin doing an Irish jig on the cobbles with the flames leaping up behind him and the men going mad with thoughts of Rhayader.

"No time!" I yelled at Flannigan, and dragged at his stirrup. "Look, the sentry!" Justin Slaughterer it was, coming straight at us like a man possessed, full gallop, and the daughters parted to let him through. Waving a scarf was Justin, bawling his head off, skidding to a stop.

"Out of it, Flannigan. Everybody out of it. Dragoons!"

We went like saints after satans, scrambling on horses, slipping, cursing, with hooves clattering and skidding on the cobbles, turbans coming off, axes dropping. Made a dive at

Randy and went clean over him and he gave me a look to kill as I snatched at his rein to steady him. The men on foot were going helterskelter, running for the cover of the woods, crashing through undergrowth, hanging on to stirrups, belly-flopping over the hedgerows head first, yelling dragoons. Bastards these dragoons if they got you cornered; sabres out, slashing, thrusting – dead men first, prisoners after, it was said – up in front of the magistrates at first light, down to Carmarthen gaol by breakfast and in Botany Bay for dinner. Trained men, these. We didn't stand a chance with them and they knew it. Spreadeagled on Randy I was fighting for a stirrup as they came down the street of the town. Heard the windows coming up now, saw white faces popping out in the blaze of the toll-gate. Reckon I was the last one left then, for as I wheeled Randy away I saw them clearly, no more than a hundred yards off, coming four abreast, sabres out and flashing in the red light; heard their hoarse shouts as I got my heels into Randy and went like the wind towards Laugharne. I knew I was the wrong side of the estuary but I had no option. The woods and open fields were my only chance. Give it to Randy. Perhaps he expected to die under torture at the hooves of the dragoon stallions, for he set down his flanks and went like a whippet with me hanging on. Leaping a hedge we took to the fields now, hooves thumping dully on the rich red earth, but I reined him at the edge of a wood and we stood in the shadows, watching, listening. Evil is the feel of eyes when you are hunted; every twig stirring to snap the head round, every tree whispering. Strange was that rest, lonely as the grave, with Randy standing there sweating and shining in the sudden, cursed moonlight and breathing for something to be heard ten miles. He snorted as I wheeled him and took him into the wood. God knows where the others had got to, never been so lonely before. The wood was eerie, shafting moonlight, with the overhanging branches snatching to bring me off. Thicker now, so I got off and walked, gripping Randy's head, hushing him quiet. Had to get east of the town, I knew it – would have to swim the river somewhere, but Randy liked a swim to cool him down. South first to get clear of the town, then east before the river got too broad. On, on, standing square to the swinging smack of branches, plunging knee deep in peaty places, scrambling out on all fours with Randy making the worst of it, wallowing and rearing and rolling his eyes at me for the outrage. Lost, I checked him and looked through the pattern of branches above. Brilliant were the stars though the moon was hiding, thank God, and the billowing clouds were going like hammer for the rim of the sky. The wind rose, buffeting and whining in the wood, sweeping up leaves in clouds and scraping his violins in the high rook tops that waved demented. Never been alone in such woods before, and now the panic of the dragoons had died dryness came with the cooling sweat. Things on legs I do not fear, upright or crawling; but horror comes to me in the face in the tree that smiles, the grotesque branches that clutch and hold too long, the whispers of things that should be dead. Through the wood now and I mounted and galloped towards Whitehill, with Randy taking the hedges in his stride, dying for his head and the barn at Cae White. Reaching the road just short of the Taf I reined him, approaching slowly for fear of a patrol, but the road was deserted. Crossing it at a canter, we went into the undergrowth again and down to the bank of the river, and, as if awaiting me, the moon came out. Darkness one moment, bright as day the next and I cursed it as Randy waded in, forelegs feeling for the plunge. Icy the water that rose to my knees and Randy was steaming as something afire and snorting and tossing. For days now the river had been in flood and it carried us downstream towards the estuary. Scrambling out on a sandy bed we struck out again for the open country and the upper reaches of the Tywi at Llangain. Randy was drooping a bit by now so I turned him to a tiny wood, entered it, dismounted and tethered him. And as I stood there light flared behind me and the pistol ball carved the bole of the tree a foot above my head. Went flat, squirming for cover, eyes peering, heart thumping, and Randy flung up his head and neighed with shock. One in the belly to quieten him as I went back on elbows and knees deeper into the wood.

The soldier rode up, dismounted, tied his horse and approached the wood. Cool customer, this one, though few

Rebeccas were armed save with useless powder-guns. He took his time; a big man, over six feet, with the pistol lying in his palm. Castlemartin Yeomanry by the look of him, a long way from home and dying for the skin of the hatred Rebecca. His every action was casual as he stood there reloading, unconcerned, it seemed, that he was outlined against the stars. I heard the metallic click of his powder flask, the snap of the hammer as he thumbed it back and secretly cursed myself that I had given him time to reload. It seemed he knew he had me, for he jumped the ditch and parted the branches, took a look at Randy and came in stooping, pistol held out. Held my breath, watching, then lowered my face as he turned my way, and my heart nearly stopped. Trailing from Randy's stirrup was Morfydd's old petticoat that I had torn off riding five miles back and thought I had flung away. This the reason for the shot without so much as a question. The wind was blustering still, drowning my retreat as I eased my body backwards, feeling for stones. A brook was behind me, gurgling and splashing, and I slid down the little bank and into it in a little shower of stones and plops. Saw the soldier wheel, and he came at a trot, swerving to branches, leaping lithely, the pistol rigid. Only one chance for me – to empty the pistol; best to empty it while he was running and I rose with a yell and flung stones, going flat. God knows how he missed me; heard the ball strike inches from me and go whining away and clattering through branches. His rush took him on me, swinging with the pistol, catching me on the shoulder and spinning me round, and next moment we were locked. Other side of the ditch now, arms and legs entangled, gasping, grunting; a farmer by the sound of him and as strong as Abel Flannigan. We were clasped as lovers as we went down the bank again, and into the brook, me uppermost. Splashing, threshing, we fought like cats, no rules, no honour. I had him by the throat now, holding him down while the water flooded over him and he gasped to breathe, but he brought up a knee and took me over his head, and we floundered and slipped, scrambling for the bank. Drenched, mud-covered, I clawed out first and stood awaiting him, eyes measuring him, switching to his hands for a knife.

"Right, you bloody swine Rebecca," he gasped, and dived at my legs, but I leaped away and he went past sprawling, and waited for next time. Big as a horse he looked in that moonlight, confident, trained to a hair with his yeomanry service; not much older than me by the look of him; farmer probably, I remember thinking – farmer fighting farmer, gentry against the people. Armlocks, headlocks, everything in his armoury, no doubt, and he came head on now, hands clenched for the swing. More my line. I ducked it and hooked him solid and I saw the shine of his eyes and his teeth bared white as his head went back and I caught him with another as he skidded against a tree. No use to him this. Every time he came in diving I hit to drop him, but he still kept coming, and I saw him more clearly as he circled for an opening. More like thirty he looked then, curly-haired and handsome; a bad age to quarrel with; full strength, full stamina, and I would have to finish him quick in case there were others. Diving, he got me, pinning me against a tree, and we slipped down the bole, punching short, rolling around the roots, but I was up first, swinging blindly and the fool ran into them. I felt the pain leap to my elbow and my hand went numb as the blow took him square. Feet up soldier now, landing on his shoulders, legs waving, rolling in leaves, and I leaned against the tree gasping, praying he would lie still and put an end to it, but not this one. Face elbowed against boots, he got to a knee, staggered upright and swayed towards me swinging blind. I ducked the first easily, the second grazed my chin and crashed against the tree with every pound of his weight behind it. In a flash of the moon I saw his face, one eye shut tight, blood from his mouth, black stains on his tunic and he opened his mouth and screamed like a girl to the agony of his broken hand. No honour in this. Fighting for life. I measured him, sighted the chin and hit it crisply, and he clutched at the tree and went down it slowly, rolled over once and lay still at my feet. With my hands to my face I swayed above him. I do not remember him catching me square, but there was blood on my fingers when I drew them clear. Gasping, I leaned against the tree above him with the world of moonlight spinning above me, with no sound but the bluster of wind and the gasping breaths of the soldier below me. I got to the brook and knelt in the water, letting the coldness flood over me, bringing back life. The soldier was stirring as I left him for Randy, his buttocks arching to the fighting spirit within him, his hands clutching as he rolled in the leaves.

Had to get going. With this one not knowing what a beating is he would start the same business within seconds of consciousness. Blinded with weariness, my shoulder like fire from the thump of his pistol, I spreadeagled myself on Randy, snatched up the petticoat and stuffed it in my pocket. By the time I reached the Tywi my strength was coming back. No more dragoons between Kidwelly and Cae White, thank God, and when I reached home we were into a gallop again. Opening the barn I shoved Randy in. Damned near dawn. Cocks were crowing from Bayleaves Farm as I rubbed myself dry and got into the bed, awaking an instant later, it seemed, in bright sunlight.

No mam to contend with, just dull looks from Morfydd and Mari. Not so bad in the mirror, really; nose, that was all, half way over my face, and skinned.

"Justin Slaughterer again by the look of it," said Mari, banging down the plate. Only the three of us now not counting Richard and Jonathon.

"More like the yeomanry – good beak-busters, them – the colonel himself, was it?" Morfydd now, acid curious, frightened. I saw her trembling hands.

"Second-in-command," I said.

"Good grief," she replied, "we are coming down the scale," and turned to Mari. "Make the most of your brother-in-law," she said. "We will not have him long."

Inclined to agree with her at this rate.

# CHAPTER 25

WALDO BAILIFF caught it that June, got it proper from Flannigan's daughters, though I had no hand in it, more the pity.

"Terrible, disgusting," whispered Mari at breakfast next day.

"Waldo Bailiff you speaking of, or Rebecca?" asked Morfydd.

For the first time since Cae White their eyes met in challenge over the table.

"Took him through on the pole, saw it myself," said Richard, his eyes like saucers. Growing fast, this one, regular man.

"Hush," said Mari. "It is too indecent to think about."

"Ask Gipsy May," said Morfydd, chewing. "Indecent all right. Things are coming improper indeed when a man pays a shilling for a child, though I hold no grief for Gipsy. Cross her palm with silver, turn her out. Do you call that justice?"

"A public exhibition. Better horsewhip him in private – never have I seen the like of it," said Mari. "It has a bad effect on the children."

A bad effect on Waldo, too.

The rumours varied but I knew the truth of it. Flannigan and ten of the daughters went up to the Reach and caught Waldo sprucing himself for his Saturday outing with Betsi Ramrod. Heading for marriage these two, arm in arm, large as life, peas in a pod in their treatment of Gipsy. Lucky for Betsi she wasn't carried, too. Trial, sentence and punishment, all within the hour, and they brought him through the village on the pole near midnight; staghung, naked but for his trews, screaming for a pigsticking, begging for mercy, while windows went up and doors came open and Betsi Ramrod weeping and tearing out her hair when they dumped him in the taproom of Black Boar tavern. Six pounds savings they found under the bed, six pounds for Gipsy May, said Flannigan to me later, though the trouble was getting it to her. Wonderful to see Flannigan in Chapel next day with Dai Alltwen Preacher roasting Rebecca up in the pulpit for dastardly attacks on God-fearing people; not a hair out of place had Abel Flannigan, and Toby Maudlin sitting next to him beating his breast for the sins of the village and Justin Slaughterer giving his bass Amen. That was a week back and not a daughter recognized: recognized, no doubt, but nobody dared breathe a name, and not a soul had seen Waldo since. Still going, said Flannigan. Thank God, said Morfydd.

"You ready?" she asked me now.

"Aye," I said, rising from table.

It was three days or so since I had tangled with the soldier and my bruises were going down and my nose coming normal. I had been lying low of late though every Rebecca and daughter in the county were out doing overtime on burning ricks and gates, and the victory was practically gained. The Trusts had lost all heart for rebuilding and the splintered remains of gates littered the highways, the charred timbers of the tollhouse rafters grinning at the summer sky. Due on shift at Gower's pit that morning, Morfydd and I took the endless road to coal. Strangely, she was looking better since Mam had left; as if the constant suppressing hand of my mother had lifted, leaving her free of criticism, but I knew the truth of it when we were half way to Ponty on that bright June day.

"I am bringing Willie O'Hara home tonight, Jethro. D'you mind?"

She glanced at me sideways and I winked.

"None of that," she said. "Respectable is Willie, never mind the tales – a woman could do worse."

"Handsome devil, I'll say that for him."

"Knows how to treat a woman," and she smiled. "Opening doors, closing gates, and he wants me."

"Are you in love with him?" I asked.

"Take me out of coal, mind."

"I am doing that," I said. "The end of this month. I asked if you loved him."

"I will only ever love one," she said. "I am thinking of my

son. His father for the next world, if there is one. Willie O'Hara will do for this."

"He wants to marry you, this Willie?"

She did not reply. Still beautiful she looked with her shawl over her shoulders and the wind catching her hair, still young enough to be loved.

"Bring him home, girl," I said. "We will make him welcome."

We walked on, leaping the brooks, taking the short cuts over the fields on the paths we knew so well. Years it seemed since we first came to Cae White. Willie O'Hara had come into her life at a time I feared for her sanity, and I was grateful to him, and relieved. For Morfydd was the one reason why I stayed on at Cae White. Much as I longed to get to America there seemed no chance with Morfydd around, and I knew that Mari would never leave her alone to fend for Richard.

"The trouble is you and Mari," said Morfydd. "Hardly fair, is it, to walk out of the place with Willie and Richard and leave the pair of you alone – not fair on Iestyn, come to that."

"No," I answered.

"Queer old life, isn't it?"

I nodded, taking her hand over a stream. Brilliant that early morning sunshine with the mist billowing down the river and the rooks screaming in the tops of the trees. Every detail of that last walk together to the pit is impressed on my mind, cut in deep grooves as with the knife of the woodcutter; every second of that morning I hear: the gurgling rush of water over stones, the coloured darts of the kingfishers I see, as if it was yesterday instead of through the mist of years.

"Mari and me will be all right," I said.

"O, aye?"

"You go and make a home with Willie, do not study us."

"No, Jethro," she said. "Not till Iestyn comes back."

"Three years," I said, watching her, wondering. . . . But I knew she thought him still alive when I saw her smile.

"God, I know how Mari feels," she said. "Three years more, that is all, and then I will see him."

Less than three hours.

I knew of a ship at Saundersfoot; a three-masted barque that was lying at the quay; waiting for the flood of immigrants from the north – people coming down on foot, it was said. Two weeks or longer she had laid at Saundersfoot with her sails trimmed down and smoke drifting from her galleys, and her captain was taking the fares at the gangplank, five pounds a head steerage, fifteen pounds a head cabins. Bound for the port of Philadelphia: a leap from there to the town of Pittsburgh and the flaming ovens of the iron. White in the deck, black-tarred her hull, a leviathan of a ship of two hundred tons, stalwart, braced in the bows for ploughing Atlantics, with pigtailed Plymouth men manning her and her captain with the face of Neptune himself, bearded and sideboarded and a gold-buttoned tunic. God, how I longed for that fifteen pounds, for Mari, Jonathon and me. Saving every penny now in the black box under the bed. No more quarts in Black Boar tavern, skimping on this and that, coming the Welsh Jew, longing for the feel of the deck beneath me, with Mari one side of me and Jonathon on the other, turning my back on the labour I hated. Last fall I had ploughed and sown Cae White, doing it spare time after a full Ponty shift, and the corn was standing high now, begging for the reapers – full price and profit for corn now the gates were nearly down. Like a longing for Mari it grew within me, this yearning for the land of promise, to make a decent life. This very morning Rebecca was marching on Carmarthen city, but I was sick of fighting. Led by Rebecca John Harries of Talog Mill thousands of the daughters were marching on the city to burn the workhouse down, they said; burn it to the ground and succour the starving, and God help the man who stands in our path. Flannigan would be there, Toby and Justin, Matthew Luke John and even Tom the Faith – scores of others I knew, fighting for justice. For this was Rebecca triumphant, showing her strength now the gates were down; pitting her numbers against the sabres of the yeomanry, spitting on dragoons, constables and magistrates. Fighting, fighting – four years of it, me – and for what? Not for gates. Fighting for Mari and the ship that was lying at Saundersfoot Quay. I would hang in her rigging, unfurl her sails, tar her from bow to stern while she rode at sea, scrub her white, labour in the galleys, bow and scrape to the dining gentry – just to hear the song of her, feel the roll of her, the buck and toss of the swell beneath her and listen to the whine of the Atlantic gales that drove her west to Philadelphia. Fifteen pounds between me and freedom – saving it now at two shillings a week – take me three years at this rate. And in three years time Iestyn would come back – tiptoeing over the waves from Botany Bay, his fingers clutching for Mari, invading her life.

I had to get away.

Lying in the seam in Number Three now, coal-grimed, sweating in inches of water, with the pick reaching in to the two foot roof. Liam Muldooney beside me mouthing the Bible, intoning deep about Kabzeel; his grandpa; grumbling and grunting about lions in snow. Worse than ever was Liam these days, what brain the coal left him was deserting him fast now: stupifying his body with unending labour, and God knows for what for he didn't need the money. The tram-towers and basketers were labouring behind us, coming in a queue from the ladders to the seams where fifty men or more lay side by side with us. I stopped for a breather and turned on my back, arms behind my head. Saw Morfydd next one up with a tram and an Irish girl shovelling it full like a man, singing above the bedlam of wheels and chinks some plaintive song of home. Pretty it sounded to its backcloth of thumps, the grunting of men, grumbling shovels, the wounding picks that echoed in the gallery to the shaft of the pit where Gower was bellowing. Pretty little Irish woman, too, come to that, coming upright now, leaning on her shovel and giving me a wink.

"Right, girl," she said to Morfydd. "Switch road, this one – through Number Six," and Morfydd nodded and crawled down to hitch up.

I got Liam Muldooney with an elbow. "Since when has Gower been using the switch road through Six?" I asked.

"Every fourth tram – Foreman's orders."

"To hell with Foreman," I said. "It isn't even propped." I sat up, hitting my head on the roof and cursing.

228

"Sit down, sit down, man," said Liam. "There's enough props by there to hold up government – they got them all in on last night's shift. Would I let a little woman go where I wouldn't go myself. Firm as Moses' rock that roof."

"That roof was dropping plugs not a week back," I said.

"And they fetched the plugs down, you satisfied? You start looking to your own business, little man, and leave me to mine. Shall I tell you of my grandpa now, and put your mind at ease?"

"To hell with your grandpa."

"Then would you rather have a chapter from Galatians?"

"O, for God's sake!" I said, for I was watching the end of Morfydd's tram, watching the glint of the backboard steel as it curved down the line to the switch road on Six, smaller and smaller in the lights of the tallow lamps.

"Sharp enough to cut yourself this morning," said Liam. "Rest you in God, little man, He will care for your Morfydd. No satan shall snatch at her in the presence of the Lord. Now give proof of your faith in Him, *bach* – tell Him what you know of the Book of the King, just to please Liam and take your mind from fear. How many books in the Old Testament, for instance?"

"Thirty-nine," I said. "Liam, I am afraid...."

"And the New Testament, little man?"

"Twenty-seven. Liam...."

"Hush you," said he. "It is not fear but the Devil wreaking his vengeance for the burning of the gates. And eight hundred and thirty-eight thousand three hundred and eighty letters in the New Testament all told, and do not argue, man, for I have taken the trouble to count them. Man, be calm."

"I am away to see Gower," I said, crawling, but he caught my wrist and twisted me back.

"Peace! The shortest sentence in His Book, if you please. ...?"

"Jesus wept," I murmured.

"Aye, aye, for the likes of you and me, Jethro. Would you take a fist to me and sweep me aside when I tell you your girl will be safe?"

Just looked at him. This the saint of faith; such men as this have prayed to their God with their bodies alight.

Liam was smiling.

"Trust you in Him," he whispered. "Do not put your trust in props, for I have prayed and the golden Lord has answered. On, now. What is the middle verse of the Book of our God, boy? Think now, shiver up the herring-roes. Shall I tell, is it? The eighth verse of the hundred and eighteenth Psalm. And how many times does the word *Lord* occur? Forty-six thousand two hundred and twenty-seven, and there is no word therein more than six syllables, and the word *Reverend* occurs only once, as if the Lord just remembered to slip the thing in. How now do I stand in the knowledge of my God?" He gripped my hand. "Forsake all wickedness. Stand you firm in the countenance of the Father, and He will protect you and those whom you love."

"As Towey." I raised my face.

"Is she not with happiness now, man? And the boy from Spain?"

"I want Morfydd living, not dead."

"So you put your faith in a four-inch prop when He can shift a mountain with His finger? O, Jethro, *bach*, do you listen to old Liam. Battered and addled I am, my body despoiled, but my soul is with glory and yours with dust. Conflict with the kings of the earth is conflict with God, for did He not teach humility to men? And the servants of the earthly queen is asking questions, you heard?"

This raised me again.

"What do you mean?"

"In search of Rebeccas, looking for daughters to break the march on Carmarthen – and searching for a man with broken hands – yours are not so tidy."

I heard his words but I did not care. Looking for the one who had flattened their dragoon, no doubt. I would do it again with half a chance, but quicker.

"God help him if they find him, mind," said Liam.

I heard his words as an echo, for I was trundling with Morfydd down Number Six gallery, the new shaft opened in a forest of props; couldn't rest till she got back to the seam, couldn't work, couldn't think.

"The Lord says turn the other cheek, Jethro."

"Aye? Well I am not turning mine."

"God forgive you," said Liam.

"Nothing to forgive."

"God help you, then," said he, and as he said it Number Six went down.

A dull thump first, then thunder, rocking us as with an earthquake, turning us, felling those standing, burying those lying. One moment light, next moment blackness. Props were going like twigs, bending, snapping, driving into the ground. Lying as I was, the drop took me square across the thighs, pinning me, and I fought to breathe as the pressure came greater; pinned as if nailed there, coal against my face, my chest, stretching as a mantle down to my ankles. Couldn't even gasp; lying solid in a tomb of coal, twisting, thighs bucking, screaming for breath, and the hand that clawed at my face was Liam's, groping for my mouth, knuckles arched for my first inward breath. Heard him scratching, someone screaming; trickles in my mouth as the dust filled it solid. This, the press, the shudder of a county. Liam was tearing the dust from my face now; somebody on my ankles heaving tons, and they drew me out as a thumb from a thumbscrew before the roof arch bellied and dropped flat. The place was in torment as I staggered up, half naked men and women rushing, screaming, tripping, falling, and children shrieking for lost parents. Gower was at the entrance to the gallery, his voice booming for order, but the mob that rushed the ladders rolled him down, passing over him. Leaning against the wall, spitting out coal, digging out my eyes, I looked at Liam Muldooney. He was sitting as a man dazed, gaping to the shock, mouthing some incantation, his face grimed against the white roll of his eyes, and then I remembered Morfydd.

The gallery was coming empty now, few tallow lamps were burning, but the colliers were still yelling down at the ladders, and I heard from there the cries of children, the bawling shouts of overmen trying to get order. Only fire was needed to turn it into Hell. Took one look at Liam and staggered to the entrance

231

to Number Six, snatching at a tallow lamp and holding it before me as I went down the incline. Terror was in me, sweat flooding over me. Reckoning by time she was half way through the switch road when the roof came down. A forest of pitprops here and I stumbled and hit myself against them in my swaying run down the line. Queer how you pray when you fear such loss – strange how God is neglected till the testing time, and there is no other with ears. The shouts and bedlam was dying behind me now as I plunged on, following the shimmer of the rails in the faltering light of the candle. The air was fetid here, heavy with dust. The roof was lower now, the walls with jutting biceps of rocks; ankle deep in water now. Stopping, I listened. No sound but the thumping of my heart and the trickling of water from above. I looked at the roof. Wide fissures were crazing it from wall to wall, dust cascading in sudden spurts from the pressure building up. Gaunt the shadows of the candle, only an inch or so of it left, the flame spluttering to the heavy air. Dank the smell that wafted then from some devil's hole, and I knew that I was holding in my hand the flame of detonation. Fear struck, thumping as a fist, putting me against the wall, and I dropped to my knees, staring at the blackness ahead.

"Morfydd!"

Flung back in my face in countless echoes, reverberating down the gallery, bouncing off the drop. The roof cracked like a shot behind me, the pressure begging for the least vibration to bring it roaring down. Couldn't even shout without reprisal. Spitting out dust, I lurched on.

Narrow here. The gallery was tapering. This is the hardest rock, its walls as filed from the body of the mountain, the roof still lower. Had to bend here, now go on all fours, with the candle held out, one hand gripping a line, and this was the beginning of the fall. Boulders of rock and coal were strewn over the narrow floor, coming thicker as I crept onward, stumbling, cursing as my knees pressed the flints. Had to rest, for my head was thumping with the hammer of my heart and each breath was drawn against the iron band of my chest. As a dog, I rested, tongue lolling, panting, hearing as if in dreams a dull roll of thunder far behind me, and the floor beneath me trembled to the new drop. As alive the rail sprang under my hand, transmitting its message of entombment for someone. Perhaps me. I did not really give it a thought. Past caring now: had to find Morfydd. The candle was spilling its tallow now, the wick hooked and black for the last minutes of flame, guttering, sparking. On again, the boulders coming thicker till the line disappeared. Crying aloud, I wept as a child weeps in all its tuneless sounds as I set the lamp down and clawed a path up the drop. It seemed a mountain but it was only three feet, for my head struck the roof, knocking me back. This was the end of it, this was the fall.

Turning on my back I lay against the heap with the floor at my heels and the roof against my forehead, eyes closed to the scald of the tears, hands clenched to the loss. This is the end of it then, as she had said, engrained as the leaf; becoming part of the living earth, buried alive in the filth of coal for the profits of industry and the greed of men. The candle was chittering, opening my eyes to its incandescent fire in the blackness of the pit. Didn't care now if I lived or died. Hope sprang then, shivering me awake in brief excitement, weighing the chances that she was beyond the fall, but I knew she was not. A gallery fall this, running as the drop of a stick; no isolated plug that she might have missed. I knew she was lost. And I saw in the seconds before the candle spat out a silver strand of shining braid, hanging from the splintered tip of a wooden prop, and stretched towards it and caught it in my fingers, pulling it down.

Blackness.

I put it against my face.

Gower came in for me, led by Muldooney, they said after, but I do not remember; with a twenty foot burrow through the drop I had heard, up by the start of the switch; hewing like madman, stark naked, some of them, sweating, bleeding, dropping with exhaustion to rise and hew again. God, these colliers!

Came in for me, ten men risking their lives for one, the most important man in their earth. A day and a night it took them, but they came crawling, with a tram rolling behind them – in like ants, out like things scalded. And ten hours later the whole of Number Six went down with a rumble they heard in Kidwelly, but I do not remember. Just a day and a night of dreaming for me; lying against the fall where Morfydd slept; hearing her voice raised in rebellion, hearing the whisper of her in a Willie O'Hara love-making; seeing her frown, the brilliance of her smile. A day and a night I lay with her, walking in summer with her over the green of the Coity mountain back home; standing beside her black starchness in chapel, hearing her sing. Sitting at home now, feeding her Richard, drawing up her bodice to the shift of my eyes: scolding now, going round the bedroom, swinging her fists like a man at me: innocent as a child under my mother's stare. Sister and lover.

I opened my eyes and saw Mari then; stars were about the curve of her shawl as she knelt by the hurdle and put her arms around me.

"O, Jethro," she said, and kissed me. "Jethro!"

Men turning away to bury the dead.

# CHAPTER 26

THEY GOT Abel Flannigan in bed, said Mari, on the night after the march on Carmarthen city: clanking horses and sabres drawn in his shippon, she said, heaving down the door and bursting up the stairs with Biddy screaming murder and heaving pans at them, yelling like a mad thing at Abel to hoof it through the window, but she yelled too late. Back to the wall in his nightshirt went Abel Flannigan, with a dragoon on his back and a constable on his legs, hitting off helmets with one hand and smacking them out with the other; five on the floor at one time, said Biddy, bleeding, ragged, tormented as a Spanish bull, was Abel, roaring to Biddy to saddle his mare while he settled all fifteen. They could have shot him, cut him down, but they didn't, to their credit. But they thumped him to his knees and tied his wrists behind him and booted him out on the end of a rope, haltered as a wife being sold at market. Biddy's screams could be heard from here, said Mari.

"And then?" I asked, flat.

"Then they went for Toby Maudlin."

Toby went easy, Mari said, thumped black and blue by his misery missus at the first clank of the sabres; kicked out through the door into the arms of the constables, his face still blackened, still wearing her nightdress, for he had taken a gate in his stride on the way back from Carmarthen.

"Justin Slaughterer was taken in Carmarthen workhouse," she said now. "He forced his way in there a yard behind John Harries Rebecca and two hundred following them, overturned the tables, smashed down the doors to free the inmates so they could put the place to flames. But the dragoons came galloping in and slammed the gates behind them."

"Got the lot," I said.

"Rebecca John Harries made back home," she answered, "but not poor Justin."

"A damned fine way to end a page of history," I said.

"Then they came here," said Mari, kneeling by the bed.

This raised me on the pillow.

"Six dragoons and a captain, Jethro. Looking for a man with broken hands, a man who had murdered one of their soldiers."

I stared at her.

"Found drowned in a brook in the woods near St Clears – beaten, and left to die, left to roll about, and drown."

"O, God," I said, sweating.

So small and unequal she looked standing there in profile, one hand gripping the sill. Hard on women, this business. She had lost one man to rebellion. She looked like losing another. Murder now. Sick, I felt.

"What . . . what did you tell them?" I whispered.

"What Gower told me – that you and Morfydd were dead. O, God," she said.

I thought of the ship, tranquil on the calm sea, waiting, waiting.

She said, "Then they went to the pit to get the truth of it and Liam Muldooney told them the same."

I covered my face with my hands.

"Jethro, you must get away," she said. "Every man under sixty in the village has been taken. Special magistrates are being sworn in to try them – hundreds and hundreds have been taken – even men who have never seen a Rebecca just in case. They will come back for you, you cannot stay here."

"Yes."

This was the Chartists all over again. With victory coming closer they had bungled it by moving too soon – men like my brother who had listened to John Frost; men like Flannigan who had followed the hothead John Harries. And now murder.

"Thank God Mam isn't here," she said.

"And if I go . . . what of you?"

"I will manage," she said.

"Cae White, on your own?"

"I have Richard and Jonathon for help. I will manage."

"You will starve, the three of you. You first," I replied.

"Perhaps for the good," she said, empty. "Not much of a life as things stand, is it?"

"Mari," I said, and put out my hand to her and she came obediently and stood above me, looking down, before she went on her knees beside the bed and into my arms. Just held her for a bit. I knew she was sobbing for Morfydd; that the grief was cutting as a knife. Then the door came open silently and the faces of Jonathon and Richard peeped round. Jonathon as Mari, dark as Richard was fair. And I saw in Richard's eyes the unspoken question as Mari rose like lightning and went to Jonathon. I glanced at Mari, my eyebrows raised and she shook her head and hurried Jonathon through the door.

"The soldiers came, Uncle Jethro," Richard said by the bed. "You heard one of them's been killed?"

"Yes."

"And Aunt Mari did say that you didn't do it and that you and my mam be dead, anyway, then they went away."

"Yes," I said.

Seven years old now, ten by the bite of his teeth on his lip

236

and he looked at me, his eyes large and blue, misted with tears.

"Where's my mam, Uncle Jethro?"

"Richard, come to me," I said.

Quite still he stood, hands clenched by his sides, his hair alight in a shaft of the window sun, then he lowered his face, weeping without sound.

"Richard," I said, and reached out and drew him against me.

Just held him, pressing him hard against me, feeling useless, cursing coal, the county, the country; cursing the world. No need to tell this one, no explanations begged. Just held him while he wept, thinking of the soldier.

"Aunt Mari now," I said. "Richard . . ." and I held him away, smiling. "With Jonathon for your brother, and Aunt Mari and me for your mam and dad."

"Took by the coal, is it?" Lips trembling, he faced me.

"Yes."

"Eh, the bloody old coal," he said, eyes slanting away from me. "Mam did say the coal would be the end of it, one night in prayers."

I nodded.

He said, hands screwing, "Staying with you, is it? Not going to the workhouse or the Hirings like Ianto Vaughan when his mam passed on?"

"No, Richard. We would not allow it."

"Tea now, is it?"

The simplicity of the grief of childhood.

"Yes," I said.

"Then I will help Aunt Mari bring it up."

"I am coming down," I said, getting out. "Would you have me lying for days like a lazy old lump?"

"Head bumps, is it?" he asked, feeling.

"Aye, but most of them going down. Away like a good boy while I dress, Dick."

He got to the door, turned and flashed me a smile, but I heard the stuttering breath of his sobbing as he went down the stairs.

"Jethro," said Mari when the boys were in bed, "you have got to get away. The soldiers will come back."

"Yes," I said.

Agitated, walking the kitchen for the last two hours, she was pulling at her fingers, encircling the finger that had once held her wedding ring, out of habit, for the ring was there no more. Face strained and pale she walked and turned, head switching to the slightest sound of the night.

"I have written to Mam and Tomos – Osian Hughes got it on the mail coach," she said. "Had to say both of you had gone, in case it was opened. Policemen are opening all letters, they say. When she hears of the pair of you Mam will go mad."

"But you were wise," I said.

She was wandering from window to window, pulling the curtains tighter, hands trembling, her lips dead white, and I longed to hold and comfort her.

"Mari," I said, and she turned as if struck.

"O, God," she whispered, and wept.

Up then, pulling her against me. She did not fight free as I expected but clung to me, her fingers as claws on my back. Cold her face when I kissed it and she twisted away when I tried for her lips.

"You have got to get away, do you understand? There is no time for this. O, but a damned child you are, Jethro! They will drag you off as they dragged off Flannigan and the others. Transportation, that will be the end of it."

Death, I thought.

"Talk sense," I said, pushing her off. "I have less than a pound saved – how far will I get without money? Best to wait here till things cool down."

"I have money," she said.

"You will need every penny you've got."

"I have fifty pounds all but two shillings. Fifty pounds. I told you before."

Me staring now.

"Grandfer's money," she said.

I sighed. "You kept it pretty dark."

"I told you down on the Burrows but you wouldn't believe me."

"Yes," I said, "I remember."

I sat down, sweating, trying to get the size of it. Me setting three years aside to save fifteen pounds and her standing here with fifty.

I rose. "Then come away with me, Mari. We will take the boys and leave this damned place. There is a ship lying at Saundersfoot. . . ."

"Not with you, Jethro," she said.

And she came nearer, standing above me as I sat down before her. Soft her voice now, every word as measured, her eyes unflinching on mine. "Time was when I would have gone to the ends of the earth with you, but not now. The women of you Mortymers are solid gold, Jethro, but they bring forth sons of solid iron – fighters all – one word and the blow, the fist before the word always, seeing but one side of the argument. Up workers, down gentry, isn't it – and there are gentry folk in America as well as in Wales. And where you find gentry you will find the Mortymers to stand against them to take that which is theirs by right." Her voice rose now, her eyes grew large and she swept her arm to the window. "Some damned good gentry people live in this county – not the puffed up little magistrates who have thieved ten fields – these are the people who have raised your gates, the absentee landlords who jump in to buy and jump back to London to live on their rents – these are the enemies." She folded her arms and smiled down at me. "But there are other kinds of gentry, boy – gentlefolk whose ancestors have made their roots here – who were great in this county and decent to their workers before you damned Mortymers turned an eye to light. And that is your trouble, you Mortymers. You tar and feather every gentleman in sight, never choosing, never dividing the black from the white – everything with a foot of lace or a carriage is branded by the Mortymers as enemies of the people, but you are blind. Look towards Squire's Reach – hasn't Lloyd Parry treated us decent – did you not give your love to a gentry girl? Look North and West to the great mansions that were built by the Welsh as the

239

beating hearts of the people – this is the true aristocracy who think like you, Jethro–not the jumped-up little pit-owners who have raced into Wales to drive a shaft for quick profits – hating the evil little magistrates, these gentry, aye, and taking them to law." She paused, bending above me, one hand clenched. "These people are one with you, Jethro, with all their birth and nobility, and you will never make me think otherwise, for I am one of them."

New, this Mari, as tempered by fire, commanding. I stared up at her.

"I have had too much," she said, her voice dying. "I have been hit too hard by you Mortymers, the people I love. I have a son to consider now, and Morfydd's boy now she has gone. It is a load. And the fight of the Mortymers is in these boys, I know it, but I will drive it out. I will teach them peace, not war; to love and not to hate; to make light of the injustices that is the lot of the poor and triumph over them with the help of God – Church or Chapel, makes no difference – God just the same." She knelt then, smiling in tears, and bowed her head, her fingers smoothing the knuckles of my hands. Skinned and swollen, these hands. I drew them away, and she raised her eyes to mine.

"The soldier is dead, Jethro," she said. "Do you remember?"

The sweat sprang to my face and I rose, turning from her.

"You ?" she whispered, instantly beside me.

Cool the glass of the window on my forehead. I bowed my head.

"My God," she said, and wrung her hands. "This is the end of it, then – murder."

I had lost her. The knowledge was enough to silence me, obliterating remorse. I could hear her pacing the floor behind me. Her steps ended.

"And you killed him in cold blood."

"Him or me," I said, flat. "It was a fair fight. I did not seek it. He must have rolled and drowned in the brook after I left. I did not kill him."

"And do you expect them to believe that ?" She caught my

arm and swung me round. "They will search the county. They will never give up. When they learn you did not die with Morfydd they will come back. O, what are we doing talking, wasting time. Quick, you must get away!"

Agitation gripped her again. Her face was stark white. "Quick, now – how much the fare for the ship at Saundersfoot?"

"Five pounds."

"You shall have twenty-five – half what is in the box."

This turned me. "It is one way of getting me out of your sight, isn't it? Give me five and you will have back every penny."

"O, God," she said, empty. "It has come to that? O, Jethro, can't you see that I love you? It is not the dirty old money – you can have all fifty. It is because I love you that I could not bear you to be taken."

"But you will not come with me?"

She lowered her hands as if slapped in the face. Eyes closed, she stood.

"And after I am gone – what then?" I said.

She emptied her hands at me.

"Back to Nanty with Tomos, is it, and labour in bloody coal?"

She opened large, rebellious eyes at me. "Do not swear at me," she said. Beautiful, she looked.

"Humping and heaving fourteen hours a day, ending the same way as Morfydd, and you shout to me about gentry," I said.

"Did it once before, Jethro," she replied. "Two children now, and I can do it again."

"So you will not come with me?"

"Not to America, not anywhere, to start the same fighting all over again."

"Because of the soldier, isn't it?"

"Because I want *peace* – nothing to do with the soldier!"

"Mari, I beg of you," I said.

"Jethro, for God's sake go."

"Better to stay and be taken. I have loved you for years, and

241

yet but once. What kind of a life with three thousand miles between us ?" Cold her lips when I kissed her, with no response, as if I had drained her of youth and fire. Strange the excitement seizing me at her nearness, the sudden torrent of my breathing drowning the chance of footsteps, the knock. So I held her, unable to leave her, unable to go.

"O, that Tomos was here!" she said as a whisper.

Just sweated and held her, ears tingling, fearful to move.

"Ask Tomos," I said, gripping her. "Tomos will know what to do. You are of me now, Mari, I am of you. Ask Tomos!"

She held me away, smiling sad. "Jethro, Iestyn – both the same. Loved them both the same. Queer, isn't it, they cannot do without me. He brought me home in rags, clothed and fed me, and left me for you. And while you hold me here I am dying inside, until you go."

"But you will speak to Tomos ? Mari, I beg you!"

She said softly, her eyes closed: "I will tell him that I am afraid. And I will tell of the soldier, because you have killed. I have my God, Jethro, you have yours – that is the difference. Now you will swear to me that you did not leave him dead ?"

"I swear it," I said.

"Now go. Wait at the ship. I do not promise to come, but if it is his wish Tomos will bring me, for Tomos and me have the same God. We will leave it to Him, is it ?" She turned from my arms and set her back to me. "Do not kiss me again, Jethro. I could not bear it. Just go."

I stood there, hands clenched, hearing the rustle of her dress as she went past me to the stairs, catching the scent of her. Barren of her, I died in seconds at the click of the door; listened to the creak of the stairs.

Empty that room in the dim light of the lamp. I stood looking at it, at my mother's empty chair by the fireplace, the place where Morfydd sat. And I saw, standing there, the shine of the table grow to life again, the snow of its cloth, the gleam of knives, and heard the tinkle of cups and plates. Blinding the lamp, its wick turned low; shimmering, dancing to the chatter and laughter. Morfydd's high shrieks, Mam's sharp replies, Mari's soft voice, Grandfer's snores. This the mood of the table, the centre of the family, the servant of life. Laughter, joy one minute, heads bent low to the plates the next; sidelong glances at someone in disgrace, nudges and winks. Cursed is the mind that it brings such visions, cursed the table. Swung away from it, cursing, and took five pounds from the box on the dresser and shouldered the door to the back, but turned.

"Goodbye," I said.

I could not see the table.

Out in the night now, the shippon was steaming. I ran over to the barn and whistled for Tara and she came out wriggling.

"Up," I said, and she leaped into my arms.

Randy turned and snorted hate at me as I closed the door and dropped the stick. Lonely it was, standing in the shippon with Tara against me, looking up at the blind windows, seeking a hand. Nothing. I turned.

Grandfer was right. My mind went back years. Fifty feet down, spreadeagled in the peat bog on the track to Tarn, head lolling, suspended in mud, I reckon he smiled.


## CHAPTER 27

NO STARS that night, not even a moon, thank God. The world was as black as a witch's gown, the air velvet and warm coming over the estuary. I walked fast at first, eager to get north to cross the barriers of the Tywi and Taf rivers, reckoning for a journey of thirty miles to Saundersfoot though it was twenty as the crow flies. I was heading for Llangain, taking the same route as I had done when we last burned the gates, striking north first, then south-west, keeping to the low ground, trotting at times with Tara running at my heels. Good to have Tara with me. Funny how a little dog can make up for humans; there always with her excited grinning, tongue seeking your fingers, in love with you, her eyes adoring though you are less than muck to your race, unloved by those you love, criticized and rejected. And I knelt at times in the darkness and held her to me. Queer little woman.

With the face of Mari sweeping back I stopped once before dropping to the Gwendraeth and turned, looking back. Distantly I saw Cae White, hooded and bewitched by night, one chink of light beaming from a curtain Mari had forgotten to pull, its gables and twisted chimneys outlined starkly against white, rolling clouds, and the standing corn beyond sweeping into blackness. Turned my back on it, whistled at Tara and hurried on, keeping to the tracks, seeking the safety of woods and thickets. Midnight was tolling from a blind clock as I reached the Tywi opposite Llangain, and I went down the bank to the water and stripped naked while Tara, squatting, shivered and looked appalled at me. Not fancying to travel soaked, I tied my clothes into a bundle and hung them round my neck, then waded in while Tara whined delighted. Gave her a whistle and struck out. Muzzle sweeping the calm water she swam beside me, one eye cocked at an otter that barked and dived at our approach. Out now, streaming, shivering, and I rolled in the river grass to dry myself, Tara copying, leaping to this new adventure after the years of neglect. Dressing, I started off again at a trot to warm myself, eyes skinned for every rustle of a thicket, going for St Clears and the narrow reaches of the Taf. Treating it likewise at Whitehill Down I reached the high ground above Newton, and lay there in the stubbled grass with Tara in the crook of my arm, shivering at the sky where the first grey streak of dawn was flushing up from the east. I slept, awaking in bright sunlight with Tara licking my face, encircled by rabbits, five all told. A man with a dog can conquer the universe. Kissing and scolding her, I picked up a rabbit and stuffed it into my coat, rose and ran down the hillock, leaping the boulders, alive to the joy of the newfound day of sun and warmth, until I remembered Cae White and Mari. In the shelter of jutting rocks now, a disused quarry, I gutted and skinned the rabbit, rubbed for a flame and hung him from sticks for roasting. God must have a special heaven for rabbits in return for the sacrifice of their bodies to Man. Never smelled the like of this one after a sleep in the open, and between us we put him well down with Tara running in circles sniffing and whining for more.

We stayed in the quarry all that day and crept out at dusk to the evening star. Brilliant this night with the full moon showing me across country to Windleways and Amroth, leading me south to the sea. Deserted country this, a few miles from Saundersfoot and I reached the bay at midnight and lay on the short grass looking at the stars. There, with the sea beneath me, I watched the procession of the worlds; helmeted Mars beaming at the molten Jupiter, Saturn spinning in his rings of white satin, the white-dusted Heavens of worlds beyond worlds. Uranus and his servant moons, I saw, Venus making her crucifix sign; Little Bear, Great Bear, the Plough in all its regal majesty; stars and constellation dripping white light in the obliterated eye of the Mother Sun. I dreamed, eyes half closed to the beauty of night. Strange, I thought in a moment of wakefulness, that this same earth upon which I was lying was the tissue and bones of men long dead; holding the cinders of tongues long silent in the billion years of time and space, warm under the belly of the panting Tara. Just the two of us, Tara and me, man and dog linked in friendship, lying on a cliff that had echoed the wolfhound, the screamed commands of primaeval man. How small the ambitions and the loves compared to the greatness of earth and sky, the unmeasured wastes of the sea, how pitiful, I thought. One man running, and loving; seeking the new in exchange for the old. So trivial this seventy years of living and dying; all ambitions ending the same, in earth.

After more than a week of hiding in sea caves, poaching and trapping to keep alive, I reached the hills dominating the harbour. The sea was flat calm and misted as I crested a rise and looked down to the quay. Yellow sands flashed brilliant light, fishing-boats dotted the bay. And the black hulk of the *Cestria* stretched its great length against the jetty where coal trams were rumbling from the nearby mine to a waiting schooner. Already the ship had unfurled her sails, jerseyed seamen were running her decks and the air was filled with hoarse cries; merchants' stalls were end to end along the sea wall, their vendors screaming their wares as I went down the

main street to the quay. Market day by the look of it, the place
thronged with coalmen, limemen, and labourers from the
mine, coal-grimed, weary. Women bent under loads too heavy
for men, barefooted children ran in the gutters, screaming a
Welsh I did not understand. Beggars flung up skinny arms as I
went down to the ship, fishermen lounged by their boats or
needled at nets. Excitement grew within me at the sight of the
ship, but I knew that I must not raise suspicion. Too many
fugitives were travelling these days for eagerness. With Tara
gripped against me I turned into a tavern. The room was
crowded to the doors with men, seamen chiefly, roaring, bantering, thumping the counter, the mugs going down, mugs upturned in shafts of the morning sun. Welsh here, chiefly; men
of the sea, barrel-chested, brown-faced, with the blue slits of
eyes for scanning horizons. They parted good natured as I
elbowed my way to the counter.

"A quart ale," I said, slapping down money, and got the mug
and steered it through the sailors to a corner, and set it down.

"God," said a voice.

Matthew Luke John, his corn-coloured hair standing on end.

"Lord," he breathed. "You on the same do as me, boy?"

His eyes were shadowed with the sleeping out, his face
pinched and pale with hunger.

"The *Cestria*, evening tide," I said. "You leaving your mam
to fend alone, then?"

"The old man passed on," said he. "So she sold up and got
out of farming – other ways to starve, she said. You hop out of
it, man, she said, and take the chance I missed, and she gave me
five pounds for steerage if I brought back a fortune."

"America, is it?"

"Couldn't be worse than this bitch of a place though it ought
to be God's country. Lucky my mam was poorly or I'd have
been on the march for Carmarthen. You heard about
Flannigan?"

"Yes," I answered.

"And Toby Maudlin, Tom the Faith, and . . ."

"Tom's not taken?" I asked, straightening.

"Taken like the rest of them. John Penry, Howell Jones, Will

246

Raven, Ifor Walker – could go on for weeks. The dragoons were knocking on my door within two hours of the Carmarthen business. Justin did us well."

"Justin?" I stared at him.

"You haven't heard? Turned Queen's Evidence. They booted him twice in the workhouse yard and he couldn't gabble the names quick enough."

"God Almighty," I said.

He raised his sad eyes to mine. "You reckon he's Welsh?"

"Doubtful," I said.

"Nothing you can put your tongue to, eh? Forget him. The dragoons booted him harder after it and now he's explaining to St Peter. Found dead in a well within two miles of Carmarthen."

"Do they know who?" I asked.

"Rebecca. She didn't leave notes. The world's well rid of him." He sighed. "You signed on yet?"

"The *Cestria*? Not yet."

"Nor me. These boys say the dragoons will search her any minute. I've been waiting days for them to clear her. But the captain isn't choosey, thank God. Saints or convicts, he says, five pounds steerage. I got away from the house with ten minutes to spare – saw my mam giving hell to those dragoons – so I'm not rushing things now." He drank and gasped, wiping with his sleeve. "Been mooching round here for the last ten days."

"We sail together then?"

"Wacko!" said he. "We'll give them America. Do you reckon they starve out there?"

"Not if you work, they say."

"I drink to that," said he. "You heard about Tom Rhayader?"

I saw a vision of the beloved Rhayader; square-faced, tanned, his eyes of steel, and shook my head.

"Hit out two of them and tried to escape, but they got him in ten yards. He didn't come out of it."

I closed my eyes. "And his wife and kids?"

"Carmarthen workhouse last time I heard. God knows now. You leaving that woman, Jethro?"

I looked at him.

"The nightgown woman," said he. "The one who filled that was worth while bringing," and he winked at Tara. "Poor exchange with that old bitch. She bedded?"

"Not that woman," I said.

"Has she gone fripperty with another Welsh chap, then?"

"Leave it, Matthew."

"Only asking, mind. No offence."

"Leave it," I said.

Commotion on the cobbles outside now; hoofbeats, clanks, the angry cries of vendors, shouted commands. We rose. The sailors were pressing to the windows, jugs dangling, fists clenched as the horsemen drew sabres to clear a path to the *Cestria*. With a captain leading they forced their way along the quay to the gangplank where the skipper stood, hands on his hips. Three soldiers pushed past him and went aboard. We watched, tense, but they came back in five minutes.

"Routine check," I said. "Their hearts are not in it."

"Give them an hour," said Matthew. "Wait for the evening tide. They might come back."

The nightshift colliers had started when we left the tavern primed with enough ale to make us cheeky, and I thought of the Gower pit as I passed the black-faced labourers; the dull-eyed Welsh and Irish women hauling and singing to the clank of the wheels. But one was young, vital, alive. Irish by her looks, this girl, with the same bright beauty as my Morfydd, black-haired, one eye closing at me as I passed. Morfydd this, this the shade of another, I thought; one who was lying a hundred feet down in the press and smashed props of Number Six, one in the seam, one inch thick. Was Willie O'Hara weeping? I wondered, or seeking the breast of another Morfydd now she had left him for Richard, her lover? Strange the wish to snatch at this Irish, strange the wish to grip her, and I went back slowly to the gangplank where the captain was waiting. Matthew was doing the talking, fist thumping, bargaining. Money chinked and I was elbowed for mine, but I was not really there. I was down in Cae White with the dinner coming out, with the tread-ling of Mam's wheel in my ears, listening to the swish of the shuttle, Jonathon's high shrieks to Mari, her soft voice. And I heard again the sigh of the scythe and saw the wheat falling obliquely in sunfire; heard the herons crying doleful from Kidwelly, the curlews shouting at dawn, the barking of otters from the Reach, the whispers of Tessa. Other things I heard: Mari's shout to go to Chapel, the crackling hiss of the blazing gates, Mam's contralto in *Sanctus*. Dashing into the pitprops now, screaming for Morfydd; making love to Mari down on the 'shore. I put my hand into my pocket and gripped my earth, the handful I had brought from the fields of Cae White.

"Not that, you fool," said Matthew, eyeing me. "The man wants his money."

"O, aye," I said, and fished it out.

Snow-white deck now, pigtailed seamen, the smell of tar.

I stood by the rail with my hand in my pocket and gripped the earth.

"What the hell is wrong with you, man?" said Matthew.

But I did not answer him. Just staring at Wales. Sails were billowing above me, oceans of white as they dropped and unfurled. Feet stamped the deck. Dimly I heard the creaks, the commands, the shrieking of capstans.

"Damned pixilated, you," said Matthew. "I'm going below."

I gripped it in my hand, this Wales, and bowed my head. Gripped this plot for which men died; for which my kin had stood square to invaders, mocking the whip, spitting in the faces of kings. For such small muck and pebbles men have laboured and suffered – for this proud land of the Celts, Iberians, Moors and Spaniards, Angles, Jutes, Bretons, *Welsh!* For this blessed race whose mongrel blood is stirred with the blood of nobles and princes, this land of song and greenness that has flung an empire of invaders into the sea. The ship shuddered and rocked to the swell and I raised my head. Relations and friends were thronging the quay now; weepy matrons, stalwart fathers, ancient grandfers pinned on sticks, and the dying red sun was shining on the bare heads of children. Screamed goodbyes now, sobs and laughter as the exiles jostled beside me.

"For God's sake what is wrong with you, man?" Matthew again, turning me.

Wind in the rigging now, sails slapping; ropes were curling against the evening sun. The *Cestria* heaved and bucked beneath me. Hawsers tightened and sprayed water, drooped slack and tightened again as she fought to be free. Hands clenched, I stood there holding Tara.

What is it that enters the blood and chains a man's soul to the soul of his country? What is it that pierces as a barb and cannot be drawn? O, this beloved country that has raised its sword to the fire of its persecutors and reddened its soil with beloved sons! *Wales!* What lies in your possession that you bite at the throats of those who leave you? You of the mountainous crags of Dinas, of Snowden, Pembrey and Capel Pass – you of the valleys, heaths and pastures, the roaring rivers, the village brooks – what is your golden key that turns in the hearts of your patriots; what flame sears their souls in the last good-bye?

The gap was widening. The *Cestria* strained to the bridling hawsers. Heard the captain then; saw his arms outstretched to the quay where the crowd was gathering into an informal choir, and the labouring Welsh and Irish rushed to join them – any excuse for a song; barefooted, ragged, come to sing.

"A song for the exiles, then?" roared the captain.

"*Sanctus, Sanctus!*" a woman shrieked.

"Right, you, *Sanctus!*" And he stood conducting.

The ship vibrated to the voices, the crew stopped work and sang; faces turned up, they sang, and it was glorious, but I could not sing.

The crowd was thicker now, pouring down to the harbour, emptying from the hovels and taverns. Vendors screamed their wares at us, bullying a path for their carts, elbowing at tipsy sailors. Bull-chested colliers shouldered in from the mine, bantering, quarrelling, forming a circle of stamping hobnails, clapping to the time as a skinny Irish woman did a jig on the quay, skirts up, scarf waving, her black sticks of legs raising the dust, and the child-labour, drooping in their rags, watched her with dejected eyes. A drunken foreigner now, bottle waving, screaming insults, bristling for a fight; a black-gowned priest, hand up in blessing, telling his beads. All the bedlam of it grew about us in a thundering of sails, and above all was *Sanctus* in power and majesty, pulling in the crowd until it jammed them solid before the gangplank. Only one stood alone. Bending at the stern rail, I watched her. This, the image of Morfydd I had seen earlier, cheeky with her harlot come-hitherings, lounging impish on a bollard, smoothing back her long dark hair. Hands on her hips, brazen, she smiled at me. Rags fluttering, she waved, and I smiled back. Dimly I heard the captain's voice:

"We leave in joy, good people, so do not weep. For the exile takes but his body to the sister land, leaving his heart in Wales. Last verse of *Sanctus* again, and sing it to the sky! Sing!"

The tide had got us proper, swinging us to the stern ropes. The wind was rising, the pennant standing as stiff as a bar. Impatient, the *Cestria* bucked to the swell. Screamed goodbyes now, people weeping aloud, ropes splashing silver as they were hooked from bollards. Halyards stiffening, sails billowing, the ship heeled and rolled in the wind, thumping in the waves. I looked again at the Irish Morfydd, and saw through her breast the winding road that led to Amroth where Mari might be coming, and far beyond it to Llangain and Carmarthen, Llandeilo and Senny, and I laboured up the Clydach Valley road to home. Cae White I saw, ruined, deserted, the golden sweeps of its rejected corn; the empty kitchen, the cold, dead hob. And then came a vision of Mari, sitting in Tomos's trap with Richard and Jonathon either side, dominated by the black mass of Tomos, trotting east towards Nanty, and Mari was weeping. Aye, weeping – but for me, or her Iestyn? Strange and cruel are the laws of God, that a woman cannot marry her dead husband's brother. And this, I knew, was why she had not come. Stranger, too, are the laws of women. The road to Amroth danced in my eyes, and the road was empty. The crowd was as solid as a heading of coal now, arms raised as a forest as the gap between us widened, and I smiled again at the Irish Morfydd; she who had risen, it seemed, from the smashed props of Number Six and walked the galleries through a thousand tons of rock, sent by my Welsh Morfydd, to say goodbye.

Matthew Luke John at my elbow now, hooking me to face him.

"For God's sake, man," said he, "you are weeping."

"Go to hell," I said.

"For the petticoat woman? For that one there? O, aye!" and he narrowed his eyes. "Well, there's a waste, but never you mind, for we'll tar and feather a few in the town of Pittsburgh. Eh, dry it up, Jethro. They come better in silk than rags."

He spoke again, but I did not hear him, for in turning I had seen the crimson sky. The sun was setting, blazing and red as a Dutch cheese with him, one half steaming the sea and the other half in Hades, flaring at the clouds with his furnace glow, taking my mind back to childhood and the flashes of Blaenafon. It was as if the ovens of Pittsburgh had crashed back on hinges, striking at the world with their incinerating glare, and Mari's face grew dim in that light as the sea divided us. Creaking, clanking, shuddering, the *Cestria* was lumbering before the wind, and in the magnificence of her bedlam I heard the call of the iron as men had heard it for a thousand years before me. O, brilliant was this sky! Brilliant is the flaring when the cauldron is turned and the molten streams run wild, hissing and firing in the moulds! I put out my arm and thrust Matthew behind me, hearing again the clang of the loading bays, the thump of hammers, the whine of the mills. Bedlam in the rigging now as the *Cestria* got going, with the wind singing as a puddler's hammer and the spray hissing as water in the steaming-pit. This, the cold kiss of the firing-iron, the scald of the ladle, the heat and stink and sweat and call of it in all its hobnail stamping, this the iron that no woman understands. With Tara held against me I shouldered my way through the exiles huddled in their tears, staring at home; lace-trimmed gentry, half naked beggars, half starved Welsh and starving Irish. Reaching the prow I stared at the western sky where the iron was pouring, turning but once to wave.

Standing erect, she was, and alone, her shawl held high.

Morfydd no longer now, but Mari standing there.

"Mari," I said. "*Goodbye.*"

Book Three

SONG OF THE EARTH

For Clayton Thatcher

The coming hope, the future day
When Wrong to Right shall bow.
And hearts that have the courage, man,
To make that future now.

Ernest Jones, Chartist poet

# I

I REMEMBER red light that beamed and flashed on the black clouds above Dowlais. Distantly, on the wind, came the bellow of the iron as the furnacemen built up the heat. The iron ran liquid in the moulds, and I could hear it sighing and moaning as they tore it from the rock by fire. The mountains trembled. The old workings by Pont Storehouse echoed thunder to the beat of the drop-hammers. The new rail consignment for Spain belled and clanged in the stackyards. Flinging aside the Dowlais blanket I got out of bed and ran to the window, shivering in the night-shirt my mam had cut down from my brother Ifor last Monday, before she had been taken ill. Toes crinkling to the nip of the boards, I stared into a world of frost, a land made beautiful in hoops of gold and crimson as they tapped the furnace bungs from Pontyclun to Merthyr, and the little rivers of sparkling iron hissed and leaped into shape to last a million years.

Bitter old winter, that one in 1845. Indignant to the frost the skeleton trees crouched in moody scarecrows down Bridge Street, Merthyr, and the mountains beyond were all over white like Church of England wedding-cake, and above the freezing hills of Brecon the moon was sitting on the peaks all bare and beautiful: down the red-black, flickering street the glazed China dogs of Solly Jew raised their poodle sniffs at a world of ice and fire. Daft old world, come to think of it, with the iron up there being boiled to a frizzle and us down here freezing to death.

'What you doing out there, boy?' asked Gwen, from the bed.

A minute back she was out to the wide, her red button nose snuffling over the Dowlais blanket, this being so called since my wicked old Granfer Ben Evan lifted it off a gentry bed twenty years back, and what he was doing around gentry beds is anyone's guess, said Dewi, my brother, he being an expert in this particular line himself.

'What you doing, Bryn?' asked Gwen, now beside me, all podges and bright curls, aged seven, three years younger than me: amazing how the dead will up and walk when bent on other people's business.

'Just looking,' I answered.

'Aye? Well, Dada said no looking for us, just bed.'

'I want to see our mam go,' I said.

'Gran will come in and hell will set alight.'

Setting alight now, it seemed. Dowlais again, burning and flaring on the snow, reflecting off the slate roof of Bethania, the little square cottages with their backs to the Taff withering and shrinking into strange shapes: faintly, above the thunder of the iron, I heard the beating of the accident gong. Gwen stiffened against me, finger up, eyes switching. 'Listen!'

I thought I heard the scream and scurries and for God's sake this and for Christ's sake that: legs one moment, mounds of rags and blood the next. They were always catching it up in Dowlais especially, said my father; as good as the Shambles slaughter-house any day of the week; one chopping block for men, another for animals.

'Any sign of Mam yet?' asked Gwen, and she put her arm around my neck and her hair against my cheek and I was warm and soft inside me for this sister, though you would never have thought us related. For Gwen was all wrist bangles and double chins, and I was inches taller, a herring in boots, said Ifor.

My big brothers Dewi and Ifor were sixteen, and identical twins when it came to womanising, but alike in no other respect. Six feet in socks, Ifor was a tap-room brawler, with a dent in his nose and raging black hair: Dewi, topping him by an inch, was dark, handsome and slim, with a fierce Silurian face: very hot for a revolution, was Dewi, and down with the Queen.

Gwen now, hugging herself, her breath steaming on the window.

'Cold to hell, I am, boy,' said she. 'Back into bed with us, is it, and leave Mam till morning?'

10

'By morning she will be gone,' I answered.

'Eh, dafto! Hobo Churchyard do come in daylight.'

'Coming at midnight, just to cheat us children,' I said.

'O, aye? Hobo is too frit to bury in the dark—too much on his conscience, says Sharon.'

'Listen!' I whispered. 'Is that Sharon crying down the street?'

Sleeping next door but eight was my sister Sharon, we being a bit short of room in by here.

'Not Sharon,' replied Gwen, getting in under the blanket. 'It is Mrs. Willie Shenkins.'

'Crying for our mam?'

'Crying for her Willie,' said Gwen.

Night and day, frost or shine, Mrs. Shenkins sits out the back of her Number Sixteen Bridge Street, Merthyr, hoping for a chill that will send her to her Willie. Big for his age was he and down in the low levels of the Cyfarthfa collieries since the age of six, but they brought him up last winter because his eyes were getting bad, like the ponies. And the agent sent him over to the puddlers, and the glare took him when they were tapping the bungs into the six-ton cauldron, and a puddler pulled him clear. Later, he fell again, head first, so they cooled the cauldron with Willie inside, and gave it a decent burial; Chapel and Church of England, Roman Catholic and Jew, and God be with Willie Shenkins, they sang, as Willie went six feet down, what was left of him, in the Company cauldron.

There was no sound in the room but Mrs. Shenkins sobbing.

'Do not mind her,' said Gwen. 'Not quite a full pound she isn't.'

Often I had seen the women cry in Merthyr, with their sack aprons to their faces, for a death or a drunk, but nobody ever cried in my life like Mrs. Shenkins cried for Willie.

I said, 'Gwen, you there?'

'Aye, man,' said she, her nose over the blanket.

'When Hobo Churchyard comes he will bring two black horses with feathers.'

'Aye, and the preacher and the Inspector of Nuisances.'

'Like when old Jack Curly died, remember?'

'A beautiful death had old Jack Curly,' Gwen said warmly.

11

'They cried and sang all the way to the chapel.'

I said, 'But first they burned the bedding and sprinkled carbolic on the floor of the house. Will the Inspector do that here?' I got into the bed beside her and she was hot and plump like a Christmas chicken, wings and elbows going, crying:

'Eh, hop it! Cold as ice, you are, and chattering to freeze.'

'Black horses do frit me, especially at funerals.'

'White horses for weddings are best,' said Gwen.

I did not speak to her.

'*Whisht*, you, Bryn. Do not cry,' she said.

Footsteps on the landing, open came the door. My father stood with the lantern held high, his shadow on the wall like an ape dancing, and my grandmother said:

'Do not heed them, Mostyn. Look, dead asleep for a grave, they are.'

Hand in hand we lay, Gwen and me, breathing for embalmed corpses.

'Take her, Mostyn,' she repeated.

But I was at the window when Hobo Churchyard came with a cart and a droopy black horse. Ifor and Dewi carried Mam out, and they stood in the snow with their lanterns painting circles of yellow about their feet. Later, the Inspector of Nuisances came and burned the bedding. Nose pressed to the window I watched the black cinders spread where the fire had been: up the stairs came the smell of the carbolic. Gwen said from the bed, 'It do not seem right to put carbolic where our mam has been.'

I was watching the road and the undertaker's cart moving black and squat along the road to Vaynor. Gwen said, 'Has Mam gone, then?'

'Aye.' There were black wheel-ruts in the snow, I remember.

'Come on in, boy.' She held the blanket wide.

Hobo Churchyard had gone. And behind the Castle Dowlais went on fire again, lighting the room with furnace glow.

I bowed my head to the flashing light of the window.

'It will be a good death tomorrow, mind,' said Gwen, 'with singing and crying and plenty to eat.'

# 2

NEXT morning, after my mam had gone, it was as if she had never existed, save that Gran laid her place at table. Otherwise everything was much as usual, with Ifor and Dewi side by side at the bosh, shaving, braces dangling, holding up nose-tips and making faces at the razor. Most mornings I would stand on the chair without a back and look into the mirror they looked into, this being about seven foot up, but no sign of whiskers rooting yet, black, fair or ginger, said Dada. This morning, however, my father said little, being in a chapel-quiet and with pew-dust in his heart, said Gran.

Gorgeous was my gran, but more of her later.

'There is a beautiful day, Mostyn, isn't it?'

Silent he sits, fist on knee.

'Chilly, mind, but beautiful.'

There is no sound but the scur of the razors and the scrape of hobnails on the flags of the kitchen.

'A decent meal when we get back, son, and your slippers by the fire, eh?'

'Dada,' I said, coming down from the bedroom.

'Leave him, Bryn,' whispered Gran.

'You heard Mrs. Ten Benyon has another one developing?' asked Dewi.

'Please do not be indelicate,' said Gran from the hob.

Bacon on the go now, sizzling sweet and brown, the pig playing a large part in our existence, said Dada, servant and master, and no wild flower do smell as beautiful.

'What is indelicate in having a baby?' asked Ifor.

'Indelicate when applied to Mrs. Ten Benyon,' said Gran, 'and the children are listening. Up to table sharp now, for it is a busy day coming.' For head of the house was our gran. They can say what they like about Welshmen, fighting at the drop of a hat and solid in the jaw, but their women run the households. My beautiful sister Sharon came into the kitchen then, she having slept with Mr. and Mrs. Isan Chapel next door but eight, they having a spare room because of a relative now deceased, there being no room in our house for fourteen-year-old sisters with ten-year-old brothers peeping over bed-clothes; and she winked at me as she pulled her chair to the table. Wicked in the eye was she, and Welsh dark, with long black hair in waves on her shoulders to drive the boys mooney in town, like Mrs. Ten Benyon must have looked about half a century back, said Dewi, when the Irish unloaded themselves at Fishguard. Three of them came to Merthyr, one after the other, and they all collected Mrs. Ten Benyon, and in her good time she saw the boots off and the shrouds on all three of them, but they got their own back by landing her with ten boys. 'Eh, dear me,' Mrs. Ten used to say, 'thirteen men I have known in all lengths from six inches to six-feet-six—men, all men, I am, pestered in the breast and loins.'

'There is a slut for you, mind, talking like that,' said Gran, forking the bacon, 'and us decent Chapel people. Fourteenth on the way, is it?'

Prim as a poke-bonnet one moment, scandal very sweet the next, for Gran.

'The new agent Man Arfon been seen in the vicinity, they say,' said Sharon.

My father stirred at the grate. 'Do you think we could have a little more hospitality towards Mrs. Ten Benyon and a little less of the scandal, considering it is a rather special day?' and this put us all quiet since my father was gentle when it came to women labouring in mine or childbirth, never passing one in town without knocking up his hat. I scrambled up to table then but Gran pulled me out of it.

'You been out the back?'

'Not yet.'

'Then out and see to it and back here with hands washed.'

It is astonishing to me how people arrange such matters, me being the best to know the call or not, and, anyway, Gwen was out there all dopey from the bed, and once I opened the door in haste and she came out head first, curled up on my boots and slipped off again without a sigh.

'Hurry up,' and I took my fist to the panel.

'Hop it,' said Gwen.

14

The dawn mist was curling smokey fingers round the back; the old tin bath on the nail crying at being out all night, and drips from the water-spouts freezing teeth in sockets as I broke off an icicle and sucked, waiting for Gwen. All down the wall the colliers and furnace-workers were getting up in shouts and groans, and I saw in the eye of my mind six hundred bare elbows sawing on bread boards and cheese being hunkered for doorsteps and small-beer and ale being poured into flagons for the scourers, rodders and rollers of Cyfartha. Dogs were fighting for breakfast scraps, cats belting each other down alleys, babies shrieking. Hairless and wrinkled, the aged teetered from the beds out of habit or to let a shift-worker in: like Mr. Isan Chapel next door but eight, aged eighty. Blinded by a furnace blow-back, was Mr. Isan Chapel, poor soul, and every morning trying to find his way down the garden path to the little seat that hung over the river, and no help from his bull-dog missus either, she being upper class since collecting third prize for a sampler from Lady Charlotte Guest, and she thought nothing of hammering poor old Isan if he didn't behave. Only five feet high was he, and never got used to the blindness, but wandering, arms out, with no sense of direction, said Dada, and he could even remember Bacon the Pig of Merthyr selling cannon to America in the War of Independence, whatever that might be. Seeing him, I vaulted the garden wall and went to guide him, for I would never forgive myself if he fell in the Taff as he did last autumn, and half the neighbourhood floundering around with ropes and clothes-poles, trying to fish him out until my dada arrived and waded into the river and carried him to the bank.

'Eh dear, you poor little soul,' said my father.

I will always remember him kneeling there with Mr. Isan Chapel held against him. And the circle of faces above them was the dregs of the community, not one of them Welsh; stamping, guffawing, until my father rose, facing them.

'Because you live like animals do you have to act like them?'

Half-drowned was Mr. Isan Chapel.

I said now, steadying him, 'You all right, sir?'

'As right as I will ever be, child, if it wasn't for the

15

indignity,' said he in Welsh, for he came from King Arthur stock up in the beautiful Prescelleys.

I got him on the seat. 'Shut the door, is it, Mr. Chapel?'

Often he left the door open facing the river, which was daft, for the Pont Storehouse urchins would arrive and heave clods at him, trying to hit him off the seat. And there was no point in me showing him respect if he was going to sit there heading off clods.

'Bryn,' called Gran from the back.

'Ay ay!'

'What you up to, then?'

'Helping Mr. Chapel.'

'Good lad. Come now, the bacon is leathering,' she cried, and I was away sharp for the bacon, for if there is anything I cannot stand it is old age and its indignity, and I only helped to make a good impression on Dada: clods it would be from me also, given half a chance.

Cut my throat before I end up as helpless as that.

'A good boy you are, Bryn,' said he, 'helping Mr. Isan Chapel.'


After breakfast, my father said, 'No work today, no school. We are going up to Vaynor, to be with Mam.'

Strange, come to think of it, that our mam should be Church of England, she having the blood of the Cornish tin-miners in a place called Bodmin, while on my father's side the family have been Methodist since Job was a comforter. Up in the room with Gwen I got into Dewi's best home-spun trews cut down, boots to shave in, a shirt front with no arms and tail and a starched collar under my ears. With my hair smoothed down and watered like the mountain fighters I stood rigid because of the creases, waiting for Gran.

'Am I pretty?' asked Gwen, turning in her funeral dress, and I did not spare her a glance, for you can dress a County Cork porker in a crinoline and never make him presentable. I would prefer her seventeen, for girls of seven I do hate, all wriggles and giggles and baby fat, with her black-buttoned boots to her knees and red bows in her long, plaited hair. 'A throw-back, this one,' said my father, 'we are dark and she is

16

fair, her blood coursing from the old Brythonic plains. But she is a Celt, remember—same as you.'

'Bows out,' said Gran, coming up the stairs. 'It is your mam's funeral you are attending, not Michaelmas Fair.' She hooked me closer for inspection. 'Face soaped up, washed behind the ears. Eh, my!' And a great softness sprang into her eyes. 'There is a sight for a dead mam, and your Granfer Ben proud in the stomach to see you so respectable.'

Stuffed and cooked we had this Granfer Ben, for breakfast, dinner and tea.

'Yes, Gran.'

'Be a good boy now, leave the crying to the women.'

'Yes, Gran.'

'And Bryn...'

I turned back to her and she did a queer little sniff and pulled me hard against her. 'Away,' she snapped, heaving me off. 'Are we standing around all day?'

Worth a mention, this gran.

A big-fleshed woman, she was, vigorous in the breast and glorious in the brow, looking seven foot high with her hair piled up on a comb, the same as Queen Victoria, and the best layer-out this side of Brecon. Five sons she bore my wicked old Granfer Ben, every one but my father being taken by the Top Town cholera. On my mother's side, apparently, things came respectable. The worst thing that happened in her branch was when my Uncle Waldo went a semi-tone flat exalting every valley in the public hall in Dowlais in 1835, and within a week he was emigrated to North America on the end of a boot, the Welsh being a trifle sensitive when it comes to disrupting Handel. Aye, practically gentry on my mother's side, said Gran, the men collecting shiners through turning the other cheek to the bruisers, which is a bloody stupid thing to do in Dowlais at the best of times, said Ifor. Three times to church every Sunday, the men in top hats and frock coats, the women in bonnets and crinolines with bowed good mornings left and right and alcohol and fisticuffs a long way down their list, and fornication something that was practised in London only, mainly Whitechapel.

'But,' said Gran that talkative day, 'your people on my side

17

of the family do not stand deep examination.' And she told of
Granfer Ben who was large in the copper-works band down
the Vale of Neath and singing the *Messiah*, sounding the
trumpet double bass while shaving with the cut-throat, being
glorious in the lower registers. Handsome devil, apparently,
handy with the mountain fighters and spare-time on the
females.

'But best of all with the Penny Gaffs on Fair Day?' cried
Sharon.

'Played in the company of Siddons, give him credit,' said
Dada, 'and under Macready of the Swansea theatre!' and he
cried, taking off Granfer Ben, ' "For beauty, starv'd with her
severity, cuts beauty off from all posterity. She is too fair, too
wise, wisely too fair to merit bliss by making me despair." '

'Romeo and Juliet!' shrieked Sharon, who was strong for the
Penny Gaffs and people like Taliesen the Poet who had long
hair, and I wouldn't trust him with a maiden aunt as far as I
could throw him, let alone the likes of Sharon.

Most artistic, my family—Dada and Sharon mainly, while
Dewi, Ifor and me were more bent on thick ears and ale and
saw-dust. Gran said:

'Eh, grief, he was a born actor—this Shakespeare chap was
clay in his hands, and very keen on the opposite sex—did my
best, but no woman on earth could suffice him. And when
Brigham Young's people came to the Top Towns on speculation, he was off to Salt Lake City and the Latter Day Saints.
No sight nor sound of him since—must have died of women, I
reckon.'

'There are worse ways of dying,' said Dewi, and I saw my
father give him a queer old look and a sigh.

'Oh, he must have been exciting, exciting!' cried Sharon,
and she picked a piece of herring out of Gran's pan and sucked
it reflectively, her actress eyes, large in her high-boned face,
going dreamy in the lamplight.

Excellent with the herrings was my gran, doing acres of
them in the big, black pan on the shining, black-leaded grate;
all sizzling and sending up a silver perfume, glad to be out of
that murky old Baglan Bay and into the bellies of Mostyn
Evan and fighters. Ach, I do love the nights of the herrings,

with Sharon at the ironing and Gwen on the samplers and Gran kneeling by the hob with the big wooden spoon out of the wash-tub.

'Damned old reprobate he do sound to me,' observed Ifor, who, on times, could be solid marble between the ears.

'Who, now?' asked Gran, looking up from the herrings.

'Granfer Ben,' said Ifor, all unsuspecting, and I saw my father open the *Cambrian* and get well down behind it, always a sign of trouble afoot.

'As God is my judge, I'll not be responsible,' said Gran, putting her spoon under Ifor's nose. 'You sit there passing lewd remarks . . .'

'But, Gran . . . !'

'Don't you gran me, you useless big oaf, scandalising your own grandfather,' which sounded Irish, and was, for Gran always went Limerick when under deep provocation.

'Sorry, Gran,' cried Ifor, backing off.

'And you big louts also—you hear me?'

'Oh, yes, Gran!' Dewi and I shouted in chorus.

'No finer man than your Granfer Ben walked in twin boots, and there's no apology for a man here fit to clean them!'

'Yes, Gran,' we all said, including Sharon and Gwen, and my dada stirred at the fire, took out his pipe, and grumbled:

'Smitten with the tongues of angels, we are. Why the hell we have to have Granfer Ben every time we have herrings do beat me,' and he rose. 'We will wash all tears from eyes. My father, Ben Evan, was the finest Falstaff in the Swansea theatre, and my mother, Ceinwen Evan, is the best cook in Christendom. All wounds healed. Up to the table sharp, sharp, sharp!'

And now we were off to the funeral.

'Bryn, Gwen, Gran!' called my father from the bottom of the stairs. 'It is half past ten and we are off directly.'

'Coming, Mostyn,' Gran called back, and took our hands in hers, saying, 'No tears, remember. Your dada is dying inside and is covering it with smiles. I will not have him brought down, you hear me?' She swallowed hard and cried deep in her throat. 'You hear me, children?'

19

'Yes, Gran,' we said, hand in hand now.

And she led the way down to the pony and trap.

She could have been going to a wedding for all the pomp and size of her, and when she stepped on the back step of the trap the pony up in the shafts, but we did not giggle, we did not even speak.

This is living on the tip of tears, on the breath between grief and laughter.

But often, I believe, Gran cried for Granfer Ben.

Some mornings, when she came down, her face was pale and proud and riven with unshed tears, and her lips were as red as cherries as if she had been kissed in sleep.

Aye, well, let me gabble on about grans and granfers and funeral suits and herrings and Latter Day Saints, for while I am doing this I am not thinking about my mother.

And forget the day in November when we put her six feet down in Vaynor.


# 3


COME spring, I was still at school on Tramroadside, for although most children were down the mines before the age of ten, my father reckoned that I was a bit of a scholar and ought to be given a chance. So it was one and sixpence a week with me and down to the private school run by Miss Bronwen Rees of Abergavenny and become a professor in an American university.

I do love the spring and her bright colours, and the lambs doing cart-wheels down in Fair Meadow, which is what they called it until the ironmasters got hold of it and plundered and spoiled it.

But up above Vaynor the country was sweet and green, and there I would go most Sundays after Chapel and lie on my ear on the earth and listen to its music. For the earth speaks, says my teacher: the stones talk to the clay, the loam and pebbles give their opinion. For what is earth, says she, except the tongues of men gone to dust?

In love, me.

In love with Miss Bronwen Rees.

'Hurry!' cried Gwen, 'we are late!' And away down Bridge Street she went, fair hair flying, very keen, though she was not too special between the ears and twice two are seven.

'Good morning, Bryn!'

''Morning, Mr. Waldo Phillips.'

'Another scholar for Miss Bronwen Rees, is it?' This from Mrs. Ten Benyon hanging out of her top window, very flourishing, as ladies are when they are making babies.

'Ay ay, Mrs. Ten!' Very fond of me was Mrs. Ten since I had been giving private lessons after school to her Owain and Cynfor; taking in Granfer Ben's books and reading aloud to the family about how point five is half of one and the Union Jack is the colour of blood and if you put down a shilling the change out of three pints is ninepence at the New Inn but watch it at the Vaughan in Neath. And I reckon my granfer was the only drover in Wales who knew about places like Pola and Treviso and Roman generals like Ostorius Scapula.

'Here are more of his books,' my father used to say. 'Learn, Bryn, learn. A scholar is worth ten labourers—anyone like me can lead a barge-horse.'

Spelling and making up poetry I am good at, but arithmetic, said my brother Ifor, who couldn't count up to fifty, is mainly learned to help the masters make a fatter profit. Dewi, also, was dead against anybody making a profit, and he spent all his spare time reading papers by a chap called Engels and back copies of *The Trumpet of Wales* and pamphlets by William Lovett and Feargus O'Connor. And my gran used to get her fists up and shout about the flames of Hell and disbelief in God; though why this Engels boy and God should disagree on anything beat me, for both are bent on feeding the hungry, which was more than the masters were about this time on The Top.

Down Bridge Street after Gwen now, weaving through the gangs of colliers coming from the levels on the old canal, lovely with their noise and banter, many being Irish from the famine ships of Fishguard, and in rags: women were out on their doorsteps, scrubbing their little half-circles of purity into the world; others brooming away the night-soil tippling down the gutters, for there was no place in Bridge Street for it save fling it out of the window, and the whiff of it curled your nose first thing in the morning. In ranks five abreast went the colliers on shift, cold tea under their arms, picks and shovels on their shoulders, and the language they were raising must have stripped the paint off the door of Bethania half a mile south. Into their ranks I slipped, stretching my thighs to keep up with them.

'*Bore da' chwi*, Evan, lad!'

' 'Morning, Mr. Shonko!'

'Off to school, is it?'

'Ay, man!'

'Make the most of it before old Crawshay gets hold of you.'

'Yes, thank you, Mr. Shonko.'

'That lovely sister of yours still activating?'

'Sad for your mam I am, my son,' said Mr. Noah Morgan.

There was Afron Shavings, the carpenter, Bili Jones and Wil Shout, the old pack-horser, all down Crawshay's canal levels, and Dai Central Eating with one tooth in his head: very partial to my mother, was Dai, in the Sunday School she took each week in the old Bethania, and I loved them all with their backslaps and insults.

I ran like a hare for the next half mile, through Pontmorlais, up to the school door: turn the handle; stand there gasping.

See her standing there in beauty, Miss Bronwen Rees of Abergavenny.

'Good morning, Miss Rees.'

'Good morning, Bryn Evan.'

Although she was Welsh speaking, she never spoke Welsh. Her grandfather, it seemed, though Welsh in name, was born fifty yards over the Hereford border, and she had an uncle living in London who was a quarter English, on his mother's side. Besides, in fifty years Welsh will be a foreign language, said she, so anbody talking it in by here I will hit to Cyfarthfa and back return journey.

But Welsh or English, one day I will set up house with Miss

Bronwen Rees. I will build this house four square to the wind; boarded floors I will give it, two rooms up, two down. And I will make a track from the mail-coach road through the Beacons, with flowers either side and more around the door. Nine boys and one girl I will fetch from Miss Bronwen Rees, God willing.

'Take your seat, please, Bryn Evan. Do not stand there staring.'

There is a voice to drive the chaps demented.

I took my place at the back with the scholars—people like Joey Randy whose da took the big stallion once a week up to Penyard, behind Cyfarthfa, and collected six guineas, and living on immoral earnings as plain as your face, said Dewi. There was Owen Bach, spit and image of the Wild Welshman who tamed the mad bulls down the Vale of Neath, and Davie Half-Moon who was bats round the chimney, like his poor old mam and dad. Mick O'Shea of Connemara was there, thicker in the mouth than a Chinese, and girls, too, though none worth a mention, our Gwen being the best in sight with her seven teeth missing in front, and ghastly when smiling. For me, indeed, there was only one female there—Miss Bronwen Rees.

Sit with your chin on your hands and watch from the back of the class.

Small, she was, large at the top and small at the bottom, and with a fine dignity. Black was her hair, flowing either side of her face in waves of mystery. And her face I have seen but once before when my father took me fishing down to Giant's Grave. Calm and pure was that face in the shop window. The Madonna, Dada explained, but did not tell more, though I recall that she had a baby in her arms and her red heart outside her dress, but it was her eyes.

It was her eyes.

'Bryn Evan, kindly pay attention.'

'Yes, ma'am.'

Dewi, who kept a list of all the useful females, had her age down as seventeen, my Bronwen. This would make her twenty-two when I was sixteen, the marrying age, and I have heard of wives much older. Take Mrs. Alfo Morgan, for instance—she took her Alfo to the altar on the day he was thirty, and she was knocking sixty, though both were Church of England, and any damn thing can happen in that lot, said Gran. But very happy, these two, with good morning kisses on the doorstep when Alfo left for mule-skinning at the tannery, and good evening kisses when he came home at night. And after a good beef dinner they would kiss good night and Alfo would slip down to the Castle Inn for a moonlight with Rosie Carey, the bar-maid, and often enough come home at dawn. 'Suits me,' Mrs. Alfo Morgan used to say, 'let Rosie begin where I leave off—she gets Alfo and I get the wages.' Not such a fool as she looks, says Gran.

But this, as my father said, is a wreck of a marriage, and I had planned it more convenient for me and Miss Bronwen Rees of Abergavenny.

'You listening, Bryn Evan?'

'Yes, ma'am.'

Gwynedd and Gwent it was again this morning. Miss Rees always started the day with some pathetic yarn before getting down to the horrible business of twice two are twenty-six. For some ten days now we had been on this yarn about Gwynedd and Gwent, a pair of twins, girl and boy, and how they got lost in a forest, according to Gwen, for, to be truthful, I never heard a thing when my Bronwen was speaking. Apparently, they were taken by a witch to a gingerbread house which had a sugar chimney and in bed there was a dog dressed up as a gran. I never really got the hang of this Gwynedd and Gwent pair, because every time my Bronwen mentioned them Gwen would swing her pig-tails in the front row and grin horribly with no teeth, and this would set me bored and heaving, for anything that took my mind off Bronwen was unwelcome.

'Bryn Evan, are you ill?'

I gripped my hands in my lap. 'No, ma'am.'

'You are making some astonishing expressions—you realise this?'

'No, ma'am.'

Very educated, she was, with a voice of gold, and sometimes, although she said she was English, she was really Welsh inside, for she'd get the pastor's *hwyl* up her red dress and wave her arms about, going to the window to face the sun with tears glittering in her eyes, which is perfectly understandable, for if you've got a heart as large as Miss Bronwen Rees you'd very likely be affected by beautiful children such as this Gwynedd and Gwent getting lost in a forest with dogs and witches. I used to weep with her, I remember, fist on the desk, the tears running hot on my cheeks.

'Is there something wrong with me, Bryn Evan?' She stood back, examining herself.

'No, ma'am.'

'Then why are you staring?'

'Not staring, ma'am.'

'What was I talking about?'

'Pardon, ma'am.'

'I was talking about Gwynedd and Gwent, wasn't I?'

'Yes, ma'am.'

'Right, you. If Dyfed is Pembrokeshire and Brychain is Brecknock, what parts of Wales are the old Welsh kingdoms of Gwynedd and Gwent?'

Well.

Here is a terrible bloody situation.

'Stand up when I speak to you, Bryn Evan.'

Sweating cobs, I stood, and I heard Billie Softo giggle next to Gwen and saw her thump him, for though I treated her rough, she would die for me, our Gwen.

'Very well,' said my Bronwen. 'I suspected that you were not listening at all, so now please tell me what you know about Gwent and Gwynedd.'

I began to shiver. Accusing faces were turned to mine. Distantly, I heard the thunder of Cyfarthfa Works: through the single window streamed a shaft of golden light. I thought: O, sun, O, *sun*!

'I am waiting, Bryn Evan.'

And out it came, in a stuttering rush of words; of dogs and witches and a gran; of sugar chimneys and a door of honeycomb, and Miss Rees listened, her face stricken.

I closed my eyes to the perfume of her as she drew nearer.

Eh, dear me, females smell beautiful.

Gwen smells of stew, the stains being on her pinafore: Sharon smells of spices. My gran has a plum-pudding smell,

25

and of lavender from the little blue bags she sews into the lining of her cloak. But the best smell of all comes from my mother, this being a cowslip smell, as if she had been sitting all day in their fields above Merthyr, and made chains of them and put them in her hair. And so did Miss Bronwen Rees smell good that day as she stood beside me tapping my desk with her ruler: this, as I say, is an April smell and comes with walking hand in hand with your mother.

'Oh, Bryn, look! Beautiful, they are. Cowslip time is best of all—could the whole world be as pure and lovely!' said the ghost of my mother.

'Talking I am to you, Bryn Evan, remember!' said Bronwen.

'Take my hand and we will run,' cried my mother. 'We will go from this dirty old place down to the forest of Rheola. You ever seen the Vale in cowslip time?'

'I am asking you for the last time, Bryn Evan. Bryn *ap* Mostyn, indeed! The *ap* is not acceptable to English law since the Act of Union in 1536, and you know it. Dogs and witches and grans, indeed! Sugar chimneys and doors of honeycomb, indeed! I will blutty teach you to stare at me!'

'*Cariad Anwyl!*' cried my mother. 'Oh, my precious, what a beautiful day!'

'Take that, and that, you blutty little Taff!' cried Bronwen.

Distantly, through the thumping pain of the ruler, I heard Gwen shrieking. Very surprising, it is, to be thumped by your mam in a cowslip field after all that loving.

We went home hand in hand that day, Gwen and me, made whole by the same pain; she having collected a couple that were meant for me, and stripes on her little fat behind that sent Gran raving, fists clenched, and it took Dewi and Ifor to drag her back from the door.

'Now, now, my lovely,' said my father, smoothing her, 'the children are not decapitated. I will have a word with Miss Rees this evening after Chapel, see.'

'By God, Mostyn, if she lays hands on these children again... !'

'Mind, she didn't really mean it, Gran,' I said.

'Didn't really mean it! Look at your sister's bottom,' and she up-ended Gwen to show me.

'Never mind hers, look at his,' said Dewi. 'Like a Carmarthen slaughter-house. What was she hitting you with, man, pig iron?'

Gran said, 'Mostyn, you will see her tonight, for if I go, as God is my judge...'

'Shall I slip down, Dada?' asked Dewi, innocently.

'Let the punishment fit the crime,' said my father, 'she has not committed murder. Ointment on bottoms and enough hatred for today—I will visit Miss Bronwen Rees. Removal of the *ap*, indeed! I will give her 1536 and the English Act of Union.'

I was glad he didn't go.

Ridiculous, come to think of it—a daft old pair like Gwynedd and Gwent coming between me and Miss Bronwen Rees of Abergavenny.

# 4

ABOUT this time, when I was eleven, the workers were trying to form a decent Union, and were coming pretty skinny with anyone who would not help them to do this, such as belting into anyone who decided to work on when the Union said to stop. New Benefit Clubs, which were the beginnings of the movement, were springing up left and right in Merthyr about this time, and since the intention of the Union was to get a rise in wages, masters like Crawshay and others naturally took exception to the idea, and formed a Union of Masters themselves. Thereafter, anyone suggesting a shilling a week extra was naturally assisted out of the job by the boot, and anyone who suggested forming a Union of Workers was accused of a crime against humanity. Generally, the way this was stopped was by sending round a list of names called a blacklist of trouble-makers, and this, I heard say, was perfectly understandable. For higher wages, said the masters, only resulted in drunkenness and debauchery and idleness, and this was against the law of God. So much against the law of God was this that pulpit preachers, Chapel and Church of England, were slipped a couple of sovereigns to condemn the Unionists from the Big Seat, and special gates of Hell were erected for any man going in the same direction as the Tolpuddle Martyrs, for this lot, apparently, were absolute sods. This scared the workers, and many pulled the forelock in front of Cyfarthfa Castle and Dowlais-Manor, hoping the masters would raise them a penny an hour, but all they succeeded in getting was a cut of five shillings a week since the price of iron had gone down a week last Sunday. Right, you, said the Union: we will make you more scared of us than you are of the masters, so they invented the Scotch Cattle. These were very special Unionists who dressed themselves up in skins and put cowhorns on their heads, and roamed the mountains after dark lowing and bellowing and visiting the homes of scabs and blacklegs and breaking their fingers and burning their furniture. I remember lying in bed with sweating dreams of my beloved Bronwen skirts up and rushing over Hirwain Common with about five hundred Bulls after her shouting improper suggestions, but mostly they confined themselves to putting the boot into simpering workers.

'It is a scandal that men should have to resort to such intimidation,' said my father.

'It is a scandal that they cannot get decent wages without having to beg or fight,' said Dewi.

'Hush now,' said Gran, 'there's a good boy.'

Dewi was always getting hot under the collar about now, talking about the greed of the employers and places like Liverpool and Bristol having been built on the slave trade by clergymen wearing out their knees on hassocks and the bishops set up in six-course dinners in their palaces while the children of the factories starved. But it was mostly the slave trade that got him agitated, though this was finished, said my father: talking about black brothers and white bastards and places like India being built on blood, and if he had his way he would nip the tabs off every collar back and front and tie bombs on the carriage of Queen Victoria, though none of this was her fault personally, apparently, for the wool was being pulled over her eyes.

Sharon said at her book of Shakespeare, ' "So I told him, my lord; and I said I heard your Grace say so: and, my lord, he speaks most vilely of you, like a foul-mouthed man he is, and he said he would cudgel you." ' She looked up. 'If it is not Queen Victoria's fault, then why tie bombs on her?'

'Because she is a symbol, stupid,' replied Dewi, scowling.

'What is a symbol?' asked Ifor, lying face down on the horse-hair sofa, salt-pickling his fists, for the railway navigators were in the district again, and anything under six inch rocks they took on the chin without so much as a blink.

Gran said, 'Praise her on the harps and cymbals, is it?' and she went on peeling her spuds.

'Oh, God,' exclaimed my father.

Dewi said earnestly, 'It is political, Gran—nothing to do with music.'

'Religion I am talking, mind,' said she.

'Then you are the only one,' said Dada.

'Oh, aye?' Up with her then, sparring at the bosh. 'But I am the only one talking decent! The house is full of fist-picklers and revolutionaries, and I will praise who I like on the harps and cymbals without asking anyone in by here.'

Dewi said, bitterly, 'And do not talk to me about religion. They shout the cause of the masters in the name of God, they bless anything they can get their hands upon for an extra half a sovereign. That Parson Williams—he hands out the rights of God's little creatures and goes rook-shooting every Sunday morning after the service, the swine.'

'Aye, but he is Church of England,' said Gran warmly, and my father groaned aloud, saying:

'We started off with the Scotch Cattle and the Unions. How the hell we have got into harps, cymbals and rook-shooting I do not know. I'm trying to read the paper—do you think we might have some peace?'

Ifor said, 'Up at Nanty, day 'fore last, a mule kicked a packer and knocked him dead. So the drovers loaded it and loaded it, until they broke its back.'

'Oh, Christ,' whispered Dewi, 'it is nothing but cruelty, cruelty. . . .'

Bang, bang on the back, and I nearly fainted with fright. Gwen opened the door and Pietro Bianca stood there, five foot two of teeth, hair and burning eyes. Mexican by nationality, anarchist by nature was Pietro, and he was only here because of my father's free-thinking. I am having no rules and regulations in this house, he used to say: each to his own, each to his whim: free expression do mould the nobler characters. Dewi leaped up, crying:

'Come in, come in, Pietro, boy!'

'Long live Mexico!'

'Long live Santa Anna!' cried Dewi.

'Death to President Polk,' said Sharon, at her Shakespeare. And Gran said:

'Take Pietro down to the cellar, Dewi, there's a good boy, and try to keep the bangs within reasonable limits.'

'The bomb he made last Tuesday brought the bedroom ceiling down,' said Dada. 'And do not shoot up, man: there are already two holes in the kitchen table.'

'Will you sing for us again tonight, Pietro?' begged Gwen, for when Pietro got going on his mandolin it was as good as any Welsh harp: and he would sit by the grate with tears on his face, singing patriotic songs about what the bloody Americans were up to in his beloved Mexico, and how Santa Anna, his national hero, would hit hell out of the savage invader, while he, Pietro Bianca of Veracruz, would personally attend to the barbaric American President Polk.

Strange brothers I had, come to think of it. There was Dewi the poet, the revolutionary; tall, lean and calm. There was Ifor, all fifteen stones of him, no sooner the word than the blow, his eyes brooding malevolence for anything six foot in boots. And romancers and hard drinkers, both; fighters both, their shirts open in winter frost, chests sprouting black hair, and my father kept them on a leash like chained tigers. Keep these two apart until Gran or I come, he used to say. Hit them with the nearest thing handy, but keep them apart in the name of God.

But Dewi was his cross. And what the devil Pietro Bianca

was doing in Merthyr at a time like this was beyond my father's comprehension, though there are some queer old folks in the place about now. He will lead Dewi to the gallows.

'Your fault, mind,' Gran used to say. 'Since we had the free-thinking we have had to drag them to Bethania, and the house is full of Shakespeare, pugilists and revolutionaries—I don't hold with it, Mostyn!'

For my part it amazed me how Pietro used to turn up on the nights we had the stew.

No women, I think, should be loved for mere beauty, for you can pick that up at sixpence a time. By stew they should be judged, and because of stew, married. Lovely, the smells a good cook can bring to a house, and I personally do not mind if Irish stew lingers a while, though Gran acted very strange over this—leaping from the table the moment the meal was finished, throwing open doors and windows and beating it out with swipes of a rag. Stew is all right in its place, said she—on the hob or in the stomach, but I am not having it sitting around the house for days after.

'This stew I smell all the way from here to Old Berhania,' cried Pietro.

'That means he wants some more,' rumbled Ifor.

'It is Irish stew made by a Welsh cook, and she is wonderful!' And he leaped from the table and embraced Gran, smacking her a kiss on both cheeks. 'This is the most wonderful cook from Nueces to Grand River!'

'Oh, go on with you, Pietro,' said Gran, very pretty with her. 'Another helping for Bryn, is it? Get plenty under your belt, boy—first day at work tomorrow.'

I will always remember that year of 1846, because this was the year I began work with Dada and the twins up on the Old Cyfarthfa.

Coal was in our hearts, for we came of a long line of coal, but we Evan family were never colliers: it was pack-mules and rafting in the old days, it was barging and flat-boats now, yet there was also sunshine in our bodies, for our Granfer Ben was born on Welsh wool down Carmarthen way, at Llanstephan by the sea, and was soft with the little lambs come

31

spring, with milking and shearing with his dad, and growing a bit of wheat till the gentry cheated them of their land by the act of enclosures, and sent them packing on a donkey. Down to the Cynon Valley they came and settled there as porthmen, which is the trade of drover, and every summer they would work the Welsh fairs and gather the cattle in batches, driving them across the mountains as far as the borders of Kent.

'Big men, remember,' said my father, 'working with people like Richards the Drover, and you can see his grave today in Aberdare Old Churchyard.'

'*Whee!*' Sharon sighed, for Richards the Drover was more important in the Merthyr valley than Queen Victoria.

'And your Granfer Ben was a specialist, too,' said Dada, warming to his pipe, 'and he held court at Abercynon Basin, shoeing the cattle for the long marches to England, and tightening the leather pads on the geese.'

'Aye?' I was breathless, hypnotised by the romance of my Granfer Ben.

'Pads I have seen on chickens walking over Mexico,' said Pietro Bianca.

'Aye,' said Dada. 'But geese are cunning old things, preferring to laze away their lives to walking three hundred miles into England, and they used to knock off their pads ten miles out so your granfer had to carry them. . . .'

The wind is doing his tonic-solfa in the eaves; a night-owl is shrieking from the hills of the Beacons. Red the firelight flickering on my father's face.

'. . . a couple of geese he could manage, but when he was fifty miles out and eight up and couldn't be seen for beaks and feathers, your Granfer Ben started getting ideas.'

'Necessity being the mother of invention,' said Gran.

'Aye, so he warmed pitch on the march and drove the geese through it on the hop, and then, adding insult to injury, he chased them through a bourne of sand, and when they came out they were soled and heeled.'

'Wonderful!' we all cried.

'Marvellous!' shouted Pietro.

'Thereafter, not a lot of notice was taken of geese limping on the march to England, and any important protests were assisted along by Granfer's boot. Very famous he became between the Old Bridge and Castle Inn, Abercynon, and Swansea, it being said that you could hear his army of geese coming a mile off, their pitch boots clattering on the flinted road, playing hell to each other about drovers in general and your Granfer Ben in particular.'

'It do take a man and a half, mind,' said Gran, 'to get the upper hand of geese—are they the same in Mexico?'

'They are the same, but bigger in Mexico,' said Pietro.

'Everything is bigger in Mexico,' said Ifor. 'And then?'

My father continued, 'But when the wit is out the ale is in, and what with fighting for right of way on the mountains—which was the habit of the old drovers—and stopping at every mountain inn between here and the city of London, you great-granfer became less than normal, and died. Alone, your Granfer Ben landed in Dowlais, in coal.'

'Down at the Starvo, and he worked deep,' whispered Gran, reflectively.

'Aye, a dirty old mine was the Starvo,' said Dada. 'You remember Richard Griffiths, who owned it?'

'I do,' answered Gran, 'since my mam scrubbed for him. Took a thousand pounds off old Sam Homfray while we were starving in Hollybush Level—a thousand pounds, mark me, on the turn of a card.'

'You should have a revolution!' cried Pietro.

'We have had a revolution,' said my father, 'and it has been crushed. We have had our riot of bread or blood, and that was also crushed—as you will be crushed in Mexico, Pietro Bianca.'

'Never!'

'It sings the same tune, Pietro—in Merthyr or Veracruz: the weak go to the wall, the strong flourish. They own too much, their power is too great for us, they are backed by the Church and guns. We had our Frost, you have your Santa Anna—a hundred years from now their names and movements will be dead.'

'Never, never! Mexico will come through the fire, Mexico will rise again!'

'Give him some more stew,' said Ifor.

33

They spoke more, but I did not hear them, for I was sick in my stomach in the face of Pietro's pride of race, and his rejection. I left them to their reflections, I remember, and went out the back, and the stars were like little lamps in the redness of iron-making, with Pontyclun and Penydarren mushrooming with light as the cauldrons were stirred. The soil of the garden trembled beneath my feet. Queer, I think, is talk of coal, for it reaches out fingers of rags and bones. And I thought, standing there, that below me gaped the caverns of the past, and in these lonely places lay the bones of men, women and children long dead, as one with coal: in darkness, in the rat-runs, in the metallic plonks of dripping water; in the Cyfarthfa levels in a feast of greed. The door opened behind me and the kitchen light cut the back with a yellow sword. My father said:

'The revolutions are dead for now, Bryn—remember this. One day it will come on the flood of the world; but the petty fights, the squabbles, the thousand dead are as nothing, and greater than this will not come in your time, or your son's, or his son's. Work, I say, forget the revolutions.'

'In coal, Dada?'

Square and handsome was his face in that strange, rosy light.

'Coal is in our blood, Bryn. Coal is in your heart from the day Granfer went down the Starvo, and to the fourth generation it do put the strain. Bed now, is it? Leave the coal to granfers.'

# 5

ALTHOUGH the Old Canal at Cyfarthfa went out of general use some years back, my family had been employed there as drainers and pulling an occasional tub-boat through it with slack coal from the tips. But the night before I was due to start work with Crawshay he transferred my father and brothers to the big Glamorgan Canal running from Merthyr to Cardiff.

'We start as hauliers, Bryn, and we end as contractor—you wait!'

Out at first light and on to the cobbles with us, Mostyn Evan and three sons, and we went down the murky street with our hobnails hitting sparks off the kerbs of Bridge Street. Boots out we went, in a barge-man silence, with mouse-trap tins under our arms and Gran's oatmeal inside us, and enough to freeze you solid as we went past Thomas Street and over the Iron Bridge by the ironworks for a last haul on a tethered tub-boat and take him down to the Dynefor Arms. This done, we collected Nell, our Cyfarthfa mule, and took her down to Fishpond and the head of the canal, for there was a big consignment of rails going down to Abercynon, and this was us—special delivery.

The wharf was thronged with ragged Irish; men and women just come in from Fishguard with droves of children, and now waiting for casual labour on the wharf loading rails, and not enough strength in twenty of them to raise a ten foot length, poor souls. Still as dark as winter curtains as we pushed a path through the hungry Irish and a voice boomed from the darkness in Welsh:

'Any Taffs by here?'

'Aye!'

Mr. Ephraim Davies we found, the agent, writing on a box. Excellent, this agent, not to compare with Man Arfon, his sub-agent, who was an unborn bastard when it came to the poor Irish.

'Mostyn Evan and three sons,' said my father.

'*Diawch!* Breeding, are you? For now, is it?'

'Three and a half,' said Dewi, pushing me up, and I stood level with belts and stomachs, seeing above me ringed the starving faces of the Irish, pinched and pale in the first streaks of dawn.

'Name?'

'Bryn Evan.'

'There's a lovely old Welsh name. Age?'

'Eleven, sir.'

'Do not call me that, young man—reserve it for the English. Address?'

35

'Fifteen Bridge Street, Merthyr.'

'Now there is a select community. Educated, I expect?'

'He is the scholar of the family, Dewi excepted,' said Dada. 'Miss Bronwen Rees, and six-inch stripes on his rear to prove it went in.'

'Nothing like it,' said Mr. Davies. 'And I could do with a bit of education from her myself, if I could manage it. Three-pence a week extra for reading, writing and arithmetic, thank God for generous employers. Hauling, is it, Mostyn?'

'We will teach him the run of it, Ephraim,' said Dada. 'This time tomorrow he will have the hang of the mule.'

'Three and threepence a week if he runs it, if not—out! By God, here is another giant of industry to stick it up the workers,' and he swept me in with thick arms, shouting, 'Welsh, any more Welsh?'

'Irish, mister!'

'In the name of the Holy Mother, man, get us in!'

'Away!' roared Ephraim, arms folded.

They pressed about him in their rags, they held their shivering babies to his eyes, they begged, pleaded. Ephraim cried:

'And would you employ the starving Welsh in Ireland, man?'

'All one nation—Celts.' This from a skinny Irishman, his head black curls, and I pitied him. 'Not bloody English, mind—*Irish*.'

'Then give me English if I am to sink to damned Irish. Who do you think you are, you people—brothers and sisters?'

'Aye, under God.'

They pulled at his sleeves; a woman knelt before him. A young girl came up, her dress ragged; about Sharon's age, and still beautiful under the hunger.

'Take her for wages. We starve, man, we starve!'

Ephraim Davies bowed his head. 'Go and beg of Crawshay, do not beg of me.'

'You damned Welsh swine!'

'And do not blame me—do not even blame Crawshay, you stupid fools. You should have thought of this before you left Ireland!' He stood on the box, crying, 'Welsh, any more

36

Welsh out there?' and they raised before him a forest of arms.

'Man in Heaven,' said my father, and pushed me on. 'Never have I seen so many.'

'It is the new famine, God help them,' said Dewi.

'They would take the bread from our mouths,' whispered Ifor.

'They'd need a ten pound hammer to get at yours,' said Dewi.

They eyed each other, like dogs hackled for fighting.

It was the same in most families these days: one side cursing the agents for keeping the Irish out, the other cursing Crawshay for bringing the Irish in. Like a flood they were pouring into the Top Towns with their crucifixes and holy water, their lovely little Madonnas propped up in the little square windows, and bleeding hearts were ten a penny between here and Pontypool: their glorious women of the long black hair and peaches and cream, if fed; or little scrags of humans burned out by men and hunger before they were twenty. But work, mind—grant them that—work till they drop, and for a crust, not money, and this was the trouble, for they undercut the Welsh wages. But once they got a sovereign or three in their belts they were mad sods for the ale-houses and the fighting. And since the Welsh were not backward in this re-spect, either, it was the fists and boots on Saturday nights, especially after the six-week-pay, with Welsh scum this and Irish bastard that and Chapel botherers here and Popish swines there, though it was the women, any nationality, who usually got the thin end of it. Blame not the starving Irish, or the poor little harlots on the doorsteps of Chinatown, said my father: blame the masters for allowing such conditions to exist—blame them for bringing in the walking ballast that will work till its stomach is lying on its back-bone; blame Guest for the cholera and Charlotte for no decent water supply; blame Hill of Plymouth for his belief in upright living while children withered and died on his porch; blame the iron-masters of Penydarren and Pontyclun, the Butes of Aberdare, the owners of Mountain Ash, Hafod, Dinas and Pontypridd— blame the whole rotten lot of them from north to south and east to west of Glamorgan and Monmouthshire who came to Wales for easy pickings and bulbous profits: and blame the Welsh masters also, said Dewi, for we are not blameless.

As we left the Irish on that first day of work I saw an Irish boy standing on a tump, watching me as we passed: thin as a Handel lute, he was, and his arms, bare to the shoulder, were blue with cold. There was only me and him in the world just then, and to cheer him I smiled and gave him a wink. For answer he drew himself up and the pride burned fierce in his eyes. His lips moved.

'Welsh bastard,' he said.

No matter, for I would rather be a bastard than hungry, and it was away with me, Dada and the twins to the wharf where the barges were waiting, their giant snouts biting into the grey, winter dawn. All around us the rails for Spain were tolling and clanging as the levers got under them: bedlam here, with men and women stripped to the waist in the frost, rushing overmen yelling orders, mules neighing under the whips and women arguing, fists up, like an Irish Parliament, everybody talking and nobody listening.

'Yours, Bryn,' shouted my father, and tossed me the mule's traces, and I had no sooner got them than she rounds with her rear and comes hooves up, trying to catch me a fourpenny one, so I slammed her one in the chops to quieten her and brought my knee up into her belly, and at this she grinned, as mules do, wagged her head and came after me like a spring lamb.

'That is better,' I said.

Jed Donkey came next, he being billeted with a hundred other donkeys, and I went round the stamping ends, looking for him, and found him instantly, which wasn't difficult since Dewi always insisted in plaiting the tail of the donkey himself with red, white and blue ribbon, which, if you stop to reflect, is the colour of the Union Jack. Getting in beside him I gave him the elbow to start with, and he gave me a look to kill since I smelled of work, and work was something this particular Jed had never been guilty of. Little wonder that this pair went broody when Dewi was around, with him nuzzling them and feeding them sugar, and them saving hind-leg belts for any-

38

thing in trews who happened to be passing, including Dada.

'Get over, you swine,' I said, and I had him out in the dawn before he knew what day it was. Harness them up, Nell and Jed Donkey, unwind the thews for barge-towing, get them up on the snout.

'Number one!' shouted Dewi above the clanging of the rails, and pointed.

'That means us,' I said, and ran them to the front barge which was deep in the stomach in finished iron: there I shackled them up, Jed leading.

'Checker out!' yelled my father, and put fingers to his mouth, whistling.

'Ay, ay!'

'Strain up, strain up!' bawled Ifor, jumping along the iron.

'If you can do any bloody better you come down here,' I said.

'No offence, man—just strain up—take the weight.'

I gave Nell my fist and the traces tightened.

'Man Arfon coming,' said Dewi.

'Room for him, too,' rumbled Ifor, thick and swarthy and stripped to the belt despite the wind. Eh, dear, here is a Hercules for you, thick in the arms and shoulders and thicker between the ears, and there wasn't a man on the wharf that morning who would have looked him over.

'Well, what have we, Mostyn Evan?'

By the light sound of his soprano voice, this one must have been standing sideways. Man Arfon, the famous. Five feet nothing in canvas leg-breeches and boots like gentry: brutal in the face also, with barn door shoulders, and there wasn't a virgin Irish safe within a mile of him, for he fed on them, said Dewi, as a hog feeds on flowers, taking them in the midst of their hunger: if this one was ever found in a ditch with a knife, the knife would be Irish, though not all the Welsh are parton saints, nor do all the pigs live in styes: given six inches' height and half a chance I would have this sod for every weeping Irish mother.

'What you got here, Mostyn?'

I would give him bloody Mostyn, if I was my father.

39

'Twenty-five ton for Abercynon,' answered Dada, coiling a fall. You could always tell when my father had head pains and tingling knuckles, being cold in the face when mixing with scum. Man Arfon said, 'The driver I am talking of, man, not the iron,' and he rocked back on his heels, his little eyes watching me from the folds of a shattered face.

'Leave him,' mumbled Dewi, going past me with a band-strap, and this he flung over our load and my father snatched it in the air, and knelt, anchoring, and flung it over to Ifor, and Ifor put his boots on the gunwale and heaved, his brown arms bulging while Dewi stepped over him and kicked down the trace.

'Snatching them from their cradles soon, I am thinking,' said Man Arfon.

I spat on my hands and took an inch on Nell's girth, watching the checker over my shoulder: he looked stiff in the head to me, and I began to want him. He said:

'A couple more his size and Crawshay will be scratching a beggar's arse, eh? Ho, ho!' and he boomed, stamping the dust.

He was trying me for temper, which was the way with agents and overmen, and only one in twenty were Welsh. This was the way of the ironmasters and coal-owners. They brought in the Staffordshire men first, the men of Scunthorpe, those trained in the trade of iron: from Doncaster and Worksop they brought down the English bargees of the Northern and Midland cuts. And these lorded it over us, sewing their noses to our business, wagging their tongues at the agent meetings. Bad tempers were watched; meetings of more than four Welsh were reported, and at the first whisper of a Union a man and his family could be black-listed by every master on The Top and sent packing over the mountain or into the workhouse. And the few Welsh agents and overmen were the black sheep of the fold, the worst of the lot: men like Man Arfon who was Welsh to his boots but betray his mates, his country, his religion, to curry favour with the English owner. 'My God,' my father once said, 'we come of the blood of princes, but when we are bad we are a stink to the name of Welsh; a blackness in the brain that spawns the first-rate Judas.'

Sometimes, for these few, I could weep for my country.

'Cast off, Ifor. Take her, Bryn!' called my father, and I cracked the whip over Nell's head and flicked Jed with the butt, and they put down their haunches and cranked to the load, hooves skidding.

'Has he handled mules before?' asked Man Arfon.

'Half mule he is, boyo—look at his ears.'

The overman put his thumbs in his belt, sidling along beside me as I got Jed moving. 'A cheeky little brat, I am thinking, and insolent in the eye with him.'

'What else do you expect for three shillings a week?' asked Dewi.

I think I hated them all, even my father at that moment. To this they bowed and scraped, the half-Welsh: to this men sent their little baskets of bribe potatoes. If this was Baptist, then they were Baptist, or Church of England, or anything going—kneeling in the pews with Beast, not God.

'You watch him,' said Man Arfon, as I straightened with the load.

'No,' replied my father, jumping down from the iron, 'you do the watching, Man Arfon. A couple of years from now he'll be looking for his first man, and half Welsh half English will do as good as any.'

I grinned at Dada.

Off his ale for weeks, was Man Arfon: fist on the bar and calling for rye at the very mention of the Evan family. Enemies, said Dewi later, are not worth having unless you make them properly.

But later we knew the size of the enemy in Man Arfon the Checker.

# 6

DOWN to the Basin with us then, with the crippled trees flaring at a leaden sky: a blue-eared morning, this one, with the hedges dripping icicles and the ice-breakers labouring up the canals and the big Camarthen drays skidding their hooves down the tow-paths, breaking it up. Aye, a wicked old winter, this one, and now well into March. The Irish were dying of cold in the cellars of China, Merthyr; father this and brother that pulling them out as stiff as boards for last rites. But, as Gran said, they'd come back to life the moment the sun came up, their laughter ringing from their hovels: pouring out of Pont Storehouse where they slept four to a bed, with Blind Tim here and Red Shaun there dancing on the cobbles to the music of the fiddles, though what they have to be joyful about beats me, said Dada. My father was always worrying about the Irish, and I wonder their God didn't do more about them, for they paid Him enough in sanctity and bribes.

''Morning, Mrs. Hanman!' cried Dada now, and her lock cottage slid up alongside. A giant Staffordshire puddler, this one, now aged sixty, her white hair tumbling in swathes down her back and tied with black ribbon for Thor, her seven foot man who died years since.

'A pail o'tea for you and the lads, and welcome, Mostyn Evan.' And she lifted her soapy arms from her wash-tub and I saw beyond her door the little black grate and the red flash of her fire: snow-white her cloth, her table bright with knives and forks.

'No time, lady,' cried Dada. 'Got iron for the Basin, and we are running late.' He turned to us. 'Line up,' he said.

And we came to him and lined up beside him, staring up at the lip of the wharf where Mrs. Hanman stood, hands on hips, and we said in chorus:

'Good morning, Mrs. Hanman.'

Respect will be shown, said my father, especially to widow ladies.

Last week Mrs. Hanman was down in Neath, and Dai Half-Moon got caught with the rowdies, till Mrs. Hanman came up. And she stepped him under her skirts and got stuck into the rowdies, and when she stepped off him, said little Dai, the rowdies had vanished and she was licking her knuckles.

With Mrs. Hanman in her cottage now, Dewi stepped off stern as we passed, and tried to lift her wash-tub and dolly which she emptied at a single heave, and he reckoned it was screwed to the flags.

On, through Quaker's Yard, on to Abercynon, the clearing house of iron for the world. Here the great warehouses and offices where half-starved clerks were bending over ledgers: on down the brick-cut and the fields where little children laboured on the frosted land; on to Lock One, the most important in the Basin. Jane Rheola, aged eighteen, is half out of her bedroom window in Lock Six Cottage, her hair hanging either side of her face, dressed pink in her new Swansea nightie.

'Oi, oi, Dewi Evan!' she shouted.

'Back into bed, girl, I am just coming up!' shouted Ifor.

There is disgusting.

'Enough of that!' cried my father, quite rightly.

'Dead you will be when you get back down, mind,' called Jane, going cuddly. 'There's beautiful, mind, a little bit of love.'

'Steady on that pole, Dewi!' roared my father. 'Dewi, lay off stern.'

'Ay ay!'

'Do not strain him, for God's sake,' said Jane.

Hot and bothered, me, by the time we got by: very attractive is Jane Rheola, but more so first thing in the morning, in pink, I reckon.

'You get about coiling those falls,' commanded my father. 'Dear me, I do not know what is happening to the modern generation.'

Found in Rheola woods by old Canal Tom when she was six weeks old, was Jane, and raised by him without a woman, and girls like this do naturally drop the tone of a decent community, said Gran.

On, on to the loading wharves where hundreds of horses were towing drams heaped with the coal and iron of The Top Towns, and as we drew closer to the Basin platforms the explosions of iron-making grew about us: great rainbows of light flooding over the skies above Hirwain and Aberdare. It was the firework display of the mountains; the music of the Crawshays and Guests, the Hills of Plymouth, the Foremans of Penydarren. The barge slid on.

'By God, they are collecting profit today,' said my father, but I could not count the profit: I saw only the loss. A tattered army of labouring Welsh and Irish, I saw; the empty sleeves, the trouser-legs tied with string. Queer old business, the more I think of it, this brotherhood of man. Dada cried, up on the prow:

'Right, Bryn, take us in!' and I gave the elbow to old Nell and took her alongside Charlie Smith's wharf where coal and lime-stone was coming in like a flood to the shovels of the teeming Irish. Here we tied up, with the sun overhead, and I unharnessed Jed Donkey and Nell and led them clear of the road. For the labouring Irish were coming for us in droves, swarming over the barge, unshackling the chains and letting under the rails with levers, and they were starting a foreman's song as we got clear, their chanting voices sweet and clear in the blustering wind.

'What do you think of Abercynon, *bach*?' asked Ifor.

'Makes your hair stand on end.'

'Some queer old customers work round here, mind,' said Dewi.

Above the thunder of the labour, the rattle of trams, the clang of steel, I heard the roaring banter of men from the Inn, and the shrieks of Scottish sopranos. Spanish labourers went by with their lovely women; gold rings in their ears, six inch stilettoes strapped to the calves. French sailors from the coasters of Brittany lounged in the weak sunlight, waiting for finished loads to take down to the Cardiff flats, and they eyed us, hating us.

'Away out of here if we want to keep our legs,' said Dada, for the rails were toppling off the deck for the stackyards. 'You got the nose-bags?'

'Aye,' I said, nose-bags being my business. And I followed them to a quiet place of trees and grass where other workers were resting, and put Jed and Nell out to grass. Here Dewi lit a fire to thaw us out, and we squatted around it, chewing vacant, unspeaking, as men do after labour.

At length, my father said, 'You see the Penydarren dram-road?'

A new-fangled Trevithick engine was fussing up and down it, pulling trucks.

'What of it?' asked Ifor.

'It sings a song of death for the barge,' said Dada.

'Eh, daft! They have been running those clumps for the past fifteen years and we are not dead yet. There will always be work for the barge.'

'Aye?' My father bit deep into his loaf, and chewed, eyes narrowed to the weak sun. 'Twelve years back John Guest put the *Powerful* and *Eclipse* on the Dowlais dram-road and worked a hundred thousand tons a year up to the rack and pinion. It takes three horses ten hours to pull a hundred tons up to Dowlais Top: the *Powerful* pulls a hundred tons up there in six. Haven't you noticed the horses shortening?'

'The horses is out, the steam engine is in,' muttered Dewi.

'Steam do evaporate, remember,' said Ifor with a burst of brains.

'Oh, God, listen to it,' said Dewi.

'You taking the mick from me?' asked Ifor, getting up.

'Already taken.'

My father said, 'Ifor, sit down.'

'All day long he do take the water from me!' Trembling, he stood, hands clenched while Dewi lounged, straw in mouth.

Trouble was coming between these two, and it was Dewi's fault mainly, for when a person is concrete between the ears it is not polite to mention it a couple of times a day. Dewi said, indolently, 'See sense, man. Is it good business to feed a horse to pull a ton when you can feed an engine to pull a hundred? It is not economic.'

'And what do that mean, economic?' I asked.

Dada said, 'Economic means cheaper, but Dewi uses the big words to take it out of Ifor.' He rose. 'Listen, you two—listen

45

all three of you. Skinny times are coming, and we will have to fight. But we cannot fight to live all the time we fight each other.' He levelled a finger at Dewi. 'Brains are all right in the head, Dewi, but they are useless chewing in the mouth, you hear me?'

'Yes, Dada,' said Dewi, frozen, for though my father never laid a finger on us there was no saying he would never start. He swung to Ifor, saying:

'And you watch your temper—save it for the ring, or I will belt you black and blue.'

'Yes, Dada,' said Ifor, head bowed.

Excellent, I thought, and I nodded approval and chucked Dada a wink.

'And don't you make capital out of it, or I will take you first!'

'Yes, Dada,' I said.

Mind, I couldn't think of any man in the county likely to take my twin brothers in pairs, except, perhaps, the Black Welshman, the terror of the Vale of Neath; nor could I think what was coming between Dewi and Ifor these days, unless it was Rosie Carey, the bar-maid of the Castle Inn. Apparently, Rosie had been moonlighting Dewi pretty hard until Ifor slipped in the back door and beat him to it, and Dewi was now losing sleep on Rosie Carey, which given half a chance I was prepared to do myself, but at the moment, of course, she wasn't a patch on Miss Bronwen Rees, for whom I was prepared to die if needs be. Nor was Dewi the only one lamenting, for according to Dai Central Eating, whom I met at Sunday School last Friday, my Bronwen had been seen on the mountain with Taliesen the Poet, which was all right with me providing he confined himself to poetry. My father was talking earnestly, but I scarcely heard him, being busy just then cutting the throat of Taliesen the Poet.

Then I heard him say, 'We can see which way the wind is blowing. Ten years from now the barges in this valley will begin to fail.'

'In any valley,' said Dewi, glancing up.

'No—in this one, for the railway has not yet come to the Vale of Neath.'

This set us back a swallow, because a move on the Vale of Neath just now might be inconvenient, all three of us being committed to Merthyr in one way or another, this being the country of Rosie Carey and Bronwen Rees.

The workers were coming in from the wharves and tram-roads to the Old Navigation Inn.

In their hundreds they came; the colliers of the distant levels, mule-drivers, loaders, haulers, cutters, engine-men and labourers: Welsh, Irish, Spanish, they came in an army, each to his camp on the grass; division defined by nationality, a border-post nobody crossed. The Welsh came to us, and these we knew. Flinging down their tools they sprawled on the tumps, eyes heavy with labour, and knocked off the tops of their flagons and drank, gasping. The Irish went to the Irish, eyeing us as they wolfed down their bread and water: the Spanish, no more than a hundred, went to the Spanish camp, watching the Welsh and Irish with equal suspicion. In Spanish they told their beads and cut hunks of mouse-trap with their long stilettoes, their dark eyes burning in their Latin faces. A woman, Dada said she was from Cordova, dropped down her hair, and this she began to comb in the sun, singing as she did so in a rich contralto, a plaintive melody in a minor key. The song of the earth was stilled; there was no sound but that woman singing, and on her voice stole the hatreds: the hatred of Irish for Welsh and Welsh for Irish, the hatred of both for the Spanish, and they for us. And I thought, sitting there listening to that woman singing among the switching eyes, that come Sunday the lot of us would be dusting knees in church or chapel before gilded altars or plain black cloth; praying to the same Jesus Whom we clothed in robes or rags, as the fancy took us.

'I agree,' said my father when I mentioned this, 'and I would not like His Opinion of us.'

And he sat in a holy quiet, as he always did at the mention of Jesus.

Later, when we were through the nose-bags, Dada rose, saying, 'And so, if the canal in this valley is dying, we must go where the canal is alive and kicking, and this, for me, is the Vale of Neath.'

'A move from Merthyr, then?' asked Ifor, askance.

'A move from here to Resolven, next valley over.'

Dewi said, 'But the Bargee Union is going strong in Resolven. You try to buy a barge on the Neath Canal and the bargees will break your head.'

'Can't get a barge on that canal,' said Ifor, 'it is against the Union rules, remember,' and my father replied:

'I know all this, it is not news. But there is more than one way of getting round the Union. Is there any law against buying a barge here and sailing it down to Cardiff, and from Cardiff through Baglan Bay and up the Neath Canal at Briton Ferry?'

'Take a barge to sea?' I gasped.

'It has never been done before,' whispered Ifor.

'It is time it was,' said Dada. He knocked out his pipe. 'Come.'

The contralto's song was severed as with a knife as we walked through the workers, following Dada: hands rigid in the air, she froze: all eyes watched as we took a track that led us through deep undergrowth.

'Where are we going?' I asked.

'Into a new future, into a new life,' said my father.

On a stricken door, at the end of a disused wharf, Dada knocked, and the door was opened by an aged, withered little man.

'Mostyn Evan, by the gods. You're having it?' he cried.

'I am having it,' replied my father. 'And I have brought my three sons to see it. Safe and sound, is she?'

'Safer than death,' said Mr. Eli Cohen. 'Hold hard a minute and I will take you down.'

Scarecrowed by age, jack-knifed by labour, Mr. Eli Cohen, barge-builder of Abercynon, stopped on the track and croaked:

'Six daughters and a wife, I have—seven females in all. You ever stopped to think, Mostyn Evan, what it is like with seven women stitching and darning and talking soprano, and no bass voice of a son to hold in your heart?'

'Three decent sons I have, all things considered,' said Dada.

We walked down the track in file, Mr. Cohen leading,

stamping with his stick. 'Aye, seven women I have, and four are married and living at home—three have children, two sets of twins and three singles. And all girls. Fourteen females, Mostyn—I am surrounded by women, talking women, weeping women who have quarrelled with their husbands, screaming women in napkins—women feeding and women on the breast, another at this moment in childbirth. Hey, you!' and he caught Ifor by the buttons of his shirt. 'Here is a man of strength and hair. Speak bass to me, son of Mostyn: whisper bass in my ear, for the love of God!'

'Dear me, man, you are in a state,' said Ifor, and I loved him for his gentleness, which Dewi, for all his cut and style, did not possess.

'Is the barge finished, Mr. Cohen?' asked Dada.

'Finished, you ask?' The old man teetered on his corns. 'With me aged eighty and all my labour gone? Landed with fourteen women and another expected? Finished, man? She is not even started. In reeds and damp, she is, and I am old,' and he shivered on the edge of the grave. Dada said, eagerly:

'Look, Eli, we will finish it. How much?'

'Ten pounds.'

'A sixty-foot iron loader for ten pounds?'

'If you finish it,' said Eli.

'Easy, man, if you tell us how,' cried Dada. 'We can fire the planks and bend them steamed to curve; we can get the iron forged private up in Cyfarthfa, for I know tame benders: we can pickle the timbers, make the bolts and nails. We can ballast her to a ten-inch draft with pig from the old bloomeries, but it is the planning and brains we are short of. Will you consider it, Eli?'

'Tools I have, mind, but too weak to lift them....'

'We will use them, Mr. Cohen,' cried Ifor.

And old Eli looked wearily around him. 'Could be done, but it will take time. Timber is here in plenty, if you pay extra. Dog-spikes and drifters, seamers and caulkers—tar and wool; all is available. All I have lacked till now is sons.'

'You have sons now, Eli Cohen!'

'Launch her in July!'

'Three months come Monday!'

'Sail her on mock canvas down the Old Glamorgan to Cardiff,' shouted Dada, 'and round to Baglan up to Aberdulais —Rheola and Glyn Neath!'

Our own barge!

Mostyn Evan and Sons at last!

Hell to pay rent to, mind, when we break the news to Gran.

# 7

CHAPEL next morning, being Sunday, for it is right to let your God know what is happening, and with an effort He might even decide to sweeten Gran.

'Not a word from anybody, remember,' said my father. 'This Cohen removal is a very delicate operation, and she is much more malleable after communication with the Lord.'

Oh, how I used to love those Sunday mornings, with people turning out mothballs and climbing into new stays, hooking black bombazine on bed-rails, with clean shirt-fronts being ironed and how do I look now, turning in circles. Eh, I adore it when the family is under one roof. In the kitchen, combing for a quiff in the cracked shaving mirror, I said, 'Dear me, Gran, I am looking forward to Bethania this morning!'

'Oh, aye? What is going on, then?' Her hand suspended on her cameo brooch of Queen Victoria, and she went to the stairs, crying, 'Mostyn, what is happening that I do not know about?'

'Did you call, my precious?' Six-foot-two of him lumbering down the stairs.

Grand my dada looked in Sunday black, the serge groaning over his wide shoulders, his waist slim, his cut-throat up around his side-boards: black, black his hair, parted in the middle, and when he walked in town the Merthyr pugilists seemed otherwise engaged, but he was scared to death of Gran, his only woman. Sad, it is, to see a man like this left without a wife, and Gran once said:

'You three bruisers get used to the idea sharp—a man like your father has need of a wife—now, don't start huffing and heaving—there is more to a woman than you have in mind. There is cooking and mending, and boots by the fire, and when it comes to good-night kisses wives are preferable to grans and mothers. And it cuts both ways, remember, for I have had my fill of men and you lot in particular. Close your mouth when you're eating, Bryn.'

'Ach, leave the chap alone,' replied Dewi. 'He is happy enough with you, and we are not having another woman cluttering up the place.'

'I am not having another mam,' said Ifor, fist on the table, and he bowed his head, his eyes bright: took it heavy over mam, did Ifor.

I was with Ifor on this. Personally, I think it is indecent to have a new wife billing and cooing in bright colours while the old one lies sobbing in black under the daffodils up in Vaynor. And I reckon the wind must have been blowing in a certain direction, for Gran could always read us like a book. She said now:

'Mostyn, this boy do not look forward to Bethania without a good reason. Something is afoot, so out with it.'

Dada replied, fingers waffling on the seams of his trews, 'It is his first girl, Mother—sweet on a girl, isn't it, Bryn lad?'

'Aye, that is it,' I answered.

'God help us,' said Gran. 'Eleven years old and he is sparking. Who is she, how old is she, what is her name and where does she come from?'

'Miss Bronwen Rees of Abergavenny,' I said.

'Well!' Gran beamed, and I was heady with her perfume as she pulled me hard against her. 'There is beautiful, the lady school-teacher, and coming to Bethania this morning to hear Mr. Emlyn Hollyoak, I hear. Church usually, unfortunately, but we can't have everything.'

'No, Gran.'

She patted and fussed me, straightening my collar and smarming down my hair. 'There is smart he is! Never be indifferent to your appearance, boy. And clean underwear is as important as a clean suit, and a man is tidy if he is clean on the skin, the collar and the boots, isn't it?'

'Aye, Gran,' replied Judas.

'Clean underwear especially, see, since you never know when you are going to have an accident.'

This accident business had been going on ever since I could remember, and by rights every man jack of us should have been down six feet. With this she held me tightly against her, rocking and humming, which could be twice as dangerous as a run-away tram after the first two minutes of being buried in Gran. I was half-way up the stairs and gasping when my father collared me, drawing me slowly down on to his bunched fist, whispering:

'Listen, you. Nobody has trained you as a diplomat, so stop hinting. One word about the Cohen barge to Gran and you will have me to account to—understand?'

'Yes, Dada,' I said, and was nearly upended as Gwen came dashing down the stairs and flung herself into his arms. And he whisked her aloft, whooping and kissing her in circles, which I think is daft. Bloody *daft*, I call that, for I cannot stand slobbering at the best of times—showing his fist to me one moment and kissing her the next. I agree, of course, that Gwen was becoming a bit more presentable, losing some of her baby fat and with a few of her front teeth back in, but if you wanted beauty you had to go to Sharon. Smooth and haughty, this big sister Sharon, now sixteen; the image of my mother with her Welsh darkness and peaches and Irish cream. The very sight of her was sending the Town lads demented, with Robert Crocker and Albert Johns and Willie Dare sitting on the wall like tom-cats, the last-named giving me the shivers. Lots of girls were getting into trouble about this time, being hauled into the aisles in the chapels, and my father always got edgy if Sharon was five minutes late coming back from the Band of Faith; going to the window and isn't it getting dark, Gran, and do you think I ought to slip out to meet her, Gran? But the climate and the darkness have nothing to do with it, Gran always used to say, for they will do in the frost what they will do in the sun, so do not fret, Mostyn, my son.

'Speak to her, Mam, speak to her! It is difficult having no wife, and she is such a child.'

'Oh, aye?' Up with her darning. 'Do not bother yourself, boy. I am quite satisfied that in sixteen years she has collected more information on the subject than me. Stop worrying. We have brought her up decent, and this will stand by her under provocation. All right, Bryn, that is all you are getting, do not mooch about out there.'

Most embarrassing when people pass remarks like that just because you happen to be passing.

'That is the one you should be worrying about,' said Gran. 'With looks like that he will be your cross in five years' time, if I am not mistaken.'

Off to Chapel on Sundays was a treat, and we always made an impression on the neighbours. About this time the churches and chapels were full in Merthyr, for they filled or emptied according to the rate of the cholera, which had picked off quite a few in Town recently.

Amazing to me how popular God becomes when the death-rate rises.

The trouble lay in the water supply, said my father, for paupers were going down in four-foot graves, and some of the coffins were floating. The birth-pangs of the '49 cholera were beginning now, although we did not know it then, and the religious jumpers were at it in the chapels and fields, though thank God Mr. Emlyn Hollyoak of Bethania did not go in for such exhibitions, said my father.

In the kitchen with us now, under inspection, tallest on the right, Gwen on the left, with Dada and Gran on a tour of inspection of ears and boots.

'Am I right, Dada?' Ifor, beetle-browed and wide, turning in a circle.

'As right as you will ever be, my son,' and dusted him. 'Just a bit of scurf on the collar, and do not snort in the pews, man, for you are not mountain-fighting.'

Me next, and get your hair cut by next Sunday, for we are not growing poets, and I hated this, for it meant sitting out the back under a basin and Ifor cheeping with scissors while I prayed for ears. Next Dewi, easy and confident, and let's get this lot over and quick, for I am meeting Pietro Bianca who is arranging two tickets for Mexico to fight for freedom, for this damned country is finished now it is toadying to the English aristocracy. Bombs were going off in the cellar these days, the idea being to develop a decent one from the shotblast powder that would put paid to an American General called Taylor, who was playing hell in a place called Buena Vista. No, Mother, I am not interfering, my father used to say: Dewi has his beliefs, and it is Dewi's neck, not mine.

'You realise he's bringing the pictures down in the second bedroom?'

'Aye, well, it is a small price to pay for complete free-thinking.'

'This free-thinking will be the death of us,' said Gran, tying bonnet-streamers. 'All ready, is it?'

And off we went in bombazine, serge, poke-bonnets and streamers, and doors came ajar and window curtains were parted for a look at the family of Mostyn Evan.

Of course, half the trouble with Bridge Street was that we were really a cut above the neighbours, though, as I have said before, there are no snobs among the working-class: really, I suppose, it was trades superior and trades inferior, and with about two-pounds-six total falling into Gran's weekly apron, we could have moved to something better. Until now, of course, my father had been saving for his own barge. Mind, had there been any justice in the world it would have hooked old Crawshay out of Cyfarthfa Castle and put him in Bridge Street for a fortnight with his back to the Taff. I suppose, in a century or so, the tame historians, said Dewi, will write about the snug little cottages of the workers and how the good employers always did the best for them under trying circumstances, but the main difficulty was that they were dealing with animals and not decent people.

'Oh, aye?' said Dada.

Aye, said Dewi, but the trouble with history is that only the ruling classes can write—like the University fops they have sent into Wales to write the Blue Books, the parsons and magistrates, the landed Members of Parliament and their lackeys, the Man Arfon traitor Welsh.

Hot, was Dewi! but I agree that Bridge Street was in a

particularly bad state that morning, after the Saturday night.

'Hush, there's a good boy,' said Gran. 'The neighbours are watching us.'

With Gran, Sharon and Gwen leading, we went, picking our way through the garbage, for it came anything from night-soil to dead cats in the Merthyr streets about now: mud streets, of course, six inches deep, with cart-tracks; narrow openings through the rows of terraced houses, and you had to keep an eye cocked in case something came out of a window. With our house it was not so bad, since it backed on to the Taff River, and all our soil and refuse was thrown into that—the same river which others tapped for drinking farther down. The houses on the Glebe Land side backed on to coal tumps, so their soil and suchlike went into the middle of the road, which was better than some, for they had gutters that ran with blood from the Shambles slaughter-house. Drains we had none, water likewise, and every day Sharon used to walk two miles with a pail up the mountain, wait for an hour in a queue and then walk back home with a pail half full by the time she got there. Sometimes, in drought, the people used to wait at the water-spouts all night, with fighting and brutalising when they thinned to a trickle, and more than once Sharon came home with an eye filled up, which sent my father and brothers raging among the spouts for the woman who had pasted her. The main trouble with the water was that the Works took priority, and the children suffered most, mortality of those under two years old being about forty per cent. Down near Coedcae Court there was a very tasty spout that ran under a burial yard, and the Irish drank from that.

'We will put a stop to it,' said Dada, 'it is only a question of time.'

'Then take your time, do not mind me,' replied Gran, 'for I have been living in this filth either here or in Dowlais ever since I can remember, and I cannot bunk to Canford Manor every time the cholera comes, like Lady Charlotte Guest.'

'She is coming round,' said Ifor, delighted. 'The Vale of Neath is over the horizon, she is coming round—boots up for Resolven.'

*       *       *

55

Into the chapel pew now, into a smell of well-hung clothes and tiger nuts, and the creak of stays and braces: up off your knees next minute, stricken with conscience for the week of dissipation; nervous coughs and smiles as Mrs. Ten Benyon came in with her brood ranging from Owain who topped six feet and Cynfor who was two-foot-six and whose name meant Sea Chieftain, and you couldn't see Cynfor for pew. Mr. and Mrs. Alfo Morgan were there, with Rosie sitting between them, pretty well back, being in the publican and sinner business; labourers in the rear, tradesmen up front, and if we'd had an ironmaster he would have been sitting on the rail. Up on our feet now, and I heard the congregation gasp, for a Zion minister took the Big Seat, not our usual Mr. Emlyn Hollyoak, and this new chap gave an explanation as to how his butty had been taken with the gout, or something, and that he would be standing in for a few Sundays. Deep my father sighed behind me, for this new Zion preacher's name had been linked with the Revival Jumpers up on Adulum Fields, and Dada was strong for proper nonconformity. First hymn now, to the words of Billy Twice, and there is lovely it is with Mrs. Afron Shavings on the harmonium. Bass I do like best, mind, and will be one, for I am inclined to be suspicious of throaty tenors, and it can prove injurious if you get too fervent in the higher registers, says Dada.

Now there is a commotion at the back, for Dai Half-Moon is on his ear letting somebody in, and there is a clattering of walking-sticks and falling hymnals just as we were about to land on Canaan's side. And then my heart stopped beating, and I stared over Gran's shoulder, for Miss Bronwen Rees was coming in as large as life and as pretty as a picture, all done in black, with a summer hat about four feet diameter on her head tied over the top with a sort of net outrigger that knotted under her chin. And now she is stuck between Dai and the pew, with excuse-me-pleases and trying to hold her hat on, and Little Dai all bows and shivers since he has never been in such close proximity to anything as gorgeous as Miss Bronwen Rees, says Dewi, and he is not as daft as he looks.

Sharon put her elbow into my ribs. 'Stop wagging. Dada is behind you.'

If Old Nick had been behind me it would have made no difference, now that I was under the same roof as my Bronwen, and my eyes began to smart with joy as I knew a marvellous communion of the spirit. Another peep. Now she is safe in the pew, Dai staring at her, jaw dropped, and finding her place in the hymnal. And suddenly seeing me she smiled brilliantly, lowering her dark lashes on to her cheeks as if in acquiescence to some wonderful secret.

Dear me. I began to sweat.

My father, 'Do you mind turning round, Bryn, for you are being watched.'

'The Zion preacher has his eye on you,' hissed Sharon. 'Turn round!' and when I did so the new pastor was fixing me with a terrible eye, his massive brow furrowed with condemnation, and I began to sweat more because you could not trust these boyos once they were in the Big Seat, and they thought nothing of hauling out bad behaviour for public examination. So I smiled purely at him and took into the hymn again, and the last verse of Williams beat about me in glory.

Boots scraping, coughing, books slapping, sit down again, await events.

They came sooner than most expected.

After a few notices about Sunday School and the Penny Readings and I hope every young person will come, the new Zion preacher stood up in the Big Pew, his white beard trembling with indignation, and he brought his fist down on to the mahogany with a crash that hit them off the seats in the Ebenezer Baptist.

'Are there drinkers among you?' he roared.

Well, there is a stupid question to ask, with half the male population good for twenty pints at a sitting. Toes curling, we sat.

'Are there drunkards here?' and I risked a peep behind at Dewi and Ifor to see how they were sticking it.

'For, if the sons of Baal are abroad, let them listen . . .!'

Very powerful in the vocal chords, this one, even for Zion; the boom of him battered off the faded walls: silence: the tragedy of Merthyr moaned suddenly in a little wind from the hills. The preacher shouted:

'For the drinkers will be the losers, mind! The Big Man will henceforth farm the land himself, and fair play to him, it is his property. He will turn the briars into vineyards of wine, the pure wine of everlasting life, and Satan will go to the wall. Alone will he travel in his vanity and corruption, drinking ale at the beerhouses—no more convivial company for Baal, for he must drink alone! Do I hear a confession?' The preacher glared round at us.

There was no sound but Mrs. Shenkins sobbing at the back, in the seat where her Willie used to sit.

The pastor threw his skinny hands to Heaven, crying, 'I look about me and find dust, but there is a jewel in the dust of the chapel. Is there not one man present ready to deny Baal and all his works? Must you go unsober in the days of feasting? Must you run helter-skelter at the name of the Lord?'

I was with him on this, of course, for the beer-houses were a disgrace to the whole community, with men staggering home laying into their wives. And all the time the Zion was hitting at the drinkers I was most concerned, though any moment he might start becoming personal about coveting oxen and asses, and I was a bit involved in this respect with my beautiful Bron. I took a deep breath when he shouted:

'But beer and gin do not stand alone as areas of iniquity. Does not Baal in all his glory stroll the Coedcae Spout at night, among the pails and pitchers and pots? Is there not one man, woman or child here this morning guilty of a debased thought?' He paused in the pin-drop silence. 'For if there is not one so guilty, then let him stand and claim now, and I will throw him high that he might hover like a crow in the vaults of Heaven! I cry again—let innocence stand! It is not enough to claim that innocence exists—let it stand!' And his great head with its white, flowing mane turned to me.

'You, lad—you!'

I slid my trews on the pew and got my head well down into my collar.

'You, boy!' A pause, then. 'Stand, my son, stand!'

Rigid, eyes clenched but peeping, I lay under the glare of his eyes.

'You he is talking to, mind,' hissed Sharon, digging me.

Six inch coach bolts had me screwed to that mahogany.

My father rustled in the dust-mote silence, his hand gripped my shoulder. 'Stand, Bryn—do as he says. I am here, do not be afraid.'

Shivering, I rose, and the preacher cried:

'How old are you, my son?'

Words steam-dry in the dust-bowl of the throat; the chest convulses, the tonsils sag. 'Eleven, sir.'

Opening his arms, he beamed. 'Eleven, eleven! Oh, that I might for ever feast mine eyes on such innocence!' And I heard Dewi groan aloud. 'Eleven years old. A little child shall lead them! Oh, make us all as pure as he, the golden wheat of Life! Would that this little boy's life stay unshadowed by the evils in our midst: that religion could dethrone impiety, the drunkard be sobered, the lame made to dance!'

The people were murmuring about me, a few weeping openly, others beating their breasts and sniffing, most staring up at me in open adoration of innocence. I stood a few inches higher in the magnificence of the man of Zion, his melodious voice breaking about me like waves over a rock: it seemed to snatch me up, transporting me to realms higher than the Old Bethania. And as more and more worshippers began to weep aloud the pastor cried, his arms thrown upwards:

'The day will come, and mark this, when innocence will prevail: when the miserable creatures now buried in their caverns of lust shall rise and be cleansed with the white robe of sianthood, and the cairns of Satan shall be emptied at a stroke! Hallelujar!'

'*Hallelujar!*' I shrieked, leaping on to the pew, fist trembling.

Dead silence.

Not a sound. The vaults echoed.

Clutching myself, I stared around, seeing the shocked, white face of Sharon, Gwen's mouth gaping and Gran's eyes so big that they threatened to drop from her cheeks. Suddenly, the pastor shrieked:

'Hallelujar, the boy is right. Hallelujar!'

As if ignited, the congregation jumped. Women fainted

away in the pews, burly men openly wept, children were screaming, and through the wailing and sighs the Zion cried, 'Behold! A mighty, pentecostal wind shall fill the house of the world. All tears shall be wiped from your eyes!'

'Hallelujar!' I yelled.

'Who shall be the first to confess before the congregation, who will be upstanding?'

I was just about to inform him about me and Miss Bronwen Rees when Dai Half-Moon jumped up at the back, croaking in tears, 'My sins are beyond forgiveness, pastor, they are beyond forgiveness!'

'Do not talk twaddle, man! Your sins, placed beside the Plan for Redemption, is like hitching a porridge-pot to the stern of a man o' war. Listen! The Great Revival is coming, good people, it is coming! The cock-fighting pitch shall be stilled; banished the foul game of pitch and toss. And if there are still devils among you I will prise them out of you with these two hands—every hoof, every horn! See now, the Lord, in my image, is aiming at you!' And he took aim at us as a soldier aims a musket, one eye closed. This did it. Pews were overturned, boots went up: people were crying for mercy, others pleading on their knees and the pastor's voice boomed on like the toll of Doom:

'The Revival shall come like the flash of a swallow's wing heralding the arrival of summer. Leap for joy! We will set the summer cornfields alight with our ardour like Samson's foxes!'

Somebody was blowing on his fingers like a hunting-horn, women were pulling down their hair to cover their faces, others starting the Revival Jump.

'*Hallelujar!*' It was a repeated cry now, taken up in chorus.

Gwen was shrieking with fright, Sharon up and dancing along the pews. Gran was up on a chair waving her hat with ostrich feathers, shouting something about when she was seventeen up in Dowlais, with Dewi trying to get her from behind, and as Dada come for me I fought him off, waving my arms for balance.

'Let that child stand!' roared the Zion pastor. 'Let him not be allayed! Is he not the implement of a giant purpose? Did he not fire us all with the first hallelujar?' and in a second of awed silence following this, Gran cried from the other side of the room:

'The ark has returned from Philistia, the ark has returned from Philistia!'

Going pretty solid was Gran, her hat off and cheering in tears, and swiping with ostrich feathers anybody trying to collar her.

'Leap for joy, good people!' yelled the pastor. 'Leap for joy!' and the place began to thunder as people got going. Down at the back Dai Half-Moon was prancing along the aisles with his missus swiping at him, but then, she was always inclined to the Established Church, and Miss Bronwen Rees was up on the Sideman's Pew leaping and landing flat-footed with her skirts above her knees and her summer hat over her eyes, the outrigger flying. And the Zion pastor roved among us like a great, white patriarch, his arms waving, as Moses must have looked when he was breaking the tablets.

I was half-way down the chapel, vaulting pews in pairs to get at Miss Bronwen Rees, when my father brought me down. In the shelter of a pew, hard in his arms, I heard him whisper, 'Quiet now, Bryn. Hush quiet, I have got you.'

And the harder I fought to be free the harder he held me, till I could scarcely breathe. 'Dewi, Ifor,' he shouted then, and the face of Ifor appeared above us.

'The place is with madness,' cried Dada. 'Go and get Gran!'

'Sharon and Gwen at it too, mind,' said Ifor.

'I do not want a report—go and get them, and sharp!'

Cold as ice in the chapel porch, with corpses lying round and people fanning and rubbing backs of hands and sprinkling water. Miss Bronwen Rees was brought in and laid beside me: through a hedge backwards was my Bron, with her hat bashed in and shrieking confessions that were a bit warmer than I had been led to believe, and I pitied her the indignity, blue in the face and sobbing. Gran came with the next half-dozen, in a state of collapse over Dewi's shoulder in a fireman's lift, with Ifor running beside them patting her hand, and the moment she was laid on the flags she raised her head, and shrieked:

'A match has been applied to the isolated tufts. The conflagration is ascending. Leap for joy, leap for joy!' and the corpses in the porch got up and started it all over again, so we rushed the door and got her out in the street where she crowed like a hen and went out like a light. Sharon and Gwen came out next, weeping and fighting, but Dada soon fixed them. Dewi said, squatting in the road, holding Gran:

'Will you tell me what is wrong with the human race?'

'No inquests from you, please,' replied Dada, fanning.

'Dead, is she?' whispered Ifor, white-faced, staring down.

'I doubt it,' answered my father, 'they rarely die at Revivals.' He turned to me shivering beside him. 'You all right now?'

'Yes, Dada.'

'He ought to be,' said Dewi, 'it was him who bloody started it, remember.'

'Stop that bad language,' said Gran, opening her eyes, 'for I will not stand for it. Will somebody please tell me what I am doing down here?'

'It is the Revival,' said Dada. 'Remember, you were attacked the same on Dowlais Top in '33?'

'Bring me Bryn,' said she, and I stood before her.

'Raise me, child.' She slapped Dewi's hands away. 'Raise me, Bryn, lad. Ach, I'd never have believed that I would live to see the joy of it—a child of Ben's flesh and blood leading a new Revival.' She put out her big hands to me and I hauled her to her feet. 'Aye, long may this stand amid the nest of disbelievers. Home now, for dinner, and Bryn shall take my hand. I have enjoyed every minute.'

With Sharon still unstable and our Gwen bawling aloud, we took the roads back to Bridge Street, all spare hands supporting the invalids, and Gran would not allow me from her sight. My father said inaudibly, 'And a little child shall lead them. Wait till I get you home, Bryn Evan, and I will warm your trews.'

'Aye!' said Ifor, vicious.

My father added, 'And this is the very last time Bethania receives me without Mr. Emlyn Hollyoak in the Pew. I have

62

had sufficient of that big Nantyglo preacher to last me a life-time, and his Revival in particular.'

'Hallelujar,' said Dewi, giving me a look to kill.

# 8

THREE months Eli reckoned it would take to complete the half-finished barge in the reeds at Abercynon, but it was more like three years before we laid the last coat of tar; the time-table coming adrift largely because we lived in Merthyr and Eli lived seven miles south. Man Arfon, checker, was the main cause of the delay, since he devised the roster system for the runs to Abercynon, and when he knew we were keen to be down there, he charged my father a pound a run.

'No more runs to the Basin this week, Mostyn, lad,' he would say.

'But you are sending iron to Cynon twice a week!'

'Aye, man, but the economics have changed a trifle, don't you see? There is a lovely English word now—Economics.'

My father said, 'I am paying you a pound a run now, Arfon, you are not getting more. Does it matter to you what barge takes the load?'

'It does now,' said the checker, 'since you are prepared to pay for the privilege.'

'Give him another ten shillings and a thump in the ear,' said Dewi.

'The temptation might be great,' said Man Arfon, 'but it would land you on the black-list, and then you would not see the sky over Abercynon. Be reasonable, man—do I favour you free? Think of the risk I take with Ephraim Davies. Besides, it is against Company regulations to carry private goods on Company water.'

To be fair, the checker had a point there. He added, 'A bedstead with brass balls is a very prominent object, remember.'

What we were doing, of course, was gradually slipping the household goods down to Abercynon into Eli's sheds. Dada said, 'It is against regulations to accept bribes, yet you are doing it, and a bedstead with brass balls is an excellent example of Cyfarthfa iron, for it was fashioned there.'

'But I am drawing the line at Welsh dressers, mind,' said Man Arfon, 'and unless I am mistaken there is one coming now. Another ten shillings, if you please, Mostyn Evan.'

As long as I live I will remember that summer dawn, on the day I was fourteen, when we shipped Gran's Welsh dresser down to Abercynon. In moonlight, like smugglers, we carried it on a wheel-barrow along Bridge Street with fearful looks at windows, and when we got to the head of the wharf where the chief agent, Ephraim Davies, was lurking, we lifted it on to Ifor's back to save the clatter of the barrow. Very strange it was to see that dresser sliding down the wharf with Ifor's boots walking under it, and Gran, Dewi and me trying to look unconcerned. Dada came from the shadows of Number Two Shed followed by Man Arfon, a barrel in knee-breeches and bandy for letting through pigs. 'Well, well,' said Arfon. 'There is a very strange object, a Welsh dresser with boots. Travelling, is it?'

Gran said, 'It is the oldest dresser in Cyfarthfa, for Owain Glyndawr himself hung his cups on it, and it is going down to Abercynon or I am staying on in Merthyr.'

'Ay, ay. I was only wondering—do not take offence. May I know who happens to be under it, for it looks all of a couple of tons from by here.'

'Aye, solid mahogany, it is,' said Gran, patting it, 'and a good man carrying it, isn't it, Ifor, boy. You all right?'

'I will be that much better with this load off my mind,' said Ifor, jack-knifed underneath it.

'Is that the lot, then?' asked Man Arfon, nervous.

'It is not,' answered Gran. 'There is the tin bath, kitchen tables and chairs, the horse-hair sofa, and the commode in case of sickness from the second bedroom. My son is paying you for patience, Man Arfon. What you got there, Sharon, my love?'

'Chicken house, Gran.'

'God help me,' cried Man Arfon. 'Not chickens also?'

'Mattresses, chest of drawers, wash-tub and fender coming in the hearse, and half a ton of coal.'

'Coal to Abercynon?' asked Arfon, shocked.

'Not leaving it,'. said Gran. 'The people coming in are Church of England.'

Man Arfon said, 'A hearse unloading on Company water! Sudden death I will have if Mr. Ephraim Davies catches me transporting this lot.'

'Worse than death you will have if it do not arrive intact,' said Gran. 'Do not strain yourself, Bryn, what you carrying?'

'The mangle, Gran.'

'Oh, aye. Put it on the dresser by here, son, for you can easily pull a rupture.' She peered under the dresser. 'You all right, Ifor?'

'Right as rain, Gran, and I know you will get going as soon as you are able.'

Clop clop in the dawn darkness, and up came Hobo Churchyard with the coal and there was a lot of pushing and barging, with Man Arfon becoming difficult about stowing things in the hold, and back we all came to the dresser and Ifor.

'Right, my beauty, all aboard,' said Gran. 'Bryn, Sharon, Gwen—lend a pound on this dresser and we will give Ifor a breather—lift on the corners—*up*!' and we heaved to take the weight off Ifor and there was a roar like a bull from under it and Ifor was arse up and ears down and blue in the face and what the bloody hell is happening.

'Giving you a pound, we are,' said Gran. 'Lift again, and easy does it—*up*!' and there was a ripping like sail canvas and Ifor bellowing and stamping hobnails.

'Anything wrong, son?' asked Gran, hands on knees now, looking under.

'It is the shelf hooks, I suspect,' said Ifor. 'Into my bottom proper they are, Gran, and begging your pardon for the language.'

'Dear me,' said Gran, 'the shelf hooks are in Ifor. It might be lighter if we took off this mangle. Dewi, Mostyn!'

'What is wrong?' asked my father, coming up.

'It is the shelf hooks,' shouted Ifor. 'They are three inches up and two with cups on,' and Dada went under for a look: very pale he was when he came out.

'Ifor is solid on the hooks,' said he, 'and it can be important to a man, so take the weight gently.'

'Is there blood with him?' asked Man Arfon, peering interested.

'Not at the moment,' said my father, 'but the gutters will run with it the moment he is free from under the thing. Steady a minute, everybody rest. I will consider this situation,' and he took out his pipe, thoughtful, while we waited breathless.

'Too late,' said Dewi. 'Look what is arriving.'

'Dear God,' said Man Arfon.

Mr. Ephraim Davies, it was, striding down the wharf, and what the hell is happening on Number Two at this time of the morning.

'Mostyn Evan and family moving,' said Man Arfon, bravely, 'and this Welsh dresser stuck its hooks up one of the sons.'

'Dear me,' said Mr. Davies, compassionate, 'there is a situation,' and he stooped, squinting under. 'To the left a bit, man. Is it getting heavy with you under by there?'

Sparks came from Ifor's hobnails, and the language that flew up sent Gran sheet-white, and shocked.

'Easy, easy with the language, you under there,' commanded Mr. Davies. 'Ashamed you should be—your poor old gran is up by here, remember.'

'God help me,' said Ifor, and my father knelt, saying:

'It is not an easy situation, son, but Mr. Ephraim Davies has arrived now, and he is technical. Meanwhile, keep the language within reasonable bounds or Gran might take exception.'

Already taken,' said Gran. 'When he comes out by there it will be six-inch meat hooks, not Welsh dressers.'

With the rest of the family taking the weight, my father went off for a confab with Man Arfon and Mr. Davies, and when they returned, he said, 'A decision has been made. The women and children will have to leave, the trews are about to be removed from Ifor.'

And they went under and there was a lot of ripping and

66

sawing, with Ifor bawling, and eventually my father crawled out with pieces of belt and trews and Ifor went like a hare coursing in the opposite direction while Mr. Davies tore strips off Man Arfon for carrying private goods on public water.

Lots of people left Merthyr about this time; like Rosie Carey who boozed the ironmasters on the day Dic Penderyn was hanged—she left and bought the Old Plough above Glyn Neath, and rumour had it that Mrs. Alfo Morgan dug deep for this, to make sure of her Alfo. Mr. and Mrs. Dai Half-Moon emigrated, too, on the boot, and were seen staggering along the road to Aberdare with bundles and their idiot son, being pelted with clods by every urchin under Pont Storehouse: Dai Central Eating, my mam's favourite at Bethania Sunday School, he left Merthyr also, being sparked by an Eli Cohen woman, and becoming keener. Mr. and Mrs. Afron Shavings, the carpenters, left, too, for Mrs. Afron started getting visions, seeing a double coffin travelling at high speed over Cyfarthfa Castle in the company of angels led by Mr. Tom Thomas, conductor of the band, blowing on a silver trumpet. Others went to the four winds when the Great Cholera came, and are not recorded—some even to England, so you can tell the panic. But one only really remembers the people with close ties to the family, like Mrs. Ten Benyon and her brood, and Mr. and Mrs. Isan Chapel next door but eight, and Man Arfon on the end of the boot of Mr. Ephraim Davies, which was poetic justice, said Dada. Last, and not least, Miss Bronwen Rees took up as mistress at a private school near Aberdulais, by the waterfall, and I had just got my teeth into a celebration quart when news came that Taliesen the Poet had been seen wandering in the same vicinity, which set me back a swallow. Robert Crocker, Albert Johns and Willie Dare also came to the Vale of Neath, their lives being practically empty, so they said, now that Sharon had gone. Mrs. Shenkins, the mother of Willie-who-died had lately been sitting out at her back in a bath of six inches of water, in desperation: but she also came to the Vale since Willie used to fish down there in the Nedd. Many, many others left when the cholera came to The Top. Away from this accursed place, said my dada. Take a chance and starve, but away, and leave the filthy place to its monumental greed that will stand for the Crawshays, the Guests and the Butes and their like to the end of Time.

Away, said Gran, to Abercynon. Now that Mr. Emlyn Hollyoak is back in the Big Seat and that wonderful preacher has returned to Zion, it will never be the same in the Old Bethania.

*Abercynon!*

Down to the Basin with us, and we were off that dirty old Merthyr barge sharper than monkeys and trundling down to Eli's wharf with the furniture with Dewi under the dresser this time, Ifor being with bandages, and Nell and Jed loaded to the forelocks, and at the back was Gran between the wheelbarrow shafts. Ifor was humping the tin bath, me with the mangle and Dada and the girls coming after with the chest of drawers and linen, Gran making sure that this was well presented since it came from Camarthen and was best quality. And there was Mr. Eli Cohen waiting outside his cottage door with his fifteen women shrieking and chattering hind legs off donkeys, a couple of the matrons getting the vapours when Dewi came from under the dresser, and please come in, Mrs. Evan, for the tea is ready and the kettle will be crying directly.

Invitations and introductions all round then, with Sharon and Gwen dropping their new English curtseys, and Ifor being dragged out for presentation—all fingers and fumbles at the sight of so many women, though I think it was more blood-pressure than shyness for those Welsh-Jew girls were beauties with their brown, haughty faces and glorious red hair.

And one, Rebecca, aged seventeen, came from the back, one hand on her hip and her lips bright red in her smile, and I saw in a flash that Ifor, my brother, was done over fifteen rounds. So we left him to his fate, and me, Dada and Dewi went down to the wharf, and there was that Cohen barge all shining black and stacked with the furniture for the voyage round to Baglan. Three years we had worked for this; you get out of the soil what you put into it, said Dada.

'Got a good prow on her,' cried Eli. 'She is an inch above the water-line with the household effects. The mast is spruce, the sail is best Mary Walters down in Neath Arches. Float her in an hour, and with luck you catch the high tide at Cardiff before the bore runs out.'

'God bless you, Eli,' said my father.

'And God bless you, too, Mostyn, for I am back to fourteen now that Rebecca and Ifor have met up again.'

'Ach, no!'

'Like a sis, he is,' I said. 'Eh, look at it.'

Very girlish was Ifor, turning up his boots under the apple tree and Rebecca Cohen coming the Delilah on him, and holding hands like a fairy instead of a thick-eared pugilist.

'Come on!' roared Dewi, disgusted.

Astonishing how Dewi treated women: disdainful, his dark eyes smouldering fire, his lips uncaring, and yet they died for him in their ravishing glances.

Second cup of tea for Gran, and can I slip out the back, Mrs. Cohen, and she was ready, and old Eli lined his women up on the dancing lawn in front of the cottage and snapped his fingers, and down they all went in their folds and crinolines, heads bowed, elbows wide, skirts out, and I could have shouted at the beauty of it.

'Sail aboard!' shouted Eli, and we all trooped down to the wharf, with Ifor and Rebecca lagging behind arm in arm and staring into each other's faces.

'Beautiful women you got here, Mr. Cohen,' said Gran. 'And best kept clear of this rabble of fists that I am landed with.'

'We will get together, ma'am,' chortled Eli. 'With your lot and my lot we could build a Welsh Jerusalem down the Vale of Neath, you think?'

'Many a true word said in jest, mind,' said Gran. 'See if we can manage it, for I would like to see all my boys wedded and bedded to the right women before I go under,' and she looked at my father, her eyes bright with unshed tears.

'Away to go, we are,' said Dada. 'We will not early forget the Cohens of Abercynon, and there will always be a welcome in Resolven, remember, especially at Michaelmas Fair!' and he helped Gran aboard the Cohen barge.

'Ifor, we are off directly!' cried Gran, and he came running with Rebecca flushed and watery behind him: mind, this had been going on for a month or two to my certain knowledge, though supposed to be a secret.

I got Nell and Jed Donkey shifting, and we glided through the Cohen Lock, waving and shouting to the Cohen tribe clustered on the bank, and down they all went again in their curtsey. Beautiful, they looked, clustered about Eli.

'May your Jew-God possess you, Eli Cohen!'

'His hands above your house, Mostyn Evan, I will miss your sons!'

'Dear me! *Dammo*, what lovely people,' sobbed Gran, wet and dabbing.

'If you get a tribute from a good woman again, you have her bear a son for me, Mostyn Evan?' called Eli, and this put us all pretty dull, me especially, for the thought of my father with another woman always brought me sick inside. These things are all right being joked about, but a véry different kettle of fish when they happen, I say.

On, gliding along the canal, harness jingling, and Jed and Nell with eager hoof-beats, sensing that they wère leaving dirty old Merthyr for good. Straight into the Old Glamorgan canal we went from the Cohen wharf, into a line of wage-slave bargees, and we were big in the chest: Mostyn Evan and Sons it was now, for we had collected out last pay-day from Crawshay and from now on it was private enterprise. And we had just run into the Abercynon Basin when Abe Sluice, the swimming pig, came up ahead and jumped on his stern, shouting:

'Where you off to, then, Evan?'

'Resolven, on the Neath Canal.'

'How the hell can you do that, without going over land?'

Dada cried, 'Down to Cardiff, into the Channel and along to Port Talbot!'

'In that thing?' Abe hooted laughter. 'Wet and dead you will be, you idiot, if you go to sea in that contraption.'

'It has been done before,' said Dada.

'Oh, aye? If the sea don't get you the Neath union will. You heard they're breaking the heads of the new bargees signing on for the Neath Canal Company?'

'Depends what you've got for a head, Abe Sluice,' bawled Ifor.

'For God's sake,' said Gran, 'do not bandy words with the unwashed, for you can always stoop to pick up rubbish. What is this about breaking heads?'

'Man's business,' said Dada, 'leave it.'

'Is it, now? If anybody is breaking my head I want to know about it. Very secretive you have been about this move, Mostyn; tell me more about Resolven, for I am just considering it. Three up and four down, isn't it?'

'And a two-acre patch, a paddock for horses, a wharf, a stable for Nell. Like a country seat, it is.'

'I can well believe it for fifty-two pounds ten.'

'Just needs a bit of repair here and there, of course,' said my father uneasily, 'but I reckoned anything would be better than Fifteen Bridge Street.'

'Well, down with my head,' announced Gran, 'for I am coming numb in the nut. Call me when we arrive at your father's paradise in Resolven.'

The sun burned down, the country shimmered and glowed with incandescent fire. The cut rippled and sang as we carved along in waving bindweed and petals, the still-water seeded with gold lace from overhanging ferns. And alongside us the poor old Black Taff, who once had watered the Romans, leaped her black arms down her oily banks. This river, as my father said, was the source of the cholera, and for months now the skeleton in rags and tatters had been wading in her depths, stalking the hovels of the Top Towns for practice, picking off a child here, a whole family there. And at night he sat on the banks of the sewer, his skull clasped in fleshless fingers, watching as the poor Irish drank from the river and the Welsh from the putrid spouts. And a month back he sent the Guests away to Canford Manor, sharpened his scythe and came swinging into Chinatown, cutting the workers down in hundreds.

It is not so much the death that counts, said my father, it is the indignity, and the evaporating agony: to die of the cholera is to die a filthy death.

And now it was all behind us. Beautiful indeed, this side of

71

the Basin, for, though the land was still ripped and torn, the sulphurous stink of the iron-making had gone, the glowing heaps of slag vanished as in a cool dream.

'What time you reckon we'll hit the sea, Dada?' I asked over Jed's ears.

He pulled out Granfer Ben's gold watch and chain. 'According to Eli we'll be bogged in the Narrows and slowed in the Tunnel at Melly. Given a two-hour sleep we should get to Cardiff at midnight, and fetch the morning Bore.'

Excitement grew within me.

At Melingriffith I would lie on my back in darkness and push with my boots along the dripping ceiling, and in oil and black water we would run, with the ghost bugguts crouching in foul weirs, claws open for the unwary hand, or leg. Eh, *diawl*! Tunnels do frit me. But also, the sea was calling me. For beyond Tiger Bay was a thirty-mile run round the coast to Baglan and Neath, working out on the swill of the Severn Bore: I sniffed the golden air, and it was salt.

I heard Dewi say, fingering the sail canvas, 'Where did Eli buy this?'

'Mary Walters, Neath chandlers, so he said,' replied Dada.

'Then the quality must be good. Who cut it?'

'Eli Cohen.'

Dewi nodded. 'And old Eli ran the clippers up the China run, didn't he? I thought so, this is a junk sail.'

'The sail of a Swiss man o' war,' said my father, 'as long as it gets me through Baglan Bay.'

Dewi flung the canvas down. 'Five shillings that we never see the sky over Baglan, and another five that the life-boat puts out from Swansea—that will cost a pretty penny.'

'Taken,' said Dada.

'Just struck me,' said Dewi, fingering his chin now. 'You ever been to sea before?'

'I am about to go,' said Dada. 'You hold Gran steady when the Seven Bore comes and leave the sails to me.'

We entered Cardiff sea-pound that led into the Bristol Channel at nine o'clock next morning. Sail up now, and we fetched Jed Donkey and Nell Mule aboard for the sea-trip.

With the wind set fair we slid gently through the moored colliers and flat-boats taking on coal from the Top Town barges, and the port about us blustered with life: coaches and horses clattering into cobbled courtyards, flunkeys bowing right and left to fine city gentlemen; ladies in hooped crinolines walked with gentry disdain before their little golden blackamoors. And among the teeming crowds of the waterfront marched troops of soldiers, their red coats flashing brass; muskets shouldered, eyes wary for the rebel Welsh, for our ancient Prince did not die in vain. He did not die in vain, said my father, and we are having him replaced by no English substitutes. Buxom serving maids with swelling tops and bustles were ladling from steaming tureens, and I watered at the mouth at the sight of those fat, city merchants forking up beef and swilling it down with quart ale pewters.

'They do themselves pretty well in the city, strikes me,' muttered Ifor.

But the mooching poor went by in droves, hands outreached to us, begging for bread. Urchins, as naked as bones, ran in circles of savage joy around a butcher's bull being led to the baiting-ring and the iron-jawed dogs. Doleful in the stocks, heaped high with refuse, a drunkard sang a dribbling song, bare toes wriggling the time. In a forest of masts, the square-rigged barques of Spain heaved at their moorings. Broken-nosed and grinning, French matelots lounged on the rails of the Brittany coasters, impounded for harbour dues, said my father, and they spat at Ifor's cheeky wave and talk of frogs.

'Where you bound for, Welshman?' This from a bearded face over a rail, the accent posh English. Dada swung his hook, grappled the ship's side, and slowed us, shouting up.

'We make for Baglan Bay, and the Neath Canal.'

'Bad weather rising in the Channel, you realise this?'

'We wait for good weather round this head and we wait all our lives, Captain.'

'You'll catch the Severn Bore, you know this?'

'That is the idea. Is the wind following?'

'Following brisk, and so will the Bore. What stern freeboard have ye?'

'Two feet.'

'Right, but keep her stern-on to the Bore or it will cost you your life.'

'Right, you,' said my father.

'Thank God for your stupidity, Welshman, though I've seen it done before. God go with you, Taff!' and the face disappeared.

'Don't sound healthy, that,' said Gran, glum.

'You batten down,' said Dada, 'and leave the sailing to sailors.'

Harlots and harpies padding along the waterfront beside us now; drunkards already rolling out of the inns, with the riff-raff quarrelling on the doorsteps and meaty clumpers flying in the smacks of fist on flesh, and the language steaming in Gran's direction was hot enough to boil Baal. In the noonday sun the last wharves slid up; the aprons facing the Bristol Channel were stacked high with the loot of the Welsh Top Towns. For nearly a million tons a year was being dug out of the mountains, a golden hoard of wealth being shipped to a hundred ports in the world: never had I realised the staggering loot that was being cut out of my country by the speculators, leaving nothing behind but hunger, poverty, disease and a ravaged land.

A million tons of loot a year from the valleys of Wales, and this was only the beginning of the tide.

I thought of my generations of farming Welsh, who had paid the price of sitting on a fortune. In the great wounds of the mountains, the sealed, fiery caverns, the places of dark, rushing water, lay the refuse of my people. In grotesque attitudes they lay, where roof fall, tram or explosion had pinned them. In the jammed ventilation doors of the galleries, lipped by flood-water or incinerated by fire, sat the husbands, wives and children, trapped in the same instant, the same scream. Upturned pit-ponies and donkeys lie in company, their flesh preserved, embalmed by the last pressure of the crush in unknown salts and stinks. Hoof and hand entwined, they lie, the refuse of a foreign profit that was shovelled out with the furnace slag, by a foreign hand, of a thousand furnaces and bloomeries from Hirwain to Blaenafon and Cyfarthfa to Swansea. Let the patriot Welsh remember Cardiff docks, the pus of the ulceration which men call profit, gained at the cost of pure Welsh and Irish blood.

'You all right, Bryn?' called my father.

I nodded.

Strange, I thought, that I should remember my people at a time like this, as if they had been borne along before my eyes on the flood of black diamonds that were pouring into the holds; and their death-knell, it seemed, was the tolling of the rails being loaded for Argentina and Peru, France and Spain.

Industry, progress—yes: but not at the price as high as this.

I saw a tattered generation of dead that day. Six abreast, they came across the sky: the wizened colliers, the tattooed miners with their head-bumps and scars; the furnacemen scalded by the iron flash, the cancerous breasts of the women of the tin-plate picklers and the jack-knifed children of the lower levels, who, with the accord of an English Church, had been used in the two foot mine levels, where only children could crawl for coal, setting their bones for ever in crippledom. Across a landscape of engines and trams, coal and pig-iron, tin-plate and copper, they marched on a cloud, this stricken army of my Welsh dead.

'Wait for me,' said a voice.

We were through the sea-pound lock now, and Dewi and Ifor were back on board. My father's face was expressionless in the vicious light of the sun. The barge swung as the sea hit her along the shanks, the white-topped rollers hissed and sprayed from the Severn lying east.

'You'd best get the legs out from under that donkey, Mostyn?' shouted Gran.

'There'll be no panic, if you let him stand. He knows what's happening.'

'Got one foot in my bath of washing now, mind.'

'Ach, don't bother me, you should see to your washing!'

'And I'm getting as wet as a herring down here, remember!'

Dada rose at the tiller. 'Dewi, Sharon—cover your Gran—don't stand there mooning—see to her!' He grinned up at the marching host. Glorious they looked in their thousand, marching across that summer sky. 'Wait for me,' he said.

I stared at him from the prow, and the sea leaped, hissing wet on my face.

Behind my father I saw the sea-lock dying into the land, and behind that I could see the day-shift iron beaming on the clouds above Dowlais as the bungs were tapped: I heard the faint thunder of it, bellowing and reverberating over the sea. All this I saw through the image of my father's face, through the humped shadows of his eyes, through his transparent cheeks and hair. And he winked at me and looked again at the sky, for the sun was glowing in a new majesty, breaking over the earth a single shaft of golden light, and in that beam the army marched. I shivered, gripping myself, watching my father as he cupped his hands to the flare of his pipe, smiling at the sky.

I heard his voice, not in echo, but loud and clear above the hammer of the wind and the tramping hobnails of the marching dead.

'Wait for me,' he said.

And I knew then that the vision I had seen would one day be real to me, and on that day my father would be safe and dead, leaving me to suffer it.


# 9


OUTSIDE the pound the wind sweetened into pleasant whispers, content now we were in her parlour, and the sky opened wider and poured the summer morning over us: a zephyr fanned from the east of the Severn, and the ribbed canvas of the sail rose and fell like the breast of a sleeping woman. Laden on the wind came the tea-smells of the Asian clippers, the spices of India, cinnamon of the South Seas and ground coffee from the bubbling fire-pots of the Brittany coasters. In full flight were noses that morning off Cardiff sea-pound. Dear me, there is a strange thing is a nose, stuck upside down on the face to keep out the rain, and with holes · yet beautiful in some degree, according to the occupant—smooth and graceful, like Sharon's, for instance, or broad-beak and busted like Ifor's, spelling manhood. But it is the soul behind the nose that speaks—nostrils flaring in the lover, put sideways for kissing, and very windy in passion. Or twiddling to the scent of fried bacon, itchy when smeared with butter, but best of all when in repose, like now—drinking great draughts of autumn woodland and salt flung high from the caverns of the drowned.

Danger, it tells of, also. I saw my father raise his great head and sniff at the wind, which is the sniff of the savage to the rustle of undergrowth.

But, of, there were some glorious whiffs off Penarth that day. Very fancy is Penarth, but she do turn out some very strange smells: pot-herbs and onions from the Italian cargobummers, garlic from the bunged-up French, curry from the Indians, turbanned and jewelled. Persian tobacco drifted under my nose from the hubble-bubble hookahs of the grimy bunks, and there is only one way to smoke, said my father, and that is through a tin bath for purity. Had God given me a choice between a tongue and a nose, I would have chosen the latter. For the tongue can betray for the taste of money, as Judas for silver; can speak evil, can be seduced into corruption, or scornful, inarticulate with fury or as smooth as buttered honey with insincerity. But the snitch is noble, silent in service, its only crime being to turn itself up occasionally. And through the glorious plunder of the nose that morning knifed the Severn tang as the plug came out of the Bore, and there was spray in the wind as we swam easily around Penarth Head towards the white-foaming Flatholm and Lavernock.

'We got there yet?' Gran had loosened her buttoned boots and stays and was sitting with her feet up, her hat over her eyes, bulging black.

'Got there, woman? We are not even started,' replied Dada.

And nor were we, for there was a great wastefulness on the sea, with the sail flapping anger, and every time the barge rose at the prow the Welsh dresser went along on its rollers and hit Jed Donkey a butt in the rear, and rather this dresser than me, for he was hind-hoof-happy under less provocation. Gwen and

Sharon were going green round the gills as we ran goose-winged and free on the Bore in a world of buck and roll, and the white horses of the Head neighing after us as the basin emptied between Clevedon and Newport.

'Stand by with the paddles to steady her,' said Dada, for we were starting to go like a feather in a puddling-pit in hisses and roars.

'Five knots, you reckon?' asked Ifor.

'If we keep at this rate we will shoot past Neath,' said Dada.

Everything appeared normal at this stage, with Gran very perky and actually singing sea-songs about being down among the prawns and winkles with cockles for dinner and sea-weed for a bed, though inclined to be wet, wet, wet, with Dewi and Ifor, the idiots, bawling the chorus. Personally, I think this is tempting Providence, and I reckon Davy Jones lifted the lid of his locker and took note of the landlubbers, for next moment the wind came down in howls and the sea leaped up in fury.

'Paddles out, lads,' roared Dada. 'Hold her steady!' And Dewi and Ifor swung out the big oars.

'Bryn—drift anchor away!' came next, and I flung it out as Eli had told us, but personally I was becoming frit to death. For white-maned seahorses were after us now and people were hanging over the side, and suddenly, to my horror, I saw that my gran was head down and boots up underneath the horse-hair sofa.

'Bryn, see to your gran!' yelled Dada, cranked over the tiller, and I jumped into the hold, a little shocked, also, for one rarely thinks of grans with lace-frilled drawers and real knees, they being mainly floor-length people. And every time I heaved to have her out the bloody sofa rolled up and hit her back under again, and the stuff she was turning up must have taken the stain and varnish off every Big Seat from here to Port Talbot.

'Dewi, Ifor,' she shrieked, 'get me from here!'

But they were on the oars, so I took a grip on Gran's heels, eyes clenched for modesty, braced my toes against the Welsh dresser, and heaved, and her high-buttoned boots came off and I was arse over ear in the scuppers, still holding boots, and I reckon they heard my gran up by Tusker Rock, and just then Nell Mule wandered up and sat on the end of the sofa while Jed Donkey started hitting hell out of the Welsh dresser.

'Bryn, for God's sake, what are you doing to Gran?' yelled Dada.

'Stuck under the sofa with Nell on the end,' I shouted, 'and Jed Donkey by here belting up the dresser.'

'He is doing what?' cried Gran, peeping out, shocked and pale.

My father came down then, flinging chickens aside and heaving up the henhouse, and I couldn't see either of them for feathers, but he got Gran under the armpits and lifted her out and sat her on the kitchen table: very unhappy she looked with her hat down over her ears, and the moment she got her boots back on she swung one into Jed Donkey's rear.

'Not fair,' I cried. 'The dresser started it, mind.'

'Look, woman!' said my father. 'Will you stop this palaver about dressers and donkeys? D'you realise, if the sea comes any higher we're likely to swim for it?'

'And I hold you responsible, remember!' cried Gran. 'Not my idea, coming on this mad-brained voyage down the middle of the ocean.'

'What is that?' I asked, finger up, listening, for there was a strange hissing noise above the roar of the sea and chattering of chickens.

'That do sound ominous, Mostyn,' said Gran. 'Sprung a leak, have we?'

'Stop that Jed Donkey!' bawled Ifor from aft, and we swung round. And there, as large as life, with one hoof up and the other in the bath, was Jed Donkey piddling over Gran's weekly wash, and this all damp and rolled for ironing.

'Now, now, no recriminations,' cried Dada, soothing her. 'Donkeys are more important that ironing, and we will see to him later.'

'Ay ay,' said Gran, evil. 'See to him I will. This barge will be half a ton lighter if that Jed Donkey crosses my path.'

'Do not be ungenerous,' said my father. 'He is a house-trained ass, but he had to go somewhere. Bale!' and he went double-bass, so we baled, for when this happened we knew which side our bread was buttered.

*Well!* If the Danes had been off Aberavon in long-boats that evening, they would have bolted back to Skagerrak at the sight of us blazing along in Swansea Bay. Rolling, pitching, shipping it, trying to beat the turn of the tide, we ran into the mouth of the Neath River, poled and towed past Giant's Grave and up to Neath Abbey, which was smoking and flaring her ironworks like a place demented, and out came the puddlers and rollers and scarecrow Irish, all waving and cheering us, for it is not every day of the week that a twenty-two-ton coal loader runs up to Red Jacket with a sail in tatters, its crew at the oars, a mule and donkey aboard and fowls in the rigging, to say nothing of three women hanging out starboard and baling with chinas.

'Make a good impression, remember,' cried Dada, rushing about and tidying up, 'these Red Jacket canal folks come very smart.' *Ach,* wonderful my father looked that summer evening as we took the sea-lock into the crosscut that joins the river and canal: stripped to the waist on the prow he stood, bantering with the lock-keeper, his muscles bulging like an ancient Phoenician who had been this way before, and Ifor and Dewi naked to the belts, faces straining skywards as they heaved on the oars. On, on in a clang of drop-hammers as dusk came down, with Lord Vernon's Briton Ferry behind us mushrooming fire and hundreds of furnacemen working like dancing dervishes against the exploding fire-balls of redness and the clouds flashing and glowing to the streams of scarlet and yellow. Live ash rained down into the cut beside us; worse than Merthyr, I thought, but soon came the moon over a lovely land.

'Right,' said Gran, 'spruce up. Shirts back on, bonnets tied, tidy now, like your father says,' and she hauled up her kitchen table and tin bath and started pulling canal buckets to flood out her washing.

'Can't you wait an hour or so, woman?' demanded Dada. 'It'll still be light at the Old Navigation.'

'Things need sweetening because poor old Jed miscalculated,' said she, and this heartened me because five miles back he was due for the knacker-yard, and now he was one of God's little creatures and we are all caught short at one time or another.

The colliers were thronging down the path for Cadoxton pit as we slid past the town all twinkling fairy lights in the gathering gloom, and the stars came out, stepping above the alders arched against the sky, and I saw, reflecting on the clouds from Swansea to Pontardawe, the bomb explosions of the iron and copperworks and heard the shriek of engines and the whine of mills.

'Worse then stinking old Merthyr, I am thinking,' said Ifor.

'What we got for a change from dirty old Dowlais, then?' asked Gran.

'You will see,' said my father.

The cut grew quieter, the banks garlanded with summer flowers: coloured birds began to dart and sway over the water as we got deeper into the fair country, and the people were more countryfied, the men very stiff in good suits and dubbined boots, the women prim in poke-bonnets and whispering behind their hands shyly at the sight of strangers, and every other minute Gran was pulling Sharon and Gwen up on the stern, and the three of them going down in deep curtseys to families strolling along the tow-path. Now we reached the aqueduct at Aberdulais mill, the junction of the Tennant and Neath, and a woman came out of Lock Cottage with her daughter to work the paddles. Welsh dark and beautiful, this pair, and with a fine dignity, their black hair flowing free as they ran the wheel. The paddle jammed, which was an act of God, said Sharon, and my father jumped ashore and freed it, and I saw a soberness in him for this woman, with bows and please allow me to do it and think nothing of it.

'Dear me,' whispered Dewi, rubbing his face.

'You leave him be!' commanded Gran, suds to the elbows and flinging water.

Through the lock now, into a golden land where coo-pidges were whimpering and willows weeping, and the bright cut winding through a country of honey and milk and great swathes of green over the glorious mountains, and Ifor cried as the Aberdulais lock receded, '*Dammo di!* You see her, Dewi? I would rather be chased round a mulberry bush by

that than rushed by a couple of dozen, eh, man?' and my
father swung instantly to him, saying softly:

'Mind your mouth, or wash it. You keep those remarks for
the beer-houses, for one day you'll know the difference between a lady and a slut.'

And Ifor, to my astonishment, grinned at this, and leaped
down to the path, elbowing me out of it, walking saucy, his
boots punching out.

'Did you hear me?' shouted my father, growing horns.

'Yes, sir,' said Ifor, instantly, back in his place.

'The woman heard you—back and apologise.' On the tow-
path with him now, flinging Ifor back. I saw Gran make a face
at Sharon, and lend a secret wink.

Very strange is fate, I think, that a man can search the earth
and never find a mate, yet sharpens his boots on a path over a
valley, and there she is waiting.

I swung the tiller now for a second look at the daughter of
the beautiful lock keeper, and Gran whistled a tune at the
sky as she hung out her smalls.

'Manna from heaven, isn't it, boy. You at it, too?'

Don't miss a thing, this one.


But when we started to pass the barges running down to
Neath, murder took a hand, with the local bargees looking
down their noses and their women looking the other way, and
eyes were glowering in dark, Silurian faces: blood and race do
not count a lot, said Dewi, when the bread is being eased out of
the mouth, and we were strangers. But the tin-plate workers
from the Works above Aberdulais on the Nedd gave a welcome, strangers or not; straight from the Dandy-fires, their
cheeks patched red with the heat, they clustered in their white
smocks, the melters, picklers, tinners and branders, and waved
and shouted, and Gran lined up with Sharon and Gwen and
went down in curtseys while we got up and bowed, for there is
nothing the Welsh like better than good manners.

'My, there is an industry!' said my father. 'If they can
make tin we can carry it, and not likely to dry up, either—they
have been feeding tinned beef to the Army since the time of
Waterloo.'

A canal overman in breeches called from the bank, 'Mostyn Evan, is it?'

'Aye!' replied Dada.

'Come in from Neath on special ticket?'

'That's us!'

'Welcome, Evan. Report to the Company early, remember, to get clearance.'

'First thing tomorrow, sir,' said my father. And he turned, not interested, staring back in the direction of Aberdulais. Got it terrible bad, my dada.

On, on, with Ifor panting up red in the face and sweating, and my father put a hand on his shoulder as he jumped aboard. On along the cut now, free of the river lock—on past Gollen and Clyne and Melin, on to Resolven.

# IO

THE Old Navigation!

Here is a tumbledown; a ragged, rickety three-storey canal inn, used by the early bargees and drovers, with a rusted, creaking sign twenty feet up to prove it. But no drovers drank here now, for their bodies were dust with the souls of people like Granfer Ben, though their obscene shouts still echoed along the tracks above Sarn Helen, the old ones say: no bargees rested here on the way to Neath Abbey, for many were drowned at sea and down twenty fathoms off Scarweather and Tusker, or lay faint in the old canal grave-yards. But the Old Navigation still stood as their tombstone, ancient with her memories of coloured crinolines and knee-breeches in the days of Dadford and Jonathan Gee, though Tom Sheasby built the upper lengths, and was arrested before he finished it, while working over at Swansea. It is necessary, said my father, to know who gave this heritage.

'I don't now who built it, Mostyn,' said Gran, hands on hips, doing a tour, 'but the chap who charged you fifty-two pounds ten ought to be arrested also, for you have been fiddled.'

'What the devil did you expect, then? Buckingham Palace?' asked Dada.

'Outwitted, Mostyn—that is the word,' Gran persisted, and good reason for such statements, for there was scarcely a window whole in the place, sheep very comfortable in the tap-room and not a slate in sight on the north aspect. On we went on the tour of inspection, Gran in front, everybody following, including Nell and Jed Donkey, they naturally being inter-ested, and out the other side faces were longer than kites. Gran finally said, 'Well, I will hand you the odd two pounds ten for it, boy, and you can keep the fifty instead of the heritage.'

No soul in some people, mind. Dada said:

'Stables at the back for the donkey and mule, remember.'

'I do,' replied Gran. 'And with their permission I will move in there and they can come in by here, for this place is not fit for pigs, let alone decent Chapel people,' and to my astonish-ment she began to cry.

Panic all round at this, with Gwen and Sharon also bucket-ing, and everybody but my dada patting and smoothing them, and for heaven's sake dry up, said Ifor, or you will start me, too.

'Mop up,' said Dada, stern. 'Are you Welsh? Do you expect a new life to be a bed of roses?' In contempt, he sniffed. 'Dry as bones you would all be on the coffin ships before you reached Boston. Can you imagine Granfer Ben dissolving in the eighteen inch bunk on the ship that hauled him to Salt Lake City?'

'Ach, yes,' answered Gran, drying up. 'It do put a different complexion on things when explained like that.'

'It do,' said my father. 'Meanwhile, get shifting, for there are enough women here to eat the place. Sharon, Gwen—away for the buckets, pails and mops and get one room presentable —and heave out those sheep. Dewi and Ifor will haul in the furniture—all sleep together tonight. I will bed the animals.'

Strange, my father: one moment a dutiful son, with yes, Mam, no, Mam: next moment a husband.

'*Cariad anwyl*, my Mostyn!' whispered Gran, adoring him.

'Aye,' replied Dada, 'and your job's the cooking—get mov-ing, for I am hungry.'

84

The only way to treat them, mind: females work better after taking a belting.

'That might even come later,' said my father.

But trouble was upon us within a couple of hours of arrival. The tap-room had been scrubbed out, Dewi and Ifor were getting the barge tarpaulin over the roof of the north aspect; two rabbits I had clouted for supper were on the boil; dusk was having a word to a hunter's moon when I went with Dada over the bridge and into Resolven village for groceries.

'And do not be all night about it,' called Gran, in her element. 'The buns are in with spuds, the table laid, and I want this over before candles.'

'Back in half an hour latest. Come, Bryn.'

There is a pretty little village, this Resolven, half asleep in the dusk and with smoke from the miners' fires standing as straight as brooms against the clear, blue night, and the stars pale, but big enough to pick from the sky with fingers. We had just got to the start of the village street when Alehouse Jones Pugilist hove in sight four sheets in the wind, being a sailor, and put his thumbs in the slips of his trews, barring right of way.

'Into the gutter,' he said.

Let me be clear on a point. The road was about fifty feet wide at Resolven Square, but his request meant changing direction. We stood, the three of us, just looking, and Alehouse said, 'Strangers, is it?'

'Mostyn Evan and son, just arrived in Resolven, sir,' said Dada, sweet, 'and been sent for groceries, so kindly let us pass.'

The colliers started coming off shift, jumping off the drams that were clattering into the village, even from afar as the big pits of Cadoxton and Brynoch: out of the inn came Evans Brewer: Eynon Shinbone left his shop with knives and sharpeners dangling on his blue and white apron; urchins by the score were eyeing me. And my father did an astonishing thing then; he knelt on the road, saying softly, so only I could hear, 'This is a man who fights for sport. Never fight for sport, Bryn, only for honour. By now, your brother Ifor would be mixing it—and to what end? Do you give or take a broken nose for fun? And pity this poor man, for he is heavy in the head. First we will try him with reason, eh?' and he rose, saying to the bruiser:

'I am not a fighting man. Yet must I sell my honour to save myself a hiding? Let us pass, and I will buy you a quart in the public.'

The blood rushed hot to my face, and I closed my eyes; the gall was bitter in my mouth. Terrible when, at his first trial of strength, you realise that your father is a coward. To lose my shame I took myself with my brothers down to the Old Ironworks outside Merthyr last spring, and you Welsh swines *out*, before we shift you! Ifor, Dewi and me, and the three of us flattened against a tram with furnacemen coming at us with ladles: swerving to boots, shouts of gusty laughter, and I heard Dewi's voice in a dream, 'Run for it, Bryn lad, run!' and we went like devils after saints with half the Staffordshire men after us.

Now, I opened my eyes and looked up at my father.

'Coward,' said a woman, and the smile left his face.

Dada said, 'Of course, when you are called this you do not step in the gutter for anybody, including God Almighty,' and he stripped off his coat, putting it into my hands. 'Home to Gran, son, and tell her I might be a few minutes late with the groceries.'

The mountain fighter was swinging back for room, spitting on his hands, the crowd was buzzing with excitement, and joy.

'Dada . . .'

'Go,' said my father, and stooped, thrusting me through a forest of legs and belts, and I ran, but when I reached the river I ran up the bank and stared back. The canal is nearly empty now, for the railway strangled it of life; the lovely locks are rusted with years of forgetfulness, the runs which I shall always love are narrowed with silt, as if Nature had done what she can to heal the knife-wound in her breast. Yet sometimes, even now, as I stand in this place at dusk, I see my father again as I saw him then a lifetime ago: handsome in his white shirt, he stood, his head black curls, waving me off, and he was smiling.

I ran like a hare coursing. Along the tow-path I went, skidding over the wharf, up to the Old Navigation and hammered through the door, to slide to a stop on the flags, staring, gasping for breath. Everybody was up on Gran's white cloth with their knives and forks set, waiting for supper, and Gran was at the top with a pair of boiled rabbits lying like naked babies on the big white and blue dish before her.

'And what time do you call this?' she asked.

I cried in agony, 'A seventeen stone mountain-fighter has got Dada in the crowd down in Resolven, and bets are being laid and blood is running in the gutters!'

Nothing happened. Ifor grinned, Dewi looked bored, Sharon tossed her head and Gwen went on playing with the cloth.

'Alehouse Jones Pugilist?' asked Ifor.

'Aye!'

Gran said, 'Up at the table sharp, Bryn. It is bad enough one being late and I will talk to him later. How can we eat boiled rabbit without salt and bread?'

I stared at her, and she added, closing her eyes and putting her hands over the rabbits, 'For what we are about to receive make us truly thankful, and may God have mercy on this Alehouse Jones Pugilist.'

Aye, the Neath canal is a barren river of Time now, the Old Navigation where I made love to Rhiannon is just a pile of old stones: no longer it stands rubbing shoulders with beautiful Resolven, stark black against the stars with the wind doing his tonic-solfa in the eaves which Ifor mended; no longer the screech owls of Rheola let fly on the ridge that Dewi mended. For a man came with a telescope and tripod and set it up in the valley and peeped on cross-hairs and brought down his hand, and a banderole went in, then a centre-line peg. And next came the navigators of Limerick and Lancashire with railway lines and sleepers, and they took the main line through the garden and a branch through the tap-room and out of the kitchen where Gran laid her table. Then, first in singles and later in pairs, the big Corsair saddletanks of Brunel raced through it at twenty miles an hour. Most of our dreams went when the Old Navigation came down, but you can't tear the soul out of a place where people have lived: demolish it, ransack it, but the wealth is still there on the breast of the land, said Gran; the people are still there in mist; the lovers like Rhiannon and me still go up the back stairs hand in hand.

Ghosts now, most of us who once lived in the Old Navigation.

*Listen.*

The land is sick of it, and so am I. We are all sick to death of being second best, of quality being booted out by quantity, of honour by greed, of Wales being milked dry by the few in the face of the many, and we are sick, too, of the tap-room patriots on high benches who wheedle for English favour, and we have been in bed with these, said my father, since the iniquitous Act of Union. If the canal must be strangled in the stupid name of Progress, said he, then strangle it in the name of Wales, who owns it: if the land must be laid waste by ironworks, coal or new-fangled railway, then ravage it in the name of the Welsh, not the English, for the English have been plunderers from Glasgow to India and back via China, and we, the cousins of their door-step, got it early because we were nearest. Aye, to English board-rooms go the profits, he used to say—and carted there by the traitors of Wales, remember, for you do not find the English wheeling barrows. If an army of peasants had to die, if a host of children had to be starved and an ocean of tears flood the valleys, then let this happen in the name of Wales, by the Welsh, for the Welsh, not for some foreign gentry class who have never seen the skies over places like Merthyr, Dowlais and Swansea, and do not intend to.

'There is only one answer to it, mind,' Dewi remarked.

'Aye?' replied Dada. 'Well, violence is what they have preached to us and handed to us from under the skirts of their Church and Parliament. But nothing is solved through violence. You can shoot, you can bomb, but you will land back where you came from, because they are experts in the trade when the occasion arises. They will spread their words on honey, preach tolerance, invoke the gentleness of their particular Christ; but, by God, Dewi, if you threaten their profit, they will teach you the art of violence—remember the Chartists, the Luddites—have you heard of Botany Bay, their slave trades? There is no madder dog than an English country gentleman.'

Personally, I am not much concerned with the politics, save that I would hit everything English back to England if I had my way, for I remember the agony of Cyfarthfa. I am much more concerned with my Vale of Neath.

The canal, which I loved, is dying. But in her quiet places the sedgewarbler still sings, also the mavis and night-jar: still the corncrakes fly, still the herons stand on one leg in the old Nedd. But, when I was very young, the Vale was alive and singing. In the days when my father put out Alehouse Jones in eight seconds flat, the people were alive. Tough, aye, but *real*—not the milksops that Wales turns out today. Down Resolven cut the barges used to run, with Dolly this and Dolly that laying into the towropes, hooves skidding, flanks steaming, with the old summer moon lying on his back heavy with his meal of June. Smoke drifts up, in dreams now, from the hooped canopies of the bargees; hares and hedgehogs simmer, the last in gipsy clay; rabbits bubble in the big, black pots of the cabins.

Gone, all gone.

Gran has gone long since; indeed, most are gone, including my dark, sweet Rhiannon, but I see their faces clearly, as if it were yesterday: I hear again the run of the Nedd, smell again the sweet, sour earth-smell of the cut: aye, all the song of the earth is with me, and through the mist of the years I smell the perfume of Rhiannon.

I keep telling of Rhiannon, and do not mean to, for she did not come to me in those early days when the only decent road in the Vale was the canal winding through the alders, long before the Great Western Corsairs came roaring through the Vale, turning the milk sour in the pails, driving the pigs demented, aborting the cows.

Yet, such is the miracle of memory, that it only seems like yesterday that my father brought us in from the Bristol Channel and into the Neath Canal, to the lock where I first set eyes on Rhiannon, and the crumbling wharf of the Old Navigation at Resolven.

# II

FOR the next week, too, we were still at it, up sharp at dawn, the women in sack aprons like labouring Irish and swilling floors, and isn't it damned filthy and absolutely disgusting, and a passing bargee informed us that it was last occupied by a Mrs. Duffy of Cork, and I can quite believe it, said Gran, and if I could get my hands on Mrs. Duffy she would land in County Wicklow. No good trying to explain that this was about eight years back.

'You all right up there?' called Dada, for Dewi and Ifor were up in the gables mending the roof, and I was hauling up slates and tiles on a rope and pulley. Dada was bricklaying along the wharf and Gwen cleaning out the stables. Soon, with the glass back in the windows, the wind of the cut was sweetening the rooms, and we had even got the floor boards mended in the second bedroom, for Gwen, within an hour of arrival, had landed back in the kitchen in a shower of plaster and petticoats. Now she said, her eyes going big at table:

'Nine barges came down the cut today, Dada, and fifteen went up, and while doing Jed's stall, I did wave to them, but only three waved back.'

I saw my brother flick a glance at Dada, and Ifor said, 'Tub Union runs it strong round these parts, I am thinking. First he sends Alehouse Jones to give us a greeting, then he will not wave to a baby.'

'He can keep his union,' answered Dada. 'We have another here—the family, and it will take some breaking.'

'A handy size, mind,' said Dewi. 'They say he has a hundred and seventy members. We have seven.'

Sharon said, 'This morning I did speak to Betsy Small-Coal. Sick and scared they are, said Betsy, because they are poor, and we are strangers.'

'Not strangers,' I interjected. 'Welsh.'

'It do not count for much these days,' said Gran.

90

Considering that I was unimportant in the family, being in the middle, I never understood why my father selected me for discussion of points of policy.

'Dada is shouting for you, Bryn!' shrieked Sharon, and she added, whirling out of the kitchen, ' "My desolation does begin to make a better life. 'Tis paltry to be Caesar; not being Fortune, he's but Fortune's knave!" Bryn, where the devil you got to?'

'Coming now just, Juliet,' I shouted, for breakfast, dinner and tea we were into this Romeo chap. Through feathering leaves, her face patterned with sunlight, I watched her, book in hand, her face smooth and proud. Scrambling from the canal I rubbed for a glow, and she drifted on tiptoe towards me, hands floating, crying, ' "How cam'st thou hither, tell me, and wherefore? The orchard walls are high and hard to climb . . ." '

'If you will go from here, I will leg my trews on,' and I left her to her dreams and Shakespeare, and found my father leaning against the empty stable, smoking at the sun.

'Listen to her,' I said. 'Stark raving, she is—no rhyme or shape to her.'

'She is entitled to her dreams, Bryn.'

'Never make a living spouting that stuff.'

He shrugged. 'It is in the blood, and come out in Sharon. The sink awaits her, the child-bed, the endless children. Grant her Juliet, do not take her hard.'

I followed him down the tow-path, our boots polishing in the dew-laden grass, and the cut was loaded with light diamonds, the bull-rushes erect and proud, and coots skidding on their tails in panic. Reaching the Cohen barge, my father jumped aboard, vaulted into the hold, and sat, his eyes half closed to the beauty of the morning.

'I have a bit of a problem, Bryn, and need it sorted out before I pop it to the rest of the family. Sit.' He patted the gunwale, and I sat, nervous.

I was hating this, for I knew what was coming. Besides, this was Gran's business, for she always sorted the problems. After a bit, Dada said, 'Is it convenient to begin, then?'

'Aye.'

'Your nose is blown, your boots are square to the deck, the

coal is from under your back-bone?' His eyes switched under his dark brows.

'Yes, Dada,' I answered, rigid, for this appeared important. Then:

'You can remember your mother, lad?'

'Aye, of course.'

'How long has she been gone?'

I replied, 'Five years back come December.'

'A long time to be without a mother. Don't you think you could do with another?'

'Another mam?'

'We don't need one?' He was making it easy, judging my expression.

'Of course not, Dada—we've got Gran.'

A dog-fox barked from the woods of Rheola, and the vixen replied, her voice strong on a wind of perfume, for this was scything time, which is a smell of crushed apples in hayseeds, and bruised grass. We watched, unspeaking, as a barge from Glyn Neath slid past us: the bargees nodded briefly, and fine they looked with their brown, bulging arms sweating in sunlight, their flannel shirts open to the waist, and red neck-ties for taking cooling water.

'Do not look so ferocious, man,' said Dada. 'It has been done before.'

'A second wife?'

'Another wife.'

'Same thing.'

'It is not. Supposing I bring one in?'

I said, turning away. 'Gran would throw her out.'

'Gran would not throw her out, for she suggested it. Good grief, I should never have started this—too young, you are.'

'I am not!'

He jerked his pipe at a couple of Glamorgan canaries pecking in the field. 'You see those two old crows? This is the way of it—in pairs. Beef bulls and door-mice, rabbits and rodents —a man is happier, son, with a woman of his own.'

I said, getting up. 'You've got three—Gran, Sharon and Gwen.'

'How old are you?'

'Knocking fifteen.'

'You sound more like twelve. Backwards in some directions, isn't it? It was silly of me to mention it, and I'm sorry.'

I said, bitterly, 'Now you make me small because I do not agree with you.'

'That is better. Now you sound like a man.'

'It would be terrible to have another woman about,' I said desperately. 'Sort of indecent, it would be, with you and her married, and in the same bed you had with mam.'

'Is marriage only the bed, then?'

The blood was pounding in my face. I whispered, 'You make Gran lay her place at table, and now you talk of bringing in another, to take her place!'

'Whoah, man, do not take it hard!' said he, and brought his fist to my chin, pushing me sideways. 'It was only a suggestion, to get the feel of the family.'

'Who is she?'

He played with his pipe, uncertain, then smiled up. 'The little lock-keeper down at Aberdulais.'

'You seeing her?'

'Only from a distance. She's got a pretty daughter, you noticed?'

I nodded, smiling with him. Relief was claiming me; the horror was passing. The sweat ran in a little trickle on my forehead, and I wiped it into my hair. Dreadful, mind, the more you think of it. My father said:

'I heard that Miss Bronwen Rees has been seen in the vicinity.'

'Aye,' I replied, joyful. 'Gone in as school-mistress down at Aber—near the lock.'

'You still keen on that Bronwen Rees, boy?'

There are times in life when clothes go sideways, when the collar of your shirt is lying on your shoulder and the buckle of your belt is lying on your hip.

'Keen as mustard, but the age is wrong, see?'

'Have you seen her lately?'

'Not since leaving Merthyr.'

'You miss her?'

'What has that to do with getting a new mam?' I asked.

'Nothing. Just that I thought it worth a mention.'

I was warm inside for him then, eyes closed at the thought of Bronwen: excellent, it is, when people are considerate about the things you think important. Strangely sad was my father's face.

'You all right, Dada?'

'Aye,' said he, and, sighing, got up. 'I will raise the matter again when you are five years older. Back home with us now or we will both be pixilated.'

All this, I suppose, was the outcome of the new free-thinking that my father was always talking about these days. There was Sharon becoming an actress and down with the Penny Gaffs every Friday night, there was Dewi making bombs and planning a revolution in the cellar with folks like Ianto Fuses, and Ifor setting up a punch-bag in the stables, getting into form for the Black Welshman, the giant navvy who lived round these parts. And all this on top of Gwen looking up hollow trees for fairy Espionosas, and now Dada going mooney about the Aberdulais lock-keeper.

No good can come of this free-thinking, I say: since it started, me and my gran were the only folks normal.

Later that day there was a fine wind rushing down the valley, with the trees waving green along the cut, and there was a strange excitement in the air: bright and foaming the old Nedd, throwing up her arms to summer.

Special, that June day, also, for my father went on foot up to Pont Walby and came back to the Old Navigation waving a piece of paper.

'Mother!' Over the cobbles he skidded, and into her arms, and she held him away as mothers do with sons, and wagged her head, beaming.

'Oh, Mostyn, I am so glad!'

'Coal hauling—special consignment from the Company at standard rates—three trips a week from Glyn Neath to Giant's Grave!'

'What is happening?' cried Dewi, rushing in from the stables.

'A contract, a contract!' shouted Sharon, dancing.

'Three trips a week, it is a fortune!' I said.

'It is a fortune all the time you can keep the rates. Two shillings a ton free on board is fair payment; it gives a thirty per cent profit to the Company, and is about what they clear with their direct employed.'

'Then the Union has no cause for complaint.'

'You don't know Tub Union,' replied Dewi. 'It depends how he takes it.'

'On the chin, if needs be,' said Ifor. 'Does Tub Union and his mates own the Neath Canal?'

My father said, 'A lot depends on what happens when we go up to Pont Walby in the morning.'

'You will get up all right,' I said. 'The trouble will begin when we start coming down.'

'Oh, ah,' said Dewi, 'hark at that! The babies are from their long clothes at last, eh?'

'Growing up fast,' said Dada. 'We had a perfect example of it earlier this morning, didn't we, Bryn?'

It brought me ill at ease. Terrible, it is, to be at odds with your father.

Gran said, fussing and patting him, 'No trouble now, Mostyn. No difficulty with this old Union thing now, promise?'

Next morning everybody was up at first light, with Gran sawing at nose-bags and running the small-beer, and Sharon dancing around and quoting very happily, she having just got a job as live-out kitchen-maid over with the Vaughans of Rheola. I was grooming Nell and Jed Donkey, Ifor and Dewi sweeping up the barge and putting pipe-clay on the Turk's Head on the tiller: beautiful, that Turk's head, my father's joy, with its white, flowing tail and intricate patterns of laced whip-cord. Everybody was out to make a good impression and make friends all round, though it seemed that Tub Union would be the main enemy.

Not one of us gave a thought to the Black Welshman, for he was a railway navigator.

'You heard that the railway company is working on the Pencydrain viaduct, Dada?' asked Dewi as we went aboard.

'It will end like the Merthyr tunnel,' said Dada. 'I heard that has come to grief.' He took the fall from my hands and coiled it neatly on the barge prow, and beyond him the cut was all misted, with shafts of sunlight striking the run in patches of hay-seed gold. 'Eight shafts dug and Mr. Ritson, the engineer, at his wit's end, for the thing is losing money.'

'Shows the intention, nevertheless,' said Ifor, bracing off with his feet. 'You don't build a viaduct, mind, unless you intend to build a railway.'

'It will come to nothing,' said my father. 'Stephenson himself has said that a railway through this valley will never be built—the gradients are tremendous.'

'Brunel don't agree with him,' sang Ifor, teeth gritted as he thrust with his pole against the wharf. In bindweed, we slid on to the breast of the cut.

'Aye, Brunel says it can be done, Dada.'

My father spread his hands. 'All right, all right—in ten years' time. By then we will have bought up the Company and we will sell out to the Great Western for a hundred thousand pounds! Easy, easy!'

'Now I know who is Dai Dafto,' said Ifor. 'Take her, Bryn, lad—give the butt to that lazy Nell Mule. Here we come, Tub Union.'

Glyn Neath!

Going up for our first barge of coal, Dada cried, 'Take her, lad!'

For a moment he paused in labour, smiling at me, and then he winked, and I winked back. The wound was healed. Trembling with joy, eager, I turned to Nell, bawling, 'Up, up, away! Give it her, girl!' and the old mule flung her weight; the trace became a bar, spraying water on the thong: damp smells arose in the skid of hooves. 'Give it her, Nell. Lay on!'

'Fend off stern!' I heard my father shout. 'Well done, Bryn, lad!'

I cracked the whip over Jed Donkey's head, for he was walking still in his nose-bag, never reckoning to pull a pound till ten o'clock in the morning.

Eh, wonderful it is on a cut first thing in the morning, in slapping water and mist and shafted sunlight, with the air

fresh and clean blowing down the land, and behind you your
father and two big brothers, going up to Pont Walby. The
women were out on the doorstep waving, of course, but naturally, we did not spare them a glance. But very proud, me, with
my shirt open to the belt, hair parted in the middle, yorks
under my knees and a red choker knotted on my shoulder:
stepping so light in greased hobnails I hardly touched the
mud.

# 12

NEVER have I seen the like of Mr. Jeremiah Alton, the
English Pont Walby agent, with a broad-brim felt hat two
sizes up on him, a black funeral coat with buttoned alpaca
knee-breeches and a plum-coloured waistcoat suffering from a
bad attack of brewer's goitre. Cost him a fortune to get it that
size, said Dewi.

'Morning, Mr. Alton,' said my father, jumping ashore at
Glyn Neath wharf.

'You are late, Mr. Evan,' and he stared up at my father,
beef nose wrinkling under his spectacles, chin vegetating, most
luxurious, and the hum of him at that time of morning would
have flattened the small-beer in the manse. Dada said:

'With respect, Mr. Alton, it is not in the Company contract
what time I report—just that I carry three times a week from
here to Giant's Grave.'

'Your tune will change when the railway arrives, my man.
You will have to get up early in the morning to beat that.'

'When it arrives. Meanwhile, I am not your man, sir. I am
partner to a contract. Where do I load?'

Note-book out now, very official, licking a stub of pencil.
'Contracts in this valley are not very important, Mr. Evan.
Men, too, are ten a penny, which you and your kind will learn.
It is the barge, the donkey and the mule the Company fiinds
important.' Removing his spectacles, Mr. Jeremiah Alton

peered at us standing with shovels. 'Welsh fighters you got there, by the look of them.'

'Butter will not melt in their mouths.'

'I am delighted to hear it. The railway navigators are astride the road at Pen-y-Dre.' He smiled thinly. 'Led by the Black Welshman.'

'Bridge building?' asked Dada.

'Railway building, or have you not heard? And the Company does not want trouble.'

'None from us, Mr. Alton. That I can promise you.'

'Then keep that promise, or you may land back in Merthyr where you came from, for I do not like your style.'

'Nor I yours,' said my father. 'Tell me the bay and we will lift from under your feet.'

'That would be wise—also Man Arfon's, for I am leaving this very day, and he will be running the wharf tomorrow.'

I saw Dewi turn away with a groan. Strange is life. When you want to make a new start Baal comes out from under the stones with instructions for you to crawl on your belly. And now Man Arfon, sacked from Merthyr, was a top dog in Pont Walby. Mr. Jeremiah Alton turned, shouting, 'Irish, Irish!'

A ragged, burly overman ran up and I could smell his panic from here.

'Bay Five. Load priority—get this barge out of it.'

'Aye, sir!' He pulled his hair. 'Certainly, Mr. Alton, sir!'

'And report to Mr. Arfon tomorrow that it was late starting contract.'

'Yes, sir!' The overman swung, his fist high. 'Right, into it. Move, move!'

I saw shovelling labourers rise and stare; men, women, children. Dropping their shovels in a panic, they ran, pushing empty trams into a branch line, then rushed back, flung their tools high on coal tubs and seized the buffers of heaped trams, dragging them towards us.

'Stand clear!'

'Come on, come on!' shouted the agent.

'I said move, you lazy swines!' yelled the overman. In rags, sweating, their eyes and mouths white in their masks of coal, the Irish labourers flung themselves to the task with a panic born of hunger. I pitied them. With levers they tripped the trams forward to the incline, running with them and leaping aside with shouts of warning as they struck the timber baulks. The coal gushed into our barge. One tram empty, drag it into the branch: another one up with a rush, trip it, leap aside.

'Trim down the spills!' shouted Dada, and we flung off our shirts and jumped into the barge hold with shovels. I saw young girls working above me, stripped like me, their hair tied back with string, hauling on the lines, grunting like animals, their iron-studded boots hitting sparks on the concrete. Whips curled and lashed in pistol-cracks over the flanks of horses: reluctant mules were getting the butt-end or the boot.

It was a scene of Hades; of sweat, brutality, hunger, pain.

I cursed this Pont Walby agent, I cursed the masters, I cursed my country.

Pausing in the shovelling, I gasped at Dewi, 'Right mess we have landed in—Man Arfon on this wharf, and he do not like Mostyn Evan and sons. I reckon we'd have done better slogging it out in Merthyr.'

Dewi spat, wiping his mouth with the back of his hand. 'You have to kill a hundred Welshmen to get a pound of brains,' he said.


Out of the Glyn Neath wharf we came and drifted past the Nedd River with our first load of coal, and the four of us pretty sober, too, for it was news to us that Brunel had actually started line-laying down at Neath.

'The Swansea Valley might have been better to make a start,' said Dewi. 'There is no talk yet of a railway going through there.'

'We will meet the railway when it comes,' said my father. 'One trouble at a time.'

'Some coming up now, by the look of it,' I said from the tow-path.

We were on the Old Levels between Morfa and Glyn Neath, the Nedd River sparkling and lovely under the midday sun, with a string of Company barges making upstream, their animals cranked to the swim and hard under the whip: on our bank the rushes were thick, and lying among them, blocking our way, were some five coalers with their crews on the river path.

'Slow us, Bryn, it's a stiff flow—slow us!'

Leading Jed Donkey through the bargees, I brought her into the reeds. The moment Dada and the boys jumped down they were ringed by men; these were the Company hired who did not own a barge and never would. Mostly colliers once, as Ifor said later; the older ones shortened by the galleries, their head-bumps and coal-tattoos telling their old trade. But some were young, and brawny handsome.

'You the new lot from the Old Navigation?' asked one, an ox of a man, and over his eyes were the scars of fighting, not coal.

'Aye,' said my father.

'That right you got a Company contract to run from Glyn Neath to the Grave?'

'I have,' said my father.

'Got a paper to prove you can run on this water?'

Dada patted his pocket. 'The contract is in here, but you have the truth of it because I have told you.'

'We are seeing that contract, Mostyn Evan, or we are running you off this canal.'

'Then come and get it,' said my father.

Hands in my trews, I wandered closer to Dada. You could have shot holes in that silence of clenched fists and squared boots; then Ifor said, 'You want to mix it, bargee, you start with me,' and Dada said:

'You realise, man, that while we fight the owners profit? What are you stopping, right of way?'

The bargee weighed my father: this man's eyes were good —bright blue in his tanned face. He said, 'Now that the railway is coming the barges will be starved. They have cut us to two shillings a ton free on board now, and when the railway runs they will cut us again.'

'There will be enough loads for all,' said Dewi. 'If they build six railways, there will always be loads for the barges.'

'Oh, aye? Do not lecture your betters, lad, or I will be bloody livid with you. Less barges we are wanting on this canal, not more.'

'Anyway,' said Dada, 'Stephenson says they will never suc-

100

ceed in building a railway—he says the one in eighty Hirwain gradient will beat the engines.'

'And Brunel says he will build it, and we back Brunel: that is what Tub Union thinks, and I am Tub Union.'

My father showed no surprise. 'We will stand with you against the railway, remember: we will join your union, we will obey its rules. Tell us what you stand for, man?' Tub Union's voice rose:

'Against the railway, against the entry of scabs like you. We stand for the Vale of Neath bargee, for better wages, and respect for trade. And we had troubles enough before you came. Do you realise the railway navigators have a log across the cut down at Tonna? Playing pranks, while we have bread to earn.'

'What are you doing about it?' asked my father.

'What do you expect? It is the Black Welshman. He is backed by five hundred navvies and we are only a hundred.'

'Dear me, you are in trouble,' said Dewi.

'The Black Welshman!' whispered Ifor, smacking his fist into his palm.

'Aye,' said Tub Union, 'and he is going for the men, not the boys.'

'Strikes me you want more bargees, not less,' said Dada. 'Are you aiming to remove that log?'

'Talk sense,' came the reply.

'And if we remove it, will you sign us on?'

The bargees grinned, loving it. Tub Union said, 'Mister, you touch that log and the big Negro will boot you out of this vale and save us the trouble.'

'And if we do shift it, and Black Sam, too?'

'By God,' said Tub Union, 'if you beat the Negro we will sign you on.'

'Money in advance,' said Dada, and fished out four shillings. 'Is it a deal?'

'I like clean men, too,' said Tub Union, and spat on the silver. 'Cards when next we meet if you clear the log. Good luck, man. The big black will peg you down and draw the bones from your bodies.'

'It will be an enjoyable experience,' said my father.

Back south down the canal again in a drowse of morning heat, with the fields flashing green and the river leaping silver as we swam alongside, loaded to the gunwales with Pont Walby coal. The sky was a basin of varnished blue flung with billowy bed-sheet clouds from St. Peter's wash, and the great mountains dozed on their shoulders in the valley, their heads circled with little haloes of mist. Joe Stork was standing on one leg in the shallows, fishing, not the least interested in bargees, badgers crawled to earth, otters were hunting in shrill whistles. Past Melin we went in the canal, with Gran and Gwen hand in hand at Resolven, dropping in stately curtseys, all prim and mockery, and went into shrieks of laughter when the four of us lined up on the gunwales and bowed back to Dada's command, our mole-skin caps dusting our boots.

'All right, son?' called Gran.

'Dando!'

All fun and laughter, he was; hard to believe that he was going down to visit the Black Welshman, the man who had taken Owen Bach, the son of *Owen Bach y Crugau*; famous in the Vale was Owen, the mad one, as they called him, since he found men too tame to fight and used to take on wild dogs at the Lamb and Flag Bridge and in Margam Park on Sundays, from what we had heard. The Negro took him in forty seconds flat, the bargees told us, and nothing had been seen of Owen since.

The lock at Aberdulais appeared deserted when we arrived, and only when I began to swing the paddle did the door open and the keeper come out: pale and proud, she looked, smiling with cool politeness as my father bowed. Shadows were under her eyes, her hair dull, her lips colourless.

''Morning, Mrs. Mortymer,' said Dada, shifty in the boots and nervous.

'Good morning, Mr. Evan.'

'Well, are you, ma'am?'

She dropped a hint of a curtsey. 'Well enough, sir.'

I glanced around for her daughter, but the cottage appeared to be empty.

'See you coming up, more than likely, eh?'

'More than likely, Mr. Evan.'

And that was that: very dull, my dada, as we dropped back into the canal, and he did not speak again until we reached Pen-y-Dre, though I noticed Dewi and Ifor exchanging some jerked thumbs and nods of understanding.

'How much do they pay these keepers?' asked Dewi.

'The cottage and ten shilling a week.'

'Looks half-starved to me, that woman.'

And still my father did not speak.

'Here comes a handy looking lot,' I cried from the tow-path.

This was the first time we had seen the navigators at work in the Vale, though they were ten a penny up in Glamorgan Vale, where the railway came earlier. But these navvies must have been special; never in my life have I seen men such as these. They were bringing the railway end-on up towards Tonna, and they were burning out quarries to bottom up the permanent-way, we heard later, for the ground was marshy: a single line of seven foot gauge they were building, and rather them than me, for the going was tough. Stripped, like the Irish, the navigators laboured, amid the clatter of the trams hauling up the stones and muck, the horses rushing pell-mell and neighing in shrieks, galloping, then swerving free, the horse to the right, bridle-lad to the left—slipping the hooks a second before the tram struck the tripping-baulk. Up went the tram, out came the muck, spilling down the embankment: men go in with shovels to spread and level and rammers to consolidate.

They lose a boy a week down here on average, said my father, but there are more where they come from, horses being dearer than boys: when you see a railway in this country you are not looking at genius, he added, you are looking at blood.

And these were the men who built them, the great Stockton to Darlington, Liverpool and Manchester: men of the Shropshire quarries, tinkers from Ireland, the giants of the northern counties and the coal-bumped little colliers of the Midland pits—anyone with enough guts and strength was flocking to the navvy gangs of men like Peto and Brassey, who employed them through grasping sub-contractors.

'Take her slow, Bryn,' called my father, and the navvies

straightened, resting on their tools as we slid past them, for here the railway was coming within feet of the cut. Irish, Spanish and French were here among the English; blacks and even Chinese could be found among the navvy gangs: fighters all, hard-drinkers all; thumping for ale in the canal inns and the publics of Neath and Swansea, and they were better hunters than leopards of the women, anything from sixteen to sixty, said Dewi, leaving a trail of children for the Guardians of the Poor wherever the railway took them. With sullen looks, unspeaking, they regarded us: trouble has a strange perfume, coming in sliding eyes and tense muscles.

'There is a log across the cut,' shouted Ifor.

'That is what we have come down for,' said my father.

I am not given to easy panic, but I reckon there are certain times when one whistles and looks the other way, for there were three of us and Dada that morning, and about five hundred navvies.

'Remember what happened to Ianto Fuses,' said Dewi.

'No need to tell me,' I replied.

A week last Friday, according to gossip, Ianto Fuses came down this way and collected a log. Sixteen stone was Ianto, and a bar-room revolutionary, and he moored his barge, went up the embankment, bowed low to the navvy foreman, and would he be good enough to shift this log in the next ten seconds or hell would come loose for navvies, and their foreman in particular.

Didn't know what hit him, said Ifor. Woke up in bed with a steak on his eye and had it later that day for his dinner, not knowing if he was in Pen-y-Dre or Swansea.

'Slacken that trace, Bryn,' called my father as we came up to the log, and he leaped down on the tow-path beside me.

'Shall we come, too, Dada?'

'You three stay were you are.'

As I tethered Jed and Nell, the navvies started coming down to the tow-path. Lounging on the bank, they cut wedges of tobacco, chewing it and spitting on their boots, or rolled it and smoked, their clays cocked up arrogantly in their whiskered faces.

'You after trouble, son?'

'No,' I said.

Big and brawny, these men, yet some were quite small; wizened gnomes from Cumberland, said Dada, but graft and exploitation in the pits had condensed them in ferocity. One about this size, but young, wandered up, gave Nell one in the ribs for luck and lounged on a gate-post beside me, his eyes glowing hatred.

I recognised him instantly. He was the Irish boy I had seen begging for work of Ephraim Davies, the agent, in Cyfarthfa, nigh four years back. Glowering, he pursed his lips, making a rude noise in my face.

'Well done,' I said. 'Now do it with your mouth.'

'You after trouble, Taff?'

'Set them up,' I said, pushing Nell out of it, but my father said, pulling me away:

'Bryn, for God's sake—must you choose a time like this?'

'Begging for it,' I said.

'Then take him in your time, not mine.' He wandered through the bunched navvies, his hands on their chests, pushing them aside, as a man can do without giving offence. And through the path he made I saw the log again, lying over the canal: at the bank end a Negro was standing, and he was a foot taller and wider than any man there, including my father. Feet splayed, naked to the waist, he grinned, his teeth appearing white in his face, and flung away a shovel, putting his fists on his hips: like some primitive god he stood motionless, his great, muscled body glistening like watered coal. 'You got a log, bargee!'

Hands in his pockets, my father joined him. 'Aye, did your gang put it?'

'I put it, Taff.'

Dada nodded, scratching his chin, deliberating. 'And I shift it, eh?'

'That is the idea.'

It was the age-old song of the drovers—fight for right of way. My father lighted his pipe, very interested in this log, then suddenly hit it on his boot and dropped it into his pocket, always a sign of trouble.

More navvies came down from the embankment, their eyes

bright in their faces at the prospect of a fight; these were the men of the randies when they broke out on pay nights and drank everything in sight, who lived in their shanty hutments alongside the line, made their own creeds of honour, and fought to the death at the drop of a hat. For these there was but one form of transport—rail; barges, to them, were a joke. The Negro said:

'I put it, Taff, and you shift it, or get back home where you came from.'

My father rubbed his chin. 'A new game, is it?'

'An old one—right of way: to see what the white Welsh are made of.'

Dada nodded. 'You talk cheeky with enough to back you.' He put his foot on the log. 'And if I shift this thing do I get down the cut?'

The Negro said, 'Not so easy, man. After you shift it you tangle with me.'

My father said, 'It's the log I'm worried about, black man. I can take you any day of the week.'

The expression on the faces of the navvies changed from interest to incredulity, and the Negro scowled, made a fist of his hand and thumped it into his palm.

'By Christ, Taff, you got it comin'!'

Dada grinned, and I knew what he was up to. The temper of the Black Welshman was known throughout the Vale: he was most dangerous when he was ice-cool, and my father was rattling him. Now, waving his arms out of his shirt he tossed it over to me, gave Black Sam another happy grin for luck, and waded into the canal.

'He strips well, Sam,' called a navvy. 'You best watch him.'

Silence. Even the sun froze: the water of the canal moved in ripples to Dada's legs as he positioned himself beside the log. Suddenly, he ducked, taking it on his shoulders, entwining his arms along the bark. He splayed his legs wide to drop height, the fine muscles of his back tensed and knotted, and he grunted deep in his chest. Relaxing his grip, he ducked out again, panting, then dipped his hands into the water and flung it high, smoothing the coldness over his face and chest. Ifor shouted from the barge:

'I say leave it, Dada, it is a two-man load.'

'One-man load for a dirty black nigger with a hide like me,' shouted the Negro in sudden anger, and I saw in a flash the insults, the kicks; the brutality of the whites, and the chained labourers of the American plantations under the lash of men called human.

'Black Welsh is dirty Welsh down in Tiger Bay!' he shouted.

'Not with me, Welshman,' said my father, taking another grip on the log.

'You will do, Taff, 'cause you are nearest. You shift that log, then I'll tan your arse like a baby.'

Suddenly, the log rose, and Dada was under it. Straightening from the waist, he held it, the end waving as he fought for balance, and I saw the sinews of his thick arms corded, the great biceps bulge and vein bright blue. Sweat ran in quick flushes down his back. I held my breath. Neck cramped under the load, face scarlet, eyes clenched, my father turned slowly from the waist, a foot out, feeling for a hold. Step by step, with agonising slowness, he moved towards the bank, and the Negro went back a pace, nodding approval.

'Give the old man credit!'

'He'll need more'n that—he still got to land it!' They pestered among themselves in a rising babble of oaths and encouragement, they shoved for a better view, bawling, their faces aflame, and I hated them. The boy-navvy yelled into my face, 'If he lands that log he still got Black Sam—murder him!'

I did not answer. I was dying inside for my father. Another wading foot, feeling for a firm place, and the log was tipping precariously. Always, it seemed, he had to fight to keep up square with the rent, either masters or mates. If it was not employers, it was people like Tub Union for membership, or Alehouse Jones for the fun of it—sent by the Union, a pawn in the game of hunger. Now the navvies were turning him into a dray-horse, for right of way, before setting him up for a beating by the most brutal man in the Vale. The boy beside me said:

'When he collects his, you get yours, remember, and no scarpering for home!'

I had no time for reply. A voice cried, 'Brunel!'

The navvies moved uneasily, the name of Brunel going through them like a fire, trapped by the spectacle of courage and the arrival of authority. Brunel was their idol. I saw a trap arrive on the road above me in bowed greetings.

'Hey, Sam!'

The Negro half turned from my father.

'Watch it, Black Sam—Great Western people coming!'

'Ritson, too...!'

Three gentlemen were standing on the bank just above me: one was quite small, wearing a soiled frock coat and striped trousers and a top hat too big for him.

'Brunel,' whispered the boy navvy, 'the one in the middle.'

With an expressionless face the man on the bank watched the scene below him, and his navvies moved nervously, like schoolboys caught at a prank. This was the engineer they loved, the man of genius who was building bridges and via-ducts, aqueducts and tunnels, and driving railways all over Britain. Suddenly, he cried, 'They are gaming you, bargee. Would you rather I stopped this?'

Navvies began to tear off their hats; there was no sound but the slap and suction of the canal as my father moved towards the bank, the log waving on his shoulders. Reaching it, he crouched momentarily, then ducked, shifting his grip. With fingers spread under the log, he shouted hoarsely, butted down, and threw. The log clattered wetly on to the bank.

I can see it now: my father standing in the reeds, throwing water over his sweating body, smoothing it from his face and hair, and I can hear it again—that one man clapping. It was Isambard Kingdom Brunel, clapping for my father. And the clapping was taken up by the gentlemen, and then by the nav-vies, and it changed to cheers that echoed and resounded down the cut. The big Negro flashed a smile at the man on the bank, crying:

'Fair play, Taff, you'm a better man than I gave credit for.'

'Thank you,' said my father, gasping. 'May we pass now, or do we tangle?'

'Any time you come down this cut, you pass, man, or you

108

call for me.' The Negro turned to Brunel. 'Just a bit of fun, sir—Welsh to Welsh during the break—no harm intended.'

'And no offence taken, I hope,' said Brunel.

'None,' said Dada, and raised his hand. 'Now be good enough to ease me out of here, for I am stinking of weeds and dead cats,' and Sam, the idiot, gripped Dada's hand and braced himself for the heave.

Too late. Dada heaved first: foot against the cut, face furious with anger, he heaved, and Big Sam flew like an angel over his head and went head over heels into the middle of the canal.

Dear me.

Now there is a hell of a commotion. Men went double, bellowing laughter: they shrieked, stamping about, mopping at their eyes. The Irish lad beside me was hooting soprano, the men with Brunel were cheering, their arms up: only Brunel was silent, weighing the situation. And the bedlam grew as my father vaulted on to the bank and stood there streaming water, and the laughter changed to shouts of warning as Big Sam floundered in fury towards him, fists clenched, his massive shoulders opening for the swing. Up on the bank now, he swung a right, and Dada's thick forearm went up, stopping it: dropping at the waist, squinting up, my father shuffled in, ducked a clubbing left, and then straightened—hitting up short. The Negro took it on the point of the chin, and teetered on the edge of the cut, arms flailing. And the hook that caught him then was glorious; a wet arm flashing in the sunlight, the fist making an arc that ended in a smack of fist on flesh. The Negro took it full. Arms dangling, he turned slowly, splashing face down into the canal.

My father turned away. 'Fetch him in before he drowns on us, Bryn.'

There was no sound over Pen-y-Dre as I stood waist-deep in the canal, holding Black Sam's head above the water; then navvies floundered in, gripping him, their actions paralysed by the speed of things and their own disbelief. Hauling the Negro ashore, they cast quick, apprehensive glances at my father as he stood on the bank before Brunel, his trews soaked and stained with mud, his hair tufted and tipped yellow with the golden dross of the canal. One of the gentlemen on the bank called. 'Well done, bargee. You will have no more truck with him, I'll warrant!'

My father said, wiping water from his eyes, 'You are right, sir. And nor will we have any truck with you and your kind.' His voice rose to a shout. 'Your navvies come to this valley as if they own the place—they cut it up for your railway, and try to drive the bargees out. But you will never drive us out because we live here—this is our home. And we were in this valley or the Top Towns before you knew of Merthyr, Dowlais, or the Vale of Neath.' He swept his arm around the staring faces about him. 'You bring in the English and the Irish. You employ the foreigners at cut prices, and they drink and whore and fight—there isn't a day's peace since they came to the place. Isn't it enough that you're carving the land to hell? Do we have to fight for right of way in our own land? Do you have to bloody starve us?'

'Mind your words, Welshman.'

'And you your railway, for I tell you this. If you want a fight you can have one. For we have been fighting in these valleys before you knew there was profit in Wales. You let us pass from Walby to Briton Ferry, or by God, it will be the worse for you. And tomorrow, if a bargee comes down here and finds a log over the cut I will go to Merthyr and bring down a thousand Welshmen, and we'll tear this railway up and toss it back to Neath where it came from.' He took a deep breath, turning to Ifor and Dewi, who were kneeling beside Black Sam. 'Is he alive?'

'Just about,' said Ifor. 'Man, you hit him.'

'Rise him,' said my father, 'for time is short. I have a barge under contract for the coasters, and we are working late. Come.'

The navvies parted as we went back to the barge, though some stood rock-still, hands bunched. The Irish boy stared at us as I shouldered him aside and hooked up Jed and Nell, and as we glided off under the animals I said to him softly, 'Now you know who you're with. You call me bastard once more and I am seeing to you right when I come by here again, logs or no logs.'

110

He did not reply, but before we had gone a few yards a voice rang out loud and clear, 'We can use you, bargee—you and your sons—any time, remember.'

And Dada called back from the deck, 'With respect, sir, not until you run us from the valley.'

With this, my father touched his hair, a thing I had never seen him do to any man.

'Do not look back,' he said.

In victory, in defeat—never look back, said my father.

# 13

AND so we made our home in the Old Navigation, and it was good. We raised a new roof, we plastered, decorated; we hoed up and dug and grew vegetables, with Gran on her knees planting seeds along the wharf in spring and tending them through summer into glorious colours. A winter came and went, came again and flowered into another May. I remember with joy those bright nights by the fire, with my father reading from the Book and the canal outside all over ice and mist; the trees scarecrowed over a frozen land, and the old Resolven mountain shivering under a leaden moon. But it was warm and quick inside the Old Navigation, and at night I would lie in bed and listen to the ice-breakers thundering down the cut, the stamping hooves of the big Carmarthen dray-horses, the shouts and banter of living people. This noise of people is the song of the earth, says my father, for is not this business of living like a great chord of music? he asked. Granfer Ben used to ask the same questions, said Gran at her stitching. Is not living and dying akin to a great symphony, in which is born the lore and scholarship, and the marvellous wisdom of the aged? 'Mind,' said she, 'he had beautiful thoughts, except when he was on the beer, the women, or the trumpet in the Dowlais Silver Band,' and she sighed at the moon in the window. For my part, I do not agree with either of them, believing that the love of a man for a woman is the true song of the earth. And with beautiful thoughts like these I naturally hankered after my Bronwen, for come May I was in a terrible bother with the spring, the year I was sixteen.

Very tight and hot under the collar I come when I think of Miss Bronwen Rees, whom one day I will marry.

Saturday morning, one week in six this was free. Ifor was over at Abercynon sparking his Rebecca; Dewi was down in the cellar with Pietro Bianca: Meic Jones, the pot-boy up at the Vaughans, Rheola, had called for Sharon and Dada had taken Gwen up the cut for a stroll.

Not a sign, not a sound of the lock-keeper at Aberdulais lately, but this was no business of mine.

An afternoon adrift, me: polished up, pulled in, best suit on, boots shining, starched collar, washed behind the ears, very presentable.

'How do I look?'

Gran eased herself up from her flower-bed in cracks and groans.

'And where might you be going, pray?' Gay with primulas and celandine, bluebells and forget-me-nots, Gran's flower-beds blazed; the passing bargees doffing their hats to her, the women bowing, and what a beautiful sight it is, Mrs. Ceinwen Evan, and what a delight it is to see it all fresh and lovely amid the dirt of Pont Walby coal. Gran had green fingers, as people have, when they are in touch with God.

'There is nothing wrong with a bit of a stroll,' I said to her.

'Nothing at all, if you keep moving. Eh, you gorgeous, come by here,' she said, and I went to her and she held me, saying soft in my ear, 'Most bountiful. Ach, look at it!' She held me at arm's length. 'Grown from boy to a man. Down to Neath and put them on their ear, is it—here is one for a start!' and she kissed me a smacker. Finger up, then. 'But be good, remember!'

Easy when you're seventy.

'Yes, Gran.'

'No complications—you know what I mean?'

'Mamgu, *Mamgu*,' I said to her.

'As fizzy as potato wine I was, at your age.'

'I bet!'

'So fizz, *cariad*, but do not overflow. *Darro*. There's a life! Do I know her?'

I shook my head. Give her a name and she would have it all over the village.

'Well, anyway, be kind to her.'

'Yes, Gran.'

'Men are rough with women. Like Granfer Ben—didn't know his own strength. Gently, is it?'

'Goodbye,' I said. I left her on her hands and knees again, her hands deep in the rich, black soil that in time would befriend her, under Dada's flannel shirts weeping on her line.

I left her, but not in the direction of Rheola.

Aberdulais, me!

Miss Bronwen Rees, and going hot and cold at the thought of her.

I had timed her like a clock. Five weeks in six I had seen her, my Bron, when we went down to the Grave with Walby coal, all done up glorious, she was, making for Shoni's farm, probably for milk.

Six shillings I had in my pocket that day, and spent already in dreams. At three o'clock I would meet her; off to Neath with us on the first barge down, a shilling ride around Town, tea out like gentry, with Welsh cakes done on the stone, for I knew she loved these: back home in moonlight, stand on the school door-step: in the music of the water-fall, I heard myself say:

'Good night, Miss Rees.'

Pale her face in that moonlight, and her eyes like stars: lips black-red and parted, in hope of a kiss. 'Oh, Bryn Evan, my darling. Do not be like that—call me Bron.'

A shivering is in her; scared, no doubt: never had a man so close before, only females like Taliesen the Poet.

Her waist is slim to the hook of my arm, the moonlight shadows deep in her cheeks. 'Oh, Bryn,' she whispered, 'kiss me, kiss me!'

Bread and cheese now, and I ate her alive.

'Oh, gently, gently, with a woman, boy. Fizz by all means, but do not overflow. Eh, gorgeous you are, like Granfer Ben.'

'Right you, Bronwen Rees, I am grown up, see.'

'Oh, Bryn!'

'Ahoy, there, Bryn Evan!' In my dream I heard his bass voice: in my dream of Bronwen. Dai Central Eating, it was, in his little rowing boat: gormless was Dai, fishing in ten inches of water, and what my mam saw in him in the days of the Old Bethania Sunday School, I never did understand.

''Afternoon, Dai,' I said. Nearly scared my wits out, bawling like that in the intimacy of me and my Bronwen.

'You want a lift down?'

'Much obliged,' I said. 'What you doing now, then?'

'Sweeping up in the tin-works in Melin; time-keeping, making tea, all odd jobs, and keeping my ear to the ground.'

Better than the old *Trumpet of Wales* was Dai Central, when it came to the scandal, with his long nose over the gate or under the bed, one tooth snitching like a rabbit: biddings, beddings, births and black bunting was Dai Central Eating. But I was not very interested now that Bronwen was practically in the locker: sixteen, me; very determined: a sailor's farewell this was going to be—tonight or never. I was putting this particular point to her when Dai said:

'You heard that me and Tegwen Harriet are sparking very strong?'

'Tegwen Harriet?'

'Wake up, man—Cohen's number five.'

'Oh, aye,' I said, vacant.

'And if I snare Tegwen and your Ifor brings down Rebecca, this makes you and me sort of cousins by marriage, four times removed?'

'Good,' I said.

'And your big sister Sharon coming very hot with her over that Meic Jones, Rheola, and noses out of joint on Robert Crocker, Albert Jones and Willie Dare?'

'Ay ay.'

'Dewi and Rosie Carey also; there's beautiful, but very immoral, mind.'

114

'Very.'

'Him and Pietro Bianca still making bangs in the cellar?'

'Louder than ever.'

'Only your dada is not involved, and that will not last for ever.'

This raised my head. 'My dada?'

'The Aberdulais lock-keeper and her daughter are coming back.'

'Coming back to where?'

'Coming back to Aberdulais lock—next Friday.'

'Where have they been these last two years, then?'

'Swansea workhouse. The mother fell ill, the daughter went in with her, for debt.'

'God help them.'

The keeper was coming back. I could imagine my father's joy. Bubbling in the heart I cut across the fields short of Bryngelli, doing boot-clogs and backsteps, waving to Dai Central Eating. Vaulting gates that were not there, I made for Rheola till Dai's boat got clear, then doubled back, my hobnails two feet up in the air. Eh, I was happy for my father: after all, nothing would come of it.

Hushed in the valley of Gadlys stood Dic Shoni's farm, and beyond the farm stood Bron's school, and the little cottage she shared with her mam. Blind as a bat in sunlight was Dic Shoni, so no fear of buck-shot as I hand-sprung his gate and leaned against his barn, waiting for Bronwen to come down for the milk.

Brush yourself down, smarm back the hair, rub your toe-caps on your calves, tighten up your stock, an inch up with your trews. Heart thudding, you wait.

And on the third chime of the church bell, the cottage door came open and Bron stood there: in a snow-white crinoline and with hoops, she stood there, her floppy summer hat done over with a pink bandage. Numb, I closed my eyes to the vision of beauty, and when I opened them she had gone, as if plucked into space. High in the sky a lark nicked and sang demented; the wind of the cut fanned my face, the sun burned

115

down. Next moment I heard voices behind the barn, coming nearer.

It was the voice of Bronwen Rees.

To this day I can smell her perfume, hear that excited chattering, and her soft laugh guaranteed to make your hair curl. But fearfully now, I heard Dic Shoni's voice, too; I retreated into the depths of the barn.

Silence. Footsteps now; a man's whisper, but it was not Dic Shoni's. Trapped, I ran swiftly up the ladder to the loft, and there went flat.

Through a crack in the boards I saw them instantly below me: Taliesen the Poet, with Bron in his arms, and I closed my eyes. Pent words of love I heard then; the inarticulate sounds that spring from lovers. And amid this beauty Bron suddenly laughed, softly and treble high, as Rosie Carey might have laughed in the arms of Dewi.

I screwed up my hand, remembering the removed dignity of my mother.

Does a man ever know a woman? I wondered. Was this my mother's twin, her face of darkness, the paramour of any passing Taliesen, a slut in straw?'

I shut my eyes and pressed my hands over my ears.

Give me men.

Enough of good women to last me a lifetime.


# 14


No place like the Vale of Neath when it comes to gossip.

And the family of Mostyn Evan over at the Old Navigation were not left out of it, for the Welsh are very interested in neighbours.

Very respectable on the face of it, that Mostyn Evan and family, the bargees; twice to Resolven Zion every Sunday, with bows on all sides, and aren't they a picture, and all but one of them a credit to the community: upbringing, it is, girl, upbringing. Ach, yes—bangs in the cellar, true, but queerer things than bangs in cellars do happen in Resolven, be fair. Strange, though, that Mostyn Evan has no woman around, isn't it? And whiter than a shroud his moral integrity, they do say, missus. Only that Dewi do not stand close examination, nor that big Ifor doing his pugilistics. Eh, but a lovely girl that Rose of Sharon, aye, and biblical. But little Meic Jones Rheola will turn her into two, given half a chance: ah! hot as hell, that Meic Jones, same as his da, mind—got them running screaming down at Swansea ten years back, as fast as they could pull them from under him, Constantinople harems don't come into it, man. But nothing against that Sharon, save that Shakespeare—isn't healthy, too much Shakespeare, says our minister, though his activities do not stand examination, remember. And that Bryn not normal, you ask me, though Dewi is his dada's cross, mind, oh, aye!

Dewi, Dewi, *Dewi*...

Slander, slander, bubbling in the ale, gurgling under the aprons; invectives coming from starched white collars, whistling over the cobbles, around street corners. In the frothing bars from the Lamb and Flag up to the Plough, Glyn Neath; in pit, in kitchen, in cornfield, it was Dewi, *Dewi*!

And that little one Gwen not quite the ticket, also: sad, sad it must be for that grandmother. Talking to the teacher, I was. Given her up, see. Twice two are eight. You know what? Down the bottom of the garden she was feeding a sparrow. 'Bread for the sparrow,' she was asking for, and when her gran went with her she was feeding a viper. In touch with the Devil, I say.

But always, always it came back to Dewi.

Anarchist, agitator, and Rosie Carey, and Mrs. Alfo Morgan used to stoke the fire up at the Lamb and Flag. 'The pillows are in constant use,' she used to say, 'as Alfo rolls out one side Dewi rolls in the other. Not that I have actually witnessed it, mind, but there is always speculation. Suits me fine, girl, as long as I draw the wages. Another pint, Mr. Talfarn Davies—first one to settle the dust?'

And Gran used to say, 'That Dewi is the talk of the village, Mostyn. Not decent, I call it, sharing a woman.'

'The cheese is that much sweeter when nibbled by another mouse,' said he.

'You ought to be ashamed of yourself!'

'Better Rosie Carey than a girl like my Sharon,' said he at *The Cambrian*.

'It is all part of the free-thinking,' exclaimed Gran. 'Never in my life will I agree with the free-thinking.'

'That is the difference between you and Rosie Carey,' said Dada.

'Is it wrong to be respectable now, then?'

But Dewi apart, we were as respectable as anyone else on the canal about this time, for the bargees of Wales must not be confused with those of England. And while George Smith, the canal reformer, had his hands full up on the big Midland canals, and fighting spare-time to bring ten thousand children out of the brickfields, he never had to come down to Wales. And if we had a bad name at times, this was brought in. Men like Baccy York, for instance, he came down from Worksop with his three wives and first ran on the Swansea cut: Laddie O'Brien, handy with a knife, he came to Giant's Grave, and Beef O'Hara, one of Tub Union's men, running from the '47 Hunger in Mayo. There was Joby Canal, who beat his children every Sunday with a switch, to stripe the God out of them, and Randy Bandy who lived with his sister and had four children by her, all dribbling idiots, working up from Melin.

'None of these compare with that Abe Sluice,' said Gran.

'A swimming pig, is that Abe Sluice,' said Ifor.

'The Company would bring them in from Tokyo for a farthing a ton less, free on board,' whispered Dewi, fist clenched.

'Where is that?' asked Gran.

'It do not matter, Mam,' said my father.

'If it do not matter then why mention it?'

'It was mentioned as a figure of speech, Gran,' explained Dewi.

'That is a queer old place for anyone to come from,' said she. 'And I think that Abe Sluice came from there. But hospitable, give them credit. I was hauled aboard for a cup of tea, and I do not forget it.'

Down from Chester was Abe Sluice, drinking and fighting, and the pair of them living more by poaching and theft than carrying Company goods. This was the scum that was coming in from England—but hospitable, of course—oh, yes, said Dada—give you the top brick: pushing dead cats out of the way when filling the kettle from the cut.

'Mind, that tea tasted queer,' said Gran, reflectively.

'And I can tell you why,' said Dewi.

'Hush,' said Dada instantly, 'enough!'

Many of the foreigners had built cabins on the Company barges, and lived aboard, but most of the Welsh lived in cottages. And any day of the week you could see the English barges tied up in the passing-places along the cut, doing their debugging, and you will not believe it when they say that I have never seen a flea. Aye, sitting in long lines on the bank, these English, de-nitting their hair and bathing the yearly bath in the canal, naked as bones. And moored alongside was the barge with the cabin door and window sealed up with paper, and brimstone burning inside—ten thousand hoppers in the bunks screaming their heads off and billows of smoke rolling over Resolven.

I am not against people keeping themselves clean, said my father, but I am against the English coming down here to do it: the bugs were caught north of the border and ought to be laid out up there, not here.

In Merthyr, Dowlais, Pontypool—any place named, it was just the same: decent Welsh homsesteads before the coming of the industries, now seats of Baal in all his glory. Down one side of the street the Welsh were with bibles under their arms, going to Chapel in black serge and crinolines, very devout with their measured tread: down the other side of the street the foreign workers would be fighting and jeering and doing it in the gutter.

Dewi said, 'The product of the English system of class, the great unwashed. They would have us be like them but we will never be like them, because we are Welsh.'

Queer old characters, mind, these English bargees, and not so much their fault, said Dada, as the fault of the English canal system: up in England the canals were hundreds of miles

**119**

long, and the bargees, unlike the Welsh, lived aboard. And they were brutalised by cramped quarters and never belonging to a community. Most of the Welsh were a cut above them— like Tom Daniels' family: down to Neath he would go with a load of coal, all done up in mole-skin trousers and bowed greetings on every side to neighbours. But the English used to act like savages. The women wore cauliflower ears and broken noses and could swear like their men-folk to blister Baal. And every pay night when the agent forked out their wages in Bethel Street in Ferry, they would roll up to the Cuddlecome Inn and sink quart pewters and hell would come loose with their fighting; women biting and scratching and tearing off skirts in a ring of cheering men from the railway. An indelicate place, this Cuddlecome Inn, apparently, and therefore I was anxious to visit it. For there was talk that they had tapmaids dancing in the saw-dust with enough fore and aft to stop the heart of a mummy, and ladies flocking up from Neath and Swansea, with Cushy, the landlady, blowing on a bugle at six o'clock in the morning and back to your own beds, ladies and gentlemen, I'm having no hanky-panky business, mine is a respectable establishment.

'There is no such place,' said Dada, finger levelled at me, 'and kindly remember it.' Bang, bang, bang on the back now.

And Dewi raised his head from Fred Engels, and winked. For my part, I thought it colourful to have Baal in all his glory rampant above the door. Very fascinating, this Cuddlecome Inn.

'Come in, come in, Pietro!' shouted my father from his corner, and I saw Gwen look up from her drawing with anxious eyes.

'Aye, come in, boy!' cried Dewi, getting up.

Pietro Bianca bowing to Sharon now, hat sweeping the floor. He kissed Gran's hand. 'Just a few friends I have brought to visit, Dewi Evan, is it all right?'

'Friends are always welcome,' said Gran, 'bring them in, Pietro.'

Well.

Six came in, burly, bare-footed, ragged: like cut-throats of

120

the Spanish Main, their great dark eyes shining from the caverns of their hungry faces.

'Down in the cellar, boys,' cried Dewi. 'Bread and cheese sent down later, is it, Gran?'

'As much as they can eat,' said my father, reading *The Cambrian*.

Gran whispered to Sharon, 'Upstairs and take down the pictures in the bedroom, there's a good girl.' She swung to my father as the last of the guests disappeared. 'You are encouraging this, remember. Thieves and vagabonds. I never thought I would live to see it. Oh, Mostyn!'

'Patriots,' said my father. 'Cut them bread and cheese.' Rising, he went to the cellar door. 'Dewi!'

'Yes, Dada?'

'Reduce it to Marx and Engels if you can; keep the bangs within reasonable limits and the bullets horizontal.'

For myself I was not much one for the politics, with bombs under the Whigs and Tories and President Polk if ever he visits Grand River: being up and coming in the female stakes I naturally found more to interest myself nearer home, especially since Bronwen Rees had fallen from grace. And although Ifor reckoned that Cushy Cuddlecome's place never existed, I had noticed a few going along the tow-path down near the Tennant worth a hammering, with neat swings of their hips, which some people find delightful, and black tumbling hair and red lips. Not that I find such people over-attractive, but by the come-hithers and blown kisses they hand out while I am on the fending-poles, it would appear that they have a need. And for this reason alone, I would be prepared to sacrifice myself on the altar of womanhood once a week, as Dewi said. This, I think, is the most beautiful thing I have ever heard Dewi say, and shows that, Karl Marx and Rosie Carey apart, there is, deep inside him, a wonderful nature.

'I shall not tell you again, Bryn—forget this,' said Dada.

'You keep clear of that Cushy Cuddlecome, or you account to me,' said Gran, looking evil. 'What happened to that beautiful school-teacher?'

'Folded up.'

Ifor rumbled, shadow-boxing in the corner, 'She is walking out with Taliesen the Poet.'

'Oh, my poor, poor lad!' cried Sharon. Dressed like a fruit-seller, was Sharon, with posies in her hands, and a woven rush basket, 'How now, that you are crossed in love? Is she fair, or dark? And what fine creature wooed her from your heart?'

'Oh, go to hell,' I said.

'Bryn!' said my father, removing his pipe.

Crash, crash! from the cellar, and he leaped up and caught the Granfer Ben clock as it dropped for the hearth. Down came the pictures in the second bedroom. Plaster trickled down from the ceiling.

'Oh, my God!' whispered Gran, holding her heart.

'They are building a new social order,' said Dada, putting back the clock. 'You get on with your knitting.'

'I have drawn a pig upside down,' announced Gwen.

'Oh, coz, coz, coz,' cried Sharon, dancing around, her hands beseeching, 'my pretty little coz!'

Ifor, naked to the waist, sweating, was thumping the boxer's bag in the back, snorting and grunting with each blow. 'I will give him Black Welshman,' he said in his teeth.

Gran frowned at her knitting. 'You know, Mostyn,' she said, 'sometimes I tend to think this house is a little bit less than normal.'

'Reflect that they come from you originally.'

'I was beginning to wonder how I could be held responsible,' said Gran.

Night.
The Old Navigation sleeps.

A hunter's moon is flashing along the canal; otters are whistling from the Nedd, badgers rolling in grunts at their earths. Dai Half-Moon and his idiot son are coming through the lock at Aberdulais; the sky is afire with the glare of the tin and copper works over Seven Sisters, the clouds apple-cheeked from the ovens of Ystalafera. I was weary to death and black with a day of coaling, coming up from the Grave behind Dai Half-Moon, and the silly sod gets stuck on the river gate with the tide going out, and began barging about in the dark

122

like a hundred-ton frigate. Up on the prow went Dada, fending off, and shouted, 'Dai, get your old heap shifting so decent men can make a bed—what ails you?'

'Trouble with this gate, Mostyn, son—stuck jammed, it is.'

'Where is Jones, the Keeper?'

'Gone, man, haven't you heard?'

Tom Jones who took over the Aber lock when the beautiful keeper and her daughter left two years ago. Dada turned to me. 'You heard that Tom Jones has finished?'

'Finished this morning when the woman came back, and her daughter,' I said, looking away.

'You might have had the grace to mention it.'

'Forgot,' I replied. 'Dai Central told me last Monday—this is the first time since we've been down.'

'Where did they get to?'

'Debt,' I said. 'Swansea workhouse.' And Dai Half-Moon shouted:

'Hold up, Mostyn, while I lever the paddle. And stop butting me in the arse.'

'Mind that language,' cried Dada.

'Comes to something when we have to work the locks ourselves,' called Dai.

It was a two-barge take, this lock, and when Dada jumped ashore and helped Dai free the paddles I slid our barge in beside Dai's, and the idiot son on the knee of his mother slobbered over the gunwale beside me, and I shivered.

'The cottage is empty,' cried my father from the bank, but I scarcely heard him: black the water swirling in as we rose, the wind breathed, fanning the moonlight. On nights such as this, when idiots stare and lock-keepers vanish, the aerial creatures fly, like the Flying Viper of Nedd Fechan, which Gwen fed with bread, and the Green Lady of Craig-y-Llyn bearing her necklace of wild berries—in mid-winter Ifor saw her, and not a berry in sight on the hedges.

My father jumped back on to the barge.

'There is a smell of sweetness in the cottage, and it is clean,' said he. 'It is not a pig-sty like when Jones had it—clean as a pin, but she is gone again.'

'Can't be,' called Dai Half-Moon. 'The Sluices reckon they

saw her here with her girl midday, after you and me come down.'

'Gone again,' said my father, and sighed as a man sighs when nails go through his hands. At me, he said, 'You could at least have told me.'

The stars were as little moons as we swung past Dai Half-Moon into the open country, and the trees above us dripped silver in that madness, for it was a night of witches and besoms and canal bugguts.

There was a great emptiness in my dada for the lock-keeper, for she had torn his blood.

Stock still my father sat on the prow, disdainful of the distant brawling from the canal inns along the cut, for this was pay night when they were at their best, with drinking and whoring with the paid women they brought up from Swansea and Neath : not much time for navvies since he had hit out the Black Welshman : even less now they had brought the railway line up within sight of the Old Navigation, the centre line pegs missing the east corner by ten feet. Marvellous, it was going to be when the big saddle-tanks came snorting up the valley, trying to get a sleep after a night-shift.

Dewi said now, 'A little noisy on the cut tonight, Dada,' trying him out.

'Aye, damned disgraceful, it is.'

For there had been talk that the beautiful lock-keeper, Mrs. Mortymer and her daughter, had been up half the night since returning, never daring to step outside the cottage now that the navvies had brought the railway up above Tonna.

'I reckon they drove her out,' said Dada, fist in his hand.

'Like they will drive us out of the Old Navigation,' said Dewi.

'Oh, aye?' This rose my father, stiff on the prow, chest bulging enormous.

The navigators were a curse to the community, said he, and he was right.

Every beer-house was filled to overflowing, no woman safe on the streets, with Dai this and that knocking on the little navvy cabins that stood beside the railway, doors coming open

124

and the Welsh going in with fists and the navvies coming out with boots off, wiping split noses and holding broken nuts. Just the same down in Neath since they arrived—knocking the helmets off the policemen and hitting out English red-coats, though naturally, the Welsh had no objection to this in the main. Aye, a funny old time was the 'fifties, the more I think of it, with the Welsh dusting knees in the chapels thanking God for coal and ironmasters who were making their lives a misery, and refusing to join the Chartists, which were the only hope they had got, said Dewi. Once all was lovely here, said Dada, but now Baal was about in gorgeous raiment : the maids were up in the attics mooning about the boys, the boys were riding cock-a-hoop and very loose in the mouth; rivers of ale were flowing over the inn counters and the Devil down in the cellar trying on the girl's stays. Sad, it is, said he, when a country loses its proper disposition, and I tell you all this—I will set fire to the house before I accept a drop in standards and show you the heat of hell—and you, Dewi, are the one copying this navvy trash.

'Yes, Dada,' said Dewi.

'You and that Rosie Carey, it has got to stop!'

'Rosie Carey, Dada?'

'You know exactly what I mean. You, too, Bryn . . .' and he levelled a finger at me. 'Your old gran is right, I am beginning to believe. And you, Ifor . . . !'

'Me, Dada?' cried Ifor from the tow-path.

'It is long past time you married Rebecca Cohen or I stand shamed before old Eli—can you hear me?'

'They can hear you back down in Briton bloody Ferry,' said Ifor, grinning wide, and this made my dada grin, too, he having a voice like a fairground barker, then some, especially when he got on the subject of virtue.

Wonderful to see my father smiling again, with all the sadness of the woman keeper left behind him.

In moonlight, bright and clear, we slid along, tired to death : above us the black trees nodded together in wind whisper, trying to recall the last lovely summer : coo-pidges, early from the nest with their voices not yet broken, cooed treble from Rheola.

Running footsteps in the night.

Gusty breathing now and stifled tears.

I saw Ifor stiffen at Nell's halter, peering into the moonlight.

Into a clearing shafted by the moon she ran, faltered, and fell into my brother's arms.

Half a mile up we found her mother, the lock-keeper of Aberdulais, lying across the tow-path.

Near starved, the pair of them: Swansea workhouse had left its mark.

'Quick,' said my father.

# 15

THERE was a marvellous investment in the enjoyment of grief when we brought the Mortymer woman home that summer night, with Gran beating her breast and isn't it an absolute scandal and Gwen gushing tears as we carried the invalid through the door feet first.

'Found her on the path.'

'The lock-keeper of Aberdulais.'

'Nearly starved to death.'

'What a damned country,' whispered Dewi.

'Quick, put her here,' commanded Gran, taking charge, 'and for heaven's sake move yourselves; can't you see the woman's nearly done?'

Pale and proud, this daughter Rhiannon, aged a bit younger than me: now kneeling beside the horse-hair sofa and gripping her mother's hand, her own eyes fevered jewels, her black hair tangled with sweat.

'What happened?' whispered Gran, on her knees with a bowl and flannel, wiping the hot brow, and for God's sake don't stand there staring, you men, but put water on the boil and heat up the stock-pot for soup.

No wonder we stared, including Dada, now he had this

woman close at last: as she lay there amid all the commotion of hand-slapping she was the image of our dead mother; the red lips bright with the fever of hunger, the same classic features of the Silurian Welsh; deep the shadows in her cheeks, her skin smooth and stark white in the marble rigidity of unconsciousness. Her daughter, Rhiannon, said softly, 'For two hours only we were back at the lock cottage, and no food, and she insisted on going to Nanty.'

'Nanty?' asked Dada.

'Nantyglo, up in the Eastern Valley. My relatives live up there—my mother's people, really, for I do not know them.'

This is strange for a start, and I saw the trouble this pair had brought with them standing in a corner, his gnome face with its imp ears peeping out of his rags, his boney hands rubbing with anticipation. Sharon said, for no apparent reason:

'She is the image of my mother,' and Dewi scraped his boots on the flags, turned away, and added, 'It is as if she has loosened the shroud and walked in from her grave at Vaynor.'

From the door I watched the girl Rhiannon: and I think I knew, although resenting her, that one day she would be mine. Gran said, sharp, 'Well, stop mooning, all of you. Mostyn— upstairs and clear out Sharon and Gwen and put them in with Bryn ...'

'Oh, Gran ... !' cried Sharon.

'And you change the blankets for the visitors—you and Gwen will go in the Dowlais single and think yourselves lucky. Is that stock-pot on the hob yet?'

'Raising the fire now, Gran,' said Ifor, hands black and on his knees.

'Good. What is your name, child?'

'Rhiannon Mortymer.'

I tried it on my tongue, and it was honey-sweet, as she was beautiful: as stepped from the pages of the glorious *Mabinogion*, which my father used to read to us, in Welsh, on winter nights. Gran said, 'There is a beautiful name. Hush and dry up now, is it? Your mam is coming round.'

'Mama,' whispered Rhiannon, kissing her hand.

127

And Mrs. Mortymer opened her eyes, transforming her face.

Dear me. I have come across some beauties in my time, for I don't keep my eyes in my boots when women pass. I have seen the Camarthen girls done up in their flouncies on Maypole days, and the Gower women straight and tall, ravishing in chapel black from bunned hair to toe, wealthy in the breast and with the carriage of queens, for their blood comes from ancient princes.

But the beauty of this Mortymer woman, taken close, was of her own.

The black lashes lifted, the great eyes switched in panic, seeing Dada, Dewi and me, staring down. Gran said:

'Do not worry, Mrs. Mortymer; women are here.'

'You hungry?' asked Ifor, rumbling up from the grate, beaming black. 'Got a good shoulder of mutton needing a home ...'

'Out,' said Gran.

'Stock-pot getting hot,' said Dada.

'I told you fix the beds—out. All men out!' and she flapped at us with the flannel. 'Loafing around you frighten a woman to death. Away!'

We shuffled into the back, thumbs indolent in our belts, looking back.

I said, black moodily, 'The spit of my mam. She has no right to look like that.'

'Aye,' mumbled Ifor, knuckling his eye. 'Just seen her close, I have. I reckon it's our mam come back.'

'Bryn,' called Gran. 'Fetch coal for the hob.'

I wandered on, unhearing. All men out, is it? Then out for me, too. I saw a red hooping in the sky as the bungs were tapped; heard the clip-clop of hooves on the road to Vaynor.

'Be reasonable,' said Dewi. 'The poor bitch can't help her looks.'

Women's business, is it?

Then they can bloody sort it out.

Now they kneel beside the sofa, souping her up, and please do not take it too fast, Mrs. Mortymer, and you are all right,

128

Mrs. Mortymer, now you have landed here with us. And now we were up at table for supper, and next it was breakfast, and when we came back from Pont Walby two days later the pair of them were still in the house: first they had the woman by the fire, then she sat opposite me with her daughter, which was a crush one side since Gwen and Sharon were squashed there, too.

For nobody, you understand, sat at the end of the table opposite my father.

That place, with the empty chair, had a knife and fork laid, for my mother.

Six years she had been gone now, but her place was always laid.

And seven days later the Mortymer woman and her daughter were still in the house, and my father in his element, the fool.

At this kind of table, when there is no family joy on it, you can lose yourself in food.

Beef and mutton I like, but trout do send me demented, for in him I taste the sun of the wild places where only trout can roam. Indeed, could I have my time again I would like to be a trout, lying dozy in rushes watching ants whiskering on reed-tips and beetles in the bubbles of light-flood, sipping and shimmering in green depths or paddling in beams of sunlight.

'Sit up properly, Bryn,' said Gran.

'Yes, Gran.'

'What is wrong with you tonight?' asked my father.

I could have told him what was wrong: the Mortymer woman was there and I was here beside my mother.

Also, there was a strange sickness rising in my throat and smooth fingers clutching my stomach.

'More rice-pudding, Rhiannon?'

'Yes, please, Mrs. Evan.'

Not doing so bad this one, either—two helpings she has had already, her dark eyes watching me across the white cloth, a ghost of a smile on her red mouth. But I could not blame her going daft on Gran's rice-pudding, when cut into wads gone cold, like now, all Chinese white but brown and gooey on top;

and if anything in this world was guaranteed to bring a top set clattering down at table it was Gran's rice-pudding.

'What? None for you, Bryn?'

'No, thank you, Gran.'

'You ill, or something?' asked Sharon.

'Excuse me,' I said.

'And where are you off to?' This from my father.

I pushed back my chair on the flags. 'Just out, Dada.'

'You realise that we have not finished the meal?'

Mrs. Mortymer said, 'Oh, it is all right, Mostyn.'

'Let him go, precious,' said Gran.

Dada levelled a finger at me. 'Right, but watch where you go and the company you keep. Dai Central is down with the cholera.'

'No!' whispered Gran, her hand to her throat.

My father nodded. 'They have got him up in Glyn Neath—sixteen cases.' He added, 'And don't be late—an early start tomorrow.'

I thought: away to hell out of this; leave them to their smiles that hid the hatreds; leave them to Dewi's open hostility, to Ifor's grumbling eyes as he saw in this Mortymer woman the ghost of my mam, and Sharon's simpering, putting on her best actress accent to make an impression. Damned hypocrites: all but Dada were wishing the pair of them back at Aberdulais, for all their beauty. I was at the door when Dada called, 'Say good night to Mrs. Mortymer, Bryn.'

The handle was in my hand. On impulse, I swung the door open, went through it and slammed it shut behind me. And turned almost instantly as the door was pulled open again by my father. I saw, behind his fury, the white table, the disapproving stares of Sharon and Gran and the saucer dark eyes of Rhiannon.

'Say good night to Mrs. Mortymer!' said my father, furious.

I stood there, just staring at her, and she whispered, 'Mostyn, it does not matter.' Oh, dear me—Mostyn twice now, is it: down to bloody Christian names, and we haven't been here a week.

'Bryn,' whispered my father, 'I will not ask you again.'

I shut my eyes. 'Good night, Mrs. Mortymer.'

'And Rhiannon.'

'Good night.'

'Good night, Bryn,' they murmured, eyes lowered.

Dusk and blackbirds were falling over the land as I ran.

I found my mother waiting for me by the barge, a misty foil to the decoy that was trying to take her place in my father's heart. I sat in the barge until the moon came up, and the Old Navigation was in darkness.

In a world that is dying of hunger, I hold no brief for the odd missed meal, and that is all that is wrong with this Mortymer woman. She was supposed to stay a couple of days, but every time she and Rhiannon hooked out their bundles my father pulled them back. They saw us into May, and with June came summer clad in her gay green rags, and looking into the sparkling Nedd she painted up her face, calling the sun to warm up her bed of rushes.

Come July, they were still in the house, and every time they got up to go my father opened his shoulders and screwed them in tighter.

'Now, listen, you,' said Gran, 'I will have no more of it. Who the devil do you think you are—head of the house?'

I did not reply. Up to my elbows in my trews, head lowered, I stood out the back while Gran laced me. She cried, 'When you own a house you will say who sleeps under its roof, and not before—you hear me?'

'Yes, Gran.'

'Don't just stand there saying nothing!'

I said, 'Not only me, remember—Dewi, Ifor and Sharon— they got no time for them, either.'

'The moment he chapels her I am going from here,' said Dewi.

'Me, too,' muttered Ifor.

'Count me in.'

Gran now, face scarlet, foot tapping. 'Then go, all three of you, but I tell you this—nobody will come between them, because he deserves her. Try as you like—put the house upside down. Go to Mexico or America, go to hell, but leave my son alone.' Sinking into Dada's armchair she began to cry in gasps and wheezes, rocking herself, stays creaking: the three of us looking at boots mainly, but we did not go to her, though usually there was panic if Gran cried.

'Gran...'

She swung to the wall. 'You leave me alone!'

A bitch is that Mortymer woman: Dewi called her this, and I call her it—a damned bitch for coming in between us.

Bang, bang on the back. 'Can I come in?' cried Pietro.

'Oh, God, no!' said Gran, very damp. 'Not Pietro at a time like this...!'

'Come in, Pietro!' sang Dewi. 'Come in. There is a better revolution going on in here than ever you'll get in Mexico.'

Supper over, and I was whittling a new gaff in a corner. Dewi was mending harness, for Pietro had gone, Ifor was out gathering two sovereigns of a gentry purse up on Resolven mountain; taken on Dai Swipo of Skewen, two stone larger: even heavier in the head was Ifor, these days, bruising with mountain-fighters inches up and thicker in the beam, but a tidy little hoard was going in his chamber under the bed. Dada said over the top of his newspaper:

'You remember that Pont Walby agent I tangled with?'

'Mr. Alton, the English?'

'Aye. He died on Friday. Being buried today.'

'No loss to the Welsh,' said Dewi, 'for he hated us.'

'He was followed by a worse one—Man Arfon, and he is Welsh. You heard he is booked for a plum job with the Great Western?'

'Plum jobs for those who grovel to the owners,' I said.

I was glad Man Arfon was moving from Pont Walby. From the moment we had met we had hated each other, and I knew he was only biding his time to get even with me.

'According to Dai Half-Moon he is going as an inspector,' said Mari Mortymer from her chair opposite Dada.

'Inspector?' Dewi laughed. 'More likely as a checker, for this is his trade. Man Arfon doesn't know a rail from the arse end of a mule.'

My father glanced up. 'Easy, Dewi.'

'Well, she's talking daft!'

'I am only saying what little Dai told me,' said Mari Mortymer, softly.

'And I was there when he said it,' observed Rhiannon coldly.

Got a bit about her, this Rhiannon, and I was becoming interested.

'You believe all Dai says and you end up as skinny as him,' I said lightly.

'But a dear little man, nevertheless, and sad about his son, isn't it?'

Sharon said at her King Henry the Fourth, 'Dai Half-Moon is a little scrounger, Mrs. Mortymer. There is not an ounce of the Christian in him.'

'I am still sorry for him, and for his son.'

Dewi said, 'Little Dai gets by on sympathy and theft. He would cut his mam's throat for the price of a pint.'

'You have to get up in the morning to get the hang of Dai Half-Moon.'

'I did not know,' replied Mrs. Mortymer. 'He seemed a good little man.'

'He is a better little man than most give him credit for,' said Dada.

Terrible is the silence of a house at odds with itself: see the agitated fingers, the nervous thrusting of the needle, the switching eyes; and the room changes colour, I have noticed: from the warm pink of kindness and understanding comes a faint flush of green, and coldness, and there is a shivering and a desire to hurt. And in that silence Mari Mortymer rose, put down her sewing, gripped Rhiannon's hand in passing and began to lay the table.

'Thank you, girl,' whispered Gran.

In the cracked mirror over the bosh I watched her lay that table, polishing each knife and fork on her white apron, smoothing the cloth at my father's place. And when she laid my mother's place, she paused, face lowered, and I think she might have been with tears. Softly, she said:

'Are you up at Pont Walby first shift tomorrow, Mostyn?'

'Aye.' He puffed at his pipe in the corner, the match flaring. 'Pig iron for a change, so we will come back clean.'

'Rhiannon and I will be coming with you.'

133

He glanced up. 'What takes you to Pont Walby?'

'It is part way to Nantyglo. Leaving tomorrow, Mostyn.'

Dewi glanced up and flickered a wink at me, and in that moment I hated him.

'What's this? Who is leaving tomorrow?' asked Gran, putting down the stew.

'We cannot stay for ever,' said Rhiannon, getting up. 'A family is entitled to be a family, and not living with strangers,' and her mother added:

'It ... it is better this way, Mostyn. Anyway, I was on my way to Nanty when you brought us in, and thank God for you all. But my mother and father-in-law are expecting us, and it is time we left here.'

'But you will be coming back, Mari?'

She shook her head. 'Not coming back, Mostyn.'

Gran turned slowly to Dewi and me. 'Now perhaps you are satisfied!'

'No, it is not their fault, Gran,' said Rhiannon. 'This is a house of ghosts. At first I thought it was only Granfer Ben...'

Mrs. Mortymer gestured with empty hands at my mother's place at the table. 'It is not only Granfer Ben—it is a house where the mother has not really died. Tonight we will pack the bundles. As I said, Mostyn—it is better this way.'

I do not know why I said, 'You come from Nantyglo?'

'No, from Carmarthen—Llanstephan—the same village as your old granfer.'

'It is queer, mind,' murmured Dewi, 'that you have been here weeks and we don't know anything about you.'

'That is because you have not asked,' replied Rhiannon, her eyes on fire.

Butter wouldn't melt in this one's mouth, but I bet she was fighting Welsh when she was roused. Dewi nodded. 'That is fair. Your husband's people up in Nanty, you say?'

Mrs. Mortymer shrugged. 'They were in Blaenafon iron—I married my Iestyn in Blaenafon. Later, the Mortymers moved to Carmarthenshire, back to the farms. My husband was killed in the Chartist riots in Newport, when trying to escape capture.'

'Tell them about your son,' said Dada, his head bowed by the lamp.

'I had a son, and his name was Jonathan. He was ten years old. He was killed two years back, working with the navigators. I let him work in their cabins, for money was short—sweeping up, making tea, with oiling bolts and nuts spare time. But one day they were short of a tripper, and they put him on the embankments, and the tram spilled and trapped him, and he died.'

'Thank God you have Rhiannon,' whispered Gran, and I saw Dewi shifting his behind uncomfortably on the stool: hot as hell, me: damned swine, me.

'Rhiannon is adopted. When I first came to Lock Cottage, Jonathan found her wandering, and brought her home.' Mrs. Mortymer smiled at Gran. 'Things have not been good for me, but I thank God every day for my Rhiannon.'

Dewi rose and went to the window. 'You are right when you say that our mother has not really died, but she will die in time.'

Sharon now, up on her feet and blazing, 'That is a dreadful thing to say!'

'But it is true. It is us children who have kept her alive, not Gran, not Dada!'

'Oh, please, do not quarrel,' cried Rhiannon, and Dewi repeated, thumping his fist into his palm, 'And I am next in line to Ifor when it comes to this responsibility—it is he who demands her place be laid at table, and I have backed him.'

'At a time like this the family should be alone,' said Rhiannon, and got up.

'Please do not go, Mrs. Mortymer.' Dewi turned from the window, smiling. 'I apologise for my behaviour to you. I did not know your man died fighting with the Chartists.'

'You want to get your values straight,' said my father, and the sound of him shocked us. 'She is accepted now, is she, now you know her husband died for the spirit of revolution.' He lumbered up. 'You are right, Mari, it would be best for you to go. One day, when I have got rid of this lot, I will come to you.'

'Mostyn, for God's sake,' whispered Gran.

Not staying in this morgue for supper. Away out of this, me.

If good women are so disturbing, we will find out what the wicked ones are made of.

# 16

NOBODY can really tell you about Cushy Cuddlecome's place: you have to drink Saturday night quarts in there to get the hang of it, and Friday night is no fool either, and this was the Friday of the six-week pay.

I ran fast down the cut, and there was a strange sickness rising in me at first, so I rested when I got to the Melin lock and watched the navvies at culvert work on night shift, with their whooahs and whip-cracks as their big horses towed the pipes: some were mares, but many were wonderful animals—entire horses from the blood yards of London: great white creatures with bodies steaming in moonlight. Panting, I shivered, remembering the *Y Ceffyl Dwr* the Water-horse who lived in the foam-cascades of the Mellte, whose hooves did not touch the pastures and whose mane floated in the clouds. Bogies and ghosties do bloody scare me, mind. Blood-curdling shrieks from the cellars under Neath Abbey, vampires who get through windows and cotton on to corpses even in the death-chamber, to say nothing of the church bells tolling in the sunken city at the bottom of Llyn Crymlyn. The poison-fish of Garn, the Frog of Hepste, which is the spirit of a hanging, do frit me stupid. Frit, frit to death I come when I see the winged serpents of Erwood and the Flying Dragon of Pont-Neath-Vaughan. It is all right somebody reading what I am writing now in a hundred years or so and calling me a Dai Dafto, for they do not live in my time. I tell you, I have seen them. Ghosties and canal bugguts, which the Midlanders brought into the Vale—these I often see, and when a clawed hand reaches up from weirs and such-like, you have got to watch

136

it. I have personally witnessed the rock and water fairies milking cows, and into the milk they mix a herb potion, and go on a randy like the navvies on this stuff, dancing naked and singing in December frost: skidding on ice and playing touch-me-last, their lips stained black through eating windberries: windberries in December, mind—enough to frighten chapel folk to death. Lots of things happen in this Vale to congeal the blood: things like dancing corpse-candles, cocks crowing at midnight, pigeons perched on coal-tips, and buggy bo's and hobgoblins by the hundred, and these, remember, are not to be confused with the *tylwyth teg*, the fair and terrible ones, for these can be sods. I have known a pair of *tylwyth teg* chase Jacki Scog and Wil Screech home through the bogs after a thick night down in Neath, hanging on to their coat-tails and putting in the boot, and Jacki and Wil arriving in the Square, Resolven, emotionally done up and physically exhausted, and it took another three quarts to get some sense into them. Then take old Modryb Ann of Mellincourt; although she is not in my time, my father takes her story for gospel, since Dobi Revival, the preacher, told him, and he got it from Dai Swansea, who was second cousin to the mate on the ship that carried old Modryb Ann's nephew.

Dreadful, horrible is the story of old Modryb Ann, as told by her nephew.

Mind, all her life old Ann acted queer, with nightly visitations from a scarecrow in fetters who knocked on her lattice window round about midnight. And although the neighbours saw old Ann let him in, they were not particularly concerned since there were quite a few of the locals up to the same trick, and they were not wearing fetters.

But it was different, indeed, when Ann's nephew came home from the sea.

Bangs on the door and clanking at midnight, so naturally, he got up, and there, as large as life, was a grey mare standing on the cobbles and a skeleton standing by the door. 'Come in,' said Ann, opening it, and her nephew peeped through a crack in the floor, and watched the skeleton enter the kitchen. 'I am come for you,' said the skeleton, putting on a cloak. 'Sit a bit, boy,' Ann replied, 'I am not quite ready,' and she went into her bedroom and came back wearing a shawl. 'This is the third time of asking, remember,' said the skeleton, 'tonight I am come to claim my bride,' and even as Ann's nephew watched, his heart turning to stone, the skeleton took old Ann's hand and gripped her waist, and they danced together on the cobbles of the kitchen. 'Right, you,' said the skeleton, 'we are off directly,' and he ran old Ann through the cottage door and on to the horse and they were away, the pair of them, and not a living soul in this valley have seen old Ann since.

The only corpse in this valley that doesn't possess a grave.

I can personally guarantee that this story is true, since I got it from my dada, and he got it from Dobi Revival, who, as his name implies, tends to the religious.

Some queer old things have happened down the Vale of Neath.

But nothing as queer as Cushy Cuddlecome's.

Away from the navvies now, with their threats to the Old Navigation: away over the aqueduct at Aberdulais I went like hell's hammers, and along the Tennant canal for Skewen, and I heard through the flowering moonlight the high shrieks of tickled women and the bass roars of men, and suddenly, round a bend on the tow-path, the Cuddlecome Inn came frowning up and blazing with light from its big, bay windows.

There was a shivering in me and a wet sweating, caused, perhaps, by the running, as I crept up to a cracked pane of glass and peered within.

Here is a dreadful sight for decent people.

Gran would have thrown a fit with legs up at the view.

The tap-room was jammed with elbowing, snarling men with pewters in their fists: ragged navvies on a randy from Brunel's railway, gipsy Irish, Frenchmen, Spaniards with gold earrings, and labouring Welsh. And they were roaring a chorus at the ceiling, boots stamping the time to the music of a melodeon played by an Irish tinker in a corner. And amid this convivial company, most with their back teeth awash, danced a tap-girl in crepe and scarlet, tight in the waist and most pleasant at the top, with her black hair swinging in plaits and tied with red ribbon.

I was beginning to realise I had a fever on me, and I reckon it went up ten points.

'Got a heart of gold on her, Welshman,' said a voice beside me, and I turned to it, shivering. Dim in the yellow light stood the Irish boy navvy I had first seen up at Cyfarthfa, and later when Dada flattened the Black Welshman.

'Ay, ay,' I said, nodding.

'Though it's not the heart that matters so much,' he added, 'but the beautiful things that go round it.'

'Do not be disgusting,' I said, shocked, and got my boot on a brick for a better view.

'Ach, no offence,' said the Irish. 'But since I'm arrived to meet her after the drinking, I'm flattening every chap round here with an eye on me rightful property.'

I weighed him. He had grown a bit. But even with a fever on there's a spare Welsh hook for an Irish chin, especially round the Skewen area.

'Are you married to her?' I asked, taking him off.

'I am not.'

'Then hop it.'

'Listen here,' said he, tapping me. 'She's not me wife, perhaps, but that woman's me food and drink and me pride and comfort, and if you continue to crack that window with your eye I'll paste you one that'll land you back in Cyfarthfa.'

'Fair enough. Shall we drink first?'

'It's a bountiful idea. Will a quart suffice ye? What's your name?'

I told him. He said, 'And mine's Tai Morlais, which is Welsh in the sound, though I'm as Irish as the fiddlers of County Mayo.'

I jerked my thumb at the tap-room. 'And she's as Welsh as a leek. Can't you keep your dirty hands off other people's nationality?'

'I would if I dare,' said Tai. 'But there's few educated Irish women round these parts, an' the ale tastes the same when the women are as soft as in Mayo, and so is Sian Edwards. Will you leave her free for me?'

I saw the girl instantly, profiled in dark beauty against the swinging lamps, her lips red and open, showing the straight

139

white lines of her teeth in her sudden, tinkling laughter.

'Sure, I'll do my best,' I said, taking him off again, 'but I can't guarantee it . . . for you've got no authority, hobnobbing with decent people.'

'I'll have one on your chin at the first intimation,' said Tai.

'If you can reach it,' said I.

We shouldered our way into the bar. I was too excited to notice Dai Half-Moon cranked over a pint in the corner.

Into a swirling fug of tobacco and ale we went, elbowing a path through buckled stomachs and hairy arms, deafened by their bawdy, stamping chorus, which was all about a sweet Swansea girl who had fallen for a buck navvy from Workington, and how she shamed her dad and finished in the workhouse with her guilt, and some bargees and navvies were in tears at the thought of her, since ale, when taken in quarts, has more ways than one out of a man. And Cushy Cuddlecome, the best pillow in the Vale, was standing on the counter, her size twelves stamping the time an inch from my nose, her sack dress billowing around my ears. Mop-lace cap awry and hanging down, fat face puckered up, she was bellowing the navvy chorus, one bare arm beating the time, her fist holding a quart of Cuddlecome Special, while below her a pair of wizened Irish navvies, an inch taller than leprechauns, danced an Irish jig, arming each other around in whoops of joy, their kicking hobnails raising the saw-dust to the screeching of an Irish fiddle.

'And around again we go me lovely boyos!' bawled Cushy, and stooped, heaving a big Lancashire bargee up on the counter beside her, and the pair of them prancing up and down now, lifting their knees in whoops, overturning tankards, flattening fingers and raising curses, with roars of laughter billowing about us as she up with her sack dress and showed her red garters.

'Good heavens,' I said, for it is disgraceful what a decent community can sink to when invaded by the likes of these: no prude, me—do not start that—in fact, pretty broad-minded, all things considered, but a middle-aged lady's legs do deserve to go under tents, especially venison haunches like Cushy Cuddlecome's.

Beside me Tai was hammering the counter for service, and getting nowhere, but as the tap-girl in scarlet and crepe swept by with her tray loaded I lifted a pair of pewter pints, and I had just got my teeth into mine when the sack dress came down and I was under Cushy Cuddlecome in a tangle of bare hams and petticoats.

'Away out of this,' I said, fighting free, and we got to a corner.

'Skin off your nose.'

'Spots on your belly.'

We drank like seven-foot colliers. Dear me. There is nothing in this world like the cold douche of a strong home-brew when it takes its dive to its death: explodes the lamp-light red in your clenched eyes. Open the gullet, and tip, for practised alers never swallow: drown, and come up gasping.

'Two things Cushy is good at,' cried Tai, 'and one is brewing ale.'

Aye, I thought, and if my dada was here just now he'd be raising six-inch lumps. Thoughts of my dada quietened me: very ashamed I felt with that pint inside me.

'You hungry, man?' shouted Tai.

'Starved.'

'Got money?'

'Six shillings,' I cried.

'Enough to drown us. Six shillings is ten Cuddlecome Specials apiece and a pair of Swansea tarts.'

'What is a Cuddlecome Special?' I asked, knowing that Swansea tarts were pastries with jam in, like by gran made back home. Eh, gorgeous, those tarts, Swansea or otherwise, made special for Sunday tea, crisp and brown but puddingy at the bottom where the jam had soaked in, and biting hot to the tongue.

'Hey, Bryn!' yelled Tai, and I pushed through the drinkers to a little table where Sian Edwards was working with a carving knife, slicing slices off a leg of lamb and hitting it between hunk doorsteps of black bread.

'Strangers, is it? There's handsome!'

141

Marvellous, mind, when beauties call you that.

'Ay, ay!'

'Never seen you before,' said she, 'but I've had an eye on your brothers!'

'You know him?' asked Tai, askance.

'I do now,' said Sian, and the look she gave me then sent me cold at the knees.

'My friend Bryn Evan,' announced Tai, and bowed before her, his mole-skin hat collecting the sawdust, and while he was down there with his neck in my hand this Sian Edwards went all cuddly in the shoulders and sweetened her lips at me, and I was just removing the table to get at her when Tai came up again and steered me into a corner. There we bit deep into the lamb doorsteps.

'Any good?'

'Aye,' I replied, 'but cheese and onion I prefer, mind.' Cheese and a Spanish onion is a meal and a half, I reckon, especially in summer to keep the flies away, said Dada, for my gran made cheese with a bite in it, never allowing it on the table until it could open the larder door and climb up there by itself, and we ate it, Dada, Ifor and me, like starving pariahs.

'You dry, Bryn, lad?' asked Tai, considerate.

'Dry as a powdered bone.'

'Jebers, this can't be,' said he, and swivelled on his stool to a bench where two brawny navvies were watching a cock being dressed for the ring, and he lifted one of their quarts and put back his empty, then shared the quart with me. And we had just parted our knees and getting into it when a fight started on the bench, for it is a mortal sin in Cushy's, apparently, to sink another's pewter: and while this was on Tai filched the other quart and we drank deep and gasping.

'Free beer is alive, eh?'

'Alive and kicking,' I said.

'This is nothing, man. Dead and buried you will be before you are finished. Where you going to be when your house comes down?'

'What do you mean?' I was seeing three of him.

'When Black Sam pulls down the Old Navigation?'

'Black Sam, how many wild horses, and what regiment of Guards?' I asked.

Tai held a bargee yorker aside and spat neatly in the spittoon and it belled like the toll of Doom. 'The railway pegs go right through the Old Navigation, says Black Sam. Out of the back door and through the front, according to the pegs, for I helped lay them.'

'The pegs miss us by twenty feet,' I shouted, getting up.

'Now, now,' commanded Tai, 'do not get your bowels twisted. Just giving you the tip, that's all. Your dada flattens Black Sam and Black Sam flattens the Old Navigation: an eye for an eye.'

'My dada will kill him,' I whispered.

'And while he is at it, a couple of thousand Brunel navigators. Drink up, boy, for you look miserable to death.'

I began to sweat. Sitting there swilling it down, waiting for the Swansea tarts, I began to sweat cobs, for the fripperty women had started to come in from Neath and Swansea, and there were things going on in odd corners to make your hair stand on end, with dancing going on in the bedrooms and stop-it-Joes and please-don't-Derricks going on left and right: hollers and groans, and tables overturning in shrieks, glass crashing in tinkles and drunks teetering about on wooden legs, and hell was coming loose in a corner with the cock-fight.

Suddenly I saw my father's face: through a haze of sweat, hops and blasphemy, I saw him: Gran came next, spinning at her wheel, then Sharon, strutting about in a shawl as Desdemona.

Very strangely, also, I saw the face of Rhiannon.

'Excuse me, please, I am going from here,' I said, getting up.

'Back door only,' said Tai. 'Your hammering is waiting out the front.'

I put a sixpence on the table.

'Two more pints and don't forget the change.'

'At once, sir,' said Tai.

On my way out the back I saw the old men of the Vale clustered around the chimney-breast, their work-riven hands expressive before their toothless champings, for old men speak with their hands: and I saw in their sallow, ancient faces the peace of the cider-fields and gleanings, before the industry came in full measure, when the world was young. Leaving them to their chattering I parted a curtain and found myself in a rough flagged kitchen: here a bright fire was blazing: turning on a spit was a naked sheep; steam was billowing up, flames spearing blue and gold to his hissing fat, a martyr of Mankind.

Being about six pints aboard and now hot enough to boil a kettle on, I bowed to him because at the time it seemed polite. 'Good evening,' I said.

The spit turned his blistered face to mine, and I saw in his glazed eyes the agony of his slow roasting, and he looked to me that moment as alive as a market-day sale: hand him back his horns and hooves and he'd have been through Cushy Cuddle-come and up the mountain.

Sian Edwards appeared just then with a carving knife and a plate to remove his left leg. 'Wrong house, boyo,' said she. 'First door on the left and second turning right.'

Even in that swimming room she was beautiful: no freckled school-girl, this, with carrots for hair and a tiger-nut in her cheek: this was eighteen, I reckoned, her arms round and white, her fingernails unbitten.

'Did Tai tell you I was his girl?'

'Aye, Sian,' I said.

'Well, I am not, for I am Welsh—Gower Welsh, mind, which is real, and it is Welsh to Welsh I have in mind. Is that handsome brother of yours still putting it over Alfo Morgan up at the Lamb and Flag?'

'So they say.'

She came nearer. 'Beautiful family, mind, especially that Dewi, though your Ifor was not behind the door when they handed out bodies. See now, here is a key. If any member of your family do fancy an hour or two with Sian, they are welcome, though I naturally prefer the males.'

Kindness do come from unexpected sources, and she drew from her bodice a key big enough for Swansea jail, and it was hot in my hand as I gripped it in my pocket. She added, over

her shoulder, 'First floor, first left, first door. There is gorgeous is a midnight visitation,' and she leaned over, eyes shut,
and kissed my lips. 'And be careful lest you land in with
Cushy.'

First floor, first left, first door, and don't land in with
Cushy.

If Dewi or Ifor saw the ceiling over Sian's attic it would be
a bloody miracle.

Coming in from the back I heard a low whining from the
other side of the fire: through the half-open curtain I saw the
tap-room drinkers at it in a fury and fights were starting: the
fighting cocks were locked in a steel embrace of beaks and
spurs and blood; money chinked in saw-dust.

Again the faint whine, and I went round a board to the
other side of the chimney-breast.

On the trundling-wheel that turned the spit a little dog was
working: behind the tattered tarpaulin that was supposed to
protect her from the heat, she treadled blindly, eyes closed to
the spiking glare.

'Ay, ay, *fach*,' I said to her, and she paused to stare, then
trundled like something demented, afraid of a stick.

You keep your god of men and leave me mine.

'*Dammo*, girl, wait a bit,' I said, stroking her and she
turned her frizzled little face to mine. Picking up my ale I
tipped the pewter to her mouth and she drank madly, not
knowing ale from water, eyes rolling in fear.

'You drink,' I said. 'Anyone stopping you I will flatten.'

No sound I heard then but her gusty breathing: in a scrape
of scorched pads, tongue lolling, she started off again. Her back
was burned pie-bald where the coals had jumped; near blind,
she was, where the fat had spattered.

I wept, but I think it was the ale.

Then, as if called, a woman parted the curtains leading to
the tap-room: a woman with the body of a yard broom and a
face like a hatchet and what the hell is going on here and get
out sharp, or you will get this instead of the bitch, and she
raised a stick.

'Only giving it a drink,' I said, in sudden fury.

145

'And might ye realise the sheep's in flames next door?' Bog Irish, this one. Out, *out*! Feeding the thing beer, indeed! You'll have it as tipsy as a coot!' She stood before me in her rags and madness, her skeleton arms waving; this single-fare ticket that was the tragedy of Ireland: the ballast that could walk from the famines and unload itself at Fishguard.

I shouted, 'The thing's nearly dead, woman. If you don't water it occasionally you'll be turning the spit yourself.'

'Well, the bloody cheek of it! Did ye hear that? Beering up the tread-mill is against the regulations, and I'm hauling you up before Cushy Cuddlecome!'

Ducking under the rod, I slipped the dog's collar and hooked her off the wheel into my arms. 'Now, then,' I said, and went for the door, but she swished the stick, and I took it on the shoulder, staggering back. She shrieked:

'Take that! You put that dog back on the treads, Welshman, or as God's me judge, I'll flog the livin' daylights out of the pair of ye.' Turning, she screamed, 'Beef O'Hara, Mick O'Shea! Will you come and handle this Welsh hooligan?' and she swung another, but I ducked it.

A voice from the bar shouted, 'What's happening to the spit? Sure, the sheep's on fire and goin' to a bloody cinder!'

Crouching, I darted for the door, but the stick came down and I took it on the face. 'One move, ye limb of Satan,' whispered the woman. 'Just one more move and I'm splittin' ye skull for you!'

Back went the tap-room curtains, then a mob spilled into the room, Cushy Cuddlecome leading; shapeless, her face flushed to its rolling fat, her dress untied at the waist. 'What's up?' she demanded, gasping.

'It's this mad Welsh. He's after stealing the wee animal entirely, an' it's me for stoppin' him.

Cushy put up her fist. 'Put that tyke down, son, for I'm warning ye. Put it down or me and mine'll hand you a shellacking that'll last ye down to the fourth generation....'

'What ails ye, Bryn?' shouted Tai. 'Have ye gone demented?'

'Aye,' I said, and stopped, gripping a firing-iron. 'And if anyone wants this dog, they come for it.'

146

'I'm coming,' said Beef O'Hara, and hooked up a chair, snapping off the legs, tossing one to Mick O'Shea. 'Take him either side, boyo, by God we'll give him thieving Welshman.'

The back door went back on its hinges as I lifted the firing-iron, and it butted Cushy in the rear, sending her floundering into the others: Dewi came first, ducked a chair-leg from Beef O'Hara and laid the prettiest left hook I have ever seen on Mick O'Shea as he rushed. Pietro Bianca kicked Beef's shins and Ifor clubbed him down from above: my father came in through the tap-room, leaving a trail of dead and dying and hauling women aside. Holding Cushy at arm's length he shouted, 'What are you doing in this filthy place?'

He shouted again, but I did not hear him, but I saw him shimmering in a world of sweat and pain: I remember dropping the firing-iron, I remember the little dog howling; then nothing.

Later, I heard Dewi say, 'Soaked with sweat, he is, his shirt is sopping.'

I opened my eyes to an avenue of stars and rushing trees, and felt the strength of Ifor about me, the grip of his thick arms as he took another lift on me, and he rumbled deep in his bull chest:

'What was he doing in Cushy's place, anyway?'

'That's what Dai Half-Moon wanted to know,' said Dada.

'Thank God for Dai Half-Moon for once,' said Dewi.

In my fever I made a mental note to crack the skull of Dai Half-Moon.

'Dada . . .' I said.

'Hush, Bryn, Ifor has got you.'

Silence now: an otter whistled from Rheola. So clear I heard him, and saw his whiskered snout: urgent whispers on the tow-path as they hauled me around and I smelled the tobacco smell on my father's hair, its curls rough on my face, and heard through his loins the thumping of his boots as he carried me.

'Is he just plain drunk?'

'Don't be a fool, Ifor. Dewi, put your coat over him, he is shivering to have his bones out.'

147

'Is it a fever?' asked Dewi, covering me in my father's arms.

'Here, give a hand,' whispered Dada. 'Hurry, for God's sake. The boy has the cholera.'

The cholera. The *cholera*!

You dodge the thing in Merthyr and pick it up at Cushy Cuddlecome's.


# 17


THERE are many ways of dying with the cholera, the old people say, and this varies with the religion of the patient. Church of England folk, for instance, take it pretty hard according to the Welsh Nonconformists, being boiled to a puddle, a foretaste of things to come. Roman Catholics, considered by the Established Church to be equally misguided, rarely pull through, while disbelievers, who worship pagans like Cushy Cuddlecome, die worst of all; in froth, shrieks and speechless agony, also, these die, their spines arching to the satanic heat as a stick withers in fire, the soles of their feet touching their heads in the final paroxysms of dying.

One thing was certain. Whatever the religion, if you caught the cholera off Dai Central Eating, or anybody else in the 'fifties, you were almost surely booked for cloud eternity. However, a few did get through for one reason or another. There are some, said my father, though qualified for Heaven in some respects, were unqualified in others—such as midnights spent in tap-rooms in the company of doubtful young ladies, and others so contaminated with navvy brew that a self-respecting cholera germ couldn't get a proper hold.

And since you come into both these categories, said he, I am not surprised to see you alive on the fifteenth day, which was an important day with the Old Cholera.

I opened my eyes to bright sunlight, I remember, with the fever broken, and saw beside me the face of Mari Mortymer: sheet-white that face, the cheeks proud and humped with weariness, the eyes black in shadow, as if the cholera had entered the stable in his rags and bowed with his scythe before her.

'I am here, Bryn,' she said, and I turned towards her, seeing the agitation growing on her face. And then her eyes opened wide and she rose in the straw, ran to the stable door and flung it wide, shrieking, 'Mostyn, Mostyn!'

If she had set the barn alight she could not have caused more commotion.

Out came Dada with lather on his face, cut-throat razor waving, then Gran, already bucketing and supported by Rhiannon and Sharon. Ifor was blundering around shouting with joy, and even Dewi wandered into the yard, grinning, his thumbs in his belt. Like a family of old retainers they came to pay me court, standing strangely silent at a respectful distance, for there must have been cholera germs as big as banana spiders flying off me still. Mari cried:

'It is broken, the fever is broken. Oh, Mostyn!'

From his eyes, skidding over the yard cobbles between them, came his love for her.

'Where is Gwen?' I asked.

'Up at Glyn Neath, she will be back soon.'

Ifor shouted, 'Back down at Cushy's first opportunity, eh, man?'

'You can pick up some queer old things in Cushy's, eh?' said Dewi.

'Do not attend them,' said Mari. 'Very impertinent, they are—you have never been within a mile of that dreadful place, have you?'

A man's woman, this one. 'No,' I said.

Gran now, mainly unintelligible, blowing and streaming one moment and smiling the next, and thank God he is going to be all right now, my prayers having been answered, the special notice given out in Resolven chapel being mainly responsible. 'And down to skin and bone, he is, poor boy.'

'Mostly in the buttocks,' said Dewi. 'For a boy of his age it shows mostly in the buttocks.'

'Aye, when the buttocks sink on a man it is a sign of general dilapidation,' said Gran.

'We will have to build you up, Bryn.' My father was un-

149

usually quiet, and I put this down to his displeasure. Mari said quickly:

'Good beef broth is what he needs, eh, Gran: if you put it on a skid-tray, Rhiannon will bring it.'

'Up on your feet this time tomorrow, remember,' said Dewi, 'do not make a meal of it.'

Rhiannon came nearer and my father drew her back. 'Thank God you are better, Bryn,' she said.

And with this Sharon wept softly, her hands over her face.

It took a strange path, this cloud of relief and love hanging over the house.

I lay back with all the sounds of the stable about me, the rustling of mice, bird-quarrels, the comforting chinking of Nell's chain, the stamp of Jed's feet: all the song and smell of life flooded into me; the golden scent of straw, the acrid tang of urine, while through the open door came the reedy earth-smells of the cut. I listened for sounds of the house, but none came: as dead, that house, its laughter coffined in its relief, perhaps.

'Friend of yours, Bryn.' Mari now, kneeling beside me, holding in her arms the little Cuddlecome bitch, and it strained and whined to be near me, and pretty good somebody had done her, with her body fatter and her coat brushed clean.

'Why are you in here with me?' I asked.

She rose with a shrug. 'Somebody had to nurse you. Gran was abed when your father brought you in. Doctor Brodie came from Glyn Neath and put the pair of us in the stable to keep it clear of the family.'

The wonderful Doctor Brodie who later gave his life to cholera, for the people of Glyn Neath.

'How long have you been here with me?'

She was rolling up her sleeves and tying back her hair, being with business.

'This is the fifteenth day. Hush now, and rest. A strip-wash for you first, and then Gran's broth. Fighting fit you will be with that inside you.'

'Hey, Mari!' called Dewi from the yard, and he and Ifor carried a brimming bath and lowered it on to the skid-tray and

150

threw her the rope, and she braced herself, heaving, and skidded it into the stable.

'Everything off, remember,' called Dewi. 'You cannot do him justice all done up in night-shirts.'

'Eh, go on with you,' said she, very pretty with her.

'Every mortal stitch, remember—off!' bawled Ifor.

Yet when they turned away their faces they were not with smiles, I noticed.

I turned my eyes from her as she bent to me.

She said she was a mam, but she looked more like eighteen. Indecent, it is, to lie helpless before a woman, one so young. And there is obscenity in the body after cholera: the sunken ribs, the sagging parchment of a belly that once was ribbed with muscle, the white, scrawny loins of the aged. I clenched my hands, and she said:

'Do not make it hard, Bryn. Indecent, they are. Personally, I do not put much store on this business of privates.'

'Not proper,' I said. 'Only you and me in by here.'

'Would you have me call your dada and give him the cholera?'

She had my night-shirt in her hand and I stared at it. She said, 'Good God, man. I put it on, surely I can take it off,' and I grinned at this.

'What about you getting it, then?'

'Old boots, me, she said, sluicing water over my body. 'And I have had it once. If the scythe don't chop you in half first time, it only skins your ribs next. Front done, over you go. Much better looking that way round.'

I saw behind her the tip of Resolven mountain with her head in the clouds, and the sun raging golden down the cut where the rooks were holding the annual Parliament in quick flourishes of the wind.

'Do not go, Mari Mortymer,' I said, and though her hands paused she made no sign that she had heard me. Later, she wrapped me in a towel and I lay back as she went to the door and combed and tidied her hair. She said:

'Welcomes are like door-mats, Bryn. They wear out under the feet.'

\*     \*     \*

Dusk came, with bats, and I listened to the banter of the cut as the bargees went down to Briton Ferry: distantly, I heard the hammering of the railway navvies. Mari was sitting on a stool by the stable door, the dog was sleeping under my hand: lazily rose the Vale moon, in dripping silver. I said:

'How near is the line?'

'Gone past us—up half a mile to Rheola locks.' Beautiful her face against the rising moon. 'They missed the house by thirty feet.'

'I haven't heard the Corsairs going through.'

'There is argument about a branch line, your father says. He has been down to Neath seeing Mr. Seth Cowbum, the solicitor.'

She smiled at me in the half light, adding, 'There is a gorgeous name, Mr. Seth Cowbum!'

'Rather him than me,' I said.

'There is an agent called Man Arfon, and he wants the house down for the branch line.'

'Man Arfon!' I slowly sat up.

'Rest yourself, he will never be a match for your dada. Some dada, you have got, you realise this?'

'Yes.'

'Do not be a grief to him, Bryn. Girls like Sian Edwards are not his style.' Getting up, she wandered to my jacket hanging on a nail and fished out Sian's key, and this she held in front of me, smiling, impish. 'There is bad luck,' she said. 'Must have missed it by inches.'

Hot and cold now. A terror, this one. She said, still smiling. 'Were I a man I would give Sian a run for it, but sixteen years old is only a boy.' She emptied her hands at me. 'Drink, if you like—fight, chew, smoke if you like, but do not seek out the secrets of girls—not yet. Give it a rest for a year or so, there's a good boy.'

I did not reply, and she winked. 'Hot to melt she will be for you by the time you are twenty.'

With this she stood on the stool and put the key on the wall-plate in the eaves, saying, 'She hands out more attic keys than the flesh-pots of Gomorrah, that Sian. And even if you got past Cushy you'd find them queueing at the door.' She tucked the key out of sight. 'Sian Edwards is yours on the night you can reach it.'

Some woman, this one. I gave her a grin.

'All the time in the world, Bryn,' she said at the moon, 'all the time in the world. And now, up on your feet as soon as you like, for I'm sick to death of being cooped up in this stable while you lie there like a lazy old lump.'

'Do not go, Mari,' I said.

'Stay around here with you hooligans? Not on your life.'

'Do not go, Mari,' I said.


They said I slept for three days after that, and when I awoke I asked for my sister Gwen, but she was still up at Glen Neath, said Mari.

But it was her eyes.

Eyes, like the tongue, can betray, but they cannot lie.

'Gone, is she?' I asked.

'Yes, Bryn.'

'The cholera?'

'Aye.'

I bowed my head, 'How ... how long?'

'Last week we took her up to Vaynor, to be with your mam.'

I wept.

'Do not make it harder, Bryn; most of the tears have been cried.' She held my face in her hands. 'For the sake of Dada, and Gran ... ?'

'Aye.' I did not say more.

In the 'fifties, in Wales, we shut the door and turned the key.

Later that night my father came into the stable and wrapped me in a blanket, and carried me into the kitchen. And while they were preparing to sit at table there was a great palaver about is he too cold or too hot, and setting me straight, and Sharon fetched a pair of bricks out of the oven and wrapped them in flannel. I sat there lording it over them, stinking of goose fat.

It was the first time since my illness that Mari had been in the kitchen. I watched her smooth, proud face; saw the flushed beauty of Rhiannon, her eyes rising at me over the white, starched cloth. I saw my father's questioning glance at Mari, and saw her secret nod.

I saw, too, that Gran's lips were trembling. Sharon was sitting stiffly, her eyes red, sick of weeping: my brothers were in a holy silence.

After Gran had served the supper my father rose at the head of the table, and said, 'Grace indeed tonight, O Lord. Bless those who have been taken from us in Thy holy Name; my wife, and Gwen, my daughter; keep them in Thy heart. Our thanks to Thee for bringing my son back into this kitchen, cleansed, free of the cholera. The people of this house give thanks for the blessing of Thy holy Name, O Lord Jesus.'

Nobody moved for a bit after this, but when Mari broke her bread, my brother Dewi broke his also, his dark eyes smiling at her: there was no sound but the ticking of the clock.

I watched them.

One by one, they broke bread with Mari Mortymer, the last being my father. Then suddenly Ifor lumbered to his feet like a bear with honey. Mari and Rhiannon opened wide eyes at him as he took Mari's hand, and drew her to her feet.

In silence, my brother Ifor led her to the chair that belonged to my mother, and set her there facing my father at the head of the table.

Head bowed, she sat, unmoving, her fingers twisting in her lap. And even when Ifor took his place again, she did not lift her face.

My father picked up his knife and fork and went at his supper.

'Eat, woman, eat,' he said.

AND SO, in summer, my father took the woman Mari Mortymer to Resolven Zion and brought her out as wife. July, I
think. is a bad month for a marriage, since there hangs in this
month the threatened death of summer. *Calan Haf*, which is
what the old ones call it, is the month for me, the very birth of
the summer year. On the first day in May I will take my
woman to the pastor, for I will not parade a fruitful lady
before the gold of a dying year.

But *Calan Haf* or *Calan Gaeaf*, May or November, it was
good to have a mother back in the house again.

Never have I seen such a palaver as there was in the preparations for the bidding; everybody up at cock-shout, Ifor in
the bosh, and me, Dewi and Dada under the pump shaving
extra close and shouting for slippery eel for cuts, and for days
now the women had been prancing around in crinoline bunting, with yards of this and that over their arms and holding it
up to the light, speaking with pins in their mouths and scissors
and needles in their fingers.

'How do I look?' asked Ifor, going in a circle in the yard.

Very tarted up was Ifor, in his long white gown, coloured
ribbons pinned to his shoulder and more flying free on the end
of his long, white staff, the official uniform of the marriage-
bidder.

'What you doing tonight?' I asked, peering inside his gown.

'Gran!' he shouted. 'Bryn is sissying me again.'

Out she came with fists and threats, and you'd better get off
if you have nothing better to do, and then Dewi appeared
dressed the same, clomping over the cobbles in hobnails.

'God, no!' I said. 'Ribbons in the hair, too, is it?'

Mind, it was not fair to take the water, for this bidding
business was a pretty affair, and much better than this stupid
new-fangled post for a penny idea.

'Right, you,' said Gran. 'Quiet, everyone. We will have this
done properly, or not at all. Recite slow, clear and do it in

chorus,' and Ifor and Dewi, after a bit of boot-tapping and nicking, cried:

'Pleased I am to relate, we being bidders of a wedding between Mostyn Evan of the Old Navigation and Mistress Mari Mortymer, both residing in the hamlet of Resolven...' They faltered, staring at each other.

'Oh, for God's sake!' said my father, distressed.

'Forgot it, Da.'

He shook his head. 'Whoever suggested this pair of nitwits for the bidding...' and Mari's voice rang out:

'Come on, come on! "Back home after the wedding..."  Come on!'

I was creased with laughter, stamping about.

'Do not be a pig, Bryn!' whispered Rhiannon, eyes afire.

Fingers locked on their stomachs, eyes turned up, shoulders swaying like a pair of school-girls, they continued, 'Back home after the wedding there will be clean chairs to sit upon, a leg of mutton and home-fed pork to eat, boiled by the bride personally...'

'Boiled by me personally,' said Gran.

'Boiled by Gran personally, also for each guest a quart of Cuddlecome brew...'

'Lamb and Flag brew, if you please,' interjected Dada. 'I have had enough talk of that Cuddlecome place to last me six weddings.'

'...Lamb and Flag brew, with small-beer for the ladies and children. Please to come, then...'

'Oh, Ifor,' wailed Mari. 'Be happy for me. Glum as coffin lids you are, do not look like that!'

'Bloody daft we look, mind,' said Ifor, brushing ribbons.

'Stop that!' cried Gran. 'Dafter you will end if you do not go into it proper. Right, finish it, and remember that nothing Welsh is daft.'

'Please to come, then,' they sang, 'and bring a hen, a turkey or a chicken—even a piece of bread, which the house can afford.'

'*Anything* the house can afford,' groaned Dada, lathering up. 'Some queer old characters we will have arriving sending that cuckoo pair as bidders.' He levelled his shaving-brush at them. 'And remember one thing—do not accept money.'

'Aye, Dada,' said Dewi, and my father turned away, saying, 'I do not agree with this, Mother. You realise they will be boots up in every establishment from here to Swansea, and we won't see them till Easter.'

'One whiff—one sniff at their breath and they will have me to account to, you understand?'

'Yes, Gran.'

'And try to look happy!' begged Mari.

I stood on the horse-mount as they went off, sending mating whistles after them.

'Enough of that, you—into the house,' cried my father.

'Eh, bless St. David! That was a glorious summer day in old Resolven, and the things Ifor and Dewi brought in filled the house. There was a pair of canal ducks from Dai Half-Moon, while Mrs. Ten Benyon who was living down by Neath Abbey sent a soup bowl. Mr. and Mrs. Isan Chapel sent a painting of a child found drowned, and Eli Cohen sent a pig on the hoof, led by Willie Dare, who went all coy and simpering at the sight of Sharon. Cushy Cuddlecome had a keg of ale rolled up by Abe Sluice and sent her regrets for absence, for there were three potential customers at the Old Navigation, and Cushy always had an eye to business. Mrs. Willie Shenkins baked eight pounds of bread, and brought it personally, with congratulations to Mari, breaking down on the doorstep. There was a cracked wash-basin from Dai Central Eating, who, thank God for our Doctor Brodie, was over the cholera, and I swear the swine unloaded it on to me. Mr. and Mrs. Alfo Morgan sent kind respects and Rosie Carey a pillowcase with Valentine hearts entwined with roses, very romantic was Miss Carey: Mrs. Hanman on the Old Glamorgan came with five meat hooks and half a leg of mutton, which Gran cried over, saying she couldn't afford it. There were dozens of well-wishers, and Ifor and Dewi were loaded with gifts from folk you would never expect, like Mr. and Mrs. Abe Sluice, and even Betsy Small-Coal sent a sampler she had stitched herself with 'Together' embroidered in silk on satin, and where she got the money from for that I shall never know, said Gran.

Mind, it is when you go up in the frock coat and down in the wooden suit—this is when real friends remember you, said my father.

'Aye,' said Gran, 'that is the answer. Up and down without a stain on the soul.'

Naturally, though, we took note of the people who hadn't sent anything, for though there is good in everybody and some of the poor souls can't afford it, according to Gran, there were also a few mean bastards who could and didn't, said Ifor.

I will always remember my little marriage because it was to Rhiannon: but nobody in Resolven hamlet will ever forget the summer day in July when my dada married beautiful Mari Mortymer.

Very stiff and starched; nervous laughs and coughs, and dust on the velvet collar and a piece of cotton on the crinoline: the men of the family stood like statues in the yard: the women held their hearts with palpitations, and Gran got a fit of the vapours just before we left, and had to be fanned round.

All right to laugh, mind, but a very exacting business is a marriage.

But, oh! These two Mortymer women, Mari and Rhiannon, do take the breath.

'Slip the big one over the county border,' whispered Dewi, 'and I would wed her myself.'

'Bryn!' called my father, and I ran to him. 'You are youngest son, so your new mother will ride with you. Take the big mare Mr. Ephraim Davies was good enough to lend us,' and my heart was thumping with pride as I led lovely Mari up the mount-steps, and helped her on side-saddle, then swung my leg over the mare's back, gripping Mari with my forearms.

'Right,' said Dada, tightening the girth, 'make yourself scarce—but no risks, remember—no big fences. Injure her, and I will see to you.'

'Yes, Dada.'

'See you in Chapel, Mari!'

'God willing, Mostyn.'

Like a Greek god I felt sitting there on that big mare's back, with Mari in my arms. The wind moved over her face, and it was perfumed to my nostrils.

Do not be mistaken: I was a boy no longer. Six-foot-one in socks, a bit stringy round the flanks perhaps, but coming thick in the shoulders and thews, and a blurr of hair coming on the chest. And the yard was filled with people, every barge coming down the cut was mooring up and their crews piling ashore, standing six deep around the gate with their flannel shirts and mole-skin caps, the men touching their hair as I took Mari past with a stately tread, for this was a mare for special occasions, the women dropping down in curtseys, the little children bowing. Too much for Gran: nearly soaked, was Gran, and we had not even started. Down went Rhiannon and Sharon, fingers clasped; firm friends, these two. And as we reached the gate I looked up at the small attic window of the Old Navigation, and saw in the eye of my mind the small, white face of my beloved Gwen.

Still: dry up; enough sadness for a wonderful day.

'Eleven o'clock at Zion—don't you dare be late!' cried my father, and there was a thunder of banter and clapping in the yard.

'If you catch us first!' I cried, and gave the heels to the big grey mare, and we were away, hooves thumping along the tow-path until we came to the Nedd bridge, and here I tamed her, and we took it slow, walking in shafted sunlight and bridle jingles into the forest tracks of Rheola.

Just me and Mari in the whole world, then, walking in hoof and heart-beats in the ancient forest of Rheola.

Shon Seler Shonko, the Poacher of Rheola, was untying his snares: wild in the eye was Shon, fresh back from Van Land for taking salmon from the Towey over in Carmarthenshire, and he staggered back in his rags, the coney hard against his chest.

Good hunting, is it, Mr. Shonko?' cried Mari.

Broken mouthed, he grinned at her, and I saw on his skinny arms the lash of the blood-soaked triangles, for a clergyman-magistrate had him for a ten pound hen, and ten years Shon

Seler Shonko did, less the voyage out and back.

'Good luck, missus! Oh, ah! Good luck, I say, lady!'

He walked alongside us, hand on the bridle.

'Got to go now, Shon,' I said.

In his riven back I saw the misery of my generation.

'You take the coney, missus? Take the coney and eat it for the wedding breakfast, eh?'

'Hop it, Shon,' I said.

'No, wait,' said Mari. 'You want me to have it, Mr. Shonko?'

'Ah, missus, by Christ I do. You have it for the luck of it, comin' from a rag-tailed old sod like me—will ye take it, in good nature?'

'And pleased to, Mr. Shonko,' said she, hooking up the rabbit.

'And right good fortune to ye, missus—a good and gentle man wi' you!'

'God bless you,' she said, and pressed his filthy hand.

And she spurred the mare with her heels, shouting, 'Good-bye, Mr. Shonko. Put some speed in it, Bryn, lad—are we hanging around all day?'

'When he come a-hunting ye, I'll send him opposite way!' roared Shon Seler Shonko. 'Isn't proper that a man should transgress such an apple of a woman!'

We thundered over the moss of Rheola, swaying through the massed trees, ducking under branches, shouting with excitement, as if she was my bride being pursued, and not my father's, with Shon Shonko's rabbit in my pocket and the big mare lively beneath us.

'Stop!' commanded Mari, and turned in the saddle as I reined the mare. 'An apple of a woman, is it?' She blew out her cheeks and made herself big. 'Transgressed, is it? But it do depend, Shon Shonko, on the manner of the man doin' the transgressing!' and she shrieked with laughter.

In a stamping of hooves and quickening hearts we went past Crugau, turning south before the House of Vaughan, and there was a love in me for the woman soon to be my mother.

Heisht in Chapel now, waiting for the bride, sitting in

beams of sunlight watching the dust-motes dance. Listening to Mrs. Tref Hopkins on the harmonium with Mrs. Arfon Shavings turning her pages: coins and keys rattling, trews square on the mahogany, boots square on the floor. Dubbined toe-caps and socks with no toes in, shirt-fronts with no arms and tails, boots with no feet in come up from the pit, sleeves with no arms in pinned at the shoulder. Da Point-Five is propped in the pew, trews with no legs in, singing *All Things Bright and Beautiful* in a glorious bass. Up for the hymn now, alpaca bulging on the shoulders of the colliers, Butcher Shinbone is standing in a pool of blood. Billie Softo is standing in his rags, dreaming of bread and butter: collywobbles from Mr. Evans Brewer, dreaming of ale. Give him a glance, shift your boots on the boards, for the collies become booms and the wobbles become thunder, and he goes blue and bucolic, does Evans Brewer, and explodes in sherry scarlets and foaming fizz and frothing golden ale in a sheet of white gin and cider amber, expiring on the pew in a gentle zizz. Sure as Fate it will happen one day, says Dada.

Lovely Tom Davies is there as sidesman, and the medical profession very well-represented, with Mrs. Teague the Herbalist who did our Gwen's whitlow and cured Dai In and Out's yellow jaundice by enchantment, and he wasn't in and out of the Vaughan for a month; also good at the lobe-cutting for children with rickets, top half ears only being evident in Resolven.

'Oh, look!' ejaculated Gran, behind me. 'Here comes that beautiful Zion Revivalist!'

'You know him?' asked Rhiannon.

'She should do,' I said, 'he practically transported her a few years back up in Merthyr Bethania.'

And down the aisle came the preacher like some gigantic patriarch, white mane of hair flowing, spade beard over his waistcoat, and behind him came a young man, tall and handsome. Rhiannon whispered excitedly, 'The preacher's name is Tomos Traherne, and the young man is my cousin sort of.'

At this the young man turned and smiled at her, his fierce, dark eyes softening in his face, and I made a mental note to keep an eye on him.

161

'*Duw*,' said Sharon, 'he can be my cousin sort-of any time he likes.'

'Hush, you lot,' whispered Gran, 'here comes the bride.'

Large and handsome my father looked in his frock coat and trews hired special from Hobo Churchyard, and Mari was young and enchanting on his arm: as regal as a queen she was, her face lifted in a smile as she walked to the Seat, and we got into the I do's and sicknesses and cherishings, which brought out Gran's bedsheet handkerchief which she kept special for weddings. Then Moses Thomas gave out the bessing hymn and Mrs. Tref Hopkins opened her shoulders and we were into the *All Hail the Power*, which was Mari's selection since she used to sing it back home in Camarthenshire. A good old corker, this one, and I reckon the Lord Jesus enjoys it as much as I do, and the Resolven congregation let it fly that lovely morning of my father's wedding. Bass and tenor, soprano and contralto, in full harmony, and the rafters shivered to the blast of sound when something moved in the pocket of my coat.

Sweating, me, and I put a curse on the soul of Shon Shonko.

'You all right, Bryn?' asked Rhiannon prettily.

'Right as rain,' I said.

Back to life had come that Shonko coney and now kicking me in the ribs like a six foot collier.

Trying to sing now, as if nothing was happening, and stuffing the bloody thing back into my pocket every time it popped out.

'*Diawch!*' rumbled Ifor behind me. 'Hey, Bryn, lad,' and he tapped me.

'What?' I said, turning.

'Do not look now, man, but there is a coney sitting up in your pocket.'

'A what?' asked Sharon.

'A coney—sitting in his pocket,' said Ifor.

'Do not talk daft,' replied Sharon.

'Hey, Gran . . .' muttered Ifor, while I cursed him, stuffing the coney back.

And just then it was up and out and running along the hymn shelf hitting up people's hymnals, raising shrieks of delight

162

from the children and walking-sticks clattering as bruisers like Dai In and Out tried to hit him cold. And then, to my horror, I saw the Revival preacher fixing me with an eagle eye.

'He'll have you, mind,' said Sharon, 'bringin' coneys into Chapel.'

Now the coney was sitting petrified between Dada's boots, now snitching round the hem of Mari's dress, giving me palpitations, for the very last thing ladies love is things like mice and conies going up and under. Now he was prancing along the harmonium, and you could see he was wondering how the hell he had landed in here from the forest of Rheola, and every kid in the place was up on the pews pointing and shrieking before being dragged down and stifled. And then I went sweating cold, for one moment he was sniffing at Mrs. Tref Hopkins' boots as they went up and down on the bellows, and next moment he was under.

'Gone up Mrs. Tref Hopkins,' rumbled Ifor in my ear.

'Do what, love?' asked Gran, taking a breath for the last verse.

'Bryn's coney, Gran. Just seen it, I have. Gone up Mrs. Tref Hopkins, see.'

'Aye, indeed, son. We will have a good strong cup the moment we are back. Sing up, there's a good lad.'

I watched Mrs. Tref Hopkins in terror, for she was already off the note and in trouble with the bellows, and never in my life have I seen such an expression on the face of a lady, which is perfectly understandable because harmoniumists have a right to perform safe in the knowledge that Rheola conies will not start walking up their legs, especially in Chapel. Now the last line coming up and she hit the keys in glorious crescendo, getting the *hwyl* right up her apron, and next moment she was boots up and music down, with the coney rushing out and people kneeling and fanning her and is she all right now and for God's sake fetch Mrs. Teague the Herbalist, since Mrs. Tref Hopkins do not appear to be herself this morning.

'Excuse me, please,' I said, 'I am going from here,' for that Revivalist preacher was on his way down the aisle towards me, his staff striking the flags like a Swansea gaoler.

Bright sunlight hit me in the porch, and there, to my

astonishment, stood Shon Shonko the Poacher as large as life, grinning like a barbary ape and with a string of conies hanging from his belt.

'Just come wi' a few more, I 'ave,' said he. 'That lovely bride, she took my hand—me, old Shon Shonko, an' I reckon she's entitled to a few more rabbits for the wedding breakfast, oh, ah!'

Very fast I went down to the river, to save me the sin of murder.

'Why!' yelled Shonko, indignant. 'No call for that, young fella—that's no sort o' language, and you just received the blessin' of Chapel!'

I did not stop until I reached the Old Navigation.


# 19


THE year my father brought Mari Mortymer as wife to the Old Navigation was like a bright eye in a face of joy. A new man was he, re-born, even larger, it appeared to me; singing in the tub before the fire while she swabbed him after the Pont Walby coaling, digging in the garden, with cheery waves even to the passing men of the new railway. It is amazing to me the effect a good wife can have upon a man, and I am sick and tired of stories about shrews and harridans with six-inch tongues lashing their men into one gin-shop after another, and I am not surprised they get belted occasionally.

'Aye, well, that is it, see,' said Gran. 'It do depend largely upon what direction they are sent from. A Baal hand-maiden can be picked up in saw-dust, but you got to sweep the dust of the chapel to find the jewel that is one like Mari,' and with this she got into the moral virtues and contrary vices, adding, ' "A prudent wife is from the Lord, and whoso findeth a wife findeth a good thing, and obtaineth favour of the Lord." '

Which was a pretty sweeping statement, it was proved later.

My father had found a beautiful wife, but with her came a beautiful basket of trouble.

I suppose, looking back, you can't expect to hit out a man like the Black Welshman and get away with it, or make enemies of people like Man Arfon who was now large in the new railway, to say nothing of the uneasy peace between Dada and Tub Union for working a private contract.

Summer faded into autumn, and spring came again over the blazing land, bringing kissing-time, and this had a deep effect on the family.

'Where are you away to, then?' asked Gran.

'Taking this up to Rebecca,' said Ifor, holding his new tin ear up to the shaving glass. Glorious was that cauliflower Ifor had collected in his return with Dai Swipo, tight-screwed into a ball and shining like a sea-lantern, and I would personally slam one of mine in a door if I thought I could mutilate it as good as Ifor's.

'Time that girl was married, Ifor,' observed Mari at her stitching.

'Ah, when times get better, girl.'

'Times will not get better, only worse,' said Sharon. 'They dropped us another threepence a ton, you hear that?'

I had heard it, and it had set my father deep in his chair, furrowed; the new railway that was belting past the Old Navigation was getting bigger and the bargees thinner. Brunel, the genius, had done what Stephenson said could not be done— linked the wealth of the towns of Aberdare and Neath, and collecting the vast tonnage of Merthyr Road, Hirwain, Glyn Neath, Resolven and Aberdulais had poured it into the maws of the sea.

The opening of the line last September was a highlight, with the Crawshay band loaded on to a truck pulled by a saddle-tank, blasting martial music from Hirwain to Neath, and nearly hitting the big black clock off the mantel with Gran out in the garden shaking her fist at the trombones and tubas, for brass bands sent her raving, especially serpentines and things like that. And I remember, when she was up in Merthyr, she used to suck lemons in front of the Brass Band Cyfarthfa, which usually put paid to them, for nothing will fill up a serpentine quicker than somebody sucking a lemon while the bandsman is blue in the face and up in the top registers.

'Welsh harps it is for me,' she used to say, 'and damage I will cause blasting brass bands, especially Cyfarthfa, for it is money the workers are wanting from Crawshay, not music.'

But back to the kissing-time of the spring of '52.

Great developments were afoot between Sharon and Richard Bennet, Rhiannon's cousin sort-of. Big and handsome, this chap, with a Welsh fire-brand of a mother and an English agitator for a father, both now dead. And though he lived with his gran and Tomos Traherne in Nantyglo, he appeared to spend most of his life down here at the Old Navigation.

Very polished and educated was this Richard Bennet, with bows on the doorstep and showing his arm to Sharon, but also too bright in the eye for Rhiannon to suit me, and I didn't reckon it healthy.

A dreadful state I was in that spring over my lovely Rhiannon.

Hot and bothered, I was, when she was closer than a yard, and I nearly threw a faint every time he cast a glance in her direction.

'Good evening, Mrs. Evan.' Low he bows to Mari; then in with a stride and a white smile on his tanned face; now his hand goes out to me and Dada, and he had a grip like an elephant in gloves.

This was the Wednesday that Sharon got the vapours.

I have never seen this happen before: I have seen her hot and swearing over a chap, but never actually faint, and she was out cold for fifteen minutes.

And Rhiannon was nearly as bad. 'Oh, Richard!' cried she. 'I haven't seen you for days.'

Isn't healthy, I say: apparently he didn't work for a living. He had fine clothes, plenty of money, and didn't work.

'Don't be ridiculous,' said Rhiannon, from the bosh.

'Mind your own business,' said Dewi.

When nobody was around I looked in the mirror: see the coal-black face, the red-ringed eyes, the white mouth. Smelling of mule, too, after a day down the pit. And in comes this Bennet chap all braveries and fancies, with a buttonhole in his coat big enough to bury him, ducking his head under the door.

'Good evening, Bryn!'

'Come in, Dick, lad!' cried my father.

Later, out the back, Dada said, 'Listen, you. When a man offers his hand to you, you take it, whether you like him or not—understand?'

I leaned against the mangle, empty and unequal.

'You owe it to Sharon, you owe it to Rhiannon—I'll not tell you again.'

But it was good at home on the nights that Richard Bennet did not come to visit. Oh, I do love it when the family is all under one roof and the doors are shut tight to keep the mice out, with the stars of the cut so big that they threaten to drop out of the sky. Like tonight.

'Hold still,' commanded Gran, with Ifor's head in her lap, and her doing his excellent cauliflower ear: expert with these was my gran, having learned the art of a hot and cold compress from pay nights up in Dowlais where the average a month was one per head of the population. Rhiannon was on the hot compresses and Sharon on the cold, doing her Shakespeare acting in between. Mari was smiling at her sewing, Dada deep in his chair, legs thrust out: Dewi, book up to the lamp, was into *The Triumph of the Working Classes over the Capitalist System*, and I have a sneaking idea who it was lent him that one.

And Sharon, with Shakespeare in one arm and Richard Bennet in the other, is in form in the middle of the kitchen. ' "Oh, coz, coz, coz, my pretty little coz, that thou didst know how many fathoms deep I am in love! But it cannot be sounded: my affection hath an unknown bottom, like the bay of Portugal." '

Some queer old things this Shakespeare chap do come out with at times.

Dada said, removing his pipe and folding *The Cambrian*, 'Sara Siddons, now deceased, retired prematurely because of the competition.'

'Easy with that hot one,' complained Ifor. 'Setting the thing alight, you are, Gran.'

167

'Hot you will have to have it, son—no good lukewarm.'

'Raising lumps on it.'

'It would have been less complicated had you ducked,' said Dada.

And Sharon, dancing to Ifor with a rose in her hand is showing enough of the deep divide in her sack dress to kill a curate. ' "Ah, you poor, sweet little rogue, you! Alas, poor ape, how thou sweatest. Come, let me wipe thy face . . ." ' and she bent to Ifor, smoothing his cheek, whispering, ' "Come on, you whoreson chops—ah, rogue, i'faith, I love thee. . . ." '

'She do the acting well, don't she, Gran,' observed Ifor, beaming.

'She do it a bit too near the knuckle for my liking,' said Gran. 'Pin up a yard or two in front, there's a good girl.'

'Oh, Gran!' Flushed and stamping is Sharon, her artistry denied.

'The free-thinking do not allow you to parade half naked—pin up!'

'Ach, let her be, Mother,' said Dada. 'It is only in the family.'

'It is disrespectful to her brothers—pin up.' Gran slapped another cold poultice on Ifor's ear. 'And you keep still. Who's she supposed to be, anyway?'

'Who are you supposed to be, Sharon my rose?' asked Dada at his newspaper.

'Doll Tearsheet in Henry the Fourth Part Two.'

'Where did Part One get to, then?' asked Gran.

'Ignore that,' said my father.

'Who is this Doll Tearsheet? She don't sound savoury to me,' said Gran.

'A cheap whore with a heart of gold,' said Sharon.

'Excuse me,' cried Mari, leaping up. 'A cup of tea for everyone, is it?'

'A what?' whispered Gran, shocked and white.

'Oh, Gran, it is only in the play!' protested Sharon.

'It might be, but I am not having such language in the house.' She levelled a finger at Dada. 'This is your fault, mind, you have encouraged her!'

'My dear girl—do you realise this is Shakespeare?'

168

'Aye, and I don't like the sound of him, either. The house is going to the devil since he came into it.' She put her fist on Ifor's ear. 'Enough's as good as a feast. Let us have a little more of that coz coz thing and the bay of Portugal, and a little less of these cheap whores with hearts of gold, you hear me?'

'Yes, Gran,' said Sharon.

'And pin up!'

For my part this Shakespeare chap do sound all right to me since I prefer to look a thing in the face than hide it under banana leaves for dirty people to find. And the people this man makes do please me, the great kings and courtiers, and also the little Doll Tearsheets, for I have seen some fine ladies under parasols I would not put in the company of this Doll, who was sweet in kindness, according to Sharon, and I would heave cobbles at the hypocrites who dress like gentry and act like harpies.

'You can find dirt anywhere, if you insist on looking for it,' said my father once. 'This poet Shakespeare makes us each a lute and on this lute we can play his words to a song of our own. Each singer sings differently. You take the Song of Solomon, for instance. You can find in it glory and goodness and love: but another will tear aside its tapestry of gold and spy beneath the nakedness and lust.'

Often, to hear my father speak, you would think he came of the bards. One thing was sure: at Granfer Ben's knee he had learned of beauty, and been educated in English and Welsh, and although he was of the barges, he was no ordinary bargee. Also, but I do not wish to be unkind, I think my poor old gran was a lot to blame for Granfer Ben going to Salt Lake City: nothing, not a thing in common, said my father.

'The saint will interpret life as the saint sees it, the monk behind the sanctity of his walls: the vile will find vileness in purity; in love of the body they will see the sexual behaviour of the animal. The unctuous will always play hypocrisy, which is the cardinal sin of men: do no look elsewhere than Jesus if you want the sight of a man, and remember that he found beauty and goodness in the harlot as he smoothed his foot in the sand.'

And now, he put out his hand to Sharon, saying, 'In the Penny Gaffs of the Swansea Michaelmas Fair I have seen your Granfer Ben play the great Falstaff.'

'You know of Falstaff?' cried Sharon, kneeling at his feet, eyes wide.

'Aye, and Pistol and Bardolph, Hotspur and Mistress Quickly of the Boar's Head Tavern. Aye, girl, you are not the only one to know of the great Shakespeare—I grieve I do not know more,' and then, to our joy, he rose from his chair while Mari watched him, smiling; he cried bassly, ' "Thou art as valorous as Hector of Troy, worth five of Agamemnon, and ten times better than the Nine Worthies. Ah, villain!" ' and with his arms out he paraded the room, shouting:

' "A rascally slave! I will toss the rogue in a blanket!" cries Falstaff.'

' "Do, if thou darest for thy heart," ' shrieked Sharon, delighted, ' "an thou dost, I'll canvas thee between a pair of sheets." '

'At this point music is played, and I am a page,' said Dada, strolling and humming loud, his hand strumming a make-believe lyre.

'And I do not like the sound of that, either,' said Gran.

'What, the music?'

'The canvas and sheets bit. Now stop it, Mostyn—I wish no more of it.'

'Oh, Gran!' cried Sharon, beside her now, arms out and loving her.

'Never you mind,' said Gran. 'No more of it—and mind Ifor's ear.'

And there are some who are monsters of virtue, yet we adore them.

Everything stopped at that moment while a Corsair went through on the line with ten ballast trucks behind it for station building up at Hirwain: in smoke and steam it bellowed past the window, and the Old Navigation shook to the depth of her foundations, as if navvies were hammering dog-spikes into the soles of her feet.

'No more cheap whores with hearts of gold, is it?' said Gran at length.

'I promise.'

'Or that Doll Tearsheet?'

'No more Doll Tearsheet. Just the old coz coz business from now on.'

And so, with Sharon laying snares for Richard Bennet and me courting Rhiannon and getting nowhere fast, with the railway getting bigger and the canal smaller, we went through the golden summer of the Vale with love impending but getting no nearer, and with anxious pockets.

But with one undying consolation.

Michaelmas Fair!

I am getting that girl under cover in a wheatfield or die doing it.

# 20

GREAT were the preparations for Neath Michaelmas Fair, with people up at dawn prancing and preening in mirrors, the men yanking at trews, shaving close and polishing boots; the women rushing around half-naked, their arms crossed on their petticoat chests, taking out crackers and curling, tightening stays and pulling on stockings, and for God's sake wash under the arms for a change, you men, said Gran, for you never seem to think of such places. Even Cinders, my little bitch, got a bath, and Dewi was out in the stables most of last night tying up Nell's mane with straw and rosettes and plaiting Jed Donkey's tail with red, white and blue ribbons. Beautiful looked our barge, too, all decorated with bunting and autumn flowers, the great Turk's Head on the tiller freshly pipe-clayed by my father for the barge competition, with the long, white tail of the first stallion he had owned blowing straight and proudly in the wind of the cut.

'Bryn,' shouted Gran, 'don't stand there idling—get the things outside on the wharf!'

'Can I help?' cried Rhiannon.

'You catch this end,' I said, shifting a box, but Ifor came up then, stripped to his black trews, and lifted it clear for the prow of the barge, to sit upon: taking on the famous Alehouse Jones in the booth, said Dewi, and God help him.

'Got the small-beer and eats?' called Gran.

'By here.'

'All ready, is it?' asked Sharon, swirling in with petticoats and bright pink crinoline, her hair flying free on her shoulders, and Dada came next with Mari on his arm, Gran all bunned up in black and cameo with a tin of her cold rice-pudding under her arm, and away to go we were, with Ifor first aboard; daft as a brush he looked, sitting there naked to the waist and his fists on his knees, but this was the custom.

'Right, cast off!' called Dada, and I coiled the mooring-rope and tightened the trace and took my seat beside Rhiannon. Dewi was at Nell's head and down the cut we went in golden morning sunlight. There is lovely it is to be travelling to the Neath Michaelmas Fair, and the clouds all wispy in the October sky and your best girl beside you. Always will I remember her scented sweetness that day, her hair black curls under her poke-bonnet and down to her waist in white ribbons, and beautiful pink her crinoline, sparked with white roses. See her face patterned with shadow and sunlight, Iberian in darkness, the lips curved red, her eyes bright and strangely light. Proud as a cocker I was that day, with her hand in mine, Mari and Dada behind us and Gran and Sharon bringing up the rear, and my elephant brother half naked on the prow, biceps bulging, ready for the best in Wales.

'They are turning out for the Fair this year, right enough!' cried Mari, and so they were, for the villagers were walking in thick swathes down the valley, pouring from the cottages of Melin, Clyne and Gerwen in a medley of colour, the children scampering in Sunday best, the women in bright crinolines and bonnet-streamers, laughing shrilly under their poke-bonnets. From the lock cottages came the keepers, being flicked by their wives for hair and scurf, sons and daughters being lectured on special behaviour, and striped bottoms it would be for hobnobbing with the navvies, male or female. The cut was alive with barges as far as I could see, many of them loaded with brass and silver bands, and already blue in the face with them, the conductors standing in the prows beating the time. Choirs from the Neath and Swansea valleys were there, too, and at Aberdulais the crowds thronged in over Seven Sisters. From the tin-plate works came the melters and boxers, the sorters and branders; the men wearing the white smocks of their trade of tin, their blood mixed with the Celts of Cornwall: the fire-maintainers were clutched in groups, each man with a cheek scalded crimson from the flare of the hearth: flat-chested came the women picklers, their breasts given to the poisonous prick of the sorting knife. The blind came, too, for eyes are given in return for tin and copper: the maimed came on crutches, and a few Dais cut-in-half were carried by the wrestlers and fighters. Owen Bach I saw, in a majesty of strength, fists on hips, straight from the bull-taming in front of the Lamb and Flag, Glyn Neath. Thundering down the railway came the snorting Corsair engines of Brunel the genius, bringing down the wealth of The Top, the puddlers, rollers, rodders, furnacemen and their families, all done posh and waving greeting to the bargees, and I saw Bili Jones and Wil Shout, the drovers, standing close with Hobo Churchyard between them and he hadn't a leg under him which brought Dada up and shouting delighted, 'Good man, Hobo!'

'Oh, sit down, son,' cried Gran, 'a minister might be watching. Dear me, this family do stoop to pick up nothing.'

'Bryn, look!' cried Rhiannon, and her grip of my knee took me light in the head so I almost fainted. 'Oh, just look at that beautiful Rosie Carey!'

A very fine sight was Rosie Carey, high in the breast and short in the ankle, done up in white for purity under a big, floppy hat, bowing this way and that to the gentlemen, and smiling, her teeth flashing white against the crimson curve of her lips: gorgeous woman, and I could have eaten her with haricot beans and gravy, and I saw her mouth open in delighted surprise as Dewi came up behind her and pinched her under the bustle.

'There is a huzzy, mind,' said Gran, evil.

'Oh, no, she is lovely!' cried Mari, who was the loveliest there.

'It do go deeper than the superficial, though,' said Gran. 'Some queer things are happening at the Lamb and Flag, I hear,' and so there was, for rumour had it that Alfo had his hand in the till while Mrs. Alfo was upstairs in their big fourposter hitting up the pigs: down in the tap-room was Alfo, night-shirt billowing as he counted out the takings, 'One for you, my Rosie, one for me, none for Mrs. Alfo, and one for Coventry.'

'No smoke without fire,' said Gran now. 'Folks reckon he's got a cottage up in the Midlands all set for Rosie Carey, and I do not think it decent.'

On, on through the patterned gold of the canal, past the junction with the Red Jacket cut and down we went past the big dry dock alongside the river where the big two hundred tonners were on the high tide, all gaily decorated with streamers and bunting, and along the banks the boys and girls were gathering to give us a cheer, and among them was Sian Edwards and Jane Rheola, and Sian winked.

'Ay, ay, Bryn Evan!' cried Sian, and went all cuddly, slapping at her hands.

'Ay, ay,' I replied, sweating bricks.

'Got another, has he?' said Jane, praying. 'Should be a law against it.'

'And I bet she don't know what day it is, eh, Bryn Evan?'

There is a pair of bitches for you.

Red as a turkey wattle was Rhiannon, her fingers twisting in her lap.

'If you so much as blink, he'll have you, girl!'

Rhiannon said, lifting her eyes to mine, 'You ... you know those two?'

'Never seen them in my life.'

'Is that a fact?' said Sian, with ears like mice. 'Sinking Cuddlecome Specials with that Tai Morlais and I had to fight him off. Dear me, woman, you do not know what is coming to you!'

'Be warned!' cried Jane, her finger up as they went off. 'Last time he landed on Cushy, but you may not be so lucky!'

In a black silence we sat then, and thank heaven nobody else had heard them because of the celebrations, and I devised

174

special tortures for Sian Edwards and Jane Rheola if ever I caught them running.

'What did she mean, that last one?' whispered Rhiannon.

'Nothing. Just trying to cause trouble,' I said.

For this was a relapse I had been trying hard to forget, and it was Rhiannon's fault, anyway, making a fuss of that chap Bennet. A couple of months back I had taken Sian's key off the stable wall-plate and popped down to the Cuddlecome Inn, but I got the directions wrong and I was first floor, first right and first door, which landed me in with Cushy, and I was out following bottles and boots from Cushy screaming blue murder and the Irish Shrew and Sian, and now doing my best to live it down.

'Don't tell me you go down to the Cuddlecome Inn!' breathed Rhiannon.

'Good lord, what next!' I replied, disgusted. 'You ought to be ashamed of yourself, saying such a thing!'

'Oh, look!' she suddenly cried. 'Here comes Richard.'

If he had worked it he couldn't have come at a better time. Barbed hooks were in me as I saw him shaking hands with Dewi on the river path, and he waved, making secret signs to Sharon who whooped with joy, knowing of a tryst.

I sat in funeral cloth, my heart clutched in green fingers. Rhiannon said, as he vaulted the bank and walked away, waving, 'Ach, he's a good one that. You know his dad was English?'

'I am not surprised.'

She sighed. 'Many things he taught me when I was young and mam took me up to his gran's in Nanty. You know that hawthorn buds taste bread and cheese?'

'Of course,' I said, unaware of it.'

'That you can make pop-guns out of elder branches?'

'Everybody knows that,' I said testily, never having heard of it.

She laughed softly, and I hated her, and she said, 'He used to catch dumbledores in Canterbury bells, but I cried and he let them go.'

'Daft old things they do up in England.'

She began to shake silently with frail laughter, and the ire

175

rose in me, clenching my hands, and I saw this Bennet coney staggering back with me after him, hooking his head off: later, he was laid out in the marble rigidity of death, and Rhiannon was beside him in widow's weeds, weeping while I sat in the Petty Sessions with a gaoler either side in a malign silence, unrepentent.

Now I said, archly and uncaring, 'I suppose you will spend your time at the fair with him and Sharon?'

'I will give some thought to it,' said she with a twig of a smile, and I sat there mortified in a rising heat of blood, while she, arrogant and larkish under her poke-bonnet, did not spare me a glance to see the effect.

'Horrible, you are,' I said. 'You do not take after your lovely mam.'

'Nor do you after your da,' said she, tartly. 'I am not as thick as I look, mind. You would never get him sinking quarts down at Cushy Cuddlecome's and hobnobbing with the scarlet ladies!' and she tossed her head.

'I have never been out with a scarlet lady!'

'Easy in front there,' said Dada, his chops on my shoulder. 'No need to boast of it to all and sundry.'

'Bryn is being a pig!' cried Rhiannon.

'So I gather,' said Dada, 'but do your best to confine the battle to within family limits, for they can hear you over in Swansea.'

The streamers, the music, the laughter beat over us in a rising tide of joy and sound, and I slipped an eye at Rhiannon. She was sitting in a splendid, savage beauty, indignant to my glance.

'It do not need the penny post, remember, for things to get around,' she said at nothing.

'You are an inch-minded bloody little bigot,' I said, with ice.

At this, for no apparent reason, she began to bucket, her fist thumping in her lap, and her nose went stuffy and her eyes red and wet, and I was glad.

'Oh, Bryn!' whispered Mari, distressed.

'Will somebody inform me what is happening up there in front?' cried Gran.

'It is Bryn being a little pig to Rhiannon, and making her cry,' said Sharon.

'But this is terrible!' cried Mari, holding us together. 'You must not quarrel on Michaelmas—and look, it is such a beautiful day!'

'I hate him!' breathed Rhiannon.

Everybody coming up now, stroking her and saying how I ought to be ashamed of myself, with daggers and sighs from Dada and an arched, understanding eye from my new mother. And between us, me and Rhiannon, sat a big English lout whispering to her words of consolation and sneering his lips at me.

I sat in a numb trance, listening to his untidy, English voice, and I swore that anything English that crossed my path that Michaelmas Fair I would hit back over to London via Cardiff.

'I hate you, I hate you!' cried Rhiannon, all bunged up and soaking.

'Oh, Rhiannon!' whispered Mari, shocked.

'I do. I hate you!'

'That makes two of us,' I said.

Bloody good start to the Fair you come to think of it.

Down the cut we went, with the crowds between us and the Gnoll getting bigger every minute, with great engines thundering down the railway with flats of bawling navvies, most of them bawling improper suggestions, and I saw my father cutting his knuckles on his serge. Then a few on the opposite path started winging bottles and such-like at Ifor who was still sitting stripped on the prow, and to his credit he didn't raise an eye when cabbages and carrots started bouncing off his nut, for dignity is a hell of a thing, mind, and has to be preserved, especially since this carrying of the champions had been going on since the canal opened in 1796.

'But the sooner we get ashore the better,' said Dada, sitting starboard of Gran and fending off rotten apples and bananas, but nothing shifted Rhiannon for every time I tried a conversation she was nose up to drown in a rainstorm. Also, navvies with six-pound swedes started getting at Ifor, and as the range shortened one parted his hair like a cannon-ball and the next hit him arse over ear off the box, and this naturally raised my father's ire, since he up and shook his fist and called them a shower of bastards, and this set Mari very dull, but Gran didn't hear because she was collecting swedes. Baccy York was chewing tobacco on the bank and his three wives already pretty tipsy; also Tub Union with his bargee bodyguard, all paid up members of the Lodge, and they all came down to meet us as we tied up, their little fat women all starched and stayed in best bombazine and hats with ostrich feathers: very truculent looked Mr. Tub Union.

'A word with you, Evan,' and he removed his clay and bowed deep to Mari, and she went down in a curtsey before him.

'Not business, I hope.'

'It is business every day in the business of living. You realise that we have been dropped on the rates of haul and will drop still lower now the rail is here.'

My father sighed. 'Look, *bach*, the sun is shining and it is Michaelmas Fair—must we talk rates of haul?'

'Talk today or starve tomorrow—take your pick.'

'The old collieries will stand by us,' said Dewi.

'The old collieries will load with us until they get railway sidings, then they will leave the Company, and we will leave the Vale.'

'I say it again, Tub Union,' said Dada, quietly, 'there is work for all.'

'There is work for the Company bargee, Mostyn Evan, but work no longer for the private contractor.

'So where do we go from here, then?' asked Ifor, lumbering up.

'We go nowhere,' replied Tub Union. 'We were here before you came—you go back to Merthyr.'

'And if I refuse?' asked Dada, polite.

'Then we bloody shift you.' He bowed to Mari. 'Begging your pardon for the language, ma'am.'

'Excellent,' said my father, 'and begging my wife's pardon for the language, you are welcome to bloody try. I am running a private barge on this canal with permission from the owners, and here it stays.' He shouldered the bargee aside.

'You will regret this,' said Tub Union.

'I have been regretting things all my life,' said my father. 'Most of all, I regret joining a Union that brings a threat to a paid-up member. Now call aside your dogs and let my women pass or I will whistle up mine and clear you from this bank.'

The crowd surged about us, the children with stick windmills and tinkerbells running in scampering joy across the Big Field of Gnoll House. Great dray horses from Cyfarthfa Yard came six abreast across the meadow, a white-smocked ostler at each bridle: rattling their brass medallions they came, their hides flashing in the sunlight, their hooves stained with ox-blood, the feathers dusted with flour. And the judges fussed about them, while in the circle they had formed beautiful Arab ponies high-stepped like country dancers.

In a square of ropes the poor were being hired for the kitchens and fields of the gentry, and I pitied their wan faces; standing in their rags as the agents and farmers barged among them, feeling their muscles and crying, 'Art thou hired, lad?' and pinching the fetlocks of the mares and pressing their stomachs to see if they were in child, shouting, 'Should thou work for me, girl, thou'll work tidy,' and many had already been hired, standing like cattle with straw in their mouths. Redcoats who had marched across Sarn Helen from Brecon Garrison lounged on their muskets, eyes switching at the Silurian swine: big men of the northern counties of England who had drunk their ale between Fort Nidum and Senny, and by the grave of Dervag, the son of Justus, had slept in a night of studded shields and strange, Roman oaths. They watched us. For lately there had been rail-greasing on the Hirwain gradient, and the giant engines were sliding backwards, so the Great Western was taking no chances.

Rhiannon I saw in a gap of the crowd, but she only put her nose up.

Lost, I wandered, looking for Tai Morlais among the cheapjacks, the poultry and bread stalls where dumpling housewives were duffing up butterpats with good luck signs. Fortunetellers were there in tinker robes and bangle earrings, Welsh weavers in a swish of shuttles. In a storm of gaiety and colour,

179

in a clash of tambourines and shrieking of fiddles, I bumped into Mrs. Shenkins, the mother of Willie-who-died.

' 'Morning, Mrs. Shenkins.' I knocked up my hat to her.

' 'Morning, Evan *bach*. Seen my Willie, have you?' She turned her wet face to mine, grizzled by the rain, snow and sun of sitting in the open these past seven years, praying for the chill that would send her to her Willie.

'Not this morning, Mrs. Shenkins,' I said.

'How am I looking, boy?'

She was tanned like teak with the weather, as square and strong as a horse. I said, 'Pretty delicate, you ask me, Mrs. Shenkins.'

'You reckon I'll last another month or two?'

'Doubtful, missus. Any day now they will slam the lid and drop you to your Willie.'

'God in heaven,' said she, 'them's bountiful words. Can't live without something to look forward to, can we?'

Sobbing, she left me. Later they told me she lived to the age of ninety-four.

Dai Central Eating I hit into next, staring up at the Booth of Dentistry, tapping his big horse tooth and trying to rake up the courage.

'Painless extractions it says, mind,' said he.

'Painless or not, it is the least you can do for Tegwen Harriet,' I replied.

'Though it don't look too healthy,' he added, and neither did it, with a half-naked savage prancing around the stage with a headdress of chicken-feathers and a pair of bruisers hitting on a big bass drum, and another blowing on a serpentine.

'No good thinking about it,' I said, assisting him up, for one good turn deserves another, and this one put me on my back six weeks with the cholera.

Painless extraction it was, sure enough, since you couldn't hear Dai hollering because of the drum, and when I uncovered my eyes I was in time to see the curtains closing and Dai going through them with his boots studs up, and nobody saw him for days.

Rosie Carey I saw next, kneeling on the grass in all her frills and fancies, with her arms around Billie Softo while he got into a meat-pie big enough to stop an elephant.

Beautiful Rosie Carey looked kneeling there with her eyes closed and Softo skinny in his hunger and rags, hard against her. And I seemed to hear, about the bedlam of the crowd, the beating of her heart.

'He didn't steal the thing,' cried Rosie. 'I paid for it. You leave him be, you big, heartless bastard.'

Forlorn, I went, dying for Rhiannon but too proud to hunt for her: wandering past the sweet stalls, the tiger-nuts, gob-stoppers and Spanish juice; heart-shaped hundreds and thousands, cashous, bull's eyes, lotus-beans and mottoes, kali pink and yellow, humbugs, jelly-babies and stick-jaw. On the great beer-stained trestles stood the belted barrels of ale, and big brown drays with flowing manes and whipping tails stamped and snorted in their nosebags while their bury drivers, stripped and sweating, rolled up the casks. And in the middle of it all Cushy Cuddlecome was hitting out the stoppers and shrieking with delight as the foam ambered and hissed.

'Out wi' ye bungs and fizz, ye gorgeous whampo!' she cried, all done up in pleated crinoline and very blousy, and I swear she was six pints in the wind although the sun was not overhead. 'Throng up, throng up, me beautiful men, for the tide's never out at Cushy Cuddlecome's, can ye hear me, son?'

Mr. Emlyn Hollyoak she was addressing, and very stern the preacher looked among the crowd, sallow under his big grey topper.

'Sure to God, there's nothin' wrong wi' a drink, your gracious,' cried Cushy. 'An' there's fine value given in me inn, for what we miss at the taps we make up for in the beds!' and she howled at the sky, fist up, her great breasts shaking. 'When it comes to us Sodom and Gomorrah can put the shutters up.'

Not good enough, of course, and people took note of it, like Mr. Waldo Scully, the Inspector of Nuisances from Neath, though it is true his business was mainly burial and drains, but he instantly came up, very official, licking his pencil. 'Miss

181

Cuddlecome, this is Michaelmas Fair, not a den of iniquity, and it is my duty to warn you ...'

'Ach, bless ye beautiful soul, yer honour,' cried Cushy, going down in a curtsey, 'I'd not offend a hair of yer head, and I'm only after slaking the thirst of the community, for they're a long time dead. Will ye have one on me to liven ye?'

Roars of laughter from the crowd at this, of course, and I pushed my way out ears down in my collar. For I knew that come starlight Cushy would be knee-deep in ale and navvies and fists up, looking for a fight, and I would rather tangle with the Black Welshman than Cushy when she was man-hating instead of man-loving.

Pietro Bianca I saw next, to my astonishment, prowling on the edge of the crowd with a placard on his chest saying 'Help Free Mexico' and his cap in his hand, and I went to him instantly, for I hadn't seen him in months.

'Pietro!'

'Bryn Evan!' His face glowed, and he cried, 'Long live Mexico!'

'God help Santa Anna,' I said. 'Where you been these months?'

'The bombs I have, the money I have not. Explosions I put under the scabs and blacklegs. You spare a penny for Mexico?'

I got one into his cap. 'Aren't you with Dewi these days?'

He glanced about him. 'Dewi is with the new revolution in Nantyglo. Under Richard Bennet the Chartists will rise again. Bombs I put under strikebreakers now, but bigger ones I will put under President Polk—me, Ianto Fuses and Dewi Evan, we fight for freedom.'

'Ay, ay,' I said, and left him. From Veracruz to Grand River they could keep their Mexico: Dewi was right, there was enough trouble to feed on at home. Through the dancing, the joy of the Fair I saw, on the road to Neath, a ragged column of burned-our poor, the sallow refuse of the tin-plate works, with their few possessions clutched against them, trudging to the workhouse.

Betsy Small-Coal I saw next· shapeless was she in her sack

dress tied at the waist with rope, and very worried about her man Joby Canal.

'Seen my Joby, have you, son?'

'No, Betsy,' I answered. Bald as a gnome was her Joby, and with ants in his trews. Nine months a year he was on the navvy tramping-ticket, working up to Darlington with news of the railway building, a walking navvy newspaper. A few weeks in Swansea jail, a fortnight at home with Betsy and the kids, then off again, leaving her full with another, and him no more than four-foot-ten in his boots.

'Always at Michaelmas my Joby comes home,' said Betsy.

At night she tramped with the coal she picked off the tumps, living in a hole under Neath Abbey by the ironworks: once she had six children, now she had two, but do not worry, woman, said Joby, there are plenty more where they came from.

'A good little man is my Joby, mind,' she said, watching me.

Pickpocket, loafer, a little scrag of a waster without a single redeeming feature.

'First-rate chap, Betsy,' I said.

The crowd bustled about us in warmth and smells of hot cloth.

'Aye,' said she. 'Every night I thank God for my Joby. For although he has faults, he do not trifle with the fancy women, nor does he leather the childer these days.'

He had covered more beds on the Stockton-Darlington than a blanket factory: the only reason why he had stopped belting the children was because he was worn out belting Betsy.

Wistful, she smiled about her, and her face was beautiful. 'My, there's a lovely Fair—good to see people happy, isn't it?'

The only hope of Heaven for men, I think, is that they are made in the bodies of women.

'You talk about my Joby, you give him a good name, see, Bryn Evan.'

I bowed deep to her.

Tai Morlais was walking arm in arm with Sian Edwards

183

and Jane Rheola, in whoops and giggles and toffee-apples. 'Just off to see Alehouse Jones duff up your Ifor—you coming?' he shouted, and I shook my head.

'Took enough duffing up himself, today, haven't you, *cariad*?' called Sian.

'Poor soul, she has rejected his advances,' said Jane Rheola.

On the wrestling green I saw an English lout, and if it wasn't the one Rhiannon had been talking about, he was good enough for me. Like Atlas he stood naked to the trews in a ring of gasping people, doing a muscle control: the sun was flashing on his rippling shoulders.

'Five shilling to any man who can throw the Cumberland Strangler!' bawled a barker, strutting about, and I saw the bargees and colliers pressing the ring tighter, wiping their mouths with the backs of their hands while their women threatened with parasols and wagging fingers, and just you dare—just you *dare* make an exhibition of yourself and I am home from this fair fast.

'Five shilling, missus,' grumbled a navvy. 'Not to be sneezed at, woman.'

'Then try it—just you try it.'

It was a job for single men. Hands in trews I wandered up, weighing the wrestler, and sensing an opponent in his law of the jungle, he turned, his green eyes switching over me with the speed of a serpent.

'Where is Cumberland?' I asked a bargee.

'North of England, ye dafto,' said somebody, so I vaulted the post and landed in the ring.

'I am on,' I said.

Up came the barker instantly. 'You wrestled before, son?'

'Aye, when it comes to five shillings.'

The crowd grumbled in its throat like bulls scenting blood. The barker roared, 'Throng up, throng up! A local boy is about to tackle the Cumberland Strangler. Give heavy, good people, give heavy—pay the lad for courage!' and he passed round his top hat.

I threw off my coat and waved out of my shirt; unlacing boots, I watched the wrestler. He walked in circles now, like a caged tiger, flexing his big shoulders, his great fair head sitting square on his bull neck, his forearms cording and bulging as he opened his hands, and I knew by his marvellous set of tin ears that he came from the professional rings of the gentry. About thirteen stones I reckoned him, a couple more than me, but I gave him more than three inches in height and had ten years on him, at least. Suddenly, still kneeling, I stared through legs at Dewi's face.

'What the hell are you doing in there?' His eyes were horrified.

'Five shillings,' I said.

'You stupid idiot! D'you realise he's a professional?' said he on all fours. 'Bryn, he'll cripple you—this is wrestling, this isn't fists.'

'Then vanish before he does the pair of us.'

'I'm coming in,' he gasped, scrambling up.

I heard him land in the ring behind me, but I did not turn to him, and I could hear a lot of barging and pushing and do you realise he isn't even eighteen and you hop it before the Strangler starts on you, and next moment there was a scream from the women and cheers from the men and Dewi was spreadeagled on the grass and the Strangler dusting his hands. Back came Dewi through the legs of the crowd. 'Did you see that? I tell you, he's a killer!'

'Hop it.'

Dewi scrambled up. 'I'm going for Dada!' and he up and dived for open country.

'Right!' shouted the barker. 'The Cumberland Strangler will now assist the local lad out of this ring in two separate pieces.' He paused. 'Make a ring, gentlemen—right, boys, into it!'

I turned to face the wrestler. The noises of the fair died in my ears.

We circled, hands out, stooping, looking for a hold. Strange the eyes of a professional wrestler: as green as June grass, this one's, the brows jutting and humped with bright hair, the cheekbones criss-crossed with thin, white scars. Hypnotic, these eyes, expressionless and cruel. Licking his thick lips, he moved a hand at me and I smacked it down, still circling. Suddenly

185

relaxing, he straightened, but I saw the trap and did not go, and he spat sideways, and winked, grinning.

'Take it slow, lad,' he whispered. 'Got eight kids need feedin'.'

'I got ten,' I said.

'You drop an' you get brass just the same, Taff.'

I saw in his face the face of Richard Bennet.

'And you call yourself a wrestler?'

'Right, you want it, you get it,' he breathed, and feinted, stepping in with the speed of sparks, snatched my wrist, twisted at the waist and flung me backwards, and as I hit the ground he landed elbow down and I didn't know if I was in Neath or Nantyglo. Gasping for breath, I rolled away as he came after me like a cat, snatching and clawing on all fours, but I flung him off and scrambled up, and no sooner was I upright than he did the same bloody thing again and I was legs waving and down while he pounced and held me momentarily before I twisted from his grip, floundering across the ring.

'Six to one on the Cumberland!'

'Take fives? Fives I am taking against the Welsh!'

Bets now, money chinked, pencils being licked, men roaring and women saying it was a damned scandal because he's only a boy.

'On't ear or backside, Taff?' said the wrestler, coming like a baboon. 'Take pick,' and we closed, chest to chest, instantly locked in a finger grip: now arms entwined, now bodies straining in a sweating, gasping hold. But I was with the advantage and I heard the wrestler grunt deep in his chest: hooking my leg round his, I heaved, and we collapsed, him underneath: rolling over, I got him above me and he dropped straight into the scissors. Face turned away, gripping the grass, I pressed him, and he went sideways, staring up, groaning with the pain of it.

'Fours!'

'I'll take fours on the Taff!'

'By gum, ee's a randy kid. Do 'im, lad, do 'im!'

I bowed my head and squeezed and the Cumberland gasped aloud, arms waving. With ebbing strength I shifted the scissors to get him higher, and dug my fingers into the earth turning all my strength into the paralysing hold about his waist. He was crying aloud now in a sustained roar from the crowd, beating at the grass, and I rolled again, jack-knifing him, switching my cramped ankles.

'Oh, Bryn, please do not hurt him,' I seemed to hear Rhiannon say.

'Oh, Bryn,' cried Rhiannon, 'when you get to know him he is very sweet.'

'Oh, you Taff swine!' shouted the wrestler. 'Oh, you sod.'

Somebody in the crowd shouted. 'Evens I offer—sixpence to sixpence, bet returned.'

'How do it feel, Cumberland, takin' it instead of givin' it?'

'Aye, but he isn't done yet!'

'In the name of God!' gasped the wrestler, and I stared at him, slackening the grip of my legs.

He inched towards me, his face agonised. 'Aw, there's an evil thing in me belly, lad, and by gum, it's fair killin' me—for heaven's sake lay off!'

Instantly, I slacked him more, and he bucked high, kicking himself free and leaping upon me, his hands around my throat. Locked, we rolled, and as I threw him away he scrambled up and had me in an arm-lock, lifting from behind, and I fell face down. Somehow, I rolled upright, and he hit me with a fore-arm smash that I don't think they would have allowed up in Cumberland. Blood swam over my eyes as I clenched them to the glare of the sun, and he hit me again, bringing me to my knees. In sweating, brutal heaves he was clouting me with everything but the bucket now. Up and down like a wet sack I went with that bastard belting me. Shoulder-throws and flying mares I had, the last being very inconvenient, I discovered; also somersaults. And as I blindly pawed the air to see where the hell he had got to I collected shoulders and elbows, stomach punches and knees, and the backs of his heels every time I went down. And then, as if to add insult to injury, he began helping me along with his boot every time I was on all fours, which, when you stop to consider it, is a very humiliating thing to happen in your own home town: round and round I went with the Cumberland Strangler booting me and every boot he put in made me more angry, so I finally staggered up

187

and faced him, and when he rushed I tabbed him with a glorious left hook that sent him staggering into the barker, and the pair of them went floundering into the crowd to roars of approval from the onlookers, and the instant he was up the barker fetched me one with his bugle, and I took it and went out like a light, to awake next moment cradled in Rhiannon's arms.

'Oh, Bryn, my precious,' said she, and Dada said it was the most lovely sight he had ever seen; me lying there in Rhiannon's arms with her tears dropping on my face, the crowd sniffing and wiping and a few buck navvies actually breaking down, which is perfectly understandable when you get a battered hulk like me being cradled in the arms of a beauty like Rhiannon; it is enough to break the heart of a Swansea slaughterer.

Away we went eventually, Rhiannon supporting me, with the crowd parting and smoothing us, and when I passed the Cumberland Strangler I slipped him a wink, he having achieved in three minutes what would normally have taken me three weeks.

# 21

LOOKING back, I suppose the family fortunes began to change in that autumn when I was eighteen. The wages of colliers and ironworkers in the valleys were being cut by the masters, and although the Company truck-shops were outlawed by Parliament twenty-one years ago in '32, most towns of the Top, for instance, were still running them, and charging a quarter more for goods that could be bought on the open market. Anti-Truck societies sprang up, and were fought and closed down by the owners, who reckoned they had a right to make profit out of their workers' food when the prices on world markets went down. And although, to his credit, Crawshay never owned such a shop in Merthyr, other owners were not so particular, and defied the Government, opening shops in Abernant and Aberdare, Nantyglo and Maesteg and a score of other places. People became poorer, things became tighter, and the bargees of the Vale of Neath were some of the first to feel the draught, for the railway was collecting what trade was going faster every month. Slowly, our runs to Briton Ferry began to be cut, and Man Arfon, the new railway superintendent at Pont Walby, was in his element.

'Well, Evan,' he used to say, 'that is the pity of it—supply and demand. Who wants barges when the railway carries quicker and cheaper?'

'The railway will never run us out of business, Man Arfon. Time will show that they will always need the barge.'

'That I cannot envisage, Evan. Foresight, that is what you lack, see.' He tipped a flask to his lips. 'Like little Bryn by here—hoping to get married soon, is it?'

'Get back into the hole you came out of,' said Dewi, tying ropes.

'Got a list of names, I 'ave, down my hole, Dewi Evan. A randy old drunk, am I? Too mean to give away my hypocrisy, am I? Enemies are not worth having unless you make them properly, is it? By God, Dewi Evan, you have made one here.'

Dada said, 'We thought we'd seen the last of you, Judas. What are you doing here at Walby?'

'You got me kicked out of Merthyr, and I landed on my feet,' said Arfon. 'Overman, you might call me now—or superintendent of liaison over the canal and railway. There's a beautiful English word that—*liaison*. Judas, is it? Toadying up the English, is it—a stink to the name of Wales, Mostyn Evan?'

'I am come for coal, man,' said Dada. 'Tell me the bay.'

'There's a dear little woman is that Rhiannon, Bryn Evan.'

The sweat of fury was running down my back.

'Tell us your master, we are here to carry coal,' said my father.

Man Arfon straightened. 'Now that Jeremiah Alton is dead, I am master here.'

'Don't fool with us,' said Dewi. 'Who do we go to for coal?"

'Back to Resolven where you came from. One run a week from now—take it or leave it.' We stared at him.

It was the beginning of the end of us. The railway was collecting one firm after another with their little concrete platforms. The Canal Company shares began to drop. With haulage competition greater every day, with the railway loading free-on-board at half the rate of the barges, the bottom started falling out of the market.

In a world of private enterprise, where the Devil takes the hindmost and cuts the throat of his grandmother for a penny a ton less, the first victim of the system is free enterprise. One night Tub Union with eighty men knocked on the door of the Old Navigation. Tub Union jerked his thumb.

'Out,' said he. 'I have told you before, I will not tell you again. Out.'

'I go when the Company discharges me as a private contractor, not before,' said my father. 'I am hauling for the same cost as the union men, I charge nothing for wear and tear.'

'Out,' said Tub Union.

Man Arfon, big enough to kill us, and now Tub Union doing it final.

Things always come in threes, said Gran, and Gran was right.

'A letter for you, Dada,' said Sharon, bringing it in.

It was morning, I remember, a bright summer day. Dewi was over in Nantyglo with Richard Bennet, Sharon was dressed ready for a Penny Gaff down in Neath, Ifor was cleaning harness out the back and trying to spin out the oats for Nell and Jed Donkey.

'What is it, Mostyn?' asked Gran at the bosh.

'An order to remove,' said Dada, turning away.

'To remove what?' asked Gran.

He went to the window, staring out. 'To remove ourselves from the Old Navigation—they are bringing through a branch line, and we are on the curve.'

'But surely, the land is ours,' said Mari, coming in, her face pale.

'The land is not ours, it belonged to the Canal Company.

Now the Company's sold out to the railway, and they are our landlords for the ground rent.'

'I always said it was not worth fifty-two pounds ten,' said Gran, flicking off soap suds.

'What are you going to do, Dada?' I asked.

'I am off to Town to see Mr. Cowbum.'

'With a name like that he'll be able to work miracles,' said Gran. 'Ach, well, I always thought I'd end in the Poorhouse.' *Rock of Ages* she sang then.

'I will come with you,' said Mari, swinging her hat off a peg.

'And me,' said Sharon. 'I was just going to Neath.'

Which left Gran and Ifor and Rhiannon and I at home; the fact is important.

'Oh, God,' whispered Gran, broken, after they had gone. 'I don't know what will be the end of it.' And then she straightened and made a fist of her hand. 'The first railway navigator coming in by here to soil the place I will hit from that yard to Cyfarthfa.'

'That is much more like it,' I said.

But I think I knew, when that letter came, that it was the end of us. First Man Arfon, the traitor Welsh, then Tub Union, leader of a Lodge that turned on its members, now Mr. Seth Cowbum and into the hands of solicitors.

'Trust in the Lord,' said Gran, after Dada, Mari and Sharon had gone.

Aye? But I think he had his hands full up in places like Merthyr and Dowlais, and must have been doing up laces when the Black Welshman came up to the back door. For some time I had been expecting this visit, for you do not hit out navvy pugilists and expect to get away with it. Alone with Rhiannon in the kitchen she was making big eyes at me when I heard him at the back.

'Morning,' he said.

'Good morning, what can we do for you?' asked Gran.

'Come to knock in pegs for the railways surveyors,' replied Black Sam.

'Is that a fact?' said Gran, going Irish. 'Shall I crack your

191

skull with this now, or will you wait till me son comes home?' and she picked up the Irish shillelagh Granfer Ben used to pay the rent with up in Dowlais.

'Put that down, woman,' said Sam, 'or you will have a piece of my mind.'

'Indeed? Well, I'm always gettin' pieces of mind from people least able to afford it. Say your bit and go.'

'Surveyor!' yelled Black Sam. 'You'd best handle this, man, for I've met with a shillelagh solicitor. Shall I toss her aside?'

'You can try,' muttered Ifor, hands on hips, coming in from the stables, and his eyes were dancing bright under his lowering brows. I got beside Gran, shouldering Ifor back, and saw in the yard at least a hundred navvies armed with picks and shovels and mandrills for blasting.

'What the hell's happening here?' I demanded.

Up came the surveyor, fussy in frock coat and top hat with notebook and pencil and maps, five-foot-two in boots, and a nose as purple as the vineyards of Babylon. 'Come now, my good woman,' said he, 'it is all signed and legal and according to my papers the owner has been informed.'

'The pegs go through the back door and out the front,' said Black Sam, loving it, 'so the house comes down.'

I said, 'My father was notified about four hours ago—is this what you call signed and legal? He is down in Neath consulting a solicitor.'

'And nobody's coming in here till he gets back,' rumbled Ifor.

The surveyor tapped his papers. 'But it is all official, a legal undertaking.'

'That is the word,' replied Gran. 'I am off to fetch the shotgun. Anyone left in that yard in the next five minutes will be undertaken six feet down and without a service. Nobody touches this house till my boy comes back.'

Man Arfon now, hands in his trews, wandering up front.

'Trouble, is it?'

'I might have known you were in it,' I said. 'This branch could serve the Kerry Flat and still miss us by a hundred feet, and you know it.'

'Essential that it goes through your rooms, Bryn Evan. There is a very beautiful word now—*essential*. Will you tell me how you can stop it?'

'We cannot,' I answered. 'But I tell you this, Man Arfon. And let there be witnesses. You are superintendent, you are liaison between the railway and the canal workers. I appeal to you in the name of the workers. If you touch this house we will take you to law—you only, you, Man Arfon.'

It triggered him. He moved uneasily in his boots. The surveyor said:

'But this is ridiculous. The railway company is the sole owner . . .'

'And he is the Company representative, so we will go after him—Man Arfon,' I said. 'And if we win, Man Arfon, my father will break you.'

The agent pulled out his watch. 'I will give you three hours. At two o'clock this afternoon the drays will move in.'

I looked at the sky. The sun was an incinerating glow in an ocean of red petticoats, shafting over the green country in royal splendour, nearly overhead.

'My father will be back by then,' I said.

With muttered curses and threats, the navvy gangs moved out of the yard.

'And that has got rid of that lot,' said Gran. 'Good for you, boy!'

'Took him rigid,' muttered Ifor, fist in his palm.

'What do we do now?' whispered Rhiannon, her eyes big.

'Barricade the house,' I replied, 'until Dada gets back with the interim injunction.'

'Never heard of that one,' said Gran. 'It do not sound decent to me.'

'And if Dada is not back in time we fight for right of way, old style, to gain an hour or two.'

'The Black Welshman is mine,' said Ifor, pushing up, his chest swelling.

'I'm glad you suggested it,' I said.

We bolted the doors back and front and nailed the windows, I fetched the shot-gun down from the attic; Ifor split a barrel and handed out staves, and we brought Nell and Jed Donkey into the kitchen with nose-bags and Cinders, my little bitch, ran around whining and smelling delighted in the air of pent excitement, and in the molten heat of the afternoon, giving us an extra hour of grace, the navvy gangs came again; flinging down their tools as far away as Melin, they came to the scent of blood, for word had gone around that the Evan family would fight. They spilled into the yard from the cut, staring at the windows, their bodies stained with the yellow mud of the earthworks and streaked with sweat. I saw on the road beyond them two teams, the demolition gangs, the ten-inch timber baulk with chains, drawn by three giant dray-horses : with this tool they could slice the Old Navigation clear of her foundations.

Man Arfon, however, did not return. Opening the landing window I looked down on the big Negro and the gang surveyor on the cobbles below.

'It needs an hour still, before my father returns,' I called. 'But we will call it legal to fight for right of way.'

'It is legal enough, I will have no brawling,' cried the surveyor, instantly agitated. He knelt with a chalk. 'First peg here, Black Sam. Knock me a peg.'

'The first man who does so gets this,' I said, bringing up the gun. 'But if you have anything to fight with, we will send a man down.'

I saw Black Sam lick his lips. Like an animal that hungers, he stared up at Ifor and me.

'I need an hour,' I said, 'and I've got the champion of the Vale.'

'Not while Ah'm standing,' said Black Sam, grinning.

The surveyor pestered about him, fuming, threatening; the navvies pressed about him, urging him on in banter and threats.

And my brother will hand him the same he got off my da,' I said, to fume him. The Negro grinned wider and unbuttoned his coat, flinging it away. Magnificent he looked in height and strength, then, the sun flashing on his great body. Beside me Ifor was trembling with excitement. Below us the navvies were

194

packing in droves into the yard, bawling, shoving, yelling up at us.

'Make a ring, Black Sam!'

'I give threes on Sam!'

'Taken.'

A Welsh voice shouted from their ranks, 'You'd best get it over quick, Sam, before his dada gets back.'

'Is he coming down or do I come and fetch him?' asked the Negro.

'Give me a knee, Bryn?' asked Ifor.

'Aye.'

Gran cried then, 'Oh, God, the black savage will kill him!'

'More than likely,' I whispered back, 'but it should take half an hour, and by that time Dada will be back.'

In the kitchen I filled a bucket with water and followed Ifor out into the yard: seeing the bucket, knowing that soon the bright spring water would run red, the mob rumbled in its maw, thirsting. And as we came mid-ring the surveyor rushed up to Ifor, squabbling in protest in a falsetto whine, and Ifor stooped and seized him and threw him high into the fists of the crowd.

'Right, you, Black Sam,' said Ifor a moment later, and he lifted from my knee and wandered towards the Black Welshman, grinning, his black-maned head thrust out, inviting a blow. Thick, heavy and tall though he was, my brother looked a pigmy as he circled the Negro giant.

'Good afternoon,' said Sam.

There was no sound in the world just then but the padding feet of the fighters.

Ifor was in first; a snap left, and the Negro slipped it, grinning back. Cagily, they circled, left fists out, right hands cocked. Suddenly hunching his thick shoulders, Ifor shuffled in, flatfooted, shooting up a stream of lefts to Sam's face, ducked a right counter and hooked a vicious right to the body and swung the same fist to the chin: the blow was square and on the point, and I think I knew the outcome, for Black Sam hardly blinked. But then, with the speed of light, Ifor stepped back and hooked a glorious overarm right flush to the head, and as

195

Sam fell forward, he swung heavily to the midriff. The Negro gasped, and went on a knee, then, amazingly, buckled up and sat on his haunches, grinning stupidly.

'What's thou doin' on t'arse, Black Sam?' cried a navvy.

'Well done, Taff!'

The crowd mumbled and mawed, swaying for the sight of blood.

'Up and do 'im, Sam!'

A North Country roared, 'Stay on backside, Black Welshman: half a bar I got on the White Welsh!'

Ifor sat on my knee as Sam got up and swayed back to his second.

'You watch him, man,' I whispered.

'He do hit easy, mind,' said Ifor.

'And so do you. Keep him off, for God's sake, till Dada comes.'

'To hell with Dada,' said Ifor. 'This baby is mine.'

A man shouted then, 'Three to one against the Welsh lad!'

'Taken.'

'Milk-sops, these bargees. He'll be on his back next round, as God's me judge. Will anyone give me sixes against him?'

'I will,' cried Gran from the back door. 'Milk-sops, is it?' cried she, going Irish. 'If the granfer were here except the grandson your black baby would be half-way over Swansea. Sixes I'm taking, man,' and she came out into the ring with Granfer's mole-skin cap on her palm.

Banter and roars at this, with the navvies loving it.

'Gran, back in the house!' I shouted.

'Indeed, I will not. Sure, there's enough of your granfer in him to eat this big fool!' and she gripped Ifor's shoulder, yelling, 'If ye tangle with the blood of Ben Evan, then you pay for it. I'm taking six to one against me grandson, and I have the money here to prove it,' and the sovereigns leaped in her hand.

'Time!' roared somebody.

'To the devil with the time, I'm taking the bets,' cried Gran, and went round the ring of kneeling navvies with the money flowing into her mole-skin cap.

196

'Gran!' shouted Ifor. 'Out of it!' and he rose, gripping her bustle, but she slapped him away and fetched him one on the side of the head that nearly buckled him. 'Six to one I'm offering, are ye taking?'

'You're on, missus!' bawled a ginger navvy, dancing her in a circle, and they came from the crowd, pushed Black Sam aside and linked hands, dancing her in a ring, fists up in the air, their clogs raising the dust and whooping like a tribe of Cherokee Indians, while Gran, her skirt lifted, swept in and out of the howling navvies with her cap spilling copper and silver.

'Dear God, it's terrible,' said Ifor, close to tears. 'She's spoiling my life's ambition.'

'Rhiannon!' I shouted. 'Come and fetch Gran out of it!' and Rhiannon came scuttling into the yard and started pushing and heaving, and just then Ifor left my knee, went into the crowd, fended Gran off with one hand and hit Black Sam with the other, and he was head over heels among hobnails, and when he got up he was breathing murder, switching his stance as he rushed. Ifor waited, then let fly with a glorious right-hander, which is the way to beat the right-hand-forward. Sam took it square, tottered and fell. Ifor turned and came back to my knee. He had not been absent ten seconds.

'And what d'you think of that?' cried Gran. 'Is it still sixes, ye sons of heathens?'

Hats were going up, money was spilling, odds were being shrieked as Rhiannon managed to tow Gran back into the house, and I reckon they could hear the row up in Bethel Street, Glyn Neath. For the yard was now filled like mackerel in a barrel, every corner of it jam-packed with ragged men and boys, the refuse of the mountains spewing from their holes in the embankments and culverts. From the cooking-pots of the navvy shanties came the whores and mistresses, the crones and beauties of the cut and railway. Ifor whispered, 'There's some ripe ones arriving now, Bryn. Any sign of Dada?'

'Come on, lads!' yelled Gran from the back door. 'Cover your mouth with your money. Six to one I'm taking on me grandson. It's the best chance of easy money since me husband duffed up Dick the Drover outside the Plough in Clyne,' and

197

she dangled the frying-pan and hit it with a hammer. 'Out and finish it, Ifor, boy!'

'Time!' I shouted, and lifted Ifor under the ribs, and Black Sam met him with a looping right swing that took Ifor's legs from under him, and the moment he was up fetched him another that would have pole-axed an ox.

Bedlam now, as I ran out, hauled Ifor to his feet and started slapping his chops to bring him round, and Gran and Rhiannon ran out and helped to get him on my knee and every time they did he rolled sideways like a drunk, and there was Black Sam sparring up before us shouting insults above the roar of the navvies while Ifor was rocking around on my knee not knowing if he was in Resolven or Swansea.

'Did he hit me?' asked Ifor, dazed.

'He did,' said Gran, 'and he'll do it again unless you get up and square off to him.'

'You ought to be ashamed of yourself,' I shouted at her.

'Where is he?' asked Ifor.

'Big as a barn door, he is,' cried Gran. 'Oh, me son, won't you lift off and see to him in the name of Granfer Ben? For you're fighting for right of way. It's the drover's fighting, you see, and legal. Just up and hit him, lad.'

'The big black one in the middle, is it?' asked Ifor.

'Time!' she yelled, and hit the frying-pan, but instead of getting up my brother Ifor just flopped about, going in circles on my knee with his eyes crossed and the Black Welshman towering above us shouting insults on the family and the navvies bellowing for Maniac Square, shouting for their bets. And just when the commotion was gathering height Gran suddenly stooped, lifted the waterbucket and swung it at Black Sam's head and he lay back into the crowd with his arms wide and his feet up, and as if this wasn't enough she flung Rhiannon aside and dived among the crowd, swinging the bucket and not losing a drop, and everywhere she went she left a trail of dead and dying behind her. Very undignified it was, to see Gran laying into people with a full bucket, putting them out right and left with Rhiannon on her bustle being towed along behind her. And there was Ifor, the Champion of the Vale, still on my knee and flopping about from the fourpenny Black Sam had caught him. Very ashamed I felt, and I closed my eyes, and when I opened them again Gran was still at it and gathering speed and my father was coming through the crowd by the stable door in a very fancy trap with a pony and a fine gentleman, and will somebody please explain what the hell is going on as he vaulted over the side.

I got Ifor on to his feet and left him swaying and ran over to my father, crying, 'It is Black Sam and Man Arfon came with surveyor's pegs, so Ifor fought for right of way until Gran started into them with a bucket.'

'I can see that,' said my father, 'and it appears she is still at it,' and so she was since she was right in the middle of them now and swinging like mad and navvies were ducking and howling and the slow ones going down like pit-props, and the language steaming up was driving Gran into a frenzy. And just before my father got to her they were raising Black Sam on to his feet, so she lay back and swung him another and he was down again with six on top of him.

'Mother, for God's sake!' cried my father, shocked, for though he basically had nothing against anyone hitting out navvies this does not make much of an impression on a Swansea solicitor of the grade of Mr. Seth Cowbum, who was standing in the middle of the yard now, watching the slaughter with sad eyes through his pince-nez glasses.

A God-fearing type was this Mr. Seth Cowbum, and very severe he looked as he examined my Gran, in his high starched collar, his goatie beard munching, and the place was filled with shrieks and screams as the navvies started spilling out of the stable yard with Gran after them screaming like a caged lunatic.

'Mother!' bawled my father in his fair-ground voice, and she stopped dead, did Gran. With her hair down to her waist and her eyes on fire, she dropped the bucket and stood guilty before him. Pitying her, I ran to her and gripped her hand and we stood together before his wrath.

'A most disgraceful exhibition, I must say,' breathed my father, his face stern.

'Not her fault, mind,' I said. 'Fighting for right of way, I told you.'

'Quiet, you!' said Dada. 'I do business with a Swansea solicitor and bring him here to avoid violence, and I find it already on the go. To say the least, I am most ashamed.'

'Injunctions do not keep the house up,' I cried. 'If Gran had not slammed in they would have had the roof off.'

Very sorry for herself my Gran looked, standing there with her fingers hooked before her and her eyes cast down, but up came the Swansea solicitor with his hand up and very benign, standing there like a string-bean, smiling.

'Mostyn Evan,' said he, sonorous, 'there are times when court injunctions are issued over the ashes of burning property, and they are useless when they arrive late. Force, sometimes, must be met with force, and proves more effective than legal scraps of paper. Would it avail us if the house was down?'

'No, sir,' said Dada, looking simple.

'Would you,' said Mr. Cowbum, all collar and whiskers, 'would you have looked with pride on a cowardly woman who had sat within, and wept?'

'I suppose not, sir,' said my father, standing sideways in his boots. 'Very sorry, I am.'

'Excellent.' Mr. Seth Cowbum, the solicitor very eminent in Swansea, bowed low before my gran and swept off his topper. 'Good woman, may more like you bring forth your kind and build the Empire, and in passing save the time of the legal profession, which invariably arrives too late. With your kind permission, ma'am, I will escort you back to the house.'

'Oh, sir!' cried Gran, undone, and she backed off and went down in her best gentry curtsey, and just then Rhiannon came back from the house and went down, too. Beautiful it looked, you know, with that revered gentleman all side-whiskers and frock coat doing his professional bow and my gran at his feet, her head bowed, her skirt a black stain on the cobbles, and the navvies that were left in the yard were dumb with enchantment, doffing their mole-skins and lowering their faces, for good manners do get the best of us, even those who do come from pigsties.

'Your son apologises, ma'am,' said Mr. Seth Cowbum. 'And I will take the problem from your capable hands, and if the Great Western Railway encroaches on your property henceforth, it will be the last illegal thing it does.'

Straight he stood then, in grace, his arm hooked, and my gran got up and took it and away they went, the pair of them, stepping like a brace of Arab stallions, nodding and bowing to all and sundry, through the stable yard and round to the front entrance.

'Sod me,' said my father. 'I am two sovereigns lighter on a legal injunction and she gets it free with her boots and a yard bucket.' Deep he sighed. 'She has been doing this kind of thing for years, and she always do finish with the upper hand.'

# 22

AUTUMN blustered into winter, and the branch line came through, missing us, like the main line, by about twenty feet. Icicled, frosted, piled with snow, the Old Navigation sat in the throat of the railway and the giant Corsairs of Brunel rattled through, belching their steam and smoke into the kitchen on their way to Aberdare, flinging soot and sulphur into the bedrooms along the branch to Rheola. Standing square to the onslaught, the old inn groaned and rasped her timbers as thousands of tons of coal, iron and limestone thundered past her foundations. Cracks appeared in her walls, hair lines that widened into crevices from ceiling to floor: the roof began to sag, and we shored it; the windows jammed and we took them out, eased and replaced them; the doors would not close. And at night we lay wide awake in our beds and listened to the wheel-spins and snorts from as far up the gradient as Pont Walby and Pencydrain. Below us the loading bays of the Clydach tram-road roared and thumped on the night shifts, the black diamonds of Resolven, our own colliery, rushing in a sea into the jaws of the trucks while our barge was tied up empty on our wharf. One trip after another was cancelled, one contract after another was stopped. By the time spring was blowing her warm winds over Sarn Helen the barge rates dropped lower still, the hauls became fewer, the canal shares cheaper still. It was two a month now, and lucky to get it from a sneering Man Arfon.

But I do not remember the year of '53 because of the skinny times, but because it surely must have been the most romantic in the history of the hamlet since 800 years and the times of the Normans. Dai Central Eating started it by leading Tegwen Harriet down to Aberdulais Baptist, the new chapel, which sent old Eli cackling with delight, but he cackled a different tune some eight months later when Tegwen rose like a ship under sail and, landed him twin girls. Then Ifor stood before Tomos Traherne, the big Revival in Zion, Resolven, with Rebecca Cohen on his arm, and not before time, said my father, for Rebecca came so hot that particular June that you could boil an egg on her, said Gran, and with Ifor not knowing what day of the week it was, the attic was cleared and the bundling bed laid out. On wet Sundays, when Rebecca visited, it was upstairs sharp with the pair of them on twin pillows and Ifor with his boots on and Rebecca done up to the ears in mail bags and sail canvas, which I firmly believe is the most beautiful Celtic custom, though with Ifor's hair standing on end when they came down for supper it do not do a great deal for the blood pressure. 'I cannot get that pair up past Lyons Row quick enough,' my dada used to say, and the following year he achieved this and nine months to the very day Rebecca's hair went redder still and she came even lovelier in the face with her and gracious with curves, especially in the front, and Eli went down to Neath for special Benediction, and when she propped up a girl he went to the very edge of his grave. Gran reckoned she had the answer to this, of course.

'Mind,' said she at tea-time, 'I have known herring exactly the same—only one roe in five million is male—right in the middle of the soft ones. This Cohen family is doomed to the breast and the womb and old Eli had better make the best of it.'

'It is an attractive theory,' said Dada, getting up from table and putting his feet up with the *Cambrian*.

'Of course,' said Gran, 'it could well be that those Cohen

girls are not doing it properly. There are the rights and wrongs of going about these things.'

Mari said swiftly, 'Another cup, Gran? Yours is stone cold.'

'Eh, no,' said Ifor, munching, 'you come wrong about that—my 'Becca knows everything about those matters.'

'Aye, but there are certain antics you got to perform, and you know it, Mostyn.'

'Excuse me,' said Sharon, spluttering in her tea, and going out.

My father said, sighing and putting down his paper, 'Do you think we might change the subject, Mother? We have had Ifor's assurance that Rebecca is well informed on these things, and from what I have seen I am also quite satisfied.'

'It is the bustling and corseting that is mainly the answer, mind,' said Gran.

'The what, darling?' whispered Mari, her face bright with love.

'High in the front for a girl, broad in the beam for a boy, see: bustling and proper corseting is the way to make the selection.'

Other romantic things happened. Mrs. Ten went up to eleven on Man Arfon, though I never did understand what that was supposed to mean. Jane Rheola and Meic Jones, the pot-boy once sweet on Sharon, should have kept going in Rheola Forest, but didn't, which was a happy thing, I think, for a lively little girl was Jane and it was only a public duty to turn herself into two, in or out of wedlock. Taliesen the Poet married Miss Bronwen Rees and had a son they called Algernon, for there is nothing like keeping the Welsh flavour when you are in love with Wales, like her, said Dewi; he still extremely keen on night visitations to the Lamb and Flag, Glyn Neath, and he do not arrive up there for washing his socks, said Sharon, who was still going strong on the travelling players and the Neath Penny Gaffs.

Also, we had a funeral at the Old Navigation that spring, though nobody died, but more of this later. Nevertheless, it do go to show what a queer old place the Vale was about this period.

Finally, my butty, Tai Morlais, married Sian Edwards in his navvy shanty in Lower Dulais, where Mr. Brunel was forming a base for the building of a new railway in the Swansea valley, and Tai and Sian jumped over a chair, which was about the closest the navigators got to a wedding service. On that great day, after receiving the invitation, I climbed into my best suit and my tallest collar; spruced up, broomed down and polished, and intended to hobnail it over Seven Sisters, but Fate intervened.

'You mind what you're up to,' said Gran. 'Evil folk, these navigators, remember.'

'Oh, no Gran, please,' interjected Mari, shocked. 'You are speaking of his friend!'

'Not evil, when you know them,' I said.

Mari said, at her stitching, 'You going alone, boy?'

'Aye, Mari.'

'Good excuse, is it, with Richard coming this evening?'

'As good as any,' I said, rubbing boots. 'A pretty good pair, with Mr. Seth Cowbum coming, too.'

'You leave Mr. Cowbum out of it,' said Gran, pointing with a comb.

In fact, some very strange things happened that spring, with Dewi out most nights with the new Chartist movement up in Nantyglo, and Gran acting queer.

'Rhiannon might like to come with you, Bryn,' whispered Mari.

'She's got Richard Bennet,' I said, gruff.

Drive you daft, see, what with one and another of them. Aye, very pulled in and perfumed was my gran these days, curling with hot irons before the shaving mirror, patting and preening, and how do I look, and would I pass in a crowd: not that I care either way if he comes, or not, for Mr. Seth Cowbum must lead his own life—anyway, he'd drop me at the nearest lamp, for he has yet to see me in fierce sunlight or on an off-day, for every woman over seventy has an off-day. And my father, lighting his pipe in the corner by the grate, would wink and eye Gran sideways as he folded up the *Cambrian*.

'Rhia would come if you asked her, Bryn.'

'Aye,' and I kissed her face; the only mother I had ever had, this one, and, in passing, the most beautiful woman in Wales.

I was just getting old Nell into the saddle in the yard when Rhiannon flew up to me all black curls, peaches and cream and crinoline; flushed and breathless with her: 'Oh, Bryn, take me with you!'

'But you haven't been invited, woman!'

'But Tai and Sian would not mind. Oh, take me!'

'What about Richard Bennet—isn't he arriving here?'

'That is why I want to be with you. Oh, Bryn!'

Nearly in tears.

You know, bloody daft are women, and I do not understand them. For months now I had this Bennet chap stuffed and cooked for breakfast, dinner and tea.

'Pretty rough, these navvies, remember—curse to make your hair curl.'

'Oh, my precious, I would not mind!'

'Right. Hurry up, then.'

And she was away shrieking, to come back a full hour later all done up gorgeous with her hair piled in ringlets and a pink crinoline and a big, white, floppy hat lying on her shoulders, and red and blue bonnet streamers flying.

'There is a good boy now, waiting for Rhiannon,' said she, wagging a finger, and stood waiting until I caught her at the waist and put her side-saddle on Nell, who rolled an evil eye at us, for there is no romance in the life of mules, as is widely known.

Honeyed and dark, this new Rhiannon, with the wonderful mystery of her womanhood swelling at her breast, and great was her dignity, chin up, smiling down. And I was just clip-clopping out of the stable gate with her held before me when Gran came dashing out of the house, yelling:

'Bring her back this minute, you hear me? Navvy weddings are not fit for virgin women. Bring her back, I say!'

So I gave Nell the heels and we were off down the cut at a gallop, shrieking, with my father's bass laughter and Mari's contralto echoing behind us.

There is beautiful it is to be clip-clopping along on a mule with the sap rising in tree and manhood, and the one you love obedient in your arms, and all the green of a new year falling about you, the April banks swarming with buttercups, celandines, and the woods behind hazed with bluebells and bee-hum and shafts of gold emblazoned in the glades. Sweet and warm was the wind, perfumed on my face by the breath of Rhiannon. Carelessly, I said:

'Why this sudden need to be with me? Usually, when Richard is down from Nanty I do not get a sniff.'

'I am afraid of Richard,' said she, her eyes cast down. 'Besides, I have always wanted to see a navvy wedding.'

'End up in bed with the groom, unless you're careful,' I said, and tightened the rein, determined that she would not trifle with me, for she was often bunned up and skinny with me, while she was the water on my throat. I swung old Nell along the drovers' track below Sarn Helen and across the Dulais Valley, and the sun was all hot and merry with him at the thought of summer and larks were diving and trilling in a sky of varnished blue. The great country of March-Hywel, stained with its blood of warriors, swung up before us in a blaze of morning, with great haloes of cloud-smoke flowing over our heads. Here, fifteen hundred feet above the shimmering Bristol Channel, Neath and Swansea were patterned in fire and smoke below us, with Skewen and Morriston blazing like hells demented in mushrooms of flame and sulphurous billows. Taking Nell short on the bridle, I lifted Rhiannon down into my arms, and held her, and such was the strength in me that I could have tossed her high in gay laughter and not snatched at a breath.

'Like a bull elephant you are,' said she, commanding. 'Put me down, Bryn Evan!'

Nineteen and fourteen stone and six-foot-two, I was, and looking for trouble. With one hand I could have held her still, but could not, because I loved her.

'Eh, dear me,' I whispered, and reached for her after laying her down, but she twisted away with the speed of a serpent and was on her feet in a gust of laughter, skirts up and flying down the mountain in a rhythm of ankle-drawers trimmed with lace, the huzzy. Hobnails pounding, I went after her and caught her below the hill of Caru, collapsing her in a tangle of petticoats and curls, and we lay together, Rhia and me, snatching at breath, and I kissed her amid gasps and protests.

'Hei up!' she cried. 'You are eating me alive.' She showed her arm. 'And look, the bruises!' Flushed and panting she was, and not all come with the running. 'Bread pudding, am I? Biting out lumps, you are.'

'I am sorry.'

'I am not,' said she. 'Let us have more of it, for you are not exactly greased lightning, Bryn,' and she closed her eyes and pouted her lips for kisses, but I turned from her.

I turned from her because often, when Richard came to visit, she was frugal with me, and tarty, like gooseberry pie without the sugar in, and when he was around I heard but the whisper of her, and never her song. It is always astonishing to me how beautifully God put the body together, yet took such little care when he stitched up the soul.

Her eyes were troubled when she said. 'As restless as an old cow's tail, you are, man. Is it angry with me, boy?'

'Bloody daft you would call me, were I to explain it.'

At this she reached out mothering hands, and held my head, swaying me and humming, which is the mother in the lover when I wanted her as a girl. I pulled myself away, and got up.

Wandering away, pushing old Nell aside, I went to the top of Caru and stared down over a golden land, seeing the cut lancing silver through the hills and the Nedd all flashing white and gleaming through the rocks of Clyne and Tonna. Lying on an elbow, I thought of the Roman legions which had rested here, the kisses taken and given by fierce Silure and Italian; the Spanish lovers of the lost decades in tears of birth and dying: here, in the place of sun and wind that I call Wales. Oh, beautiful Wales, I thought, on whose breast we are lying, you and me, Rhiannon, whose blood is noble and has coursed through ancient princes. 'Do you understand, Rhia?'

'It is all a bit complicated for me,' said she, coming up and lying beside me. 'Tell me, Bryn, tell me what you are thinking!' and she caught my hand and pressed it against her breast, and the softness of her stilled me. Still lying, I said:

'You will not laugh if I tell you of a story my mother told me, when I was ten years old? You want to hear how God made the earth?'

'Aye,' said she, in warmth and secrets.

I said, holding her, and looking down on Wales, 'In six days God made the earth, and on the seventh day he rested, as is told in Genesis. You listening?'

'Ears shivering,' said she, eyes closed.

'And he went from his workshop to his couch, and slept. But the wind moved over the land, stirring open his door. And God looked into his workshop again and saw that his task was not yet finished since he had a small barrel of clay and a large barrel of vision and enterprise left over. "I will make another nation," said he, getting up, "and because I am at the end of the alphabet, I will call them *Welsh*." You still with me?' I asked her.

'I can hear the beating of your heart,' said Rhiannon, like a cat in cream.

I continued, 'So he made the Welsh, and because he had put little clay, he made them small in stature, to get more of them. And he put them down on a plain and watched them mate and bring forth, and this they did readily, said my mother, because their blood was of the hot Iberian. And then, five hundred years later, which to God was a moment of Time, he looked again, and they had come to thousands.'

I got up, looking over the land, and said, 'But although they were fierce in love and war they were uncultured, and God knew then his only mistake, and said, 'Of course! How can a people of small stature, filled with vision and enterprise, see into distant places when they live on a plain? So I will make their country with mountains. Snowdonia, and Dinas and the Black Mountains and the Beacons!' You hear me, Rhia?'

But she was sleeping, not given to poetry, and I went from her to a quiet place of bushes and stood there filled with a great excitement, looking down on my mother, my girl. For a man can mate with a country, make no mistake. There, on that April day up on March-Hywel, I heard the cry of the bards. In sword-clash, I heard the song of a lost age of princes, the cries of the feudal lords, and saw the skin of the beast Lee and heard his talk of felons: the hammering of scaffolds, I heard, up from the Marcher Lordships; the squalid poetry of Tudur Aled, whom my father hated. My eyes filled with tears and I

208

began to tremble, and I knelt on the soil that bore me and thrust my fingers deep into its earth, and listened to the song. In all my dreams of possessing Rhiannon, in all the stuttering panic of lips and heart and loins, there was a greater need in me than Rhiannon, and a greater, deeper love. This was a mother of haughty pride; a land cleansed by her rejection of the conqueror.

I got up. The wind was cold on my face, I remember, and I looked at my hands. The fingers, the hands, the wrists were stained with her soil, where I had driven them. And there was a great joy in me, a calm in me: one with my country.

Rhiannon was lying asleep where I had left her; the mule grazed nearby.

And I went to Rhia, and knelt, touching her foot, and at this she awakened instantly, starting in panic, then smiling, her hand to her throat.

'You come back to me, Bryn?' she asked, softly.

'Aye, Rhia.' I was cool with her, having no need of her now.

'You believe I love you?'

I did not reply, and she said, looking away:

'You want me to prove that I love you, Bryn Evan?'

So beautiful she looked, lying there, with the redness flying in her cheeks and her eyes dark in her face. I seemed to hear her voice as from a great distance:

'You want me bad, you take me, Bryn, for I am your girl.'

I remember only that I held her, and she said, in gasps:

'Oh, God, Bryn. Oh, God, you hold me!'

Even on the best of us, says Gran, some rust do stain the mechanism of the soul. With a little human assistance it do easily polish off, though.

'Up a dando, quick,' I said, lifting her to her feet. 'Up quick, before you are in trouble. No chapel up by here, no Methodist preacher up on Mynydd March-Hywel. Done decent, it will be, with a ring and proper service, because I love you.' My hands were soiled, I remember, and I held them to my face.

'And I love you, too, Bryn, *cariad*,' she said. 'For all the

Richards coming and going, I do love Bryn, my sweet, my precious. Up away, and dando! Last one down to Hendre is a maniac,' and she was off again down the hill with skirts up and me after her, dragging Nell Mule.

It is not really much good trying to tell of a navvy wedding, when they go on a randy: you have to be there yourself to witness it. And the randy they turned up south of Crynant on the day Tai Morlais, my butty, married Sian Edwards, is talked off in the Dulais Valley to this day.

'I'm frit,' said Rhiannon, as I wheeled Nell down the last slopes above Crynant and we approached the encampment.

'If that's all that happens to you, I'll be thankful,' I said. 'You realise randy navvies are hot enough normal, without you setting fire to them?'

'You shouldn't have let me come,' said she, pert and nose up.

There is no sense in some people, so I did not answer, but clamped her with my arms and reined Nell Mule through the hutments of the compound, and doors came open and windows blew out and craggy faces and hair appeared and look what's coming, for God's sake.

One moment peace and quiet, next a commotion, with dogs bounding up snarling and cats going like bullets, and the earth street a clamour of ragged children and shrieking crones.

On we went, with Rhia white-faced but waving and bowing with brightness, and a few of the women curtseyed, give them credit, and a group of old navvies pulled off their caps on doorsteps as we passed.

'Where you bound for, mister?' This from a hulker naked to the trews, washing in a barrel, hair tuddled up, wet flesh gleaming.

'Tai Morlais' wedding breakfast!'

'Straight through, and best you come early, for Tai won't have a bloody leg under him in an hour.' His hands paused and his eyes traced Rhiannon from toe to face and back again. Like a wet tiger he looked, standing there watching.

'Bryn, love, you won't leave me, eh?' Shivering, she was.

'Depends how you behave. By the time the wedding is over

they won't know you from Sian Edwards. Just act natural and keep close.'

Cheap-jacks and hucksters were unfolding travelling stalls outside the rough huts, and as we rode deeper into the compound the music of fiddles and squeeze-boxes greeted us. The crowds grew thicker; thick-stemmed, hairy men, all stripped to the waist, were rolling out barrels of ale or tossing them high on to their brown shoulders: boy-navvies rushed past with piled loaves and pails of butter from the crowded tommy-shop on a corner. Black-dressed and bunned-up, the navvy wives watched in lounging unconcern as we passed: a dogfight under Nell's very nose now, and a fist-fight in one of the huts, by the sound of it, with furniture over-turning and glass splintering in coarse oaths and shrieks from a woman.

'Don't look very healthy,' said Rhiannon, shivering, and gasping.

'Didn't I warn you? Anything Welsh in skirts they have for dinner, and you look tasty done up like that.'

'A pig you are, Bryn Evan. Dear me, look at this!'

Flouncy women now, six of them, done up in red and blousy, waving fists and gin bottles, and doing mock curtseys to Rhiannon as we trotted by, and up with them, shrieking hoarsely, and the language floating up on the gin sent me sheet-white and shocked, and I'd heard some in my time.

By a well in the middle of the encampment a great bonfire was burning and a whole calf was turning on a spit, with a swaying crowd of navvies and their women laying out benches for the celebrations, and a butcher, beefy and red, sharpening knives; people shouting in a score of dialects from Scotland to the Welsh border, and wizened old navvies already dancing in circles to the music of a melodeon, their arms going up like dervishes. Now a gipsy dancer in a scarlet skirt and bangle earrings, her long, black hair flying as she spun and swayed to the screech of Irish fiddles. And behind her I saw Tai Morlais, fists on his hips and staring. Gone was the boy, this was a man. Deep-throated, he called:

'Bryn Evan!'

'Ay ay!' I shouted.

Through the people he came, swinging men aside. 'Bryn Evan, Bryn Evan!'

'So you got her, eh?' I shouted in the commotion, and slipped off Nell and lifted Rhiannon down, and he gripped me with big hands: fine and handsome he looked, did Tai; all done up in mole-skin trews with red stockings and high-laced boots, and the finest velveteen coat over a scarlet waistcoat with pearl buttons, and his tammy, bright blue, with a sleeping-bobble swinging on his head.

'Where's Sian, then?' I yelled above the clamour.

'Ach, do we need her when there's crackling like this around?' Low he bowed to Rhia. 'A woman should be full in the haunch and firm in the calf, so you're the loveliest dinner I've seen since the old days of Cushy Cuddlecome.'

'She's me friend, Tai,' I said, taking off his Irish. 'She's gentry stock, and delicate in the ears, so please water the language.'

'I will, for sure, man.' He was staring at Rhiannon. 'You'll forgive the bad manners, for I'm bog Irish, lady. And it's just that I'm unsure if I'm on me arse or me elbow, for the beauty of ye is undoin' me. Ach, it's beautiful. Will ye step this way, ma'am, and I'll show ye me bunk, though the trouble is that I'm only a buck navvy, and ye'll be sharing it with another thirty, or so.'

'Can I come, too?' I asked.

'Sure, you're welcome. It's too rough for a lady, being out here and every dirty old Lancashire and what-not givin' her the eye. Come and meet Sian,' and he tossed Nell's reins to a lad and caught Rhiannon's hand and was away through the crowd with her to a hut beyond the roasting animal, and the cheers and roars that followed him deafened me. After them I went, and just in time got a glimpse of Rhia's pink crinoline as she disappeared into the hut on the end of him.

In the hut Sian was sitting on her bed, being prepared for her wedding: very off-the-shoulder was Sian, and beautiful, sitting there in her Welshness and a strange piety as the women dressed her. Bangle earrings for Sian; pale and smooth her face, but rouged in the lips where the navvy wives had painted; red was her dress, and her shoes were laced above her ankles. In simple grace she sat, unspeaking, her face in profile against the single window while the ragged wives scuttled about her.

'Sian, are you listening?' Tai bent before her, screwing his tammy. He drew Rhiannon forward, whispering, 'There's no talking in her, ye see, girl. She'll likely be a shrew after the wedding, so there's no talking in her before she jumps the chair, ye understand. It's a virgin quiet, see. An' I have her word on it, so I'm lucky.' He bent to Sian, who sat motionless, as if deaf, blind and mute. 'I'm bringing me friend and his woman, Sian. You remember Bryn Evan down at Cushy's? You recall the night he came and swiped Cinders, the wee bitch? Well, he's come over the mountain to wish us well, an' it's six sons he'll be wishin' you, woman, for although he's a Taff, he's a right good fella. Can ye hear me, Sian? It's plentiful that he's hoping for us, an' that's good friends indeed.'

No sign, not a movement she made; straight over his shoulder she looked as the women oiled her hair, which was plaited either side of her head and reached to her waist.

'I have brought a gift for you Sian,' I said and gave a sovereign to Tai.

He opened her fingers, closing them upon the sovereign. I said, leaning towards her, 'The money is split between me and Rhia. And last week I took it up to Pont-Nedd-Fechan and put it under a boulder, and when I went up for it last night the fairy offering was there, in twelve white circles of paper, but I would not take the exchange.'

'Blessed, it is,' said Rhiannon, touching her hand, 'for he did not take the exchange.'

'Dear God,' said Tai. 'There is lovely friends we do have, isn't it?'

Sian did not reply.

'No turnings and no breeches I wish you,' said Rhiannon. 'Easy births, Sian, and sons I will have for you.'

'Go now,' said one of the women, and I straightened, looking around the hut. There were about forty beds lining the rough, mud walls, some single and a few double. About twenty navvies were in there, some sitting on their beds, some in them, sleeping after shift, for they were working on the tunnel drainage, and some farther up on the Merthyr, which had been a thorn in Ritson's side from the day he constructed it. In the double beds men and women were sleeping; one bed held a family of four, and the woman was awake, with a child at her breast, sucking noisily in the strange silence, fists waving. In the middle of the room was a stove and on the fire a big black pot, and stirring it, like a witch over a brew, was a ragged, skinny old woman. Hanging out of the pot were lengths of string, each with a name tied to the end: a coney in the pot for Redbonce, explained Tai afterwards; a piece of stolen beef for Sour Billo, a quarrelsome navvy who hailed from Cork; half a hare for Dirty Tom and a squirrel for Parson, the new English boy, who prayed.

'Right the first evenin' he come in, he prayed,' said Tai, 'and Boxer came in with ten quarts aboard and let fly with his boot, and the boot hit Parson and cut his face, and the blood ran down through his fingers, but still he prayed, kneeling by the bed.'

'But he does not pray now,' said Rhiannon.

'Oh, aye, he does still,' said Tai. 'Next night he prayed the same, and Boxer threw the boot again and it knocked Parson over on his ear, and when he came round he started praying again, with one eye filled up. And on the third night he come in Boxer left his own bed and sat on Parson's, while he prayed with a special one for Boxer because he was a bastard, behaving like that. And he still sits there. Anyone throwing at Parson now gets the boot from Boxer.'

My father says there is more honour under oil-lamps than under chandeliers.

Tai said, outside the hut, 'Did you see my Sian cry, Bryn Evan?'

'Aye.'

'She cries because I'm only a navvy, and a buck Irish one, at that, and my Welsh name do make no difference.'

'Up to you, Tai, to see she do not cry in future,' I said.

But at the dancing Sian did not cry.

In a whirl of colour Sian danced in the middle of a ring of clapping, cheering navvies, with her Irish fiddlers playing for

214

her and Tai as he armed her round in circles. Cushy Cuddlecome was there, too, with her Irish stew, standing on a dray
cheering and bawling, urging the customers to drink deep, and
I made sure there was something about sixteen stones between
me and Cushy, for she would give out some past history as soon
as look at me. The afternoon wore on into dusk, and at the first
stars the celebrations stopped.

'Bring out the chair!'

The cry was taken up. 'Bring the chair, bring the chair!'
The brawny creatures sho had rafted the bogs of Chat Moss
linked hands, chanting:

'The chair, the chair!'

I watched them.

These were the men who drove the terrible Woodhead
tunnels in Cheshire, in '45 and last year: men such as these,
childish in their joy now, were those who braved the terrifying
barrow-runs of the London to Birmingham; whose comrades
died under earth falls and borehole explosions, or in upset
buckets in the tunnel air-shafts. Who built the Paris to Rouen
railway and ate with Brassey at the Feast of Maisons the year
before last: these giants, now chanting falsetto and clapping at
the wedding of a little Welsh serving-maid, were those who
knew no law but labour; who, by their sweat, had changed the
face of Britain and raised monuments greater than the Pyra-
mids; these were the men who, within a few years, were to
save the ragged, beaten British army of the war in the Crimea.
I saw them anew, not as men who were taking away my birthright of the barges, but as the new heroes of my generation.

'The chair!' The chant was taken up to a thunder, and a
little gnome of a navvy rushed into the ring and placed one
down.

Silence. Not a whisper. The wind blew softly from
March-Hywel, fanning our faces. Rhiannon's hand was gripping mine. I see her face now, her lips parted, expectant, and I
feel the tenseness of her body beside me. In the ring Tai
Morlais and Sian Edwards stood motionless, as carved from
stone; twin splashes of colour against the green of the mountain.

And then Tai moved. Going first, he leaped over the chair,

skidded to a halt, and turned, his arms wide. Sian curtseyed deep to him, her face lowered, and then, straightened, lifted her skirts to her waist and ran, bounding over the chair and into his arms, and they fell together on the grass in a joyful tumble of limbs as he kissed her to a bellow of cheers from the navvies. Instantly, the ring was broken. Turning, shrieking, hand in hand, they ran, Tai and Sian, and got about ten yards before the navvies caught them, carrying them shoulder high to the hut where Sian had been prepared for the wedding.

'But when is the wedding?' demanded Rhiannon, flushed in the milling crowd.

'That was the wedding,' I said.

'But they had no minister.'

So beautiful she looked standing there among the pushing, barging people, that I kissed her.

'They do not need a minister, girl, all the time they have got a chair,' I said.

'Good God,' she said, fanning, 'and where are they taking them now?'

'Give you three guesses,' I said.

# 23

IT was bat and curtain time as we clopped along the tow-path past New Inn towards the Old Navigation and the blaze of Rheola, and old Nell was dozy after her descent of March-Hywel and the spin and colour of Tai's wedding, now far behind us.

Sweetly, a hymn sounded then, coming to us on the clear April air, and there drifted upon us a bass unison song of men; a music that entered our dozy dream, as Nell was dozy, of a pale moon, stars and a stamp of hooves. Rhiannon, half asleep against me in the saddle, stiffened, and her eyes were large and startled in the strange light.

'What is that?'

I reined Nell to a halt, and we stood there amid the spring whispers of the cut. A night-jar sang in a frenzy of joy: on the far bank a badger, as blind as a bat, was nosing the soil for his musk, the scent of his earth.

'*Heisht!*' whispered Rhiannon. 'It is hymn-singing from Rheola House.'

Tense, we listened, and heard the words clearly:

> *Abide with me, fast falls the eventide.*
> *The darkness deepens, Lord, with me abide....*

Often, especially on Sunday nights, the Vaughans of Rheola would come up from Aberdulais aqueduct in barges with choirs, and beautiful it was to hear the full harmony of the ancient hymns, and always they sang in Welsh.

'Not Rheola House,' I said. 'It's coming from the Old Navigation.'

'Aye,' replied Rhiannon, breathing again. 'Got enough there today for a full choir—Tomos Traherne and Richard, Mam Mortymer and Mr. Cowbum come to visit Gran....'

'Counting them all that makes eight, if Sharon is home. That is a choir of men, and more like a hundred.'

Shivering was in us; there was an enmity in the night, with the hunchback trees of the cut crouching about us now, like animals for the spring. Nell, too, was trembling beneath us, and snorting, her eyes rolling white.

Opposite Crugau Farm the singing was louder. As the Old Navigation grew into shape under the Rheola moon, it came in a full throat-chorus of tenor and bass.

'For God's sake, what is it?' breathed Rhiannon.

'We will soon find out,' I replied, and gave Nell the heels and we galloped past Crugau straight and I wheeled Nell and reined her short outside the stable yard. In a blast of sound, the singing was about us now.

> *Where is death's sting? where, grave, thy victory?*
> *I triumph still, if Thou abide with me.*

Sliding off Nell, I lifted Rhiannon down, ran to the stable gate and swung it wide into the yard.

Packed in a tight circle in the middle of the yard were over a hundred men, and not one head turned to me at the crash of the gate. Bare-headed, they sang as men sing at funerals, dressed in their Sunday best.

'For God's sake what is happening?' I barged into their ranks, spilling and humping them before me, and they did not resist me, but sang on. Beef O'Hara I recognised first, then Mick O'Shea, the Cuddlecome drunk. Laddie O'Brien I shouted at, but he did not answer. Abe Sluice and Ditch Fielder I swung aside, furious and frightened. In the middle of the ring, standing on a rough trestle, was a pauper's coffin, and in letters stark white on the tar was painted my father's name. Mick Spit, the Midlander, I saw then, his face grieved; Bargey Boy and Dutch, Job Moses came next, their handkerchiefs held to their faces.

And Tub Union stood by the coffin in funeral black. With a Prayer Book in his hands, he turned to face me.

'Accept the Union's condolences on the death of your beloved father,' said he, deep. 'We grieve for you in this tragic loss, Bryn Evan.'

Distracted, her face stark white and sweating, Rhiannon burst through into the circle then, and gripped me, but she made no sound.

I bowed my head and the horror of it swept over me in waves, and I knew a cold and awful sickness; the bile rose in my throat, and I swallowed it down. Tub Union said, turning to the men:

'Last verse, now, and give it reverence, for this was a good man, and a brother,' and they sang, in glorious harmony:

> Hold Thou Thy Cross before my closing eyes;
> Shine through the gloom, and point me to the skies...

Tub Union then turned to me, and said, 'Try anything, lad—one move, and we will pull you to pieces.'

Trembling, I stood there.

It was the mock burial of the scab: it was the burial, by his brothers, of a brother unwanted: the shifting of one who had refused to shift. This was the punishment for working on when

218

the Union said stop. It was the revenge reserved for the traitor Welsh, men like Man Arfon on their way to high places in English business or government.

It was also a forecast of death for one, like my father, who was under-cutting the bargee rates by a penny a ton.

Up in Nantyglo and Blackwood, in Merthyr and Tredegar, the Scotch Cattle would scotch a man by breaking his leg when he worked on when the Union said strike. But the *Funeral of the Scab* was worse than mutilation, for it spelt the death of the soul: a Church of England service for a nonconformist man. And after the service that man was dead to the community. At Market, the wives would console his wife, and send her flowers; wreathes would arrive at the door. At school the children would play at weeping, with his children.

'God help you, Tub Union,' I said, and I turned to my father's voice, for he had heard the mule.

'Is that you, Bryn? Bring Rhiannon in, please.'

Shouldering aside men, I pulled her after me and thrust her into the kitchen; Dada slammed the door.

Hands clenched, I stared around the room.

Dewi I saw first, sitting with legs splayed, butting his fists together in his agony, his face raging and dark: Ifor was sitting in my father's chair by the grate, rigid under his command. Gran, her arms folded on the table, was quietly weeping within them, and Mr. Cowbum, the solicitor, stood with his hand on her shoulder in bewildered timidity. One by one, I saw them as Rhiannon ran into Mari's arms: Tomos Traherne I saw, magnificent in presence, hands gripping the window-sill, his white beard trembling, indignant and helpless. Richard Bennet I saw last, sombre and angry, pacing like a caged tiger, and he raised glowing eyes at me as I said:

'What the hell is happening here?'

'The little boys are playing their games—don't tell me you need it explaining,' said my father.

'You join the Union, you keep its rules,' interjected Richard.

'When I was a member of the Union I kept its rules,' replied Dada. 'When it would not take my subscription, I made my own.'

'Whose side are you on?' I said to Richard.

'Oh, for God's sake!' cried Mari, her hands over her face.

My father did not go to her, and Tub Union's voice stole into the room.

' "Man that is born of woman hath but a short time to live, and is full of misery. He cometh up, and is cut down, like a flower; he fleeth, as it were a shadow, and never continueth in one stay." '

Dada said, lighting his pipe, 'It would not be so bad, mind, if I could go down as a Methodist. Do you realise Tub Union's got a collar on back to front and I have to put up with Church of England?'

In my agony outside I had noticed this. Mari said:

'Oh, please, Mostyn, I cannot bear this!'

'You will have to, woman. They can bury me as deep as they like, remember, but I will go down six feet when my time is come, not a moment before.'

'One way or another, they are burying you, and you know it.'

My voice seemed to echo in the room, and my father said:

'Right, assume this. Now will somebody tell me what I can do about it?'

'You can shift him outside with them, for a start,' I shouted, pointing at Richard, and Dewi was instantly on his feet:

'*Diawch!* You leave him out of this or I will not be responsible!'

My father came into the middle of the kitchen. 'They will bury me alive before they bury this family. The only fighting in here will be done by me, remember it. Let Richard remember his conscience and you two remember that you are brothers, or I will take a hand.'

'I am not with the bargee Union,' said Richard, eyeing me.

'And is there a difference?' I cried. 'For long enough you have been spouting the need for Unions, of everybody being brothers and charters of decency—is this what they turn out for a penny a week?'

Mari said, wearily, 'Oh, Bryn, for God's sake stop it!'

'If they work for savages, can you blame them if they behave like savages?'

'As long as you count me out,' I said. 'I've had enough of

you and your bloody Unions to last me a life-time.'

My father said, 'Bryn, sit down and shut up, and mind your language. Listen to them for a bit: there is more and more humour in it the more you hear of it.'

Tun Union said, ' "I heard a voice from Heaven, saying unto me, Write. From henceforth blessed are the dead which die in the Lord: even so saith the Spirit; for they rest from their labours. Lord have mercy on us." '

' "Christ have mercy on us," ' said the men in bass chorus.
' "Lord have mercy on us. Our Father, which art in Heaven. . . . " '

Dada grinned wide. 'Dear old Moses Shon should have heard that one. Missed his vocation, did Tub, bless him. Moses would have put him up for Lampeter Theological.' He put his arm round Mari's shoulders. 'Make a pot of tea, girl. We have got a long way to go. It is loam and shale in that yard, and they will be in here borrowing picks in the next ten minutes.'

'I say fight, Dada,' said Ifor, lumbering to his feet. 'Bryn is right.'

'And I say fight,' said Tomos Traherne, and the shock of his voice turned us all. 'They outrage the word of God: force, at times, must be met with force, as He whipped them out of the Temple.'

'Tea, Mari,' said Dada, 'for I am thirstier than a desert, being dead.' He nodded towards Tomos. 'With respect to your cloth, man, this is my house, so I will do the fighting. And let something be understood in here before we lose the sense of proportion. If I am going down in theory I am not having my face booted in before it in practice. Nor am I going out there with a mandrill to beat sense into men who are my comrades in misery. You, Mr. Cowbum, earlier talked of the virtue of Welsh beliefs, but there is no virtue in a belief unless you back it with bread. It is all right for you, sir, because you and yours are eating. But were I to take the food from your mouth you would be worse than savage in a week.' He smiled at Tomos. 'You called them mad an hour back, Pastor, and you are right, for they are mad with fear. It is a world of rip and claw, and if we live in a jungle we accept the jungle law. Today Tub

221

Union is eating me because I haul to Ferry for a penny a ton less than Union rates: tomorrow he will be eaten because he is doing the same, to feed his children. So do not anybody here talk of force or the union of ideals or the virtue of beliefs. Do not talk to me of anything save the will to change things, as Richard Bennet is trying o do, in the name of God; and do not talk to me of Jesus, Pastor, until they change.' To Mari he said, 'Now hurry the pot, woman, for I am not given to tap-room speeches and I am drier than the wife of Lot.'

After this we did not speak much, but drank the tea Mari made us and sat in lamp-light and silence, listening to the soprano chinking of the picks and the baritone grouse of the shovels; later we heard the rope-creak lowering of the coffin, and a bit to your right, for God's sake, or you will have him over: then stones and earth were thrown on wood and bass voices talked about ashes and dust.

They timed it to the stroke of midnight, and they raised the cross over the mound and left us in peace, and I left the room and went out to see what was written so that always would I remember it, this indignity and cruelty of men to men.

In the light of the moon I saw it, chalked white.

MOSTYN EVAN
SON OF BEN THE DROVER
DIED APRIL 24TH 1854
BURIED BY HIS COMRADES
IN THE UNION

When I got back into the kitchen only Dada and Gran were left, and she called to me and I went to her, standing before her like a child.

'You see it, Bryn?' she asked, mopping up.

'Aye, Gran.'

'And you will always remember it?'

I nodded.

'Right,' said she. 'Remember this too. There is a time to weep and a time to spit in their faces, and that is now. Take a shovel and dig it up. Take it far, so women do not see it, for the sight of it could dry a womb. Then return and fill the place. Fill the place in the yard, and I will look next morning.

If I see a sign of ground disturbed God help you; this is your task, for you are youngest son.' She faltered then, hand to her heart.

'And then?' I got up. 'You all right, Gran?' She nodded, smiling.

I looked at my father: strangely aged, he seemed, as if Tub Union had come in with the men and taken funeral fingers to his cheeks.

'Then what?' asked Gran, with business.

'Do we move from here?'

At this she straightened, hand on hips, but her face was pale.

'A message for Tub Union, and you will deliver that, too. Tell him that we fight for right of way. That yesterday, had he asked respectable, we might have considered it. Now not even cannons and fuses will shift us from the Old Navigation, me especially.'

'It is a mistake, Mother,' said my father, looking at nothing.

'Me and him,' said Gran, jerking her thumb. 'For we are of drover blood—me and him: us, especially. Tell Tub Union he can pull the roof down over our heads, he can dig up the foundations, he can bring through another branch line, he can burn us alive. But never, as long as I live will I leave the Old Navigation. Business as usual, it is—you and Dewi and Dada, up to Glyn Neath for the haul at dawn tomorrow.'

For all the defiance there was a sudden sickness in them, especially in Gran. Trembling, she sat there, and I cursed Tub Union.

# 24

GETTING into the Old Navigation that June was like trying to enter a besieged town, with the main line one side of it, the Rheola branch line on the other and its back garden specially selected by Man Arfon for a rail and sleeper stacking compound. When the navvies came and built a signal box on Gran's front patch the only entrance left to us was along the tow-path. Slowly, as convolvulus strangles a tree, the railway strangled us. Now its cracked windows stared blankly on to the embankments and rails and sleepers; Gran's flower garden was now withered under layers of soot and coal-dust. And as the railway flats and trucks thundered past us with greater loads at higher speeds, the hair-cracks of our walls widened to crevices and the crevices deepened into fissures that ran in crazy patterns from eaves to foundations. The Old Navigation was dying on her feet, and we knew it. And we were dying, too. As officially dead as if he was six feet under, my father would wait outside the Canal Company office in Bethel Street down on Briton Ferry for the occasional tossed-in haul from Glyn Neath to Giant's Grave. Defying Tub Union, he dropped his rates per ton again, and the Company snatched momentarily at the higher profit; but as the barge hauls came less and less, as colliery after colliery built access tram-roads or blasted deep into the rock for cuttings and platforms, our savings dwindled to nothing. Also, since Dewi, Ifor and me were working part time in Resolven colliery now, my father could not take a barge haul even when it was offered. Come autumn Ifor went to live with Rebecca in Abercynon, and the house was empty of his stumbling bass manners: Sharon, too, was never in the place; preferring the Penny Gaffs and travelling players, and just earning enough to keep herself. And when Dewi was not over in Nantyglo with Richard planning another anti-Truck society, he was out with Ianto Fuses and Pietro Bianca greasing the railway lines and spinning the Corsairs on the Glyn Neath to Hirwan gradient.

Which night after night that winter of the Crimean War, left in the kitchen Dada, Mari, Rhiannon, me and Gran.

And with Mr. Seth Cowbum becoming extremely bright in the eyes the following spring, it appeared to me that soon we would be more.

In a drooping, creaking, crumbling Old Navigation that bright spring day we awaited with pent excitement the coming of Mr. Cowbum.

Courting very hard was Seth, bless him. All brown topper

and kid gloves, black frock coat tight at the waist over his corsets, mother-of-pearl buttons on a scarlet waistcoat, button-holed and whiskered, his moustache waxed wickedly at the ends: polished and pruned, he came trotting from Neath in his pony and trap. And Gran was rushing about from window to window as happy and flushed as a young maid, and he can please himself if he comes or not for I am not bothered either way: then up in the shaving mirror with her, smoothing the wrinkles under her eyes, patting up her beautiful hair. Straight as a ruler was she, and proud in carriage: this coming from the dignity of her youth, wet or fine, down at the water-spout behind Ynysbiben Inn, to come back with the pitcher on her head. I can see her now as I write this, seven foot tall was she and in bombazine black, with the setting sun red behind her over Rheola, a Welsh woman of Samaria.

'A word to you quickly, before she gets back,' said my father now, and we came from our chairs and lined up before him.

In the old days up in Cyfarthfa, when we were half pints, we used to do the same, I recall. Ifor would be on the right, then Dewi, Sharon, me and Gwen; all dressed in our sack night-shirts, ready for bed; lined up for the de-nitting—Gran with the fine comb on the hair, Dada after ears, and after that performance mouths would be prised open for great dollops of brimstone and treacle, and it was up at first light rushing out the back with people hollering and dancing in the kitchen. And I can see my little Gwen now, her toes curling to the nip of the winter flags, being done, with letters stamped across her back-side, 'When empty, please return to Pontypool.'

Sweet was the sound of Gwen in my heart. My father said now:

'A word, please, about Gran and Mr. Seth Cowbum,' and we circled him like assassins, after the scandal. Said he, 'Beds for the mistresses, altars for the wives, the saying goes, and courting at any age brings fun and banter. But there will be none of it with this pair, you understand? This is neither courtship nor marriage, but mere friendship. Mr. Cowbum has asked my permission for Gran to stay at his home. Amazingly, he is a lonely man, and if she agrees to go, then it is none of our business. So no jokes at their expense, please, for Gran is our mother, and it is from her we come. You understand?'

'Yes, Dada,' we said, in chorus.

'He will be here within the hour and bringing his daughter; who knows? If everything runs smoothly, Gran might even finish up as his housekeeper.'

'What, no wedding?' ejaculated Sharon.

'Not that I am aware of,' replied Dada. 'Chalk and cheese, this pair. But it is two women in one kitchen in by here, says Gran, and she is right. Old folks understand each other, so let them be. Tidy up and make a special effort, and anybody with a foot in the wrong place will have me to account to later. You listening, Ifor?'

'Aye, Dada.'

Gran came back just then, all very casual about the visit, and people were coughing discreetly behind their hands and talking about the weather, and the moment Gran's back was turned again we all dashed upstairs in a fever, pulling out best Sunday serge, with creases to cut your throat, and polishing up boots. Rhia and Sharon were flapping about in chemises and curlers, with stays going on and people kneeing backs and hauling on strings. And in the middle of it Rebecca arrived with Ceri, their baby girl, and most beautiful Rebecca looked standing there in the yard while old Eli and his missus drove off in the trap.

Strange the emotion of sadness I knew whenever I saw Rebecca; strange the mystery of her eyes as she lifted them to mine as I came into the yard and raised the shawl from her baby's face. Fifteen months old was Ceri now, and lusty, and 'Becca still feeding her, and you can keep your old goat's milk, Gran used to say, for there is nothing better than mother's, and Betsy Small-Coal suckled all hers up to the age of five, and Betsy knows what she's about, said Gran. Rebecca's great dark eyes moved over my face.

'Seth Cowbum and his daughter coming now just, you heard?' I said to her.

She did not answer, and Mari came up with Ifor, crying, 'Here they are, 'Becca and baby Ceri!' And she took the baby from its mother's arms and nuzzled and cooed it, whispering to Ifor, 'Sit and watch, eh, lad? Do not talk unless spoken to directly, eh? There's a good boy.'

And Rebecca sat in my father's chair by the grate with Ceri on her breast, her dark eyes cast down, and I saw in her gipsy face the lost tribes of Israel, the wanderers of the Red Sea, which are the true Welsh who settled in the Vale of Neath at the time of the Romans. In a moment, for me, she was the Rebeka, one with Moses and the pillar of cloud: in her I knew the ragged wanderings of Migdol and the starving encampments of Baalzephon: she raised her eyes to mine in the mirror, and I knew with my brother's wife a strange and terrible affinity and was with her in the dust-storms and seawaste of Pihahiroth.

Momentarily, I closed my eyes in the mirror and heard her breathing in the scur of the razor.

'Cool, lad,' said my father in passing, 'mind you do not cut yourself.'

Mr. Seth Cowbum and his daughter Miss Penelope arrived for tea at four o'clock, and there was a dreadful palaver then, with people still rushing about wiping at things with dusters and for God's sake, Ifor, try to look intelligent and no funny business from you either, Dewi, for it is a tea-party and not anti-Truck politics, and Gran running her finger around the dresser for dust. Sharon, fair and beautiful in pink, whirled into the kitchen, delighted, crying:

' "Is this the son of a friendly nation who entereth the gate? Ah, Pericles, see—he brings his regal daughter! Let honour be paid to them, sir, since soon their blood will mingle with the blood of this house." '

'Oh, for God's sake, sit down, woman,' cried my father in a panic. 'Mari!'

Always, when in terror, he called for Mari.

'Aye, Mostyn?'

'They are in the yard—where is Gran, for Heaven's sake?'

'Coming!'

'*Darro* me,' said Dada. 'All fingers and thumbs, I am. Mari, you lead the way. Rebecca, you come next with Ceri, and pin up your front, there's a good girl. Rhiannon, Sharon—best

227

curtseys, please—no half-downs. And you three...' He eyed us.

Out into the yard now as Mr. Cowbum clattered his pony and trap to a halt, and we were low in curtseys and stiff with bows, and Penelope, Mr. Cowbum's daughter who had come to look Gran over, sank down at her feet and stayed there until Gran raised her, which I thought was beautiful.

If girls of eighteen do stir the blood, then hand me women of thirty.

Beautiful, this Penelope, her head bright curls, her brightness enhanced by Rhiannon's darkness, and her English eyes were blue and sparkling.

'How do you do, Mrs. Evan?' said she.

'How are you?' asked Gran. Precious, I think, is the tapestry of life: birth, nationality fade in the shine of good breeding; muslin and lace can match side by side on the velvet of good manners. Gran said then:

'Mostyn, my son; Mari, my daughter-in-law; Rebecca and Ceri; Sharon, Dewi, Ifor, Bryn and Gwen, who is dead. Come you in, the pair of you; thirsty as salt-cellars you must be, for it is puddling weather,' and she led the way into the house while I unharnessed the pony and put it in with Nell and Jed Donkey, and Cinders whined and leaped at me from the straw in joy.

Take a deep breath, take a hole in on the belt, into the kitchen, sit at table. Stiff at the starched cloth, you sit amid the coughs and whispers and discreet smiles of the visitors, everybody with their hands folded in their lap, and it is so quiet that stays are creaking and tums cobbling and the Granfer Ben clock on the mantelpiece in the bedroom upstairs is ticking like a death-watch beetle. Sideways in your suit, you sit, with your boots on back to front and your collar on your ear, with all the cups and saucers gleaming on their best behaviour, the spoons for afters polished and tinkling treble as people shift, the knives flashing bright from the board. This is when a table speaks, I think, dying to play its part of making the good impression for the loved one: this is when the kettle cries its best tears, the milk is cream for the first two cups, the bread smiles brown and crisp and the tea has all the scented musk of India. Mari came in with the tea-pot just then, thank God, smiling, her eyes dancing, crying, 'It is good of you to come, Miss Penelope. Long enough your father has been talking of you.' She settled herself down, with business, embracing us all. 'Been this way before, have you?'

'Often—to parties at Vaughan Rheola, and Aberpergam. Oh, it is beautiful!'

'You know the Vaughans Rheola well, I expect?'

'Once or twice I have been for harp playing, and poetry readings, and there met Mr. Thomas Stephens, the historian.'

'Well now! Anglo-Welsh, have we?'

'Hampshire English, Mrs. Evan,' said Mr. Cowbum, 'but we come as friends.'

'Interested in Welsh literature, though?' asked Dada, finding his tongue.

'Aye, but not a word you will get from me, sir,' cried Miss Penelope, and I was stricken with terror when she turned on me, and said, 'You think Rheola house is beautiful, Bryn?'

Fingers screwing, face like a turkey's wattle. 'Aye, ma'am.'

'It ought to be,' said Dewi, chewing, 'the money they spent on it.'

Sharon announced gravely, 'The grapes of Rheola are the finest in the county!'

'So I hear. And you were lucky in Resolven, for the cholera did not come below Crugau Farm?'

'We had it,' said Dada, 'but we picked it up at Skewen, and that is another story.' Mr. Cowbum said, then:

'When my wife was alive we often used to come to Rheola for the grapes. Unfortunately, she died of the cholera a year after Doctor Brodie.'

'A good man, that Doctor Brodie,' said Mari.

Silence. Words steamed dry in remembered grief. And in that silence two others came in and sat at table: my darling Gwen, and the wife of Mr. Cowbum.

'My father tells me your sons are working for Mr. Lyons now, Mr. Evan.'

'Aye. All three down Resolven colliery—but Ifor only part-time—three days a week, until Rebecca and Ceri come to live by here.'

'So you are no longer a private bargee?'

'With the railway here, the future is dim for the barges, Miss Penelope.'

'Already? With the increase in coaling, I would have thought you were safe for another twenty years.'

'That is where you run into loss of profit,' said Dewi suddenly, 'and when you get loss of profit, nothing is safe.'

Gran came in with the kettle then, crying, 'A good strong cup, for God's sake. Thought she would never boil. Warmed the pot have you, Mari, my love? See this old pot, you two? Had it since my dear husband was down the old Starvo—hot water we used to have them days, and pretend it was tea. Pass the bread and butter now, make yourselves at home, do not be backward.'

Like a starting-gate going up, things fly off when Gran comes in, with plates sliding about and arms crossed in offerings, and no-thank-you's and yes-please's flying up and mouths being crammed with tremendous relief, for once the chops are going the tongue cannot talk. Strange and beautiful it is, I think, this quaint shyness of God's creatures. Dewi said:

'New seams are opening up above Glyn Neath; iron is slipping, coal is taking over. They say it began with Letty Shenkins up in the Aberdare Valley. You are right, ma'am. There ought to be enough for the bargee for the next twenty years, but when the speculators start cutting each other's throats it is the common people, not the gentry, who bleed to death.'

'It is nothing to do with speculation,' said my father. 'Dewi is young, therefore he is hot. In this case the fight is among the workers, not the masters; I am a private contractor, and the Union is easing me out.'

'Then that is the fault of the Union, not the owners, surely,' said Mr. Cowbum.

'Aye, on the face of it,' answered Dewi. 'But the quickest way to kill a union of brothers is to bring in outside competition, and this the owners know, so the effect is exactly the same.'

'Right,' said Dada. 'Now remember that this is a tea-party

230

and not a political platform. Any more bread and butter, any-body?'

Cinders was lying across my boot and pushed her nose up my trews and began to lick my shin: very strange, it was, to be sitting there making polite conversation with the bitch's muzzle half-way up and licking my knee. But stranger still is life, that you can sit like this in the security of afternoon tea and yet be balanced on the tip of disaster. Rebecca's eyes were lowering and lifting at me from the other side of the table when Sharon said, for no reason:

'There was a ball at Vaughan Rheola last Friday night. Passing on the road between the lodges, I did see them, sitting on the lawns after the dancing. The moon was over the forest, the stars were beautiful, and Llewellyn Nicholas was playing on the harp.' Dreamy, she stared past me at the window.

'Trained by Miss Jane Williams, was young Nick,' re-marked Dada. 'Often, up at New Inn, I have heard him play for Watkin the Weaver.'

'Beautiful looking chap, too, mind,' said Rebecca, with a burst of intelligence. 'Best looking chap this side of Briton Ferry, I reckon.'

'Aye, lovely looking,' said Sharon warmly.

'Like I told Ifor here,' said Rebecca. 'Pimply he do send me just to look at him, and he can wash his socks in my pudding basin any time he likes.'

'Indeed,' whispered Mr. Cowbum.

'Expressive, that is the word for it,' said Dada. 'Expres-sive.'

'Mind,' said Gran, 'a wonderful instrument is the harp. Harps I do like because they are respectable.'

'Being played by angels, that is bound to be,' observed Ifor.

'But I do not hold with balls, though.'

'Really,' said Mr. Cowbum.

With an effort, I said, 'The harp ... is the spirit of Wales. Plinlimmon and Craig Rhos, I see, when I hear the harp. And John Morgan of Rhigod Plough plays better than Nicholas, though he gets only a shilling a night.'

'Aye,' replied Gran, 'but poor old Nick is not himself these days—too much dancing—wearing himself out, like that Blodwen Davies, Ephraim's girl.'

'Does she go dancing?' asked Sharon. 'I thought her legs were bothering her.'

'They never bothered anybody else,' said Dewi.

Swiftly, Mr. Cowbum interjected, 'I was fortunate enough to hear Miss Jane of Aberpergam play to Charlotte Guest, at Abergavenny.'

'Just the same with her, though,' said Gran.

'Who, dear?' asked Mari with sweetness.

'That Blodwen Davies—all she thinks of is balls—breaking old Ephraim's heart, she is.'

'Sharon has hopes of becoming an actress,' said Dada, like something stunned.

'How very interesting,' cried Miss Penelope. 'Now, I was wondering where I had seen her before—was it in Hamlet?'

'Ought to be ashamed of herself, that Blodwen Davies,' said Gran, munching.

'As Desdemona she is a demon,' said my father, instantly. 'She played to a full house a week last Saturday in Swansea, and Mr. Macready has very high hopes of her.'

'More cake, Seth?' asked Gran, up and bustling.

'He do like that cake, Gran,' remarked Ifor. 'Two pieces he do have already, mind.'

'Well, just a very small piece, to please you, Ceinwen,' said Mr. Cowbum.

'Aye, and take the outside bit, man, and eat it slow, for it sat in the middle. Tends to raise a bit of wind, I find, when it sits in the middle. Bit for you, too, Rhiannon, my love?'

And Rhiannon took it, flashing me a promising smile: warm and together, these days, Rhiannon and me, and Richard Bennet very far over the horizon.

'Cake and fat food is the same, of course,' said Gran, blowing her tea. 'Indeed, an excess of anything can be a curse.' And my father said, quickly:

'You ... you have met Jane Williams of Aberpergam House, Seth?'

'I happened to meet her at a Llanover reception—Penelope was with me. She is both gifted and beautiful.'

'Aye, but the bane of poor old Ephraim's life, mind,' said Gran.

It is sad when the old ones begin to fade.

My father said with deliberation, 'It is Miss Jane Williams we are discussing, Mother, not Blodwen Davies.'

'Aye, well I have said it once and I say it again—balls will be her downfall, for she thinks of nothing else—losing her head to the young bucks of the county.'

'Excuse me,' said Dewi, and he was up and away and I heard his boots stamping in the yard. My father closed his eyes, fingers pinching the bridge of his nose, and Mari said with speed:

'Another cup for anybody—come on, Mr. Cowbum, you are as dry as a bone, you are. More bread and butter for Ifor, too, is it?'

'Aye,' he rumbled, for he had been eating solid from the moment he sat down and had nearly cleared a loaf. Gran got up, crying:

'Indeed not, Mari—you entertain the guests and I will see to it.'

A big saddle-tank thundered through then, with twenty tons of lime and grain for the upland farms, and the place shuddered to the thumping impact of the wheels: flakes of plaster drifted down from the ceiling as the flats whined away towards Pont Walby and the signal outside crashed the clearway. Ceri awoke, screaming and kicking, nuzzling Rebecca for feed.

'Eh, my lovely, my precious baby,' said Ifor in his boots, digging her.

'A lusty child, to be sure,' observed Seth Cowbum.

'Just needs feeding,' said Ifor, and I held my breath.

Rhiannon cried, 'Shall I take her, Rebecca, while you finish your tea?'

'With me, *cariad*?' said Mari, opening her arms and clapping to Ceri. 'Upstairs to the bedroom till mam comes, eh?'

Ifor said, darkly, 'Everybody in by here eating, except Ceri.'

Too late.

Watch them all as Rebecca, who knows no difference, unbuttons the bodice of her dress, her dark eyes lowered in the majestic action of motherhood: see Ifor's grin of relief as he helps her with her petticoat, one strap coming down: now a discussion of importance between them, in secret whispers while Seth Cowbum sat with his hair on end:

'Not that one, 'Becca.'

'Aye, it is.'

'Empty, woman—she had that one for dinner.'

'Eh, dafto! I should know—look, ten gallons, it is.'

I switched a glance at Rhiannon, and she was staring at the ceiling, hands gripped, busting inside. My father's face was a study of quiet resignation. Mari, smiling beautifully, watched as Rebecca bared her breast to her baby, and Ceri fought it, fists waving as Gran came in with the bread and butter, crying delighted, 'Why, there's lovely! Ceri having tea, too, is it? That's right, my precious—baby's being left out, was it? Forgetting all about our little Ceri?'

And Rebecca sat there in majesty, as in some ancient Pharaoh market-place, her dark eyes shining as she watched her baby suck in noisy desperation.

Later, when the moon rose over Rheola, Mr. Cowbum rose and said with dignity, 'And so, on the advice of your father, I come with my daughter to break bread with you and ask permission to carry your grandmother off to my home in Swansea. . . .'

'As housekeeper?' asked Dewi.

'We will come to that later, young man.'

'Sit down,' said Dada, as Dewi got up, protesting.

Mr. Cowbum continued, unperturbed, 'One fool at a time on the floor, sir, your turn will come later. If this is the custom of the Welsh, I ask for an uninterrupted hearing.' He strolled the room like a court-room barrister, thumbs in the armholes of his waistcoat, jabbing at us with spectacles to make a point. 'This being a house of free-thinkers, where the opinion is sought of all, not one, I come before you to ask for her company in my home on Kilvey Hill, convinced, perfectly convinced that she is wasted here . . .'

'Shame, shame!' cried Dada.

'What are you talking about—wasted?' demanded Ifor.

'I repeat it—wasted. Can such a cook, for instance, receive the credit that is her due after fifty years of service?'

'Oh, go on with you, Seth,' cried Gran, loving it.

'Father,' said Miss Penelope, 'don't make a meal of it.'

'Indeed not, I am coming to the point. I claim that familiarity breeds contempt. In this house there are many other women capable of cooking, scrubbing and cleaning—you are loaded with women, and I have none. No, do not look at Penelope, for she does not live at home. Would you believe it when I say that I cook for myself in this lonely bachelorhood, that I darn my own socks, make my own bed, sweep out my own chambers . . . ?'

Shouts of derision at this, because we knew he had three servants and two gardeners in his mansion overlooking the Tawe.

'Ill-matched,' said Dewi.

'Ill-matched, sir? In what respect? In age we are the same; in wealth also, for we can only sit on one chair at a time, farmhouse or Chippendale. She is richer than I, for she has grandchildren, and all I have is a daughter.'

'Wrong nationality,' I said.

'Because she is Welsh, and I am English? Cannot love bridge the gap of all nationality, especially a love like mine, for I will have you know, sir, that I am older than Methuselah, like her, and we are wise in the ways of nationalities.' He paused, strolling the floor, and in that silence a black bear of shape must have moved over the flags on soundless boots; Granfer Ben had left the wild herds of Sarn Helen and come to sit with Gran. And she rose, then, gathered her skirts and left the room, and I heard her feet heavy on the stairs. Undaunted, Mr. Cowbum continued:

'In culture only you might have me at a disadvantage, since on all sides I hear talk that you are the lost tribe of Israel, though with my knowledge of your history I claim this as open to doubt . . .'

'Stick to the point, sir,' cried Dewi.

'I will indeed, and I will confound you, since I claim to know more of your history than you do yourselves.' He rocked on his heels, grinning at us.

'I doubt that,' said Dada.

'It is a popular misconception, for instance, that the Ancient Britons were conquered by the Romans ...'

'It is an historical fact,' shouted Dewi.

'It is history's lie, sir, and I will prove it. You claim that the Romans left these shores, and that the Saxons arrived and drove the Ancient Britons into a land called Wales, and that the Principality was founded after the Battle of Chester in A.D. 617?'

'That is correct.'

'It is factually wrong, Mostyn Evan. See now, I am better suited and more worthy of this woman than if I were Welsh by blood. The Battle of Chester played no important part in the history of this country. Your history began in A.D. 50 with the invasion of Flintshire by a Roman general, but his name escapes me.'

'Ostorius Scapula,' I said.

'Correct, young man. And then, in A.D. 296, the emperor Diocletian divided the province of Britain into Secunda, Flavia, Maxima and Britannia Prima, the capital of which was Cirencester. And that, ladies and gentlemen, was how your history began.' He bowed. 'Now who claims that we are ill-matched?'

I said, 'It began a thousand years before that, sir,' and they turned their faces to mine. 'It began before the Romans and Saxons, even before the Celts, when the Iberians came from the east, from Pola and Treviso, Rapallo and Tarragona, in Spain.'

'Good gracious,' cried Cowbum. 'If time permitted ...'

'Time does not permit,' said Penelope.

'Take him away!' shouted Dewi.

'Give him Gran to get rid of him,' rumbled Ifor, grinning.

'Where is she, then?' asked Sharon. 'Oh, isn't he marvellous!'

My father went to the foot of the stairs, crying, 'Mother, Seth is waiting!'

No reply. The house tingled with silence. Dada said, 'I expect she's packing. I will fetch her.'

Now there was a great commotion of finding coats and hats, and we thronged out into the moonlit yard, and I remember that there was a scent of burning pine in the air from the night fires of the vagrants.

The stars were like little moons over the mountain when my father came back to the yard.

'Seth!'

We turned to him, stricken by the urgency of his voice. Dada stood in the doorway, hands clenched, his face pale, and we stared at him as he said, quite simply:

'My mother is dead, sir.'

His voice echoed strangely in the night. Mari gripped my arm, leaning against me, and my father added:

'She is sitting in Granfer Ben's chair. She is holding the mantel clock he left her. And she is dead.'

# 25

GRIEF is ill-remembered.

I could cant and cry down by here, but I will not. I could write the whole rigmarole from the lying-in and night-watches with candles to the incantation via floral tributes, and the end would be the same.

I had a lover, and she died.

My father had eleven pounds ten in the tea-caddie, and he spent eight pounds fifteen of it. We buried her with ham and cloves, which was the way she wanted: we had every neighbour and friend in the community to see her off—also enemies: from Dai Half-Moon and Alehouse Jones Pugilist to Betsy Small-Coal and Rosie Carey minus Alfo, by Dewi's special request. We had Seth Cowbum and Penelope and Miss Jane Williams of Aberpergam House; Eli Cohen came with his harem, also Mr. Ephraim Davies and Blodwen. Richard Bennet came down from Nanty with Mam Mortymer, and Tomos Traherne officiated at Zion, Resolven. She went on manse cloth in varnished oak with brass handles, two each side, and one fore and aft, and with Granfer Ben's black mantel clock ticking at her feet, which she once requested. She was officiated by Hobo Churchyard, and laid out by Mari.

Not even Gran would have asked for more.

And Seth Cowbum wept at the gave in shuddering grief, and had to be supported.

But my father, who had known her over forty years, he did not weep, though some others did.

But all the tears are wept now, this autumn; all the pillows are dried. Strange is grief: really self-pity, when you get down to it. Yet nothing could fill the void of our emptiness, no rallying of the spirit, no dogma of common sense could make us whole again.

Empty, we were, in the Old Navigation.

Do you know this emptiness?

By night the Rheola moon hunted in the windows; by day the August sun warmed us: yet we were as people dead: living, talking, moving, we were not alive, because she had gone from us.

We took her up to Zion, Resolven, on that hot day in June, two months back. And it seemed to me, standing there bare-headed, listening to the lovely Welsh of Tomos Traherne, that two small arms of earth reached up to embrace her as they lowered her into darkness, beside my Gwen.

And my gran was not the only one to leave home that year. Six weeks after she died Sharon dressed herself up in frills and fancies, and a coach full of Swansea Players waited on the road above Crugau Farm, and we came in a stream from the Old Navigation, loaded with a trunk and baggage, with Mari and Rhiannon very damp with lace handkerchiefs, and at the last minute Sharon got a touch of the vapours, which was the right way to go, I suppose, she being an actress, though by the standard of some of the long-haired randies she was travelling with she would more likely become a mother. Actors and actresses I do not particularly hold with, there being too much hand-kissing and bowing for my liking, and long hair on men tends to make me suspicious, while from men with perfume, like these, I would run a mile. Although, there is no general rule in this case either, apparently, since the biggest outing Dewi ever took was handed him by a lace and powder pansy with golden hair on his shoulders and smelling of ashes of roses, the first thing he smelled when he came round.

'Be a good girl,' said my father, embracing her. 'And if you fail in this, come back to me, for me and the family are your friends.'

We stood above Crugau—Dada, Mari, Dewi, Rhiannon and me, and watched the coach and four galloping along the top road towards Rheola.

And my father wept, I remember. For the death of his mother he did not weep, but he wept for the going of his beautiful Sharon, his rose.

That night, in kitchen dusk, my father said, 'Soon we will go from this place, I think.'

'Aye,' I said, at the bosh, just off shift from the Gwidab level.

'Nothing to keep us here now,' said Dewi, elbows on the table.

Stripping off my shirt, I added, 'You seen the ceiling in Sharon's room? If Rhiannon coughs twice it will be down round her ears.'

'And there is a crack in the front wall you can put a fist in,' said Mari.

Kneeling at the bath before the grate was she, stray hairs lying on her sweating face, having just swabbed Dewi down—all but his back, and now awaiting me. As I tossed my shirt away Rebecca came in with Ceri in her shawl and sat by the back window, staring down the track that led to the dram-road where Ifor would be coming. Silence was in Rebecca; the calm and quiet of her generations dead lay on her face: only her eyes spoke at times, great and liquid, like black orbs in her brown, high-cheeked face.

'Oi, missus!' I said, and jerked my thumb, and she turned her great eyes in my direction and looked at me as Jez must have looked at Jehu, and she did not go.

'You ready, boy?' asked Mari.

Black as a sweep, I was, just a sambo, with great white rings for eyes and mouth. Last week I had come under a fall, working with Ifor in a heading when a plug dropped, and Ifor yelled and pushed me clear, but a rock splinter fractured and tore my hip, and every night now Mari dressed the wound, three inches long and gaping. Night after night, it was naked in the bath with Mari, for there was no other way to do it, with her at me with a brush, scraping out the dust and poison while I chewed on a rag.

Six weeks now I had been down the Resolven drift and it seemed like six years. Dada said, glancing up from his newspaper:

'Away upstairs, 'Becca. Any fainting in here will be done by Bryn, please.'

'Too thick between the ears,' said Dewi, still chewing. 'Where there is no sense there is no feeling.'

'Come on, come on,' said Mari, waiting on her knees.

'Still got my trews on.'

'Then take them off, man.'

'Not decent. Rebecca is still here.'

Dewi said, 'Got a special. Got it cheap off the hucksters down Neath. Hinges, it do, in the middle of his back.'

'Please do not be vulgar,' said Dada.

'Oh, Bryn!' cried Mari. 'In, in—'Becca is not interested.'

Not much. I swear Rebecca was watching me in the window while I got into the bath, and it do strike me as awkward that men are expected to parade naked in front of matrons and sisters while Hell would pay rent if you asked them to show an inch of ankle. Dewi said:

'Did you go to see Mr. Lyons today, Dada?'

'Aye. Starting Monday, I am.'

'What you think of Lyons?'

My father shrugged. 'A coal-owner. You can tie them up in bundles of ten, but he is paying a shilling over the odds.'

'He gets it back in his Company shop. Did you try for pay in cash?'

'Was it worth trying?'

'A worker is entitled to the coin of the Realm!'

'Tell that to Queen Victoria.'

I said from the bath, 'You can get cash if you ask for it, but it will cost you five per cent.'

'What is that, for God's sake?' asked Ifor, coming in. 'I know the five, mind, but that per cent part do beat me.'

'Shilling in the pound,' said Dewi, drinking.

'Ay, ay, *bach*!' Bending, Ifor hit me sideways. 'Being bathed by aunty, is it?' He held my chin, making sweeting noises. 'There's beautiful, my baby.'

'Do not be bloody daft!'

Dada said, 'Lyons is not alone, mind. Every other coal and ironmaster in the country is at it—when the cost of coal on world markets goes down the price of food goes up—it is the law of supply and demand.'

'It is a bloody scandal,' said Dewi, fiercely.

'Do you think we might have a few less bloodies?' said Mari, at me with the brush.

'Oh, Christ,' I whispered.

'And a little less of that! *Duw*, what a house!'

'Rubbing holes in him you are, woman,' rumbled Ifor. 'Here, *bach*, take another bite,' and he took a knot in the rag and I bit, sweating cobs.

'Moses' tablets he has got in here,' said Mari, 'and they have got to come out. Oh, my precious, I am dying for you,' and she kissed me, and started brushing again, her fingers red. 'Convenient, mind, to have a Truck Shop in the village.'

'It would be convenient if the goods were cheaper,' said Dewi, sparring up.

'Can I come in?' cried Rhiannon, knocking the door.

'No,' I cried back.

'Aye, let her in, Mari,' said Ifor. 'What is wrong with a bit of bares?'

'Educational,' said Dewi. 'She's got to know some time, see?'

'Do not mind me,' I said, 'bring in the whole damned village.' The room began to shift around me, and I gripped the bath.

'You all right, boy?'

'No.'

'Good lad, here is another piece,' said Mari.

Dada remarked, 'If the goods were cheaper than the Tai Shop and Sam Jenkins Ton, it would not be a Truck Shop.

241

You pay in cash at the Tai or Ton and the cost comes out the same.'

'And Lyons collects the double profit,' said Dewi. 'The anti-Truck law was passed by Parliament fifteen years back and we've still got bloody Truck Shops—what do you make of it?'

'It is quite simple. There is one law for the English and another for the Welsh.'

'Oh, no, Dada,' said Dewi, 'that is wrong. If you want to know what they do to their own, you read the reports coming out of Lancashire.'

Distantly, I heard Mari say, 'Mostyn, I think Bryn is going out. Will you come by here and steady his head?'

Excellent was Mari when it came to this kind of thing, she having learned the art of chop and sew from her sister-in-law up in Monmouthshire, she said, and with no doctor in Resolven it was up to the women: only like doing ribs of beef, really, she used to say, but this version do make a great deal more palaver.

Now, later, there was a thinness in us, for autumn had come and gone in gold-dust and sepia and great flocks of migrating birds had wheeled over the Vale before October. Skinny is God, I think, that he do not issue autumn all the year round; sitting on a golden throne, with a charcoal burner under His waistcoat and sending blustering winds and ice and sleet down on us. Winter came, and they slept on the burning slag-heaps of Dowlais for warmth, and died of sulphur: under Neath Abbey the scare-crowed vagrants died, including the eldest of Betsy Small-Coal, which left her with the baby. The riff-raff of the navigators died in the culverts of the embankments and were pulled out feet first, stiff as ram-rods, for it was a blue-nose, coughing winter, this one, with the earth hammered into iron and the thatched roofs of the cottages all over frosty and sparkling white diamonds. Ragged and wheezy the trees of the cut and the alders began creaking rheumatic and asking each other where the hell spring had got to, with the ice-breakers thundering their steel prows down the cut, tumbling the little glaciers before them, and the great English drays straining and skidding under the lash, and one tore a hoof off outside the Old Navigation, and even the railway saddle-tanks were spinning their wheels on the Hirwain gradients and shouting for extra sand and double-headers. And the double-headers put an end to the Old Navigation, opening her wounds wider, bringing down the bedroom ceilings, kicking away the foundations of the out-house.

When the first, weak rays of spring sunlight filtered over a frozen country and the great Van Rocks of the Beacons lifted their shining heads to the distant trumpet of the sun, we were finished in the Old Navigation, and we knew it.

'We are going from here,' said my father.

'Not before time,' said Dewi. 'It is falling round our ears.'

'When are they coming for the barge?' I asked.

'Any minute now.'

'Man Arfon, more than likely?'

My father said, frowning up the cut, 'God in Heaven, he do not have that much cheek!'

'You do not know Man Arfon,' said Dewi.

Hobo Churchyard arrived late, which meant he was sober. A very good friend was Hobo, attending on the family for corpses and removals, but he could be greased lightning also, after a few good quarts. Like in the snow-drifts of the winter of '39 when he sledged the vicar down Ponty mountain: sitting on his chest, was Hobo, and whooping like a Cherokee Indian, with his top hat in one hand and a flagon of gin in the other, doing eighty over the hedges, they reckoned, and the vicar with flowers under his chin and not even screwed: the fastest trip of his life, said Dada.

Dada said, now, 'We will be better off in Big Street; play fair to Mr. Lyons, he has given us a house.'

'For which he is receiving rent,' said Dewi.

'A bit crowded, though,' added Mari, 'two up, two down.'

Tethering Nell and Jed, I went into the bare kitchen and up the stairs, instantly smelling Gran's lavender. Here, back in the kitchen, was the leaded grate with its firing irons, the snow-white counterpane of the hearth. Here, out the back, was the rusty tin bath hanging on the nail; there the cracked seat of the earthly throne, and watch yourself on that, Dada once said; the sheaf of the *Cambrian*, dated January 1856, hanging on string behind the door. Now the smells of dinner, the dismal sop of the drying-up cloth, the sud-frothing copper on wash-day Mondays. A house, to me, is a ship tossed on the endless sea of human emotions: its walls are the bulwarks, the kitchen its galley, the attic is the bridge.

'Bryn, you there?' called Rhiannon. 'Man Arfon is coming. Quick!'

'God help him,' I said.

Large as life came Man Arfon, thumbs in his trews, with the swagger of a man in triumph. And with him came a bodyguard of four—two tough railway men and two bargees—Tub Union and Beef O'Hara, who knew the time of day.

'Well, well, Mostyn Evan—off directly, I suspect?' asked Man Arfon.

'That is correct, sir,' said Dada, and I groaned within, knowing this mood.

Instantly, Mari said, 'Late already we are, Mostyn; don't keep Hobo waiting, eh?'

'When we have finished this transaction,' said Dada. 'You have come for the barge, Superintendent?'

Very plum was Man Arfon today, done up in riding breeches with a crop, a gentry waistcoat canary yellow and brown gaiters. 'Aye,' said he, 'I 'ave. Dear me, Mostyn Evan, there is a tremendous pity—bringing a fine barge like that all the way from Cyfarthfa, and now got to sell it.' He stolled up and down the wharf, kicking it.

'A tremendous pity,' repeated my father. 'You have the bill of sale?'

'Aye, by here—all three copies, and I have the money, too—sixteen pounds?'

'That is strange. I have the fourth copy, and mine says nineteen.'

'*Diawch!* There is queer. Must be a clerical error.'

'It will be,' replied Dada, 'unless I receive nineteen pounds.'

'Sad at leaving, Mostyn Evan?' He drew closer, slapping his gaiters with the riding-crop.

244

'Aye, man, sorry in my heart.'

'Put your every penny into it, eh? but the foresight was lacking, you must agree. Very strange, I was only thinking last night—you get me booted out of Merthyr as a sub-agent, and I land up here as a superintendent: you leave to make your fortune as a private contractor, and end up as a collier. You know what you lack, Mostyn Evan?'

'Tell me,' said Dada.

'Economic anticipation. Well, there is a lovely English sentence—economic anticipation. Don't it drip off the tongue?' He beamed. 'It do make all the difference, mind, for we are living examples. Either you got it, or not. If you have, then you finish at the top, like me. If you haven't, then you end like you, on your arse.'

'Mostyn, for God's sake,' whispered Mari, drawing near to him, but my father only grinned wide.

'The money now, sir, if you please,' he said, and held out his hand.

And Man Arfon pulled out a purse and counted nineteen sovereigns into his palm.

'Thank you,' said Dada, and turned. 'You there, Dewi?'

'Aye, Dada.'

'The money is paid and we take nothing lying down. Mari, take Phiannon and go and find Rebecca.' He tapped Man Arfon's shoulder. 'Bryn, you have always wanted this one, you have got him now. Tub Union is mine and he is going on an outing. Dewi—the railway men are yours. Anyone spare in the next ten seconds can take this fat fool O'Hara,' and he moved, pulling Man Arfon towards me as I let fly the hook. And as Arfon staggered back, shrieking, I saw my father bend at the waist, shuffling in, taking Tub Union square with fist after fist. One moment country-quiet, next it was bedlam, with Man Arfon on one knee shrieking like a stuck pig, and I dragged him upright and fetched him another and the two railway men galloping knees up and popping on the end of Dewi's boot, and in seconds he was back and into Beef O'Hara, fighting soundlessly, the image of my father with his Welsh, hooking stance. They succeeded in nothing, they took everything, simultaneously dropping cold: Tub Union moved once, rising on an elbow, then fell flat again. My father stood over him, licking his knuckles.

'Where's that other bastard?' he said.

'By here.' I was holding Man Arfon up by his waistcoat and I tossed him against my father. 'You do him,' I said. 'It is like beating up Rhiannon.'

And my father seized the superintendent by his leg and shoulder and raised him high above his head and walked slowly to the canal, and stood there, poised, with Man Arfon ten feet up and screaming like a woman.

'By God, there's only a few of you,' cried Dada, 'but when the Welsh come trash they stink of the gutter. Economic anticipation, is it? Aye, well here is the damp variety. There is more than one way of ending up on your arse, Man Arfon,' and he stooped and threw him high and he fell, spreadeagled, arms flailing, into the canal.

'Excellent,' said Hobo Churchyard. 'Do I raise the corpses first, Mostyn, or do you prefer the furniture?'

'Big stuff on first, and mind you go easy with the dresser. Dewi, Bryn—fetch the bedsteads, then the table and chairs. By God, we will wash our hands of this accursed railway. Back to coal where we came from, for the love of God.'

'Sixteen Big Street, Resolven!'

The sun was high when we trundled the hearse away up past Crugau and along the road to the Biben Inn and took left over the river and into Resolven. Past the canal loading bay we went and along by New Inn, with men raising hats at the hearse and women dropping curtseys; up past the Square to Lyon's Row, and down to Number Sixteen where our women were waiting, and people were hanging out of windows and gossiping in doors and look what is arriving now, good God.

A new life: a new village with a name that stood square to the world, its chin hazed with the blue of manhood, with hair on its chest and a hook in either hand.

*Resolven!*

THE TOP TOWNS began to smoulder. They went on fire seventeen years back with the rise of the Chartists, said Dewi, and we shall rise again.

Dewi was right, I reckoned, probably for the first time in his life.

Like a giant hand laid on Wales, the valleys of the Rhondda, Merthyr, Aberdare and Rhymney clenched their fingers into a fist, inwardly seething to the inrush of the new labouring population. The great famine rushes were being repeated and the starving Irish were again being landed secretly on the coasts and begging their way to the new industry of coal. In came the south-west English, the over-spill tin-miners of Cornwall, the Staffordshire specialists, the sawn-off timber-fellers of Yorkshire and Lanarkshire: from all points of the compass they came for coal, marching in battalions down the Welsh lanes, and the coalmasters cornered them, divided them, flung up mile after mile of little terraced homes, and housed them, and then drove them underground on a seventy-hour week at one and a penny a ton, tools and candles found. The Mines Act of fourteen years back which outlawed female and child labour was flung overboard by the very men who made it, and the Truck Shops, closed by the same law, were re-opened. In the glow of the new get-rich-quick, foundering under the raw potential of flesh and blood, the owners sank coal pits on every side, deeper and bigger: new drifts were driven into the bowels of the country and the coal hewn out and trucked and barged, regardless of safety precautions, and the slag and rubbish that accompanies blood on coal, spilled towering tips and dumps over the blazing land. Ignoring social conditions, the owners shafted and dug, broke into old workings and exploited them, cut wages to increase profits and cut each other's throats in a razoring competition for rail and port and barge. And, doing so, laid acres of white headstones and new cemeteries where once was pasture. The child labour again sagged at the ventilation doors; special dwarfs were employed in the three foot seams, the eight- and ten-year-olds of a new generation, their spines set into crippledom by crawling underground, and a new generation of mothers hauled and bucketed under Glamorgan and Monmouthshire and gave birth at the face. And the obscenity is, said Dewi, that those in high office who once opposed these wrongs are now the leaders of the new merchant aristocracy. And not all merchants, either. Among them, a root of the cancer, was the old Welsh gentry, the ninety per cent traitors to the cause of the Welsh, whose ancestors had fussed and fooled with the English for favours since the iniquitous Act of Union: the gentry clergy who put on collars back to front and invoked the name of God in support of an English Church and Throne: the gentry magistrates who cried their disgust of all things Welsh, and sentenced men like Shon Shonko in a foreign language. Let their names be written on the scroll of Welsh dishonour, said Dada: let their lackey social jumpers and tame historians bolster the crime with lying pens and tongues—the Lingens, Symons and Vaughan Johnsons of the dirty books of 1847.

'Excellent,' said Dewi, 'I didn't know you had it in you.'

'I am sick to death of what they are doing to my country,' said Dada.

'Then what are you going to do about it?'

My father said, 'Better men than me have tried, and failed. Remember the Chartists?'

'Aye. And I tell you this, they got closer than you think,' replied Dewi. 'If God had not been on the side of the masters, as usual—if an officer and twenty men had not been in the Westgate, the government of Britain would have been run from the tap-room of the Coach and Horses, Blackwood. If it had not been for a man in a glazed hat . . .'

'What kind of hat?' I interjected.

'A glazed hat.'

Mari, sweeping up the grate, sat back and wiped stray hairs from her sweating face. '*Duw*. I've seen some hats in my time, but never a glazed one.'

'A spy, sent special down into Wales, to make the Chartists move before their time . . .'

'You ever seen a glazed one, Mostyn?'

'Oh, Christ!' whispered Dewi.

'And watch that language!' Finger up, she rose, the image of my gran in her wrath, and her beauty still turned every head in Resolven. 'And let me tell you this, Dewi Evan—God is on the side of goodness in the outcome, remember that.'

'It would not appear so,' said Dewi, bitterly.

'Oh, boy!' she whispered, gripping his hair. 'Do not tear yourself to pieces for people. The owners are rich and we are poor. What do you expect your dada to do?'

'Fight.'

Mari shut her ears with her hands and closed her eyes. 'For Heaven's sake give us a rest from it. I lost one man to the Chartists, would you have me lose another?' Bright and fierce were her eyes.

'If needs be,' said Dewi softly. 'What do you expect men to do—sit on their backsides and whine? Every damn Sunday you go on your knees to a Tory God in a working-class hell, and this is why you've got these social conditions.' He got up from the table and wandered the room, hackled, thumping his fist into his palm.

'Gently with Mari, lad,' said my father.

'Force must be met with force, violence with violence!'

'My God,' said Mari. 'I wonder where I have heard that before?'

Silence. Very uncomfortable, with people loosening collars and smoothing pinafores: first time Dewi and Mari got stuck across each other. I winked at Rhia over the white, starched cloth, and she lowered her eyes, great black circles in her face, and the colour flew to her cheeks: amazing, it is, how women can read thoughts.

Not much time to bother with the politics, me, save that I knew the owners were a shower of sods. Twenty-one come Sunday, me, and in need of a wife; and so full of life that I could have put my fist through the carving on the top lodge, Rheola, and not skinned a knuckle. Personally, as far as I am concerned the bloody politicians can stuff themselves under glass with aunty's feathers, and the Chartists, Lodges, Unions and Scotch Cattle can assist each other individually, with broken bottles. Chasing the women more in my line, bending the men over five foot eleven, no quarter asked and three pints made one quart, one in each hand. The only reason why I didn't slip down to see the Black Welshman now he was lodging at Pentre was because I reckoned he was past it. I topped Dewi by a stone and Dada by an inch. Not really room for you in by here, Mari used to say, sweeping up the kitchen, hold your legs up: the place for baby elephants is under brattice-cloth tents: out, *out*! said Rhiannon. I winked at her again.

A terrible effect this do have on them, mind.

Said Dada, watching me, 'Do not pester Rhia.'

'And a good example he is,' said Dewi, jerking his thumb at me. 'With the place sliding from under him all he can think of is ale and women.'

'Ay ay!'

'Thick as iron, he is—solid from the hat down.'

'Aye, man, you like to try me?'

'Any time you like!'

'Now, now!' cried Mari, finger up.

So I winked at Rhia again, and she went all cuddly and wriggling, and I could see that though she was red round the chops she was giggling inside. This is the way to get them, mind, when they start giggling.

'Will you behave yourself?' asked Dada, getting up.

Eh, dear me. Gorgeous is life.

*Darro!*


Mind, although I loved that Old Navigation I loved this Big Street in Resolven better, for it is good to have people living closer about you, with their smells of cooking in your kitchen and their warmth and sounds coming into your heart. And houses joined together in rows I do like especially, since they are like a gang of colliers going out on a razzle, arms linked in warmth, and here is Polly Poppit's petticoats on the line and there is Dobi Revival's new chapel shirt, and the smoke from the chimneys floats up merrily and the kids are playing hop-scotch and Devil-at-the-window. Actually, I am sorry in my heart for the owners sitting in their company parks trying to keep their loot now they've made it. For it do beat me how they expect to find human beings under all those starched shirt-front and crinolines, and when you get rid of all the palaver and rigmarole they go to bed for loving and babies just the same as us, though they would never admit it. Amber and gold is a good home-brew and excellent for the bowels, as is widely known, but all after-dinner port is good for is sparking toes on merchant bankers, says Dada, and serve them bloody right, says Dewi.

Give me a street of colliers, you can keep the mansions. Very exciting things happen down our Big Street, Resolven, and the same sweet wind that blows on Mr. Lyons, the owner, blows on us. But he do not get the dinner smell of Mrs. Pudding's steak and kidney, or see the smile on Da Point-Five's face as he shuffles along on his leather thigh-pads to bow good morning to old Sam Tommer, the overman, every day of the week.

' 'Morning, sir,' says Da Point-Five. 'Thank you, Mr. Tommer.'

' 'Mornin', Da,' says Sam, 'do not mention it.'

For when the bell-stone dropped two years back and pinned Da to the thighs, old Sam came up with an axe, and cried, 'The roof will fall in the next two minutes and it'll take half-an-hour to get you out. Do you want to live, man, or do you want to die?'

'Chop me clear, Foreman,' said Da, and Sam threw him a rag to chew on and chopped him in half, staunched him in the heading and carried him clear, and the next minute the stall went down.

'Best friend a man ever had, though he's English,' said Da. 'Took guts, see.'

Aye, wonderful things happen in Resolven. Here comes Moses Up, the sidesman, walking with Davey Down, the undertaker, in funeral black, never apart; lodging in the same bed with a bolster down the middle, respectable. Fine folk, these, and always ready to assist the community in a positive direction, said Dada.

' 'Morning, Moses!'

'Good morning, Bryn Evan. Off on shift, is it?'

'Ay ay! 'Morning, Davey Down!'

251

'Good morning to you. Very healthy you are looking, all four of you!'

'Healthy as little fleas.'

Usually pretty glum was Davey Down, which was natural, I suppose, considering his occupation, and he had never been the same since the cholera didn't get south of Crugau. Also, times were skinny for Moses Up until the new Zion went up in '63, this one being only twenty by thirty and holding a handful. And rumour had it that Mrs. Hanman, the big Staffordshire puddler, was keeping them both for six shillings a week and them only eating on alternate days, with Davey on the egg and Moses doing the bacon.

Bright the sun that spring morning, going on shift, and our boots clattered on the flags as we went up the Row, and the little gardens set neat and trim, different to dirty old Cyfarthfa. Mrs. Thrush Morgan is singing in Number Thirteen, giving the tonic-solfa a going over while she makes the beds for her two Irish lodgers Tim Dunnit and Bill Blewitt who are down the level on nights. Disappointed for the Swansea opera, was Mrs. Thrush Morgan, and now inflicting it on us, and any more of this and I am writing to the Inspector of Nuisances, said Dada, for I cannot bear sopranos who are sharp in the higher registers. Now he added:

'I hear that Siloa Congregational, Aberdare, expelled a sidesman for trying to break a strike? Hefty, the colliers are coming up there, isn't it?'

'They are not even started,' replied Dewi.

'They say half the congregation are Scotch Cattle, you heard?'

'You can never tell with the Cattle,' said Dewi. 'They get in pubs and pulpits.'

'Bombing blacklegs and breaking arms, is it?' asked Ifor.

'For working on when the Union says stop.'

'There are no Unions,' I said, 'only mountain meetings and benefits and lodges.' One all sides there was talk of Unions, but I had never met one.

'Because Unions are outlawed, that doesn't mean you haven't got them,' answered Dada. 'The South Wales Ironmasters re-formed theirs last week.'

252

'Flogging and burning their mates?' I said. 'If these are the Union boys you can give me the Benefits.'

'One day you will learn that the the heroes of the working classes are the Scotch Cattle,' said Dewi.

'Aye? Then let them come down by here and try it.'

On, on, up the mountain road to the level, with the dew sparkling on the short, green turf, Dada and Dewi in front now, then Ifor and me leading Nell Mule and Jed Donkey, whom we worked at the face. With my father employing little Bill Softo as mule-leader, this gave us three drams, and Lyons covered his wages in the standard three sovereigns a week we got in tokens. Ne need for Scotch Cattle in Resolven, for we were making our fortune with a four-man team, and although Lyons took your boots he didn't reckon to skin your heels in his shop, which was better than some I could mention. In two headings we worked—Dada and Dewi in one, me and Ifor in the opposite. We would take it in turns, Ifor and me, in face-cutting and pillars for one while his mate packed the roof, and every so often Bill Softo would come in with Jed or Nell and draw out the coal one side for the engine house and the slag for the tip. Doing better these days, and sleeping in the barn at Crugau with a sheep called Daisy, who was his friend, and every Friday Mari would hook him in to our house and feed him a meat meal to drop a rhino, and I had heard that odd times found him with his boots under Mrs. Hanman, and with Rosie Carey still hugging him to the ample breast, little Biflie, now thirteen, wasn't doing so bad.

Up on the track to the level Dobi Revival was doing his washing, soap to the elbows in his tin bath, and he called to us as we passed, crying:

'Blessed are those who walk the path of righteousness, for they will sail to the throne of Heaven as a white dove flung into the sky by the hand of God.'

'Ay ay!'

' 'Morning, Dobi!' cried my father.

Very hairy, was Dobi Revival, Chinese moustache and revival beard, and his fine hair in shining waves to his shoulders: every Friday morning Dobi would be washing out his

253

smalls on the mine level, greeting the colliers coming through, and it was harps and clouds or molten fire with Dobi, and no in-betweens.

'See now!' cried he, holding up a dripping shirt. 'Are your four souls as white as this, Mostyn Evan?'

'I doubt it,' said Dada. 'Please to let us pass, there's a good man.'

But Dobi barred the way and bared his chest of rags, crying, 'There is a guilty conscience in every sinner's breast!' and he gripped me. 'Like a tinderbox, it lies. And Heaven will strike a match and the soul will flare in torment for everlasting!'

'Oh, give over, man,' I shouted, pulling away.

'Strange, nevertheless,' said Dada, 'how Dobi can select those most in need.'

'It is a democracy of the purse and privilege,' said Dewi, pushing Dobi aside. 'It is a God uncaring, one worshipped by the insane.'

'Watch it, man, watch it!' warned Dobi, soapy fist raised high.

'You watch it,' said Dewi, 'or I'll head you into your own bloody washing.'

'Poor soul, pity him, Dewi,' said Dada.

'You are now to enter the bowels of the earth!' cried Dobi, standing in his bath. 'Filth on you, Dewi Evan, filth indeed! May Baal reach out fingers from the old workings and blister you for the blasphemy, may you sink to your bowels into the lower regions.'

And we went down the dram-road followed by threats and clods from Dobi.

But it was not all coal and politics and religious insane.

There were barge outings and country fairs and patsais and decorating the graves at Easter, and with Richard Bennet dug in up at Nanty now that Sharon had gone for the acting, there was, for me alone, Rhiannon.

*Rhiannon!*

The main trouble, I find, is that in the business of living together it is not the eating that matters, or the chapelling, the strolling, the talking; it is the sleeping together that do count for a lot, and no nearer that than I was some seven years back when I first marked her down for this performance. Most ladies, I find, being blessed with certain possessions, do tend to hold on to them, which I think is a pity, for things as beautiful as these ought to be shared. And there are some, like Jane Rheola and Rosie Carey and Cushy Cuddlecome, who have the right idea in this respect, and when it comes to sharing, most men can show women the way home; like splitting a plug of tobacco or an eating-tin, or a quart. And apparently, it isn't any good asking politely, as Dai Central Eating discovered when courting Tegwen Harriet. Frisky as a spring lamb was Tegwen, that day on the road to Tonna, according to Dai—going all girlish and chase-me-sailor, which naturally gave Dai confidence. But when he popped the question, she lay back, opened her shoulders and hit him boots up into the heather.

Unfortunately, the women I come across tend to the same view, with Rhiannon no exception. Very severe about herself was Rhia, and although she did once draw the curtains on that afternoon up on March-Hywel, she had changed her mind since, with a lot of slapping and shoving and how would you like somebody doing this to your sister, which is guaranteed to set any chap back a mile, for the thought of anyone even contemplating such a thing with Sharon I find absolutely disgusting.

It is unhappy being marrying age, with parents saying 'Don't you dare' and every woman in the place threatening to lay into you, to say nothing of pastors and preachers wagging their fingers and threatening hell fire, although these don't seem to miss a lot as far as I can see. And even if you did manage to collect a Jane Rheola or Rosie Carey or Cushy Cuddlecome, and came unstuck, all the God-fearing got up off their knees and put out the flags and declared it a Roman holiday.

Lately, in the absence of anything else, Polly Poppit, the new English girl, was lying on my pillow, but only in dreams. Very ample was Polly Poppit, bright fair was her hair, and very dimply when she smiled, but Dai In and Out beat me to it and laid siege to her one warm night in September. But he got the street wrong, did Dai, and also the date, apparently, when he climbed through a window one midnight and laid his

255

head on Polly's chest. And he got the number wrong, too, for when he woke next morning he was sleeping on Mrs. Pudding. Naturally, this caused a stir, for it is coming to something if virtuous ladies like Mrs. Pudding cannot sleep with their windows open without characters like Dai In and Out climbing in and curling up on their chests.

At this point it is only fair to point out that Dai In and Out is so named because he spent most of his life in and out of the Bottle and Glass on the road to Neath. People took note of it. Not good enough. What is right for the Bottle and Glass is not necessarily the ticket for Mrs. Pudding, though I must say she's been smiling ever since.

'Why?' asked Rhiannon.

'Just thought you'd like a walk, that's all.'

'What for?'

Never had she been so beautiful as on that particular May day, all dished up in pink and white, with the sun burnishing her hair, and there was a merry flavour in her I could taste on the tip of my tongue, it being my intention to eat her alive given half a chance and the flutter of an eye.

'Where to, then?' she asked, looking pert.

I said, 'Oh, lovely it is walking up the Bont, along Sarn Helen.'

'When a boy's face shines, look behind his ears,' said she.

'Nobody's going to murder you, woman!'

'It's not murder I'm scared of.'

'You coming, then?'

'Ay ay. But put one finger on me and you will not see me for dust.'

Got the prettiest girl in the Vale; got summer in all her beauty; got eight pounds in the tea-caddie for marriage, but got to wait until December, according to Dada. 'You cannot marry on a penny less than fifteen pounds ten,' he used to say.

Fifteen pounds ten. Might just as well be fifty. Can't wait. Along the lane that led to the mountains I took Rhia's hand in mine, and there was a need in me to be one with her. In a place of white blossom we stopped in the heat of the climb, and I hooked my arm about her waist and her lips were red when I drew from her, and her hat fell off, I remember, and she stood gasping in my arms and staring, having never been kissed like that before, so I kissed her again.

'Eh, I do love you, Rhia . . .'

'Loose me,' said she, pushing. 'In several pieces I am; mad apes are about on Sarn. Time for dinner, is it?'

But she did not mention this again as I stooped and lifted her in my arms, and the valley echoed her laughter as I laid her down at the foot of the wild apple tree, and the blossoms showered in the wind, and fell, pink and white about us, and fluttered in her hair.

'Bryn,' she said, like a woman.

Through a rift of her hair I saw the distant Vans spearing a sky of glittering blue, and the great Sarn Helen winding her snake of centuries through the hills of the Roman legions. And I thought that perhaps, in this place, some dark-browed ensign had lain: that the kisses I was giving to Rhiannon had been given by him, two thousand years ago, to a bondmaid Celt or following concubine: that my Welsh Rhiannon, so quiet to my touch, was one whose name was Cleo or Subara.

'Eh, Bryn, my sweet,' she said.

And in the radiance of that day I heard about us the tramp of men whose mothers hailed from Thrace and Macedonia, the white-paved streets of Rome: I saw the majesty of a passing army, and the flood-gates of our youth beat about us in a world of sun and wind and a forging of strength.

'*Diawch!*' said Rhia, sitting up and pushing away.

'What is it?'

'Dear me,' said she, 'that was a near miss. What do you think I am, man, iced cucumber?'

'I am sorry,' I said.

'I am not,' said she.

All the sounds of the earth were about us now; the sigh of the wind from Brecon, the showering petals, the larks high above us: down in the valley by Walby an ox lowed bassly and there was a smell of milk from the farms. And beside me lay Rhiannon, as if sleeping.

Bending, I kissed her, and what began in tenderness ended

257

in quick breathing, because I loved her, and I could not let her go. Here, I thought, but for the evil of money, we would go, Rhiannon and me: in this place of loveliness we would run, with the sky for a roof, free of the stain of coal, the scream of the trapped foot, the mangled hand. And at night, in the red glow of a cave fire, we would be as it was planned we should be, united in this gift of love, which men deride and elders call shameful: and there would be no conscience in this union, no accusing fingers, and nothing of tears.

'*Cariad* . . .' she whispered.

I heard the sound of her not on the hills of Sarn, but from across the sea, before the world was ice: I heard her amid the savageries of Gorizia. In this woman I knew delight. In a penned marriage by capture she spoke again, and her breath held the perfume of musk, which I have smelled before in the market place of Treviso: lithe was she, and quick, and her arms were swift about me as once before, when her garments were gold and her sheets saffron. There was a little woman of my blood, I remember, and she had no breasts, and she died young. How beautiful, then, this woman under the stumbling hands of my childhood. Darkness was in her face, her mouth was sweet to mine, my friend and companion.

And I knew her on Sarn Helen as I had known her before on the blood-stained marble of Corinth, before the coming of the Goidelic horde.

And now the sun blazed about us, the sheep called from the Mellte, and when I opened my eyes from the dream she was yet one with me.

'Oh, God,' she said, and her eyes were wide and startled.

I held her in strength, and she said, 'Bryn ... you said strange things; you spoke in a Welsh I did not understand.'

'You were dreaming, Rhia.'

She said, her face turned away, 'Now we are in trouble.'

'More than likely.'

About me the land was flowing with a new brightness. Fan Lia was rearing skyward; Pen Milan of the crags was trumpeting in sunlight, and away to the east the pennants of Glas Forest were stained with red. Rhiannon said, her lips against mine:

258

'I do not care, for I love you. You are my man, Bryn Evan. I do not care.'

I put her face against mine, and held her fast.

# 27

COME autumn, the old River Nedd was alive and swirling with trout, and the salmon so thick at the weirs that they were rubbing their fins off. Folks were strolling innocently through Resolven with two-foot tails sprouting out of the backs of their collars and the women were dropping aniseed in the gutters before boiling salmon, for the bailiffs had six-inch noses when it came to smelling out the poachers, and houses were being searched for gaffs and nets. More than one went to transportation from the Vale, since God has laid it down, according to the Church of England, that salmon belongs to the gentry and is far too good for the working classes. Old Shon Seler Shonko, for instance, he got another seven years from a gentry clergyman, although Mari and my father travelled to Swansea Sessions to plead for him, for poor old Shonko was spiders between the ears without a doubt. But he went to transportation just the same, swung aboard the prison hulk in Swansea docks like a scarecrow linnet fluttering in a cage.

'Goodbye, mistress!'

'Goodbye, Mr. Shonko.'

'Going back to my old gran,' he cried to Mari. 'Don't you worry about me, missus,' which was true enough since his old gran was whipped through the streets and taken in chains to the plantations nearly a hundred years ago, for stealing a six-penny petticoat, in the Christian town of Haverfordwest.

Sent on the Grand Tour by a clergy-magistrate who owned the water, and that was the end of Shon Shonko, and Mari wept, I remember, her apron to her face, in great sobs, for she loved old Shon, and she would not be comforted.

But happy things happened, too, that particular autumn.

Old Mrs. Scales in the Truck Shop was sent down the road by the mine company, and nobody wept over that: Ifor made another little seed-cake in his beloved 'Becca, and how he managed this I shall never know, since he slept with me and Dewi in the back bedroom. Number Sixteen was a decent little house, mind, and a palace to some of the shacks up The Top, with Mari and Dada in the room next to ours and Rhia, Rebecca and Ceri downstairs, there was only one room left for living and eating. I can see Mari now as she opened her arms to Ceri on the afternoons when Ifor was off shift:

'Come with your old gran, is it, precious? Come with me and I shall show you beautiful things, and a bag of sweets, too, from Mrs. Scales? And your mam and dada can have a little stroll up the mountain?'

And Rebecca of the flaming hair and dark face would raise her lovely eyes over the table at her husband.

And I can hear my father now, 'Mr. Lyons has done us well. The rent is low. But it is just not big enough for three families. When we get a bit more in the caddie we will shift from here, and get another bedroom, for it is not good that a family be divided.'

He need not have bothered.

Aye, in came September and set herself up on Resolven mountain with her spinning-wheel between her knees and wove great carpets of gossamer over the hedges, and the thick-eared fraternity were out every morning gathering it into match-boxes for cuts: cold and damp those misty dawns when we went to the mine, and the grass brushed back our boots and the rushes and spears gobbed soap-suds over our trews. Always, on these glorious mornings, I would take great chests of the strong mountain air, before going into the swirling dust of the mine, and I was never one for the pipe. I recall my gran used to say, 'If God had meant you to smoke he would have put a chimney on your head.' And nor do I care much for the chew and spit, believing this to be a dirty habit, but Dewi was not so particular. With Ceri in my arms I took her to the top of the Row for sweets, and Dewi spun up a sixpence, and I snatched it.

'Pick me up a plug, man,' he said, so we went into the Truck, my Ceri and me, while Dada, Ifor and Dewi dawdled up to Zion.

'Good God!' I said.

For Rosie Carey was behind the counter, not Mrs. Scales, and she was like a flower, even at that time of the morning.

'Came last night,' said she. 'Took over from Mrs. Scales. Does Dewi ever come to buy?'

'Outside now just,' I said. 'Shall I fetch him?'

'No,' said she, proud. 'Do not fetch him. Tell him that Alfo has gone to Coventry and I would not go with him. If Dewi Evan is interested, he will come in here, but tell him that I am second best.'

Lines of weariness were telling round her eyes, the matron of her thirty years having raised her knocker and come in, and Alfo Morgan, with Blodwen's till in his pocket, reckoned them that much sweeter under twenty-five.

'Mrs. Alfo turned me out,' she said then.

'Less than you deserved, Rosie.'

Deep she sighed. 'Not much good, am I?'

I shrugged. 'A plug of Raleigh for Dewi and a ha'peth of tiger-nuts for Ceri by here. One thing about it, at least we'll get the right weight.'

I saw her against the shelves, the bottles, the cheese-cuts, and saw that she was bright to tears, and with a great sadness. She threw in a nut for luck, which was more than you'd collect from Ma Scales, and I once stood with Ceri for five minutes while she sucked one to make the weight, the old sod.

'Ifor's baby, is it?' she smiled at Ceri now. I nodded, and she said:

'You come to Auntie Rosie, for a little minute?'

Ceri buckled and shifted in my arms, turning her face.

'Sorry, Rosie,' I said, taking the sweets and tobacco.

She smiled brilliantly, her head back. 'Kids are my trouble, I expect. Down by here, in this shop, I'll get hundreds.' She held herself, saying, 'One day I will have one, you see, Bryn Evan. One day.'

'More than likely. Thank you, Rosie.'

'To help me—you will tell Dewi?'

'Aye.'

'You reckon I'm worth having, boy?'

'No, ma'am.'

'At least you are honest.'

'Aye, but some don't agree with me,' I said, 'Billie Softo, for one.' The bell tonged like the toll of doom for Rosie as I went through the door, and I saw in the mind of my heart a tiny, drab room with a sacked window, and Rosie sitting there waiting to pay the rent, and her hair was white and her face aged, and past her window thronged the ghosts of her hundred lovers.

I put Ceri down and told her to run and the others were tapping their boots and where the hell have you been, outside the Tai Shops.

I did not tell Dewi as I gave him the plug: no business of mine. People have to sort it out, like me: up to them, their comings and goings, their sadness and their loves. I'd have handled it different, had I known what was coming.

Billie Softo, talk of the devil, was harnessing up Nell and Jed Donkey as we arrived up at the engine, and he was naked to the belt in a set of ankle-length pink drawers, with lace round the boots. He looked like a Turkish Delight but with nothing at the top, and seeing the spacers I froze with fright.

'Very attractive, Softo,' said my father, 'when did you collect them?' and he fingered the material, nodding approval.

'Couple o' months back, zur,' replied Billie. 'Found 'em up on Sarn.' He grinned at me with a naked mouth. 'Under a wild apple tree, they was, and blowin' as large as life.'

'Dear me,' I said, sweating, for you could never tell where Billie Softo was directioning from minute to minute. Dada said then, thoughtful:

'You know, Dewi, I could swear I have seen these spacers somewhere before.' He rubbed his chin, frowning.

'Put a sovereign on it,' replied Dewi, and Ifor said, reflectively:

'Mind, spacers do arrive in very queer places. You remember Randy Bandy, over at Cynon?'

'Like my brother,' said Dada.

262

'He reckoned he saw a muslin set going over Neath at two thousand feet followed by flying bandsmen on trombones and tubas, and one leg was yellow and the other purple.'

'Couldn't 'ave been this pair, zur,' cried Softo, merrily, 'for these is pink, see. Ah, a fine lady and gentlemun come up to Sarn, an' I did see 'em, and they left him special for me, Billie Softo.'

'You know this lady and gentleman, Billie?' asked my father.

'Oh, ah!' Wide he grinned at me, landing me a wink.

'But you must not tell their names, Billie—you understand?' He took from his pocket a sixpence and put it in Billie's hand. 'There now. But if you tell that lady's name, I will take it from you. You promise, man?'

'Ay ay!'

Molten lead it would be for Softo the moment I got my hands on him, and Dewi said idly, as we walked to the mine, 'You get about a bit, boy—you ever seen those pinks on a fireguard?'

'Do not talk daft,' I said, sweating cobs.

Mrs. Willie Shenkins was basketing at the door as we went into the level, sobbing as she hauled the baskets on the skip, and her coal-black face was riven with tears.

''Mornin', Mrs. Shenkins,' I said.

'My little Willie's working down Two Heading, you heard?'

'Aye,' I called.

'Mr. Lyons very pleased with him, too. Strong as a horse and twenty-one yesterday.'

'Send him happy birthdays,' cried my father, and added, 'She is a different woman, mind, since she brought him back. Good morning, Mr. Morgan!'

'Ah, Mostyn Evan!' Mr. Thrush Morgan on his haunches in the six-foot stall, and cutting happily with an Irish lad packing and dramming on him, and thank God I am away from Welsh sopranos, for he was only happy when he was in the seam. We stood against the wall as two drams went by and took the turn-out, and behind us came Billie Softo with our four drams and Jed Donkey. Alehouse Jones Pugilist lumbered by on his way

263

to his stall; always worked alone, did Alehouse, and he touched his hair to my father as he went, very respectful.

The gallery shafted here, and my father and Dewi, taking a grip on their tools and candles, turned for Number Four while Ifor and me took Six Heading, which led to the old working where Da Point-Five had caught it.

'A word with you, Bryn?' called Dada, lifting his candle-tack.

'Now?'

'No—any time—say first hour. Eight o'clock, by here?'

'Aye.' Cool the draught as Haf Benyon, aged seven, pulled the vent door, and cold on my sweating face, this sounding official. Sweet and bright was Haf's smile in the light of my candle as she sat there with her rag doll, the last of Mrs. Ten's brood, before Man Arfon's; but Owain and Cynfor, her big brothers, always worked her stall and would not let her from their sight, to their credit.

'You all right, precious?' thundered Ifor, bending to her and stroking her face, and she beamed at him, for all the mine children loved Ifor and he always carried a sweet for them; kneeling, stroking their faces upwards, like now.

Through the door and into the heading, and we crawled past Owain and Cynfor, the long and the short of it, for Cynfor had never topped five foot and he was well into the seam with his brother wedging the props.

'Come on out of it,' I said, slapping his leg, and he eased himself under the roof, gasping.

'Watch her. All bloody night she's been moaning.' He hit up with his pick haft and the coal trickled.

'Safe as a bank,' said Ifor. 'Heave over, Owain, that hole won't take two of us.' And Owain gave him some dirty old back-chat and wriggled out and Ifor wriggled in, saying, 'Tell Softo to open through—he should be here by now, what the hell is he up to?'

'Wait, you,' I said, and Ifor crawled off and sat on his haunches by the pillar, and I lighted my candle and clayed it on a board. Slipping down into the hole I smelled for gas, and it was strong. Gwidab was a good level, being damp and shallow, and although many of them got it on the chest, few died of this. But she was a bugger for damp in holes, and it had to be cleared.

'Is Haf clear of the door?' I called to Ifor.

'Aye.'

'I'll fix this. Keep Softo out.'

Ifor grunted reply, so I coiled the rope and wound it on my arm and pulled the trap over my head, then reached up and pulled the candle forward, shielding my face. The gas lit instantly, running a red flame round the face, and ended in a dull explosion above me. Rocks and stones showered on the trap.

'Right, Ifor,' I called.

He came on all fours towards me down the shaft, coughing and spluttering in the smoke, like a great, white bear coming to devour me, and he said:

'You'll bloody kill yourself one day, doing that.'

'Maybe,' I replied, 'but I'm not breathing gas.'

'That's what Da Point-Five said, and now he's got no legs.'

'Get in and cut, man, and think yourself lucky.'

'First ton for my 'Becca,' said Ifor, and spat on his hands, and swung.

Up came Billie Softo then, his face through the vent door, his candle flickering red shadows on the face. I cried, 'You shift your arse, Softo, or I'm kicking it up to Glyn.'

'You boot me, mister, and I'll tell 'em what you left up there by the Bont!' He cackled, then, holding his sides, boots waving.

'What's he laughing in doubles about?' gasped Ifor, spitting.

'You get on with your cutting.'

The last thing I do, I'm braining that damned Softo.

We drammed out after I took a run, and Ifor packed the roof and the pillars were solid, and this was good. Some colliers reckoned to shave the pillars that held the roof, but not me. You want coal you get it off the face, old Sam Tommer, the English overman, used to say; Lancashire or Wales, makes no odds. You shave the pillars and you've got trouble; any collier shaving under me goes down the road. And Sam was right. Gas-flashing he did not mind, and if he wanted speed he would thin out on the props, but the coal stayed fast in the pillars. I crawled out and cried, 'Softo, come in by here and pack for Ifor, I'm going up the heading.'

My father was waiting for me up in the gallery clear of people, sitting on a fall, long legs thrust out, smoking in the light of his candle.

'Ay ay, Dada.'

He motioned with his pipe, saying, 'Sit you down, lad, I want a little word with you.'

'Yes, sir,' I said.

Taking his time over this one, and I saw his face square and strong in the light of the candle. He was over fifty now, which was young for a collier, for there were some turned eighty—men like Cobler Johns—still working on the drams. But coal was taking its toll; his cheeks were marked, where the pit was cutting its pattern, his hair was white at the temples, and although he had not been down long, the dust was taking his chest, though the muscles of his back and shoulders bulged and knotted to his every movement.

'Time you were wed, son.'

I closed my eyes as the blood leaped into my face, and was glad of the dark.

He said, 'You reckon Rhia will have you?'

'Maybe.'

'You'd better find out, eh? If you take too long over it she'll more than likely line up another. You love her?'

I was sweating like a Spanish bull now, for I knew what was coming. 'Yes, Dada,' I replied.

'You pick and choose how you like, lad, but I want you up at Zion. May be you won't be so lucky next time. Next time you take some piece up the mountain and somebody peeps, it won't be Billie Softo. And where does that land a decent girl like Rhia?'

I raised my face to his and the drams went by in rattling thunder within inches of us, and his eyes did not falter.

'How much you got saved?'

'Ten pounds five.'

'I'll knock this up to fifteen ten, then you can wed—no, I'm not having any more of these biddings, I've only just finished paying for the last one. When will you speak to her?'

'Tonight.'

'Right.' He rose. 'And now, no more of these mountain hops, Bryn, you do youself no justice. If you are going to make Rhiannon your wife you shouldn't be up the Bont sparking another.'

I did not reply, and he said, 'You don't make it easy—standing there saying nothing. You know what I'm trying to tell you?'

'Yes, Dada.'

He wiped his mouth with the back of his hand, and said, 'Save the rough stuff for the men—gently does it, lad, when you go with the women. God made them with His left hand, remember, so they are weaker than us.'

I nodded, thankful for the darkness.

'And don't try those tricks on a lady like Rhiannon, or I am having a hand in it—you understand me?'

'Yes, Dada.'

'Now away back to the stall and get those trews off Billie Softo or you will never hear the end of it.'

# 28

WITH the rest of the day shift we came down the mountain that dusk—Dada, Ifor and me, for Dewi had left straight for Nantyglo for a Lodge meeting, and could not spare time for tea. With tools clanking, we came down past the brook and the Tai Shops into Big Street.

Lovely, it is, to live in a street, I say, with all the excitement of the men coming home and the women sitting outside their backs and handing out all the cheek in the world. Smoke from the chimneys stood as straight as bars and the air was perfumed with the scent of burning pine, and the mist was falling with September over the Vale. Children were playing

267

hop-scotch along the flags, the wizened granmas framed their dried-prune faces in the upstairs windows in toothless smiles of greeting, and ailing granfers crossed their boots and cocked up cheeky clays and nods.

This is when I love my people best, when the family is two hundred.

Have a peep in Number One. Here is the top dog, old Sam Tommer of Lancashire, sitting in the tin bath by the fire, like a Chinese joss, all bald head and stomach, blowing at the suds : there is his skinny missus, a shin-bone in black stockings and a face for chopping fire-wood, and not very fond of the heathen Welsh, being a cut above them, really, as wife to the overman. Mean as a razor and twice as sharp was Mavis Tommer, and every night when poor old Sam came back from the Vaughan after his glass, she would march him up and down the kitchen flags bare-footed, for some unknown reason, and this very bad for his arches, as Polly Poppit used to say. Dai In and Out was skidding along to New Inn with his seven o'clock penny; trying hard to cut it down, and all credit to him, but you could tell the time by Dai with his pint every hour from six o'clock to chuck.

'I didn't realise it was so late,' said Dada, consulting his watch, and he knocked up his hat to the Truck. 'Good evening, Miss Carey.'

'Evenin', Mostyn Evan. Seen Dewi, have you?'

'Just slipped up to a Lodge meeting, Miss Carey, but back later tonight.'

Anxious and worried looked Rosie. 'You told him, Bryn?'

I nodded the lie. Dada said, 'Nice to have you in the village, Miss Carey.'

'Welcome, I'm sure, Mostyn Evan.'

On, on down the Row, with women hanging out washing, pegs in mouths and shouting banter and others carrying steaming pails for the kitchen baths, men stepping out of trews behind neat lace curtains, starched clothes being flapped on the table for tea. In the window of Mrs. Hanman, the gigantic Staffordshire puddler, Davey Down is spooning up the stew, scrag end from Eynon Shinbone in the Tai, while Moses Up watches glum, it being his turn on the bread, and hoping for a sop. Jane Rheola is leaning against her gate, hands on hips, eyes under her fluttering lashes, lips pouting red, for Meic is on nights. Mrs. Thrush Morgan is sitting Dafydd on the White Rock again, and got him a semitone under the top G sharp, and I saw my father's agonised face, with Tim Dunnit and Bill Blewitt sitting entranced, either side of the piano. Mrs. Pudding is chopping suet on her board; cherubic and comely, Lovely Tom Davies is chopping sticks; starched up and bottled in Ancient and Modern, Mrs. Afron Shavings and Mrs. Tref Hopkins are off for hymn practice, hating each other, arm in arm; Mrs. Ten Benyon is changing her baby, safety-pin in mouth, and say what you like, says Mari, she is a wonderful mother.

On, on, boots thrusting out, abreast we go, Dada, me and Ifor, and as we reach the gate Ceri comes tumbling out and runs into Ifor's arms and he swings her high in booming laughter, kissing her face.

'Got soldiers in our house,' says Ceri.

'We got what?'

'Wait.'

Da Point-Five was reading the *Cambrian* on the flags and he turned up his ravaged face to the sun.

'Steady, Mostyn.'

'What the hell is happening in there?'

'Routine questioning—easy, man. Nobody is being executed . . .'

Ifor said, cold, 'When . . . when did they come?'

'Two of them—an hour back. They slipped in like mice, and I'm the only one who saw them. Dewi, they're after.'

'By God, I'm not taking this,' said my father, and screwed up his hands, striding away, but Da hung on to a boot.

'Cool, Mostyn, cool—it is the only way. You lay a finger on one of them and you'll be in Brecon barracks by sunset.'

'Da is right,' I said, gripping my father. 'Easy does it.'

We followed him down the back and into the kitchen.

Mari, Rhiannon and Rebecca were sitting side by side, and Ceri ran to her mother and Rebecca lifted her on to her knee, and she sat there, wide-eyed. Standing before them was a Brecon sergeant, and there was a great size to him, resplendent in his red and brass; he was young, his face square and strong and his eyes bright blue in his tanned face. Behind the door as we opened it was a soldier of the line, his musket held loosely before him. My father said:

'What the hell are you doing in here?'

'You are Mostyn Evan, the father of Dewi?'

'Have you permission to enter this house?'

The sergeant said, and I admired his coolness, 'You are the tenant. Permission has been given by Mr. Lyons, the landlord.'

'Now I am here you will need mine,' said my father. 'What you want to know you will ask outside, or do you make a trade of frightening women?'

'Oh, Mostyn, for God's sake!' whispered Mari, broken.

'Outside if you prefer it, Evan,' said the sergeant. 'We can parade the Row, if you wish, but thought you would like this done quietly.'

'We will bolster the neighbours, man. I have nothing to hide.'

They went out the back, the sergeant leading, and I felt Ifor tense his body as they passed, and I gripped him. 'You stay here with 'Becca, man.'

'Like hell,' said he, and followed us outside.

Out the back quick, and now there is a to-do, with every kid in the Row staring through the gate, fingers in their mouths, and the neighbours hanging on the fence like string-beans, and it is astonishing to me how much washing needs pegging out in these predicaments, and windows going up and doors coming open and what the hell is happening in Number Sixteen? The sergeant said:

'Your son lives in this house, Evan?'

'He does.'

'Where is he now?'

'I saw my son last an hour back on the Gwidab dram-road.'

'And why did he not return here with the rest of you?'

'My son is twenty-seven. Does he have to account to me for his every movement?'

'Do you know where he has gone.'

'I do not.'

'Do you?' The sergeant nodded towards Ifor and me. Dada said:

'Neither do they. I am head of this house and I speak for my son.'

The Redcoat smiled and shifted his feet. There was about him a quiet authority more usually found in their officers, and he was not without charm. He could have handled this in a much more brutal way, for he held the power of life and death over the Welsh workers. In the Top Towns, where the owners called in the military to break a strike, I have seen the Welsh flung out of their homes, their women man-handled. Time was, in Crawshay's Merthyr, when a troop had only to cut a dog in half to get obedience, or hang an innocent Dic Penderyn. But the Bread or Blood riots of '31, and the rise of the Welsh Chartists in '39 had changed the face of their authority. Yet they still demanded instant loyalty to their puppet Queen, and this, usually, was the test of Welsh fidelity. The sergeant said now, 'You are aware that your son is a member of illegal organisations?'

'If he is, then he is responsible.'

'The Chartists, for instance.'

'According to the *Cambrian*, they do not exist.

'And an anti-Truck society up in Aberdare.'

Dada grinned. 'He ought to get a medal for that. Didn't your own Parliament outlaw Truck nearly fifteen years ago?'

'It is an offence punishable by transportation to be a member of a Scotch Cattle herd.'

'God help him,' said Dada, 'he appears to have had a busy time. I wonder he managed to do a seventy-hour week. Look, man, we are tired. Say what you want of us, and go.'

'Dewi Evan.'

'Then name a charge.'

'There is no charge. He is wanted for questioning.'

'On what grounds?'

'The death of a black-leg up at Abernant.'

'That is not special, soldier. They are dying every week.'

'In the death of this one you think your son is not implicated? Perhaps you are right, but it is your duty to tell us where we can find him.'

271

'I have no duty to you,' said my father.

From the gate Da Point-Five called, 'Careful, Mostyn, in the name of God.'

The sergeant straightened, and I knew him instantly for a trainee officer: no fool, this one; he had carefully laid the trap, and we knew now what was coming. This was how they divided the patriot Welsh from the traitor Welsh. If they wanted a man for questioning, and could not get him, this was how they took the hostage. The sergeant said, taking out his note-book. 'One last question, Mostyn Evan, and be careful how you reply. You agree that you are answerable, on oath, to the Queen, to whom you owe allegiance?'

'I owe allegiance to none save my Welsh Prince,' said my father, 'and he died at her hands six hundred years ago.'

'Excellent,' said the sergeant, replacing his note-book. He nodded to the soldier by the gate. 'Take him,' he said.

'Mostyn, you fool,' said Da Point-Five.

Mari wept, and would not be comforted.

And on the third day after his going, Ifor and I waited outside Brecon Barracks, which was the place of questioning, and the gates opened and closed and my father stood there on the cobbles. His eyes were blackened, his lips were split, but there was no weariness in him.

'Is it well with Mari?' he asked.

'Aye, Dada,' I said.

'And Dewi is not home?'

I shook my head.

Ifor cried at the gates then, his fists high, 'You bastards, you bloody English bastards!'

'There is no point in rubbing it in,' said my father. 'Home now—come, Ifor—home, the three of us.'

We took the road to Sarn Helen, and we did not speak again, as far as I can remember.

## 29

NEXT April blossomed into May and the Vale flowered in petals of pink and white, with the big sweet chestnut up by Crugau showering its beauty of the generations and the lime trees in their seventh year flower: along the cut the bluebells swarmed, and even the primroses, normally shy of humans, blazed their yellow clusters on the banks.

And Dewi did not come.

Up in Blind Shoni's field on the road to Tonna the bees were going demented; lambs were cartwheeling in the meadows of Rheola and rams playing leap-frog. Bright as a barber's pole was that month of May, and the redcoat troops painting it up, their scarlet uniforms moving into the valley, though it was amazing how many bent nails they found on the roads. Brass bands were playing on market-days, one even arriving in Resolven square outside The Ton, come all the way down from Cyfarthfa to happify the Welsh, but it is astonishing how quickly a couple of kids sucking lemons can put paid to a set of bugles, trombones and tubas.

Off shift, my father would stand by the window, looking over the fields.

'Not seen hide nor hair of him,' whispered Rosie Carey.

'He will probably come to you first, Miss Carey. You will not keep him to yourself?'

'Not much good, perhaps, Mostyn Evan, but I would not come between father and son.'

'God bless you, woman.'

Rebecca said, putting her stomach on the table, 'Sorry in my heart for that woman, I am, mind.'

There was, between Rosie and Rebecca, an affinity.

Very flourishing was Rebecca with her second, and Ifor fumbling and fussing her, and mind the corner of the grate, love, in case you injure the brain.

'Same as everything else,' said Rebecca. 'What you don't 'ave you don't miss, but you go short of a fella and it do bring you broody.'

'It is one way of putting it,' said my father, blowing his tea.

'Gets right up my nose, it do, the way people treat her.'

'A bit up to a dream she is, though,' mumbled Ifor. 'Always mooning through the window. Quack-quack daft, I reckon.'

'The only one who is quack-quack daft is you in by here,' said Rebecca, sawing at the bread. 'Honest as an oat-grain is Rosie Carey, which is more than I can say for some I could mention.'

'No need to get nasty,' said Ifor.

'Aye? Well, there's no call for it. A sod you are, calling her daft!'

''Becca!' said my father.

'There you are, then,' said Mari. 'That is over. No quarrelling, you two, when you have so much to love.'

'Stuck up damned virtuous, he is,' said Rebecca. 'Before I tinged his nose he was sowing his boots all over the country. Men are all the same. One rule for them and another for people like Rosie.'

'Dear me,' said Ifor, glum, 'you do go on, don't you?'

'A lot of damned old soaking about virtue and motherhood, and off to New Inn to kill the quarts.' She added, 'And the first yard of skirt . . .'

Which was a bit unfair, for very temperate was Ifor these days, with nothing more than ten pints or so at a sitting, and as far as I knew he was on the tack on garters.

My father said, 'Hush it down a bit, if you please, 'Becca.'

'Don't know what's got into her these days,' grumbled Ifor.

She began to cry then, did Rebecca, in great heaving sobs, her apron to her face, and immediately Mari and Rhiannon were up and about her, whispering and comforting her, but she was in a hell of a state with her red hair down, cheeks scarlet and soaking, with Rhiannon sending Ifor looks to kill though he had scarcely said a word.

'I do not want this baby!' shrieked Rebecca.

My father rose. 'Hush, Rebecca!'

Ceri began to cry now, trying to climb on her mam, and Ifor took her on his knee and she fought him, screaming.

Damned good tea, this one, with women bawling and men shouting, and there, to my horror, was Dan Double-Yoke standing out the back with the milk from Crugau, as large as life, taking it all in. Three pairs of twins had Dan Double-Yoke.

'Oh, God!' sobbed Rebecca. 'I do not want this baby!'

'Dan Double is outside, mind,' I said.

I give the family credit. Whether it was weddings, motherhood or death, nothing could dry us up quicker than handing it to the neighbours. Rebecca mopping up now and everybody on their feet clearing the table and 'Good morning, Dan Double. Beautiful day, isn't it—different from last week—ridiculous weather for May—no shape to it. Only three eggs, is it?'

'All I can spare, Mrs. Evan—running down on hens, see. The cock got bad feet—rushing round for eight years, chasing the widows.'

'No need for the details, Dan,' called my father.

Very stitched up was Dan Double, and butter would not melt in his mouth, and his long, thin face half-soaked; but he managed to tickle up the women and Mrs. Pudding used to roll round shrieking when Dan got loose.

'Aye, Mostyn,' cried he, 'but the cock 'ave got to be dominant, see, or the girls go off the lay. How's your system, Mrs. Evan?'

'Healthy as a flower, thank you, Dan Double.'

'And beautiful!' He pinched Mari's cheek. 'All over blooming? *Ach*, oh! Give me girls knocking forty, and ample. All sizzling come summer, after a little bit of sun.' He danced Mari in a circle, his hat held high, and did a hobnail hopscotch on the flags.

'Right,' said Dada, coming out the back. 'We have had enough of you.'

'Eh, Mostyn Evan, for shame! Would you bury her alive?' He flung out his hands to Mari, eyes closed. 'The eggs are free, woman. Just give a thought to old Dan Double if this one here is taken prematurely. Wide, wide would I fling you into a universe of men. Seen Dewi, have you?'

'If I tell you that you'll be as wise as me,' said Dada.

'Lots of people looking, though.'

Night after night the redcoats wandered through the street, and very interested, apparently, in Number Sixteen.

275

Dan went, bowing backwards through the gate and blowing kisses to Mari.

Rebecca, I noticed, was smiling again.

Sick and tired to death of the carrying. God, I pity women: I reckon Eve must have been up to worse tricks than Genesis booked her for in the Garden of Eden, for the serpent has been at her ever since. Mari said now, holding Rebecca:

'It is a difficult time, Ifor. She will be all right soon. Try to understand.'

'Aye,' mumbled Ifor, who knew nothing of such things.

At least he kissed her when he went on dawn shift with Billie Softo.

Dada and I were working the nights, so we stayed at home.

'Thank God she kissed him,' said Mari.

Looking back, it might not have happened had Dewi been home and the shifts stayed normal. But with the heavier stall of the two, Dada linked with me, and left the inside one for Ifor, Billie Softo and Jed Donkey.

It was a mistake, for there wasn't two ounces of brains between the three of them.

Alehouse Jones, who was in the next stall, said it was a bellstone. Manuel Cotari, the Italian, said it was a face-slip that trapped them first, then took the roof. To this day Owain and Phylip Benyon reckoned that Billie was clearing the gas with a cover board and candle, like I used to do, and the stone dropped as Ifor came in with Jed Donkey.

Whatever it was, it laid sixteen tons on them, and when they roped Ifor's feet for the haul-out he would not come, said Albert Crocker, for his arms were wrapped around Billie Softo.

'She liked that,' said my father. 'Miss Carey liked that. . . .'

In the coal-blackness of my dream, I heard Rhiannon's voice from the kitchen, and its panic entered my growing consciousness; the room made shape as I slowly opened my eyes and I flung back the bed-clothes as her feet hammered on the stairs.

'Bryn!' She burst into the room. 'Accident!' she gasped.

'Where?' I was stepping into my trews.

I gripped her and we listened, and there was no bell.

My father flung open his door then and came in to me, doing up his shirt.

'Accident,' whispered Rhia, and her eyes, wide and bright, stared at me.

'Where is Mari?'

'Up the Truck. 'Becca is over The Ton.'

'Is it Fach or Gwidab?' I asked.

'Mrs. Hanman has just come down from the Tai. She reckons it is one of the Benyons. Maris Tommer says it is Cynfor.'

'God help him,' said my father.

'That's next stall to us,' I replied. 'But I didn't hear the bell.'

We were downstairs in the kitchen when Da Point-Five put his head through the gate, and shouted, 'Up the Gwidab, Mostyn—you heard?'

'Aye, now just. Did you hear the bell?'

'Not ringing it any more. Bloody thing's worn out.'

They did not ring the accident bell. It saved the panic of the whole village tearing up the mountain. Over at the Cymer colliery last July they had the same, it was said. The fire-damp went round the face, and of a hundred and fifty-six below ground a hundred and fourteen were killed outright and the rest seriously injured, and women and children were lifting the brattice-cloth and screaming, trying to kiss them back. And Cymer was only one. Men were dying in scores; every day of the week women and children went down the pits and did not come back.

So no more accident bell, said Mr. Lyons, and he was right, said Dada: let the stretcher speak, though it has no tongue.

'But old Sam Tommer don't agree, mind,' said Da Point-Five. 'He reckons the women are entitled to the bell, so they could get shawled up and down to the pit. Very musical, too. Two good legs I left under a ten ton bell-stone down the Gwidab, but I got a toll longer than the Kingdom Come.'

'Stretchers coming now,' said Rhiannon.

Mari came running then, her hair down, her eyes wild.

277

Dada said, holding her, 'It is young Cynfor Benyon caught it, and maybe Owain—we do not know for sure. Where is Rebecca?'

'Over at the Ynysfach Inn.'

'Best she stays there,' I said.

It was four of them: Ifor, Billie Softo, Cynfor Benyon, and old Sam Tommer. For Sam caught it half-an-hour later, they said, when he was trying to get the first lot out, and another plug dropped.

They came slow down Big Street.

Ifor came first, then Cynfor, then Billie Softo, and Sam came last because he lived at Number One: four men to each stretcher, they came, in a black procession, and there was no sound but the tramp of their boots on the ruck.

The women were standing outside their backs with their children about them, I remember. Beside Mavis Tommer they laid Sam down, and left him, and she said nothing, but stood with clenched hands staring at the sky, for this was the second man she had given to the earth. Billie Softo belonged to nobody, so they put him outside the Truck for Rosie Carey, and she came out and knelt beside him. Ifor and Cynfor they brought on, and I could hear the women sighing as they shepherded their children indoors, for it was not their turn. Mrs. Ten Benyon, with her brood clustered about her, gave her baby to Mrs. Morgan.

'Cynfor, is it?' she asked, for it could have been any of three others she had down the Gwidab.

'Aye,' said Owain.

'Dear me,' said Mrs. Ten, and knelt, lifting the stretcher-cloth.

On came Ifor, and I bowed my head and splayed my boots on the stones.

Alehouse Jones, Albert Crocker, Lovely Tom Davies and Mr. Herbert the builder brought him, and they laid him at my father's feet, and stood there, empty. Then somebody said:

'It got him on the gob-stone, Mostyn—him and Billie; quick as death.'

'Thank you,' said my father.

278

We stood in an aimless clutch, staring at nothing, and I saw on the slope of the mountain the trees turning up their leaves to each golden rush of the sun.

Mrs. Tommer came up then. She said, 'I got the boards in the house, Mari Evan. You give me a hand with mine, I give you a hand with your'n. Big men, see, in the turning.'

'Yes, Mrs. Tommer,' said Mari.

'Got old blankets, have ye?'

'Aye.'

'Do yours first, shall we?'

'If you please, Mrs. Tommer, thank you, Mrs. Tommer,' said my father.

'I do him,' said Rebecca, and we swung to her as she came up with Ceri.

Mrs. Tommer was kneeling, untying the brattice-cloth, and Rebecca cried, coming closer:

'You leave him, you bloody leave him, Mrs. Sam!'

I picked Ceri up and held her against me as Rebecca pushed her way to the stretcher, and knelt.

She lifted the brattice-cloth and sweat was on her face.

'He's my chap, so I got to do him.'

The wind was warm on our faces: distantly, I heard the clatter of the railway.

'Better get him in, then,' said Rebecca.

# 30

I HOLD no brief for the evangelical Ikes, and I reckon old Tomos Traherne up at Nantyglo was one, but luckily we only needed him for births, weddings and funerals.

God, to my mind, do have a pretty rough time round these parts, and at times He can't know which way to turn, what with one and the other of them.

'Behold thy servant, Ifor!' cried Tomos Traherne that day in Zion when we put Ifor down. 'In all his manhood and

279

purity he lived, attendant on the Word. And now he has flung his goodness into the lap of the Vale!'

This dampened quite a few of them, but not my father, nor my sister-in-law, Rebecca.

My brother Ifor was what he was, and for this I am thankful.

And when he reaches the golden gate of the biggest seat of all, St. Peter will see him coming and uncork a bottle of the best stuff, knowing that only the strong brew would be good enough for Ifor.

In promise to Rebecca, my father took us from Number Sixteen, Big Street, Resolven, in the middle of May, and I was sad.

Sad, sad I was to leave my sweet Resolven.

The trouble with me, I think, is that I fall in love with houses. Damned near in tears, I was, when we left Big Street. No longer would I see Jane Rheola undressing at the window, but you dare not stop for a gaze, of course, or Meic would be out with a chopper, and he once chased Dan Double from The Ton to New Inn, swiping and missing him by inches: very reserved was Dan these days when Jane was in the window. No longer would I see Davey Down sopping up the fat of Moses Up's morning bacon, or hear Mrs. Thrush Morgan sharpening up the Gentle Lark and the savoury, mouth-watering smell of Mrs. Pudding's steak and kidney would no longer go strutting down the street in hobnails.

'Goodbye, Da Point-Five.'

'Ay ay, man. See you later, see.'

Bow to Mrs. Hanman, bow deep to her six-foot-two against the sun.

'Goodbye, Mrs. Hanman.'

'God go with you, Bryn Evan.'

Eynon Shinbone and Evans Brewer, bulging bulbous, stand side by side.

'*Cofion Cynnes!*'

'Aye. Goodbye, Eynon, goodbye, Evans.'

Weeping is Evans Brewer, and God knows why, for I always treated him bad.

Mrs. Afron Shavings and Mrs. Tref Hopkins now, coming with books and music, and Alehouse Jones Pugilist trundling the Zion harmonium down to the square on a hand-cart. And we stood in the middle of them all, my father and the family, and did not speak while Alehouse set it down and Mrs. Afron set the music up and people let fly.

Mr. Herbert the builder was coming with Lovely Tom Davies, and behind them along the Neath Road thronged a great crowd of people. From near and far they were coming: from the tram-roads of the levels, the colliers and miners, the deacons, the drunkards. The bargees were coming, too, rounded up by Ehpraim Davies, the old Cyfarthfa agent, and very poshed up and refined looked Ephraim, with his daughter Blodwen on his arm. And behind the people came the ponies and traps, headed by Eli Cohen and his flaming women, and Eli was up and waving his sticks. Mrs. Willie Shenkins was sobbing and mopping, but rushing round organising everything, and even Tub Union and the bargees—people like Laddie O'Brien, Abe Sluice and Beef O'Hara—were arriving.

'Good God!' ejaculated my father. 'Look what is coming!'

Resplendent in an outsize trap drawn by a brown dray came Cushy Cuddlecome with the Irish Shrew beside her and Ditch Fielder and Bargey Boy, their new fancy men, like ram-rods on the tan seats in brown hats and whiskers. Very done up was Cushy in her big summer hat, built like an hour-glass and blowing with pink and white ribbons, and behind her came the riff-raff of the Cuddlecome Brew, the Irish dancers with melodeons, the wizened Lancashire navvies and the bull-chested Irish: linking arms they came with all their bawdy banter, and even Bronwen Rees with Taliesen the Poet and their three children, and carrying for triplets was my Bron, by the circumference of her and here he is now, and isn't he gorgeous—just think I used to teach him English grammar over at Tramroadside! Aye, and this is his girl, the beautiful Rhiannon! And the fame of our going must have spread as far as the Swansea valley where Brunel was planning the big new railway, for along came old Tai Morlais and Sian on his arm in bright, gipsy colours.

'*Hie,* Bryn, lad!'

'Tai! Sian!'

In they came, fighting their way towards us amid the shoving, laughing swaying of the crowd, and he gripped Rhiannon and kissed her. In came Evans Brewer, rolling a barrel, and the ready navvies tapped it and handed out foaming pewters: in came Mrs. Pudding and Mrs. Dai Half-Moon with plates of cold rice-pudding and Welsh bake-stones, and Albert Crocker and Willie Dare set up on the pavement with a bugle and trombone, with Sam Jenkins Ton on the bass drum, and the morning was split with Welsh airs. There was Bili Ynysbont come from Tonna in case anybody fainted and Mrs. Teague the Herbalist from Cymla, and even Polly Poppit, the English girl, with her husband five foot up and seven stone odd, said Tai, and no wonder she is generous, said Sian, looking gorgeous.

'Serve out the taps, me lucky lads!' bawled Cushy. 'We'll hand them something to remember us by. Everybody welcome at the Cuddlecome, feet up and ale down,' and she stood up in her trap and beat time to the band. Mrs. Ten Benyon came, despite her loss, with Man Arfon's subscription toddling; towering and string-bean came Owain and behind him Tegwen Harriet and Dai Central Eating. Everybody came. I cannot think of one who was left out.

'Sorry to death I am about your son,' said Tub Union, gripping my father's hand. 'Bygones are bygones, Mostyn Evan?'

'Ay, indeed, mart. Met my missus, have you?'

'Ach, yes—that Michaelmas Fair, remember?'

Everybody shoving over for Da Point-Five; rushing around their ankles carrying a plate in one hand and a pint in the other. Tim Dunnit and Bill Blewitt were carrying our furniture out of Number Sixteen, and I noticed a few of the village sorcerers wiping it for quality, and it would be all round the village the moment we were gone.

Mari cried, 'Remember the train is off at half-past-ten, Mostyn!'

To Mr. Ephraim Davies, my father said, 'Sir, this is the

282

wife of Sam Tommer, our overman. She is coming with us as far as Aberdare.'

Lanky and tight-fisted Mrs. Mavis Tommer stood, hanging on to tears.

'God bless you, woman,' said Ephraim Davies, bowing.

'It is a cleaner death than some,' said Mavis Tommer.

Mrs. Isan Chapel was wandering lost, looking for Isan, so I collected her and gave her to Rhiannon. Rosie Carey stood alone; I pitied her.

'No news of your Dewi, Mostyn?' asked one.

'All in good time,' said my father. 'He will turn up, like the bad penny.'

I shouted, up on a chair, 'They even told Seth Cowbum, Dada—look!'

Trotting on a little piebald mare came old Seth, sweeping off his hat to Mari, very gallant, and seeing her eyes fill with tears, I left them and all their tears and laughter, and walked up the Tai, to Zion.

' 'Becca,' I called. I opened the grave-yard gate.

In the Yiddish tongue she was speaking to him; it was the incantation of her race. And she knelt closer to the grave and turned her face to the sky and cried aloud, but she did not weep.

'Going now, 'Becca,' I said, drawing her up.

She said, eyes closed, 'I loved him, mind.'

'Ay, ay . . .'

'I . . . I was a bitch to him at times, but I loved him. You believe that?'

'Yes, girl.'

'God, what a world!' She straightened in my arms. 'Just look at this stomach.'

'Rather you than me.'

'You seen my Ceri?'

'Mari had her now just,' I replied.

Empty she shrugged, looking around. 'Oh, well. Away now, is it?'

'Aye. To Aberdare.'

Heaving down on her knees in grunts and groans, she kissed the earth.

'Got to go, boy,' she said. 'Goodbye, my precious.'

I helped her up. Hand in hand we went down the hill to The Ton.

# 31

LIKE a mighty Pentecostal wind, the Big Revival began sweeping over the mountains that early summer, and as we travelled north to Aberdare it blustered past us down the Vale of Neath.

In a great and unfathomed accord, driven by suffering and new ideals, a harvest of souls began, gathering in small tributaries from the Big Seats of Salem to Bethania, Ebeneezer to Calfaria. Almost every denomination of the Nonconformist Church was involved; Baptist and Congregational, Unitarian and Calvinist Methodist, Wesleyans, Presbyterian and Independent, and others. And the black-clad disciples of God in the new garment trickled from the pews of Zion and Soar, Providence and Carmel: the trickle of tributaries merged into a river and the river into a flood of rhetoric bulging with Welsh *hwyl*: fists raised in barn, cottage, mountain top and valley, the new revivalists poured forth a torrent of words. Led in popularity by the great David Morgan, the wind of Heaven blew like a prairie fire over The Top. Converts flocked to the new cause. The Sunday schools were packed. Banished was the foul game of pitch and toss; prize-fighters became outcasts, drunkards were denounced from crag and pulpit, malefactors were pulled out into the aisles for torments, harlots chased through the streets with bibles and sticks. Hard-liners who had not seen a pew since baptism were now powerful on their knees most of Sunday; wool was growing on the shoulders of publicans and sinners.

Mind, until we steamed into Aberdare station that evening, I was under the impression that the coming Revival was confined to the Welsh.

'I must say I do not see how it can affect the Irish,' said my father.

'Perhaps things are different in the city,' suggested Mari.

'Can't think why we haven't heard more about it,' said Rhiannon, which, as it turned out, was the most sensible remark of the night.

Anyway, with excuse-me-pleases and mind-your-backs and whispered requests for shifting room, we managed to get all the furniture off the railway flats and set among the little crowd on the platform.

'What happens now, then?' I asked my father.

'Wait a bit and get the size of this, for I don't understand it,' said he.

So we stood on tiptoe at the edge of the crowd and listened to the fervent Revival speaker. On the platform roof he stood, a ragged, bearded bone of a man, with flowing hair and wild eyes, and he shouted:

'The dew of heaven is falling among the corn-stalks of Aberdare, sure to God! Do I see a few ears flourishing under the bonnets and hats? Lads and lassies of the great new Revival, the Lord has had a fine time tonight, indeed. For he only catches the wee fishes, d'ye see. It is the likes of us that have to salt them. Am I glowing?'

'You're the brightest light in the city, your honour,' shouted a broad Irish voice. 'You're flaring brighter than the ironworks of Aberaman and including the Gadlys, from here.'

'Could you turn up the wick a bit for us, parson,' shouted another, 'for you're still a bit dim here at the back.'

'Is that so? Then I'll turn me up an inch. Sure to God, it makes me burn the brighter, the things that are happening. D'ye know what? I was up in Higher Miskin this very day outside the Boot, and there was a Welsh friend there crying, "Milk, milk, milk!" And this very week I heard the same chap shoutin', "Cream, cream, cream!"—but that was before his conversion to the true dissenting faith. Now, don't ye think that's wonderful? To be under the influence of the chapels instead of wallowing in the poitheen like us heathen Irish?'

Cheers and clapping at this, from a crowd as ragged and

unkempt as the French Revolution, and a few looked back-teeth-floating to me.

Mari said warmly, 'What a lovely thing to say—Oh, beautiful people are the Irish.' My father said, with business:

'If I bide here all night I will not get the hang of it. Look, Bryn—you stay with the women while I knock up the Lletty Shenkins agent. ....'

'Number six down Blind Man Groping Lane, yer honour!' somebody cried.

'Thank you,' replied Dada. 'And remember,' he said to me, 'don't let a stick of that furniture out of your sight.'

'You want to find a fool in the country, you bring him from the town,' I said.

Rhia sighed. 'Thank heavens for Mr. Lyons, recommending us to the Lletty Shenkins.'

'Don't be too keen till you get there,' I replied.

'Hey, you down there!' shouted the preacher. 'You, the fine big Welsh lad—can ye hear me, son?'

'Me?' I asked, thumbing my chest.

'Aye, indeed,' cried he. 'Ach, may God be praised, there's a wonderful specimen of manhood. Welcome to Aberdare, boyo, for Welshmen are only good Irishmen who have never learned to swim. Aye, a right welcome to you and your pretty women, including the one carrying the tub. Are ye come as neighbours?'

'Aye!' Very embarrassed I felt.

'Then you've landed among friends right enough. For the Irish and Welsh have been Celts in arms since the first landing of the Beast Cromwell at Wexford, and his right hand man, the very same year, knocked off your Prince Llewelyn up in the country of Builth. Am I correct, now?'

'Sure, you are, Patrick, me love!' shrieked a woman. 'Isn't he a wonderful fella on the history o' the exploited people!'

'Which brings me to the point, young Taff. Are ye after shifting your household goods this minute?'

'My father is coming back with a hand-cart, now just,' I cried, wishing him to the devil.

'He's doin' no such thing, me boy,' shouted the preacher, and bawled at the crowd, 'Can we stand here and watch our

286

neighbours trundlin' their goods and chattels—one man and three women, an' us not lifting a finger to help?' Roars and cheers at this, and he cried down at me, 'Where are ye bound for, son?'

'Green Fach,' I said, and could have bitten off my tongue.

'Right, me lucky lads! We'll be delaying the Revival sermon for a bit while we all give a hand with the Welsh furniture—are ye on?'

'Oh, dear,' whispered Mari, 'we ought to wait for Dada.'

I managed to collar the Welsh dresser in the rush, for one moment we were furniture and the next we were Irish, with eager hands lifting the bed and somebody else on the mangle, and out of the corner of my eyes as I jack-knifed under the dresser I saw the commode with the Revival preacher, and it was going like the hammers of hell. And as I galloped along with Mari and Rhia steadying the thing, the tin bath went up one side street and the bed up another, and by the time we were fifty yards down Station Street, all we had left was the dresser. *Well.*

Ten minutes later my father wandered up with his thumbs in his trews, and with him came the Lletty Shenkins agent, a sunflower wearing spectacles sitting on a high, starched collar.

'It would appear, Mr. Evan,' said this agent, examining us, 'that they have met up with our Patrick Revival, the furniture remover.'

Mari said, clutching me, 'You cannot blame Bryn, Mostyn. He seemed such a nice man and he did sound very generous.'

'So shall I,' said Dada, and turned to me. 'If you want to find a fool in the country, you bring him from the town, is it? You big, useless gunk of a Welshman. You congenital bloody idiot.'

'Yes, Dada,' I said.


You have to see this Aberdare to believe it.

I thought I had seen some places up in Merthyr, but Bute Street and Wigan Row where the north country English lived was as bad as anything I had seen up The Top, and Hirwain and Club Row were not fit for pigs—and all owned by Lord Bute. Acres of the bright, clay soil were ponds of human filth: the cess-pits, where they existed, had overflowed and in some houses at Cobblers Row, near the vicarage, the night-soil in the ground floor rooms was inches deep.

People came out of their cottages to watch us as we passed; thin, weary creatures with dark hollows for eyes, and many of the old were shaking with ague in their tattered clothes. Filthy, emaciated children, the refuse of greed, stood in the gutters and stared at the strangers. Two men were fighting in the street outside the Royal Oak, nearly naked, snarling like dogs as they rolled in the garbage, clawing at each other and shrieking oaths.

'Oh, God,' whispered Rhia, and I gripped her hand and hurried her on. With Mari on one arm and Becca on the other, my father picked a path through the indescribable filth, and as we went we were followed by boisterous laughter, with naked children tiptoeing after us, aping our movements.

'In the name of Heaven, what have we come to?' whispered Mari as I passed her.

'It will be better down in Green Fach,' I replied.

'It do sound pretty, don't it?' observed Rebecca.

If you have seen Green Fach in the 'fifties up in Aberdare; if you have smelled Green Fach as we smelled it that summer dusk, you would have known something worse than the slums of Asia, said my father.

On, on we went, the Lletty Shenkins man leading us, and thank heaven we left the dresser in his yard, said Mari, for we would never have got it over the great mounds of garbage. And the inns and taverns were full to the windows, with elbows going up and quarts going down and men and women staggering out arm in arm and the air was split with the shriek of Irish fiddlers and the blast of melodeons and thumping tambourines. In the gutters sat beggars, men and women who were the burned-out slag of the ironworks, the refuse of profit that was shovelled away by the likes of Wayne of Gadlys and Bailey of Aberaman, and all to no end, for his works, built ten years back, was never a success. Here sat the evicted poor of the Bute rents, the crippled young and trembling aged. Here lay the young collier with the broken back, head cradled in his wife's arms; the girl-mother with her baby at her breast. Here

I passed, in tears, a ravaged generation of Welsh who were being broken on the wheel by a system of wealth and privilege that was countenanced by Church and State.

'By the Christ,' said my father, 'I heard it was bad, but I would not have come within a mile had I known it was as bad as this. One day, in return, they will hand us an English prince.'

'Dewi showed us the seven year sanitary report, but we would not believe it,' I said bitterly.

'Now we learn the hard way.'

We went on, nearing Green Fach in a glare of pulsating light, for the blast furnaces of Tye and Bryn David were tapping the bungs and salvoes of hot air rushed about us in dull cannonades, and a pillar of brilliant light shot high into the clouds with incinerating brightness, illuminating the black, forbidding country about us, the lowering hills, the crooked, squalid streets and leaning cottages. The earth beneath us trembled to the shot-firing underground. The wind was acrid with the tang of sulphur.

Rhia said, clutching my hand, 'Bryn, Bryn. . . .'

I gave her a grin. 'A little paradise, girl—wait till you see it in daylight.'


They told us that Number Five, Green Fach had only been up twenty years, but it looked more like two hundred with its stained walls and the piles of refuse at the front and back, with no garden save a pond of stinking cess-pit overflow along its unpaved street, and no light came into the rooms save red flickerings from the distant ironworks, and there was nowhere big enough to swing a cat.

'Take it or leave it,' said the agent. 'If Mr. Lyons hadn't recommended you, you wouldn't get a house at all.'

'The rent?' asked my father, mooching around the crumbling floor.

'Five shillings a week.' His strange, round eyes, bright with the inner fever of his goitre, moved over Rhiannon in quiet assessment.

There was no particular evil in him. The old French custom of *Droit du Seigneur*, of which my father had warned our

289

women, might have died with the French Revolution in France, but it had not died in Wales. Part of the perks of Man Arfon's agency used to be the virgin Irish; this one, apparently, preferred the Welsh. It was a simple question of supply and demand; the English had the money and the Welsh had the women. Masters, sub-agents, even overmen had power over the family. In a world of skin and scrape the weakest went to the wall. Many a Welshman has starved on the drift to keep the virtue of a wife or daughter.

'Did you see the way he looked at me?' whispered Rhia, fearful.

My father said, 'No, Mr. Batey, my women prefer the pit to house-hold scrubbing. In any case, they have enough in here to keep them occupied.'

'As you wish,' said Mr. Batey.

A shadow moved over the window a moment after he had gone.

'Somebody out the back,' said Rebecca.

I flung open the door. The Revival preacher stood shivering on the threshold.

'Is this the house of Mostyn Evan and family, by any chance, yer worship?'

'You know damned well it is,' I said, and reached out, gripped him by the collar and steered him into the room.

'Where is my furniture?' thundered my father.

'Ach, sir, the situation's a wee bit complicated, if ye get me. . . .'

'It will be if that furniture is not back in the next ten minutes.'

Patrick Revival screwed his cap. 'You see, yer worship, a misunderstanding's at the bottom of it. Me friends got the accommodation mixed, and a lot of it's being delivered at various addresses in the town.'

'I can well believe that,' I shouted.

'But if you'll give me a day or two, I'll guarantee to round it up. The commode I've got here, an' the bed I can put me hands on, for I know the fella setting his aunty in it.'

'Oh, my God,' whispered Dada.

'Every stick you'll get back, sir. And what you lose I'll pay for in good money. For I'm working decent shifts down the Lletty Shenkins, Mostyn Evan, an' I wouldn't be missing a shilling a week or so.'

'How do you know my name?' asked Dada, suddenly interested.

Patrick Revival shifted his feet uncertainly. I slammed the back door shut.

'Tell us,' I said.

Strangely, I pitied him standing there in his rags. Hunger and fear was strolling in the caverns of his face and his eyes were large and fevered.

'I bumped into a fella in Royal Oak, and he was sent by your son.'

'My son, Dewi?'

'Aye, sir.'

'You know my son?'

'God in Heaven,' whispered the man. 'Everybody in Upper Miskin knows Dewi Evan, including the military. Didn't ye know he's Scotch Cattle?'

My father turned away to the window. The Irish said:

'There's not much happening round here that Dewi Evan don't know about. He's a power in the land, I can tell ye.'

'Go now, Irish,' I said, opening the door.

'An' there's a price on his head big enough to bury the entire community. What the hell d'ye think I'm doing rushing back with your furniture? It was he who sent the command.'

'Out,' I said.

After he had gone, Mari whispered, 'Oh, Mostyn!'

My father did not move from the window.

'He needs to keep away, then,' I said. 'If he comes round here he'll only land us in trouble,' and Dada turned to me, saying:

'Look at this place. Isn't he right, and aren't we wrong? I say good luck to him, for he's got more guts than the rest of us.'

We did not speak more, but stood there in the dusk of the empty room: things were changing from minute to minute. I had never heard my father speak like that before.

## 32

THINGS changed a great deal for us after Ifor died.

Rhia and I were supposed to be getting married in August, latest, in Zion Resolven, but that had gone by the board. Now it would be Calvinistic Methodist at Bethel, Hirwain. But it does not matter a lot which pew you select, said Mari: you could splice up at St. Joseph's, Mountain Ash, as a Roman Catholic, or stand up in Salem as a Penpound Baptist.

On our second week of working at the Lletty Shenkins, Dada said:

'Buying the old sticks of furniture has set us back a bit, boy, but we will get you and Rhia fixed up the moment we can.'

The four of us off to work at dawn that day, I remember— Dada, me, Rhia and Mari; with 'Becca left behind in Five Green Fach to do the house and cooking.

'She is near her time,' said Rhia. 'Should she be left alone?'

'Rough north country is Mrs. Robinson next door, but a good neighbour, and handy with the deliveries,' said Mari.

'No need for you to come working,' I said bitterly.

'Leave her, Bryn,' said Dada. 'It is what she wanted.'

Mari said, 'Now, what would I do sitting home in Green Fach all day, eh? 'Becca has Ceri for company, and if we are wanted she can run down to the mine. Leave it now, we have been through it all before.'

Either side of the road, men, women and children were hurrying to shift; most for the Abernant blast and forge, others for the Aberdare Iron Company, which, with the Gadlys Furnace Works, were sending every year nearly fifteen thousand tons to Cardiff. Doors were opening and slamming in the panic of the late-for-work, slops were pouring from windows, chambers being emptied in the road. Redcoats from Brecon Garrison were on the cobbles in fours, or lounging on street corners, bayonets flashing in the weak dawn light, while the people of the occupied country went to work.

'Never thought we'd drop to a Top Town pit,' I said, bitterly.

Dada laughed. 'Quite well off as a collier, though. Ten years back a roller was on an eighty-shilling week, now he's on thirty-five, and a railstraightener is cut by more than half.'

'Which is still more than we pick up.'

'That is why you have got to have me,' said Rhia. 'The third dram lifts us to thirty-seven, and we need forty to live decently.'

'Take me below and you've got a fourth dram,' said Mari.

'You stay on top,' I replied. 'Bad enough Rhia coming down.'

The trouble here was that we were paid on the dram system —the more drams per man, the higher his wages, since a cutter could cut faster than his mate filled the trucks. All over The Top about now the colliers were taking their children down the pit, for another head meant another dram. In some pits babies of two and three years of age were going into the cages on their father's shoulders and, once below, were laid to sleep or set to play while older children were put to work on the ventilation doors.

'Things will improve when the Union comes,' said my father.

'When it comes,' said Rhiannon. 'Meanwhile, I want to get married, and there is six pounds seven under the bed.'

Ifor dying had pulled us down. A very expensive thing is death.

'God, what a place,' I whispered.

For wounded soldiers from the Crimea were begging along the road to the Lletty Shenkins mine, their eyes stricken in their riven faces, their tunics pinned at the elbows, their trousers tied with string. We did not spare them a glance more than passing.

With the wages of the colliers the same that day as they were thirty years back, even a glance was costly, and the prices in the coal and ironmasters' Truck Shops were going higher every month, for industry was running down now the war was over.

'Strike action is the only way to raise wages,' I said as we went. 'Dewi said that and he was right.'

'But you cannot use strike action to get an increase,' said my

293

father. 'You strike to resist a reduction in wages.'

In the history of the Welsh coalfields until the year 1871, long after my family ceased to exist in Aberdare, not a single strike of any importance was for a wage increase.

What we did not know as we went to work that first day in Aberdare, was that a strike of two months was about to begin against a fifteen per cent reduction. And at the end of the strike the Aberdare colliers would have to accept a further five per cent reduction to compensate the owners for the losses incurred.

See them on their knees in Chapel come Sunday; see them at communion in Church and wearing out their souls for larger profits: giving sixpenny purses for the Bible Penny Readings and silver purses for the Abergavenny eisteddfods.

Give me pigs and I will give you coalmasters.

A queer old place this Lletty Shenkins mine, and Resolven colliery was a bakestone with jam on, compared with it. Redcoat cavalry were patrolling its approaches; foot soldiers were guarding the entrance to the cage.

The cage faced me.

Drift mines and levels, where you walk into the mountain, I can stand, but ever since I can remember I have been afraid of the cage. I cannot stand the slam of the gate, the sooted cram of the sweating humanity, the sickening drop into earth: down, down to the pin-drop light a thousand feet below, in whines and shakes and rattles. Less chance of getting out, too, come flood or fire-damp. And bad on the chests, especially in Number Two stall where we were working; for every ton of coal we cut we were running out half a ton of gob.

'I am afraid of the cage,' whispered Rhia, and clutched my hand.

'Nothing to it,' I said. 'Stand on your toes and hold up your stomach.'

The colliers shoved over for her as she got into it. Leaving Mari with the croppers on the top.

I watched Rhia's face that morning, so as never to forget it. I traced every line of her, and cut it in my eye.

In plain sack-cloth she was dressed; still beautiful, though her hair was bunned and tied back with string, because of the machinery. Her smock was laced about her neck high, and about her waist was a rope girdle; to her ankles her dress reached, but her arms were bare to the shoulders. Like a pale flower she stood among the Welsh colliers of the cage, though some were hefty Irish and already stripped to the belt, the smudges of coal across the shoulders and the pallor of their faces telling their trade: other women were crammed in, two being the hags of the early seams; as broad and strong as men, these, their faces blunted and brutalised by the orgy of the underground, their womanhood long vanished in the years of dramming and filling. A few little children stood at their fathers' belts, their great, wide eyes staring up at Rhiannon.

'This way,' said Dada as the cage opened at the bottom. With Rhia between us we thronged along the road to our heading with the rest of the colliers in a clanking of picks and shovels, and I watched Rhia's face as we passed the night shift stalls where the fillers were still on; men and women filling drams and packing up the roof to a chanting song of labour, their coal-stained bodies riven with sweat and flashing in the light of their candles. Ike Winchester, the road overman, was standing at the fork in the rail.

'Got another head,' said my father.

'A pretty one at that,' said Ike. Solid good English north country was old Ike, and he spoke like a Welsh, having come down to the industries years back and worked with the navvies on the Pencydrain viaduct, so he had a soft place for us. For six months he held his missus in a six foot culvert, but the second winter chilled her, and she died, so he buried her in Melincourt Chapel and left the Vale, and, like us, came north to Aberdare. My father said:

'Pretty or not, she's a dram, and I want it. Book us a third, Ike. I've got another back home in child, and she's eating for six.'

He smiled at Rhia, his fading eyes suddenly lighting up in his face, and said to me, 'A third it will be, but keep her in sight, son.'

'You watch me.'

'Your little woman, is it?'

'Aye.'

'Keep her out of the dust; women are bad on the dust.'

'It's a wet seam, or she would not have come.'

He followed us down to Two Stall, hands on hips as we stripped off our shirts and crawled under the roof. 'You got gas here, by the smell of it.'

'We have got water,' said my father, spitting on his hands.

'Aye, I noticed—give her a hole, Mostyn.'

'I will do it,' I said, and knelt and swung the pick into the face, and it took, and held, and when I prised it out the water trickled. Ike pushed in his fingers and tasted it, shrugging; there was a difference between an underground spring and the still water of an old flooded working.

'Could be anything,' said my father. 'You know this heading?'

Ike said, 'Not this far. The records don't show. But if there's pressure there you would have had it before now. Pit it and I'll send down a hand-pump. Very wet on the drawers, is it?'

Rhia said, 'Shall I come back with you for the dram, Mr. Winchester?'

He did not reply, so my father stopped swinging, and looked at him.

'No, girl,' answered Ike. 'A special chap is bringing it, but it might be an hour or so.'

'Do not be long,' said Dada, 'and stand away so decent men can earn their money. Rhia, if he's starving us on a two-dram shift, better bring one up.'

'I will help you with the first one,' I said, and I took her up to the turn-out. Against the dram I held her, seeing the whiteness of her eyes in that black place, and there was a taste of dross on her lips when I kissed her.

'I love you, Rhia.'

'Ah!'

'For everlasting.'

'Eh, my sweet one,' she said against my throat.

I held her. In the distant clumping of the ponies of the higher level, in the faint whine of the cage and the iron rattle of the drams, I hold her, and her sack dress was coarse under my hands.

'That must be the deepest kiss in the county of Glamorgan.'

I said, 'The moment we can get a start we will collect another Billie Softo, then you will go from this place.'

'Ach, no!' she protested. 'It is cheaper with me, and we need money for 'Becca. Besides, I have got you down by here.'

I said, gripping her hands, 'Watch the roof. Keep your feet out from under the dram, is it?'

'One coming now—look.' She pointed down the road. A dram was coming in the flickering glow of the lamps. I turned, shouting:

'Third dram coming now, Dada.'

'Do not mind me,' he called back. 'You take your time with the woman while I dig up Glamorgan. What the hell is happening, Bryn?'

'We'll fill the third first—easy on the turnout,' I said, and we hauled the other two out of it while the third came up.

I stared in disbelief.

My brother Dewi was pushing behind it. Reaching out, he pulled Rhia hard against him, then gripped my shoulder in passing. Without a word, he pushed the dram up to the face where my father was picking out.

'Dada,' he said, and stood there in the candlelight.

Instantly knowing the voice, my father threw down his pick without even turning in the stall. 'You have been a long time about it, Dewi,' he said.

'I came when I could. They would have taken me if I had come before.'

'Which is what follows when you spend your life shattering creeds and breaking idols. Do you even know about Ifor?'

'Oh, Jesu,' said Dewi, his head bowed, 'do not talk to me about Ifor.'

'Sorry too bloody late, isn't it?' I said, coming up with Rhia.

'Oh, *hisht*, Bryn!' she said, holding me, and he jerked his thumb at her.

'Did you really have to bring her down?' he asked, bitterly.

'Got to keep the family alive till you form the Union,' I said.

My father eased himself out of the stall. 'Right, Bryn, you've had your say; now shut it.'

I looked at Dewi in the flickering candlelight: it was not more than eight months since I had seen him, yet he looked eight years older: about him was a chunky strength, something of Ifor; a man made bigger by the yellow light on his sweating body, but weariness lay in the humped shadows of his eyes.

Sitting back on the gob I gripped my hands, knowing a blind and violent anger. Rhia was hauling a third dram to feed Rebecca decent, so she could make her child, and it should have been Dewi. My father said, filling his pipe:

'They tell me you are a wanted man. Come on a bit since the old days of the free-thinking, haven't we?'

'Scotch Cattle,' I said, 'the scum of the Union. God help you if you think I'm dropping twopence a week to the likes of them.'

'Get out of Aberdare, Dada,' said Dewi, ignoring me.

I said, 'Something wrong with the comradeship of men if you have to break their legs and smash their fingers to get them in the club.'

'For God's sake get out, Dada,' whispered Dewi.

Sir John Guest of Dowlais had a herd of Scottish cattle; strong, fierce animals with black faces and curved horns. And from this the men who were enforcing the rules of the new Union took their name. They roved in herds of hundreds over the mountains, burning furniture and beating the scabs and blacklegs who worked on when the Union said strike.

Dada lighted his pipe, saying, 'One place is as good as another in this hell. Can you name a pit where I would get higher rates, with coal going down?'

'Resolven. Lyons would take you back. With old Sam Tommer dead you might even make overman.'

'Lyons employs English overmen, not Welsh. Besides, we cannot go back because of 'Becca.'

'Get out before you starve, Dada.' Dewi's voice rose. 'We are kicking out the Irish and calling the town to strike. A week from now not a ton of coal will run from Aberdare valley, for we are fighting the new wage reduction—you even heard about that?'

Dada nodded, and Dewi cried, making a fist, 'Fifteen per cent—not five, not even ten—*fifteen*!'

'The price of coal is dropping on world markets,' I said.

'You damned idiot!' he swung to me. 'Do you believe every bloody thing they tell you?'

'Now, don't start rising tempers,' said Dada.

'The owners are acting like savages!'

'And you reply by breaking the legs of your fellows. If they are savages, what does that make you?'

'If the swines go to work when the Union says strike, they take what is coming. Anyway, we do not give the orders, they come from London.'

'Then tell London to come down and starve with Aberdare,' said Dada. 'They will bring in the troops—remember Merthyr. It is a crime to strike, and you know it.'

'It is the right of every man to withhold his labour. Do they own you body and soul?'

'Damned near,' I said, 'and we realise it.'

'You're doffing your hats to them and they've got their feet in your faces. By God, these times don't breed men!'

My father frowned up. Rhia made a sweet lamenting noise beside me, her hands to her face, and Dewi cried:

'The town will stand by us. It will be a total strike, and if the Irish give out, God help them, for we'll run them from the valley.'

'Aren't the Irish people, too?' asked Rhia, softly.

'There must be a goal, woman. You must have an ideal and strive for that ideal—die for it, if needs be. This town will be in rags come winter, and still the Irish pour in, under-cutting Welsh wages. To hell with the foreigners, we fight for the Welsh. If you stop to consider individuals you become a sentimental slave.'

Dada said, 'You are too hot for reason, Dewi. Time was I thought you would make something of yourself, but I do not think so now.' He levelled his pipe. 'They will bring in troops and shoot you down as they shot you down in Newport . . .'

'We will fight to the death, you will see.'

'They will transport the likes of you and Pietro and Richard Bennet—all the little men, as they transported Frost, Williams and Jones. And the big men like O'Connor, Lovett and Plaice will go free, as they went free before. The State is expert in handling revolution because it learned from France. Listen, son, listen. The owners are the State; they created it for their own convenience, they run and maintain it. And you are threatening their wealth. You can rape their daughters and get away with it, but if you touch a shilling of their money they will burn you alive.'

'*Nefoeddwen!* Then isn't it right to fight such an evil?'

'When you have something to fight it with.'

'With our bare hands, if necessary!'

'Right, then, but not with me, for I am sick of fighting. I have too many women and children, in the kitchen or in the stomach, to think of fighting.' Rising, he knocked out his pipe and pushed Dewi gently aside. 'Now away, son, for we have coal to cut and God, we need the money.'

Dewi whispered, his face white, 'So you will sit on your backside and whine about exploitation while others do your fighting for you.'

'If needs be, under present circumstances, for I have no option. Fire your belly, Dewi, but do not heat your brain—see sense.'

'If you don't give a sod for this generation, what about the next one?'

My father turned to him wearily. 'You get yourself a load of kids and then you would change your tune. Too much to lose, for us, but you have everything to gain. The next generation will have to manage while I see to this one.'

'It is your kind of selfishness that has brought us to this!'

'Away to your Workingmen's Union, son, let ordinary people work.'

'And cowardice.'

If I had not been guarding the dram he would have struck his head: Dewi dropped against me to Dada's fist, and I knelt, lowering him gently to the floor. Climbing up, he shoved me aside, staring at us. Blood ran from his mouth, trickling down his chest, and he wiped it away with the back of his hand.

'Goodbye, Dada,' he said.

I turned away: I could not bear the sight of my father's face.

Turning, Dewi left us: Rhia was bowed against the dram, in disordered weeping.

# 33

COME the end of that June the whole of the Aberdare valley between Hirwain and Mountain Ash was out on strike. First the Wherfa closed, then the Middle and Upper Dyffryns; the Aber Nant-y-groes and Aberaman followed, and after half-a-dozen others came the Lletty Shenkins. Short of coal for their fires, the ironworks began to blow out their furnaces, beginning with the Gadlys up to the big Aberdare. Five thousand colliers in pits big and small, in drift and level and mine, struck in the valley against the fifteen per cent reduction in their wages. The towns, villages and hamlets died that summer. Bright as a blue-bag was the sky over The Top; no smoke sullied the wash-day clouds, the gigantic cumulus that flowered over Aberdare; no longer soot and sulphur stained the summer wind; a new sweetness bloomed on the mountains, with the heather all gay in her purple dress again and the little brooks boasting clean and white from the caverns of the hills and cascading in beauty down the crags to the floor of the valley.

In July, from Aberdare to Abercynon, the children, always the first, began to die, and the little yellow coffins went trailing up the hillsides: the sick and aged began to follow, then the vagrants. They died in scores from the small-pox; of typhoid and cholera. They died in the sink-pits of Wigan Row, Hirwain Row and Club Row, and Bute Street, which is named after the landlord. Of under-nourishment and the lack of good water, they died; from the fever spouts of the Maes y dre and Darran; through drinking from the River Dare and the Cynon, and the Vicarage Well; from epidemic, endemic and contagious diseases, they died, it was officially said.

But they did not die, they were murdered, said my father.

They also died from boredom, and this I believe, for I saw them. I saw them sitting on their hunkers on street corners, staring into space; or aimlessly playing pitch and toss for pebbles, or fighting bare-knuckle with a friend to break the monotony.

They were not alone in this, of course. Up in Crawshay's Merthyr, for lack of a decent water supply that would have cost a thousand pounds, they died like flies eight years back; seventeen hundred men, women and children in four months.

In filth, in the cess-pits that their masters called comfortable little cottages, they died while masters like Bute and Crawshay were building their castles and mistresses like Lady Charlotte Guest were running for their country manors, frightened to death of the cholera.

Let further generations despise the tame historians, the crooked lackeys of the subscriber histories; those who wheedled for favour and the owner's purse to set down the lie of how my generation died.

At the hands of coal and ironmasters who couldn't afford to lay a decent water supply in a land abundant with water, or lay a decent drain in a land of slope and incline; this is how they died.

On the second week of the strike 'Becca put her fist on the table and bowed her head and clenched her eyes, and Mari rose instantly, whispering:

'Rhia—sharp upstairs with the towels and sheets. Bryn, away quick to the spout for water. Mostyn, you help—water, *water*! And boil it, remember; for God's sake do not forget to boil it.'

And Rebecca rose, shapeless in Nature's joke, and shambled wearily up the narrow stairs of Green Fach, for labour.

'Where has Mam gone?' asked Ceri, now four.

'Up to rest,' said Dada. 'You are going next door to Mrs. Robinson.'

Black-haired and olive skinned was Ceri, her eyes like great brown jewels in her high-boned, Jewish face, and dainty in the mouth. Yet there was in her the same heavy clumsiness of my dead Ifor.

It do seem like yesterday, sitting there at the table in Green Fach, listening to Mari's consoling voice upstairs, the stifled screams that floated down, the drumming of Rebecca's heels on the boards above us. Hour after hour it went on, and I can see now the bright sweat on my father's face. All that day he and I had pitchered the water the four miles return from the mountain spout, for we dared not trust the ones in Town for fear of infection, and even then it was floating wigglers and red things with ears on. At nine o'clock that night I could stick it no longer and I handed it over to 'Becca.

'Off out,' I said, hitching up.

'At this time of night?'

'Got a pain in my stomach, and it's fair crippling me.'

'I got one in my back,' said Dada. He went to the foot of the stairs, calling, 'Mari, the pair of us slipping out, you need us?'

Rhia came down the stairs, I remember, her hair tangled, her eyes bright.

'Oh, my God,' she whispered, staring at me.

'Is she coming normal?' asked Dada.

'Aye, but ... oh, it is terrible.'

'Now you know what you have got coming,' I said.

'Give us half an hour,' said Dada, 'we are both in a hell of a state.'

'I will mention it to 'Becca,' said Rhiannon.


The Irish were collecting it on the streets of Aberdare that night.

Sorry in my heart, I am, for the poor bloody Irish.

In the vagrant lodging houses, for one, they were getting it: the Welsh going in and beating them out with sticks and boots, and I pitied them cowering under the threats, hands up in terror as they stumbled down the street half-dressed.

'If anything goes wrong, the Irish get it first,' said Dada, strolling along.

'Mind, the vagrants are a disgrace,' I said.

A few years back we had five or more vagrant houses in Town, and the charge was threepence a night for a single and sixpence for a family. And with the landlords evicting the Irish right, left and centre, whole families were wandering practically destitute, and mainly the Irish. So a family would buy a sixpenny bed at the vagrant and put the family on the mattress, which sometimes laid five or six, getting them head to toe, of all sexes and sizes and most as naked as moles, to make more room; the ceilings so low in one house they couldn't sit up in bed.

'One landlord a night,' said Dada, 'smack in the middle.'

'And a coalmaster under the bed,' I said.

Blacklegs were being marched to work by the military, and a few of them Welsh, by the look of it, for they were colliers, and few Irish worked underground. I hated and pitied them; the redcoats forming them up, halting them in the road until they were joined by another or two; leaving their homes and their women and children to the scowling neighbours.

'God help them when the military leave,' said Dada.

'God help them if the Cattle get hold of them,' I said.

Red torches were flashing on the mountains, rockets were soaring into the star-lit sky: distantly, on the wind, came a faint bass lowing, like an animal in pain. The choice was not easy, said Dada; it is the torture of the Cattle or the agony of seeing your children starve.

'How much have we got left between us?' I asked.

'Twelve sovereigns all round, according to Rhiannon, counting yours.'

I nodded.

'It won't take long to dish up another twenty, the moment the strike is done, lad.'

'Aye.'

'Worth waiting for, a decent girl like Rhia.'

I nodded.

Not waiting. Not now. These days my Rhia was as much a wife to me as Mari was to my father. It had gone too long, we had been tried too far.

Not on your life. She was my woman; no more waiting.

'Try and keep decent, Bryn,' said my father.

'Ay, ay, don't worry about me, man.'

Two little pigs do live in English sties, said Rhiannon, and this little pig is in love with another. You tell me what is left to us if we do not have each other. God do understand.

Well, well. Don't see enough of Him round the Aberdare direction to know if He did or didn't.

Got my Rhia, and life was bearable. A few years from now, with the exception of life around twenty-one, I would get round to thinking about the everlasting fire, and the evangelical Ikes can make what they like of it.


They were breaking Irish windows down High Street and Irish shrieks were coming from the Boot area. For the Irish were strike-breaking when the Welsh said strike, and good Irishmen were either dead or back in County Clare direction.

'You don't have to be English to be a hooligan, mind,' said Dada. 'I know a few good Welsh ones, and there should be no nationality in street or pulpit.'

'You agree with them breaking strike, then?'

'I do not, but I understand the reasons why they do it—things come different when the children begin to starve.'

'Then you would do it if Ceri hungered?'

'I am Welsh, not Irish. If other Welsh children are at it, then Ceri starves, too; this is the law.'

'Queer old situation, if we did strike—Dewi breaking our nuts for us.'

He said, deep, 'It has happened before, it is what the owners hope for; the belly can split husband against wife and father against son. But we have twelve pounds before we sink to the level of the poor Irish.'

'The money will see us through six weeks,' I answered. 'We will be back at Lletty Shenkins long before that.'

'I hope you are right.'

Down Canon Street the Welsh mob was howling and waving cudgels. A barrel of ale was rolled over the cobbles down Commercial Street and another filched from the Bute Arms where windows were being smashed. And these they set up and foaming mugs were passed round, and in the Castle tap it was

305

running under the doors. Down Wind Street a brass band came marching, with Redcoat cavalry prancing either side of it, and the Irish came up from Bute Street and met them in hundreds, for we saw it; a surging wave of screaming humanity, sticks and cudgels raised, and the trombones and tubas and kettles took it head on, with a six-foot Irishman putting his boot through the big bass drum, which is enough to send any decent Welshman mad and raving.

'God, what a sight!' whispered Dada as we flattened ourselves against the wall of the Black Lion. Fists were going up and cudgels coming down, with special constables going in with batons and coming out wiping cuts and holding bruises, and everybody trying to hit out the military, which is natural. Shots were clattering through the medley of shrieks and curses as the Welsh and Irish fought it out, and then a wing of the Irish mob tore off and flew down Monk Street and another made off towards the station, hitting out Welshmen with every tool God has provided since the Creation. A scene of Hades, this, with shawled Irish women racing along the gutters and little children falling among the flying boots of the colliers. One young woman stumbled amid the Irish, and lay still, her hands over her head, and immediately Dada was into the mob, flinging Irishmen aside, while I went in after him kicking at shins, for there is nothing like a good old hop to take your mind off the business in hand.

Dragging her out, we sheltered her against a wall while the mob flooded past us. I whispered into her white face, 'You all right, Irish?'

She opened fevered eyes at me, bright jewels in the pinched hunger of her cheeks, and shrieked, 'Keep away from me, ye filthy scalpeens. Dirt on ye souls for what you're doin' to me people, ye Welsh heathen!'

A voice above us cried bass:

'Are there reinforcements up at Gadlys, sergeant?' He was an officer, bright-haired and English, and he sat his horse well as it pranced the cobbles, his sabre held high.

'Only a platoon across Green Street, sir!'

'You'll need a company, for they are after the Wayne furnaces. Away to it, man!'

As the girl scrambled away my father made large eyes at me, and I shared his fears.

'Run, run!' he cried, and hammered into the mob.

We got into the back of our Number Five as the Irish mob, turned from wrecking the furnaces, came piling through the street window without opening it. And as I ducked a stick and caught an Irish jaw square in the passage I saw Rhia at the top of the stairs with something in her arms, and her face was white and terrified. Screams and shrieks were coming down the row as Welsh and English front doors went down and glass shattered, and Mrs. Robinson was hanging out of her window in her nightdress dropping coal on the invaders and yelling to go easy since her dada was born in Kerry, and Patrick Revival never lost a wink, it was said, though Mrs. Regan next door but seven lost two china dogs and a double hair mattress because her old man was Staffordshire, which was reasonable when you consider it. But it was pretty unreasonable if you were like us, as Welsh as Irfon Bridge.

Within the first minute the Irish confetti took every window fore and aft, said Rhia afterwards, and with at least twenty Irish in the kitchen and only two of us, it was naturally a little inconvenient. Side by side and hooking short, Dada and me, for you daren't swing in case you collected the dresser. And in the latter stages Mari and Rhia came down and assisted County Clare folk and Limericks through the front door with chair legs. Actually, I thought we were doing all right until an Irish navvy ducked a left hook from Dada and I stepped into it and went out like a light. And when I came to I was sitting in three feet of wreckage with my jaw sideways and Rhia kneeling beside me dabbing me with cold water and my father raging and tying up knuckles, the knots in his teeth.

'How are you?' he demanded.

'I'm lovely,' I said.

'You look it,' said he. 'How many times have I told you I'm inclined to drift on the left? If it happens again for God's sake keep on the right.'

Not an Irishman in sight now, and the town was quiet under the stars, weeping in the smashed kitchens, rocking itself with hunger. We got things more or less ship-shape and went upstairs to see 'Becca. Sitting up in bed as large as life, was she, and chewing willow bark for a headache. But she loosened her tears when I took her baby boy in my arms, and my father said from the end of the bed, 'Sometimes I think that God is sitting on the boards of the coalmasters, but at times like this He is sitting in by here, in Green Fach.'

'Becca whispered in her throat, 'Looks just like my Ifor, he do, standing there.'

'Downstairs, you,' said Mari, elbowing me. 'Give Mama's Ifor to me; squeezing the stomach from him, you are, Bryn.'

Downstairs, by the grate, I listened to Rebecca sobbing and the breathless squalling of the new Ifor Evan, and I clenched my hand for my brother. Through the smashed window of the back I watched Gomer Taff, the Gadlys collier and his three mates carrying Wil Wicker down to the New Inn on his platter, for this was Saturday night. And Saturday night, wet or fine, peace or riot, they took him, broken back included, down to the tap, and brought him back to his missus as tight as a pair of stays, and there are advantages, mind, Wil used to say, in living horizontal, for the old hen don't know if it's two pints or twenty.

'Good night, Bryn,' he cried, as I leaned on the back gate now.

I got up off the gate as he passed, and stood decent for him.

'Good night, Wil Wicker,' I said.

The Black Dare of Gadlys was going in sucks and whirls and gurgles to her underground bed of cholera: the pit-head and wheel were stark against the moon. The stars were big over Aberdare, and the wind, I remember, was weeping.

Rhia called in pent breath from the kitchen, 'You there, Bryn?'

'Aye.'

She came to me in frozen mood, her fist against her face, and stared, speechless, at me.

'What is it, woman?'

'The money is gone. Mari just found the caddie. It ... it is empty!'

Dada came then, hands clenched. 'You ... you heard? Rhia told you?'

The bile rose to my throat and I swallowed it down.

'In the name of God,' whispered Mari, coming out, 'what shall we do?'

Empty, we stood, looking at each other, empty.

All down the Row the lights were going out: faintly, the new Ifor cried on 'Becca's breast. Mari said:

'He is Ifor's boy, Mostyn, and he is not starving, like the baby Irish.'

'It will not come to that.'

'Before it does,' said Mari, 'I will go to work.'

Hands clenched, she faced him.

'You will go to work when I say,' whispered my father.

'Understand us now,' replied Mari. 'When Rebecca thins on milk for Ifor's child, Rhia and I break strike.'

'You are usurping the command of my house.'

'Call it what you will, Mostyn.'

'You leave here to work without my permission, woman, and you need not come back.'

'So be it,' said Mari, and gathered Rhiannon, and they went into the kitchen.

I touched my father.

'Leave me,' he said.


# 34


On the seventh week of the colliers' strike Aberdare looked more like a town under military occupation than a Top Town coalfield. But the strikers were still defiant: burning the truck shops, bombing the houses of the black-legs and hoisting men to the top of the pit-head wheels as punishment for sneaking on to shift under Company protection. Under the threat of the fifteen per cent reduction, under the heel of the coming Union and the boot of the military, my town slowly died, leaving in its bare rooms the gnaw and pallor of hunger.

'Seven fat years, seven lean ones,' said Tomos Traherne in his beard, 'it be the law of God,' and he raised his palms upwards in our kitchen, crying, 'But the wind of Heaven is blowing over the mountains. In the death of the body through our own transgressions we are in the midst of a glorious revival of the soul. *Selah!*

'Selah,' whispered Mari, her eyes cast down.

'Selah,' I said, wishing him to the devil privately, for it was fourteen fat ones for Tomos Traherne if his stomach was a pointer.

Sad was my town, my dirty, rambling, silent, ugly little Aberdare. No longer the children kicked the pig's bladder along the flagged terraces in all their shrieks and laughter; no longer the women sang from their kitchens the high, sweet sadness of the Welsh sopranos; no longer was heard the fumbling bass and soaring tenor. In the bake of summer the town steamed. The brooks were dried in their calcined beds. Down in the Spanish and Italian houses the foreigners fingered their rosaries; the starving Irish keened and wailed in the nights. In the rake of her derelict chimneys and blown-out furnaces, in the stilled blur of her pit-head wheels, Aberdare died.

And Ifor, the son of my brother, wept at Rebecca's daily sugar and bread, for his milk was thin. So 'Becca rested. In bed most of the day to hold her strength, she stared over the sun-drenched fields, looking for Ifor. By day, while Dada and I went up the mountain to fetch water from the clean spouts, Mari and Rhia would gather the fleece off the hedges. This they spun on the wheel that belonged to my gran, making children's vests for selling in Abergavenny market, and for these a cart came once a week. Of canal reeds we wove baskets and panniers, as Mari taught us; from hazel we fashioned pegs, and Rhiannon took these gipsy style down to Skewen and Morriston, selling at the doors, and even over Sarn Helen to Brecon where they wash very white.

I remember the idleness, the boredom, the hunger of that seven-week strike against reduction. But most of all, in detail, I remember the night that the agent Mr. Batey came.

'The Spanish have broken the strike up in Merthyr, you heard?' asked Rhia.

Thin and pale she looked, her lips bloodless; yet her eyes, large and shadowed in the pallor of her face, burned with a strange, inner fever.

'It is a rumour sent out by the owners,' said my father.

Mari rose. 'It is true. Ike Winchester I saw today, and he told me.'

'Ike Winchester?'

'He is come over from Lletty Shenkins to run the Gadlys Pit when the strike is over.' Bending, she lifted Ceri against her, and there was a great silence in her for my father: scarcely a word had passed between them since the night of the Irish riots.

Tomos said, 'I heard Mr. Batey, the General Agent, has finished with Lletty, too. He is going round the Rows trying to persuade people into the Gadlys.'

'Because it is easily protected,' I said.

He nodded heavily, muttering, 'I never thought the time would come when the workers of this town would need protection from my Richard Bennet and your Dewi, and their like.'

'It is a sign of the times,' said Dada. 'I never thought the time would come when I would need protection from the greed of coal-owners.'

'Oh, God, listen to it!' whispered Mari.

'Aye, listen!' said my father. 'For you have closed your ears too long. Dewi was right and we were wrong. Force must be met with force, violence with violence.'

Sick to death of it all, I got up and went to the back door, opening it and staring out. And Tomos Traherne said, bass, ' "It is the vengeance of God on the ungodly for the wickedness of the people. ..." '

My father got up. 'Out,' he said.

'Mostyn!' cried Mari, turning.

' "For it is the day of the Lord's vengeance," ' shouted Tomos, beard trembling, ' "and the year of recompenses for the controversy of Zion. And the streams thereof shall be turned into pitch, and the dust thereof into brimstone ... the

311

cormorant and bittern shall possess it; the owl also, and the raven shall dwell in it ...!" '

'Out!' shouted my father, gripping him and heaving him up, and I opened the door as Dada assisted him through it on to the cobbles, and Mari was shrieking behind him as Tomos raised his staff and held it high, crying aloud:

'This is the judgment of the Lord on those that fly in the face of authority! Here shall the great owl make her nest, and lay and hatch! Here shall the vultures also be gathered, each with his mate ... !'

'Ay ay,' I said, throwing his hat after him and slamming the door, and Dada shouted, his hands to his head:

'I've stood that God-botherer long enough. Christ is weeping out there for the people of the town and he is sitting in by here roasting us for not going back to work. What kind of religion is that?'

'Is it religion to sit in idleness while 'Becca's child is dying for want of milk?' cried Mari.

'Oh, God, it is too big for me,' said my father, covering his face.

'But not for me!' cried Mari, bending over him. And she put her hands in her hair and pulled it about her face, and cried, 'Now I have stopped begging. It has gone on long enough, it is time the women took a hand.' She began to cry then, in gasps and wetness, and I went and held her.

'Hush, you,' I said, 'the world is crying enough. Soon it will be over, soon it will come right between you and Dada.'

'Not between us now. Oh, God, I have ploughed those hopes underground a long time ago. We are strangers.'

'Dada, for heaven's sake,' I said, turning to him.

In a sudden panic, Rhiannon said at the window, 'Heisht, Mama, *heisht*! Mr. Batey, the agent, is coming!'

'And he will go the same direction as Tomos Traherne,' cried my father.

'Oh, please, please let him speak,' begged Rhia.

No sense in this. One moment a good old-fashioned family palaver with men shouting and women crying and preachers going out head first, and next minute everybody rushing around slapping the furniture and for goodness' sake try to make the place presentable. No time for more discussion, he was in.

On the step he stood, six feet up and skinny, with his hat on his ears and his collar cutting his throat. His eyes, bulging behind his spectacles, moved slowly around the kitchen : resting on Rhia, he said :

'Good evening, Mostyn Evan.'

'Say your business and go,' said Dada, fist on the table, turned away.

'It is simple. The strike is broken.' He entered softly.

'Thank God, thank God,' whispered Mari, tightening her shawl.

Dada said, 'Now let us have the truth. If the strike were broken there would be dancing in the streets. What do you want of us?'

'It is what you want of me, Mostyn Evan.' From his pocket he brought a handful of golden sovereigns, and these he held over the table. 'What chance have you got? The owners can spill these along the streets, and here you sit without a glass of water.'

'Shift him, Bryn,' muttered my father.

'You dare!' whispered Mari, bending at the waist, her eyes on fire.

Batey said, 'You put a finger on me, Mostyn Evan, and I will run you from these mountains. I tell you, the strike is broken. In Aberaman they are going back, at Cwmdare; and the furnaces are alight at Abernant. Mr. Robinson is starting in the morning, also Gomer Taff, and the Irish will be going up in hundreds with the Spanish and Italians. Now then!'

'I will believe this when I see it,' said my father.

'You will see it soon enough,' said Mari, 'because Rhia and me are starting in the morning.'

'Well done, Mrs. Evan,' said Mr. Batey. 'You are respected in Green Fach. If you go in the Gadlys Pit will open.'

'If she goes in she leaves this house,' said Dada, getting up.

'I am with Dada,' said Rhia. 'I am with Dada because I am with Bryn. When Bryn says work, I work, and not before.'

The shock of her voice turned us all. Mari sat down slowly. She said :

313

'Let the baby die, then. I can do no more.'

My father said softly, 'And now get out, Batey. There is only one strike-breaker here and she can be discounted. Time was, tell Wayne, that I would have been with her, but not now. Time was I would have been first into Gadlys, for the greed of the workers is the same as the masters. But I will not break strike now, although I am not with the Union. I will not break strike, Batey, because the owners are showing worse than greed. This is a strike against a reduction, not for an increase. It is a strike against the owners who are cutting on wages to flush up their profits. And they are bringing in the foreigners to cane the backs of the Welsh: they are bringing in the starving to get their fifteen per cent. The swine can watch a two foot coffin go up Cemetery Road without the lift of a hat, for I have seen them. Now get out and look in Town for English black-legs, for you will not find them among the Welsh.'

Mr. Batey bowed slightly. 'As you wish. Good night, Mr. Evan.'

I shut the door behind him.

Mari said, 'If Gran were here tonight it would have been a different tune.'

'Aye,' replied my father, 'for she was Welsh.'

Faintly, from the room above, came the sound of Ifor crying.

Near midnight I awoke, rising up in the bed, hearing a sound.

A footstep had slurred the boards of the landing. Getting out, I opened the door. Rhiannon, fully dressed, was going silently down the stairs. I listened. The lock of the back door grated. Now, at the window, I saw her floating over the cobbles of the Row, and the moon was bright down the street where no lights burned, and the town lay silent, because of the curfew.

'Rhia!' I whispered, but she did not hear me.

I clenched my hands, knowing where she was going.

Dressing swiftly, I ran down into the deserted street and along the banks of the Dare, crossing it into High Street and along to Bute.

Now along the high pavement, flattening in the doorways, for soldiers were forming at the end by Maerdy House, and I doubled back into Cardiff Road towards Sunnybank and Blind Man Groping Lane.

Snatching at breath, I went swiftly up to the house of Batey, the agent, and there I found her.

As carved from black stone Rhiannon was standing there by the gate, and beyond her, working in his lighted window, was Mr. Batey.

A madness was in her face when she turned to me, and yet there was in her no surprise.

'Bryn,' she said.

'Aye, girl.'

I held her and she was thin in my arms, and trembling.

Suddenly she held me away, and in that light her eyes were stark white, the pupils glittering, and strange.

'You been here before, Rhia?' I whispered, and I shut my eyes to the pain of fire in me, and in the nearness and warmth of her there was comfort.

'Aye. Once before I came, but he was not here. So I waited, and he did not come. Got to have money, see, for 'Becca's baby.'

'Yes,' I said.

'You wait for me, Bryn? Mr. Batey said to come. A sovereign, it is, mind. You know Beth Regan, the Irish . . . ?'

I bowed my head against her.

'Got to have money, says 'Becca, for Ifor's son.'

I held her and would not let her go.

'Who is there?' cried a voice.

Batey was standing in his door-way, his lamp held high.

'Come,' I said. 'Come, Rhia.'

'Who is it?' called Batey.

I did not look back.

To save me the sin of murder, I did not look back.

In the kitchen I got her back into her night-dress, hushing and kissing into silence her excited chatter: sweat was on her, running in streams over her body.

After a bit, cradled in my arms, she slept, and I went up the stairs to my father's room, and knocked, and Mari came to the

315

door, clutching her night-dress to her throat.

'My girl is ill,' I said.

My father came then, his hair awry. 'What is happening, Bryn?'

'Rhia is ill,' I replied. 'It is the fever of the starve.'

With wild eyes Mari pushed past me and ran down the stairs, and then the door of Rebecca's room came open and she stood there with Ifor in her arms.

'Dada, for God's sake,' she said.

Turning, my father put his face against the wall, saying, 'The house is split from top to bottom.'

'Death will split it more,' I answered. 'A month from now the people of this valley will be working, and ours will be dead. I am breaking strike tomorrow.'

# 35

AND SO, on the fiftieth day of the strike we stood in the Row of Green Fach and awaited the coming of the protection military.

Dada, Mari and I waited outside our back for the dawn shift, and we did not speak. All down the Row the word went round, and doors started coming open and windows shooting up, and dear me, Mrs. Jones, I would have to see it with my own eyes before I would believe it.

Mostyn Evan and family breaking the strike.

Their amazement changed to dumbness and their dumbness to silent fury. And breeding in the fury was their despising, and their hatred.

In a trickle from their gates, buttoning their coats, tying their aprons, they came white-faced and staring, and ringed us, and did not speak, at first.

There was old Ike Winchester from Lletty Shenkins, come down to work the Gadlys when the strike broke: Mr. and Mrs. Robinson, our north-country English neighbours, handy in the mouths but with hearts of gold: there was William Williams called Billy Twice, the old Cardie collier, now burned out by shallow seams down the Garn, and dust. Peg Skewen, the Park Pit coal-cropper, came with Noah Morgan of the Forge, Abernant. Gomer Taff from Number Ten, said:

'In the name of Heaven, Mostyn Evan, I never would have believed it.'

Standing at the back was Penrhy Jones, the minister of Siloa, Gadlys, who was our Big Seat, and staying in Number Three with his sister. Strong for his God, the Revival and for whipping them from the Temple, the men of greed, was he. With hurt eyes he regarded us, and this was the deepest wound of all.

Ike Winchester shouted, 'Mostyn, give them a week and we will all be back!'

My father did not reply. Side by side, we stared down the Row.

'And I took you for a four-square man, Evan!'

'About as straight as a scythe-handle.'

'Scab!'

'Blackleg!'

And as their tempers heated the dawn blew soft about us: sweet was the perfume of my valley after the smokeless solace of the night. Upon us they heaped dirt and insults, and when the military came marching down the Row they raised their fists and shouted in our faces. And we did not move.

About forty other scabs came, mainly Irish and Spanish, and they marched in threes with eight foot redcoats either side, muskets shouldered, bayonets fixed, and ahead of them was a sergeant. Seeing us, he halted, crying:

'You for Gadlys, Welshman?'

My father nodded.

'Line in, then!' Leaving his column, he drew his sabre, forcing a path through the neighbours, and we trooped after him to the column.

'Wait,' said my father. 'I have sick people, and I need protection.' He jerked his thumb at the house and I saw a flash glimpse of Rebecca standing with Ceri at the window.

'I can spare you one,' said the sergeant.

Penrhy Jones called, 'That is the second fool talking. He

317

needs no protection, his people will be safe.'

'You guarantee this, pastor?' shouted the soldier.

'Get about your business, man. Leave the Welsh to the Welsh.'

With Mari between us, we marched off at the back of the column. I looked at my father; erect he went, his eyes dead in his face. Mari's face was chalk-white and her hands clenched to the growing clamour of the mob who were piling out of their doors to greet the dawn-shift scabs.

Down Unity Street and Ty Fry the strikers were lining the road three deep, racing up from Canon and Commercial and Bute, buttoning up and belting up and smoothing straight from the bed. And in the red-tinged light of dawn they lent their bawled insults to the workers of Gadlys, forming an avenue down which we walked. Here were soldiers in scores, sabres drawn, their horses plunging among the tattered buildings of the ironworks of Wayne, their nostrils snorting mist amid the panic of the shoving crowd. On, on we went along the avenue of hatred and threats, their fists an inch from our faces as the soldiers fought to keep them back. Enveloped by their fury and insults we went, and I felt for Mari's hand and gripped it; the howling reached a new thunder as we neared the shaft of Gadlys; cold as ice that hand, and I chanced a look at her. Blood was on her face from a flung stone and her eyes were closed, the lashes ringed black on the drawn parchment of her cheeks.

On the last twenty yards to the cage the soldiers were facing the crowd; men of the Glamorgan military, their numbers swollen by the Workmen Volunteers, the traitor army loyal to the owners, and six Swansea dragoons on horse-back were anchored around the Head, their eyes switching about them nervously.

'Right into it, into it!' Musket-butts at the ready, they ringed us, with a flogging on the end of it if they lost us to the crowd.

The Spanish went first, herded like sheep, and the cage descended: then went the Irish, spitting back the insults of the ragged army of strikers thrusting about us and bawling the blackleg song. And in the moment before the drop of the cage

318

I saw, down the cinder slope of the pit, the face of my brother Dewi. And even as I stared the crowd about him swayed and broke. Richard Bennet I saw, too, dressed as a labouring Irish in a tam-o'-shanter and scarlet neck-tie, and I raised my hand, crying, 'Dewi, Dewi!'

Clearly he saw me, I knew this by his face. Putting his hands on his hips, he turned away, and spat.

The cage dropped into the pit blackness of the butcher's shop they called Gàdlys.

To a pin-prick of light five hundred feet below, we dropped. And with the slam of the cage door went from there in a babble of foreign tongues to the Victorian parting, which is the division where the main gallery sweeps away to avoid running under St. John's Parish Church in the light above.

A man was issuing picks and shovels here, and I recognised him instantly despite the wavering light of the pit candles.

It was Pietro Bianca, as if stepped straight from the days of the Old Navigation, and he did not speak.

'Pietro . . . !' whispered Mari, peering, but he made no sign that he knew her.

My father gripped her arm, drawing her on with the colliers. 'Come, Mari,' said he. 'Times have changed. It is not your Pietro Bianca.'

On we went down the drift for Forge Side, the Spaniards leading in a clank of tools, and I feared for Mari, who had not been below before.

A swine was this Wayne Gadlys: she began in the drop beside St. John's and ran in a mile drift down to Fothergill, the beating heart of Abernant and the mushrooming scarlet of the furnaces of Forge Side. And the workers of Colliers' Row and Engineers' Row knew Gadlys for the bitch she was. So when the women asked the Truck for six penn'orth of accidents for a minced beef Sunday they were talking of the shambles of Fothergill; but owners don't know the difference between minced beef and chopped colliers, they said, and only the women knew what was coming up next on the stretchers of Gadlys.

And if the bell-stone and dram and hoof and engine don't

319

get you down Gadlys, the chances are that water would, for she was loaded to the gunwales in underwater ponds and streams and old, flooded workings.

'Watch the water,' said my father.

We went on, wading now in twelve inches, and it was evil black and oily, with Mari tying up her dress to her knees.

Now there was a great softness in my father for his wife, and I was glad.

I waded on, glancing back, and saw with joy that he was again one with her, for under the lamp of a heading he had her against the rock, and was kissing her. The overman shouted:

'First in. Mostyn Evan, the son, and the woman. Where are they?'

'Shift over,' I said. 'I am here, the others are coming,' and I threw down the tools and stripped off and there was a strange coldness in the air which, down a pit, stinks of water.

Dada said, coming up with Mari, 'Wet, isn't it?'

'Wet enough for bath night.'

Mari said, 'What was Pietro doing back up there, Mostyn?'

I winked at Dada. 'Breaking strike, like us.'

'I am not such a fool as I look,' said she.

'It has happened before,' said my father, tossing his coat and tightening. 'The lark is to stay down; you never break strike if you don't come up. The Spaniards are at it, why not the Mexicans?'

She shrugged, went back up, unshackled a dram and kneed it, spragging it along to the face for filling while me and Dada wandered round with candles belting the roof for bell-stone, though she looked solid enough by the time the overman came back: broad and teak-tough, this one, a Cardie Welsh with doormats on him fore and aft, a busted beak, and all he lacked for a cave-man was a cudgel, said Mari.

'You all right by here?'

'Another six inches and you will drown us,' said Dada. 'You got pumps?'

'We had pumps until the strike, this is seven weeks' water.'

'It will come hard on the woman—you got a spare animal?'

'The ponies are over in Park, but I got half a donkey.'

320

'Half a donkey is better than none,' I said.

'Come and fetch him,' said the foreman, and I liked his style.

In ten minutes I was back, racing with him down the gallery and yelling:

'Jed Donkey. Dada, Mari, look! Jed Donkey!'

Ragged, skinny, weary, worked out and blind as a bat. But Mari went on to her knees in the pit-water and put her arms around his neck, and cried, 'Oh, my little precious, my little Jed Donkey!'

'*Duwedd!*' cried my father. 'Last time I heard of you, you were up for the knacker-yard!'

'Sent by Gran,' said Mari, loving him, and I saw old Jed grin, as donkeys do. 'Now things are going to change.'

She was right.

But I do not think Gran had a hand in what came after that.


For three days we worked from the Gadlys, taking the drift mine to Abernant, coaling out on to Forge Side for the furnaces, for these were alight again, though only in half-blast and an eighth production which was turning Fothergill's hair grey, they said. Daily money we took home to 'Becca, and daily we faced the mob around Siloa Baptist. But Ifor strengthened and my Rhiannon rose in the bed, though not speaking. And nor did we feel so bad about the strike, for the Quakers were abroad on the streets with their Irish soup-kitchens. Often I had heard my father say that he would be mighty interested in the God of animals, and, personally, I would not dream of entering a heaven that didn't have dogs, cats, mice and Quakers, for these four are one with the greatest purity.

Conversely, I am doing my best to keep out of the hell that will be especially stoked by Welsh furnacemen for ironmasters with coal supplied by Taff colliers for coalmasters, preferably anthracite.

I sat on Rhia's bed. 'Got Jed Donkey back,' I said. 'You hear me, Rhia? Got Jed Donkey back.'

And she gave me a ghost of a smile that was once so gay.

'The fever is broken,' said Rebecca, 'be thankful for that.'

321

And I kissed her, I remember, and went out that day for the fourth dawn shift down the lower drift of the Gadlys.

To this day they do not know who shot-fired in Four Heading when we already had more coal in the seam than we could handle. Between the four of us we were pulling out ten tons a day, with Dada and me hewing and Mari and Jed on the drams, and we were doing this in ten inches of water.

When the ceiling came down in Four it took the shaft of the old working with it. Before the smoke was cleared we were up to our middles in flood.

'Round the top pillar!' shouted my father, and hooked his arm round Mari's waist and bent her to the weight of water coming down the shaft. 'Bryn, Bryn!'

'Coming!'

Jed was up to his haunches, and I ducked under water and knocked out the pin and the hook came free, and he shrieked and plunged for the opening of the stall with me after him, and came clear into the gallery where the flood was pounding. In the spluttering lamps this took him high, and he cartwheeled over in the blackness, his hooves cracking on the roof as the wave bore him down. Bracing myself to the flood, deafened by the earsplitting roar of water from the old working, I shouted till I was hoarse. Higher up the gallery I could see the lights of the Spaniards and above the dull roar I heard their cries of alarm as the water searched them, forcing them to climb the drift.

'Bryn!' With surging joy, I heard my father again.

'Dada!'

'Can you get round?'

With the wave splashing against the roof, the lamps were going out on the ledges above me; only one burned in wanes and splutters on the high face of Two Stall behind me. I yelled above the thunder, 'Try to get back. What the hell are you doing in there?'

'The water took us.' His voice was fainter. 'Can you hand Mari round the pillar?'

'Aye, push her round!'

Bracing my feet to the swell of the gallery flood, I clung on

322

to the coal. The flood was still rising up my chest yet I could see the Spanish lights up the drift and their racing figures as they climbed higher. Momentarily the water flowed across my eyes and I instantly leaped, cracking my head on the roof.

'Dada, hurry! Hand Mari round!'

Nothing but the roar of the flood as the old workings let it go. Driven by unknown pressures, the static water found life, bounding and free as it took over the new stalls. Panic began to hit me as it rose to my throat, but it was settling now, after its first onslaught, and I shifted round the pillar, trying to get into Four Stall.

'Dada!'

No reply.

With the flood dying, I stamped round the pillar, ducked under the water and dived into blackness, groping my way around the pillar into the flooded drift. But when I straightened for air the roof hit me down, and I knew the flood was solid. Gasping, swallowing water, I cranked my body around the pillar again, and straightened into six inches of air.

'Dada! Mari!'

The roof of the cave echoed, the flood washed over my face. With death threatening, I did not recognise it: it seemed impossible, with the gallery but feet away, that anybody would die, least of all my father, who was indestructible; or Mari, who was in his care. Taking a deep breath against the roof, I ducked under the water again and crawled round the pillar into Four Stall once more, taking the middle this time, hands sweeping out for a hold. Something brushed my searching hand and I plunged deeper into the blackness. Here a fresh surge of colder water enveloped me from the old working, and I swayed towards it, feeling the rock face, trying desperately to keep direction. And suddenly Mari's dress streamed over me, caressing my face, my naked chest. Gripping it, I pushed backwards, falling to my right, and I struck the coal pillar. Up now, into air, gasping and retching. With one hand gripping the dress and the other pulling me round the pillar, I collected into Two Stall, and ducked under the flood again, dragging Mari upright against me, lifting her face into air.

'*Mari!*'

The lamp was flickering now as I shrieked her name and clutched her against me. Wading along the pillar, I pulled her to the wall. In two foot of air I laid her on the gob face down and leaned on her, and the water gushed from her in a great sickness. On her I turned, crying at the roof, 'Dada, Dada!'

In the gutting light of the last lamp, I stared about me at the coal and bit my knuckles and began to cry and call his name. Then Mari stirred under my hand, and I hauled her up against me, smoothing her hair from her face and whispering things I can no longer remember.

I do not know how long I sat there with Mari in my arms, now in pitch darkness, for the last lamp had gone out. And although the flood had not risen higher than my chest, there was a great pressure in my ears and it was difficult to breathe. I knew then that it was only the air lock that was saving us. The first penetration to free us would allow the air to escape and the water to rise to the roof. And I saw, as I lay there on the high gob, the faint glow of the gallery at the end of the stall, a six inch slit of redness reflecting in the flood.

I also knew, seeing this, that my father was dead, for the next stall, being lower on the drift, would have filled to the roof. In darkness I lowered my face against Mari's, and wept. Hearing this, she stirred in my arms.

'Whisht, *whisht*,' I said, and rocked her against me.

There was no sound then but our breathing and a faint trickling of water.

They say I must have slept, because it was over two hours later that I heard distant knocking. Louder, louder it sounded, beating me into alertness. Raising a lump, I knocked back, and sat waiting, breathless, for the reply.

It came. The colliers were at it.

They came in fire, in gas, in flood: for hero or blackleg, they always came. And I saw in my mind the panic of the houses and the measured speed of the teams: from near and far they would be coming, the firemen, stretcher-men, the miners, the strike forgotten.

The knocking became louder, developing into thumps that shook the stall. Dust began to trickle in patters down the wall

324

where they were coming through from Six Stall, I could hear it hissing into the water. And this overman knew his job, for he was taking it high above the level, by the sound of it. Coal began to fall in noisy plops, and I heard the growing hiss as the air began to escape from the trap, and felt the water rise up my chest. I listened. Faintly, I could hear them plugging the air hole, and there came the duller thuds as they picked it lower down.

'Mari,' I whispered; I could not see her face in that blackness, and she could have been dead, but for her gusty breathing.

And then I heard a voice.

'That you in by there, Evan?' From a place beyond the grave, that voice.

I yelled back, 'Bryn Evan, the son. And Mari, my mother.'

'Any Spanish?'

'None.'

'They got Spanish holed up in Number Four.'

'Nobody else in here except my father, and he is dead.'

'We are coming through, lad.'

'It is air-locked, mind!'

'Aye, we know. How much ceiling you got?'

'Two feet.'

'You need more with the woman—have you tried for a hole?' It sounded to me like Ike Winchester.

'Wait, you,' I shouted, back. 'I'll try now.' Laying Mari back on the gob I shifted in the water, feeling the roof, for Dada, I remembered, was working it high, as usual. Some picked low, but he always took it high, never trusting the undercut. Beside the wall the roof sloped up. Gathering Mari against me, I elbowed along, and the air was sweeter. I cried:

'Got another six inches.'

'Get into it, and listen—can you hear me?'

'Aye.'

'Breathe easy, for we need an hour. They're building the lock-wall behind us, but it takes time.'

The dull hammering began again as they took in under the flood, and I gathered Mari in my arms, and she said suddenly, her voice clear and strong:

'Mostyn!'

I clung to her.

'Do you ... do you kiss me, Mostyn?' she said.

Bending, my face against hers, I did not dare to move, for she believed me to be her husband.

'Kiss me, Mostyn,' she whispered.

I put my lips on hers, and kissed her, and there was no sound in her when I set her free, as if the kiss had taken the life from her body. But she spoke again, in Welsh, which was her mother tongue, saying:

'*Fy annwylyd, fy nghariad Cu; Cedwais fy nghalon ti aros i mi!*'

Later, they dropped the wall and I tied down her skirt with my belt and lifted her into the air-lock, and the men took her.

They put her on the stretcher under the brattice-cloth when they set her down for the cage, but I would not have the stretcher because my father would have carried her, had he lived.

I held her against me in the cage going up. In sunlight I held her as I stepped on the cinders. And with her in my arms I walked down the line of white-faced people who, but a few hours before, had cursed us. And at the end of the people Rhiannon was standing, so I knelt before her and laid Mari at her feet.

'Your mam, my dada,' I said, and Rhiannon did not speak.

# 36

THERE was a great peace in me, standing here in the garden of the Old Navigation. And in the brilliance of that summer evening, it seemed to me that all her wounds were healed, and she was filled with a strange, urgent new life. With coal and culm the barges glided past Gran's overgrown garden; the long lines of trucks rattled and snorted up the gradient towards Glyn Neath; the house of Rheola flashed her astonishing whiteness along the road that led to Tonna.

Idly, I walked through the sagging rooms; up the stairs to Sharon's bed, and in the sweet decay of memories heard again her voice, saw again her strutting postures and fierce declamations.

Beneath the piled cinders of the kitchen grate the hearth was still with a snow whiteness. This, I remembered, was Ifor's job every Saturday, and he laid it clean with canal brick-dust. I used to brighten the knives, I remember, gliding them up and down the gritty board, and Gran would not take them unless they were shiny enough to shave in. The smell of fish on forks, said Mari, can be cured by driving the prongs into the earth.

Here is the cracked shaving mirror above the bosh; there is the punch-bag hanging from the ceiling of the back that Ifor used for the pugilistics, and I feinted and hooked it with the right as I went past, and patted it in the name of Ifor.

It was warm in the garden, the sun was brilliant, and the cut was all over golden with seed-dust and glowing in her banks with water-lilies.

Here is the Espianoza tree which held Gwen's treasure: here, in my hand, are the pearls and little glass beads she stole from Gran's needle-work box; the white rings of paper, which was the fairy money.

A barge glided by in shafts of sunlight, the bargee waved.

'Ay ay!'

'How are you?'

I got up, holding these things in my clenched hand. Standing there in all the moving beauty of the day I seemed to hear them all again: the ardent protests of Dewi, the laughter of Mari, the bass commands of my father.

Rhiannon I heard, too, her voice ringing in the room.

The kitchen was shafted with sunlight as I wandered round touching the places they had touched, listening to the music of a life now past. There was no particular sadness in me; most of the grief was now spent. I had come back here because I was complete in this place, one with the family in unity and love. It was the law of life itself that change should come about; it was the law of God that life went on.

I went down the stairs into the cellar, thinking of Dewi: of the nights when Pietro and Ianto Fuses used to come; the revolutionary pamphlets, the speeches, the free-thinking my father insisted on. And it was strange that I knew with Dewi a new affinity. In the scattered books and papers, in the rabid broadsheets of the Chartists, the wood-cuts of O'Connor and Frost he had pinned on the walls, I knew my brother standing there in the face of his past better than ever I did in the old days of his present. He, more than anything, had encompassed the death of the family in his idealistic fight to give it a new future. The very ruin of the Old Navigation seemed, to me, to relate the decay of his principles, the dust of his ambitions.

And then I saw it, pinned to the cellar door: a page he had torn from one of Sharon's books. Swinging the door into the sun, I read:

'In certain parts of the island there is a people called Welsh, so bold and ferocious, that, when unarmed, they do not fear to encounter an armed force; being ready to shed their blood in defence of their country, and to sacrifice their lives for renown.'

*King Henry V of England*

For a long time I stood reading this again and again.

The words, in the act of repetition, seemed to catch me up. I took the page down, screwed it up in my hand and held it against me.

The words seemed to burn against my fingers, and I became aware of a new and great excitement. I went up into the kitchen and from there into the garden. And with the paper gripped harder, I looked over the land as I looked upon it on that summer day up on March-Hywel with Rhiannon, on the day of Tai and Sian's marriage.

The excitement grew within me, stronger and stronger, and I began to tremble. In my great emptiness there came a new vitality, a strength that flowed through me. And I saw before me not a land of defeat and exploitation, but a land of triumph. I saw in the scarred landscape and the tunnelled mountains not a desecration but the glory of their wealth. And I knew, standing there, staring up to The Top, that the smoke of this year of cruelty and oppression was the bonfires of future generations, that the old order would be swept away, the old slaveries buried in the mountainous heaps of slag that one day would be green again; that the rivers now black with furnace-washings would cleanse themselves for the lives of men and women yet unborn.

It was as if I myself had become re-born, that the spirit of my country had moved in me, making me one with her in all her stubborn courage. And as she now stood purified by the flames of adversity and was strengthened and refined, so was I drawing into me the strength and determination of her greatness.

I began to walk away from the Old Navigation, drawn once more to Rhiannon. I began to run. Stupidly, obsessed with this new-found joy, I called her name.

'Rhiannon!'

I did not stop running until I reached Crugau. The train was gathering speed, a snorting Corsair pulling a new-fangled contraption of trucks and low-loaders for the industries of The Top, and I ran alongside it and scrambled aboard one, lying there gasping, staring at the astonishing blue of the sky with the clatter of the rails thumping through my shoulders as we gathered speed. And in the very power of the new inventions the joy in me grew, filling me with an exuberance I had never known before. I scrambled up, splaying my legs to the swaying flat with the wind whistling through my hair and flattening my clothes. The Corsair belched smoke, flying soot struck my face in little needles of pain, but I rejoiced in the action and movement and strength of it all. Over Pencydrain viaduct we went, rattling, bucking, with a hundred-foot drop into the valley below, and over my shoulder I saw the flowing land of the Vale of Neath in all its summer beauty. Resolven mountain I saw, and the wooded slopes of the Forest of Rheola, and in the heart of it the old Nedd was leaping down to the sea and the canal cut a staggering needle of silver through the summer gold and green down to Aberdulais. The beauty of it caught my breath, and I could have shouted with the joy of it. Now, turning, hanging on with the flat clattering and leaping under me, I saw The Top coming up in a cleft of the mountains. And the furnaces were alive again in Hirwain, the billowing scarlets and golds of their bungs cannonading across the black, burned land. The pit-wheels were revolving in blurs of light; colliers and miners were thronging through the narrow streets of TreGibbon. Smoke was billowing in black and yellow sulphurous banks across the white-washed cumulus of the Brecon Beacons, and beneath them Cader Fawr and Garn were flashing green, rearing skywards in the stricken sunlight.

On the corner of Market Street and Duke old Penrhy Jones, our Siloa minister, was ranting at the crowd: golden in the mouth and with God on his shoulder was our Penrhy, and a spade was a bloody spade, and just you look out. No Devil-shaker, this one; no false doctrines or heaping hypocrisies were his. Gasping from my mitch on the flat, I skidded along the cobbles, pausing to listen, and Penrhy cried, his fist at the sky:

'There comes to a man and a country in the greatest need a great revival of the spirit, you hear me? Then shall the caverns of darkness spew open and the light enter, and that time is now. Listen, *listen*!' He tossed back his white, flowing mane of hair and set his squat body rigid in the crowd. 'God is our salvation, and He is walking these mountains. You called upon Him in your distress and He has answered and will redeem you and pluck you to His breast as he plucked and held the people of Moses in the plague of boils and blains. Are you with me?'

And the crowd roared and swayed about him, calling his name.

'As He drowned the enemies of the people in the time of Pharaoh, so will He strike your enemies now. He comes in His great ship on the sea of His Revival. In the mouth of David Morgan, He comes. His word is in the hearts of the children, and He will feed them. The strike is over. Food will flow to your kitchens. And it is not a day of defeat, you hear me? It is a day of victory. From this time on Wales will begin to live. I see a great vision. Look, look to the west, and there shines a golden sun!'

They wept, they clasped their hands before him, they laughed with joy.

'Aye, a golden sun is shining, and it is the light of God. On what we build today will stand the new generations. Great buildings will rise, and new institutions. In this suffering we will build an empire of new learning, and great universities. And we will flow like a river to many lands, for we have gifts to bear them, being Welsh.' His voice rose to a cry, and he flung his blue-veined hands upward. 'I see an age of kings, I see a time of glory. On all sides the chapels will rise and the denominations will exalt, not in their individual glory, but in the greatness of His name!'

Stricken by his vision, I stood rooted, staring up at him. And still he spoke, holding them on the tips of his fingers, drawing them up from the dirt and squalor into the light of promise. And, standing there, jostled, shoved by the massing crowd, I seemed to see behind him a slow rent in the clouds. And from this rent a glorious light began to shine. In this light I saw the torn centuries of the past and on a great stairway walked the lost generations of a land despoiled; the blinded, the maimed by iron. The scarred colliers of the pits I saw, the women haulers, the children of the ventilating doors : all these I saw clearly, as I saw them once before outside the sea-pound of the Old Glamorgan, on the barge to Resolven; a thousand years ago, it seemed, when I was a child. And as the *hwyl* of the preacher beat about me, I turned my face to the sky. Gwen, I saw, in cloud; and then Gran, taking her hand. Ifor next, and I saw him clearly, calling to my dead mother, who was his adored. And then I saw my father, magnificent in strength, and he was laughing. For Mari was running towards him, her hand upraised, and I heard her voice above the roar of the Market Street crowd.

'Wait for me!' she called. 'Wait for me!'

And Penrhy cried, his voice vibrant, 'For the new Revival will herald the next summer like the flash of a swallow's wing. Mark me, mark me!'

Turning, I fought my way through the crowd; shouldering through their laughing, excited faces. And I saw before me the straight lines of the chimneys belching flame and smoke and the whole scurry and tear of it, the clatter of the cobbled streets, the squalid, smoke-grimed buildings, the colliers going on shift in their noisy banter, for the soldiers had gone.

They were building a railway in the Swansea valley. The navvies were flooding in again, rolling down from the English north-country or marching in on the tramping-ticket; Irish, Spanish, English, Welsh, to pay a new obeisance to the great Brunel and Stephenson. In their hundreds they were coming, many with their wives and children, to fling up their wooden shanties along the line. Anything over six feet in socks they took without asking. Uncertain, I stood on the edge of the people, not knowing whether to run to Green Fach first or down to the station to sign on.

Away out of coal, me: enough of coal to last me a generation.

Penrhy cried then, 'This is the time to live, the time to die is passed. With God we will take the land forward into her new life! In the genius of our people, in the name of the new inventions!'

I ran; got a few yards and turned to Rhia's voice behind me.

'Bryn!' Gasping, she seized my hands. 'Oh, where have you been? The strike is over, it is over. Did you hear our Penrhy?'

'Aye!'

She cried, clutching me, 'Eli has just come and taken 'Becca and the children back to Abercynon. There is only me; the house is empty.'

'There is only you,' I said.

The sickness had gone from her with food, and there was a new, dark beauty in her, a new womanhood, and it could have been Mari standing there.

I said, 'I am signing on the railway for Swansea, I am getting out of coal. . . .'

'Oh, God, to get out of coal,' she whispered.

'Good money with the navvies, see, and Tai and Sian will be there. You coming?'

'And jump over a broom?' She held herself, smiling sad. '*Duw*, there is a great pain for you in me. You take me?'

'Got to do it proper,' I said. 'How much money you got?'
'One and sixpence.'
'I've got three shillings. What about Gran's dresser?'
'Worth ten shillings of anybody's money.'
'We have got to do it decent,' I said, 'for Gran's got her eye
on us. Two and sixpence for the service down in Zion, Re-
solven, and a shilling for sidesman Moses Up?'
'That do leave one shilling,' said Rhiannon, making faces at
the sun.
'Then we can afford to keep the dresser, which will put the
curlers in Gran,' I said. 'If I'm signing on with the Great
Western, the least they can do is carry the furnishings.'
'Tai Morlais, is it?'
'Tai and Sian. Now we will build things instead of knocking
them down. You ready, woman?'
'Aye, man.'
And off we went arm in arm, for in Wales, in the 'fifties,
you slammed the door on death. And as we went we heard the
great Penrhy Jones shout to the crowd, 'There is no way back,
my people. Henceforth, the way is forward. I see before me a
great revival of the spirit, new horizons of glory, and the land
shall be blessed! "Behold, the tabernacle of God is with men,
and he shall dwell with them, and they shall be his people, and
God himself shall be with them and be their God!"'
Aye, down Duke and across Commercial we went, arm in
arm, and even down Station Street, in nudges and whispers
and pointing, and jaws dropping right and left, and I heard
Penrhy cry:
'On the burned out slag of this generation we will build a
new Jerusalem, for the Great Revival is here. New temples
shall rise for the land of our fathers!'
'Amen,' murmured the crowd, and I heard it bass, like a
great wind beating about us.
*Amen.*

# HOSTS OF REBECCA – ALEXANDER CORDELL

*HOSTS OF REBECCA* continues Alexander Cordell's brilliant trilogy of mid-nineteenth century Wales, which began with *RAPE OF THE FAIR COUNTRY.*

This is a brawling colourful novel of nineteenth century Wales, with all the passion, humour and Celtic sadness of RAPE OF THE FAIR COUNTRY.

It is the story of a people's struggle : slaves of the coal mines by day, under cover of dark, men unite in a secret host who burn and fight to save their families from starvation. It is the story of young Jethro Mortymer, striving to keep his family alive, and tortured by a terrible guilty love for his brother's wife.

'Running over with lust and strength . . . sin and righteousness'

*The Times*

'Magnificent . . . will provide hours of delight. These Mortymers are unforgettable'

*New York Times*

## CORONET BOOKS